D1248255

ALEXANDRE DUMAS

Known as 'the elder', born at Villers-Cotterets on 24th July 1802. Early life spent in poverty, but playwriting obtained for him the position of librarian of the Palais Royal. Left Paris in 1832, travelled abroad; returned to journalism and to write historical novels. Assisted Garibaldi at Naples in 1860. Returned to Paris in 1864 and died at Puys on 5th December 1870.

EVERYMAN, I will go with thee,

and be thy guide,

In thy most need to go by thy side

ALEXANDRE DUMAS

The Forty-five

INTRODUCTION BY
MARCEL GIRARD

DENT: LONDON
EVERYMAN'S LIBRARY
DUTTON: NEW YORK

© Introduction, J. M. Dent & Sons Ltd, 1968

All rights reserved
Made in Great Britain
at the
Aldine Press · Letchworth · Herts
for
J. M. DENT & SONS LTD
Aldine House · Bedford Street · London
First included in Everyman's Library 1907
Last reprinted 1968

NO. 420

SBN: 460 00420 4

INTRODUCTION

The Forty-five is a sequel to *Marguerite de Valois* and *Chicot the Jester*, especially to the latter, and it is difficult to follow the plot or to understand the characters without bearing in mind the earlier episodes. The three novels together form a huge chronicle of the reigns of Charles IX and Henri III, from 1572 to 1585, that is to say from the Massacre of St Bartholomew to the death of the Duc d'Anjou; a terrible epoch, well suited to inspire a novelist.

Why did Alexandre Dumas break off at that date? Surely the assassination of Henri III, last of the Valois, in 1589 would have made a much better ending to a period of history. Those four years of struggle between the king and the League, tragically terminated by the murder of both protagonists, offered material for no less exciting a tale. Moreover, some of the secondary intrigues covered by *The Forty-five* are not concluded, and we remain a little hungry. Internal evidence suggests that Dumas had not had time to finish; and in fact the Revolution of 1848 called him to other activities—politics and journalism—which led him ultimately to ruin and exile. We shall therefore never learn from his pen what became of Chicot, or whether the beautiful Duchesse de Montpensier yielded to the advances of young Ernauton de Carmainges. Never mind! The curious reader can always refer to the usual history books.

For history—need we say it once again?—is the raw material of the novel, and provides Dumas with his brilliant title: *The Forty-five*. Nothing so intrigues and excites a reader as those numbers which skilful authors use as titles for their works. Balzac had led the way with his *Story of the Thirteen*. Forty-five can equally pass as a cabbalistic number. The Duc d'Epernon himself explains to the king why he has chosen just forty-five noblemen to protect him against murder and conspiracy. Notice that grouping, at once magical and tactical:

' I will explain, Sire. The number three is primordial and divine; furthermore, it is convenient. For instance, when a cavalier has three horses, he is never reduced to going on foot. When the first is weary, the second is at hand; and the third replaces the second in case of wounds or disease. You will always have, then, three times fifteen gentlemen—fifteen in active employment, thirty resting. Each day's service will last

twelve hours, and during those twelve hours you will always
have five on the right hand, five on the left, two before and
three behind. Let any one attack you with such a guard as
that!'

Those forty-five Gascon nobles, who present themselves at
the gates of Paris on the day of Salcède's execution in October
1585, are a strange collection. Badly dressed, empty purses,
mouths full of astonishing Gascon oaths (*mordieu! parfandious!
cap de Bious! Ventre saint-gris!*), mounted on old farm-horses,
they are a fair embodiment of those age-old types of young
provincials who 'go up' to the capital in search of fame, love
and money. They are so many copies of the most famous of
all Gascons, d'Artagnan, as we see him arriving in Paris at the
beginning of *The Three Musketeers*; or, again, of La Mole and
Coconnas who make their entry in the first pages of *Marguerite
de Valois*. Indeed those sensational arrivals illustrate a theme
of the nineteenth rather than of the sixteenth century. Here
too Balzac, with his Rastignac, has shown the way. The pity
is that Dumas has not given his Forty-five more prominence,
more unity, more *esprit de corps*. A few members of the group
we come to know fairly well: Loignac their captain, Sainte-
Maline, Chalabre and one or two others—above all Ernauton
de Carmainges, so handsome and so gentle. But the group *as a
group* we hardly know at all; we seldom see it living and acting
as a collective reality. The real interest of the Romantic Age
centred upon individuals only: the hour of Unanimism had
not yet struck! Despite the title, Dumas makes us share much
more in the thoughts and feelings of Henri de Bouchage, for
example, and above all of Chicot, who is here, as in the earlier
volumes, his spokesman and, so to speak, his other self.

The historical situation is the outcome of a ten-year struggle
for power between four political forces; a hypocritical contest,
stealthy, delivering its blows with velvet-gloved hands, making
more use of poison and calumny than of the sword. It is none
the less a fight to death.

First we have the king, Henri III—'Henriquet', as the
common people nicknamed him from contempt. Aged only
thirty-four, but prematurely old, effeminate and tortuous, he
has bequeathed to history a sorry reputation. Modern hist-
orians, however, tend to rehabilitate him, and even Dumas
presents him here in a more favourable light than in the
previous volumes. Despite caricature and shady jokes, he
embodies the reason of State against faction, political intelligence in the service of national unity. Delicacy, fairness—
yes, and a measure of courage—appear in his conduct, and I
find him possessed of a certain charm, owing perhaps to his
dark character of fallen angel condemned without a hearing

Like Chicot, I would be tempted to follow and serve him—
even while loading him with blame—because he represents
in Paris the only valid force that can prevent the realm from
disintegration.

The Guise party, forming what is called the League, is an
assembly of all the 'factious' who, under pretext of serving the
Catholic faith and opposing the Reformation, seek to win for
themselves titles and lucrative employments. At the head of
the League, the three princes of Lorraine and their sister (the
Guise) mean to supplant the Valois on the throne of France.
They rely on the most fanatical elements of the clergy, those
'leaguer-monks' such as Frère Borromée, who handle a sword
more readily than a rosary and wear coats of mail under their
habits. Behind them looms the sombre figure of His Most
Catholic Majesty, Philip II, King of Spain, who would like to
use, or at least to neutralize, France in order to wage his war
against England. None of these conspirators will stop at anything. Mademoiselle de Montpensier, a madly romantic young
woman who has fiendishly allowed Salcède to be executed on
the Place de Grève, goes so far as to organize the king's removal
by employing in turn the methods of seduction, of force, of
lies, of a disordered and vain imagination. History will show
the Leaguers successful for a moment in obtaining control
of Paris—the famous *Journée des Barricades*; but Henri III
will arrange for the assassination at Blois, by his Forty-five,
of the Duc de Guise and the latter's brother the Cardinal de
Lorraine. Thus he will recover his authority, but not for long:
Jacques Clément, a young monk who appears for a moment
here, will in turn avenge the League by killing the king with a
knife-thrust to the belly. Finally, this long rivalry will profit
Henri de Navarre: the Bourbon dynasty, not that of Guise,
will succeed to the House of Valois.

The king has another and equally dangerous rival in the
person of his own brother François, formerly Duc d'Alençon
and now Duc d'Anjou. Just as Henri III succeeded his brother
Charles IX, so the ties of blood do not prevent him from plotting
under the tacitly condoning eyes of the Queen Dowager, their
mother Catherine de Médicis. We recall Anjou's cowardly
assassination of Bussy d'Amboise and his pursuit of Diane de
Méridor with his sadistic attentions. Politically he is even more
fatal and more odious. That little ill-famed man, the very
embodiment of evil as Dumas presents him, had extravagant
ambitions. First he solicited the hand of Elizabeth of England,
despite their difference in age; but Elizabeth, who in 1579 had
had the contract drawn up for political reasons, refused at the
last minute to proceed, notwithstanding two journeys to
London by her suitor. In default of England, he sought to

become sovereign of the Low Countries, and had himself proclaimed Duke of Brabant and Count of Flanders with the apparent consent of William the Silent. The Flemings, however, were against him and he had to undertake a campaign against Antwerp which is a model of ignominy. After causing the death of thousands of French noblemen, he will fly like a coward but lose none of his big-headedness. History tells us that he actually died at Château-Thierry, as in the novel, but on 10th June 1584 according to l'Estoile's *Diary*, not in the following year. Likewise, the date of the disastrous siege of Antwerp is 17th January 1583, and history says nothing on this occasion about dikes being breached and consequent floods. Dumas, in order to heighten the effect of his story, has antedated an event that took place during the wars of Louis XIV. Finally, and above all, there is no evidence that the Duc d'Anjou was poisoned, let alone by Diane de Méridor! According to her biographers Diane was at that time living quietly at the Château de Montsoreau, near Saumur, where she had rejoined her husband after the death of her lover.

Here we have a good illustration of Dumas' attitude towards history. For him, as for most romantic authors, 'artistic truth' takes precedence of 'factual truth'. There is an accepted principle that the novel must not be a mere re-presentation of events: what must appear above all else is *the idea*. Now, factual detail is often the fruit of chance; it does not enable us to sort out the real play of cause and effect, the mutual operation of characters and of circumstances. History has been transmitted to us in a state of disorder. The role of fiction, therefore, is to re-establish the true order of things, the true order of the mind. It is possible, for example, that the Duc d'Anjou died, in l'Estoile's words, 'of a serious haemorrhage, accompanied by a slow fever which had gradually weakened him and reduced him to skin and bone'. But of what importance is that? So far as Dumas is concerned, what matters is that Anjou, at the age of thirty-four, paid the penalty of unbelievable crimes of which he had been guilty no less in his private life than in his political activity. Whatever may have been the instruments employed by fate—sickness or poison—Anjou's death accords with the logic of his character and with that of his period. The hand of Diane appears as the hand of vengeance, of an almost abstract justice, which transcends the accidental circumstances of the event.

Lastly, there is the fourth, though somewhat belated, political force: the party of Henri de Navarre, king of that famous little province on the Pyrenean frontier, leader of the Protestants, the future Henri IV. It is undoubtedly with him that Dumas' sympathy lies. That intelligent Gascon, brave and libertine, the 'Vert-Galant', the 'good king' of popular song, was a political brain of exceptional quality. He was the creator of France's prosperity at the beginning of the seventeenth century, the champion of tolerance and apostle of national unity. Like Chicot, Dumas cannot but yield to the charm of that attractive and brilliant personality.

However, the hour of Henri IV has not yet come. The future hero has taken refuge in his province, which he enlarges slightly by seizing the city of Cahors; he uses rather like a hostage his own wife, sister of Henri III, the celebrated Queen Margot, whom he deceives with La Fosseuse, but who cuckolds him in return with Turenne, neither of which facts will prevent them from making common cause; in a word, he moves his pawns so that they may be in a position of strength at the right moment. In *The Forty-five*, the reader does not witness the last phase (1588–94) of that climb to power. If he wishes to know more about those events and their attendant circumstances, he will be able to consult, among other works, Michelet's *History of France* ('The Sixteenth Century', Book II, Part 3, chapters 10–15), in which the romantic historian takes over from the historical novelist, although the views of the world taken by those two writers present fundamental differences.

The world of Alexandre Dumas, as we see it at the end of this long chronicle of the reign of Henri III, has all the characteristics of a poetical world: it is created 'from the head', conjured up 'from within'. There is nothing intellectual about the mental processes of our author; they are diametrically opposed to the objective methods of a scientific mind, such as the true historian must possess. If we have several times caught him in the act of flaunting history, the fact is that his inner vision is so strong that his pen cannot submit to reality. No, reality must bow to his vision.

How did Dumas see the world? He saw it as a theatre. In the episodes provided for him by ancient sources, he does not look, in the manner of an historian, for social, religious, economic or strictly political causes: as on the stage, he sees only the confrontation of personalities. The historical actors play their parts, good or evil, with their personal ideas and passions.

This kind of 'psychomachy' is wholly within the romantic tradition, which conceives society as a juxtaposition of individuals. Men and women speak, move, lay plans, succeed or fail, as in the theatre; history is made by and through them. A naïve and popular concept, but one that will always please the

majority of readers more than will today's habit of recon-
structing history in the light of ideologies.

The psychological level of this theatre is not very high.
André Gide went so far as to describe its performers as mere
'puppets'. That is rather unfair: Dumas' puppets, after all,
are endowed with minds and hearts, though it must be admitted
that their motives are over-simplified. The truth is that
everything happens as if each scene were based upon a picture;
and indeed at that period *genre* painting was highly favoured
in all countries. Dumas' text might serve as a commentary
upon the great compositions of, say, Paul Delaroche, his
contemporary, whose 'Princes in the Tower' or 'Assassination
of the Duc de Guise' are contemplated with a shudder by
visitors to the Louvre or the Musée de Chantilly. When you
read Dumas' account of the death of the Duc d'Anjou, you
receive the impression that he is describing the attitudes of
the persons concerned as they might have appeared on canvas.
'Henri was sitting beside the head of the couch whereon his
brother was extended. Catherine was standing in the recess in
which the bed was placed, holding her dying son's hand in hers.
The Bishop of Château-Thierry and the Cardinal de Joyeuse
repeated the prayers for the dying, which were joined in by all
who were present, kneeling, and with clasped hands.' In this
way the story unfolds like a succession of 'historical scenes',
which, as I have elsewhere remarked, correspond to the several
numbers of a serial novel.

Such a design from another pen would give a completely
static effect. Fortunately, Dumas' nature is so strong that it
animates all he touches. His concept is saved from 'wooden-
ness' by what we may call his prodigious instinct for life. That
vigour which, in the last resort, is the master quality of
Alexandre Dumas, grips the reader, convinces him and compels
his willing and confident assent. Consider, for example, that
unlikely pursuit across Flanders and northern France, where
we see Diane de Méridor and her faithful Rémy, amid fearful
perils, trying to overtake the Duc d'Anjou and wreak revenge.
How can the modern reader, who is generally sceptical,
consent to walk in the footsteps of those two determined
shadows? Because Dumas leads him firmly by the hand,
obliging him to follow; and such is the constraint that never
for a moment can he decide to close the book and leave his
heroes, who through war and flood have become his friends,
until he reaches that forest, where of course Rémy will cut
Aurilly's throat, and until he comes to the palace of Château-
Thierry, where of course Diane will poison the infamous duke.
The movement of the story is like that of destiny—it sweeps
us along: we cannot escape.

That inevitability ,however, does not weigh heavy and oppress the reader as it does in most novels of the romantic era. All is saved by the liveliness of the story. Oddly enough, Dumas is a gay author—which certainly does not mean a comic author. He is a happy author and makes us happy because he has a sense of humour. This humour enables us to accept situations that would otherwise be intolerable. It is he, for instance, who lightens the dreadful scene in the 'Corne d'Abondance', that cheap lodging-house from which we know that one of the two adversaries, Chicot or Borromée, will not come out alive. True, we are present at a scene of veritable butchery; but through the narrative, among the wine bottles and the repartee, there moves a breeze of refreshing gaiety which lessens its horror. That humour is like the air that sustains life. Dumas does not take himself too seriously, and there perhaps lies the reason for his remarkable success.

There is only one human activity about which he never jests: love. Love indeed plays an important part in *The Forty-five*, no less important than that of politics and war. It is in fact the driving force, for it will determine the inner motives of the actors. Even those who have no share in it, either because they do not love or because they are not loved, will use the love of others to achieve their ends, to set their snares, to organize conspiracy and to forge the links of alliance. The crazy love of Henri de Bouchage for Diane de Méridor; the unclean love of the Duc d'Anjou for the same Diane; the loving friendship of Rémy le Haudoin for Diane again, which we guess to be very strong; the desperate love of Ernauton de Carmainges for the beautiful but Machiavellian Duchesse de Montpensier; the ironic and frivolous love of Henri de Bourbon for La Fosseuse; the scandalous loves of Marguerite de Navarre; and lastly the mournful love, reaching beyond the grave, of Diane for her murdered lover—all those happy and unhappy passions sustain the interest of the historical narrative, breathe into it their warmth and emotion, endow it with more humanity.

Humanity: here at last is the key-word that alone can explain the enduring popularity of Dumas' novels after more than a hundred years. The word must be understood not according to its psychological but according to its moral content. His concept of man proceeds not from observation but from a sort of wager: men are good or they are evil—sheer Manichaeism! What are we to think of it? One might embark on a long and fruitless discussion of human nature. Is it simple or complex; given or acquired; responsible or irresponsible? Dumas believes that there are men naturally good and others purposely evil. Chicot, Diane, Rémy, du Bouchage, Henri de Bourbon are among the good. The Duc d'Anjou, Aurilly, the

Duc de Mayenne, the Duchesse de Montpensier, Borromée are
among the evil. The subject of *The Forty-five*, as of the earlier
volumes, is the struggle between good and evil. The heroes are
redressers of wrong: they pursue a cause or a sacred vengeance.
The moral point of view may irritate twentieth-century
readers; it is in fact the weakness of the novels of Dumas, as of
those by Victor Hugo and other romantic authors. From the
artistic and aesthetic standpoint their method is too heavy-
handed. But the public at large does not feed upon art and
aesthetics alone; it needs consolation, reassurance. In the
eternal 'combat of day and night' the ordinary man takes
sides and gets excited.

'The false and the marvellous are more human than the
true man,' wrote Paul Valéry. Alexandre Dumas verifies that
saying, for there is no writer at once more false and more
human. The false, however, is relative and open to dispute.
The human is absolute and imposes itself as a sensible reality
of the heart. That was understood by his great contemporaries,
his peers, all of whom were his friends. 'You are a force of
nature,' Michelet wrote to him. 'He is an Enceladus, a
Prometheus, a Titan,' declared Lamartine. And his work was
hymned in verse by Victor Hugo as 'glittering, numberless,
dazzling, happy, in which daylight shines'. Times have
changed, but the huge romantic massif of Dumas has scarcely
been affected by erosion. Despite the new means of escapism
and the universal triumph of the television screen, his books
are read everywhere. None will refuse assent to this judgment
of Apollinaire, which sums up all the esteem and all the friendship which this great man deserves: *The wonderful Dumas* . . .

1968.   MARCEL GIRARD.

BIBLIOGRAPHY

POETRY AND PLAYS. *Élégie sur la Mort du Général Foy*, 1825; *La
Chasse et l'Amour* (in collaboration), 1825; *Canaris* (dithyramb), 1826;
La Noce et l'Enterrement (in collaboration), 1826; *Christine* (or *Stock-
holm, Fontainebleau et Rome*), 1828; *Henri III et sa Cour*, 1829; *Antony*,
1831; *Napoléon Bonaparte, ou Trente Ans de l'Histoire de France*, 1831;
Charles VII chez ses Grands Vassaux, 1831; *Richard Darlington*, 1831;
Térèsa, 1832; *Le Mari de la Veuve* (in collaboration), 1832; *La Tour de
Nesle*, 1832; *Angèle* (in collaboration), 1833; *Catherine Howard*, 1834;
Don Juan de Marana, ou la Chute d'un Ange, 1836; *Kean*, 1836; *Piquillo*,
comic opera (in collaboration), 1837; *Caligula*, 1837; *Paul Jones*, 1838;
Mademoiselle de Belle-Isle, 1839; *L'Alchimiste*, 1839; *Bathilde* (in colla-
boration), 1839; *Un Mariage sous Louis XV* (in collaboration), 1841;
Lorenzino (in collaboration), 1842; *Halifax*, 1842; *Les Demoiselles de
Saint-Cyr* (in collaboration), 1843; *Louise Bernard* (in collaboration),
1843; *Le Laird de Dumbicky* (in collaboration), 1843; *Le Garde Forestier*

(in collaboration), 1845; *L'Oreste*, 1856; *Le Verrou de la Reine*, 1856; *Le Meneur des Loups*, 1857; Collective Eds., *Théâtre*, 1834–6, 6 vols., 1863–74, 15 vols. Dumas also dramatized many of his novels.

TALES AND NOVELS, TRAVELS. *Nouvelles Contemporaines*, 1826; *Impressions de Voyage*, 1833; *Souvenirs d'Antony* (tales), 1835; *La Salle d'Armes* (tales), 1838; *Le Capitaine Paul*, 1838; *Acté, Monseigneur Gaston de Phébus* 1839; *Quinze Jours au Sinai*, 1839; *Aventures de John Davy*, 1840; *Le Capitaine Pamphile*, 1840; *Maître Adam le Calabrais*, 1840; *Othon l'Archer*, 1840; *Une Année à Florence*, 1840; *Praxède; Don Martin de Freytas; Pierre le Cruel*, 1841; *Excursions sur les bords du Rhin*, 1841; *Nouvelles Impressions de Voyage*, 1841; *Le Speronare* (travels), 1842; *Aventures de Lyderic*, 1842; *Georges; Ascanio; Le Chevalier d'Harmental*, 1843; *Le Corricolo; La Villa Palmieri*, 1843; *Gabriel Lambert; Château d'Eppstein; Cécile; Sylvandire; Les Trois Mousquetaires* (The Three Musketeers, E.M.L. 81); *Amaury; Fernande*, 1844; *Le Comte de Monte-Cristo*, 1844–5; *Vingt Ans après*, 1845 (Twenty Years After, E.M.L. 175); *Les Frères Corses; Une Fille de Régent; La Reine Margot*, 1845 (Marguerite de Valois, E.M.L. 326); *La Guerre des Femmes*, 1845–6; *Le Chevalier de Maison-Rouge*, 1846 (E.M.L. 614); *La Dame de Monsoreau*, 1847 (Chicot the Jester, E.M.L. 421); *Le Bâtard de Mauléon*, 1846; *Mémoires d'un Médecin*, 1846–8; *Les Quarante-cinq*, 1848 (The Forty-five, E.M.L. 420); *Dix Ans plus tard, ou le Vicomte de Bragelonne*, 1848–50 (E.M.L. 593–5); *De Paris à Cadix*, 1848; *Tanger, Alger, et Tunis*, 1848; *Les Milles et un Fantômes*, 1849; *La Tulipe Noire*, 1850 (The Black Tulip, E.M.L. 174); *La Femme au Collier de Velours*, 1851; *Olympe de Clèves*, 1852; *Un Gil Blas en Californie*, 1852; *Isaac Taquedem*, 1852; *La Comtesse de Charny*, 1853–5; *Ange Pitou, Le Pasteur d'Ashbourn; El Satéador; Conscience l'Innocent*, 1853; *Catherine Blum; Ingénue*, 1854; *Les Mohicans de Paris*, 1854–8; *Salvator*, 1855–9 (the two last with Paul Bocage); *L'Arabie Heureuse*, 1855; *Les Compagnons de Jéhu*, 1857; *Les Louves de Machecoul*, 1859; *Le Caucase*, 1859; *De Paris à Astrakan*, 1860.

OTHER WORKS. *Souvenirs de 1830–42.* 1854; *Mémoires*, 1852–4; *Causeries*, 1860; *Bric-à-brac*, 1861; *Histoire de mes Bêtes*, 1868; *Memoirs of Garibaldi*, reminiscences of various writers, historical compilations, etc.; Children's Tales: *Histoire d'un Casse-Noisette. La Bouillie de la Comtesse Berthe; Le Père Gigogne.*

SELECTED BIOGRAPHIES IN ENGLISH. A. F. Davidson, *Alexandre Dumas Père*, 1902; H. Parigot, *Alexandre Dumas Père*, 1902; J. Lucas-Dubreton, *Alexandre Dumas, the Fourth Musketeer*, 1929; H. Gorman, *The Incredible Marquis*, 1929; F. W. Reed, *The Life of Alexandre Dumas Père*, 1934; Ruthven Todd, *The Laughing Mulatto*, 1939; A. Craig Bell, *Alexandre Dumas*, 1950.

CONTENTS

PART FIRST

xvi Contents

Contents

CHARACTERS

The action takes place in the period 1584–5. Many of the characters are historical; dates shown are those of birth and death.

CATHERINE DE MÉDICIS (1519–89), queen-mother, widow of Henri II

HENRI III (1551–89), king of France

LOUISE DE LORRAINE (1553–1601), queen of France, wife of Henri III

François, DUC D'ANJOU (1554–84), brother of the king

HENRI DE BOURBON (1553–1610), king of Navarre, Protestant leader, later Henri IV

MARGUERITE DE VALOIS (1553–1615), sister of the king, became Marguerite de Navarre, wife of Henri de Bourbon. Principal heroine of Dumas' novel *Marguerite de Valois*

HENRI DE GUISE (1550–88), duke of the House of Lorraine, head of the Catholic League

CARDINAL DE LORRAINE (1555–88) ⎫
DUC DE MAYENNE (1554–1611) ⎬ his brothers

DUCHESSE DE MONTPENSIER (1552–96), their sister

DIANE DE MÉRIDOR, wife of the Comte de Monsoreau; victim of the Duc d'Anjou, who had her lover Bussy d'Amboise, assassinated. Principal heroine of Dumas' novel *Chicot the Jester*

RÉMY LE HAUDOIN, a doctor, friend of Diane de Méridor

The King's Party

Antoine d'Anglerays, called 'CHICOT' (1550–92), called also by the pseudonym Robert Briquet, Gascon nobleman, the king's jester

ANNE, Duc de Joyeuse (1561–87), grand admiral of France

HENRI DE JOYEUSE, Comte DU BOUCHAGE (1567–1608), in love with Diane de Méridor ⎫
  ⎬ his brothers
FRANÇOIS, Cardinal DE JOYEUSE (1562–1615) ⎭

Nogaret de Lavalette, DUC D'ÉPERNON (1554–1642)

COMTE DE SAINT-AIGNAN

M. DE LOIGNAC, captain of the royal guard of the Forty-five, lover of the Duchesse de Montpensier

VICOMTE ERNAUTON DE CARMAINGES, member of the Forty-five, in love with the Duchesse de Montpensier

M. DE SAINTE-MALINE ⎫
M. DE CHALABRE
PERDUCAS DE PINCORNAY
PERTINAX DE MONTCRABEAU ⎬ members of the Forty-five
EUSTACHE DE MIRADOUX
HECTOR DE BIRAN ⎭

LOUIS DE CRILLON (1543–1615), colonel of the French Guards

The Party of the Duc d'Anjou
AURILLY, confidant of the Duc d'Anjou

The Party of Navarre
M. DE TURENNE, lover of Marguerite de Navarre
M. D'AUBIAC
M. DUPLESSIS DE MORNAY
Mlle de Montmorency, called 'LA FOSSEUSE', mistress of Henri de Bourbon
CHIRAC, a doctor

The Party of the League
THE SUPERIOR of the Convent of the Hospitaliers
DOM MODESTE GORENFLOT, Superior of the Jacobin Priory
BROTHER BORROMÉE
BROTHER JACQUES (1567–89) (Jacques Clément, who assassinated Henri III in 1589)
BROTHER PANURGE
M. DE MAYNEVILLE
M. DE CRUCÉ
M. DE BUSSY-LECLERC
M. DE MARTEAU
NICOLAS POULAIN, assistant to the public prosecutor of Paris
PRESIDENT BRISSON
M. DE SALCÈDE

The Dutch
WILLIAM OF NASSAU, Prince of Orange (1533–84)
THE BURGOMASTER OF ANTWERP
GOES, a Flemish sailor

Supernumeraries
Maître BONHOMET, host of the Corne d'Abondance
Maître FOURNICHON, host of The Sword of the Brave Chevalier
Madame FOURNICHON, his wife
LARDILLE DE CHAVANTRADE, widow of Eustache de Miradoux
MILITOR DE CHAVANTRADE, her son
MITON
JEAN FRIARD
MIRON, a doctor

PART FIRST

CHAPTER I

THE PORTE ST. ANTOINE

On the 26th of October, 1585, the barriers of the Porte St. Antoine were, contrary to custom, still closed at half-past ten in the morning. A quarter of an hour after, a guard of twenty Swiss, the favourite troops of Henri III., then king, passed through these barriers, which were again closed behind them. Once through, they arranged themselves along the hedges, which, outside the barrier, bordered each side of the road.

There was a great crowd collected there, for numbers of peasants and other people had been stopped at the gates on their way into Paris. They were arriving by three different roads—from Montreuil, from Vincennes, and from St. Maur; and the crowd was growing more dense every moment. There were monks from the convent in the neighbourhood, women seated on pack-saddles, and peasants in their carts; and all, by their questions more or less pressing, made a continual murmur, while some voices were raised above the others in shriller tones of anger or complaint.

Besides that multitude of people who had approached to enter the city, special groups might have been observed of persons who appeared to have come out from it. These, instead of looking at the gate, fixed their gaze on the horizon, bounded by the convent of the Jacobins, the priory of Vincennes, and the Croix Faubin, as though they were expecting the advent of some Messiah. These groups consisted chiefly of *bourgeois*, warmly wrapped up, for the weather was cold, and the piercing north-east wind seemed trying to tear from the trees the few last yellow leaves which still remained on them.

Three of these *bourgeois* were talking together—that is to say, two talked and the third listened; or, we ought to say, the third did not even seem to listen, so occupied was he in looking towards Vincennes. Let us turn our attention to this last. He was a man who must be tall when he stood upright, but at this moment his long legs were bent under him, and his arms, not less long in proportion, were crossed over his breast. He was leaning against the hedge, which almost hid his face, before which he also held up his hand as if for further concealment. By his side a little man, mounted on a hillock, was talking to a large man who was constantly slipping off the slope of the same hillock, and at each slip catching at the button of his neighbour's doublet.

" Yes, Maître Miton," said the little man to the tall one, " yes, I tell you that there will be a hundred thousand people around the scaffold of Salcède—a hundred thousand, at least. See, without counting those already on the Place de Grève, or who are on the way thither from different parts of Paris, the number of people here; and this is but one gate out of sixteen."

" A hundred thousand! that is a large number, Friard," replied the large man. " You may be sure that many will follow my example, and will not go to see this unlucky man quartered, for fear of an uproar."

" Maître Miton," replied the small man, " be careful! you are talking politics. There will be no trouble at all, I am sure." Then, seeing his interlocutor shake his head with an air of doubt, he turned to the man with long legs and long arms, and continued, " Am I not right, monsieur? "

" What? " said the other, as though he had not heard.

" I am saying that nothing will happen on the Place de Grève to-day."

" I think you are wrong, and that there will be the execution of Salcède," quietly replied the long-armed man.

" Yes, doubtless; but I mean that there will be no noise about it."

" There will be the noise of the blows of the whip which they will give to the horses."

" You do not understand; by noise I mean tumult. If there were likely to be any, the king would not have had a stand prepared for him and the two queens at the Hôtel de Ville."

" Do kings ever know when a tumult will take place? " replied the other, shrugging his shoulders with an air of pity.

" Oh, oh! " said Maître Miton, privately, to his interlocutor, " this man talks in a singular way. Do you know who he is, comrade? "

" No."

" Then why do you speak to him? You are wrong. I do not think he likes to talk."

" And yet it seems to me," replied Friard, loud enough to be heard by the stranger, " that one of the greatest pleasures in life is to exchange thoughts."

" Yes, with those whom we know well," answered Maître Miton.

" Are not all men brothers, as the priests say? "

" They were primitively; but in times like ours the relationship is singularly loosened. Talk, then, with me if you must talk, and leave the stranger alone."

" But I know you so well that I know what you will reply, while this stranger may have something new to tell me."

" Hush! he is listening."

" So much the better; perhaps he will answer. Then you think, monsieur," continued he, turning again towards him, " that there will be a tumult? "

" I? I said nothing of the sort."

" No; but I believe you think so."

" And on what do you found your surmise? Are you a sorcerer, M. Friard? "

" Why, he knows me! "

" Have I not named you two or three times? " said Miton.

" Ah! true. Well, since he knows me, perhaps he will answer. Now, monsieur, I believe you agree with me, or else you would be there, while on the contrary, you are here."

" But you, M. Friard, since you think the contrary of what you think I think, why are you not at the Place de Grève? I thought the spectacle would have been a joyful one to all friends of the king. Perhaps you will reply that you are not among the friends of the king, but among those of MM. de Guise, and that you are waiting here for the Lorraines, who they say are about to enter Paris in order to deliver M. de Salcède."

" No, monsieur," replied the little man, visibly frightened at this suggestion; " I wait for my wife, Nicole Friard, who has gone to take twenty-four table-cloths to the priory of the Jacobins—having the honour to be washerwoman to Dom Modeste Gorenflot the abbé."

" Look, comrade," cried Miton. " See what they are doing! "

M. Friard, following the direction of his friend's finger, saw that besides the gates the closing of which had already created so much excitement, they were closing still another gate, while a party of Swiss placed themselves before it. " How! more barriers? " cried he.

" What did I tell you? " said Miton.

" It is queer, is it not? " said the unknown, smiling.

At the sight of this new precaution, a long murmur of astonishment and some cries of fear proceeded from the crowd.

"Clear the road! Back!" cried an officer.

This manœuvre was not executed without difficulty; the people in carts and on horseback tried to go back, and nearly crushed the crowd behind them. Women cried and men swore, while those who could escape did so, overturning the others.

"The Lorraines! the Lorraines!" cried a voice in the midst of this tumult.

"Oh!" cried Miton, trembling, "let us fly."

"Fly! and where?" said Friard.

"Into this enclosure," answered Miton, tearing his hands by seizing the thorns of the hedge.

"Into that enclosure? it is not so easy. I see no opening, and you cannot climb a hedge that is higher than I am."

"I will try," returned Miton, making new efforts.

"Oh, take care, my good woman!" cried Friard, in a tone of distress; "your ass is on my feet. Oh, monsieur, take care! your horse is going to kick."

While Maître Miton was vainly trying to climb the hedge, and M. Friard to find an opening through which to push himself, their neighbour quietly stretched his long legs and strode over the hedge with a movement as simple as that by which a horseman places himself in the saddle. Maître Miton imitated him at last with much detriment to his hands and clothes; but poor Friard could not succeed, in spite of all his efforts, till the stranger, stretching out his long arms, and seizing him by the collar of his doublet, lifted him over.

"Ah, monsieur," said Friard, when he felt himself on the ground, "on the word of Jean Friard, you are a real Hercules. Your name, monsieur—the name of my deliverer?"

"I am called Briquet—Robert Briquet, monsieur."

"You have saved me, M. Briquet! my wife will bless you. But, by the way, *mon Dieu!* she will be stifled in this crowd. Ah, cursed Swiss, only good to crush people!"

As he spoke, he felt a heavy hand on his shoulder; and looking round and seeing that it was a Swiss, he took to flight, followed by Miton. The other man laughed quietly, then turning to the Swiss, said, "Are the Lorraines coming?"

"No."

"Then why do they close the door? I do not understand it."

"There is no need that you should," replied the Swiss, laughing at his own wit.

CHAPTER II

WHAT TOOK PLACE OUTSIDE THE PORTE ST. ANTOINE

ONE of the groups was formed of a considerable number of citizens. They surrounded four or five cavaliers of a martial appearance, whom the closing of the gates annoyed very much, as it seemed, for they cried with all their might, " The gate! the gate! "

Robert Briquet advanced towards this group and began to cry louder than any of them, " The gate! the gate! "

One of the cavaliers, charmed at this, turned towards him and said, " Is it not shameful, monsieur, that they should close the gates in open day as though the Spaniards or the English were besieging Paris? "

Robert Briquet looked attentively at the speaker, who seemed to be about forty-five years of age, and the principal personage in the group. " Yes, monsieur," he replied, " you are right; but may I venture to ask what you think their motive is for these precautions? "

" *Pardieu!* the fear they have lest some one should eat their Salcède."

" *Cap de Bious!* " said a voice, " a sad meal."

Robert Briquet turned towards the speaker, whose voice had a strong Gascon accent, and saw a young man twenty to twenty-five years old, resting his hand on the crupper of the horse of the first speaker. His head was bare; he had probably lost his hat in the confusion.

" But, as they say," replied Briquet, " that this Salcède belongs to M. de Guise—"

" Bah! they say that? "

" Then you do not believe it, monsieur? "

" Certainly not," replied the cavalier; " doubtless, if he had, the duke would not have let him be taken, or at all events would not have allowed him to be carried from Brussels to Paris bound hand and foot, without even trying to rescue him."

" An attempt to rescue him," replied Briquet, " would have been very dangerous, because, whether it failed or succeeded, it would have been an avowal on the duke's part that he had conspired against the Duc d'Anjou."

" M. de Guise would not, I am sure, have been restrained by such considerations; therefore, as he has not defended Salcède, it is certain that Salcède is not one of his men."

" Excuse me, monsieur, if I insist; but it is not I who invent, for it appears that Salcède has confessed."

" Where—before the judges? "

" No, monsieur; at the torture."

" They assert that he did, but they do not repeat what he said."

" Excuse me again, monsieur; but they do."

" And what did he say? " cried the cavalier, impatiently. " As you seem so well informed, what were his words? "

" I cannot boast of being well informed, since, on the contrary, I am seeking information from you."

" Come, let us hear! " said the cavalier, impatiently. " You say that Salcède's words are repeated; what are they? Speak."

" I cannot certify that they were his words," replied Briquet, who seemed to take a pleasure in teasing the cavalier.

" Well, then, those they attribute to him."

" They assert that he has confessed that he conspired for M. de Guise."

" Against the king, of course? "

" No; against the Duc d'Anjou."

" If he confessed that—"

" Well? "

" Well, he is a poltroon! " said the cavalier, frowning.

" Ah, monsieur, the boot and the thumb-screw make a man confess many things."

" Alas! that is true, monsieur."

" Bah! " interrupted the Gascon, " the boot and the thumb-screw, nonsense; if Salcède confessed that, he was a knave, and his patron another."

" You speak loudly, monsieur," said the cavalier.

" I speak as I please; so much the worse for those who dislike it."

" More calmly," said a voice at once soft and imperative, of which Briquet vainly sought the owner.

The cavalier seemed to make an effort over himself, and then said quietly to the Gascon, " Do you know those of whom you speak? "

" Salcède? "

" Yes."

" Not in the least."

" And the Duc de Guise? "

" No."

" And the Duc d'Alençon? "

" Still less."

" Do you know that M. de Salcède is a very brave man? "

" So much the better; he will die bravely."

" And that when the Duc de Guise wishes to conspire, he conspires for himself? "

" *Cap de Bious !* what is that to me? "

" And that the Duc d'Anjou, formerly M. d'Alençon, has killed, or allowed to be killed, all who were interested in him— La Mole, Coconnas, Bussy, and the rest? "

" I don't care for that."

" What! you don't care? "

" Mayneville! Mayneville! " murmured the same voice.

" To be sure; it is nothing to me. I know only one thing, *sang Diou !* I have business in Paris this very day—this morning; and because of that madman Salcède they close the gates in my face. *Cap de Bious !* this Salcède is a scoundrel, and so are all those who, with him, have caused the gates to be closed."

At this moment there was a sound of trumpets. The Swiss had cleared the middle of the road, along which a crier proceeded, dressed in a flowered tunic, and bearing on his breast a scutcheon on which was embroidered the arms of Paris. He read from a paper in his hand the following proclamation:—

" This is to make known to our good people of Paris and its environs that the gates will be closed for one hour, and that none can enter during that time; and this by the will of the king and by direction of the mayor of Paris."

The crowd gave vent to their discontent in a long hoot, to which, however, the crier seemed indifferent. The officer commanded silence, and when it was obtained, the crier continued:—

" All who are the bearers of a sign of recognition, or are summoned by letter or mandate, are exempt from this rule. Given at the Hôtel de la Prévôté de Paris, Oct. 26, 1585."

Scarcely had the crier ceased to speak, when the crowd began to undulate like a serpent behind the line of soldiers. " What is the meaning of this? " they all cried.

" Oh! it is to keep us out of Paris," said the cavalier, who had been speaking in a low voice to his companions. " These guards, this crier, these bars, and these trumpets, are all for us; we ought to be proud of them."

" Room! " cried the officer in command; " make room for those who have the right to pass! "

" *Cap de Bious !* I know who will pass, whoever is kept out! " said the Gascon, leaping into the cleared space.

He walked straight up to the officer who had spoken, and

who looked at him for some moments in silence, and then said, " You have lost your hat, it appears, monsieur? "

" Yes, monsieur."

" Did you lose it in the crowd? "

" No. I had just received a letter from my mistress, and was reading it, *cap de Bious !* near the river, about a mile from here, when a gust of wind carried away both my letter and my hat. I ran after the letter, although the button of my hat was a single diamond; I caught my letter, but my hat was carried by the wind into the middle of the river. It will make the fortune of some poor devil—so much the better! "

" So that you have no hat? "

" Oh, there are plenty in Paris, *cap de Bious !* I will buy a more magnificent one, and put in it a diamond twice as large as the other."

The officer shrugged his shoulders slightly and said, " Have you a card? "

" Certainly I have one—or rather, two."

" One is enough, if it be the right one."

" But it cannot be wrong—oh, no, *cap de Bious !* Is it to M. de Loignac that I have the honour of speaking? "

" It is possible," said the officer, coldly, and evidently not much charmed by that recognition.

" M. de Loignac, my compatriot? "

" I do not say no."

" My cousin? "

" Good! Your card! "

" Here it is; " and the Gascon drew out the half of a card, carefully cut.

" Follow me," said Loignac, without looking at it, " and your companions, if you have any. We will verify the admissions."

The Gascon obeyed, and five other gentlemen followed him. The first was adorned with a magnificent cuirass, so marvellous in its work that it might have come from the hands of Benvenuto Cellini. However, as the make of this cuirass was somewhat old-fashioned, its magnificence attracted more laughter than admiration; and it is true that no other part of the costume of the individual in question corresponded with this magnificence. The second, who was lame, was followed by a grey-headed lackey, who looked like the precursor of Sancho Panza, as his master did of Don Quixote. The third carried a child of ten months old in his arms, and was followed by a woman who kept a tight grasp of his leathern belt, while two other children, one

four and the other five years old, held by her dress. The fourth
was attached to an enormous sword, and the fifth, who closed
the troop, was a handsome young man, mounted on a black
horse. He looked like a king by the side of the others. Forced
to regulate his pace by those who preceded him, he was advancing slowly, when he felt a sudden pull at the scabbard of his
sword; he turned round, and saw a slight and graceful young
man with black hair and sparkling eyes.

" What do you desire, monsieur? " said the cavalier.

" A favour, monsieur."

" Speak; but quickly, I pray you, for I am expected."

" I desire to enter into the city, monsieur; an imperious
necessity demands my presence there. You, on your part, are
alone, and want a page to do justice to your fine appearance."

" Well? "

" Take me in; I will be your page."

" Thank you; but I do not wish to be served by any
one."

" Not even by me? " said the young man, with such a strange
glance that the cavalier felt the icy reserve in which he had tried
to close his heart melting away.

" I meant to say that I am not able to take any one into my
service," said he.

" Yes, I know that you are not rich, M. Ernauton de Carmainges," said the young page. The cavalier started; but the
lad went on, " Therefore I do not speak of wages; it is you, on
the contrary, who if you grant what I ask, shall be paid a
hundredfold for the service you will render me. Let me enter
with you, then, I beg, and remember that he who now begs has
often commanded." Then, turning to the group of which we
have already spoken, the lad said, " I shall pass; that is the
most important thing. But you, Mayneville, try to do so also
if possible."

" It is not everything that you should pass," replied Mayneville; " it is necessary that he should see you."

" Make yourself easy ; once I am through he shall see
me."

" Do not forget the sign agreed upon."

" Two fingers on the mouth, is it not? "

" Yes; success attend you."

" Well, Master Page," said the man on the black horse, " are
you ready? "

" Here I am," replied he, jumping lightly on the horse,
behind the cavalier, who immediately joined his friends, who

were occupied in exhibiting their cards and proving their right to enter.

"*Ventre de biche!*" said Robert Briquet; "they are all Gascons, or the devil take me!"

CHAPTER III

THE EXAMINATION

THE process of examination consisted in comparing the half-card with another half in the possession of the officer.

The Gascon with the bare head advanced first.

"Your name?" said Loignac.

"My name, monsieur? It is written on that card, on which you will find something besides."

"No matter! your name!" repeated the officer, impatiently. "Don't you know your name?"

"Yes, I know it, *cap de Bious!* and had I forgotten it you might have told it to me, since we are compatriots and even cousins."

"Your name! Thousand devils! do you suppose I have time to lose in recollections?"

"Well, I am called Perducas de Pincornay."

Then, throwing his eyes on the card, M. de Loignac read, "Perducas de Pincornay, Oct. 26, 1585, at noon precisely. Porte St. Antoine."

"Very good; it is all right," said he. "Enter. Now you," said he to the second.

The man with the cuirass advanced.

"Your card?" said Loignac.

"What! M. de Loignac, do you not know the son of your old friend, whom you have danced twenty times on your knee?"

"No."

"I am Pertinax de Montcrabeau," replied the young man, with astonishment. "Do you not know me now?"

"When I am on service I know no one. Your card, monsieur?"

The young man with the cuirass offered his card.

"All right! pass," said Loignac.

The third now approached, whose card was demanded in the same terms. The man plunged his hand into a little goat-skin pouch which he wore, but in vain; he was so embarrassed by the child in his arms that he could not find it.

" What the devil are you doing with that child? " asked Loignac.

" He is my son, monsieur."

" Well, put your son down on the ground." The Gascon obeyed; the child began to howl. " You are married, then? " Loignac asked.

" Yes, monsieur."

" At twenty? "

" They marry young among us; you ought to know that, M. de Loignac, who were married at eighteen."

" Oh! " thought Loignac, " here is another who knows me."

" And why should he not be married? " cried the woman, advancing. " Is it out of fashion in Paris to marry? Yes, monsieur, he is married; and here are two other children who call him their father."

" Yes, but who are only sons of my wife, M. de Loignac, as also is that great boy who follows us. Come forward, Militor, and salute M. de Loignac, our compatriot."

A lad of from sixteen to eighteen years of age, came forward —vigorous, agile, and in his round eye and hooked nose resembling a falcon. A light budding moustache shaded his lip, at once insolent and sensual.

" This is Militor, my step-son, M. de Loignac, the eldest son of my wife, who is a Chavantrade, related to the Loignacs— Militor de Chavantrade, at your service. Salute, then, Militor." Then, stooping to the child who rolled and cried in the road, he added, while searching all his pockets for his card, " Be quiet, Scipion; be quiet, little one."

" In Heaven's name, monsieur, your card! " cried Loignac, with impatience.

" Lardille! " cried the Gascon to his wife, " come and help me."

Lardille searched the pouch and pockets of her husband, but uselessly. " We must have lost it! " she cried.

" Then I arrest you," said Loignac.

The man turned pale, and said, " I am Eustache de Miradoux, and M. de Sainte-Maline is my patron."

" Oh! " said Loignac, a little mollified at this name; " well, search again."

They turned to their pockets again, and began to re-examine them.

" Why, what do I see there on the sleeve of that blockhead? " said Loignac.

" Yes, yes! " cried the father. " I remember, now, Lardille sewed the card on Militor."

"That he might carry something, I suppose," said Loignac, ironically.

The card was looked at and found all right; and the family passed on in the same order as before.

The fourth man advanced and gave his name as Chalabre. His card was found correct, and he also entered.

Then came M. de Carmainges. He got off his horse and presented his card, while the page hid his face by pretending to adjust the saddle.

"The page belongs to you?" asked Loignac.

"You see he is attending to my horse."

"Pass, then."

"Quick, my master!" said the page.

Behind these men the gate was closed, much to the discontent of the crowd. Robert Briquet, meanwhile, had drawn near to the porter's lodge, which had two windows, one looking towards Paris, and the other into the country. He had hardly reached his new post of observation when a man, approaching from Paris on horseback, and at full gallop, leaped from his saddle, entered the lodge, and appeared at the window.

"Ah, ah!" said Loignac.

"Here I am, M. de Loignac," said the man.

"Good. Where do you come from?"

"From the Porte St. Victor."

"Your number?"

"Five."

"The cards?"

"Here they are."

Loignac took them, examined them, and wrote on a slate the number five. The messenger left, and two others appeared, almost immediately. One came from the Porte Bourdelle, and brought the number four, the other from the Porte du Temple, and announced six. Then came four others—the first from the Porte St. Denis, with the number five; the next from the Porte St. Jacques, with the number three; the third from the Porte St. Honoré, with the number eight; and the fourth from the Porte Montmartre, with the number four. Lastly came a messenger from the Porte Bussy, who announced four. Loignac wrote all these down, added them to those who had entered the Porte St. Antoine, and found the total number to be forty-five.

"Good!" said he. "Now open the gates, and all may enter."

The gates were thrown open, and then horses, mules, and carts, men, women, and children, pressed into Paris, at the risk of suffocating one another, and in a quarter of an hour all the crowd had vanished.

Robert Briquet remained until the last. "I have seen enough," said he; "would it be very advantageous to me to see M. de Salcède torn in four pieces? No, *pardieu!* Besides, I have renounced politics; I will go and dine."

CHAPTER IV

HIS MAJESTY HENRI III.

M. FRIARD was right when he talked of a hundred thousand as the number of spectators who would meet on the Place de Grève and in that vicinity, to witness the execution of Salcède. All Paris appeared to have a rendezvous at the Hôtel de Ville. Paris is very exact, and never misses a fête; and the death of a man is a fête, especially when he has succeeded in exciting so many passions that some curse and others bless him, while the greater number lament him.

The spectators who succeeded in reaching the Place saw the archers and a large number of Swiss and light-horse surrounding a little scaffold raised about four feet from the ground. It was so low as to be visible only to those immediately surrounding it, or to those who had windows overlooking the Place. Four vigorous white horses beat the ground impatiently with their hoofs, to the great terror of the women, who had chosen this place, or had been forcibly pushed there. These horses were unused to work; they had scarcely done more than sometimes in the pastures of their native country to carry on their broad backs the chubby children of peasants returning slowly home at sunset.

After the scaffold and the horses, what next interested the spectators was the principal window of the Hôtel de Ville, which was hung with red velvet and gold, and ornamented with the royal arms. This was for the king. Half-past one had just struck when this window was filled. First came Henri III., pale, almost bald—although he was at that time only thirty-five years old—his eyes sunk in their bluish circles, and his lips constantly trembling with nervous contractions. He entered, sombre, with eyes fixed, at once majestic and unsteady, strange in his appearance, strange in his bearing, a ghost more than a living person, a spectre more than a king—always an incomprehensible mystery to his subjects, who when they saw him appear never knew whether to say "Vive le roi!" or to pray for his soul. He was dressed in black, without jewels or orders; a single diamond shone in his cap, serving as a fastening to three short plumes. He carried in his hand a little black dog that his sister-in-law, Marie Stuart, had sent him from her prison, and on which his fingers looked as white as alabaster.

Behind the king came Catherine de Médicis, already bowed by age—for she was at this time sixty-six or sixty-seven years old —but still carrying her head firm and erect, and darting bitter glances from under her thick eyebrows. At her side appeared the melancholy but sweet face of the queen, Louise de Lorraine. Catherine came to a triumph, Louise to an execution. Behind them came two handsome young men—one of them hardly twenty years old, the other not more than twenty-five. They had each an arm around the other, in defiance of the etiquette which in the presence of kings, as at church in the presence of God, forbids that men should seem attached to anything. They smiled—the younger with ineffable sadness, the elder with enchanting grace. They were brothers. The elder was Anne, Duc de Joyeuse, and the other Henri de Joyeuse, Comte du Bouchage. The people had for these favourites of the king none of the hatred which they had felt towards Maugiron, Quélus, and Schomberg—a hatred of which D'Epernon was sole heir.

Henri saluted the people gravely; then, turning to the young men, he said, "Anne, lean against the tapestry; it may last a long time."

"I hope so," said Catherine.

"You think, then, that Salcède will speak, mother?"

"God will, I trust, give this confusion to our enemies."

Henri looked doubtful.

"My son," said Catherine, "do I not see some tumult yonder?"

"What clear sight you have! I believe you are right. I have such bad eyes; and yet I am not old. Yes, here comes Salcède."

"He fears," said Catherine; "he will speak."

"If he has strength," said the king. "See, his head falls about like that of a corpse."

"He is frightful," said Joyeuse.

"How should a man be handsome whose thoughts are so ugly? Have I not explained to you, Anne, the secret connection of the physical and the moral, as Hippocrates and Galen understood and expounded them?"

" I admit it, Sire; but I am not a good pupil. I have sometimes seen very ugly men very good soldiers. Have you not,
Henri? " said he, turning to his brother; but Henri, buried in
deep meditation, looked without seeing and heard without
understanding, so the king answered for him.

" Eh, *mon Dieu !* my dear Anne, who says this man is not
brave? He is brave, *pardieu !* like a wolf, a bear, or a serpent.
He burned in his house a Norman gentleman, his enemy; he has
fought ten duels and killed three of his adversaries. He has
now been taken in the act of coining, for which he has been
condemned to death."

" That is a well-filled existence, which will soon be finished."

" On the contrary," said Catherine, " I trust it will be
finished as slowly as possible."

" Madame," said Joyeuse, " I see those four stout horses, who
appear to me so impatient of their state of inactivity that I do
not believe in a long resistance of the muscles, tendons, and
cartilages of M. de Salcède."

" Yes, but my son is merciful," replied she, with the smile
peculiar to herself; " and he will tell the men to go gently."

" But, madame," said the queen, timidly, " I heard you say
this morning that there were to be only two draws."

" Yes, if he conducts himself well. In that case all will be
finished as soon as possible; and as you interest yourself so
much in him, you had better let him know as much, my
daughter."

" Madame," said the queen, " I have not your strength when
looking at suffering."

" Do not look, then."

The king heard nothing; he was all eyes. They were lifting
Salcède from the car to the scaffold, round which the archers
had cleared a large space, so that it was distinctly visible to all
eyes, notwithstanding its small elevation.

Salcède was about thirty-five years of age, strong and
vigorous; and his pale features, on which stood drops of blood,
were animated, as he looked around him, by an indefinable
expression, sometimes of hope, sometimes of agony. At first
he cast his eyes towards the royal party; but as if compre-
hending that death, not life, came to him from that quarter, his
gaze did not rest there. It was in the multitude, in the midst
of that stormy sea, that he searched with burning eyes, his soul
trembling on his lips. The crowd gave him no sign.

Salcède was no vulgar assassin; he was of good birth, even
distantly related to the queen, and had been a captain of some

renown. Those bound hands had valiantly borne the sword; and that livid head, on which were depicted the terrors of death —terrors which doubtless the victim would have hidden in the depths of his soul had not hope still lingered there—had conceived great designs. Therefore, to many of the spectators he was a hero; to others, a victim. Some looked on him as an assassin; but the crowd seldom despises those very great criminals who are registered in the book of history as well as in that of justice. Thus they narrated in the crowd that Salcède was of a race of warriors; that his father had fought against the Cardinal de Lorraine, but that the son had joined with the Guises to destroy in Flanders the rising power of the Duc d'Anjou, so hated by the French.

Salcède had been arrested and conducted to France, and had hoped to be rescued by the way; but unfortunately for him, M. de Bellièvre had kept such good watch that neither Spaniards nor Lorraines nor Leaguers had been able to approach. In the prison Salcède hoped; during the torture, on the car, even on the scaffold, he still hoped. He wanted neither courage nor resignation; but he was one of those who defend themselves to their last breath. He darted anxious glances towards the crowd, but constantly turned away with a look of disappointment.

At this moment an usher, raising the tapestry of the royal tent, announced that the President Brisson and four councillors desired the honour of an instant's conversation with the king on the subject of the execution.

" Good," said the king. " Mother, you will be satisfied."

" Sire, a favour," said Joyeuse.

" Speak, Joyeuse; and provided it be not the pardon of the criminal—"

" Sire, permit my brother and me to retire."

" What! you take so little interest in my affairs that you wish to retire at such a moment? "

" Do not say so, Sire. All that concerns your majesty profoundly interests me; but I am of a miserable organisation, and the weakest woman is stronger than I am on this point. I cannot see an execution without being ill for a week; and as I am the only person who ever laughs at the Louvre, since my brother, I know not why, has given it up, think what would become of the Louvre—so sad already—if I were sad also."

" You wish to leave me then, Anne? "

" Peste ! Sire, you are exacting; an execution is a spectacle of which, unlike me, you are fond. Is not that enough for you, or must you also enjoy the weakness of your friends? "

" If you remain, Joyeuse, you will see that it is interesting."

" I do not doubt it, Sire; I only think that the interest will be carried to a point that I cannot bear;" and he turned towards the door.

" Go, then," said Henri, sighing; " my destiny is to live alone."

" Quick, Bouchage!" said Anne to his brother. " The king says yes now; but in five minutes he will say no."

" Thanks, my brother," said Bouchage; " I was as anxious as you to get away."

CHAPTER V

THE EXECUTION

THE councillors entered.

" Well, gentlemen," said the king, " is there anything new? "

" Sire," replied the president, " we come to beg your majesty to promise life to the criminal; he has revelations to make which, on this promise, we shall obtain."

" But have we not obtained them? "

" Yes, in part; is that enough for your majesty? "

" No," said Catherine; " and the king has determined to postpone the execution if the culprit will sign a confession substantiating his depositions under the torture."

" Yes," said Henri; " and you can let the prisoner know this."

" Your majesty has nothing to add? "

" Only that there must be no variation in the confessions, or I withdraw my promise; they must be complete."

" Yes, Sire; with the names of the compromised parties."

" With all the names."

" Even if they are of high rank? "

" Even if they are those of my nearest relatives."

" It shall be as your majesty wishes."

" No misunderstanding, M. Brisson. Writing materials must be brought to the prisoner, and he must write his confessions; after that we shall see."

" But I may promise? "

" Oh, yes! promise."

M. Brisson and the councillors withdrew.

" He will speak, Sire," said the queen; " and your majesty will pardon him. See the foam on his lips."

"No," said Catherine; "he is seeking something. What is it?"

"*Parbleu!*" said Henri; "he seeks M. le Duc de Guise, M. le Duc de Parma, and my brother, the very Catholic king. Yes, seek, wait. Do you believe that there is more chance of rescue on the Place de Grève than on the route from Flanders? Do you think I have not here a hundred Bellièvres to prevent your escaping the scaffold to which one alone has brought you?"

Salcède had seen the archers sent off for the horses; and he understood that the order for punishment was about to be given. Then there appeared on his lips that bloody foam which the young queen had noticed. The unfortunate man, in the mortal impatience which consumed him, bit his lips till they bled.

"No one!" he murmured; "not one of those who promised me help! Cowards! cowards!"

The horses were now seen making their way through the crowd, and creating everywhere an opening which closed immediately behind them. As they passed the corner of the Rue St. Vannerie, a handsome young man, whom we have seen before, was pushed forward impatiently by a young lad, apparently about seventeen. It was the Vicomte Ernauton de Carmainges and the mysterious page.

"Quick!" cried the page. "Throw yourself into the opening; there is not a moment to lose."

"But we shall be stifled; you are mad, my little friend."

"I must be near," cried the page, imperiously. "Keep close to the horses, or we shall never arrive there."

"But before we get there you will be torn to pieces."

"Never mind me; only go on."

"The horses will kick."

"Take hold of the tail of the last; a horse never kicks when you hold him so."

Ernauton gave way in spite of himself to the mysterious influence of this lad and seized the tail of the horse, while the page clung to him. And thus, through the crowd, waving like the sea, leaving here a piece of a cloak, and there a fragment of a doublet, they arrived with the horses close to the scaffold on which Salcède was writhing in the convulsions of despair.

"Have we arrived?" asked the young man, panting.

"Yes, happily!" answered Ernauton, "for I am exhausted."

"I cannot see."

"Come before me."

"Oh, no! not yet! What are they doing?"

"Making slip-knots at the ends of the cords."

" And he—what is he doing? "

" Who? "

" The condemned."

" His eyes turn incessantly from side to side."

The horses were near enough to enable the executioner to tie the feet and hands of the criminal to the harness. Salcède uttered a cry when he felt the cord in contact with his flesh.

" Monsieur," said the Lieutenant Tanchon to him, politely, " will it please you to address the people? " and added in a whisper, " A confession will save your life."

Salcède looked earnestly at him, as though to read the truth in his eyes.

" You see," continued Tanchon, " they abandon you. There is no other hope in the world but what I offer you."

" Well! " said Salcède, with a sigh, " I am ready to speak."

" It is a written and signed confession that the king exacts."

" Then untie my hands and give me a pen; and I will write it."

They loosened the cords from his wrists; and an usher who stood near with writing materials placed them before him on the scaffold.

" Now," said Tanchon, " state everything."

" Do not fear; I will not forget those who have forgotten me; " but as he spoke, he cast another glance around.

Doubtless the moment had come for the page to show himself; for seizing the hand of Ernauton, " Monsieur," said he, " for pity's sake, take me in your arms and raise me above the heads of the people, who prevent me from seeing! "

" Ah! you are insatiable, young man."

" This one more service; I must see the condemned, indeed I must."

Then, as Ernauton still hesitated, he cried, " For pity's sake, monsieur, I entreat you! "

The lad was no longer a whimsical tyrant; he was an irresistible suppliant. Ernauton raised him in his arms and was somewhat astonished at the delicacy of the body he held. Just as Salcède had taken the pen, and looked round as we have said, he saw this young lad above the crowd, with two fingers placed on his lips. An indescribable joy spread itself instantaneously over the face of the condemned man, for he recognised the signal so impatiently waited for, and which announced that aid was near. After a moment's hesitation, however, he took the paper and began to write.

" He writes! " cried the crowd.

" He writes! " exclaimed Catherine.

" He writes! " cried the king; " and I will pardon him."

Suddenly Salcède stopped and looked again at the lad, who repeated the signal. He wrote on, then stopped to look once more; the signal was again repeated.

" Have you finished? " asked Tanchon.

" Yes."

" Then sign."

Salcède signed, with his eyes still fixed on the young man. " For the king alone," said he, and he gave the paper to the usher, though with hesitation.

" If you have disclosed all," said Tanchon, " you are safe."

A smile compounded of irony and anxiety played on the lips of the victim, who seemed to question impatiently his mysterious interlocutor. Ernauton, who was fatigued, wished now to put down the page, who made no opposition. With him disappeared all that had sustained the unfortunate man; he looked round wildly and cried, " Well, come! "

No one answered.

" Quick! quick! the king holds the paper; he is reading! "

Still there was no response.

The king unfolded the paper.

" Thousand devils! " cried Salcède, " if they have deceived me! Yet it was she! it was really she! "

No sooner had the king read the first lines than he called out indignantly, " Oh, the wretch! "

" What is it, my son? "

" He retracts all—he pretends that he confessed nothing, and he declares that the Guises are innocent of any plot! "

" But," said Catherine, " if it be true? "

" He lies! " cried the king.

" How do you know, my son? Perhaps the Guises have been calumniated; the judges, in their zeal, may have put a false interpretation on the depositions."

" Oh, no, madame; I heard them myself! " cried Henri.

" You, my son? "

" Yes, I! "

" How so? "

" When the criminal was questioned, I was behind a curtain and heard all he said."

" Well, then, if he will have it, order the horses to pull."

Henri in anger gave the sign. It was repeated; the cords were refastened; four men jumped on the horses, which, urged by violent blows, started off in opposite directions. A horrible cracking, and a terrible cry was heard. The blood was seen to spout from the limbs of the unhappy man, whose face was no longer that of a man, but of a demon.

"Ah, treason! treason!" he cried; "I will speak, I will tell all! Ah! cursed duch—"

The voice had been heard above everything, but suddenly it ceased.

"Stop, stop!" cried Catherine; "let him speak."

But it was too late. The head of Salcède fell helplessly on one side; his eyes were dilated, fixed, and obstinately directed towards the group where the page had appeared. But he could no longer speak—he was dead. Tanchon gave some rapid orders to his archers, who plunged into the crowd in the direction indicated by Salcède's denouncing gaze.

"I am discovered!" said the page to Ernauton. "For pity's sake, aid me! they come; they come!"

"What do you want?"

"To fly! Do you not see that it is I whom they are seeking?"

"But who are you, then?"

"A woman. Oh, save me! protect me!"

Ernauton turned pale; but generosity triumphed over astonishment and fear. He placed his *protégée* before him, opened a path with blows, and pushed her towards the corner of the Rue du Mouton, towards an open door. The young page leaped off and darted towards that door, which seemed to have been opened for her, and was closed behind her. Ernauton had not time to ask her name, or where he should find her again; but in disappearing she had made a sign full of promise.

Meanwhile Catherine was standing up in her place, full of rage.

"My son," said she at last, "you would do well to change your executioner; he is a Leaguer."

"What do you mean, mother?"

"Salcède suffered only one draw; and he is dead."

"Because he was too sensitive to pain."

"No; but because he has been strangled with a fine cord from underneath the scaffold, just as he was about to accuse those who let him die. Let a doctor examine him, and I am certain that he will find round his neck the circle that the cord has left."

"You are right!" cried Henri, with flashing eyes; "my cousin of Guise is better served than I am!"

"Hush, my son—no commotion! we shall only be laughed at, for once more we have missed our aim."

"Joyeuse did well to go and amuse himself elsewhere," said the king; "one can reckon on nothing in this world—not even on executions. Come, ladies, let us go."

CHAPTER VI

THE BROTHERS

MM. DE JOYEUSE had, as we have seen, left this scene. Side by side they walked through the streets of that populous quarter, which on that day were deserted, so general was the rush to the Place de Grève. Henri seemed preoccupied and sad; and Anne was unquiet on account of his brother. He was the first to speak. "Well, Henri," said he, "whither are you leading me?"

"I am not leading you, brother; I am only walking before you. Do you wish to go to any place in particular?"

"Do you?"

"Oh, I do not care where I go."

"Yet you go somewhere every evening, for you always go out at the same hour and return late at night."

"Are you questioning me, brother?" said Henri, with gentleness.

"Certainly not; let us each keep our own secrets."

"If you wish it, brother, I will have no secrets from you."

"Will you not, Henri?"

"No; are you not my elder brother and my friend?"

"Oh! I thought you had secrets from me, who am only a poor layman. I thought you confessed to our learned brother, that pillar of theology, that light of the church, who will be a cardinal some day; and that you obtained absolution from him, and perhaps at the same time, advice."

Henri took his brother's hand affectionately. "You are more than a confessor to me, my dear Anne—more than a father; you are my friend."

"Then, my friend, why, when you used to be so gay, have I seen you become sad? And why, instead of going out by day, do you go out only at night?"

"My brother, I am not sad."

"What, then?"

"In love."

"Good! and this preoccupation?"

"Is because I am always thinking of my love."

"And you sigh in saying that?"

" Yes."

" You sigh! You, Henri, Comte du Bouchage; you, the brother of Joyeuse; you, whom some people call the third king in France (you know M. de Guise is the second, if not the first); you, rich and handsome, who will be peer and duke on the first occasion—you in love, and you sigh! you, whose device is ' hilariter.' "

" My dear Anne, I have never reckoned the gifts of fortune, past and to come, as things to constitute happiness; I have no ambition."

" That is to say, you have not at present."

" At all events, not for the things you speak of."

" Not just now perhaps; but later you will return to them."

" Never, brother; I desire nothing, I want nothing."

" You are wrong. When one is called ' Joyeuse '—one of the best names in France—when one has a brother a king's favourite, one desires everything, and has everything."

Henri hung his blonde head sadly.

" Come," continued Anne, " we are quite alone here; have you anything to tell me? "

" Nothing, but that I love."

" The devil! that is not a very serious affair; I also am in love."

" Not as I am, brother."

" I also think sometimes of my mistress."

" Yes, but not always."

" I also have annoyances."

" Yes; but you also have joys, for you are loved."

" True; but I have obstacles. They exact from me so much mystery."

" They exact! If your mistress exacts, she loves you."

" Yes, she loves me and M. de Mayenne—or rather only me, for she would give up Mayenne at once if she was not afraid he would kill her; it is his habit to kill women, you know. But then I detest those Guises, and it interests me to amuse myself at the expense of one of them. Well, I repeat I have sometimes annoyances, quarrels, but I don't become sober as a monk on that account; I continue to laugh, if not always, at least once in a while. Come, tell me whom you love, Henri; your mistress is beautiful, at least? "

" Alas! she is not my mistress."

" Is she beautiful? "

" Very beautiful."

" Her name? "

" I do not know it."

" Come, now."

" On my honour."

" My friend, I begin to think it is more dangerous than I thought; it is not sadness, but madness."

" She never spoke but once before me, and since then I have not heard the sound of her voice."

" And you have not inquired about her? "

" Of whom? "

" Why, of the neighbours."

" She lives in her own house; and no one knows her."

" Ah! then she is a ghost? "

" She is a woman, tall and beautiful as a nymph, serious and grave as the angel Gabriel."

" When did you meet her? "

" One day I followed a young girl to the church of La Gype-cienne; I entered a little garden close to it, where there is a stone seat under some trees. Do you know this garden, Anne? "

" No; but never mind. Go on."

" It began to grow dark; I had lost sight of the young girl, and in seeking her I arrived at this seat. I saw a woman's dress, and held out my hands. ' Pardon, monsieur,' said the voice of a man whom I had not noticed; and he gently but firmly pushed me away."

" He dared to touch you, Henri? "

" Listen; he had his face hidden in a sort of frock, and I took him for a monk. Besides, he impressed me also by the polite manner of his warning; for as he spoke, he pointed out to me the woman whose white dress had attracted me, and who was kneeling before the seat as though it were an altar. It was towards the beginning of September that this happened. The air was warm; the flowers planted by friends around the tombs scattered their delicate perfume; and the moon, rising above the white clouds, began to shed her silver light over all. Whether it was the place or her own dignity, I know not, but this woman seemed to me like a marble statue, and impressed me with a strange respect. I looked at her earnestly. She bent over the seat, enveloping it in her arms, placed her lips to it, and soon I saw her shoulders heave with such sobs as you never heard, my brother. As she wept, she kissed the stone with ardour. Her tears had troubled me; but her kisses maddened me."

" But, by the pope, it is she who is mad—to kiss a stone and sob for nothing."

" Oh! it was a great grief that made her sob, a profound love which made her kiss the stone. Only whom did she love? For whom did she weep? For whom did she pray? I know not."

" Did you not question this man? "

" Yes."

" What did he reply? "

" That she had lost her husband."

" Bah! as if people wept like that for a husband. Were you content with such an answer? "

" I was obliged to be content, for he would give me no other."

" But the man—what is he? "

" A sort of servant who lives with her."

" His name? "

" He would not tell me."

" Young or old? "

" He might be about thirty."

" Well, afterwards? She did not stop all night praying and weeping, did she? "

" No; when she had exhausted her tears, she rose. And there was so much mystery and sadness about her that instead of advancing to her as I might have done to another, I drew back; but she turned towards me, though she did not see me, and the moon shone on her face, which was calm and sad, and the traces of her tears were still on her cheeks. She moved slowly; and the servant went to support her. But, oh, my brother, what startling, what superhuman beauty! I have never seen anything like it on earth; only sometimes in my dreams heaven has opened, and visions have descended resembling that reality."

" Well, Henri, what happened then? " said Anne, interested, in spite of himself, at a recital at which he had determined to laugh.

" Oh, it is nearly finished, brother. Her servant whispered something to her; and she lowered her veil. Doubtless he told her I was there; but she did not glance towards me. I saw her no more; and it seemed to me, when the veil concealed her face, as if the sky had become suddenly overshadowed—that it was no longer a living thing, but a shade escaped from the tomb, which was gliding silently before me. She went out of the garden; and I followed her. From time to time the man turned and saw me, for I did not hide myself. I had still the old habits in my mind, the old leaven in my heart."

" What do you mean, Henri? "

The young man smiled. " I mean, brother," said he, " that I have often thought I loved before; and that all women, until now, have been for me—women to whom I might offer my love."

"Oh! and what is this one?" said Anne, trying to recover his gaiety, which in spite of himself had been a little disturbed by his brother's narration.

"My brother," said Henri, seizing his hand in a fervent grasp, "as truly as I live, I know not if she be a creature of this world or not."

"By the pope! you would make me afraid, if a Joyeuse could know fear. However, as she walks, weeps, and gives kisses, it seems to me to augur well. But go on."

"There is little more. I followed her, and she did not try to escape or lead me astray; she never seemed to think of it."

"Well, and where does she live?"

"By the side of the Bastille, Rue de Lesdiguières. At the door, the servant turned and saw me."

"You made him a sign that you wished to speak to him?"

"You will think it ridiculous, but I dared not; the servant impressed me almost as seriously as the mistress."

"You entered the house, then?"

"No, brother."

"Really, Henri, I am tempted to disown you this evening. But you returned the next day?"

"Yes, but uselessly; and equally in vain I went to La Gypecienne."

"She had disappeared?"

"Like a shadow."

"But you inquired?"

"The street has few inhabitants, and no one knew her. I watched for the servant; but he also had disappeared. However, a light which shone every evening through the Venetian blinds consoled me by the knowledge that she was still there. I employed a hundred devices to enter the house—letters, messages, flowers, presents; all in vain. One evening the light failed to appear, and I saw it no more. The lady, wearied doubtless by my pursuit, had left the Rue de Lesdiguières, and no one knew where she had gone."

"But you found her again?"

"Chance aided me. Listen; it is really strange. I was going along the Rue de Bussy, a fortnight ago, about midnight. You know how strict the regulations are about fire; well, I saw not only light in the windows of a house, but a real fire, which had broken out in the second story. I knocked at the door, and a man appeared at the window. 'You have fire in your house!' I cried. 'Silence! I beg; I am occupied in putting it out.' ' Shall I call the watch?' I asked. ' No! in Heaven's name, call no one!' ' But can I help you?' ' Will you? I shall be very grateful;' and he threw me the key out of the window.

"I mounted the stairs rapidly and entered the room where the fire was burning; it was used as a chemist's laboratory, and in making I know not what experiments, an inflammable liquid had been spilled, which had ignited the floor. When I entered, the fire was almost got under. I looked at the man. A frightful scar disfigured his cheek, and another his forehead; the rest of his face was hidden by a thick beard. ' I thank you, monsieur,' said he; ' but you see all is now over. If you are as gallant a man as you seem, have the goodness to retire, for my mistress may return at any moment, and will be angry if she sees a stranger here.'

"The sound of his voice struck me instantly. I was about to cry, ' You are the man of La Gypecienne—of the Rue de Lesdiguières!' (for you remember that I had not seen his face before, but only heard his voice), when suddenly a door opened and a woman entered. ' What is the matter, Rémy, and why this noise?' she asked. Oh, my brother, it was she!—more beautiful by the dying light of the fire than she had appeared in the light of the room. It was she!—the woman whose memory had ever lived in my heart. At the cry which I uttered the servant looked narrowly at me. ' Thanks, monsieur,' said he again; ' you see the fire is out. Go, I beg of you.' ' My friend,' said I, ' you dismiss me very rudely.' ' Madame,' said he, ' it is he.' ' Who?' ' The young man we met in the garden, and who followed us home.' She turned towards me and said, ' Monsieur, I beg you to go.' I hesitated; I wished to speak, but words failed me. I remained motionless and mute, gazing at her. ' Take care, monsieur,' said the servant, sadly; ' you will force her to fly again.' ' Heaven forbid!' cried I; ' but how do I offend you, madame?' She did not reply. Insensible, mute, and cold, as though she had not heard me, she turned; and I saw her disappear gradually in the shade."

"And is that all?"

"All; the servant led me to the door, saying, ' Forget, monsieur, I beg of you.' I fled, bewildered and half crazy; and since then I have gone every evening to this street, and concealed in the angle of the opposite house, under the shade of a little balcony, I see, once in ten times, a light in her room —that is my life, my happiness."

"What happiness!"

" Alas! I should lose this if I tried for more."

" But suppose you lose yourself by practising that resignation? "

" My brother," said Henri, with a sad smile, " I am happy thus."

" Impossible! "

" What would you have? Happiness is relative. I know that she is there, that she lives and breathes there. I see her through the wall, or rather I seem to see her; if she left that house, if I should spend another fortnight like that which I spent when I had lost her, I should be crazy, or should become a monk."

" Not so, *mordieu !* One monk in a family is enough."

" No railleries, brother."

" But let me say one thing."

" What is it? "

" That you have been taken in like a schoolboy."

" I am not taken in; I only gave way to a power stronger than mine. When a current carries you away you cannot fight against it."

" But if it lead to an abyss? "

" You must be swallowed up."

" Do you think so? "

" Yes."

" I do not; and in your place—"

" What would you have done? "

" Enough, certainly, to have learned her name and—"

" Anne, you don't know her."

" No; but I know you, Henri. You had fifty thousand crowns that I gave you out of the last hundred thousand the king gave to me."

" They are still in my chest, Anne; I have not touched one of them."

" *Mordieu !* so much the worse; if they were not in your chest the woman would be in your bedroom."

" Oh, my brother! "

" Certainly. An ordinary servant may be bought for ten crowns, a good one for a hundred, an excellent one for a thousand, and a marvel for three thousand. Let us see, then. Suppose this man to be the phœnix of servants, the beau ideal of fidelity; yet, by the pope! for twenty thousand crowns you will buy him. There would then remain thirty thousand crowns to pay the phœnix of women delivered over by the phœnix of servants. Henri, my friend, you are a ninny."

"Anne," sighed Henri, "there are people who cannot be bought; there are hearts that the king is not rich enough to purchase."

"Well, perhaps so; but hearts are sometimes given. What have you done to win that of the beautiful statue?"

"I believe, Anne, that I have done all I could."

"Really, Comte du Bouchage, you are mad. You see a woman, sad, solitary, and melancholy; and you become even more sad, more recluse, and more melancholy than she is. She is alone; keep her company. She is sad; be gay. She regrets; console her, and replace him she regrets."

"Impossible, brother!"

"Have you tried? Are you in love, or are you not?"

"I have no words to express how much!"

"Well, in a fortnight you shall have your mistress."

"My brother!"

"Faith of Joyeuse! You have not despaired, I suppose?"

"No, for I have never hoped."

"At what time do you see her?"

"I have told you that I do not see her."

"Never?"

"Never!"

"Not even at her window?"

"Not even her shadow, I have told you."

"We must put an end to that. Do you think she has a lover?"

"I have never seen any one enter her house except that Rémy of whom I spoke to you."

"Take the house opposite."

"It may not be to let."

"Bah! offer double the rent!"

"But if she sees me there, she will disappear as before."

"You shall see her this evening."

"I!"

"Yes. Be under her balcony at eight o'clock."

"I shall be there, as I am every day, but without more hope than usual."

"Well, give me the address."

"Between the Porte Bussy and the Hôtel St. Denis, near the corner of the Rue des Augustins, and a few steps from a large inn having for a sign the Sword of the Brave Chevalier."

"Very well, then; this evening at eight o'clock."

"But what do you intend to do?"

"You shall see. Meanwhile, go home; put on your richest

dress, and use your finest perfume. This evening you shall enter the house."

" May God hear you, brother! "

" Henri, when God is deaf the Devil is not. I leave you; my mistress awaits me—no, I should say M. de Mayenne's mistress. By the pope! she at any rate is not a prude."

" My brother! "

" Pardon, good servant of love; I make no comparison between those two ladies, you may be sure, although after what you have told me, I prefer mine, or rather ours. But she expects me, and I don't want to make her wait. Adieu, Henri, till the evening."

The brothers then pressed each other's hands, and separated.

CHAPTER VII

THE SWORD OF THE BRAVE CHEVALIER

During the conversation we have just related, night had begun to fall, enveloping the city with its damp mantle of fog.

Salcède dead, all the spectators were ready to leave the Place de Grève, and the streets were filled with people hurrying towards their homes. Near the Porte Bussy, whither we must now transport our readers, to follow some of their acquaintances and to make new ones, a hum, like that in a bee-hive at sunset, was heard proceeding from a house painted in rose-colour, and ornamented with blue and white pointings, which was known by the sign of the Sword of the Brave Chevalier, and which was an immense inn, recently built in this new quarter. This house was decorated to suit all tastes. On the entablature was painted a representation of a combat between an arch-angel and a dragon breathing flame and smoke, in which the artist, animated by sentiments at once heroic and pious, had placed in the hands of the " brave chevalier " not a sword, but an immense cross, with which he hacked in pieces the unlucky dragon, whose bleeding fragments were seen lying on the ground. At the bottom of the picture crowds of spectators were represented raising their arms to heaven; while from above angels were extending over the chevalier laurels and palms. Then, as if to prove that he could paint in every style, the artist had grouped around gourds, grapes, a snail on a rose, and two rabbits, one white and the other grey.

Assuredly the proprietor must have been difficult to please

if he was not satisfied, for the artist had filled every inch of space; there was scarcely room to add a caterpillar. In spite, however, of this attractive exterior, the hotel did not prosper; it was never more than half full, though it was large and comfortable. Unfortunately, from its proximity to the Pré aux Clercs, it was frequented by so many couples prepared to fight that other couples, more peaceably disposed, avoided it. Indeed, the Cupids with which the interior was decorated had been ornamented with mustaches in charcoal by the *habitués;* and Dame Fournichon, the landlady, always affirmed that the sign had brought them ill luck, and that had her wishes been attended to, and the painting represented more pleasing things—such as the rose-tree of love surrounded by flaming hearts—all tender couples would have flocked to them.

M. Fournichon, however, stuck to his sign, and replied that he preferred fighting men, since any one of them drank as much as six lovers; so that though he should pay but half his account, there was still a gain, for the most prodigal lover wouldn't pay as much as three fighting men. And besides, he would add, wine is more moral than love.

In reply to this Dame Fournichon would shrug her plump shoulders in a way which indicated her ideas on the subject of morality.

The Fournichon affairs were in this divided state, and the Fournichons were vegetating in the Rue de Bussy as they had previously vegetated in the Rue St. Honoré, when an unforeseen incident changed everything, and brought victory to the opinions of Maître Fournichon, to the greater glory of that worthy sign on which every kingdom of nature had its representative.

About a month before the execution of Salcède, the host and hostess, all of whose rooms were then empty, were looking out of the window sadly, and were watching the exercises of some soldiery on the Pré aux Clercs, when they saw an officer, followed by a single soldier, advancing towards their hotel. He was about to pass when the host called out loudly, " Oh, wife, what a beautiful horse ! "

Madame Fournichon replied in an equally audible voice, " And what a handsome cavalier ! "

The officer, who did not appear insensible to flattery, raised his head and looked first at the host and hostess and then at the hotel. Fournichon ran rapidly downstairs and appeared at the door.

" Is the house empty ? " asked the officer.

"Yes, monsieur, just at present," replied the host, humiliated; "but it is not usually so."

However, Dame Fournichon, like most women, was more clear-sighted than her husband, and called out, "If monsieur desires solitude, he will find it here."

"Yes, my good woman, that is what I desire at present," said the officer, who dismounted, threw the bridle to the soldier, and entered the hotel.

He was a man of about thirty-five years of age; but he did not look more than twenty-eight, so carefully was he dressed. He was tall, with a fine countenance and a distinguished air.

"Ah, good!" said he, "a large room and not a single guest."

Maître Fournichon looked at him with astonishment, while Madame Fournichon smiled at him significantly.

"But," continued the captain, "there must be something either in your house or in your conduct that keeps people away."

"Neither, monsieur," replied Madame Fournichon; "only the place is new, and we choose our customers."

"Oh! very well."

Maître Fournichon condescended meanwhile to nod his head in approval of his wife's answers.

"For example," she continued, "for a person like your lordship, we would send away a dozen."

"That is polite, my pretty hostess; thank you."

"Will monsieur taste the wine?" asked Fournichon.

"Will monsieur visit the rooms?" added his wife.

"Both, if you please."

Fournichon descended to the cellar.

"How many people can you lodge here?" asked the captain of the hostess.

"Thirty."

"That is not enough."

"Why so, monsieur?"

"I had a project; but we will speak of it no more."

"Ah, monsieur, you will find nothing larger, except the Louvre itself."

"Well, you can lodge thirty people?"

"Yes, doubtless."

"But for a day?"

"Oh! for a day, forty, or even forty-five."

"Forty-five! *parfandious!* that is just my number."

"Really? You see, then, it is all right."

"Without making a commotion outside?"

"We have often eighty soldiers here on Sundays."

" And no crowd before the house—no spying by the neighbours? "

" *Mon Dieu!* no! our nearest neighbours are a worthy *bourgeois,* who meddles with no one, and a lady who lives so retired that although she has been here for three weeks I have not seen her."

" That will do excellently."

" So much the better."

" And in a month from to-day—"

" That will be the 26th of October."

" Precisely.   Well, on that day I hire your inn."

" The whole of it? "

" Yes, the whole.   I wish to give a surprise to some countrymen, officers—or at least soldiers; they will be told to come here."

" But if it be a surprise—"

" Oh, if you are curious or indiscreet—"

" No, no, monsieur," cried she.

Maître Fournichon, who had heard what had been said, added, " Monsieur, you shall be master here, and there will be no questions; all your friends will be welcome."

" I did not say my friends; I said countrymen," replied the officer, haughtily.

" Yes, monsieur, it was my mistake."

" You will give them supper."

" Certainly."

" If necessary they will sleep here."

" Yes, monsieur."

" In a word, give them all they want, and ask no questions."

" Very well, monsieur."

" Here are thirty livres in advance."

" Well, monsieur, these gentlemen shall be treated like princes. Will you assure yourself by tasting the wine? "

" Thank you; I never drink."

" But, monsieur, how shall I know these gentlemen? "

" That is true; *parfandious!* I forgot. Give me paper, light, and wax."

When they were brought, the captain made a seal on the paper with a ring he had on his finger. " Do you see this figure? " said he.

" A beautiful woman."

" Yes; a Cleopatra. Well, each of these men will present a similar one, on which you will receive him. You will have further orders afterwards."

The captain then descended the stairs and rode off, leaving the Fournichons delighted with their thirty livres in advance.

"Decidedly," said the host, "the sign has brought us good fortune."

CHAPTER VIII

THE GASCON

WE dare not affirm that Dame Fournichon was as discreet as she had promised to be, for she interrogated the first soldier whom she saw passing as to the name of the captain who had conducted the review. The soldier, more cautious than she, asked her why she wished to know.

"Because he has just been here," she replied; "and one likes to know to whom one has been talking."

The soldier laughed. "The captain who conducted the review would not have entered this hotel," said he.

"Why not? Is he too great for that?"

"Perhaps so."

"Well, but it is not for himself that he wanted the hotel."

"For whom, then?"

"For his friends."

"He would not lodge his friends here, I am sure."

"*Peste!* how you run on, my brave fellow! Who, then, can he be who is too grand to lodge his friends in the best hotel in Paris?"

"Well, my good woman, he who conducted the review is simply M. le Duc Nogaret de Lavalette d'Epernon, peer of France, and colonel-general of infantry. What do you say to that?"

"That if it was he, he did me great honour."

"Did you hear him say '*parfandious*'?"

"Oh, yes!"

We may now judge if the 26th of October was impatiently expected. On the evening of the 25th a man entered, bearing a heavy bag, which he placed on Fournichon's table.

"It is the price of the repast ordered for to-morrow," said he.

"At how much a head?"

"At six livres."

"Will they have only one meal here?"

"That is all."

"Has the captain found them a lodging, then?"

" It appears so," said the messenger, who departed, declining to answer any more questions.

At last the much-desired day arrived; half-past twelve had just struck when some cavaliers stopped at the door of the hotel. One, who appeared to be their chief, came with two well-mounted lackeys. Each of them produced the seal of Cleopatra's head, and was received with all sorts of courtesies, especially the young man with the lackeys. Nevertheless, excepting this young man, they all seemed timid and pre-occupied, especially when they mechanically touched their pockets. Most of them went out, however, until supper-time, either to swell the crowd at the execution of Salcède, or to see Paris.

About two o'clock a dozen other travellers arrived, in small parties. One man came in alone, without a hat, a cane in his hand, and swearing at Paris, where he said the thieves were so adroit that they had stolen his hat as he had passed through a crowd, without his being able to see who had taken it. However, he said he was himself to blame for wearing a hat ornamented with such a superb diamond. At four o'clock forty people had arrived.

" Is it not strange? " said Fournichon to his wife; " they are all Gascons ! "

" Well, what of that? The captain said they were all country-men, and he is a Gascon. M. d'Epernon is from Toulouse."

" Then you still believe it was M. d'Epernon? "

" Did he not let slip three times the famous ' *parfandious* ' ? "

" He let slip the famous ' *parfandious* ' ? " asked Fournichon, anxiously; " what sort of an animal is that? "

" Imbecile ! it is his favourite oath."

" Ah ! "

" There is only one thing to be surprised about, and that is that we have only forty Gascons, when there should be forty-five."

But about five o'clock the five other Gascons arrived, and the number of guests was complete. Never was such surprise painted on so many Gascon faces; for an hour nothing was heard but " *sandioux !* " " *mordioux !* " and " *cap de Bious !* " and there was such noisy joy that it seemed to the Fournichons that all Poitou and Languedoc were collected in their room. Some knew and greeted each other.

" Is it not singular to find so many Gascons here? " asked one.

" No," replied Perducas de Pincornay; " the sign is tempting for men of honour."

"Ah! is it you?" said Sainte-Maline, the gentleman with the lackeys; "you have not yet explained to me what you were about to do when the crowd separated us."

"What was that?" asked Pincornay, reddening.

"How it happens that I met you on the road between Angoulême and Angers without a hat, as you are now."

"It seems to interest you, monsieur?"

"Faith! yes. Poitiers is far from Paris, and you came from beyond Poitiers."

"Yes, from St. André de Cubsac."

"And without a hat?"

"Oh! it is very simple. My father has two magnificent horses; and he is quite capable of disinheriting me for the accident that happened to me."

"What was that?"

"I was riding one of them, when it took fright at the report of a gun that was fired close to me, and ran away; it made for the bank of the Dordogne and plunged in."

"With you?"

"No; luckily I had time to slip off, or I should have been drowned with him."

"Ah! then the poor beast was drowned?"

"*Pardioux!* you know the Dordogne—half a league across."

"And then?"

"Then I resolved not to return home, but to go away as far as possible from my father's anger."

"But your hat?"

"The devil! my hat had fallen off."

"Like you?"

"I did not fall; I slipped off."

"But your hat?"

"Ah! my hat had fallen. I sought for it; it was my only resource, as I had come out without money."

"But how could your hat be a resource?"

"*Sandioux!* it was a great one, for I must tell you that the plume of this hat was fastened by a diamond clasp that his Majesty the Emperor Charles V. gave to my grandfather when, on his way from Spain to Flanders, he stopped at our château."

"Ah, ah! and you have sold the clasp, and the hat with it. Then, my dear friend, you ought to be the richest of us all; and you should have bought another glove. Your hands are not alike; one is as white as a woman's, and the other as black as a negro's."

"But listen; as I turned to seek my hat I saw an enormous crow seize hold of it."

"Of your hat?"

"Or rather of the clasp; attracted by the glitter, and in spite of my cries, he flew away with it, and I saw it no more. So that, overwhelmed by this double loss, I did not dare to return home, but came to seek my fortune in Paris."

"Good!" cried a third, "the wind has changed into a crow. I heard you tell M. de Loignac that the wind had carried it away while you were reading a letter from your mistress."

"Now," cried Sainte-Maline, "I have the honour of knowing M. d'Aubigné, who, though a brave soldier, writes well, and I recommend you to tell him the history of your hat; he will make a charming story of it."

Several stifled laughs were heard.

"Ah, gentlemen," cried the Gascon, "do you laugh at me?"

They turned away to laugh again.

Perducas threw a glance around him, and saw a young man near the fireplace hiding his face in his hands. He thought it was to laugh, and going up to him, struck him on the shoulder, saying, "Eh, monsieur, if you laugh, at all events, show your face."

The young man looked up; it was our friend Ernauton de Carmainges, still stupefied by his adventure at La Grève. "I beg you will leave me alone," said he, "I was not thinking of you."

"Oh, very well," Pincornay grumbled, "if you were not thinking of me, I have nothing to say."

"Ah, monsieur," said Eustache de Miradoux to Carmainges, with the most conciliatory intentions, "you are not polite to our compatriot."

"And what the devil have you to do with it, monsieur?" replied Ernauton, more and more irritated.

"You are right, monsieur," said Miradoux, saluting; "it doesn't concern me." And he turned away to rejoin Lardille, who was sitting by the fireplace.

But some one barred his passage. It was Militor, with both hands in his belt, and a sly smile on his lips. "Say, then, step-father," said the scamp.

"Well?"

"What have you to say about it?"

"About what?"

"The way in which that gentleman silenced you?"

" Eh? "

" He shook you off in fine style."

" Ah! you noticed that? " said Eustache, attempting to pass Militor. But the latter defeated the movement by a step to the left which brought him in front of Eustache.

" Not only I," Militor continued, " but every one else. See how they are laughing all around us."

In fact, they were laughing, but not more at that than at anything else. Eustache turned red.

" Come, come, step-father," said Militor, " don't let the affair grow cold.

Eustache assumed a lofty air and approached Carmainges. " It is said, monsieur," said he, " that you have intended to be particularly disagreeable to me."

" When was that? "

" Just now."

" To you? "

" To me."

" Who says so? "

" Monsieur," said Eustache, indicating Militor.

" Then monsieur," replied Carmainges, dwelling ironically on the title—" *Monsieur* is a goose."

" Oh, oh! " said Militor, furious.

" And I beg him," continued Carmainges, " not to come here troubling me with his impertinence, or I shall recall the opinion of M. de Loignac."

" M. de Loignac did not say that I was a goose, monsieur."

" No, he said you were an ass; do you prefer that? It is of small consequence to me. If you are an ass, I will strap you; if you are a goose, I will pluck you."

" Monsieur," said Eustache, " he is my step-son. Treat him more gently, I beg you, for my sake."

" Ah! that is how you defend me, step-father! " cried Militor, in a rage; " I can defend myself better alone."

" Go to school, children! " said Ernauton; " go to school! "

" To school! " cried Militor, advancing with raised fist on M. de Carmainges; " I am seventeen years old, do you understand, monsieur? "

" And I am twenty-five years old," said Ernauton, " and I shall therefore punish you according to your deserts." And seizing him by the collar and belt, he lifted him from the ground and threw him, as if he had been a package, through the window into the street, while Lardille yelled at the top of her voice.

" Now," said Ernauton, quietly, " step-father, step-mother,

step-son, and all the rest, I will make mince-meat of any one who disturbs me again."

"Faith!" said Miradoux, "I think you are right."

"Ah, there! say, then, do they throw men out of the window here?" said an officer, entering. "What the devil! when one indulges in such amusement, he ought at least to cry, 'Out from under!'"

"M. de Loignac!" cried twenty voices.

"M. de Loignac!" repeated the Forty-five.

At that name, known through all Gascony, every one arose and was silent.

CHAPTER IX

M. DE LOIGNAC

BEHIND M. de Loignac, Militor entered, bruised by his fall and crimson with rage.

"Servant, gentlemen," said M. de Loignac; "we are making a good deal of noise, it seems to me. Ah! Maître Militor, it appears, has been vicious again, and his nose has suffered."

"I shall be paid," muttered Militor, shaking his fist at Carmainges.

"Supper, Maître Fournichon," cried M. de Loignac; "and from this moment let all be friends, and love one another like brothers."

"Hum!" said Sainte-Maline.

"That would be difficult," added Ernauton.

"See," cried Pincornay, "they laugh at me because I have no hat; and they say nothing to M. Montcrabeau, who is going to supper in a cuirass of the time of the Emperor Pertinax, from whom it probably descended. See what it is to have defensive arms."

"Gentlemen," cried Montcrabeau, "I take it off; so much the worse for those who prefer seeing me with offensive instead of defensive arms." And he gave his cuirass to his lackey—a man about fifty years old.

"Peace! peace!" cried Loignac, "and let us go to table."

Meanwhile the lackey whispered to Pertinax, "And am I not to sup? Let me have something, Pertinax; I am dying of hunger."

Pertinax, instead of being offended at this familiar address, replied, "I will try; but you had better try to get something for yourself."

"Hum! that is not reassuring."

"Have you no money?"

"We spent our last crown at Sens."

"The devil! then try to sell something."

A few minutes after a cry was heard in the street of, "Old iron! who wants to sell old iron?"

Madame Fournichon ran to the door, while Fournichon placed the supper on the table; and to judge by its reception it must have been exquisite. Fournichon, not being able to sustain all the compliments addressed to him, wished his wife to share them; but he looked for her in vain—she had disappeared. He called her, and she did not come. "What is she doing, then?" he asked a servant.

"Oh, master," he replied, "she is selling all your old iron for new money."

"I hope not my cuirass and arms," said he, running to the door.

"No," said Loignac; "it is forbidden to buy arms."

Madame Fournichon entered triumphantly.

"You have not been selling my arms?" cried her husband.

"Yes, I have."

"I will not have them sold."

"Bah! now that we are at peace two stewpans are worth more than an old cuirass."

"Nevertheless, the trade in old iron must be rather languishing since the king's edict which M. de Loignac just mentioned," said Chalabre.

"On the contrary, monsieur," said Dame Fournichon, "for a long time that same merchant has tempted me with his offers. Faith! to-day I couldn't resist, and finding the opportunity, I have seized it. Ten crowns, monsieur, are ten crowns; and an old cuirass is never more than an old cuirass!"

"What! ten crowns?" said Chalabre; "so dear as that? the devil!"

"Ten crowns! Samuel, do you hear?" said Pertinax, looking for his valet; but he was not to be seen.

"It seems to me," said Loignac, "that this man carries on a dangerous trade. But what does he do with all that old iron?"

"Sells it again by weight."

"By weight! and you say he gave you ten crowns—for what?"

"A cuirass and a helmet."

"Why, even if they weighed twenty pounds, that is half a crown a pound. This hides some mystery."

The party became more animated, thanks to the Burgundy wine, of which Fournichon's spices increased the consumption. The voices mounted to a higher pitch; the dishes rattled; heads were filled with vapours through which each Gascon saw everything in rose-colour, except Militor, who thought of his fall, and Carmainges, who thought of his page.

"Here are a good many joyful men," said Loignac to his neighbour, who happened to be Ernauton—"joyful without knowing why."

"Nor do I know," replied Carmainges. "But then, I am an exception; I am not joyful at all."

"You do yourself wrong, monsieur, for you are one of those persons for whom Paris is a mine of gold, a paradise of honours, a world of happiness."

Ernauton shook his head.

"Very well! we will see."

"Do not laugh at me, M. de Loignac."

"I do not; I distinguished you at once, and that other young man also who looks so grave."

"Who is he?"

"M. de Sainte-Maline."

"And why this distinction, if this question be not too curious?"

"I know you, that is all."

"Me! you know me?"

"You, and him, and all here."

"It is strange."

"Yes, but necessary."

"Why?"

"Because a chief should know his soldiers."

"And all these men?"

"Will be my soldiers to-morrow."

"But I thought that M. d'Epernon—"

"Hush! do not pronounce that name here, or rather do not pronounce any name here. Open your ears and shut your mouth. Since I have promised you all favour, I begin by giving you that advice as part of the account." Then, rising, M. de Loignac said, "Gentlemen, since chance unites here forty-five compatriots, let us empty a glass of wine to the prosperity of all."

This proposal gave rise to frantic applause. "They are almost all half drunk," said Loignac; "it would be a good opportunity to make them repeat their histories, but we haven't time enough." Then, raising his voice, "Holloa! Maître

Fournichon, dismiss from the room all women, children, and lackeys."

Lardille retired grumbling; she had not finished her dessert. Militor did not move.

"Did you not hear, M. Militor?" said Loignac; "to the kitchen!"

There remained only the forty-five men, and M. de Loignac then said, "Now, gentlemen, each knows who called him to Paris. Good! that will do; do not call out his name. You know also that you have come to obey him."

A murmur of assent came from all, mingled with astonishment, for each one knew only what concerned himself, and was ignorant that his neighbour had been moved by the same influence.

"Very good!" continued Loignac. "Later you will become acquainted with one another. You agree that you have come here to obey him?"

"Yes, yes!" they cried.

"Then, to begin, go quietly out of this hotel to the lodgings prepared for you."

"For all?" asked Sainte-Maline.

"Yes, for all."

"We are all commanded, are all equal here," cried Perducas, whose legs were so unsteady that he had to put his arm around Chalabre's neck.

"Yes," replied Loignac; "all are equal before the will of the master."

"Oh!" cried Carmainges, colouring; "I did not know that M. d'Epernon would be called my master."

"Wait!"

"I did not expect that."

"Wait, hot-head! I did not tell you who was to be your master."

"No; but you said we should have one."

"Every one has a master; and if you are too proud to acknow-ledge him we spoke of, you may look higher. I authorise you."

"The king!" murmured Carmainges.

"Silence!" said Loignac. "You have come here to obey; obey, then. Meanwhile, here is an order which you will please read aloud, M. Ernauton."

Ernauton took it and read these words:—

Order to M. de Loignac to take command of the forty-five gentle-men whom I have summoned to Paris with the consent of his Majesty.—NOGARET DE LAVALETTE, Duc d'Epernon.

They all bowed at this.

" Thus," continued Loignac, " you have to follow me at once. Your equipages and servants will remain here. M. Fournichon will take care of them, and I will send for them afterwards; but now be quick! the boats are ready."

" The boats!" cried all the Gascons; " we are, then, to embark?"

" Certainly; to go to the Louvre we must go by water."

" To the Louvre!" they cried joyfully. " *Cap de Bious!* we are going to the Louvre."

Loignac made them all pass before him, counting them as they went, and then conducted them to the place where three large boats were waiting for them.

CHAPTER X

THE PURCHASE OF CUIRASSES

As soon as the valet of Pertinax heard the words of Madame Fournichon, he ran after the dealer in old iron. It was already late; and doubtless the dealer was in a hurry, so that he had gone some distance when Samuel went out from the hotel. Samuel was therefore obliged to call to him. He appeared to hesitate at first; but seeing that Samuel was laden with merchandise, he stopped.

" What do you want, my friend?" said he.

" *Pardieu!* I want to do a little business with you."

" Well, be quick!"

" Are you in a hurry?"

" Yes."

" When you have seen what I bring you, you will be willing to wait."

" What is it?"

" A magnificent piece, of which the work—but you do not listen."

" Yes; but I am also looking round."

" Why?"

" Do you not know that it is forbidden to buy arms?"

Samuel thought it best to feign ignorance, and said, " I know nothing; I have just arrived from Monte de Marsan."

" Oh, that is another thing; but you have just arrived, and yet you know already that I buy arms?"

" Yes, I know it."

" And who told you?"

" *Sandioux !* no need for any one to tell me; you proclaimed it loud enough a little while ago."

" Where was that ? "

" At the door of the Brave Chevalier."

" You were there, then ? "

" Yes."

" With whom ? "

" With a crowd of friends."

" A crowd of friends ? No one is there usually. But whence come all these friends ? "

" From Gascony, like myself."

" Are you for the King of Navarre ? "

" Come, now ! we are Frenchmen, heart and soul."

" Yes; but Huguenots ? "

" Catholic as our Holy Father the Pope, thank God ! " said Samuel, taking off his hat. " But our business is not about that; it has to do with this cuirass."

" Well, come under this portico; it is too public in the street. Now let me see this cuirass," said he, when they were under the portico.

" See," said Samuel, " how heavy it is."

" It is old and out of date."

" A work of art."

" I will give you six crowns."

" What ! six crowns ! and you gave ten just now for an old thing—"

" Six, or none."

" But look at the chasing."

" Of what use is the chasing, when I sell by weight ? "

" The gilding alone is worth ten crowns—"

" Well, I will give you seven."

" You bargain here; and at the inn you gave anything. You go against the law, and then endeavour to cheat honest people."

" Do not call out so loud."

" Oh, I am not afraid," said Samuel, raising his voice; " I am not engaged in unlawful commerce, and nothing obliges me to hide myself."

" Come, then, take ten crowns and begone."

" I told you the gold was worth more. Ah, you want to escape; I will call the guard."

At the noise a window opposite was opened. The dealer was frightened. " Come," said he; " I see I must give you what you want. Here are fifteen crowns; now go."

" That will do," said Samuel; " only these are for my master. I want something for myself."

The dealer half drew his dagger.

" Yes, yes, I see your dagger," said Samuel; " but I also see the figure in that balcony watching you."

The dealer, white with terror, looked up and saw a man who had witnessed the whole scene. " Oh!" said he, affecting to laugh, " you get all you want out of me; here is another crown. And may the devil strangle you!" he added in a low tone.

" Thanks, my good friend," said Samuel; and he made off.

The dealer began to take up his wares, and was also going, when the *bourgeois* opposite cried out, " It seems, monsieur, that you buy armour."

" No, monsieur," said the unlucky dealer; " this was a mere chance."

" A chance that suits me."

" In what respect, monsieur?"

" I have a heap of old things that I want to get rid of."

" I have as much as I can carry."

" But let me show them to you."

" It is useless; I have no more money."

" Never mind, I will give you credit; you look like an honest man."

" Thank you; but I cannot wait."

" It is odd, but I seem to know you."

" Know me?" cried the dealer, trembling.

" Look at this helmet," said the *bourgeois*, showing it from the window.

" You say you know me?" asked the dealer.

" I thought so. Are you not—" he seemed seeking for the name—" are you not Nicolas—"

The dealer looked frightened.

" Nicolas Trouchou, ironmonger, of the Rue de la Cossonnerie?"

" No, no!" cried the man, breathing more freely again.

" Never mind; will you buy all my armour—cuirass, sword, and all?"

" It is a forbidden commerce."

" I know that; he whom you dealt with just now called it out loud enough."

" You heard!"

" Yes, all; and you were liberal. But be easy; I will not be hard upon you. I have been a trader myself."

" What did you sell?"

" Never mind; I have made my fortune."

" I congratulate you."

" And consequently I like to take comfort; I sell all my old iron because it is in my way."

" I understand that."

" And there are the thigh-pieces and the gloves."

" But I have no use for all that."

" Nor I."

" I will take only the cuirass."

" You buy only cuirasses, then? "

" Yes."

" That is odd, for if you buy and sell by weight, one sort of iron is as good as another."

" That is true, but I have preferences."

" Well, then, buy only the cuirass, or rather—now I think again—buy nothing at all."

" What do you mean? "

" I mean that in these times every one wants his arms."

" What! in perfect peace? "

" My good friend, if we were in perfect peace, there would be no such demand for cuirasses, *ventre de biche !* "

" Monsieur ! "

" And so secret too."

The dealer made a movement to go away.

" But really, the longer I look at you the more I think I know your face. You are not Nicolas Trouchou, but still I know you."

" Silence ! "

" And if you buy cuirasses—"

" Well? "

" I am sure it is for a work agreeable to God."

" Be quiet ! "

" You enchant me ! " cried the *bourgeois*, stretching out a long arm over the balcony, and seizing the hand of the dealer.

" Then who the devil are you? " cried he, who felt his hand held as if in a vice.

" I am Robert Briquet, the terror of schismatics, the friend of the Union, and a fierce Catholic; and now I positively recognise you."

The dealer turned white.

" You are Nicolas—Grimbelot the currier."

" No, you are mistaken. Adieu, Maître Robert Briquet; delighted to have made your acquaintance." And the dealer turned his back to the balcony.

" What! you are going away? "

" You see that I am."

" Without taking my old iron? "

" I have no money with me, I told you."

" My valet can go with you."

" Impossible."

" Then what shall we do? "

" Why, remain as we are."

" *Ventre de biche !* that doesn't suit me; I have too great a desire to cultivate your acquaintance."

" And I to escape from yours," replied the dealer, who, resigning himself to abandon his cuirasses and lose everything rather than be recognised, took to his heels and ran away.

But Robert Briquet was not a man to be foiled; he jumped from his balcony and speedily overtook the dealer.

" You are mad! " said he, putting his large hand on the poor devil's shoulder. " If I were your enemy, I have but to cry out, and the watch is in the next street; but you are my friend, and now I know your name."

This time the dealer began to laugh.

" You are Nicolas Poulain, lieutenant to the provost of Paris. I knew it was Nicolas something."

" I am lost! " murmured the man.

" No; you are saved. *Ventre de biche !* I will do more for the good cause than ever you would."

Nicolas Poulain uttered a groan.

" Come, come, courage! " said Robert Briquet; " recover yourself. You have found a brother—Brother Briquet. Take one cuirass; I will take the two others. I give you my gloves and the rest of my armour for nothing. Come on, and Vive l'Union! "

" You accompany me? "

" I will help you to carry these cuirasses which are to conquer the Philistines. Go on; I follow."

A spark of suspicion lingered in the soul of the lieutenant, but he thought, " If he wished me ill, he would not have acknowledged he knew me. Come on, then! " he added aloud, " if you will."

" To life or death! " cried Briquet, and he continued to talk in this strain till they arrived near the Hôtel Guise, where Nicolas Poulain stopped.

" I fancied it would be here," thought Briquet.

" Now," said Nicolas, with a tragic air, " there is still time to retire before entering the lion's den."

"Bah! I have entered many. *Et non intremuit medulla mea!*" exclaimed Briquet. "But pardon me; perhaps you do not understand Latin?"

"Do you?"

"As you see."

"What a catch!" thought Poulain—"learned, strong, bold, and rich!" Then he added aloud, "Well, let us enter," and he conducted Briquet to the door of the hotel. The court was full of guards and men wrapped in cloaks, and eight horses, saddled and bridled, waited in a corner; but there was not a light to be seen. Poulain whispered his name to the porter, and added, "I bring a good companion."

"Pass on."

"Take these to the magazine," said Poulain, handing the cuirasses to a soldier.

"Good! so there is a magazine," said Briquet to himself. "*Peste!* what an organiser you are, Monsieur Provost!"

"Yes, yes, there is judgment in it," replied Poulain, with a proud smile. "But come, let me present you."

"No, I am very timid. When I have done some work, I will present myself."

"As you please. Then wait here for me."

"What are we waiting for?" asked a voice.

"For the master," replied another.

At this moment, a tall man entered. "Gentlemen," said he, "I come in his name."

"Ah! it is M. de Mayneville," said Poulain.

"Ah, really!" said Briquet, making a hideous grimace which entirely changed his appearance.

"Let us go up, gentlemen," said M. de Mayneville; and he ascended a staircase leading to an archway.

All the others followed; and Briquet brought up the rear, murmuring, "But the page! where the devil is the page?"

CHAPTER XI

STILL THE LEAGUE

At the moment when Robert Briquet was about to enter, he saw Poulain waiting for him.

"Pardon," said he; "but my friends do not know you, and decline to admit you to their councils till they know more of you."

"It is very just; and you know my natural modesty had anticipated that objection."

"I do justice to you," said Poulain; "you are an accomplished man."

"I retire then," said Briquet, "happy to have seen in one evening so many brave defenders of the Catholic Union."

"Shall I reconduct you?"

"No, I thank you; I will not trouble you."

"But perhaps they will not open for you; yet I am wanted."

"Have you not a password?"

"Yes."

"Then give it to me. I am a friend, you know."

"True. It is ' Parma and Lorraine! ' "

"And they will open?"

"Yes."

"Thanks; now return to your friends."

Briquet took some steps as if to go out, and then stopped to explore the locality. As a result of his observations, he conjectured that the archway ran parallel to the exterior wall, and terminated in a hall where the mysterious council from which he had been excluded was to assemble. What confirmed him in this supposition was that he saw a light at a barred window, pierced in the wall, and guarded by a sort of wooden pipe, such as they placed at the windows of convents and prisons to intercept the view from without, while the air was still admitted. Briquet imagined this to be the window of the hall, and thought that if he could gain this place he could see all. He looked round him; the court had many soldiers and servants in it, but it was large, and the night was dark. Besides, they were not looking his way, and the porter was busy preparing his bed for the night.

Briquet rapidly climbed upon the cornice which ran towards the window in question, and ran along the wall like a monkey, holding on with his hands and feet to the ornaments of the sculpture. Had the soldiers seen in the dark this figure gliding along the wall without apparent support, they would not have failed to cry, "Magic!" but they did not see him. In four strides he reached the window, and established himself between the bars and the pipe, so that from the inside he was concealed by the one, and from the outside by the other.

He then saw a great hall, lighted by an iron lamp with four branches, and containing piles of armour of all sorts. There were enough pikes, swords, halberds, and muskets, to arm four regiments. He gave less attention, however, to the arms than to the people engaged in distributing them; and his piercing eyes sought eagerly to distinguish their faces.

"Oh, oh!" said he, "there is Maître Crucé, little Brigard, and Leclerc, who dares to call himself Bussy. *Peste!* the *bourgeoisie* is grandly represented; but the nobility—ah! M. de Mayneville presses the hand of Nicolas Poulain; what a touching fraternity! An orator too!" continued he, as M. de Mayneville prepared to harangue the assembly.

Briquet could not hear a word; but he thought that the speaker did not make much impression on his audience, for one shrugged his shoulders and another turned his back. But at last they approached, seized his hand, and threw up their hats in the air. But though Briquet could not hear, we must inform our readers of what took place.

First, Crucé, Marteau, and Bussy had complained of the inaction of the Duc de Guise. Marteau was spokesman, and said, "M. de Mayneville, you come on the part of M. le Duc de Guise, and we accept you as his ambassador; but the presence of the duke himself is indispensable. After the death of his glorious father, he, when only eighteen years of age, made all good Frenchmen join this project of the Union, and enrolled us under this banner. We have risked our lives and sacrificed our fortunes for the triumph of this sacred cause, according to our oaths, and yet in spite of our sacrifices, nothing progresses— nothing is decided. Take care, M. de Mayneville, Paris will grow tired; and then what will you do?"

This speech was applauded by all the Leaguers.

M. de Mayneville replied, "Gentlemen, if nothing is decided, it is because nothing is ripe. Consider our situation: Monsieur the Duke and his brother the cardinal are at Nancy. The one is organising an army to keep in check the Huguenots of Flanders, whom M. d'Anjou wishes to oppose to us; the other is expediting courier after courier to the clergy of France, and to the pope, to induce them to adopt the Union. The Duc de Guise knows, what you do not, that the old alliance between the Duc d'Anjou and the Béarnais is ready to be renewed; and he wishes, before coming to Paris, to be in a position to crush both heresy and usurpation. But in the absence of M. de Guise we have M. de Mayenne, who is both general and counsellor, and whom I am expecting every moment."

"That is to say, your princes are everywhere where they are not wanted," said Bussy. "Where is Madame de Montpensier, for instance?"

"She entered Paris this morning."

" No one has seen her."

" Yes, monsieur."

" Who was it? "

" Salcède."

" Oh, oh! " cried all.

" But," said Crucé, " has she, then, become invisible? "

" Not at all; but unseizable, I trust."

" And how does any one know that she is here? " asked Nicolas Poulain. " I presume Salcède didn't tell you."

" I know that she is here," replied Mayneville, " because I accompanied her to the Porte St. Antoine."

" I heard that they had shut the gates."

" Yes, they had."

" Then how did she pass? "

" In her own fashion."

" She had the power, then, to open the gates of Paris? " said the Leaguers, jealous and suspicious, as the common people always are when allied with the great.

" Gentlemen," said Mayneville, " something took place at the gates of Paris this morning of which you appear to be ignorant. The orders were to open only to those who brought a card of admission,—signed I know not by whom. Immediately five or six men, some of whom were poorly clothed, passed with these cards before our eyes. Now, who were those men? What were the cards? Reply, gentlemen of Paris, who promised to learn everything concerning your city."

Thus Mayneville, from the accused, became the accuser, which is the great art of an orator.

" Cards and exceptional admissions! " cried Nicolas Poulain, " what can that mean? "

" If you do not know who live here, how should we know who live in Lorraine, and spend all our time on the roads to join the two ends of the circle called the Union? "

" How did these people come? "

" Some on foot, some on horseback; some alone, and some with lackeys."

" Did they belong to the king? "

" Three or four had the appearance of beggars."

" Were they soldiers? "

" There were but two swords among the six."

" They were strangers? "

" I think they were Gascons."

" Oh! " said several voices, in a tone of contempt.

" No matter," said Bussy; " were they Turks, they must

receive our attention. We must find out about them. M. Poulain, that is your business. But all that throws no light on the League's affairs."

"There is a new plan," replied M. de Mayneville. "You will know to-morrow that Salcède, who had betrayed us and would have done so again, not only did not speak, but retracted on the scaffold,—thanks to the duchess, who, in the suite of one of these card-bearers, had the courage to penetrate the crowd even to the place of execution, and made herself known to Salcède, at the risk of discovery. At this sight Salcède stopped his confession, and an instant after, the executioner stopped his repentance. Thus, gentlemen, you have nothing to fear as to our enterprise in Flanders; this secret is buried in the tomb."

It was this last speech which had so pleased all the conspirators. Their joy seemed to annoy Briquet; he slipped down from his place, and returning to the court, said to the porter, "Parma and Lorraine!" The gate was opened, and he left.

History tells us what took place afterwards. M. de Mayneville brought from the Guises the plan of an insurrection, which consisted of nothing less than to murder all the principal people of the city who were known to be in favour with the king, and then to go through the streets crying, "Vive la Messe! death to our enemies!"—in fact, to enact a second Saint Bartholomew, in which, however, all hostile Catholics were to be confounded with the Protestants. And in so doing they would serve two gods,—the one who reigns in heaven, and the one who wished to reign on earth; the Eternal and M. de Guise.

CHAPTER XII

THE CHAMBER OF HIS MAJESTY HENRI III.

IN a great room at the Louvre sat Henri, pale and unquiet. Since his favourites, Schomberg, Quélus, and Maugiron, had been killed in a duel, Saint-Mégrin had been assassinated by M. de Mayenne; and the wounds left by their deaths were still fresh and bleeding. The affection he bore his new favourites was very different from what he had felt for the old. He had overwhelmed D'Epernon with benefits; but he loved him only by fits and starts, and at certain times he even hated him and accused him of cowardice and avarice.

D'Epernon knew how to hide his ambition, which was indeed

vague in its aspirations; but his cupidity governed him completely. When he was rich he was laughing and good-tempered; but when he was in want of money he used to shut himself up in one of his châteaux, where, frowning and sad, he bemoaned his fate, until he had drawn from the weakness of the king some new gift.

Joyeuse was very different. He loved the king, who, in turn, had for him almost a fatherly affection. Young and impulsive, he was perhaps somewhat egotistical, and cared for little but to be happy. Handsome, brave, and rich, Nature had done so much for him that Henri often regretted that she had left so little for him to add.

The king knew well these two men, and loved them, doubtless, by force of contrast. Under his sceptical and superstitious covering, Henri concealed a depth of philosophy which, but for Catherine, would have been developed in useful directions. Often betrayed, Henri was never deceived.

It was, then, with this complete understanding of the character of his friends, with this profound acquaintance with their faults and their good qualities, that, remote from them, isolated, sad, in that sombre chamber, he meditated upon them, upon himself, upon his life, and contemplated in the shadows those funereal horizons already outlined on the future to many eyes less clear-sighted than his own.

"After all," he said to himself, "why should I be uneasy? I have no further wars to encounter. Guise is at Nancy, Henri at Pau; the one is obliged to keep his ambition to himself, the other has none. The enterprising spirits are quiet; no Frenchman has seriously contemplated that impossible enterprise,— to dethrone his king. That third crown promised by Madame de Montpensier's golden scissors was but the freak of a woman wounded in her vanity. My mother alone dreams always of that phantom of usurpation, without being able to show me the usurper. But I, who am a man; I, who have a young head notwithstanding my sorrows,—I know what course to take with the pretenders whom she suspects. I will make Henri de Navarre ridiculous, Guise odious; and sword in hand I will break the foreign leagues. *Par la mordieu!* at Jarnac and at Moncontour I was not stronger than I am to-day. Yes," he continued, letting his head fall upon his breast, "but meantime I am lonely; and it is horrible to be lonely. Eh! there is my only, my real conspirator,—ennui; and my mother has never spoken to me of that. Let me see; will any one come this evening? Joyeuse promised to be here early. He amuses himself;

but what the devil does he do to amuse himself? D'Epernon,—
ah, he does not amuse himself, he sulks; well, faith, let him
sulk at his ease."

"Sire," said the usher, "M. le Duc d'Epernon."

All those who have known the weariness of waiting, the
accusations it suggests against the person awaited, the readiness
with which the cloud is dissipated when the person appears, will
understand the eagerness with which the king ordered a chair to
be brought forward for the duke. "Ah! good-evening, duke,"
said he; "I am enchanted to see you."

D'Epernon bowed respectfully.

"Why were you not present at the execution of Salcède? I
told you there would be room at my window."

"Sire, I was unable to avail myself of your Majesty's kindness."

"Unable?"

"Yes, Sire; I was busy."

"One would think that you were my minister, coming to
announce with a long face that some subsidy had not been
paid."

"Faith! your Majesty is right. The subsidy has not been
paid; and I am penniless. But it was not that which occupied
me."

"What then?"

"Your Majesty knows what took place at the execution of
Salcède?"

"*Parbleu!* I was there."

"They tried to carry off the criminal."

"I did not see that."

"It is the rumour all through the city, however."

"A groundless one."

"I believe your Majesty is wrong."

"On what do you found your belief?"

"On the fact that Salcède denied before the people what he
had confessed to the judges."

"Ah! you know that already."

"I try to know all that interests your Majesty."

"Thanks; but what do you conclude from all this?"

"That a man who dies like Salcède was a good servant, Sire."

"Well?"

"And the master who has such followers is fortunate."

"You mean to say that I have none such, or rather that I
no longer have them. You are right, if that be what you mean."

"I did not mean that; your Majesty would find, I am sure,

were there occasion, followers as devoted as the master of Salcède found him."

"The master of Salcède! Call things by name! Who is this master of Salcède?"

"Your Majesty should know better than I."

"I know what I know. Tell me what you know."

"I know nothing; but I suspect much."

"Good!" said Henri, annoyed. "You come here to disturb me and to say disagreeable things, do you not? Thank you, duke; I recognise you well in that."

"Now, then, your Majesty is unjust to me."

"Just, I think."

"No, Sire, a devoted man may give a warning that proves to have been erroneous; but none the less the man does his duty in giving the warning."

"These are my affairs."

"Ah! since your Majesty thinks so, you are right, Sire; we will say no more about them."

A silence ensued, which the king at length interrupted. "Come," said he, "don't oppress me, duke; I am already as gloomy as a Pharaoh in his pyramid. Enliven me."

"Gaiety cannot be forced, Sire."

The king struck the table angrily. "You are a bad friend," said he; "I lost all when I lost my former ones."

"May I dare to say to your Majesty that you hardly encourage the new ones?"

The king looked at him with an expression which he well understood.

"Ah! your Majesty reproaches me with your benefits," said he; "but I do not reproach you with my devotion."

"Lavalette," cried Henri, "you make me sad—you who are so clever, and could so easily make me joyful. It is not your nature to fight continually, like my old favourites; but you are facetious and amusing, and sometimes give good counsel. You know all my affairs, like that other more humble friend, with whom I never experienced a moment's ennui."

"Of whom does your Majesty speak?"

"Of my poor jester, Chicot. Alas! where is he?"

D'Epernon rose, piqued. "Your Majesty's souvenirs to-day are not very amusing for other people," said he.

"Why so?"

"Your Majesty, without intending it perhaps, compared me to Chicot, which is not very flattering."

"You are wrong, D'Epernon; I could only compare to Chicot

a man who loves me and whom I love. He was a faithful and intelligent servant."

"It was not to make me resemble Chicot, I suppose, that your Majesty made me a duke?"

"Chicot loved me, and I miss him; that is all I can say. Oh, when I think that in the same place where you now are have been all those young men, handsome, brave, and faithful; that there, on that very chair on which you have placed your hat, Chicot has slept more than a hundred times—"

"That may have shown a great deal of mind," interrupted the duke; "but certainly it was not very respectful."

"Alas! he has now neither mind nor body."

"What became of him?"

"He is dead, like all who have loved me."

"Well, Sire, I think he did well to die; he was growing old—much less, however, than were his jokes—and I have heard that sobriety was not one of his virtues. Of what did the poor devil die—indigestion?"

"Of grief."

"Oh, he told you so, to make you laugh once more."

"You are wrong; he would not sadden me with the news of his illness. He knew how I regretted my friends—he, who had so often seen me weep for them."

"Then it was his shade that came to tell you?"

"No; I did not even see his shade. It was his friend, the worthy prior Gorenflot, who wrote me this sad news."

"I see that if he were alive your Majesty would make him chancellor."

"I beg, duke, that you will not laugh at those who loved me, and whom I loved."

"Oh, Sire, I do not desire to laugh; but just now you reproached me with want of gaiety, *parfandious!*"

"Well, now I am cooled down; now I am in the mood in which you wanted to find me when you began the conversation with your sinister hints. Tell me, then, your bad news, D'Epernon. The king has always the strength of a man."

"I do not doubt it, Sire."

"And it is fortunate; for, badly guarded as I am, if I did not guard myself, I should be dead ten times a day."

"Which would not displease certain people of our acquaintance."

"Oh! against them I have the arms of my Swiss."

"I could find you a better guard than that."

"You?"

" Yes, Sire."

" What is it? "

" Will your Majesty be so good as to accompany me to the old buildings of the Louvre? "

" On the site of the Rue de l'Astruce? "

" Precisely."

" What shall I see there? "

" Oh, come first! "

" It is a long way, duke."

" We can go in five minutes through the galleries."

" D'Epernon—"

" Well, Sire? "

" If what you are about to show me be not worth seeing, take care."

" I answer for it, Sire."

" Come, then," said the king, rising.

The duke took his cloak, presented the king's sword to him, then, taking a light, preceded his Majesty.

CHAPTER XIII

THE DORMITORY

In less than five minutes they arrived at their destination. The duke took out a key, and after crossing a court, opened an arched door, the bottom of which was overgrown with long grass. They went along a dark corridor and then up a staircase to a room, of which D'Epernon had also the key. He opened the door, and showed the king forty-five beds, and in each of them a sleeper.

The king looked at all this with a troubled curiosity. " Well," said he, " who are these people? "

" People who sleep to-night, but will not do so to-morrow night, except, of course, by turns."

" Why not? "

" That your Majesty may sleep in peace."

" Explain yourself. Are these your friends? "

" Chosen by me, Sire; intrepid guards, who will not leave your Majesty, and who, gentlemen all, will be able to go wherever your Majesty goes, and will let no one approach you."

" And you thought of this, D'Epernon? "

" I alone, Sire."

" We shall be laughed at."

" No, we shall be feared."

" But they will ruin me! "

" How can a king be ruined? "

" I cannot pay my Swiss."

" Look at these men, Sire. Do you think they would be very expensive to keep? "

" But they could not always live like this; they would be stifled. And look at their doublets! "

" Oh, I confess they are not all very sumptuously clothed, but if they had been born dukes and peers—"

" Yes, I understand; they would have cost me more? "

" Just so."

" Well, how much will they cost? That will perhaps decide me, for in truth, D'Epernon, they do not look very inviting."

" Sire, I know they are rather thin and burnt by our southern sun, but I was so when I came to Paris. They will fatten and whiten like me."

" How they snore! "

" Sire, you must not judge them to-night; they have supped well."

" Stay, there is one speaking in his sleep; let us listen."

Indeed, one of the gentlemen called out, " If you are a woman, fly! "

The king approached him softly. " Ah, ah! " said he, " he is a gallant."

" What do you think of him, Sire? "

" His face pleases me; and he has white hands and a well-kept beard."

" It is Ernauton de Carmainges, a fine fellow, who is capable of much."

" He has left behind him some love, I suppose, poor fellow. But what a queer figure his next neighbour is! "

" Ah! that is M. de Chalabre. If he ruins your Majesty, it will not be without enriching himself, I answer for it."

" And that one with such a sombre air; he does not seem as though he dreamed of love."

" What number, Sire? "

" Number 12."

" M. de Sainte-Maline, a brave fellow, with a heart of bronze."

" Well, Lavalette, you have had a good idea."

" I should think so. Imagine the effect that will be produced by these new watch-dogs, who will follow you like your shadow."

" Yes, yes; but they cannot follow me like a shadow in that

garb. My body is of good style; and I will not have it disgraced by its shadow, or rather by its shadows."

" Ah! we return, Sire, to the question of money."

" Did you expect to avoid it? "

" Not at all; on the contrary, it is in all affairs the fundamental question. But about this also, I have an idea."

" D'Epernon! "

" My zeal for your Majesty doubles my imagination."

" Well, let us hear it."

" If it depended upon me, each of these gentlemen should find by his bed to-morrow morning a purse containing a thousand crowns, as payment for the first six months."

" One thousand crowns for six months; six thousand livres a year! You are mad, duke; an entire regiment would not cost that."

" You forget, Sire, that they are to be your Majesty's shadows; and you have yourself said that you wish your shadows to be decently clad. Each will have to take from his thousand crowns enough for arms and equipments. Set down fifteen hundred livres to effect this in a manner to do you honour, and there would remain forty-five hundred livres for the first year. Then for subsequent years you could give three thousand livres."

" That is more reasonable."

" Then your Majesty accepts? "

" There is only one difficulty, duke."

" What is it? "

" Want of money."

" Sire, I have found a method. Six months ago a tax was levied on shooting and fishing."

" Well? "

" The tax has yielded in the first six months sixty-five thousand crowns, which have not yet been turned into the treasury, and await your Majesty's disposal."

" I destined it for the war, duke."

" The first interest of the kingdom is the safety of the king."

" Well; there still would remain twenty thousand crowns for the army."

" Pardon, Sire; but I had disposed of them, also."

" Ah! "

" Yes, Sire; your Majesty had promised me money."

" I was sure of it," said the king. " You give me a guard so that you may obtain your money."

" Oh, Sire! "

" But why that number forty-five? " asked the king, passing to a new idea.

" I will explain, Sire. The number three is primordial and divine; furthermore, it is convenient. For instance, when a cavalier has three horses, he is never reduced to going on foot. When the first is weary, the second is at hand; and the third replaces the second in case of wounds or disease. You will always have, then, three times fifteen gentlemen—fifteen in active employment, thirty resting. Each days' service will last twelve hours, and during those twelve hours you will always have five on the right hand, five on the left, two before, and three behind. Let any one attack you with such a guard as that! "

" *Par la mordieu !* it is a skilful combination, duke; I congratulate you."

" Look at them, Sire; will they not have a good effect? "

" Yes, when dressed they will not look bad. Well, so be it."

" Well, then, Sire, I have a favour to ask."

" I should be astonished if you had not."

" Your Majesty is bitter to-day."

" Oh, I only mean that having rendered me a service, you have the right to ask for a return."

" Well, Sire, it is an appointment."

" Why, you are already colonel-general of infantry; more would crush you."

" In your Majesty's service I am a Samson."

" What is it, then? "

" I desire the command of these forty-five gentlemen."

" What! you wish to march before me, behind me? You carry your devotedness to that point? You wish to be captain of guards? "

" No, I should have a deputy; only I desire that they should know me as their head."

" Well, you shall have it. But who is to be your deputy? "

" M. de Loignac, Sire."

" Ah! that is good."

" He pleases your Majesty? "

" Perfectly."

" Then it is decided? "

" Yes; let it be as you wish."

" Then I will go at once to the treasurer, and get my forty-five purses."

" To-night? "

" They are to find them to-morrow when they wake."

" Good; then I will return."

" Content, Sire? "

" Tolerably."

" Well guarded, at all events."

" By men who sleep."

" They will not sleep to-morrow, Sire. "

D'Epernon conducted the king to the door of the corridor, and left him, saying to himself, " If I am not king, I have guards like a king; and they cost me nothing, *parfandious !* "

CHAPTER XIV

THE SHADE OF CHICOT

THE king, as we have said, was never deceived as to the character of his friends; he knew perfectly well that D'Epernon was working for his own advantage, but as he had expected to be obliged to give without receiving anything in return, whereas he had got forty-five guards, he was pleased with the idea. Besides, it was a novelty, which was a thing that a poor King of France could not always get, and especially Henri III., who, when he had gone through his processions, counted his dogs, and uttered his usual number of sighs, had nothing left to do. Therefore he became more and more satisfied as he returned to his room.

" These men are doubtless brave, and perhaps will be very devoted," thought he; " and forty-five swords always ready to leap from their scabbards are a grand thing."

This thought brought to his mind the other devoted swords that he regretted so bitterly; and he sank again into that deep melancholy into which at this period he fell so often that it might be called his habitual condition. The times so inauspicious, men so wicked, crowns so loosening on the heads of kings—impressed him again with that strong desire either to die or to become animated, which the English, our superiors in melancholy, had already baptised by the name of " spleen." He looked around for Joyeuse, and not seeing him, inquired for him.

" Monsieur the Duke has not yet returned," said the usher.

" Then call my *valet de chambre.*"

When he was in bed they asked if his reader should attend, for Henri was subject to long fits of wakefulness, and was often read to sleep.

"No," replied the king. "I want no one; only if M. de Joyeuse returns, bring him to me."

"If he returns late, Sire."

"Alas! he is always late; but whatever be the hour, bring him here."

The servants extinguished the candles and lighted a lamp of essences, which gave a pale blue flame that the king liked. Henri, brave in the presence of a real danger, had all the fears and weaknesses of children and women. He feared apparitions; he feared ghosts. Following the shadows made on the wall by his light, searching with his eyes the obscure corners of his chamber, listening for the slightest noise, he at length fell asleep. But his sleep was of short duration; he awoke, thinking he heard a noise in the room.

"Joyeuse," he asked, "is it you?"

No one replied. The light burned dim, and threw faint circles on the ceiling of carved oak.

"Alone still!" murmured the king. "*Mon Dieu!* give me the strength to be always alone in my life, as I shall be after death."

"Eh, eh! alone after death? That is not certain," answered a strident voice that vibrated with a metallic ring a few feet from the bed; "and the worms—how about the worms?"

The king started up and looked round him in terror. "Oh, I know that voice!" he murmured.

"Ah! that is fortunate," replied the voice.

"It is like the voice of Chicot."

"You burn, Henri; you burn."

Then the king, getting half out of bed, saw a man sitting in the very chair which he had pointed out to D'Epernon.

"Heaven protect me!" cried he; "it is the shade of Chicot."

"Ah! my poor Henriquet, are you still so foolish?"

"What do you mean?"

"Shades cannot speak, imbecile, since they have no body, and consequently no tongue."

"Then you are Chicot himself," cried the king, joyfully.

"I have nothing to say about that; we shall see later what I am—we shall see."

"Then you are not dead, my poor Chicot?"

"Here you are, screaming like an eagle. Yes, on the contrary, I am dead, a hundred times dead."

"Chicot, my only friend!"

"You, at least, are not changed; you say always the same thing."

" But you, Chicot, are you changed? "

" I hope so."

" Chicot, my friend, why did you leave me? "

" Because I am dead."

" You said just now that you were not dead."

" Dead to some; alive to others."

" And to me? "

" Dead."

" Why dead to me? "

" It is easy to comprehend; you are not the master here."

" What do you mean? "

" You can do nothing for those who serve you."

" Chicot! "

" Do not be angry, or I shall be so also."

" Speak then, my friend," said the king, fearing that Chicot would vanish.

" Well, I had a little affair to settle with M. de Mayenne, you remember? "

" Perfectly."

" I settled it; I beat this valiant captain without mercy.   He sought for me to hang me; and you, whom I thought would protect me, abandoned me, and made peace with him.   Then I declared myself dead and buried, by the aid of my friend Gorenflot, so that M. de Mayenne has ceased to search for me."

" What a frightful courage you had, Chicot!   Did you not know the grief your death would cause me? "

" Yes, it is courageous, but not at all frightful.   I have never lived so tranquilly as since the world thought me dead."

" Chicot, my head turns.   You frighten me; I know not what to think."

" Well! settle something."

" I think that you are dead and—"

" Then I lie; you are polite."

" You conceal from me a part of the truth; but presently, like the orators of antiquity, you will tell me terrible truths."

" Oh, as to that, I do not say no.   Prepare, poor king! "

" If you are not a shade, how could you come unnoticed into my room, through the guarded corridors? "   And Henri, abandoning himself to new terrors, threw himself down in the bed and covered up his head.

" Come, come! " cried Chicot; " you have only to touch me to be convinced."

" You are not, then, a messenger of vengeance? "

" *Ventre de biche!* have I horns like Satan, or a flaming sword like the archangel Michael? "

" But how did you come? "

" Why, I have still the key that you gave me, and which I hung round my neck to enrage your gentlemen, and with this I entered."

" By the secret door, then? "

" Certainly."

" And why to-day more than yesterday? "

" Ah! that you shall hear."

Henri, sitting up again, said like a child, " Do not tell me anything disagreeable, Chicot. Oh, if you only knew how glad I am to see you again! "

" I will tell the truth; so much the worse if it be disagreeable."

" But your fear of Mayenne is not serious? "

" Very serious, on the contrary. You understand that M. de Mayenne gave me fifty blows with a stirrup-leather, in return for which I gave him one hundred with the sheath of my sword. No doubt he thinks, therefore, that he still owes me fifty, so that I should not have come to you now, however great your need of me, had I not known him to be at Soissons."

" Well, Chicot, I take you now under my protection; and I wish—"

" What do you wish? Take care, Henriquet! every time you say, ' I wish,' you are on the point of saying something silly."

" I wish that you should be resuscitated and appear openly."

" There! I said so."

" I will defend you."

" Good! "

" Chicot, I pledge my royal word."

" Bah! I have better than that."

" What? "

" My hole; and there I remain."

" I will protect you, I tell you," cried the king, jumping out of bed.

" Henri, you will catch cold; go back to bed, I pray."

" You are right, but you exasperate me. How! when I have enough guards, Swiss, Scotch, and French, for my own defence, should I not have enough for yours? "

" Let us see; you have the Swiss—"

" Yes, commanded by Tocquenot."

" Good! then you have the Scotch—"

" Commanded by Larchant."

" Very well! and you have the French guards—"

" Commanded by Crillon. And then—but I do not know if I ought to tell you—"

" I did not ask you."

" A novelty, Chicot! "

" A novelty? "

" Yes; imagine forty-five brave gentlemen."

" Forty-five? What do you mean? "

" Forty-five gentlemen."

" Where did you find them? Not in Paris, I suppose? "

" No; but they arrived here yesterday."

" Oh! " cried Chicot, with a sudden illumination, " I know these gentlemen."

" Really! "

" Forty-five beggars, who only want the wallet—figures to make one die with laughter."

" Chicot, there are splendid men among them."

" Gascons, like your colonel-general of infantry."

" And like you, Chicot. However, I have forty-five formidable swords at command."

" Commanded by that forty-sixth formidable sword called D'Epernon."

" Not exactly."

" By whom, then? "

" Loignac."

" And it is with them you think to defend yourself? "

" Yes, *mordieu!* yes," said Henri, irritated.

" Well, I have more troops than you."

" You have troops? "

" Why not? "

" What are they? "

" You shall hear. First, all the army that MM. de Guise are raising in Lorraine."

" Are you mad? "

" No; a real army—at least six thousand men."

" But how can you, who fear M. de Mayenne so much, be defended by the soldiers of M. de Guise? "

" Because I am dead."

" Again that pleasantry."

" Now, it was to Chicot that M. de Mayenne owed a grudge. I have therefore taken advantage of my death to change my body, my name, and my social position."

" Then you are no longer Chicot? "

" No."

" What are you, then? "

" I am Robert Briquet, merchant and Leaguer."

" You a Leaguer? "

" A devoted one, so that I keep away from M. de Mayenne. I have, then, for my defence (for me, Briquet, member of the holy Union): first, the army of Lorraine—six thousand men; remember that number."

" I listen."

" Then, about one hundred thousand Parisians."

" Famous soldiers! "

" Sufficiently so to annoy you much, my prince. Six thousand and a hundred thousand are one hundred and six thousand. Then there is the pope, the Spaniards, M. de Bourbon, the Flemings, Henri de Navarre, the Duc d'Anjou—"

" Have you done? " interrupted Henri, impatiently.

" There still remain three classes of people who are opposed to you."

" What are they? "

" First, the Catholics, who hate you because you destroyed only three quarters of the Huguenots; then the Huguenots, who hate you because you have destroyed three quarters of them; and the third party is that which desires neither you nor your brother nor M. de Guise, but your brother-in-law, Henri de Navarre."

" Provided that he abjure. But these people of whom you speak are all France."

" Precisely. These are my troops as a Leaguer; now add, and compare."

" You are joking, are you not, Chicot? "

" Is it a time to joke, when you are alone against all the world, my poor Henriquet? "

Henri assumed an air of royal dignity. " Alone I am," said he; " but at the same time I alone command. You show me an army; but where is the chief? You will say M. de Guise; but do I not keep him at Nancy? M. de Mayenne, you say yourself, is at Soissons, the Duc d'Anjou is at Brussels, and the King of Navarre at Pau; so that if I am alone I am free. I am like a hunter in the midst of a plain waiting to see his prey come within his reach."

Chicot scratched his nose. The king thought he was convinced. " What can you reply to that? " he asked.

" How eloquent you are always, Henri! Your tongue remains your own; that is, in fact, more than I expected, and I offer you my sincere congratulations. In your discourse I object to only one thing."

" What is it? "

" Oh, nothing, almost nothing—a figure of rhetoric, merely;
I object to your comparison."

" In what respect? "

" You say that you are the hunter lying in wait for the game,
while I, on the contrary, maintain that you are the game,
whom the hunters track to his lair."

" Chicot! "

" Well, man lying in wait, let me hear whom you have seen
approach."

" No one, *pardieu !* "

" Yet some one has come."

" Of those whom I named? "

" Not exactly, but nearly."

" Who? "

" A woman."

" My sister Margot? "

" No; the Duchesse de Montpensier."

" She! at Paris? "

" *Mon Dieu !* yes."

" Well, what if she be? I do not fear women."

" True; but she comes to announce the arrival of her brother."

" Of M. de Guise."

" Yes."

" And you think that embarrasses me? "

" Oh! you? nothing embarrasses you."

" Give me ink and paper."

" What for? To sign an order for M. de Guise to remain at
Nancy? "

" Exactly; the idea must be good, since you had it also."

" Execrable, on the contrary."

" Why? "

" As soon as he receives it he will know he is wanted at Paris;
and he will come."

The king grew angry. " If you only returned to talk like
this," said he, " you had better have stayed away."

" What would you have, Henri? Ghosts are not flatterers."

" You confess, then, that you are a ghost? "

" I have never denied it."

" Chicot! "

" Come, don't get angry, for near-sighted as you are, you will
become blind. Let us see. Didn't you say that you kept
your brother in Flanders? "

" Certainly, and I maintain that it is good policy."

" Now listen, and let us not get excited; with what purpose do you think M. de Guise remains at Nancy ? "

" To organise an army."

" Well; and for what purpose does he destine this army ? "

" Ah, Chicot! you fatigue me with all these questions."

" You will sleep better after it. He destines this army—"

" To attack the Huguenots in the north—"

" Or rather, to thwart your brother of Anjou, who has called himself Duc de Brabant, and wishes to build himself a throne in Flanders, and who constantly solicits your aid in the prosecution of that purpose."

" Aid which I always promise him, and which, of course, I shall never send."

" To the great joy of the Duc de Guise. Well, if you were to feign to send this aid; if they only went half-way—"

" Ah, yes! I understand; M. de Guise would not leave the frontier."

" And the promise of Madame de Montpensier that her brother would be here in a week—"

" Would be broken."

" You see, then? "

" So far, good; but in the south—"

" Ah, yes; the Béarnais—"

" Do you know what he is doing? "

" No."

" He claims the towns which were his wife's dowry," said the king.

" Insolent! to whom the honour of an alliance with the House of France is not sufficient, and who permits himself to claim what belongs to him! "

" Cahors, for example; as if it would be good policy to give up such a town to an enemy."

" No, indeed, that would not be good policy; but it would be the act of an honest man perhaps."

" M. Chicot! "

" Let it be as if I had said nothing; you know I don't meddle with your family affairs."

" But to return to Flanders. I will send some one to my brother. But whom can I send? To whom can I trust a mission of so great importance? Oh! now I think of it, you shall go, Chicot."

" A dead man go to Flanders? Come, now! "

" No; you shall go as Robert Briquet."

" Good! a *bourgeois*, a Leaguer, a friend of M. de Guise,

performing the functions of an ambassador near M. le Duc d'Anjou!"

" That is to say, you refuse? "

" *Pardieu !* "

" You disobey me? "

" I disobey you? Do I owe you obedience? Have you ever given me anything which binds me to you? I am poor and obscure. Make me duke and peer; erect my land of Chicoterie into a marquisate; endow me with five hundred thousand crowns; and then we will talk about embassies."

Henri was about to reply, when the door opened, and the Duc de Joyeuse was announced.

" Ah! there is your man," said Chicot; " who could make a better ambassador? "

" Decidedly," murmured Henri, " this devil of a man is a better adviser than any minister of mine has ever been."

" Ah! you agree to it, then? " said Chicot. He then buried himself in the great chair, so as to be quite invisible in the dim light. M. de Joyeuse did not see him. The king uttered a cry of joy on seeing his favourite, and held out his hand.

" Sit down, Joyeuse, my child," said he; " how late you are! "

" Your Majesty is very good," answered Joyeuse, approaching the bed, on which he sat down.

CHAPTER XV

THE DIFFICULTY OF FINDING A GOOD AMBASSADOR

CHICOT was hidden in his great chair, and Joyeuse was half lying on the foot of the bed in which the king was bolstered up, when the conversation began.

" Well, Joyeuse," said Henri, " have you wandered much about the town? "

" Yes, Sire," replied the duke, carelessly.

" How quickly you disappeared from the Place de Grève! "

" Sire, to speak frankly, I do not like to see men suffer."

" Tender heart! "

" No; egotistical heart, rather. Their sufferings act on my nerves."

" You know what occurred? "

" No."

" Salcède denied all."

" Ah! "

"You take that very indifferently, Joyeuse."

"I confess I do not attach much importance to it; besides, I was certain he would deny everything."

"But since he confessed before the judges—"

"All the more reason that he should deny it afterwards. The confession put the Guises on their guard, and they were at work while your Majesty remained quiet."

"What! you foresee such things, and do not warn me?"

"I am not your minister, to talk politics."

"Well, Joyeuse, I want your brother."

"He, like myself, is at your Majesty's service."

"Then I may count on him?"

"Doubtless."

"I wish to send him on a little mission."

"Out of Paris?"

"Yes."

"In that case, it is impossible."

"How so?"

"Bouchage cannot go away just now."

The king looked astonished. "What do you mean?" said he.

"Sire," said Joyeuse, quietly, "it is the simplest thing possible. Bouchage is in love; but he has carried on his negotiations badly, and everything is going wrong. The poor boy is growing thinner and thinner."

"Indeed," said the king, "I have remarked it."

"And he has become sad, *mordieu!* as if he had lived in your Majesty's court."

A kind of grunt proceeding from the corner of the room interrupted Joyeuse, who looked round astonished.

"It is nothing, Joyeuse," said the king, laughing, "only a dog asleep on the footstool. You say, then, that Bouchage has become sad?"

"Sad as death, Sire. It seems he has met with some woman of a funereal turn of mind. However, one may succeed as well with this sort of woman as with others, if he knows how to take them."

"You would not have been embarrassed, libertine?"

"You understand, Sire, that no sooner had he made me his confidant than I undertook to save him."

"So that—"

"So that already the cure has begun."

"What! is he less in love?"

"No; but he has more hope of making her so. For the future, instead of sighing with the lady, we mean to amuse her in every possible way. To-night I stationed thirty Italian musicians under her balcony."

"Fie!" said the king; "that is common."

"What! common—thirty musicians who have no equals in the entire world?"

"Ah, upon my word, music would not have amused me when I was in love with Madame de Condé."

"No; but you were in love, Sire."

"Madly," said the king.

Another grunt was heard, which sounded very much like a mocking laugh.

"You see that this is quite another thing, Sire," said Joyeuse, seeking, but in vain, to see whence came that strange interruption. "The lady, on the contrary, is indifferent as a statue, and cold as an icicle."

"And you think music will melt the icicle, will animate the statue?"

"I do not say that she will come at once and throw herself into the arms of Bouchage; but she will be pleased on seeing that all this noise is made on her account. If she do not care for this, we shall have plays, enchantments, poetry—in fact, all the pleasures of the earth; so that even if we do not bring gaiety back to her, I hope we shall to Bouchage."

"Well, I hope so; but let us drop Bouchage, since it would be so trying to him to leave Paris. I hope you are not also, like him, the slave of some passion?"

"I never was more free, Sire."

"Oh! I thought you were in love with a beautiful lady?"

"Ah, yes! the mistress of M. de Mayenne—a woman who adored me."

"Well?"

"Well, imagine that this evening, after having given my lesson to Bouchage, I went to see her with my head full of his love-story, and believing myself almost as much in love as he. I found a trembling, frightened woman. The first idea that occurred to me was that I had interrupted some one. I tried to reassure her; but it was useless. I interrogated her; but she did not reply. I tried to embrace her; and she turned her head away. I grew angry, and we quarrelled; and she told me she should never be at home to me any more."

"Poor Joyeuse!" said the king, laughing, "what did you do?"

"*Pardieu*, Sire! I took my hat and cloak, bowed, and went out, without once looking back."

" Bravo, Joyeuse! it was courageous."

" The more so, Sire, that I thought I heard her sigh."

" But you will return? "

" No, I am proud."

" Well, my friend, this rupture is for your good."

" Perhaps so, Sire; but I shall probably be horribly bored for a week, having nothing to do. It may perhaps amuse me, however; it is something new, and I think it high-toned."

" Certainly it is; I have made it so," said the king. " However, I will occupy you with something."

" Something lazy, I hope? "

A third grunt came from the chair; one might have thought the dog was laughing at the words of Joyeuse.

" That is a very intelligent dog," said Henri. " He divines what I want you to do."

" What am I to do, Sire? " continued Joyeuse.

" Get on your boots."

" Oh, that is against all my ideas."

" Get on horseback."

" On horseback! impossible."

" And why? "

" Because I am an admiral, and admirals have nothing to do with horses."

" Well, then, Admiral, if it be not your place to mount a horse, it is so at all events to go on board ship. So you will start at once for Rouen, where you will find your admiral's ship, and make ready to sail immediately for Antwerp."

" For Antwerp! " cried Joyeuse, in a tone as despairing as though he had received an order to set out for Canton or Valparaiso.

" I said so," replied the king, in a cold and haughty tone, " and there is no need to repeat it."

Joyeuse, without making the least further resistance, fastened his cloak and took his hat.

" What a trouble I have to make myself obeyed! " continued Henri. " *Ventrebleu!* if I forget sometimes that I am the master, others might remember it."

Joyeuse bowed stiffly, and said, " Your orders, Sire? "

The king began to melt. " Go," said he, " to Rouen, where I wish you to embark, unless you prefer going by land to Brussels."

Joyeuse bowed without answering.

" Do you prefer the land route, duke? " asked Henri.

" I have no preference when I have an order to execute, Sire."

" There, now you are sulky. Ah! kings have no friends."

" Those who give orders can expect to find only servants."

" Monsieur," replied the king, angry again, " you will go, then, to Rouen; you will go on board your ship, and will take the garrisons of Caudebec, Harfleur, and Dieppe, which I will replace afterwards. You will put them on board six transports, and place them at the service of my brother, who expects aid from me."

" My commission, if you please, Sire."

" And since when have you been unable to act by virtue of your rank as admiral? "

" I only obey, Sire, and as much as possible avoid responsibility."

" Well, then, Monsieur the Duke, you will receive the commission at your hotel before you depart."

" And when will that be? "

" In an hour."

Joyeuse bowed and turned to the door. The king's heart misgave him. " What! " cried he, " not even the courtesy of an adieu? You are not polite; but that is a common reproach to naval people."

" Pardon me, Sire, but I am a still worse courtier than I am a seaman; " and shutting the door violently, he went out.

" See how those love me for whom I have done so much! " cried the king; " ungrateful Joyeuse! "

" Well, are you going to recall him? " said Chicot, advancing. " Because for once in your life you have been firm, you repent it! "

" Ah! so you think it very agreeable to go to sea in the month of October. I should like to see you do it."

" You are quite welcome to do so; my greatest desire just now is to travel."

" Then if I wish to send you somewhere you will not object to it? "

" Not only I do not object, but I request it."

" On a mission? "

" Yes."

" Will you go to Navarre? "

" I would go to the devil, great king."

" Are you joking, buffoon? "

" Sire, I was not very gay during my life, and I swear to you I am even sadder since my death."

" But you refused just now to leave Paris."

" My gracious sovereign, I was wrong, very wrong, and I repent."

" So that now you wish to leave Paris? "

" Immediately, illustrious king; this instant, grand monarch."

" I no longer understand you," said Henri.

" You have not, then, heard what was said by the Grand Admiral of France? "

" What was that? "

" That he had broken with the mistress of M. de Mayenne."

" Yes; well, what of it? "

" If that woman, in love with a charming fellow like the duke —for Joyeuse is charming—"

" Doubtless."

" If that woman dismisses him, sighing, it is of course for some reason."

" Probably; otherwise she would not dismiss him."

" Well, that reason, do you know what it is? "

" No."

" You cannot guess? "

" No."

" It is that M. de Mayenne is about to return."

" Oh, oh! " said the king.

" You comprehend at last?   I congratulate you."

" Yes, and I begin to believe that Mayenne will return."

" Well, then, I will go to Navarre if you wish to send me."

" I wish it, certainly."

" I wait your orders, gracious prince," said Chicot, assuming the same attitude as Joyeuse.

" But you do not know if the mission will suit you.   I have certain projects of embroiling Margot with her husband."

" ' Divide to reign ' was the A B C of politics one hundred years ago."

" Then you have no repugnance? "

" It does not concern me; do as you wish.   I am ambassador, that is all; and as long as I am inviolable, that is all I care for."

" But still you must know what to say to my brother-in-law."

" I say anything!   Certainly not."

" Not? "

" I will go where you like; but I will say nothing."

" Then you refuse? "

" I refuse to give a message; but I will take a letter."

" Well, I will give you a letter."

" Give it me, then."

" What! you do not think such a letter can be written at once?   It must be well weighed and considered."

" Well, then, think over it.   I will come or send for it early
to-morrow."

" Why not sleep here? "

" Here? "

" Yes, in your chair."

" *Peste !* that is done with; I shall sleep no more at the
Louvre.   A ghost to be seen asleep in an armchair—what an
absurdity ! "

" But you must know my intentions concerning Margot and
her husband.   My letter will make a noise, and they will question
you; you must be able to reply.   What the devil ! you represent
me; I don't want you to appear like a fool."

" *Mon Dieu !* " said Chicot, shrugging his shoulders, " how
obtuse you are, great king !   Do you think I am going to carry
a letter two hundred and fifty leagues without knowing what is
in it?   Be easy; at my first stopping-place I shall open your
letter and read it.   What! have you sent your ambassadors for
ten years to all parts of the world and know no better than that?
Come, rest in peace, and I will return to my solitude."

" Where is it? "

" In the cemetery of the Grands Innocents, great prince."

Henri looked at him in astonishment again.

" Ah! you did not expect that," said Chicot.   " Well, till
to-morrow, when I or my messenger will come—"

" How shall I know your messenger when he arrives? "

" He will say he comes from the Shade."   And Chicot disappeared so rapidly that the superstitious mind of Henri
doubted whether it was in fact a body or a shade which had passed
through that door without a sound, under that tapestry without
moving a fold.

CHAPTER XVI

THE DEATH OF CHICOT

CHICOT, in actual substance—we grieve to disappoint those
of our readers who favour the marvellous to the point of believing
that we should have the audacity to introduce a ghost into this
story—Chicot, then, had taken his departure after saying to the
king, under the guise of badinage according to his custom, all
the truths that he wished to declare.

This is what had happened.   After the death of the king's
friends, after the troubles and conspiracies fomented by the
Guises were entered upon, Chicot had reflected.   Courageous,

as we have seen him to be, and indifferent to events, he was yet disposed to make the most of all the incidents of experience, and find amusement in them, as do all men of superior endowments; for it is only the addle-brained who become weary of this world and seek diversion in the other.

Chicot's reflections led him to the conclusion that M. de Mayenne's vengeance was likely to prove more efficacious than the king's protection; and he said to himself, with his own characteristic philosophy, that in this world nothing can annul material fact; and, therefore, all the king's halberds and all his courts of justice could provide no remedy for an opening—even though almost imperceptible—which the blade of M. de Mayenne might make in Chicot's jacket. Besides, he was weary of playing the part of a jester, and of those royal familiarities which seemed to be leading him straight to destruction.

Chicot began, therefore, by putting between his own person and M. de Mayenne's sword the greatest possible distance. To that end he set out for Beaune, with the threefold purpose of getting away from Paris, embracing his friend Gorenflot, and tasting the famous wine of 1550, which is so warmly discussed in the letter which closes our story of *La Dame de Monsoreau*. It must be admitted that the consolation thus sought was sufficient to him. At the end of two months he could see that he had conspicuously increased in bulk, and reflected that in this way he was effectually disguised. But at the same time he observed that as he became more rotund he was coming to resemble Gorenflot more than was fitting for a man of intelligence. With him spirit still dominated matter.

After Chicot had imbibed the contents of several hundred bottles of the famous wine of 1550, and had devoured the twenty-two volumes comprised in the library of the priory—in which the prior had found the Latin maxim, *Bonum vinum lætificat cor hominis* [1]—he was aware of a great weight in his stomach, and a great void in his head.

" I might become a monk in good earnest," he said to himself; " but with Gorenflot I should be too much the master, and in any other abbey I should be not masterful enough. To be sure, the frock would conceal me for ever from the eyes of M. de Mayenne; but, by all the devils! there must be other means, less commonplace, worth seeking. I have read in another book, not included in Gorenflot's library: *Quere et invenies*." [2]

Chicot sought, therefore, and this is what he found. Under

---

[1] Good wine rejoices the heart of man.
[2] Seek and ye shall find.

the circumstances it was sufficiently original. He made a confidant of Gorenflot, and persuaded him to write to the king under his dictation.

Gorenflot wrote with difficulty, it is true; but he managed to state that Chicot had retired to the priory; that his sorrow on being obliged to separate from his master, when the latter had become reconciled with M. de Mayenne, had affected his health; that he had struggled against his regrets, but his grief had proved to be greater than his strength, and he had finally succumbed.

Chicot also wrote a letter to the king. This letter, dated in 1580, was divided into five paragraphs. These paragraphs were written from day to day, and reflected the progress of his disease. The first paragraph was written and signed with a firm hand; the second betrayed his faltering strength, and was signed in a tremulous hand; at the end of the third he wrote " Chic—; " at the end of the fourth, " Ch—; " at the end of the fifth only " C," with a scrawl.

That scrawl from the hand of a dying man produced on the king a painful effect, and explains his taking Chicot for a ghost.

We would gladly here present to our readers the letter of Chicot; but Chicot was, as we say nowadays, a very eccentric man. The style is the man; and his epistolary style was so very eccentric that we dare not reproduce his letter here, however effective we might expect it to be.

At the end of that letter, lest Henri's interest should grow cold, Gorenflot added that since the death of his friend the priory of Beaune had become odious to him, and he would prefer to live in Paris.

This postscript Chicot had with much difficulty drawn from Gorenflot's fingers; for Gorenflot was well satisfied with his situation at Beaune, as was also Panurge. He piteously begged Chicot to remember that wine is always adulterated, unless one is on the spot to choose it for himself. But Chicot promised the worthy prior that he would himself come every year to provide him with choice wines; and as, on this point among many others, Gorenflot recognised Chicot's superiority, he at last yielded to his friend's persuasions.

In reply to Gorenflot's letter and Chicot's words of farewell, the king wrote with his own hand as follows:—

MONSIEUR LE PRIEUR,—You will give a sacred and poetic burial to poor Chicot, whom I regret with all my heart; for he was not only a devoted friend, but was also a gentleman of rank, though unable to trace his genealogy beyond his great-great-grandfather.

You will surround him with flowers, and arrange so that he shall lie towards the sun, which he especially loved, being from the South. As to yourself, whose grief I honour the more since I share it, you will leave your priory of Beaune, according to the desire which you have expressed to me. I have too much need at Paris of devoted and intelligent men to allow you to remain at a distance. I therefore appoint you prior of the Jacobins, with a residence near the Porte Saint-Antoine, in Paris, a neighbourhood to which our poor friend was especially attached.—Your affectionate   HENRI,

Who begs you not to forget him in your holy prayers.

It may be easily imagined that an autograph like that, a letter written entirely by a royal hand, made the prior open his eyes; that he admired the power of Chicot's genius, and hastened to take flight toward the honours that awaited him. For ambition had already, as may be recalled, started one of its tenacious off-shoots in the heart of Gorenflot, whose name had always been "Modeste," and who, since he had become prior of Beaune, was called "Dom Modeste Gorenflot."

Everything took place according to the desires of the king, and those of Chicot at the same time. A bundle of sticks, designed to represent the corpse physically and allegorically, was buried in a sunny place, in the midst of flowers, beneath a flourishing vine. Then, once dead and buried in effigy, Chicot assisted Gorenflot in his preparations for removal.

Dom Modeste was installed with great pomp in the priory of the Jacobins.

Chicot slipped into Paris under cover of night. He purchased, near the Porte Bussy, a small house which cost him three hundred crowns. When he wished to visit Gorenflot he had three routes: that by way of the city, which was the shortest; that along the bank of the river, which was the most romantic; and that which followed the walls of Paris, which was the most sure. But Chicot, who was a dreamer, chose generally the route along the Seine; and since at that time the river was not yet confined between walls of stone, the water came, as says the poet, to lap its sloping shores, on which the dwellers in the Cité could often see Chicot's long shadow outlined by the bright light of the moon.

Once installed in his new abode, and having changed his name, Chicot gave himself to the task of changing his appearance. He called himself Robert Briquet, as we have already seen, and as he walked, was bent slightly forward. Moreover, anxiety and the lapse of five or six years had rendered him nearly bald; the black and curly hair of other days had withdrawn, as the ebbing sea retires, from his forehead back towards the nape of his neck.

We have already said that he was an adept in the art, so prized by ancient actors, of changing by skilful contractions the natural play of the muscles and the habitual expression of the features.

By dint of assiduous practice, Chicot was able, even in broad daylight, to become at will a veritable Robert Briquet,—that is to say, a man whose mouth was stretched from ear to ear, whose chin went up to his nose, and whose eyes were crossed in a way to make one shudder,—all this without grimace, but not without interest to the lovers of change; for Chicot's face, delicate, long, and angular as it was, became broad, ruddy, dull, and sodden. His long arms and legs he could in no way contrive to reduce; but by perseverance he managed, as we have said, to acquire a curve in his back, and that made his arms seem almost as long as his legs.

To these various exercises Chicot joined the precaution of avoiding intimate relations with any one. For however disjointed he might be, he could not keep himself in the same posture eternally; but how could he appear humped at twelve o'clock when at ten he had been seen upright? What excuse can you give a friend who sees you suddenly change your face because while walking with him you happen to meet one you suspect?

Robert Briquet adopted therefore the life of a recluse,—a life which agreed, moreover, with his inclination. His sole diversion was to visit Gorenflot and consume with him that famous wine of 1550, which the worthy prior had taken good care not to leave in the cellars of Beaune.

But vulgar souls, not less than great, are subject to change. Gorenflot changed. He beheld, fallen within his power and discretion, the man who thitherto had been the arbiter of his destiny. Chicot, coming to dine at the priory, seemed to him a Chicot in bondage, and from that moment Gorenflot thought too much of himself, and too little of Chicot.

Chicot noticed the change in his friend, but was not offended; the changes he had met in his companionship with King Henri had taught him to bear such things philosophically. He put himself more on his guard, and that was all. Instead of visiting the priory every day, he began to go there only once a week; then he went once a fortnight, and finally only once a month. And Gorenflot was so puffed up that he appeared to perceive no difference. Chicot was too philosophical to be sensitive; he laughed in his sleeve at Gorenflot's ingratitude, and scratched his nose and chin as usual.

"Water and time," he said, "are the two most powerful resolvents that I know: the one breaks rock, the other self-conceit. Let us wait."

Chicot waited; and while he waited those events happened which we have recited, and from the midst of which there seemed to him to arise certain new combinations which portended political catastrophe; and, therefore, since his king, whom he still loved,—dead though he was,—seemed to him, in the face of coming events, to incur certain dangers similar to those from which he, Chicot, had already rescued him, he took it upon himself to visit the king in the rôle of ghost, with the sole purpose of revealing to him the future.

We have seen how the announcement of M. de Mayenne's approaching arrival—an announcement involved in the return of Joyeuse, and which Chicot had sagaciously evolved—had caused Chicot to be transformed from ghost to flesh and blood, and from the condition of a prophet to that of an ambassador.

Now that all which might seem obscure in our narrative has been explained, by our readers' permission, we will follow Chicot as he goes from the Louvre and takes his way to his little house in Bussy Square.

CHAPTER XVII

THE SERENADE

FROM the Louvre Chicot had not far to go to his home. He went to the bank of the Seine and got into a little boat which he had left there.

"It is strange," thought he, as he rowed and looked at the still-lighted window of the king's room, "that after so many years, Henri is still the same. Others have risen or fallen; while he has gained some wrinkles, and that is all. He has the same weak, yet elevated mind; still fantastical and poetical; still the same egotistical being, always asking for more than one has to give him,— friendship from the indifferent, love from the friendly, devotion from the loving—and more sad than any one else in his kingdom. I believe, in fact, that I am the only one who has fathomed that strange compound of debauchery and repentance, of impiety and superstition, as I alone am acquainted with the Louvre, through the corridors of which so many favourites have passed on their way to the tomb, to exile, or to oblivion." He breathed a sigh, rather of reflection than of melancholy, and applied himself vigorously to his oars. "By the way," he said suddenly, "the king did not speak of giving me any money for my journey; that proves at least that he thinks me a friend." And he laughed quietly.

He soon arrived at the opposite bank, where he fastened his boat. On entering the Rue des Augustins, he was struck by the sound of instruments and voices in a quarter usually so quiet at that late hour. "Is there a wedding here?" thought he. "*Ventre de biche !* I had only five hours to sleep, and now this will keep me awake."

As he advanced, he saw a dozen torches carried by pages, while thirty musicians were playing on different instruments. The band was stationed before a house that Chicot, with surprise, recognised as his own. The invisible general who directed the affair had disposed musicians and pages in such a manner that all had their faces turned towards the house of Robert Briquet, and gazed at his windows in ardent contemplation. On observing that, Chicot was for a moment stupefied. Then, slapping his thighs with his bony hands, he said, "But there is some misunderstanding. All that noise cannot be made on my account." Approaching nearer, he mingled with the spectators who had been attracted to the scene, and looking attentively around, he became satisfied that all the light of the torches illumined his house, as all the harmony surrounded it; no one in that crowd was giving attention to the house opposite or to any others in that vicinity.

"In fact," Chicot said to himself, "it is for me! Has some unknown princess fallen in love with me?" But that idea, flattering as it was, did not satisfy him; and he turned towards the house facing his, but it showed no signs of life.

"They must sleep soundly there," said he; "*ventre de biche !* such a noise is enough to wake the dead. Pardon me, my friend," said he, addressing himself to a torch-bearer, "but will you tell me, if you please, for whom all this music is designed?"

"For the *bourgeois* who lives there," replied he, pointing out to Chicot his own house.

"Decidedly, it is for me!" thought he. "To whom do you belong?" he asked of a tambourine player, at that moment unoccupied.

"To the *bourgeois* who lives there."

"Ah! they not only come for me, but they belong to me— still better. Well, we shall see;" and elbowing his way through the crowd, he opened his door, went upstairs, and appeared at his balcony, in which he placed a chair and sat down. Without appearing to notice the laughter which greeted his appearance, he said, " Gentlemen, are you sure there is no mistake? Is all this really for me? "

" Are you M. Robert Briquet? " asked the director of the orchestra.

" Himself."

" Then we are at your service, monsieur," replied the Italian, with a movement of his baton which started a new outbreak of harmony.

" Certainly it is unintelligible," thought Chicot. He looked around; all the inhabitants of the street were at their windows, excepting those of the opposite house, which, as we have said, remained dark and quiet. But on glancing downwards, he saw a man wrapped in a dark cloak, and who wore a black hat with a red feather, leaning against the portico of his own door, and looking earnestly at the opposite house. The leader of the band from time to time left his post and spoke softly to this man. Chicot instantly understood that here lay all the real interest of the scene, and from that moment gave that person all his attention. Suddenly a gentleman on horseback, followed by two squires, appeared at the corner of the street and pushed his way through the crowd.

" M. de Joyeuse! " murmured Chicot, who recognised at once the Grand Admiral of France, booted and spurred in obedience to the king's order. The crowd dispersed; the music ceased. The cavalier approached the gentleman under the balcony. " Well, Henri," said he, " what news? "

" Nothing, brother, nothing."

" Nothing? "

" No, she has not even appeared."

" They have not made noise enough."

" They have roused all the neighbourhood."

" They did not cry, as I told them, that it was all in honour of this *bourgeois*."

" They cried it so faithfully that there he is, sitting in his balcony, listening to the serenade."

" And she has not appeared? "

" Neither she nor any one."

" The idea was ingenious, however," said Joyeuse, disappointed; " for she might, like the rest of the people, have profited by the music given to her neighbour."

" Ah, you do not know her, brother."

" Yes, I do; or at all events, I know women, and as she is but a woman, we will not despair."

" Ah! you say that in a discouraged tone, brother."

" Not at all; only give the *bourgeois* his serenade every night."

" But she will go away."

" Not if you do not speak to her, or seem to be doing it on her account, and remain concealed. Has the *bourgeois* spoken? "

" He has addressed the orchestra; and there he is, about to speak again."

In fact, Briquet, resolved to bring the matter to an explanation, rose to address once more the leader of the band.

" Hold your tongue up there and go in! " cried Joyeuse, out of humour. " What the devil! since you have had your serenade, you have nothing to say; so keep quiet! "

" My serenade! " replied Chicot, in his most polite manner; " but I should like to know at least to whom my serenade is addressed? "

" To your daughter, imbecile! "

" Pardon, monsieur; but I have no daughter."

" To your wife, then."

" Thank God, I am not married! "

" Then to yourself; and if you do not go in—" cried Joyeuse, urging his horse towards the balcony.

" *Ventre de biche !* but if the music be for me—"

" Old fool! " growled Joyeuse. " If you do not go in and hide your ugly face, they shall break their instruments over your head."

" Let the man alone, brother," said Henri; " the fact is, he must be very much astonished."

" And what right has he to be astonished, *morbleu ?* Besides, if we get up a quarrel, perhaps she will look to see what is the matter. So let us pommel the *bourgeois ;* let us burn his house, if necessary; but, *corbleu !* let us make a commotion! "

" No, for pity's sake, brother, do not let us force her attention! we are beaten, and must submit."

Chicot had not lost a word of this last dialogue, which had thrown some light on his still confused ideas. He therefore mentally prepared for his defence, knowing the humour of him who attacked; but Joyeuse yielded to his brother's request, and dismissed the pages and musicians. Then he said to his brother, " I am in despair; everything conspires against us."

" What do you mean? "

" I have no longer time to aid you."

" I see now that you are in travelling-dress; I did not remark it before."

" I set off to-night for Antwerp, by desire of the king."

" When did he give you the order? "

" This evening."

" *Mon Dieu!* "

" Come with me, I entreat."

" Do you order me, brother? " said Henri, turning pale at the thought.

" No; I only beg you."

" Thank you, brother. If I were forced to give up spending my nights under this window—"

" Well? "

" I should die."

" You are mad."

" My heart is here, brother; my life is here."

Joyeuse crossed his arms with a mixture of anger and pity. " If our father," he said, " begged you to let yourself be attended by Miron, who is at once a philosopher and a doctor—"

" I should reply to our father that I am well, and that my brain is sound, and that Miron cannot cure love-sickness."

" Well, then, Henri, I must make the best of it. She is but a woman, and at my return I hope to see you more joyous than myself."

" Yes, yes, my good brother, I shall be cured; I shall be happy, thanks to your friendship, which is my most precious possession."

" After your love."

" Before my life."

Joyeuse, deeply affected, notwithstanding his apparent frivolity, interrupted him.

" Let us go, brother," said he.

" Yes, brother, I follow you," said Bouchage, sighing.

" Yes, I understand—the last adieux to the window; but you have also one for me, brother."

Henri passed his arms round the neck of his brother, who leaned down to embrace him.

" No! " cried he. " I will accompany you to the gates." And with a last look towards the window, he followed his brother.

Chicot continued to watch. Gradually every one disappeared; and the street was deserted. Then one of the windows of the opposite house was opened, and a man looked out.

" There is no longer any one here, madame," said he; " you may leave your hiding-place and go down to your own room." And lighting a lamp, he gave it into a hand stretched out to receive it.

Chicot looked earnestly; but as he caught sight of her pale but sublime face, he shuddered and sat down, entirely subjugated, in his turn, by the melancholy influence of the house.

CHAPTER XVIII

CHICOT'S PURSE

CHICOT passed the remainder of the night dreaming in his armchair. " Dreaming " is the proper word, for they were dreams, rather than thoughts, that occupied his mind. To revisit the past, to see clearly in the light of a single glance an entire epoch almost effaced from memory—that is not to think. Chicot dwelt that night in a world already left by him far behind, peopled by shades illustrious or gracious, whom the glance of a pale woman, like a faithful lamp, showed to him passing one after another, with their trains of remembrances happy or terrible; so that he who on returning from the Louvre regretted his lost sleep did not even think of going to bed. When the dawn began to silver the glass of his windows, " The hour for ghosts has passed," he said; " it is time to think of the living." He rose, girded on his long sword, threw a cloak over his shoulders, and with the firmness of a sage, examined the bottom of his purse and his shoes. The latter seemed to him in good condition for a campaign; the former deserves particular attention.

Chicot, a man of an ingenious imagination, had made in the principal beam which ran through his house a cavity, a foot and a half long and six inches wide, which he used as a strongbox, to contain a thousand crowns in gold. He had made the following calculation: " I spend the twentieth part of one of these crowns every day; therefore I have enough to last me for twenty thousand days. I cannot live so long as that; but I may live half as long, and as I grow older my wants and expenses will increase. This will provide for twenty-five or thirty good years, and that is enough." He was therefore tranquil as to the future.

This morning, on opening his store, " *Ventre de biche!* " he cried, " times are hard; and I need not be delicate with Henri. This money did not come from him, but from an old uncle. If it were still night, I would go and take one hundred crowns from the king's pocket; but it is day, and I now have no resource but n myself or in Gorenflot."

This idea of drawing money from Gorenflot made Chicot smile. "It would be odd," thought he, "if Gorenflot should refuse a hundred crowns to the friend through whom he was appointed prior to the Jacobins. Ah!" he continued, shaking his head, "he is Gorenflot no longer. Yes; but Robert Briquet is always Chicot. But that letter from the king—that famous letter which is to kindle a conflagration in the court of Navarre —I was to go for it before day; and here it is day already."

Chicot replaced the board which covered his hiding-place, and fastened it with four nails; then, ready to depart, he looked for the last time around that little chamber, in which for many happy days he had been inaccessible and safe. Then he gave a glance to the house opposite. "Those devils, the Joyeuses," he said, "are quite capable of burning my house down some night to attract the lady to her window. And my thousand crowns! really, I think it would be better to hide them in the ground. However, if they burn my house, the king shall pay me for it."

Thus reassured, Chicot left the house, and at that moment saw at the window of the opposite house the servant of the unknown lady. This man, as we have said, was completely disfigured by a scar extending from the left temple over a portion of the cheek; but although bald and with a grey beard, he had a quick, active appearance, and a fresh and young-looking complexion. On seeing Chicot, he drew his hood over his head, and was going in; but Chicot called out to him, "Neighbour! the noise here last night has disgusted me with my house, and I am going for some weeks to my farm. Will you be so obliging as to look after my house a little?"

"Willingly, monsieur."

"And if you see robbers?"

"Be easy, monsieur; I have a good arquebuse."

"I have still one more favour to ask."

"What is it?"

"I hardly like to call it out."

"I will come down to you."

He came down accordingly, with his hood drawn closely round his face, saying, as a sort of apology, "It is very cold this morning."

"Yes," said Chicot, "there is a bitter wind. Well, monsieur, I am going away."

"You told me that before!"

"Yes, I know; but I leave a good deal of money behind me."

"So much the worse. Why not take it with you?"

" I cannot; a man is duller and less resolute when he has to save his purse at the same time with his life. Therefore I leave my money here; but I leave it well hidden—so well that I have nothing to fear but fire. If that should happen, will you who are my neighbour watch the burning of a certain great beam, the end of which you can see there on the right? Watch it and search in its ashes."

" Really, monsieur, you embarrass me. This confidence would have been far better made to a friend than to a stranger, of whom you know nothing."

" It is true, monsieur, that I do not know you; but I believe in faces, and I think yours that of an honest man."

" But, monsieur, it is possible that this music may annoy my mistress also, as well as yourself; and then she may move."

" Well, that cannot be helped; and I must take my chance."

" Thanks, monsieur, for your confidence in a poor unknown! I will try to be worthy of it; " and bowing, he went into the house.

Chicot murmured to himself, " Poor young man! what a wreck! and I have seen him so gay and so handsome! "

CHAPTER XIX

THE PRIORY OF THE JACOBINS

THE priory which the king had bestowed upon Gorenflot in recompense for his loyal services, and especially in recognition of his brilliant eloquence, was situated near the Porte St. Antoine. This was at that time a quarter much frequented, for the king frequently visited the Château de Vincennes, and several noblemen had built charming residences in its neighbourhood.

It was a good position for the priory, which arose proudly on the road to Vincennes. The priory was built on four sides of an immense court, planted with trees; it had a kitchen-garden behind, and a number of out-houses, which made it look like a small village. Two hundred monks occupied the dormitories situated at the end of the court, while in the front four large windows, with a balcony before them, gave to the apartments of the priory air and light.

Like a city prepared to stand a siege, the priory was maintained by its own resources and dependencies; its pasture-land fed a troop of fifty oxen and ninety-nine sheep—for by some traditional law, no religious order was allowed to possess one hundred of anything—while certain out-buildings sheltered ninety-nine pigs of a particular breed, which were most carefully reared and fattened. The espaliers of the priory, which were exposed to the midday sun, furnished peaches, apricots, and grapes; while preserves of these fruits were skilfully made by a certain Brother Eusèbe, who was the architect of the famous rock constructed of confectionery which had been presented to the two queens by the Hôtel de Ville of Paris at the last state banquet which had taken place there.

In the interior of this paradise for gourmands and sluggards, in a sumptuous apartment on the first floor, whose balcony overlooked the high-road, we shall find Gorenflot, ornamented with an additional chin, and characterised by that sort of venerable gravity which the constant habit of repose and good living gives to the most vulgar faces. Half-past seven in the morning had just struck. The prior had profited by the rule which gave to him an hour's more sleep than to the other monks, and now, although he had risen, he was quietly continuing his sleep in a large and luxurious armchair. The furniture of the room was more mundane than religious. A carved table, covered with a rich cloth; books of religious gallantry (that singular mixture of love and devotion which we meet with only at that epoch of art); expensive vases; and curtains of rich damask—were some of the luxuries of which Dom Modeste Gorenflot had become possessed by the grace of God, of the king, and especially of Chicot.

Gorenflot slept, as we have said, in his chair, when the door opened softly, and two men entered. The first was about thirty-five years of age, thin and pale, and with a look which commanded even before he spoke; lightnings seemed to dart from his eyes when they were open, although their expression was generally softened by a careful lowering of the white eyelids. This was Brother Borromée, who had been for the last three weeks treasurer of the convent. The other was a young man about seventeen or eighteen, with piercing black eyes, a bold look, of small stature, but well-formed, and whose turned-up sleeves displayed two strong arms quick in gesticulation.

" The prior sleeps still, Father Borromée," said he. " Shall we wake him? "

" On no account, Brother Jacques."

" Really, it is a pity to have a prior who sleeps so long, for we might have tried the arms this morning. Did you notice what beautiful cuirasses and arquebuses there were among them? "

" Silence, Brother! you will be heard."

" What a misfortune!" cried the young man, impatiently, stamping his foot; " it is so fine to-day, and the court is so dry."

" We must wait, my child," replied Borromée, with a feigned submission which the fire of his eyes contradicted.

" But why do you not order them to distribute the arms? "

" I order! "

" Yes, you."

" You know that I am not the master here; there is the master."

" Yes, asleep, when every one else is awake," replied Jacques, impatiently.

" Let us respect his rank and his sleep," said Borromée, overturning a chair, however, as he spoke.

At the sound Gorenflot looked up and said sleepily, " Who is there? "

" Pardon us," said Borromée, " if we interrupt your pious meditations; but I have come to take your orders."

" Ah! good-morning, Brother Borromée; what orders do you want? "

" About the arms."

" What arms? "

" Those which your reverence ordered to be brought here."

" I! and when? "

" About a week ago."

" I ordered arms? "

" Without doubt," replied Borromée, firmly.

" And what for? "

" Your reverence said to me, ' Brother Borromée, it would be wise to procure arms for the use of the brethren; gymnastic exercises develop the bodily forces, as pious exhortations do those of the soul.' "

" I said that? "

" Yes, reverend prior; and I, an unworthy but obedient brother, hastened to obey."

" It is strange; but I remember nothing about it."

" You even added this Latin maxim, *Militat spiritu, militat gladio.*"

" What!" cried Gorenflot, immeasurably astonished, " I added that maxim? "

" I have a faithful memory," said Borromée, lowering his eyes.

" Well, if I said so," Gorenflot replied, gently moving his head up and down, " it is because I had my reasons for saying so, Brother Borromée. In fact, that has always been my opinion, that it is necessary to exercise the body; and when I was simply a monk I fought with the word and with the sword —*militat—spiritu.* Very good, Brother Borromée; it was an inspiration from the Lord."

"Then I will finish executing your orders, reverend prior," said Borromée, retiring with Jacques.

"Go!" said Gorenflot, majestically.

"Ah!" said Borromée, "I had forgotten; there is a friend in the parlour who asks to see your reverence."

"What is his name?"

"Maître Robert Briquet."

"Oh, he is not a friend—only an acquaintance."

"Then your reverence will not see him?"

"Oh, yes! let him come up; he amuses me."

CHAPTER XX

THE TWO FRIENDS

WHEN Chicot entered, the prior did not rise, but merely bent his head.

"Good-morning," said Chicot.

"Ah, there you are! you appear to have come to life again."

"Did you think me dead?"

"Of course; I saw you no more."

"I was busy."

"Ah!"

Chicot knew that before being warmed by two or three bottles of old Burgundy, Gorenflot was sparing of his words; and since, considering the time of the morning, it was probable that he was still fasting, Chicot sat down to wait.

"Will you breakfast with me, M. Briquet?" asked Gorenflot.

"Perhaps."

"You must not be angry with me if it has become impossible for me to give you as much time as I could wish."

"And who the devil asked you for your time? I did not even ask you for breakfast; you offered it."

"Certainly I offered it; but—"

"But you thought I should not accept."

"Oh, no! is that my habit?"

"Ah! a superior man like you can adopt any habits, Monsieur the Prior," replied Chicot, with one of those smiles that were peculiarly his own.

Gorenflot looked at Chicot; he could not tell whether he was laughing at him or speaking seriously. Chicot rose.

" Why do you rise, M. Briquet? " asked Gorenflot.

" Because I am going away."

" And why are you going away, when you said you would breakfast with me? "

" I did not say I would; I said ' perhaps.' "

" You are angry? "

Chicot laughed. " I angry! " said he, " at what? Because you are impudent, ignorant, and rude? Oh, my dear monsieur, I have known you too long to be angry at your little imperfections! "

Gorenflot, astounded by that naïve sally on the part of his guest, remained with his mouth open and his arms extended.

" Adieu," said Chicot.

" Oh, do not go! "

" My journey will not wait."

" You travel? "

" I have a mission."

" From whom? "

" From the king."

" A mission from the king! then you have seen him again? "

" Certainly."

" And how did he receive you? "

" With enthusiasm; he has a memory, king as he is."

" A mission from the king! " stammered Gorenflot.

" Adieu," repeated Chicot.

Gorenflot rose, and seized him by the hand. " Come! let us explain ourselves," said he.

" On what? "

" On your irritability to-day."

" I! I am the same to-day as on all other days."

" No."

" A simple mirror of the people I am with. You laugh, and I laugh; you are rude, so am I."

" Well, I confess I was preoccupied."

" Really! "

" Can you not be indulgent to a man who has so much work on his shoulders? Governing this priory is like governing a province. Remember, I command two hundred men. I am at the same time manager, architect, intendant—all that without including my spiritual functions."

" Ah! it is too much indeed for an unworthy servant of God."

"Ah! you are ironical, M. Briquet. Have you lost all your Christian charity?"

"I had Christian charity, then?"

"I think that you are envious. Be careful; envy is a capital sin."

"Envious! of whom?"

"Why, you say to yourself, Dom Modeste Gorenflot is rising; he is on the ascending grade."

"While I am on the descending grade, I suppose?"

"It is the fault of your false position, M. Briquet."

"M. Gorenflot, do you remember the text, 'He who humbles himself shall be exalted'?"

"Nonsense!" cried Gorenflot.

"Ah! now he doubts the Holy Writ—the heretic!"

"Heretic! it is the Huguenots who are heretics."

"Schismatic, then."

"Come, what are you trying to say, M. Briquet? Really, you bewilder me."

"Nothing, but that I am setting out on a journey, and that I have come to make you my adieux; so good-by, Seigneur Dom Modeste."

"You will not leave me thus?"

"Yes, *pardieu !*"

"A friend!"

"In grandeur one has no friends."

"Chicot!"

"I am no longer Chicot; you reproached me with my false position just now."

"But you must not go without eating; it is not wholesome. You have yourself told me so twenty times. Come, let us breakfast."

"Oh, you live too badly here."

"Badly here!" murmured the prior, in astonishment.

"I think so."

"You had to complain of your last dinner here?"

"The horrible taste is still in my mouth; phew!"

"Of what? speak!"

"The pork cutlets were burned."

"Oh!"

"The stuffed ears did not crackle under your teeth."

"Ah!"

"The capon was soft."

"Good heavens!"

"The soup was greasy."

" For pity's sake!"

" The gravy was covered with oil, which yet floats in my stomach."

" Chicot! Chicot!" sighed Dom Modeste, in the same tone in which Cæsar, dying, said to his assassin, " Brutus! Brutus!"

" And then you have no time to give me."

" I!"

" You said so, did you not? It only remains for you to become a liar."

" Oh, I can put off my business; it was only a lady who asks me to see her."

" See her, then."

" No, no, dear M. Chicot! although she has sent me a hundred bottles of Sicilian wine."

" A hundred bottles of Sicilian wine!"

" I will not receive her, although she is probably some great lady. I will receive only you, dear M. Chicot. She wishes to become my penitent—that great lady who sends bottles of Sicilian wine by the hundred. Well, I will refuse her my spiritual counsels; I will send word to her to choose another director."

" You will do all that?"

" To breakfast with you, dear M. Chicot; to repair my wrongs towards you."

" Your wrongs spring from your savage pride, Dom Modeste."

" I will humble myself, my friend."

" From your idleness."

" Chicot! Chicot! beginning to-morrow, I will mortify myself by joining my monks in their exercise."

" Your monks in their exercise!" said Chicot, opening his eyes. " In what exercise—that of the fork?"

" No, of arms."

" Arms!"

" Yes; but it will be fatiguing to command."

" Who had this idea?"

" I, it seems."

" You! impossible!"

" Yes; I gave the order to Brother Borromée."

" Who is he?"

" The new treasurer."

" And whence comes this treasurer?"

" M. le Cardinal de Guise recommended him."

" In person?"

" No, by letter."

" Is it he whom I saw down below? "

" That is the man."

" He who announced me? "

" Yes."

" Oh, oh! " said Chicot, involuntarily; " and what qualification has he—this treasurer, so warmly recommended by the Cardinal de Guise."

" He reckons like Pythagoras."

" And it is with him you decided on these exercises of arms? "

" Yes, my friend."

" That is to say, he proposed to you to arm your monks? "

" No, my dear M. Chicot; the idea was entirely mine."

" And for what end? "

" To arm them."

" No pride, hardened sinner; pride is a capital sin. That idea did not originate with you."

" Oh, I do not know. And yet it must have been mine, for it seems that I pronounced a very good Latin text on the occasion."

" You! Latin! Do you remember it? "

" *Militat spiritu—*"

" *Militat gladio.*"

" Yes, yes; that was it."

" Well, you have excused yourself so well that I pardon you. You are still my true friend."

Gorenflot wiped away a tear.

" Now let us breakfast, and I promise to be indulgent."

" Listen! I will tell the cook that if the fare be not regal, he shall be placed in confinement; and we will try some of the wine of my penitent."

" I will aid you with my judgment."

CHAPTER XXI

THE BREAKFAST

GORENFLOT was not long in giving his orders. The cook was summoned.

" Brother Eusèbe," said Gorenflot, in a severe voice, " listen to what my friend M. Briquet is about to tell you. It seems that you are negligent; and I hear of grave faults in your last soup, and a fatal negligence in the crackling of your ears. Take care, brother, take care! a single step in a wrong direction may be irremediable."

The monk grew red and pale by turns, and stammered out an excuse.

" Enough," said Gorenflot; " what can we have for breakfast to-day? "

" Eggs fried with cocks' combs."

" What else? "

" Mushrooms."

" Well? "

" Crabs cooked with Madeira."

" Those are all trifles; tell us of something solid."

" A ham, boiled with pistachios."

Chicot looked contemptuous.

" Pardon! " cried Eusèbe; " it is cooked in sherry wine."

Gorenflot hazarded an approving glance towards Chicot.

" Good, is it not, M. Briquet? " said he.

Chicot made a gesture of half-satisfaction.

" And what have you besides? "

" You can have some eels."

" Oh, we will dispense with the eels," said Chicot.

" I think, M. Briquet," replied the cook, " that you can taste of my eels without regretting it."

" What! are they rarities? "

" I nourish them in a particular manner."

" Oh, oh! "

" Yes," added Gorenflot; " it appears that the Romans or the Greeks, I forget which—a people of Italy, in short—nourished their lampreys as Eusèbe does his eels. He read of it in an old author called Suetonius."

" What! Brother Eusèbe," cried Chicot, " you give men to your eels to eat? "

" No, monsieur; I mince the intestines and livers of fowls and game with a little pork, and make a kind of sausage-meat, which I throw to my eels, and they are kept in soft water, often renewed, in which they become large and fat. The one which I shall offer you to-day weighs nine pounds."

" It must be a serpent! " said Chicot.

" It swallowed a chicken at a meal."

" And how will it be dressed? "

" Skinned and fried in anchovy paste, and done with bread-crumbs; and I shall have the honour of serving it up with a sauce flavoured with garlic and allspice, lemons and mustard."

" Perfect! " cried Chicot.

Brother Eusèbe breathed again.

" Then we shall want sweets," said Gorenflot.

" I will invent something that shall please you."

" Well, then, I trust to you; be worthy of my confidence."

Eusèbe bowed and retired. Ten minutes after, they sat down, and the programme was faithfully carried out. They began like famished men, drank Rhenish wine, Burgundy, and Hermitage, and then attacked that of the fair penitent.

" What do you think of it? " asked Gorenflot.

" Good, but light. What is your penitent's name? "

" I do not know; she sent an ambassador."

They ate as long as they could, and then sat drinking and talking, when suddenly a great noise was heard.

" What is that? " asked Chicot.

" It is the exercise which is beginning."

" Without the chief? Your soldiers are badly disciplined, I fear."

" Without me! never! " cried Gorenflot, who had become excited with wine. " That cannot be, since it is I who command, I who instruct; and stay, here is Brother Borromée, who comes to take my orders."

Indeed, as he spoke, Borromée entered, throwing on Chicot a sharp and oblique glance.

" Reverend prior," said he, " we only wait for you to examine the arms and cuirasses."

" Cuirasses! " thought Chicot; " I must see this," and he rose quietly.

" You will be present at our manœuvres? " said Gorenflot, rising in his turn, like a block of marble on legs. " Your arm, my friend; you shall see some good instruction."

CHAPTER XXII

BROTHER BORROMÉE

WHEN Chicot, sustaining the reverend prior, arrived in the courtyard, he found there two bands of one hundred men each, waiting for their commander. About fifty among the strongest and most zealous had helmets on their heads, and long swords hanging to belts from their waists. Others displayed with pride rounded cuirasses, on which they liked to make a noise with an iron gauntlet. Brother Borromée took a helmet from the hands of a novice, and placed it on his head. While he did so, Chicot looked at it and smiled. " You have a handsome helmet there, Brother Borromée," said he. " Where did you buy it, my dear prior? "

Gorenflot could not reply, for at that moment they were
fastening a magnificent cuirass upon him, which, although
spacious enough to have covered Hercules Farnese, painfully
compressed the undulations of the flesh of the worthy prior.
" Not so tight! " cried he. " I shall stifle; stop! "

" You asked the reverend prior, I believe," said Borromée,
" where he had purchased my helmet."

" I addressed that question to the reverend prior, and not
to you," Chicot replied, " because I presume that in this convent,
as in all others, nothing is done except on the order of the
superior."

" Certainly," said Gorenflot, " nothing is done here but by
my order. What were you asking, dear M. Briquet? "

" I ask Brother Borromée if he knows where that helmet was
obtained."

" It made part of a lot of armour that the reverend prior
bought yesterday to arm the convent."

" I! " said Gorenflot.

" Yes; do you not remember that they brought several
cuirasses and helmets here, according to your reverence's
orders? "

" It is true," said Gorenflot.

" *Ventre de biche!* " thought Chicot; " my helmet is much
attached to me, for after I carried it myself to the Hôtel Guise,
it comes, like a lost dog, to find me at the priory of the Jacobins!"

At a sign from Borromée, the monks now formed into lines,
while Chicot sat down on a bench to look on.

Gorenflot stood up. " Attention! " whispered Borromée to
him.

Gorenflot drew a gigantic sword from the scabbard, and
waving it in the air, cried in the voice of a stentor, " Attention! "

" Your reverence will fatigue yourself, perhaps, in giving the
orders," said Borromée, softly; " if it please you to spare your
precious health, I will command to-day."

" I do indeed wish it," said Dom Modeste. " In fact, I am
suffering; I am stifling. Go on."

Borromée bowed and placed himself at the head of the troop.

" What a complaisant servant! " said Chicot. " That fellow
is a jewel."

" He is charming; I told you so."

" I am sure he does the same for you every day."

" Oh, every day! He is as submissive as a slave."

" So that you have really nothing to do here—Brother
Borromée acts for you? "

" Oh, *mon Dieu*, yes ! "

It was wonderful to see Borromée with his arms in his hands, his eye dilated, and his vigorous arm wielding his sword in so skilful a manner that one would have thought him a trained soldier. Each time that Borromée gave an order, Gorenflot repeated it, adding, " Brother Borromée is right; but I told you all that yesterday. Pass the pike from one hand to the other ! Raise it to the level of the eye ! A half-turn to the left is exactly the same thing as a half-turn to the right, except that it is just the contrary."

" *Ventre de biche !* you are a skilful instructor ! " said Chicot.

" Yes, I understand it well."

" And you have in Borromée an apt pupil."

" He understands me. Oh, yes ! he is very intelligent."

While the monks went through their exercises, Gorenflot said, " You shall see my little Jacques."

" Who is Jacques ? "

" A nice lad, calm-looking, but strong, and quick as lightning. Look ! there he is with a musket in his hand, about to fire."

" And he fires well."

" That he does."

" But stay—"

" What is it, then ? "

" But if—but no ! "

" Do you know my little Jacques ? "

" I ? not at all."

" But you thought for a moment that you did ? "

" Yes, I thought I had seen him in a certain church one day, or rather one night, when I was shut up in a confessional. But no, I was mistaken ; it was not he."

This time, we must confess, Chicot's words were not exactly in accordance with the truth. He was too good a physiognomist ever to forget a face that he had once seen. Meanwhile Jacques loaded a heavy musket, and placing himself at one hundred yards from the mark, fired, and the ball lodged in the centre, amid the applause of the monks.

" That was well done ! " cried Chicot.

" Thank you, monsieur ! " said Jacques, whose cheeks coloured with pleasure.

" You manage your arms well, my child," added Chicot.

" I study, monsieur."

" But he is best at the sword," said Gorenflot; " those who understand it say so ; and he is practising from morning till night."

"Ah! let us see," said Chicot.

"No one here, except perhaps myself, is capable of fencing with him; but will you try him yourself, monsieur?" said Borromée.

"I am but a poor *bourgeois*," said Chicot; "formerly I have used my sword like others, but now my legs tremble, and my arm is weak."

"But you practise still?"

"A little," replied Chicot, with a smile. "However, you, Brother Borromée, who are all muscle and tendon, give a lesson to Brother Jacques, I beg, if the prior will permit it."

"I order it," declaimed the prior.

All the monks came to make a ring around the pupil and the professor. Gorenflot leaned towards his friend and naïvely said, "It is almost as interesting as to chant vespers, is it not?"

"That is what the light-horse say," replied Chicot.

The two combatants prepared for the trial. Borromée had the advantage in height and experience. The blood mounted to the cheeks of Jacques and animated them with a feverish colour. Borromée gradually dropped all appearance of a monk, and was completely the master of arms. He accompanied each thrust with a counsel or a reproach; but often the vigour and quickness of Jacques triumphed over the skill of his teacher, who was several times touched. When they paused, Chicot said, "Jacques touched six times, and Borromée nine; that is well for the scholar, but not so well for the master."

A flash, unperceived by all but Chicot, leaped from Borromée's eyes, and revealed a new trait in his character.

"Good!" thought Chicot, "he is proud."

"Monsieur," replied Borromée, in a tone which he endeavoured to render calm, "the exercise of arms is a difficult one, especially for poor monks."

"Nevertheless," said Chicot, "the master ought to be at least half as good again as his pupil; and if Jacques were calmer, I am certain he would fence as well as you."

"I do not think so," replied Borromée, biting his lips with anger.

"Well, I am sure of it."

"M. Briquet, who is so clever, had better try Jacques himself," replied Borromée, in a bitter tone.

"Oh! I am old."

"Yes, but learned."

"Ah! you mock," thought Chicot; "but wait." Then he said, "I am certain, however, that Brother Borromée, like a wise master, often let Jacques touch him out of complaisance."

"Ah!" cried Jacques, frowning in his turn.

"No," replied Borromée; "I love Jacques, certainly, but I do not spoil him in that manner. But try yourself, M. Briquet."

"Oh no!"

"Come, only one pass!"

"Try," said Gorenflot.

"I will not hurt you, monsieur," said Jacques; "I have a very light hand."

"Dear child!" murmured Chicot, with a strange glance followed by a smile. "Well!" said he, "since every one wishes it, I will try;" and he rose slowly, and prepared himself with about the agility of a tortoise catching flies.

CHAPTER XXIII

THE LESSON

FENCING was not at that time the science that it is now. The swords, sharp on each side, were used almost as often to strike with the edge as to thrust with the point; besides, the left hand, armed with a dagger, was at the same time offensive and defensive, and hence resulted a number of slight wounds, which in a real combat kept up a continual excitement. Fencing, then in its infancy, consisted in a multitude of evolutions, in which the actor moved continually, and which, on a ground chosen by chance, might be continually impeded by the character of its surface.

It was common to see the fencer throw himself forward, draw back again, or jump to the right or left; so that agility, not only of the hand, but of the legs and of the whole body, was one of the first conditions of the art. Chicot did not appear to have learned in this school, but seemed to anticipate the modern style, of which the superiority and grace is in the agility of the hands and immovability of the body. He stood erect and firm, with a wrist at once strong and supple, and with a sword which seemed a flexible reed from the point to the middle of the blade, and an inflexible steel from the middle to the guard.

After the first passes, Jacques, seeing before him this man of bronze, whose wrist alone seemed alive, gave some impatient passes, which merely made Chicot extend his arm, and at every opening left by the young man, strike him full on the chest. At each of these strokes of the button, Jacques, red with anger and eagerness, made a leap backwards. For ten minutes he displayed all the resources of his wonderful agility; he flew like a tiger, twisted like a serpent, and bounded from right to left. But Chicot, with his calm air and his long arm, seized his time, and putting aside his adversary's foil, still sent his own to the same place, while Borromée grew pale with anger. At last, Jacques rushed a last time on Chicot, who, parrying his thrust with force, threw the poor fellow off his equilibrium; and he fell, while Chicot himself remained firm as a rock.

" You did not tell us that you were a pillar of the fencing-school," said Borromeé, biting his nails with vexation.

" I, a poor *bourgeois !* " said Chicot; " I, Robert Briquet, a pillar of the fencing-school! Ah, monsieur! "

" But, monsieur, to manage a sword as you do you must have practised enormously."

" Oh, *mon Dieu !* yes, monsieur, I have sometimes held the sword, and have always found one thing."

" What is that? "

" That for him who holds it, pride is a bad counsellor, and anger a bad assistant. Now, listen, Jacques," he added; " you have a good wrist, but neither legs nor head. You are quick; but you do not reason. There are three essential things in arms —first the head, then the hands, and then the legs. With the first you can defend yourself; with the first and second you may conquer; but with all three you can always conquer."

" Ah, monsieur," said Jacques, " try Brother Borromée; I should like to see it."

" No," said the treasurer; " I should be beaten, and I would rather confess it than prove it."

" How modest and amiable he is! " said Gorenflot.

" On the contrary," whispered Chicot, " he is stupid with vanity. At his age I would have given anything for such a lesson; " and he sat down again.

Jacques approached him, and admiration triumphing over the shame of defeat, " Will you give me some lessons, M. Briquet? " said he; " the prior will permit it, will you not, your reverence? "

" With pleasure, my child."

" I do not wish to interfere with your master," said Chicot, bowing to Borromée.

" Oh, I am not his only master," said he. " Neither the honour nor the defeat is wholly due to me."

" Who is the other, then? "

" Oh, no one ! " cried Borromée, fearing he had committed an imprudence.

" Who is he, Jacques ? " asked Chicot.

" I remember," said Gorenflot ; " he is a little fat man who comes here sometimes—a well-appearing man, who is a good drinker."

" I forget his name," said Borromée.

" I know it," said a monk who was standing by. " It is Bussy Leclerc."

" Ah, a good sword ! " said Chicot.

Jacques reiterated his request.

" I cannot teach you," said Chicot. " I taught myself by reflection and practice, and I advise you to do the same."

Gorenflot and Chicot now returned to the house.

" I hope," said Gorenflot, with pride, " that this is a house devoted to the king's service, and good for something, eh ? "

" *Peste !* I should think so ! " said Chicot. " One sees fine things, reverend prior, in visiting you."

" And all this in one month—in less than a month."

" And done by you ? "

" Done by me, by me alone, as you see," said Gorenflot, straightening himself.

" It is more than I expected, my friend; and when I return from my mission—"

" Ah, true, dear M. Chicot; let us speak of your mission."

" The more willingly because I have a message to send to the king before I go."

" To the king, my dear friend ! You correspond with the king ? "

" Directly."

" And you want a messenger ? "

" Yes."

" Will you have one of our monks ? It would be an honour to the priory ? "

" Willingly."

" Then you are restored to favour ? "

" More than ever."

" Then," said Gorenflot, " you can tell the king all that we are doing here in his interest."

" I shall not fail to do so."

" Ah, my dear Chicot ! " cried Gorenflot, who already believed himself a bishop.

" But first I have two requests to make."

" Speak."

" First, money, which the king will restore to you."

" Money! I have my coffers full."

" Faith! you are fortunate."

" Will you have a thousand crowns? "

" No, that is far too much; I am modest in my tastes, humble in my desires, and my title of ambassador does not make me proud; I conceal it rather than boast of it; therefore one hundred crowns will suffice."

" Here they are; and the second thing? "

" An attendant."

" An attendant? "

" Yes, to accompany me; I like society."

" Ah, my friend, if I were but free, as formerly."

" But you are not."

" Greatness enslaves me," murmured Gorenflot.

" Alas! " said Chicot, " one cannot do everything at once. But not being able to have your honourable company, my dear prior, I will content myself with that of the little Jacques; he pleases me."

" You are right, Chicot; he is a rare lad, who will go far."

" I will begin by taking him two hundred and fifty leagues, if you will permit it."

" He is yours, my friend."

The prior struck a bell, and when the servant appeared, said, " Let Brother Jacques come here, and also our messenger."

Ten minutes after, both appeared at the door.

" Jacques," said Gorenflot, " I give you a special mission."

" Me? " cried the young man, astonished.

" Yes, you are to accompany M. Robert Briquet on a long journey."

" Oh! " cried he, enthusiastically, " that will be delightful. We shall fight every day, shall we not, monsieur? "

" Yes, my child."

" And I may take my arquebuse? "

" Certainly."

Jacques bounded joyfully from the room.

" As to the message, I beg you to give your orders. Advance, Brother Panurge."

" Panurge! " said Chicot, to whom the name recalled certain pleasing remembrances, " Panurge! "

" Alas! yes," said Gorenflot; " I have chosen this brother, called Panurge like the other, to make journeys as the other did."

" Then our old friend is out of service."

" He is dead."

"Oh!" said Chicot, in a tone of sympathy; "but then he must have become quite old."

"Nineteen years, my friend; he was nineteen years old."

"That is a case of remarkable longevity," said Chicot; "it is only in convents that one finds such instances."

CHAPTER XXIV

THE PENITENT

PANURGE advanced. There was certainly nothing in either his moral or his physical character that entitled him to receive the name of an ass; he resembled a fox rather, with his small eyes, pointed nose, and projecting jaw. Chicot looked at him a moment, and in that moment measured his value as a messenger of the convent. Panurge remained humbly near the door.

"Come here, Monsieur the Courier," said Chicot. "Do you know the Louvre?"

"Yes, monsieur."

"And in the Louvre a certain Henri de Valois?"

"The king?"

"I am not so sure about that; but people generally call him so."

"Is it to him that I am to go?"

"Precisely; you will ask to speak to him."

"Will they let me?"

"Yes, till you come to his *valet de chambre*. Your frock is a passport, for the king is very religious."

"And what shall I say to the *valet de chambre*?"

"Say you are sent by the Shade."

"What shade?"

"Curiosity is a vice, my brother."

"Pardon!"

"Say then that you are sent by the Shade."

"Yes."

"And that you want the letter."

"What letter?"

"Again!"

"Ah! true."

"My reverend," said Chicot, turning to Gorenflot, "decidedly I liked better the other Panurge."

"Is that all I am to do?" asked the courier.

" You will add that the Shade will wait for it, going slowly along the road to Charenton."

" It is on that road, then, that I am to join you? "

" Exactly."

Panurge went to the door and lifted the *portière* to go out. It appeared to Chicot that in lifting the *portière* Brother Panurge had unmasked a listener. Chicot's acute mind was satisfied that Brother Borromée was listening.

" Ah, you listen," thought he; " so much the better, I will say something for your benefit."

" So," said Gorenflot, " here you are, honoured with a mission from the king, dear friend? "

" Yes, confidential."

" It relates to politics, I presume."

" So do I."

" What! you don't know with what mission you are charged? "

" I know that I am to carry a letter, that is all."

" A state secret, probably? "

" I think so."

" And you have no suspicion? "

" We are sufficiently alone for me to tell you what I think, are we not? "

" Speak; I am a tomb for secrets."

" Well, the king has finally decided to send aid to the Duc d'Anjou."

" Really? "

" Yes; M. de Joyeuse was to set out last night for that purpose."

" But you, my friend? "

" I go towards Spain."

" How do you travel? "

" Oh, anyhow; on foot, on horseback, in a carriage—just as it happens."

" Jacques will be good company for you."

" Thanks, my good friend. I have now, I think, only to make my adieux."

" Adieu; I will give you my benediction."

" Bah! it is useless between us."

" You are right; but it does for strangers;" and they embraced.

" Jacques! " called the prior; " Jacques! "

Borromée appeared.

" Brother Jacques! " repeated the prior.

" Jacques has gone."

" What! gone? " cried Chicot.

" Did you not wish some one to go to the Louvre? "

" Yes; but it was Panurge," said Gorenflot.

" Oh! stupid that I am," cried Borromée, " I understood it to be Jacques."

Chicot frowned; but Borromée appeared so sorry that it was impossible to say much. " I will wait, then," said he, " till Jacques returns."

Borromée bowed, frowning in his turn. " By the way," said he, " I forgot to announce to your reverence—and I came up for that—that the unknown lady has arrived and desires to speak to you."

" Is she alone? " asked Gorenflot.

" No; she has a squire with her."

" Is she young? "

Borromée lowered his eyes.

" Good! he is a hypocrite," said Chicot to himself.

" She appeared still young," said Borromée.

" My friend," said Gorenflot, turning towards Chicot, " you understand? "

" I will leave you," said Chicot, " and wait in a neighbouring room or in the court."

" It is far from here to the Louvre, monsieur," said Borromée; " and Jacques may be delayed, or they may hesitate to confide an important letter to a child."

" You make these reflections rather late," replied Chicot; " however, I will go on the road to Charenton, and you can send him after me." And he turned to the staircase.

" Not that way, if you please," said Borromée, " the lady is coming up, and she does not wish to meet any one."

" You are right," said Chicot, smiling; " I will take the little staircase."

" Do you know the way? "

" Perfectly." And Chicot went out through a cabinet which led to another room, from which led the secret staircase. The room was full of armour, swords, muskets, and pistols.

" They hide Jacques from me," thought Chicot, " and they hide the lady; therefore, of course I ought to do exactly the opposite to what they want me to do. I will wait for the return of Jacques, and I will watch the mysterious lady. Oh, here is a fine shirt-of-mail thrown into a corner; it is much too small for the prior, and would fit me admirably. I will borrow it from Gorenflot, and give it to him again when I return."

And he folded it together and slipped it under his doublet. He had just finished when Borromée entered.

Chicot pretended to be admiring the arms.

" Is monsieur seeking some arms to suit him? " asked Borromée.

" I! *mon Dieu!* what do I want with arms? "

" You use them so well."

" Theory, all theory; I may use my arms well, but the heart of a soldier is always wanting in a poor *bourgeois* like me. And then my breath fails me, and my legs are execrable; that is my principal defect."

" Permit me to observe, monsieur, that that defect is even more important in travelling than in a passage-at-arms."

" Ah! you know that I am travelling? " said Chicot, carelessly.

" Panurge told me," replied Borromée, colouring.

" That is queer; I thought I hadn't spoken of that to Panurge. But no matter; I have no reason to conceal myself. Yes, my brother, I am making a little journey; I am going to my own country, where I have property."

" Do you know, M. Briquet, that you have procured Brother Jacques a great honour? "

" That of accompanying me? "

" Yes, but especially that of seeing the king."

" Or his valet; for it is quite probable that Jacques will get no farther."

" You are, then, on intimate footing at the Louvre? "

" Oh, most intimate, monsieur! It is I who furnish the king and the young noblemen of the court with hosiery."

" The king? "

" I had his custom already when he was Duc d'Anjou. On his return from Poland he remembered me, and made me furnisher for his court."

" It is a fine acquaintance you have there, M. Briquet."

" The acquaintance with his Majesty? "

" Yes."

" Every one wouldn't say so, Brother Borromée."

" Oh! the Leaguers? "

" Every one is more or less a Leaguer now."

" You, surely, are not much of a Leaguer? "

" I? why do you say that? "

" When one knows the king personally."

" Eh, eh! I have my politics, like every one else."

" Yes, but your politics are in harmony with those of the king."

" Don't be too sure of that; we often dispute."

" If you disagree, how is it that he intrusts you with a mission? "

" A commission, you mean."

" Mission or commission, it is the same; the one or the other implies confidence."

" Pshaw! if I know enough to take my measures, that is all the king expects."

" Your measures? "

" Yes."

" Political or financial measures? "

" No, measures of cloth."

" What! " said Borromée, stupefied.

" Certainly; you can easily comprehend."

" I listen."

" You know that the king has made a pilgrimage to Notre-Dame de Chartres."

" Yes, to obtain an heir."

" Exactly. You know there is a sure way of arriving at the result which the king desires."

" It appears, at any rate, that the king does not employ that method."

" Brother Borromée! "

" What is it? "

" You know well that the only question is to obtain an heir to the crown by miracle, and not otherwise."

" And that miracle they seek— "

" At Notre-Dame de Chartres."

" Ay, yes! the chemise? "

" Yes, the king has taken her chemise from that good Notre-Dame, and has given it to the queen; and in exchange for that chemise he wishes to bestow a robe like that of the Notre-Dame de Toledo, which is said to be the most beautiful and the richest robe of the Virgin in the world."

" So that you are going— "

" To Toledo, dear Brother Borromée; to Toledo, to take the measure of that robe and make one like it."

Borromée appeared to hesitate whether he ought to believe or not the words of Chicot. After mature reflection, we are authorised to think he did not believe.

" You can judge, then," continued Chicot, as if not suspecting what was going on in the treasurer's mind, " how agreeable to me must be the company of men of the Church under such circumstances. But time passes, and Jacques cannot be long delayed; I will go and wait for him at the Croix Faubin."

" I think that will be best."

" Then you will tell him as soon as he comes? "

" Yes."

" And send him after me? "

" I will not fail."

" Thanks, Brother Borromée; I am enchanted to have made your acquaintance."

He went out by the little staircase, and Borromée locked the door behind him.

" I must see the lady," thought Chicot.

He went out of the priory and went on the road he had named; then, when out of sight, he turned back, crept along a ditch, and gained, unseen, a thick hedge which extended before the priory. Here he waited to see Jacques return or the lady go out.

CHAPTER XXV

THE AMBUSH

Chicot made a slight opening through the hedge, that he might see those who came and went. The road was almost deserted as far as he could see; there was no one but a man poorly clothed measuring the ground with a long pointed stick. Chicot had nothing to do, and therefore was preparing to watch this man, when a more important object attracted his attention.

The window of Gorenflot's room opened with folding-doors upon a balcony; and Chicot saw them open, and Gorenflot come out, with his most gallant manner and winning smile, leading a lady almost hidden under a mantle of velvet and fur.

" Oh! " thought Chicot, " here is the penitent. She looks young; it is very odd, but I find resemblances in every one I see. And here comes the squire. As for him, there is no mistake; I know him, and if he be Mayneville—*ventre de biche !* —why should not the lady be Madame de Montpensier? And, yes, *morbleu !* it is the duchess! "

After a moment, he saw the pale head of Borromée behind them.

" What are they about? " thought Chicot. " Does the duchess want to board with Gorenflot? "

At this moment Chicot saw M. de Mayneville make a sign to some one outside. Chicot looked round; but there was no one to be seen but the man measuring. It was to him, however, that the sign was addressed, for he had ceased measuring, and was looking towards the balcony. Gorenflot continued his courtesies to the penitent. M. de Mayneville whispered something to Borromée, and the latter began immediately to gesticulate behind the prior, in a manner unintelligible to Chicot, but apparently clear to this man, for he went to another place, where, on a new sign from Borromée and Mayneville, he remained fixed like a statue. After a few seconds, upon another sign made by Brother Borromée, he began a sort of exercise which engaged Chicot's attention the more, because he could not divine its purpose. He began to run quickly towards the gate of the priory, while M. de Mayneville held his watch in his hand.

" The devil! " said Chicot; " all this looks suspicious. The enigma is well put, but perhaps I could solve it, could I but see the face of that man of measures."

At that moment the man looked around; and Chicot recognised Nicolas Poulain—the man to whom he had sold his armour the day before. Shortly after, they all re-entered the room and shut the window, and then the duchess and her squire came out of the priory and went towards the litter which waited for them. Gorenflot accompanied them to the door, exhausting himself in bows and salutations. The curtains of the litter were still open, when a monk, in whom Chicot recognised Jacques, advanced from the Porte St. Antoine, approached, and looked earnestly into it. The duchess then went away, and Nicolas Poulain was following, when Chicot called out from his hiding-place, " Come here, if you please! "

Poulain started, and turned his head.

" Do not seem to notice, M. Nicolas Poulain," said Chicot.

The lieutenant started again. " Who are you, and what do you want? " asked he.

" I am a friend, new but intimate. What I want will take long to explain; come here to me."

" To you? "

" Yes; here in the ditch."

" What for? "

" You shall know when you come."

" But—"

" Come and sit down here, without appearing to notice me."

" Monsieur! "

" Oh! M. Robert Briquet has the right to be exacting."

" Robert Briquet! " cried Poulain, doing as he was desired.

" That is right; it seems you were taking measures in the road."

" I? "

" Yes; there is nothing surprising that you should be a surveyor, especially as you acted under the eyes of such great people."

" Great people! I do not understand."

" What! you did not know? "

" What do you mean? "

" You did not know who that lady and gentleman on the balcony were? "

" I declare—"

" Oh, how fortunate I am to be able to enlighten you! Only imagine, M. Poulain; you had for admirers Madame de Montpensier and M. de Mayneville. Do not go away. If a still more illustrious person—the king—saw you—"

" The king? "

" His Majesty, yes, M. Poulain; he is very quick, I assure you, to admire, and recompense labour."

" Ah, M. Briquet, for pity's sake! "

" If you move, dear M. Poulain, you are a dead man; keep still, therefore, and avoid that disgrace."

" But in the name of Heaven, what do you want with me? "

" Your good—nothing else; have I not said that I am your friend? "

" Monsieur," cried Nicolas Poulain, in despair, " I do not know what wrong I have ever done to the king, or to you, or to anybody! "

" Dear M. Poulain, my ideas may be wrong, but it seems to me that the king would not approve of his lieutenant of the provosty acting as surveyor for M. de Mayneville; and that he might also take it ill that you should omit in your daily report the entrance of Madame de Montpensier and M. de Mayneville yesterday into his good city of Paris."

" M. Briquet, an omission is not a crime; and his Majesty is too good—"

" M. Poulain, I see clearer than you; and I see—"

" What? "

" A gallows."

" M. Briquet! "

" And more—a new cord, four soldiers at the four cardinal points, a number of Parisians around, and a certain lieutenant of my acquaintance at the end of the cord."

Nicolas Poulain trembled so that he shook the hedge. " Monsieur! " cried he, clasping his hands.

"But I am your friend, dear M. Poulain, and I will give you a counsel."

"A counsel?"

"Yes; and very easy to follow. Go at once—at once, you understand—to—"

"Whom?"

"Let me think. To M. d'Epernon."

"M. d'Epernon, the king's friend?"

"Exactly; you will take him aside—"

"M. d'Epernon?"

"Yes, and you will tell him all about that measuring of the road."

"Is this madness, monsieur?"

"It is wisdom, on the contrary, the highest wisdom."

"I don't understand."

"It is clear, nevertheless. If I denounce you as the man of the cuirasses and measures, they will hang you; but if, on the contrary, you disclose all with a good grace, they will reward you. You do not appear convinced, however. Well, that will give me the trouble of returning to the Louvre, but I do not mind doing that for you;" and he began to rise.

"No, no; stay here! I will go."

"Good! But you understand—no subterfuges, or to-morrow I shall send a little note to the king, of whom I have the honour —such as you see me, or rather such as you do not see me—to be the intimate friend; so that if you are not hanged till the day after to-morrow, you will only be hanged the higher."

"I will go," said the lieutenant, terrified; "but you strangely abuse—"

"Eh, dear M. Poulain, erect altars to me. Five minutes ago you were a traitor, and I make you the saviour of your country. Now, go quickly, for I am in a hurry! The Hôtel d'Epernon; do not forget."

Nicolas Poulain ran off with a despairing look.

"Ah, it was time!" said Chicot, "for some one is leaving the priory. But it is not Jacques; that fellow is half as tall again."

Chicot then hastened to the Croix Faubin, where he had given the rendezvous. The monk who was there to meet him was a giant in height; his monk's robe, hastily thrown on, did not hide his muscular limbs, and his face bore anything but a religious expression. His arms were as long as Chicot's own; and he had a knife in his belt.

As Chicot approached, he turned and said, "Are you M. Robert Briquet?"

" I am."

" Then I have a letter for you from the reverend prior."

Chicot took the letter and read as follows:—

My dear Friend,—I have reflected since we parted; it is impossible for me to let the lamb which the Lord has confided to me go among the devouring wolves of the world. I mean, you understand, our little Jacques Clement, who has been received by the king and has fully performed your errand. Instead of him, who is too young, I send you a good and worthy brother of our order; his manners are good and his humour innocent, and I am sure you will like him. I send you my benediction. Adieu, dear friend.

" What fine writing!" said Chicot; " I will wager it is the treasurer's."

" It was Brother Borromée who wrote it," said the Goliath.

" In that case," said Chicot, smiling pleasantly at the great monk, " you will return to the priory, my friend."

" I? "

" Yes; and tell his reverence that I have changed my mind, and intend to travel alone."

" What! you will not take me, monsieur? " said the man, with astonishment, mixed with menace.

" No, my friend, no."

" And why, if you please? "

" Because I must be economical, and you would eat too much."

" Jacques eats as much as I do."

" Yes; but Jacques is a monk."

" And what am I? "

" You, my friend, are a gendarme, or a foot-soldier."

" What do you mean? Do you not see my monk's robe? "

" The dress does not make the monk, my friend; but the knife makes the soldier. Tell Brother Borromée that, if you please."

The giant disappeared, grumbling, like a beaten hound. As to our traveller, as soon as he had seen the man enter the great gate of the convent, he hid himself behind a hedge, took off his doublet, and put on the fine shirt-of-mail which we have mentioned. Having done that, he struck across country for the road to Charenton.

CHAPTER XXVI

THE GUISES

ON the evening of the same day on which Chicot set out for Navarre, we find again, in a large room at the Hôtel Guise, the person who, disguised as a page, had entered Paris behind Carmainges, and who was also, as we know, the penitent of Gorenflot. On this occasion no precaution had been taken to disguise her person or her sex. Madame de Montpensier, elegantly dressed, her hair glittering with precious stones, was waiting impatiently for some one.

At last a horse's step was heard; and the usher almost immediately announced M. le Duc de Mayenne. Madame de Montpensier ran to her brother so hastily that she forgot to proceed on the point of the right foot, as was her habit, in order to conceal her lameness. " Alone, brother? " said she; " you are alone? "

" Yes, my sister," said the duke, seating himself, after kissing the duchess's hand.

" But Henri; where is Henri? Do you know that every one expects him here? "

" Henri has nothing to do here, and plenty to do in Flanders and Picardy. We have work to do there; and why should we leave it to come here, where our work is done? "

" But where it will be quickly undone, if you do not hasten."

" Bah ! "

" Bah as much as you please, brother; I tell you the citizens will be put off no longer; they insist upon seeing their Duc Henri."

" They shall see him at the right time. And Salcède? "

" Is dead."

" Without speaking? "

" Without uttering a word."

" Good ! and the arming? "

" Finished."

" And Paris? "

" Is divided into sixteen quarters."

" And each quarter has the chief whom we have appointed? "

" Yes."

" Then let us live in peace; and so I shall say to our good *bourgeoisie*."

" They will not listen to you."

" Bah ! "

" I tell you they are furious."

" My sister, you judge others by your own impatience. What Henri says, must be done; and he says we are to remain quiet."

" What is to be done, then ? " asked the duchess, impatiently.

" What do you wish to do ? "

" Firstly, to take the king."

" That is your fixed idea; I do not say it is bad, if it could be done, but think how often we have failed already."

" Times are changed; the king has no longer defenders."

" No; except the Swiss, Scotch, and French guards."

" My brother, when you wish it, I will show you the king on the road with only two lackeys."

" I have heard that a hundred times, and never seen it once."

" You will see it if you stay here only three days."

" Still another project? "

" A plan, if you please."

" In that case, tell me about it."

" Oh! it is only a woman's idea; and you will laugh at it."

" God forbid that I should wound your pride as an author! But let me hear the plan."

" You are laughing at me, Mayenne."

" No, I am listening."

" Very well; in four words it is—"

At this moment M. de Mayneville was announced.

" My accomplice," said the duchess; " let him enter."

M. de Mayneville entered, and approaching the Duc de Mayenne, kissed his hand. " One word, monseigneur," said he; " your arrival is suspected at the Louvre."

" How so ? "

" I was conversing with the captain of the guard at St. Germain l'Auxerrois, when two Gascons passed."

" Do you know them? "

" No; they were quite newly dressed. '*Cap de Bious !*' said one, ' you have a magnificent doublet; but it will not render you so much service as your cuirass of yesterday.' ' Bah!' said the other; ' however heavy the sword of M. de Mayenne may be, it will do no more harm to this satin than to my cuirass;' and then he went on in a series of bravadoes, which showed that they knew you were near."

" And to whom did these men belong? "

" I do not know; they talked so loudly that some passers-by approached, and asked if you were really coming. They were about to reply, when a man approached, whom I think was

Loignac, and touched them on the shoulder. He said some words in a low voice, and they looked submissive, and accompanied him, so that I know no more; but be on your guard!"

"You did not follow them?"

"Yes, but from afar. They went towards the Louvre and disappeared behind the Hôtel des Meubles."

"I have a very simple method of reply," said the duke.

"What is it?" asked his sister.

"To go and pay my respects to the king to-night."

"To the king?"

"Certainly. I have come to Paris; I bring him news from Picardy—he can have nothing to say against that."

"The idea is good," said Mayneville.

"It is imprudent," said the duchess.

"It is indispensable, sister, if they indeed suspect my arrival. Besides it was the advice of Henri that I should go at once and present to the king the respects of the family; that once done, I am free, and can receive whom I please."

"The members of the committee, for example, who expect you."

"I will receive them at the Hôtel St. Denis on my return from the Louvre. You will wait for us, if you please, my sister."

"Here?"

"No; at the Hôtel St. Denis, where I have left my equipages. I shall be there in two hours."

CHAPTER XXVII

THE LOUVRE

THAT same day, about noon, the king came out of his cabinet and called for M. d'Epernon. The duke, when he came, found the king attentively examining a young Jacobin, who blushed and lowered his eyes under the searching scrutiny of the king.

The king took D'Epernon aside. "Look, what an odd-looking monk!" said he.

"Does your Majesty think so? I think him rather ordinary."

"Really!" Then to the monk the king said, "What is your name?"

"Brother Jacques, Sire."

"Your family name?"

"Clement."

"Good! You have performed your commission very well."

"What commission, Sire?" said the duke, with his wonted familiarity.

"Nothing!" said Henri. "It is a little secret between me and some one you do not know."

"How strangely you look at the lad, Sire! You embarrass him."

"It is true; I know not why, but it seems to me that I have seen him before; perhaps it was in a dream. Go, my child; I will send the letter to him who asks for it. Be easy. D'Epernon, give him ten crowns."

"Thanks, Sire," said the monk.

"You did not say that as if you meant it," said D'Epernon, who did not understand a monk despising ten crowns.

"I would rather have one of those beautiful Spanish knives on the wall," said Jacques.

"What! you do not prefer money?"

"I have made a vow of poverty."

"Give him a knife, then, and let him go, Lavalette," said the king.

The duke chose one of the least costly and gave it to him. Jacques took it, quite joyful to possess such a beautiful weapon. When he had gone, the king said to D'Epernon, "Duke, have you among your Forty-five two or three men who can ride?"

"Twelve, at least, Sire; and in a month all will be good horsemen."

"Then choose two, and let them come to me at once."

The duke went out, and calling Loignac, said to him, "Choose me two good horsemen, to execute a commission for his Majesty."

Loignac went to the gallery where they were lodged, and called M. de Carmainges and M. de Sainte-Maline. They soon appeared, and were conducted to the duke, who presented them to the king. The duke then withdrew, and the two young men remained.

"You are of my Forty-five, gentlemen?" said the king.

"I have that honour, Sire," said Sainte-Maline.

"And you, monsieur?"

"And I also, Sire," replied Carmainges; "and I am devoted to your Majesty's service, as much as any one in the world."

"Good! Then mount your horses, and take the road to Tours; do you know it?"

"We will inquire."

"Go by way of Charenton."

"Yes, Sire."

" And proceed till you overtake a man travelling alone."

" Will your Majesty describe him? " said Sainte-Maline.

" He has long arms and legs, and has a large sword by his side."

" May we know his name, Sire? " asked Carmainges.

" He is called ' the Shade.' "

" We will ask the name of every traveller we see, Sire."

" And we will search the hotels."

" When you find him, give him this letter."

Both the young men held out their hands.

The king remained for a moment embarrassed. " What is your name? " said he to one of them.

" Ernauton de Carmainges, Sire."

" And yours? "

" René de Sainte-Maline."

" M. de Carmainges, you shall carry the letter; and you, M. de Sainte-Maline, shall deliver it."

Ernauton took the precious charge, and was going to place it in his doublet, when Sainte-Maline stopped him, kissed the letter, and then returned it to Ernauton. This made Henri smile. " Come, gentlemen," said he; " I see I shall be well served."

" Is this all, Sire? "

" Yes, gentlemen; only our last recommendation. This letter is more precious than the life of a man. Upon your lives, do not lose it. Give it secretly to the Shade, who will give you a receipt for it, which you will bring back to me; and above all, travel as though it were on your own affairs. Go."

The two young men went out—Ernauton full of joy, and Sainte-Maline full of jealousy. M. d'Epernon waited for them, and wished to question them, but Ernauton replied, " Monsieur the Duke, the king did not authorise us to speak."

They went to the stables, and the king's huntsman gave them two strong horses. M. d'Epernon would have followed them, but at that moment he was told that a man wished to speak to him at once.

" Who is he? " he asked.

" The lieutenant of the provosty of Paris."

" *Parfandious !* am I sheriff or provost? "

" No, monsigneur; but you are a friend of the king, and, as such, I beg you to hear me," said a humble voice at his side.

The duke turned. Near him was a man bowing perpetually.

" Who are you? " asked the duke.

" Nicolas Poulain, at your service, monseigneur."

" And you wish to speak to me? "

" I beg for that favour."

" I have no time."

" Not even to hear a secret? "

" I hear a hundred every day, monsieur. Yours would make a hundred and one; that would be one too many."

" But this concerns the life of his Majesty," said Poulain, in a low voice.

" Oh, oh! then come into my cabinet."

CHAPTER XXVIII

THE REVELATION

M. D'EPERNON, while crossing the antechamber, addressed himself to one of the gentlemen who stood there. " What is your name, monsieur? " said he.

" Pertinax de Montcrabeau, monseigneur."

" Well, M. de Montcrabeau, place yourself at that door, and let no one enter."

" Yes, Monsieur the Duke;" and M. Pertinax, who was sumptuously dressed, with a blue satin doublet and orange stockings, obeyed. Nicolas Poulain followed the duke into his cabinet. He saw the door open and shut, then the *portière* fall over the door, and he began to tremble.

" Now let us hear your conspiracy," said the duke.

" Oh, Monsieur the Duke, it concerns the most frightful crimes."

" They wish to kill me, I suppose."

" It does not concern you, monsieur; it is the king. They wish to carry him off."

" Oh, again that old story," replied the duke, disdainfully.

" This time the thing is serious, Monsieur the Duke."

" On what day do they intend to do it? "

" The first time that his Majesty goes to Vincennes in his litter."

" How will they do it? "

" By killing his two attendants."

" And who will do it? "

" Madame de Montpensier."

D'Epernon began to laugh. " That poor duchess! what things are attributed to her! "

" Less than she projects, monsieur."

" And she occupies herself with that at Soissons? "

" No; she is in Paris."

" In Paris! "

" I can answer for it."

" Have you seen her? "

" Yes."

" That is to say, you thought you did."

" I have had the honour of speaking to her."

" The honour! "

" I am wrong; the misfortune."

" But, my dear lieutenant, the duchess cannot carry off the king."

" With her associates, of course."

" And where will she be when this takes place? "

" At a window of the Jacobin priory, which is, as you know, on the road to Vincennes."

" What the devil do you tell me? "

" The truth, monsieur; all is prepared to stop the litter at the gate of the priory."

" And who made the preparations? "

" Alas! "

" Finish quickly! "

" I did, monseigneur."

D'Epernon started back. " You, who denounce them? "

" Monsieur, a good servant should risk all in the service of the king."

" *Mordieu !* you risk hanging."

" I prefer death to infamy, or to the death of the king; therefore I came. And I thought, Monsieur the Duke, that you, the friend of the king, would not betray me, and would turn my news to good account."

The duke looked fixedly at Poulain. " There must be more in it," said he; " resolute as the duchess is, she would not attempt such an enterprise alone."

" She expects her brother."

" The Duc Henri? " cried D'Epernon, with the terror one might feel on the approach of a lion.

" No, monsieur; only the Duc de Mayenne."

" Ah, good! " said D'Epernon; " now I must set to work to counteract these fine projects."

" Doubtless, monsieur; it was for that I hastened hither."

" If you have spoken the truth, you shall be rewarded."

" Why should I lie, monseigneur—I, who eat the king's bread? If you do not believe me, I will go to the king himself, and will die, if I must, to prove my words."

" No, *parfandious !* you shall not go to the king; you shall
have to deal with me alone."

" So be it, monseigneur; I said that only because you seemed
to hesitate."

" No, I do not hesitate; and to begin with, I owe you a
thousand crowns, and you shall keep this secret between you
and me."

" I have a family, monsieur."

" Well! a thousand crowns, *parfandious !* "

" If they knew in Lorraine that I had spoken, each word
would cost me a pint of blood; and in case of any misfortune, my
family must be able to live, therefore I accept a thousand crowns."

" To the devil with your explanation! What matters it to
me for what reason you accept, so long as you do not refuse?
The thousand crowns are yours."

" Thank you, monseigneur."

The duke approached a coffer. Poulain thought it was for
the money, and held out his hand, but the duke only drew out
a little book and wrote, " Three thousand livres to M. Nicolas
Poulain." " It is as if you had them," said he.

Nicolas bowed, and looked puzzled.

" Then it is agreed? " said the duke

" What is agreed, monseigneur? "

" That you will continue to instruct me? "

Nicolas hesitated; it was the office of a spy that was imposed
on him.

" What! has your noble devotion vanished already? "

" No, monseigneur."

" Then I may count on you? "

" You may."

" And I alone know this? "

" You alone."

" Now you may go, my friend; and, *parfandious !* let M. de
Mayenne look to himself! "

When D'Epernon returned to the king he found him playing
at cup and ball. D'Epernon assumed a thoughtful air, but
the king did not remark it. However, as the duke remained
obstinately silent, the king raised his head and said, " Well,
Lavalette, what is the matter? Are you dead? "

" I wish I were," replied D'Epernon; " I should not see
what I do see."

" What, my cup and ball? "

" Sire, in a time of great peril the subject may be alarmed
for the safety of his master."

" What! again perils? devil take you, duke!"

" Then you are ignorant of what is going on?"

" Faith! yes, perhaps."

" Your most cruel enemies surround you at this moment."

" Bah! who are they?"

" First, the Duchesse de Montpensier."

" Yes, that is true; she came to see Salcède. But what is that to me?"

" You knew it, then?"

" You see I did, since I tell it to you."

" But that M. de Mayenne has arrived, did you know that also?"

" Yes, since yesterday evening."

" What! this secret?" cried D'Epernon, with a disagreeable surprise.

" Are there, then, any secrets from the king? You are zealous, dear Lavalette, but you are slow. This news would have been good at four o'clock yesterday, but to-day—"

" Well, Sire, to-day?"

" It comes a little late, you will admit?"

" Still too soon, Sire, it seems, since you will not listen to me."

" I have been listening for half an hour."

" You are menaced; they lay ambushes for you."

" Well, yesterday you gave me a guard, and assured me that my immortality was secured. Are your Forty-five no longer worth anything?"

" Your Majesty shall see what they are."

" I should not be sorry, duke; when shall I see?"

" Sooner perhaps than you think."

" Ah! you want to frighten me."

" You shall see, Sire. By the way, when do you go to Vincennes?"

" On Saturday."

" That is enough, Sire." D'Epernon bowed and withdrew.

CHAPTER XXIX

TWO FRIENDS

WE will now follow the two young men sent by the king. Scarcely on horseback, Ernauton and Sainte-Maline, determined that one should not get before the other in the gateway, nearly crushed each other in the gateway. The face of Sainte-Maline became purple, and that of Ernauton pale.

" You hurt me, monsieur," cried the former after they had passed through; " do you wish to crush me? "

" You also hurt me, only I did not complain."

" You wish to give a lesson, I believe? "

" I wish to give you nothing."

" Ah! " cried Sainte-Maline, urging forward his horse so as to be nearer his companion, " pray repeat that."

" You are seeking a quarrel, are you not? " replied Ernauton, quietly; " so much the worse for you."

" And why should I wish to quarrel? I do not know you," answered Sainte-Maline, disdainfully.

" You know me well, monsieur; for in the country from which we come my house is but two leagues from yours, and I am well known there, being of an old family. But you are furious at seeing me in Paris when you thought that you alone were sent for; also, because the king gave me the letter to carry."

" Well," said Sainte-Maline, white with anger; " I admit all that you say; but there is one result."

" What is it? "

" That I do not like to be near you."

" Go away, then; *pardieu*, I do not want to keep you."

" You appear not to understand me."

" On the contrary, I understand perfectly. You would like to take the letter from me and carry it yourself; but unfortunately you must kill me first."

" And who tells you that I do not wish to do that? "

" To desire and to do are two different things."

" Descend with me to the banks of the water, and you will see that with me they are the same."

" My dear monsieur, when the king gives me a letter to carry, I carry it."

" I will tear it from you by force."

" You will not force me, I hope, to shoot you like a dog."

" You! "

" Yes; I have a pistol, and you have not."

" You shall pay for this."

" I trust so, after my commission is over; but meanwhile I beg you to observe that as we belong to the king it is setting a bad example to quarrel."

Sainte-Maline was furious, and bit his fingers with rage.

" There, there, monsieur! " said Ernauton, " keep your hands to hold the sword when we shall come to that."

" Oh, I shall burst! " cried Sainte-Maline.

" A task less for me," said Ernauton.

It is impossible to say how far the still increasing rage of Sainte-Maline would have carried him, for suddenly Ernauton, in crossing the Rue St. Antoine, saw a litter, and uttering a cry of surprise, stopped short to look at a woman half-veiled. " My page of yesterday! " he murmured. The lady gave no indication that she recognised him, but leaned back in her litter.

" *Cordieu !* you keep me waiting," said Sainte-Maline, " and that to look at women! "

" I beg pardon, monsieur," said Ernauton, resuming his course.

The young men now rode on without speaking. Sainte-Maline soon discovered, to his chagrin, that his horse was not as good as Ernauton's, and could hardly keep pace with him. This annoyed him so much that he began to quarrel with his horse, and he so tormented him with whip and spur that at last the animal started off and made for the river Bièvre, where he got rid of his rider by throwing him in. One might have heard half a mile off the imprecations of Sainte-Maline, although he was half stifled by the water. By the time he scrambled out, his horse had got some little way off. He himself was wet and muddy, and his face bleeding with scratches, and he felt sure that it was useless to try and catch it; and to complete his vexation he saw Ernauton going down a cross-road which he judged to be a short cut.

He climbed up the banks of the river, but now could see neither Ernauton nor his own horse. But while he stood there, full of sinister thoughts towards Ernauton, he saw him reappear from the cross-road, leading the runaway horse, which he had made a *détour* to catch. At this sight Sainte-Maline was full of joy and even of gratitude; but gradually his face clouded again as he thought of the superiority of Ernauton over himself, for he knew that in the same situation he should not even have thought of acting in a similar manner.

He stammered out thanks, to which Ernauton paid no attention, then furiously seized the reins of his horse and mounted again. They rode on silently till about half-past two, when they saw a man walking with a dog by his side. Ernauton passed him; but Saint-Maline, hoping to be more clever, rode up to him and said, " Traveller, do you expect something? "

The man looked at him. Certainly his aspect was not agreeable. His face still bore marks of anger; and the mud half dried on his clothes, the blood on his cheeks, and his hand extended more in menace than interrogation, all seemed very sinister to the traveller.

"If I expect something," said he, "it is not some one; and if I expect some one it is not you."

"You are very impolite, my master!" said Sainte-Maline, glad to find at last an opportunity to let loose his wrath, and furious besides at having afforded by his mistake a new triumph to his adversary. While he spoke, he raised his arm to strike the traveller with his whip, but he, with his stick, struck Sainte-Maline on the shoulder, while the dog rushed at him, tearing his clothes, as well as his horse's legs.

The horse, irritated by the pain, rushed furiously on. Sainte-Maline could not stop him for some time, but he kept his seat. They passed thus before Ernauton, who saw him go by without even smiling at his misfortune. When Sainte-Maline had succeeded in quieting his horse, and M. de Carmainges had rejoined him, his pride had not diminished, but impelled him to attempt a compromise. "Come, come!" said he, forcing a smile, "it seems I have fallen on my unlucky day. That man, however, bore a close resemblance to him whom his Majesty described to us."

Ernauton continued silent.

"I am speaking to you, monsieur," said Sainte-Maline, exasperated by that coolness, which he regarded with good reason as a sign of contempt, and which he was determined should give place to some definite outbreak, though it should cost him his life—"I am speaking to you; don't you hear me?"

"He whom his Majesty described to us," replied Ernauton, "had neither stick nor dog."

"That is true," said Sainte-Maline; "and if I had reflected, I should have a contusion the less on my shoulder and two holes less on my thigh. It is good to be wise and calm, I see."

Ernauton made no reply; but rising in his stirrups, and putting his hand above his eyes, he said, "Yonder is the man we seek, waiting for us."

"*Peste!* monsieur," grumbled Sainte-Maline, jealous of his companion's new advantage, "you have good eyes; I can see only a black spot, and hardly that."

Ernauton, without replying, continued to advance. Very soon Sainte-Maline also could see and recognise the man designated by the king. An evil impulse seized him, and he pushed on so as to arrive first. Ernauton looked at him with a glance that recalled him to himself, and he went more slowly.

CHAPTER XXX

SAINTE-MALINE

ERNAUTON was not deceived; the man he saw was really Chicot. He on his side had seen the cavaliers coming, and suspecting that it was for him that they came, waited for them. Ernauton and Sainte-Maline looked at each other.

" Speak, monsieur, if you wish," said Ernauton to his adversary.

Sainte-Maline was suffocated by this courtesy. He could not speak; he could only bend his head. Then Ernauton, advancing, said to Chicot, " Monsieur, would it be indiscreet to inquire your name? "

" I am called ' the Shade.' "

" Do you expect anything? "

" Yes, monsieur."

" Will you be good enough to tell us what? "

" A letter."

" From where? "

" From the Louvre."

" Sealed with what seal? "

" The royal seal."

Ernauton put his hand into the breast of his doublet and drew out a letter.

" That is it," said Chicot; " and for greater certainty I was to give you something in exchange, was I not? "

" A receipt? "

" Yes."

" Monsieur," continued Ernauton, " I was told to carry it; but this gentleman was to deliver it." And he handed the letter to Sainte-Maline, who gave it to Chicot.

" You see," said Ernauton, " that we have faithfully fulfilled our mission. There is no one here, and no one has seen us give you the letter."

" It is true, gentlemen; but to whom am I to give the receipt? "

" The king did not say," said Sainte-Maline, looking at his companion with a threatening expression.

" Write two, monsieur, and give one to each of us. It is far from this to the Louvre; and some misfortune may happen to one of us on the road." And as he spoke, Ernauton's eyes flashed in their turn.

"You are wise," said Chicot, drawing his tablets from his pocket, from which he tore out two pages and wrote on each:—

Received from the hands of M. de Sainte-Maline the letter brought by M. Ernauton de Carmainges.—THE SHADE.

"Adieu, monsieur," said Sainte-Maline, taking his.

"Adieu, monsieur, and a pleasant journey to you," added Ernauton. "Have you anything else to send to the Louvre?"

"Nothing, I thank you."

Then the young men set off towards Paris, and Chicot in the opposite direction. When he was out of sight, "Now, monsieur," said Ernauton to Sainte-Maline, "dismount, if you please."

"And what for, monsieur?" said Sainte-Maline, with astonishment.

"Our task is accomplished; we have now to converse. This place appears excellent for such an interview as ours."

"As you please, monsieur;" and they got off their horses.

Then Ernauton said, "You know, monsieur, that without any cause on my part, you have during the whole journey insulted me grievously. You wished to make me fight at an inopportune time, and I refused; but now the time is good and I am your man."

But Sainte-Maline was angry no longer, and did not wish to fight. "Monsieur," replied he, "when I insulted you, you responded by rendering me a service. I can no longer use the language towards you that I did then."

Ernauton frowned. "No, monsieur," he said; "but you think now what you said then."

"How do you know?"

"Because your words were dictated by hatred and envy, and they cannot already be extinct in your heart."

Sainte-Maline coloured, but did not reply.

Ernauton continued, "If the king preferred me to you, it was because I pleased him best; if I was not thrown into the Bièvre like you, it was because I ride better; if I did not accept your challenge before, it was because I was wiser than you; if I was not bitten by the dog, it was because I had more sagacity; if I now summon you to draw your sword, it is because I have more honour; and if you hesitate, I shall say more courage."

Sainte-Maline looked like a demon, and drew his sword furiously. Ernauton already held his in his hand.

"Stay, monsieur," said Sainte-Maline; "withdraw your last words. They are too strong, you must admit, who know me well—since, as you have said, we live only two leagues apart. Withdraw them; be satisfied with my humiliation, and do not disgrace me."

"Monsieur," said Ernauton, "as I never allow myself to get into a rage, I never say more than I mean; consequently, I shall withdraw nothing. I also am sensitive; and being new to the court, I don't want to have to blush every time I may meet you. A stroke of the sword, if you please, monsieur; it is for my satisfaction as well as yours."

"Oh, monsieur, I have fought eleven times," said Sainte-Maline, "and two of my adversaries are dead. Are you aware of that, monsieur?"

"And I, monsieur, have never fought, for I have never had occasion; and I did not seek it now. I wait your pleasure, monsieur."

"Stay!" said Sainte-Maline, "we are compatriots, and we are both in the king's service; do not let us quarrel. You are a brave man, and I would give you my hand if I could. What would you have? I am envious; it is my nature. M. de Chalabre or M. de Montcrabeau would not have made me angry; it was your superior merit. Console yourself, therefore, for my envy cannot injure you; and unfortunately for me, your merit remains. I should not like any one to know the cause of our quarrel."

"No one will know it, monsieur."

"No one?"

"No; for if we fight I shall kill you, or you will kill me. I do not despise life; on the contrary, I cling to it, for I am only twenty-three years of age, have a good name, and am not poor. I shall defend myself like a lion."

"Well, I, on the contrary, am thirty, and am disgusted with life; but still I would rather not fight with you."

"Then you will apologise?"

"No, I have said enough. If you are not content, so much the better, for then you cease to be superior to me."

"But monsieur, one cannot end a quarrel thus, without the risk of being laughed at."

"I know it."

"Then you refuse to fight?"

"With you."

"After having provoked me?"

"I confess it."

"But if my patience fail, and I attack you?"

"I will throw my sword away; but I shall then have reason

to hate you, and the first time I find you in the wrong, I will kill you."

Ernauton sheathed his sword. "You are a strange man," said he; "and I pity you from the bottom of my heart."

"You pity me?"

"Yes, for you must suffer horribly."

"Horribly."

"Do you never love?"

"Never."

"Have you no passions?"

"One alone, jealousy; but that includes all others to a frightful degree. I adore a woman as soon as she loves another; I love gold when another possesses it. Yes, you are right; I am unhappy."

"Have you never tried to become good?"

"I have never succeeded."

"What do you hope? What do you expect to do?"

"What does the venomous plant? It has flowers, like other plants, and there are those who know how to make them useful. What do the bear and bird of prey? They destroy, but certain breeders know how to train them for the chase. So shall I be in the hands of MM. d'Epernon and de Loignac, till the day when they shall say, 'This plant is hurtful; let us tear it up. This beast is furious; let us kill him.'"

Ernauton was calmed; Sainte-Maline was no longer an object of anger, but of pity.

"Good fortune should cure you," said he; "when you succeed, you will hate less."

"However high I should rise, others would be higher."

They rode on silently for some time. At last Ernauton held out his hand to Sainte-Maline, and said, "Shall I try to cure you?"

"No, do not try that; you would fail. Hate me, on the contrary, and I shall admire you."

An hour after, they entered the Louvre; the king had gone out, and would not return until evening.

CHAPTER XXXI

LOIGNAC'S ADDRESS TO THE FORTY-FIVE

EACH of the young men placed himself at a window to watch for the king's return. Ernauton, however, soon became abstracted in wondering who the woman could be who had entered Paris as his page, and whom he had since seen in such a splendid litter; and with a heart more disposed to love-adventure than to making ambitious calculations, he forgot why he was sitting there till, suddenly raising his head, he saw that Sainte-Maline was no longer there. He understood at once that he had seen the king arrive, and had gone to him. He rose quickly, traversed the gallery, and arrived at the king's room just as Sainte-Maline was coming out.

"Look!" cried he, joyfully; "see what the king has given me!" and he showed a gold chain.

"I congratulate you, monsieur," said Ernauton, quietly; and he entered in his turn.

Sainte-Maline waited impatiently until he came out again, which he did in about ten minutes, although it appeared an hour to Sainte-Maline. When Ernauton came out, he looked all over him, and seeing nothing, he cried joyfully, "And you, monsieur, what has he given to you?"

"His hand to kiss," replied Ernauton.

Sainte-Maline crushed his chain impatiently in his hands; and they both returned in silence. As they entered the hall the trumpet sounded; and at this signal all the Forty-five came out of their rooms, wondering what was the matter, while they profited by this reunion to examine one another. Most of them were richly dressed, though generally in bad taste. They resembled a corps of officers in civilian garb—the military manner being what, with few exceptions, they most affected.

The most discreet might be known by their quiet colours, the most economical by the substantial character of their equipments, and the most gay by their white or rose-coloured satins. Perducas de Pincornay had bought from some Jew a gold chain as thick as a cable. Pertinax de Montcrabeau was all bows and embroidery; he had bought his costume from a merchant who had purchased it of a gentleman who had been wounded by robbers. It was rather stained with blood and dirt, it was true; but he had managed to clean it tolerably. There remained two holes made by the daggers of the robbers, but Pertinax had had them embroidered in gold.

Eustache de Miradoux did not shine; he had had to clothe Lardille, Militor, and the two children. All the gentlemen were there admiring one another, when M. de Loignac entered frowning, and placed himself in front of them with a countenance anything but agreeable.

"Gentlemen," said he, "are you all here?"

"All!" they replied.

"Gentlemen, you have been summoned to Paris as a special guard to the king; it is an honourable title, but it engages you too much. Some of you seem not to have understood your duties; I will therefore recall them to you. If you do not assist at the deliberations of the council, you will constantly be called upon to execute the resolutions passed there; therefore the responsibility of those secrets rests upon you. Suppose now that one of the officers on whom the safety of the state and the tranquillity of the crown reposes, betrays the secrets of the council, or a soldier charged with a commission does not execute it—his life is the forfeit; you know that?"

"Doubtless," replied many voices.

"Well, gentlemen, this very day a measure of his Majesty's has been betrayed, and a step which he wished to take rendered perhaps impossible."

Terror began to replace pride in the minds of the Forty-five, and they looked at one another with suspicion and disquietude.

"Two of you gentlemen," continued Loignac, "have been heard in the open street chattering like a couple of old women, and that about grave things."

Sainte-Maline advanced. "Monsieur," said he, "pray explain at once, that suspicion may not rest on us all."

"That is easy. The king heard to-day that one of his enemies —precisely one of those whom we have been enrolled to guard him against—had arrived in Paris to conspire against him. This name was pronounced secretly, but was overheard by a soldier on guard; that is to say, by a man who should be regarded as a wall—deaf, dumb, and immovable. However, that man repeated this name in the street with a noise and boasting which attracted the attention of the passers-by, and raised quite a commotion. I know it, for I was there, and heard and saw all; and had I not placed my hand on his shoulder to stop him, he would have compromised such grave interests that had he not been quiet at my touch, I should have been compelled to poniard him on the spot."

Pertinax de Montcrabeau and Perducas de Pincornay turned deadly pale; and Montcrabeau tried to stammer out some excuses. All eyes were turned towards them.

"Nothing can excuse you," said Loignac. "Even if you were drunk, you should be punished for that; if you were only boastful and vain, you still ought to be punished. Consequently," continued Loignac, "M. de Montcrabeau, and you, also, M. de Pincornay, shall be punished."

A terrible silence ensued. Then Pertinax said, "Pardon, monsieur! we are provincials, new to the court, and unaccustomed to politics."

"You should not have accepted the honour of serving the king without weighing its responsibilities."

"For the future we will be as mute as sepulchres, we swear to you!"

"Good; but can you repair the evil you have done to-day?"

"We will try."

"It is impossible, I tell you."

"Then for this time pardon us."

"You live," continued Loignac, "with a sort of licence which I must repress by a strict discipline. Those who find the terms too hard will return home; I can easily replace them. But I warn you that justice will be done among us secretly and expeditiously. Traitors will be punished with death on the spot."

Montcrabeau nearly fainted; and Pertinax grew paler than ever.

"I shall have," Loignac continued, "for smaller offences lighter punishments, as imprisonment, for instance. For this time, I spare the lives of M. de Montcrabeau and M. de Pincornay, because they probably acted in ignorance. I do not punish them with imprisonment because I may need them this evening or to-morrow. I give them, consequently, the third punishment I shall use for delinquents—a fine. You have received one thousand livres apiece, gentlemen; you will each return one hundred. And I will use that money to reward those whose conduct I approve."

"One hundred livres!" cried Pincornay; "*Cap de Bious!* I haven't them. I have spent them on my equipment."

"Sell your chain, then. But I have a word more to say. I have remarked many signs of irritation between different members of your body; whenever a difference arises I wish the matter referred to me, and I alone shall have the power of allowing a duel to take place. Duelling is much in fashion now, but I do not wish that in following the fashion my company should continually be made incomplete. The first duel, therefore, that takes place without my permission will be punished with a rigorous imprisonment and a heavy fine. Let those of you to whom these words apply bear them in mind. You may go, gentlemen. By the way, fifteen of you will place yourselves this evening at the foot of the staircase when his Majesty receives, and at the first signal will occupy the antechambers, should the occasion arise; fifteen will station themselves outside, mingling in the train of those who visit the Louvre; and fifteen will remain at home. Also, as you should have some chief, and I cannot be everywhere, I will each day name a chief for the fifteen, so that all shall learn to obey and command. At present I do not know the capacities of any one, but I shall watch and learn. Now go, gentlemen; and M. de Montcrabeau and M. de Pincornay, you will remember that I expect your fines to be paid to-morrow."

They all retired except Ernauton, who lingered behind.

" Do you wish anything? " asked Loignac.

" Yes, monsieur," said Ernauton, bowing; " it seems to me that you have forgotten to point out to us our duties. To be in the king's service has a glorious sound, doubtless, but I should wish to know in what this service consists? "

" That, monsieur, is a question to which I cannot reply."

" May I ask why, monsieur? "

" Because I myself am often ignorant in the morning of what I shall have to do in the evening."

" Monsieur, you are placed in such a high position that you must know many things of which we are ignorant."

" Do as I do, M. de Carmainges: learn those things without being told; I do not hinder you."

" I ask you, monsieur," said Ernauton, " because, coming to the court without likes or dislikes, led by no passion, I might be more useful to you than another, without being more valiant."

" You have neither likes nor dislikes? "

" No, monsieur."

" You love the king, at least, I suppose? "

" I ought to, and I wish to, as a subject and a gentleman."

" Well, that is the cardinal point by which to regulate your conduct."

" Very well, monsieur; but there is one point which disquiets me."

" What is it? "

" Passive obedience."

" It is an essential condition."

" So I understand; but it is sometimes difficult for persons who are delicate on points of honour."

" That does not concern me, M. de Carmainges."

" But, monsieur, when an order displeases you—"

" I read the signature of M. d'Epernon, and that consoles me."

" And M. d'Epernon? "

" He reads the signature of his Majesty, and consoles himself as I do."

" You are right, monsieur, and I am your humble servant; " and Ernauton was about to retire, when Loignac stopped him.

" I will say to you," said he, " what I have not said to the others, for no one else has had the courage to speak to me thus."

Ernauton bowed.

" Perhaps," continued Loignac, " a great personage will come to the Louvre this evening; if so, do not lose sight of him, and follow him when he leaves."

" Pardon me, monsieur; but that seems the work of a spy."

" Do you think so? It is possible; but look here; " and he drew out a paper which he presented to Ernauton, who read:—

Have M. de Mayenne followed this evening, if he presents himself at the Louvre.—D'EPERNON.

" Well, monsieur? "

" I will follow M. de Mayenne," said Ernauton, bowing.

CHAPTER XXXII

THE BOURGEOIS OF PARIS

M. DE MAYENNE, with whom they were so much occupied at the Louvre, set out from the Hôtel de Guise, booted and on horseback, as though he had just arrived. He was received by the king affectionately.

" Well, cousin," said he, " you have, then, come to visit Paris? "

" Yes, Sire; I come in my brother's name and my own, to recall to your Majesty that you have no more faithful subjects than ourselves."

" *Mordieu !* " said the king, " that is so well known that aside from the pleasure your visit gives me, you might have spared yourself this trouble. You must have had some other motive."

"Sire, I feared that your regard for us might be shaken by the reports which our enemies circulate about us."

"What reports?" asked Henri, with that simplicity which made him so dangerous, even to those most intimate with him.

"What!" cried Mayenne, rather disconcerted; "has not your Majesty heard any reports unfavourable to us?"

"My cousin, know once for all that I allow no one to speak ill of the Guises in my presence."

"Well, Sire, I do not regret my visit, since I have had the pleasure of finding my king so well disposed towards us; but I will admit that my precipitation was groundless."

"Oh, there is always something to do in Paris."

"Yes, Sire; but we have our business at Soissons."

"What business, duke?"

"Your Majesty's, Sire."

"Ah, true; continue, Mayenne, to do as you have done. I know how to appreciate the conduct of my subjects."

The duke retired, smiling. The king rubbed his hands, and Loignac made a sign to Ernauton, who spoke to his valet, and then followed M. de Mayenne. There was no fear of missing him, for Pincornay's indiscretion had made known the arrival in Paris of a prince of the House of Guise, and the good Leaguers were pouring from their houses to meet him. In vain Mayneville checked the more zealous, saying, "Not so much zeal, my friends! not so much zeal! Good God! you will compromise us."

The duke had an escort of two or three hundred men when he arrived at the Hôtel St. Denis—a circumstance which made it easy for Ernauton to follow him without being noticed.

As the duke entered his hotel, Ernauton saw a litter pierce through the crowd. Mayneville approached it; the curtains were opened; and Ernauton thought he recognised his former page. The litter disappeared under the gateway, and Mayneville followed; an instant after, Mayneville appeared on the balcony, and thanked the Parisians in the duke's name, but begged them to disperse and go home.

All went away accordingly, except ten men, who had entered after the duke. These were the deputies of the League, who were sent to thank M. de Mayenne for his visit, and to entreat him to persuade his brother to come also. In fact, these worthy citizens, who were not wanting in imagination, had in their preparatory meetings contrived a number of plans which needed only the sanction and support of a chief on whom they could rely.

Bussy-Leclerc came to announce that he had instructed the

monks of three monasteries in the use of arms, and had enrolled five hundred *bourgeois* in a regiment; that is to say, had got ready an effective force of a thousand men.

Lachapelle-Marteau had worked among the magistrates, the clerks, and the lawyers. He could offer both counsel and action—the former represented by two hundred black robes, the latter by two hundred archers.

Brigard had gained the merchants of the Rue Lombards and the Rue St. Denis.

Crucé had shared with Lachapelle-Marteau the work among the lawyers, and had gained over the University of Paris.

Delbar promised for all the sailors in the port—a formidable contingent of five hundred men.

Each of the others had something to offer, even Nicolas Poulain, the friend of Chicot.

When Mayenne had heard them all, he said, " I admire your strength; but I do not see the end you propose to yourselves."

Bussy-Leclerc answered, " We want a change, and as we are the strongest—"

" But how will you arrive at this change? "

" It seems to me," replied Bussy, boldly, " that as the idea of the Union came from our chiefs, it is for them to point out its aim."

" You are perfectly right," said Mayenne; " but it is also for them to judge of the proper time for action. The troops of M. de Guise may be ready, but he does not give the signal until he thinks fit."

" But, monseigneur, we are impatient."

" For what? "

" To arrive at our end. We also have our plan."

" Ah! that is different; if you have your own plan, I say no more."

" Yes, monseigneur; but may we count on your aid? "

" Doubtless, if this plan be approved by my brother and myself."

" We believe it will be."

" Let me hear it, then."

The Leaguers looked at one another, then Marteau advanced. " Monseigneur," said he, " we think the success of our plan certain. There are particular points where all the strength of the city lies—the great and the little Châtelet, the Hôtel de Ville, the Arsenal, and the Louvre."

" It is true."

" All these are guarded, but could easily be surprised."

"I admit this also."

"The town itself, however, is defended outside, firstly, by the chevalier of the watch with his archers. We thought of seizing him in his house, which could be easily done, as it is a lonely place."

Mayenne shook his head. "However lonely," said he, "you cannot force a door and fire twenty shots without attracting attention."

"We have foreseen this objection, but one of the archers of the watch is on our side. In the middle of the night two or three of us will go and knock at the door; the archer will open, and tell his chief that the king wishes to speak to him, which would not appear strange, as he is often sent for in this manner. Once the door is open, we will introduce ten men—sailors who lodge near—who will soon finish him."

"Murder him?"

"Yes, monseigneur. At the same time we will force the doors of the other functionaries who might take his place, such as M. d'O, M. de Chiverny, and M. le Procureur Laguesle. Saint Bartholomew has taught us how to manage."

"This is all well, gentlemen; but you have not told me if you mean at the same time to force the doors of the Louvre—that strong and well-guarded fortress. Believe me, the king is not so easily taken as the chevalier of the watch. He will take to the sword; and remember, he is the king. His presence will have a strong effect on the citizens; and you will be beaten."

"We have chosen for this undertaking four thousand men who do not love the Valois enough for his presence to have on them the effect of which you speak."

"And you think that enough?"

"Doubtless; we shall be ten to one."

"Why, the Swiss are four thousand strong.

"Yes, but they are at Lagny, and that is eight leagues from Paris; and supposing they were sent for, it would take two hours for the messenger to go on horseback, and eight for them to return on foot. That would make ten hours; so that they would arrive just in time to be stopped at the gates, for in ten hours we should be masters of Paris."

"Very good; but supposing all this accomplished, the watch disarmed, the authorities disappeared, and all obstacles removed, what do you mean to do?"

"Form a new government of honest men. As for ourselves, so long as our commerce is successful, and we have enough for our wives and children, we care for little else. Some among us might desire a command, and they should have it. We are not difficult to satisfy."

"I know you are all honest, and would not suffer a mixture in your ranks."

"No, no!" cried several voices.

"Now, M. Poulain," said the duke, "are there many idlers and bad people in Paris?"

Nicolas Poulain, who had hitherto kept in the background, was now forced to advance. "Certainly, monseigneur, there are a great many," he replied.

"Can you give us an estimate of their number?"

"About four thousand thieves, three thousand or more beggars, and four or five hundred assassins."

"Well, there are at least eight thousand good-for-nothings; of what religion are they?"

Poulain laughed. "Of all, monseigneur, or rather, of none; gold is their god, and blood their prophet."

"Yes; but their politics? Are they Valois, Leaguers, Navarrais, or what?"

"Robbers only."

"Monseigneur," said Crucé, "do not suppose that we mean to take these people for allies!"

"No, I do not suppose so; and that is what disturbs me."

"And why so, monseigneur?" they asked with surprise.

"Because as soon as there are no longer magistrates in Paris, as soon as there is no longer royalty, or public force, or anything to restrain them, they will begin to pillage your shops while you fight, and your houses while you occupy the Louvre. Sometimes they will join the Swiss against you, and sometimes you against the Swiss, so that they will always be the strongest."

"The devil!" cried the deputies, looking at one another.

"I think this is a question for grave consideration, gentlemen," said the duke. "I will think it over, and endeavour to find the means of overcoming the difficulty; your interests, before our own, has ever been our maxim."

The deputies gave a murmur of approbation.

"Now, gentlemen, permit a man who has travelled twenty-four leagues on horseback in forty-eight hours to seek a little sleep."

"We humbly take our leave, monseigneur," said Brigard. "What day shall you fix for our next meeting?"

"As soon as possible, gentlemen; to-morrow or the day after;" and he left them all astounded by the foresight which had detected a danger of which they had not even dreamed.

No sooner had he disappeared than a door opened and a woman rushed in.

" The duchess ! " they cried.

" Yes, gentlemen; who comes to save you from your embarrassments. What the Hebrews could not do, Judith did. Hope, then, gentlemen, for I also have my plan; " and she disappeared through the same door as her brother.

" *Tudieu !* " cried Bussy-Leclerc; " I believe that is the man of the family."

" Oh ! " murmured Nicolas Poulain, " I wish I were out of all this."

CHAPTER XXXIII

BROTHER BORROMÉE

IT was about ten o'clock in the evening when the deputies returned home. Nicolas Poulain remained behind the others, reflecting on the perplexing situation in which he found himself, and considering whether he should report all that he had heard to M. d'Epernon, when, in the middle of the Rue de la Pierre au Réal, he ran against a Jacobin monk. They both began to swear, but looking up, recognised each other.

" Brother Borromée ! " cried Poulain.

" Nicolas Poulain ! " exclaimed the monk.

" How are you ? " asked Nicolas, cautiously. " Where in the world were you running to in such a hurry at this time of night ? Is the priory on fire ? "

" No; I was going to the Duchesse de Montpensier's hotel, to speak to M. de Mayneville."

" And what for ? "

" Oh ! it is very simple," said Borromée, seeking for a specious answer. " Our reverend prior was solicited by the duchess to become her confessor; he accepted at the time, but since then he has had scruples, and has sent me to tell her not to rely upon him."

" Very good; but you are going away from the Hôtel de Guise."

" Exactly so; for I hear she is at the Hôtel St. Denis, with her brother."

" Quite true; but why do you deceive me ? It is not the treasurer who is sent with messages of that sort."

" But to a princess ! Now do not detain me, or I shall miss her."

" She will return; you might have waited for her."

"True; but I shall not be sorry to see Monsieur the Duke also."

"Oh, that is more like the truth! Now that I know with whom your business is to be transacted, I will hinder you no longer. Adieu, and good luck!"

Borromée, seeing the road clear, hastened on.

"Come, come," said Poulain, looking after him, "there is something new; but why the devil should I want to know what is going on? Is it possible that I am beginning to like the occupation to which I am condemned? Fie!"

Meanwhile the brother and sister had been conversing together, and had settled that the king had no suspicions, and was therefore easy to attack. They also agreed that the first thing to be done was to organise the League more generally in the provinces, while the king abandoned his brother, who was the only enemy they had to fear so long as Henri de Navarre occupied himself only with love-affairs.

"Paris is all ready, but must wait," said Mayenne.

At this moment M. de Mayneville entered, and announced Borromée.

"Borromée! who is he?" cried the duke.

"The man whom you sent me from Nancy, when I asked for a man of action and a man of intelligence."

"I remember; I told you I had the two in one, and sent you Captain Borromée. Has he changed his name to Borromée?"

"Yes, monseigneur, his name and his uniform. He is now named Borromée, and is a Jacobin."

"Borroville a Jacobin?"

"Yes, monseigneur."

"And why, then, is he a Jacobin? The devil would be much amused should he recognise him under his frock."

"Why is he a Jacobin?" The duchess made a sign to Mayneville. "You will know that later," he continued; "it is our secret, monseigneur. In the meantime let us hear Captain Borroville, or Brother Borromée."

"Yes, his visit disturbs me," observed Madame de Montpensier.

"And me, also, I confess," said Mayneville.

"Then introduce him immediately," said the duchess.

As to the duke, he hesitated between a wish to hear the messenger, and the fear of failing an appointment with his mistress. He looked at the door and at the clock. The door opened, and the clock struck eleven.

"Eh, Borroville," said the duke, unable to restrain his

laughter, notwithstanding his ill-humour, "how you are disguised, my friend!"

"Yes, monseigneur, I am not much at my ease in this devil of a dress, I confess; but as it is worn in the service of her highness, I do not complain."

"Good! thank you, captain. And now let us hear what you have to say to us at so late an hour."

"I could not come sooner; I have all the priory on my hands."

"Well, now speak!"

"Monsieur the Duke, the king is sending succours to the Duc d'Anjou."

"Bah! we have heard that the last three years."

"Yes; but this time it is certain. At two o'clock this morning M. de Joyeuse set out for Rouen. He is to take ship to Dieppe, and convey three thousand men to Antwerp."

"Oh! who told you that, Borroville?"

"I heard it from a man who is going to Navarre."

"To Navarre! to Henri?"

"Yes, monseigneur."

"And who sends him?"

"The king, with a letter."

"What is his name?"

"Robert Briquet; he is a great friend of Gorenflot's."

"And an ambassador from the king?"

"Yes; I am sure of it, for he sent one of our monks to the Louvre to get the letter."

"And he did not show you the letter?"

"The king did not give it to him; he sent it by his own messenger."

"We must have this letter."

"Certainly," said the duchess.

"How was it that this did not occur to you?" said Mayneville.

"I did think of it, and wished to send one of my men, who is a perfect Hercules, with M. Briquet, but he suspected, and dismissed him."

"You must go yourself."

"Impossible!"

"And why?"

"Because he knows me."

"As a monk, but not as captain, I hope."

"Upon my soul, I don't know; that Robert Briquet has an eye that is very embarrassing."

"What is he like?"

" He is tall—all nerves, muscles, and bones; shrewd, mocking, and taciturn."

" Ah, ah! and clever with his sword? "

" Marvellously."

" A long face? "

" Monseigneur, he has all faces."

" And an old friend of the prior's? "

" From the time when he was only a monk."

" Oh, I have a suspicion which I must have cleared up. Borroville, you must go to Soissons, to my brother—"

" But the priory? "

" Oh, you can invent some excuse to Gorenflot; he believes all you say," said Mayneville.

" You will tell my brother all you know about the mission of M. de Joyeuse."

" Yes, monseigneur."

" And Navarre—" said the duchess.

" Oh, I charge myself with that! " said Mayenne. " Let them saddle me a fresh horse, Mayneville." Then he murmured to himself, " Can he be still alive? Yes, it must be he."

CHAPTER XXXIV

CHICOT, LATINIST

AFTER the departure of the young men, Chicot went on at a rapid pace; but as soon as they had disappeared in the valley, he stopped at the top of a hill and looked all round him. Then, seeing no one, he seated himself on the edge of a ditch, leaned back against a tree, and began what he called his examination of conscience. He had now two purses, for he perceived that the packet he had received contained money, besides the letter. It was quite a royal purse, embroidered with an " H " at each end.

" This is fine! " said Chicot, examining the purse; " it is charming on the part of the king. His name, his arms! no one could be more generous or more stupid. Decidedly I shall never make anything of him. All that astonishes me is that he did not have embroidered on the same purse the letter which he sends by me to his brother-in-law. Now let me see how much money he has sent. One hundred crowns—just the sum I borrowed from Gorenflot. Ah, pardon, let us not calumniate; here is a little package—five quadruples in Spanish gold.

Come, that is delicate; it is very polite, Henriquet. But the purse annoys me; if I were to keep it I should feel as if the very birds, as they flew over my head, would denounce me as a royal messenger."

So saying, he drew from his pocket Gorenflot's bag, emptied the king's money into it, then placed a stone in the purse, and threw it into the Orge, which flowed under the bridge at his feet.

" So much for myself; now for Henri," said Chicot; and he took up the letter, broke the seal with the utmost tranquillity, and sent the envelope into the river after the purse. " Now," said he, " let us read." And he opened the letter and read as follows:—

DEAR BROTHER,—The deep love which you felt for our late dear brother and king, Charles IX., still clings to the Louvre and to my heart; it grieves me, therefore, to have to write to you about vexatious things. You are strong, however, against ill-fortune, so that I do not hesitate to communicate these things to you—things which can be told only to a tried friend. Besides, I have an interest in warning you—the honour of my name and of your own, my brother. We resemble each other in one thing, that we are each surrounded with enemies. Chicot will explain to you.

" '*Chicotus explicabit,*' " said Chicot—" or rather, '*evolvet,*' which is infinitely more elegant."

M. de Turenne, your servant, causes daily scandal at your court. God forbid that I should interfere in your affairs, except where your honour is concerned; but your wife, whom to my regret I call my sister, ought to exercise such care for you, instead of me—which she does not do.

" Oh, oh! " said Chicot, continuing his Latin rendering, " '*quæque omittit facere.*' That is severe."

I advise you, therefore, to watch the communications of Margot with Turenne, that she does not bring shame on the House of Bourbon. Act as soon as you shall be sure of the fact, into which I pray you to inquire as soon as Chicot shall have explained to you my letter.

" ' *Statim atque audiveris Chicotum litteras explicantem,*' " said Chicot; " let us proceed."

It would be a grievous calamity if the least suspicion should attach to the legitimacy of your successor, my brother—a momentous consideration, of which God has forbidden me to think; for, alas! I am condemned in advance not to live again in my posterity.

The two accomplices, whom as brother and king I denounce to you, generally meet at a little château called Loignac—the pretext being generally the chase. This château is, besides, the focus for intrigues to which the Guises are not strangers, and you know the strange love with which my sister pursued Henri de Guise. I embrace you, and am ever ready to aid you in all, and for all; meanwhile aid yourself by the advice of Chicot, whom I send to you.

"'*Age, auctore Chicot,*'" said Chicot. "Here am I installed counsellor of the King of Navarre! This seems to me a bad commission, and in flying from one ill I have fallen into a worse one. Really, I should prefer Mayenne. But the letter is clever, and if Henriot be like other husbands, it will embroil him at once with his wife, Turenne, the Guises, and even with Spain. In fact, if Henri de Valois is so well informed of all that occurs in Navarre, he must have some spy there; and that spy is going to annoy Henriot. Then again," he continued, "this letter will lead me into mischief if I meet a Spaniard, a Lorraine, a Béarnais, or a Fleming, curious enough to wish to know what brings me here; and I should be very foolish not to remember that there is a chance of that. M. Borromée, above all, I suspect may play me some trick. Besides, what did I seek in asking the king for this mission? Tranquillity. And now I am going to embroil the King of Navarre with his wife. However, that is not my affair, except that I shall make mortal enemies, who will prevent my reaching the happy age of eighty. Faith! so much the better; life is pleasant only while one is young. But then I might as well have waited for the knife of M. de Mayenne. No, for there must be reciprocity in all things. I will pursue my journey; but I will take precautions, so that if any one kills me he will find on me money only, and will do harm to me alone. I will finish what I began; I will translate this fine letter into Latin, and engrave it on my memory. Then I will buy a horse, because from Juvisy to Pau I should have too often to put the right foot before the left if I walked; but first I will destroy this letter."

This he proceeded to do, tearing it into an infinite number of little pieces, sending some into the river, others into the air, and burying the rest in holes in the ground.

"Now let me think of my Latin theme," said he; and this study occupied him until he arrived at Corbeil, where he gave little attention to the wonders of the cathedral, and much to those of a restaurant whence came an appetising smell of dinner. We will not describe either the dinner he made or the horse he bought; suffice it to say that the dinner was long and the horse was bad.

CHAPTER XXXV

THE FOUR WINDS

CHICOT, with his little horse—which ought to have been a big one to carry him—after having slept at Fontainebleau, made a *détour* to the right, and proceeded towards the little village of Orgeval. He would have been glad to make some leagues farther that day, for he wished to increase his distance from Paris; but his horse stumbled so frequently and so badly that he thought it prudent to make a halt. Besides, he had seen nothing on the road to arouse suspicion. But Chicot never trusted to appearances. Before going to bed he examined with great care the house in which he was to sleep. They showed him handsome chambers, with three or four doors; but in his judgment those chambers had too many doors, and the doors were not well enough secured. The host had just finished repairing a large closet, with but one door, which opened on the stairway, and which was provided with formidable bolts on the inside. Chicot had a bed prepared in that closet, which at first sight he preferred to the magnificent chambers which had been shown to him.

Although the hotel had appeared almost uninhabited, he locked the door and placed a heavy table and a chest of drawers against it. He then put his purse under his pillow, and repeated to himself three times the translation of the king's letter. There was an extremely high wind blowing, and as it howled in the neighbouring trees, it was with a feeling of great satisfaction that Chicot plunged into a very comfortable bed. He had a lamp by his bedside; before going to sleep—and partly that he might go to sleep—he read in a very curious book which had just appeared, written by a certain mayor of Bordeaux, called Montagne, or Montaigne. This book had been printed in Bordeaux in 1581; it contained the first two parts of a work since then well known, entitled *The Essays*. It was interesting enough to read and re-read—by day. But it had the merit also of being tedious enough not to keep a man from sleeping who had travelled fifteen leagues on horseback, and had taken his bottle of generous wine at supper. Chicot had a great liking for that book, which on leaving Paris he had slipped into his pocket, and with the author of which he was personally acquainted. Cardinal du Perron had called it the breviary of honest men; and Chicot willingly took it for his breviary.

Nevertheless, in reading the eighth chapter he fell into a deep sleep.

The wind moaned about the house, sometimes like a child crying, and sometimes like a husband scolding his wife; and as Chicot slept, it seemed to him, in his dreams, that the tempest came nearer and nearer. All at once a sudden squall of invincible force broke locks and bolts, pushed the chest of drawers, which fell on the lamp, which it extinguished, and on the table, which it smashed.

Chicot had the faculty of waking quickly, and with all his senses about him; he understood at once that it would be better to slip out of bed into the recess behind than to get out in front. As he glided into the recess, his left hand seized the bag of crowns, and his right hand grasped the hilt of his sword. He opened his eyes; the darkness was profound. He listened, and it seemed to him that everything in the room was going to pieces in the battle of the four winds; chairs were falling, and the table breaking more and more under the weight of the drawers. As he understood that he could do nothing against the gods of Olympus, he contented himself with standing in a corner of the recess, with his sword held out before him, so that if any of these mythological personages approached, they would spit themselves upon it. At last he profited by a momentary cessation in the uproar to cry loudly, " Help, help ! "

Chicot made so much noise that it seemed to quiet the elements, as if Neptune had pronounced the famous " *Quos ego* "; and after six or seven minutes, during which Eurus, Notus, Boreas, and Aquilo seemed to beat a retreat, the host appeared with a lantern and enlightened the scene, which looked deplorably like a field of battle. The great chest of drawers was overturned on the broken table; the door was held only by one of its hinges, and the bolts were broken; three or four chairs were on the floor with their legs in the air; and to crown all, the crockery, which had been on the table, lay in bits on the floor.

" What ! it is hell here, then ? " cried Chicot, recognising his host in the light of his lantern.

" Oh, monsieur," cried the host, on seeing the frightful havoc, " what has happened ? "

" Tell me, my friend, how many demons have you in your house ? " asked Chicot.

" Oh, Jesus, what weather ! " replied the host, in a pathetic tone.

" But the bolts do not hold; this house must be made of card-board. I would rather go away; I prefer the road."

" Oh, my poor furniture!" sighed the host.

" But my clothes! Where are they? They were on this chair."

" Your clothes, my dear monsieur?" said the host, innocently; " if they were there, they ought to be there still."

" What! 'if they were there!' Do you think I came here yesterday in this costume?"

" *Mon Dieu!* monsieur," answered the host, at a loss for a reply to such an argument, " I know you were clothed."

" It is fortunate that you can admit that."

" But—"

" But what?"

" The wind has dispersed everything."

" Ah! that is an explanation!"

" You see."

" But, my friend, when the wind comes in, it comes from outside; and it must have come in here if it made this destruction."

" Certainly, monsieur."

" Well, the wind in coming in here should have brought with it the clothes of others, instead of carrying mine out."

" So it should, and yet the contrary seems to have happened."

" But what is this? The wind must have walked in the mud, for here are footmarks on the floor." And Chicot pointed out the traces left by a muddy boot, on seeing which the host turned pale. " Now, my friend," continued Chicot, " I advise you to keep a watch over these winds which enter hotels, penetrate rooms by breaking doors, and retire, carrying away the clothes of the guests."

The host drew back towards the door. " You call me thief!" said he.

" You are responsible for my clothes, and they are gone; you will not deny that?"

" You insult me."

Chicot made a menacing gesture.

" Holloa!" cried the host; " holloa! help!"

Four men armed with sticks immediately appeared.

" Ah, here are Eurus, Notus, Aquilo, and Boreas," said Chicot. " *Ventre de biche!* since the opportunity presents itself, I will deprive the earth of the north wind; it is a service to humanity—there will be an eternal spring." And he made such a thrust with his long sword in the direction of the nearest assailant that the latter, if he had not leaped back with the lightness of a veritable son of Æolus, would have been pierced through and through.   Unfortunately, as in making that backward leap he was facing Chicot, and consequently could not look behind, he landed on the edge of the upper step of the stairway, down which he rolled with a great noise.   That retreat was a signal for the three others, who disappeared through the opening before them—or rather, behind them—like ghosts sinking through a trap-door.   But the last to disappear had time, while his companions made their descent, to whisper something to the host.

" Your clothes shall be found," he growled.

" Well, that is all I ask."

" They will be brought to you."

" Very good.   I don't want to go naked; that is reasonable, it seems to me."

The clothes soon made their appearance, but visibly deteriorated.

" Ah! there are nails in your staircase; what a devil of a wind it was! " said Chicot.   " But no matter; it is an honourable restitution.   How could I have suspected you?—you have such an honest face."

The host smiled pleasantly.   " Now," he said, " you will go to sleep again, I suppose."

" No, I thank you; I have slept enough.   Leave me your lantern, and I will read."

Chicot replaced the chest of drawers against the door, got into bed again, and read till daybreak, when he asked for his horse, paid his bill, and went away, saying to himself, " We shall see to-night."

CHAPTER XXXVI

HOW CHICOT CONTINUED HIS JOURNEY, AND WHAT HAPPENED TO HIM

CHICOT passed his morning in congratulating himself on the coolness and patience he had displayed through his night of trials.

" But," thought he, " they never take an old wolf twice in the same snare; therefore it is nearly certain that they will invent some new deviltry to practise on me to-day, so I must be on my guard."

The result of this reasoning was that Chicot made a march that day worthy of being immortalised by Xenophon.   Every tree, rising ground, or wall served him for a point of observation. He also concluded on the road alliances, if not offensive, at least defensive. Four grocers from Paris, who were going to Orléans to order preserves, and to Limoges for dried fruits, allowed Chicot, who called himself a hosier from Bordeaux returning home, to join their company, which was rendered more formidable by four clerks, who were following their masters. It was quite a little army, and scarcely less formidable in mind than in number, so warlike a spirit had the League introduced among the Parisian shopkeepers. At all events, the proverb is true which says that three cowards together have less fear than one brave man alone. At last they reached the town fixed on for supper and sleeping. They supped, and then each went to his room.

Chicot, who had not been sparing during the repast, either of his fun, which amused his companions, or of the Muscat and Burgundy, went to bed, after having arranged to travel again with the grocers on the morrow. He thought himself guarded like a prince by the four travellers, whose rooms were in the same corridor and close to his own. Indeed, at this epoch, the roads being far from safe, travellers were in the habit of promising one another mutual aid in case of need. Chicot then, after bolting his door and striking the walls, which returned everywhere a satisfactory sound, went to bed and to sleep. But during his first sleep an event occurred which the Sphinx himself, the diviner *par excellence*, could not have foreseen; but the Devil was mixing himself up with Chicot's affairs, and he is more cunning than all the sphinxes in the world.

About half-past nine a blow was struck on the door of the room where the clerks all slept. One of them opened in a very bad humour, and found himself face to face with the host. " Gentlemen," said he, " I see with pleasure that you are sleeping all ready dressed, for I wish to render you a great surprise. Your masters grew very warm over politics at supper-time; and it seems that a sheriff of the town heard them and reported it. Now, as we are very loyal here, the mayor sent down the watch, and they have arrested your masters and carried them off. The prison is near the Hôtel de Ville. Go, my lads! Your mules are ready for you; your masters will join you on the road."

The four clerks shook like hares, ran downstairs, jumped on their mules, and took the road back to Paris, telling the host to let their masters be informed of their departure and of the direction they had taken, if they should return to the hotel.

Having seen them disappear, the host went to knock very gently at one of the doors in the corridor. One of the merchants cried out in a loud voice, " Who is there? "

" Silence! " replied the host, " and come quietly to the door."

The merchant obeyed, but before opening, he said again, " Who are you? "

" Your host; do you not recognise my voice? "

" *Mon Dieu!* what is the matter? "

" Why, it seems you talked rather too freely at table, and the mayor has been informed by some spy, and has sent to arrest you. Luckily, I thought of showing them your clerks' room instead of yours, so that they are busy upstairs arresting them."

" Oh, oh! what are you telling me? "

" Pure and simple truth. Make haste, and escape while you can! "

" But my companions? "

" Oh, I will tell them."

And while the merchant dressed, the host awakened the others, and very soon they all disappeared, walking on the points of their toes, that they might not be heard.

" That poor hosier! " said they. " It will all fall on him; but it is true he said the most."

Of course Chicot had received no warning. While the merchants were flying, he was sleeping peacefully.

The host now descended into the hall, where stood six armed men, one of whom seemed to command the others. " Well," said this one.

" I have obeyed your orders, monsieur."

" Your inn is deserted? "

" Absolutely."

" The person is not awakened."

" No."

" You know in whose name we act, and what cause we serve, for you serve the same."

" Yes, certainly. Therefore, I have sacrificed, to keep my oath, the money that these men would have spent at my house; for it is said in the oath, ' I will sacrifice my goods to the defence of the holy Catholic religion.' "

" ' And my life,' you forget that," replied the officer.

" *Mon Dieu!* " cried the host, clasping his hands. " Do they want my life? I have a wife and children."

" Your life will be demanded only if you do not obey blindly what is ordered you."

" Oh! I will obey."

"Then go to bed, shut the doors, and whatever you see or hear, do not come out, even if your house is burning."

"Oh, I am ruined!"

"I am instructed to indemnify you; here are thirty crowns."

"My house estimated at thirty crowns!" cried the inn-keeper, piteously.

"We shall not break even a window, poltroon! Bah! what poor champions of the holy League we have here!"

The host went away and did as he was told. Then the officer ordered two men to place themselves under Chicot's window, while he himself, with the three others, mounted to his room.

"You know the order," said the officer. "If he opens and lets us search, and we find what we seek, we will not do him the least harm; but if the contrary happens, a good blow with a dagger. No pistol, you understand; besides, it is needless, since we are four against one."

The officer knocked.

"Who is there?" cried Chicot.

"Your friends the grocers, who have something important to tell you."

"Oh!" said Chicot; "how last night's wine has strengthened your voice!"

The officer lowered his voice and said in an insinuating tone, "Open quickly, dear companion."

"*Ventre de biche!* how your grocery smells of old iron!"

"Ah! you will not open?" cried the officer, impatiently. "Upon him, then; break oven the door!"

Chicot ran to the window, but saw below two naked swords shining.

"I am caught," said he.

"Ah, ah!" cried the officer, who had heard the noise of the window opening; "you fear the perilous leap, and you are right. Come, open!"

"Faith! no; the door is solid, and I shall get help when you make a noise." And he began to call for the merchants.

The officer laughed. "Fool!" cried he. "Do you think we have left you their help? Undeceive yourself; you are alone, so make up your mind to it. Go on, soldiers!"

Chicot heard three blows struck on the door.

"There are three muskets there, and an officer," said he; "below there are only two swords. There are fifteen feet to jump; that is hard, but I prefer the swords to the muskets."

And tying his bag to his belt, he got on the window-sill with his drawn sword. The two men below stood ready with their swords; but as Chicot had expected, on seeing him jump sword in hand, they drew back, intending to strike him after he reached the ground. Chicot alighted on his feet, and one of the men gave him a thrust immediately. Thanks, however, to Gorenflot's coat-of-mail, the blade broke like glass.

" He has armour! " cried the soldier.

" *Pardieu!* " said Chicot, cutting open his head with a blow of his sword.

The other began to cry out, thinking now only of defending himself; but at the second pass, Chicot laid him by his comrade, so that when the door was burst open, the officer saw through the window his two sentinels lying in their blood, and Chicot running quietly away.

" He is a demon, he is steel-proof! " cried he.

" Yes; but not ball-proof! " cried a soldier, taking aim.

" No firing; no noise! You will wake the city. We shall catch him to-morrow."

" Ah! " said one of the soldiers, philosophically; " four men should have been placed here, and two only sent upstairs."

" You are a fool! " replied the officer.

" We shall see what the duke will say he is," grumbled the soldier, to console himself.

CHAPTER XXXVII

THE THIRD DAY OF THE JOURNEY

CHICOT retreated with that tranquillity only because he was at Etampes; that is to say, in a city, in the midst of a population, under the protection of magistrates, who would have arrested the officer immediately on his complaint. It was the knowledge of this which had induced the officer to withhold his men from firing and to abstain from pursuit. Therefore he retired with his soldiers, leaving the two dead men on the ground, after laying their swords by them, that it might seem as though they had killed each other.

Chicot vainly searched for his former companions, and then, supposing that his enemies, having missed their stroke, would avoid remaining in the city, he considered it good strategy to remain there himself. Nay, more; after making a *détour*, and from the corner of a neighbouring street hearing the footsteps of horses going away, he had the audacity to return to the inn. There he found the host, who had not recovered from his terror, and who let him saddle his horse in the stable, watching him with the same stupor he would have shown in looking at a ghost. Chicot took advantage of that stupor not to pay his account; and the host refrained from making any claim.

Chicot went and finished his night in the public-room at another inn, among all the drinkers, who were far from thinking that this tall unknown, who looked so smiling and gracious, had just killed two men. At break of day he started again, a prey to anxiety, which increased from moment to moment. Two attempts had failed; the third might be fatal to him. A clump of trees inspired him with apprehensions difficult to describe; a ditch made shivers run over his body; a wall, somewhat elevated, almost made him turn back. From time to time he resolved that once at Orléans, he would send a courier to the king to ask for an escort from city to city. But as the road to Orléans was passed without accident, Chicot began to think again that it was needless, and that the king would lose his good opinion of him, and also that an escort would be a great trouble. He went on therefore; but his fears began to return as evening approached. All at once he heard behind him the galloping of horses; and turning round, he counted seven cavaliers, of whom four had muskets on their shoulders. They gained rapidly on Chicot, who, seeing that flight was hopeless, contented himself with making his horse move in zigzags, so as to escape the balls which he expected every moment. He was right, for when they came about fifty feet from him, they fired; but thanks to his manœuvre, all the balls missed him. He immediately abandoned the reins and let himself slip to the ground, taking the precaution to have his sword in one hand and a dagger in the other. He came to the ground in such a position that his head was protected by the breast of his horse.

A cry of joy came from the troop, who, seeing him fall, believed him dead.

" I told you so," said a man, riding up, with a mask on his face; " you failed because you did not follow my orders. This time, here he is; search him, dead or alive, and if he moves, finish him."

Chicot was not precisely a pious man; but at that moment it occurred to him that there is a God, and he thought that God was opening his arms to him, and that perhaps in less than five minutes the sinner would be in the presence of his Judge. He stammered some prayer, serious and fervent, which certainly was heard on high.

Two men approached Chicot, sword in hand. It was easy to

discover from his groans that he was not dead. But since he made no movement to defend himself, the more zealous of the two had the imprudence to come within reach of his left hand; the dagger, as if moved by a spring, was plunged into his throat. At the same instant half of the sword in Chicot's right hand disappeared in the side of the second cavalier, who was trying to get away.

"Ah, treason!" cried the chief, "he is not dead; charge your muskets!"

"No, I am not dead yet," cried Chicot, whose eyes flashed lightning; and quick as thought he threw himself upon the chief of the troop.

But two soldiers came to the rescue; Chicot turned and wounded one in the thigh.

"The muskets, *mordieu !*" cried the chief.

"Before they are ready," cried Chicot, "I shall have opened your entrails, brigand, and shall have cut the cords of your mask, that I may know who you are."

"Stand firm, monsieur! stand firm, and I will aid you!" cried a voice, which seemed to Chicot to come from heaven.

It was that of a handsome young man on a black horse. He had a pistol in each hand, and cried again to Chicot, "Stoop! *morbleu,* stoop!"

Chicot obeyed. One pistol was fired, and a man rolled at Chicot's feet; then the second, and another man fell.

"Now we are two to two," cried Chicot. "Generous young man, you take one, here is mine;" and he rushed on the masked man, who, groaning with rage or with fear, defended himself as if used to arms.

The young man seized his opponent by the body, threw him down, and bound him with his belt. Chicot soon wounded his adversary, who was very corpulent, between the ribs; he fell, and Chicot, putting his foot on his sword to prevent him from using it, cut the strings of his mask. "M. de Mayenne! *ventre de biche !* I thought so," said he.

The duke did not reply; he had fainted from loss of blood and the shock of his fall. Chicot, after a brief reflection, rolled up his sleeve, took his large dagger, and approached the duke to cut off his head, when his arm was seized by a grasp of iron, and a voice said, "Stay, monsieur; one does not kill a fallen enemy."

"Young man," replied Chicot, "you have saved my life, and I thank you with all my heart; but accept a little lesson very useful in the time of moral degradation in which we live. When a man has been attacked three times in three days; when he has been each time in danger of death; when his enemies have, without provocation, fired four musket-balls at him from behind, as they might have done to a mad dog—then, young man, he may do what I am about to do." And Chicot returned to his work.

But the young man stopped him again. "You shall not do it, monsieur," he said, "while I am here, at least. Not in that way should such blood be shed as that now issuing from the wound you have already inflicted."

"Bah!" said Chicot, with surprise, "you know this wretch?"

"That wretch is M. le Duc de Mayenne—a prince equal in rank to many kings."

"All the more reason; and who are you?"

"He who has saved your life, monsieur."

"And who, if I do not deceive myself, brought me a letter from the king three days ago."

"Precisely."

"Then you are in the king's service?"

"I have that honour."

"And yet you save M. de Mayenne? Permit me to tell you, monsieur, that that is not being a good servant."

"I think, on the contrary, that at this moment it is I who am the king's good servant."

"Perhaps," said Chicot, sadly—"perhaps; but this is not a time for philosophising. What is your name?"

"Ernauton de Carmainges."

"Well, M. Ernauton, what are we to do with this great carcass, equal in grandeur to all the kings of the earth?"

"I will watch over M. de Mayenne, monsieur."

"And his follower, who is listening there?"

"The poor devil hears nothing; I have bound him too tightly, and he has fainted."

"M. de Carmainges, you have saved my life to-day; but you endanger it fearfully for the future."

"I do my duty to-day; God will provide for the future."

"As you please, then, and I confess I dislike killing a defenceless man. Adieu, monsieur. But first, I will choose one of these horses."

"Take mine; I know what it can do."

"Oh, that is too generous."

"I have not so much need as you have to go quickly."

Chicot made no more compliments, but got on Ernauton's horse and disappeared.

CHAPTER XXXVIII

ERNAUTON DE CARMAINGES

ERNAUTON remained on the field of battle much embarrassed what to do with the two men, who would shortly open their eyes. As he deliberated, he saw a waggon coming along, drawn by two oxen, and driven by a peasant. Ernauton went to the man and told him that a combat had taken place between the Huguenots and Catholics, that four had been killed, but that two were still living. The peasant, although desperately frightened, aided Ernauton to place first M. de Mayenne and then the soldier in the waggon. The four bodies remained.

"Monsieur," said the peasant, "were they Catholics or Huguenots?"

"Huguenots," said Ernauton, who had seen the peasant cross himself in his first terror.

"In that case there will be no harm in my searching the heretics, will there?"

"None," replied Ernauton, who thought it as well that the peasant should do it as the first passer-by. The man did not wait to be told twice, but turned out their pockets. It seemed that he was far from disappointed, for his face looked smiling when he had finished the operation, and he drove on his oxen at their quickest pace in order the sooner to reach his home with his treasure.

It was in the stable of this excellent Catholic, on a bed of straw, that M. de Mayenne recovered his consciousness. He opened his eyes, and looked at the men and the things surrounding him with a surprise easy to imagine. Ernauton immediately dismissed the peasant.

"Who are you, monsieur?" asked Mayenne.

Ernauton smiled.

"Do you not recognise me?" said he.

"Yes, I do now; you are he who came to the assistance of my enemy."

"Yes; but I am he who prevented your enemy from killing you."

"That must be true, since I live; unless, indeed, he thought me dead."

"He went away knowing you to be alive."

"Then he thought my wound mortal."

" I do not know; but had I not opposed him, he would have given you one which certainly would have been so."

" But then, monsieur, why did you aid him in killing my men? "

" Nothing more simple, monsieur; and I am astonished that a gentleman, as you seem to be, does not understand my conduct. Chance brought me on your road, and I saw several men attacking one. I defended the one; but when this brave man (for whoever he may be, he is brave), when he remained alone with you, and had decided the victory by the blow which prostrated you—then, seeing that he was about to abuse his victory by killing you, I interfered to save you."

" You know me, then? " said Mayenne, with a scrutinising glance.

" I had no need to know you, monsieur; you were a wounded man—that was enough."

" Be frank; you know me."

" It is strange, monsieur, that you will not understand me. It seems to me that it is equally ignoble to kill a defenceless man as it is for seven men to attack one."

" There may be reasons for all things."

Ernauton bowed, but did not reply.

" Did you not see," continued Mayenne, " that I fought sword to sword with that man? "

" It is true."

" Besides, he is my most mortal enemy."

" I believe it, for he said the same thing of you."

" And if I survive my wound—"

" That will no longer concern me, and you will do what you please, monsieur."

" Do you think me dangerously wounded? "

" I have examined your wound, monsieur, and I think that although it is serious, you are in no danger of death. I believe the sword slipped along the ribs, and did not penetrate the breast. Breathe, and I think you will find no pain in the lungs."

" It is true; but my men? "

" Are dead, all but one."

" Are they left on the road? "

" Yes."

" Have they been searched? "

" The peasant whom you must have seen on opening your eyes, and who is your host, searched them."

" What did he find? "

" Some money."

" Any papers? "

" I think not."

" Ah! " said Mayenne, with evident satisfaction. " But the living man; where is he? "

" In the barn, close by."

" Bring him to me, monsieur; and if you are a man of honour, promise me to ask him no questions."

" I am not curious, monsieur; and I wish to know no more of this affair than I know already."

The duke looked at him uneasily.

" Monsieur," said Ernauton, " will you charge some one else with the commission you have just given me? "

" I was wrong, monsieur; I acknowledge it. Have the kindness to render me the service I ask of you."

Five minutes after, the soldier entered the stable. He uttered a cry on seeing the duke; but the latter had strength enough to put a finger to his lip, and the man was silent.

" Monsieur," said Mayenne to Ernauton, " my gratitude to you will be eternal; and doubtless some day we shall meet under more favourable circumstances. May I ask to whom I have the honour of speaking? "

" I am the Vicomte Ernauton de Carmainges, monsieur."

The duke expected further details; but it was now the young man's turn to be reserved.

" You were going to Beaugency? "

" Yes, monsieur."

" Then I have delayed you, and you cannot go on to-night, perhaps? "

" On the contrary, monsieur, I am about to start at once."

" For Beaugency? "

Ernauton looked at Mayenne like a man annoyed by this questioning. " To Paris," said he.

The duke appeared astonished. " Pardon," said he; " but it is strange that going to Beaugency, and being stopped by an unforeseen circumstance, you should return without fulfilling the object of your journey."

" Nothing is more simple, monsieur. I was going to a rendezvous appointed for a particular time, which I have lost by coming here with you; therefore I return."

" Oh, monsieur, will you not stay here with me for two or three days? I shall send this soldier to Paris for a surgeon; and I cannot remain here alone with these peasants, who are strangers to me."

" Then let the soldier remain with you, and I will send you a doctor."

Mayenne hesitated. " Do you know the name of my enemy ? " said he.

" No, monsieur."

" What! you saved his life, and he did not tell you his name ? "

" I did not ask him."

" You did not ask him ? "

" I have saved your life also, monsieur; have I asked you your name? But on the other hand, you both know mine."

" I see, monsieur, there is nothing to be learned from you; you are as discreet as brave."

" I observe that you say that in a reproachful manner; but on the contrary, you ought to be reassured, for a man who is discreet with one person will be so with another."

" You are right! your hand, M. de Carmainges."

Ernauton gave him his hand, but without betraying, by anything in his manner, his knowledge that he was giving his hand to a prince.

" You have blamed my conduct, monsieur," said Mayenne; " but I cannot justify myself without revealing important secrets. It will be better, I think, that we carry our confidences no farther."

" You defend yourself, monsieur, when I do not accuse. You are entirely free, believe me, to speak or to keep silent."

" Thank you, monsieur; I will keep silent. I will only say that I am a gentleman of good rank, and able to be of use to you."

" Say no more, monsieur; thanks to the master whom I serve, I have no need of assistance from any one."

" Your master," asked Mayenne, anxiously, " who is he ? "

" Oh, no more confidences! you proposed it yourself."

" It is true."

" Besides, your wound begins to inflame; I advise you to talk less."

" You are right; but I want my surgeon."

" I am returning to Paris, as I told you; give me his address."

" M. de Carmainges, give me your word of honour that if I intrust you with a letter it shall be given to the person to whom it is addressed."

" I give it, monsieur."

" I believe you; I am sure I may trust you. I must tell you a part of my secret. I belong to the guards of Madame de Montpensier."

" Oh, I did not know she had guards."

" In these troublous times, monsieur, every one guards himself as well as he can, and the House of Guise being a princely one—"

" I asked for no explanation, monsieur."

" Well, I had a mission to Amboise; when on the road I saw my enemy. You know the rest."

" Yes."

" Stopped by this wound, I must report to the duchess the reason of my delay."

" Well? "

" Will you therefore put into her own hands the letter I am about to write? "

" If there is ink and paper here," said Ernauton, rising to seek for those articles.

" It is needless; my soldier should have my tablets with him."

The soldier drew from his pocket some closed tablets. Mayenne turned towards the wall to work a secret spring, and the tablets opened; he wrote some lines in pencil, and shut them again. It was impossible for any one who did not know the secret to open them without breaking them.

" Monsieur," said Ernauton, " in three days these tablets shall be delivered."

" Into her own hands? "

" Yes, monsieur."

The duke, exhausted by talking, and by the effort of writing the letter, sank back on his straw.

" Monsieur," said the soldier, in a tone little in harmony with his dress, " you bound me like a calf, it is true, but whether you wish it or not, I regard those bonds as chains of friendship, and will prove it to you some day." And he held out a hand whose whiteness Ernauton had already remarked.

" So be it," said he, smi.ing; " it seems I have gained two friends."

" Do not despise them," said the soldier; " one has never too many."

" That is true, comrade," said Ernauton; and he left them.

CHAPTER XXXIX

THE STABLE-YARD

ERNAUTON arrived at Paris on the third day. At three in the afternoon he entered the quarters of the Forty-five, at the Louvre. The Gascons called out in surprise on seeing him. M. de Loignac, hearing those cries, entered, and perceiving Ernauton, assumed a frowning expression; Ernauton approached him directly. M. de Loignac signed to him to enter a little room, where he always gave his private audiences. " This is nice behaviour, monsieur," said he—" five days and nights absent. And it is you—you, monsieur, whom I thought one of the most sensible—it is you who set the example of such a breach of discipline."

" Monsieur, I did what I was told to do."

" What were you told to do? "

" To follow M. de Mayenne, and I have followed him."

" For five days and nights? "

" For five days and nights, monsieur."

" Then he has left Paris? "

" He left that same evening, and that seemed to me suspicious."

" You were right, monsieur. What then? "

Ernauton related clearly and energetically all that had taken place. When he mentioned the letter, " You have it, monsieur? " asked Loignac.

" Yes, monsieur."

" The devil! that deserves attention; come with me, I beg of you! "

Ernauton followed Loignac to the courtyard of the Louvre. All was preparing for the king's going out, and M. d'Epernon was seeing two new horses tried, which had been sent from England as a present from Elizabeth to Henri, and which were that day to be harnessed to the king's carriage for the first time.

Loignac approached D'Epernon. " Great news, Monsieur the Duke! " said he.

" What is it? " said D'Epernon, drawing him to one side.

" M. de Carmainges has seen M. de Mayenne lying wounded in a village beyond Orléans."

" Wounded! "

" Yes, and more, he has written a letter to Madame de Montpensier, which M. de Carmainges has in his pocket."

" Oh, oh! send M. de Carmainges to me."

" Here he is," said Loignac, signing to Ernauton to advance.

" Well, monsieur, it seems you have a letter from M. de Mayenne."

" Yes, monsieur."

" Addressed to Madame de Montpensier? "

" Yes, monsieur."

" Give it to me, if you please; " and the duke extended his hand.

" Pardon, monseigneur; but did you ask me for the duke's letter? "

" Certainly."

" You do not know that this letter was confided to me? "

" What matters that? "

" It matters much, monseigneur; I passed my word to the duke to give it to the duchess herself."

" Do you belong to the king or to M. de Mayenne? "

" To the king."

" Well! the king wishes to see the letter."

" Monsieur, you are not the king."

" I think you forget to whom you speak, M. de Carmainges," said D'Epernon, pale with anger.

" I remember perfectly, monseigneur, and that is why I refuse."

" You refuse? "

" Yes, monseigneur."

" M. de Carmainges, you forget your oath of fidelity."

" Monseigneur, I have sworn fidelity only to one person, and that is the king.   If he asks me for the letter, he must have it; but he is not here."

" M. de Carmainges," said the duke, growing very angry, " you are like the rest of the Gascons—blind in prosperity. Your good fortune dazzles you, my little gentleman; the possession of a state secret stuns you like a blow with a mallet."

" What stuns me, monseigneur, is the disgrace into which I seem likely to fall—not my fortune, which my refusal to obey you renders, I know, very precarious.   But no matter!   I do what I ought, and I will do only that; and no one, excepting the king, shall see this letter but the person to whom it is addressed."

" Loignac," cried D'Epernon, " go at once and place M. de Carmainges in prison."

" It is certain that will prevent me from delivering the letter— so long at least as I remain in prison; but once I come out—"

" If you never do come out? "

" I shall come out, monsieur—unless you have me assassinated. Yes, I shall come out; the walls are less strong than my will, and then—"

" Well? "

" I will speak to the king."

" To prison with him, and take away the letter! " roared D'Epernon, beside himself with rage.

" No one shall touch it! " cried Ernauton, starting back and drawing from his breast the tablets of M. de Mayenne; " I will break it to pieces, since I can save it in no other way; M. de Mayenne will approve my conduct, and the king will pardon me."

The young man was about to execute his threat, when a touch arrested his arm. He turned and saw the king, who, coming down the staircase behind them, had heard the end of the discussion.

" What is the matter, gentlemen? " said he.

" Sire," cried D'Epernon, furiously, " this man, one of your Forty-five Guardsmen, to which he shall soon cease to belong, being sent by me to watch M. de Mayenne, in Paris, followed him to Orléans, and received from him a letter for Madame de Montpensier."

" You have received from M. de Mayenne a letter for Madame de Montpensier? " asked the king of Ernauton.

" Yes, Sire; but M. d'Epernon does not tell you under what circumstances."

" Well, where is this letter? "

" That is just the cause of the quarrel, Sire. M. de Carmainges resolutely refuses to give it to me, and determines to carry it to its address."

Carmainges bent one knee before the king. " Sire," said he, " I am a poor gentleman, but a man of honour. I saved the life of your messenger, who was about to be assassinated by M. de Mayenne and six of his followers, for I arrived just in time to turn the fortune of the combat."

" And M. de Mayenne? "

" Was dangerously wounded."

" Well, what then? "

" Your messenger, Sire, who seemed to have a particular hatred of M. de Mayenne—"

The king smiled.

" Wished to kill his enemy. Perhaps he had the right, but I thought that in my presence, whose sword belongs to your

Majesty, this vengeance would be a political assassination, and—"

" Go on, monsieur."

" I saved the life of M. de Mayenne, as I had saved that of your messenger."

D'Epernon shrugged his shoulders; Loignac bit his long mustache; the king remained cold.

" Go on," said the king.

" M. de Mayenne, reduced to one companion—for the four others were killed—did not wish to part with him, and ignorant that I belonged to your Majesty, confided to me a letter to his sister. I have this letter, Sire, and here it is; I offer it to your Majesty, who has the right to dispose of it and of me. My honour is dear to me, Sire; but I place it fearlessly in your hands."

Ernauton, so saying, held out the tablets to the king, who gently put them back.

" What did you say, D'Epernon? " said he; " M. de Carmaignes is an honest man and a faithful servant."

" What did I say, Sire? "

" Yes; I heard you pronounce the word ' prison.' *Mordieu !* on the contrary, when one meets a man like M. de Carmainges, it is reward we should speak of. A letter, duke, belongs only to the bearer and to the person to whom it is sent. You will deliver your letter, M. de Carmainges."

" But, Sire," said D'Epernon, " think of what that letter may contain. Do not play at delicacy, when perhaps your Majesty's life is concerned."

" You will deliver your letter, M. de Carmainges," said the king.

" Thanks, Sire," said Carmainges, beginning to retire.

" Where do you take it? "

" To Madame la Duchesse de Montpensier, I think I had the honour of telling your Majesty."

" I mean, to the Hôtel de Guise, St. Denis, or where? "

" I had no instructions on that subject, Sire. I shall take the letter to the Hôtel de Guise, and there I shall learn where Madame de Montpensier is."

" And when you have found her? "

" I will deliver my letter."

" Very good. M. de Carmainges, have you promised anything else to M. de Mayenne than to deliver that letter to his sister? "

" No, Sire."

" No secrecy as to the place where you find her? "

" No, Sire."

" Then I will impose only one condition on you."

" I am your Majesty's servant."

" Deliver your letter, and then come to me at Vincennes, where I shall be this evening."

" Yes, Sire."

" And you will tell me where you found the duchess? "

" I will, Sire."

" I ask no other confidences, remember."

" Sire, I promise."

" What imprudence, Sire! " cried D'Epernon.

" There are men you cannot understand, duke. This one is loyal to Mayenne; he will be loyal to me."

" Towards you, Sire, I shall be more than loyal—I shall be devoted," cried Ernauton.

" Now, D'Epernon, no more quarrels," said the king; " and you must at once pardon in this brave fellow what you looked upon as a want of devotion, but which I regard as a proof of loyalty."

" Sire," said Ernauton, " Monsieur the Duke is too superior a man not to have discovered, through my disobedience (for which I confess my regret), my respect for him; only before all things, I must do what I believe to be my duty."

" *Parfandious!* " said the duke, changing his countenance like a mask, " this trial has done you honour, my dear Carmainges, and you are really a fine fellow; is he not, Loignac? However, we gave him a good fright; " and the duke burst out laughing.

Loignac did not answer; he could not lie like his illustrious chief.

" If it was a trial, so much the better," said the king, doubtfully; " but I counsel you not to try these experiments often. Too many would give way under them. Now let us go, duke; you accompany me? "

" It was your Majesty's order that I should ride by the carriage-door? "

" Yes; and who goes the other side? "

" A devoted servant of your Majesty's—M. de Sainte-Maline," said D'Epernon, glancing at Ernauton to see the effect of his words; but Ernauton remained unmoved.

CHAPTER XL

THE SEVEN SINS OF MAGDALENE

THE king, however, on seeing the liveliness of his horses, did not wish to be alone in the carriage, but desired D'Epernon to sit by him. Loignac and Sainte-Maline rode on either side, and an outrider in front. The king was, as usual, surrounded by dogs, and there was also a table in the carriage, covered with illuminated pictures, which the king cut out with wonderful skill, in spite of the movement of the carriage. He was just then occupied with the life of Magdalene the sinner. The different pictures were labelled—" Magdalene gives way to the sin of anger;" " Magdalene gives way to the sin of gluttony," and so on through the seven cardinal sins. The one that the king was occupied with as they passed through the Porte St. Antoine represented Magdalene giving way to anger.

The beautiful sinner, half lying on cushions, and with no other covering than the magnificent hair with which she was afterwards to wipe the feet of Jesus, was having a slave, who had broken a precious vase, thrown into a pond filled with lampreys, whose eager heads were protruding from the water; while on the other side a woman, even less dressed than her mistress, as her hair was bound up, was being flogged because she had, while dressing her mistress's head, pulled out some of those magnificent hairs whose profusion might have rendered her more indulgent to such a fault. In the background were visible some dogs being whipped for having allowed beggars to pass quietly, and some cocks being murdered for having crowed too loudly in the morning.

On arriving at the Croix Faubin, the king had finished this figure, and was passing to " Magdalene giving way to the sin of gluttony."

This represented the beautiful sinner lying on one of those beds of purple and gold on which the ancients used to take their repasts; all that the Romans had most *recherché* in meat, in fish, and in fruit—dormice in honey, red mullets, lobsters from Stromboli, and pomegranates from Sicily—ornamented the table. On the ground some dogs were disputing for a pheasant, while the air was full of birds, which had carried off from the table figs, strawberries, and cherries, sometimes dropping them on a colony of mice, who with their noses in the air awaited that manna from heaven. Magdalene held in her hand one of those singularly shaped glasses which Petronius has described, filled with a white *liqueur*.

Fully occupied with this important work, the king merely raised his eyes as they passed by the convent of the Jacobins, from which vespers was sounding on every bell, and of which every window and door was closed. But a hundred steps farther on, an attentive observer would have seen him throw a more curious glance on a fine-looking house on his left, which, built in the midst of a charming garden, opened on the road. This house was called Bel-Esbat, and unlike the convent, had every window open with the exception of one, before which hung a blind. As the king passed this blind moved perceptibly; Henri smiled at D'Epernon, and then fell to work on another picture. This was the sin of luxury. The artist had represented this in such glowing colours, and had painted the sin with so much courage and minuteness that we can only mention a single feature of it, which, however, was altogether episodical: Magdalene's guardian angel was flying back to heaven affrighted, and hiding his face in his hands. This picture, full of minute details, occupied the king so completely that he never noticed an image of vanity who rode by his carriage. It was a pity, for Sainte-Maline was very happy and proud on his horse, as he rode so near that he could hear the king say to his dog, "Gently, M. Love, you get in my way," or to M. le Duc d'Epernon, "Duke, I believe these horses will break my neck." From time to time, however, Sainte-Maline glanced at Loignac, who was too much accustomed to these honours not to be indifferent to them; and he could not but feel the superiority of his calm and modest demeanour, and even would try to imitate it for a few minutes, until the thought would recur again, " I am seen and looked at, and people say, ' Who is that happy gentleman who accompanies the king?'" Sainte-Maline's happiness seemed likely to last for a long time, for the horses, covered with harness heavy with gold and embroidery, and imprisoned in shafts like those of David's ark, did not advance rapidly. But as he was growing too proud, something peculiarly annoying to him came to moderate his joy; he heard the king pronounce the name of Ernauton, and not once, but two or three times. Sainte-Maline strained his attention to hear more, but some noise or movement always prevented him —either the king uttered some exclamation of regret at an unlucky cut of the scissors, or one of the dogs began to bark; so that between Paris and Vincennes, the name of Ernauton had been pronounced at least six times by the king, and at least four times by D'Epernon, without Sainte-Maline's knowing the reason. He persuaded himself that the king was merely inquiring the cause of Ernauton's disappearance, and that D'Epernon was explaining it. At last they arrived at Vincennes, and as the king had still three sins to cut out, he went at once to his chamber to finish them. It was a bitterly cold day, therefore Sainte-Maline sat down in a chimney-corner to warm himself, and was nearly falling asleep, when Loignac put his hand on his shoulder.

"You must work to-day," said he. "You shall sleep some other day; so get up, M. de Sainte-Maline."

"I will keep awake for a fortnight if necessary, monsieur."

"Oh, we shall not be so exacting as that."

"What must I do, monsieur?"

"Get on your horse and return to Paris."

"I am ready; my horse is standing saddled."

"Good; go then straight to the room of the Forty-five, and awaken every one. But excepting the three chiefs, whom I will name to you, no one must know where he is going, nor what he is about to do."

"I will obey these instructions implicitly."

"Here, then, are some more: leave fourteen of these gentlemen at the Porte St. Antoine, fifteen others halfway, and bring the rest here."

"Yes, monsieur; but at what hour must we leave Paris?"

"When night falls."

"On horseback or on foot?"

"On horseback."

"Armed?"

"Fully; with daggers, pistols, and swords."

"With armour?"

"Yes."

"What else?"

"Here are three letters—one for M. de Chalabre, one for M. de Biran, and one for yourself. M. de Chalabre will command the first party, M. de Biran the second, and yourself the third."

"Good, monsieur."

"These letters are not to be opened till six o'clock; M. de Chalabre will open his at the Porte St. Antoine, M. de Biran his at the Croix Faubin, and you yours on your return."

"Must we come quickly?"

"As quickly as possible, without creating suspicion. Let each troop come out of Paris by a different gate—M. de Chalabre by the Porte Bourdelle, M. de Biran by the Porte du Temple,

and you through the Porte St. Antoine. All other instructions
are in the letters. Go quickly from here to the Croix Faubin,
but then slowly; you have still two hours before dark, which
is more than necessary. Now do you well understand your
orders?"

"Perfectly, monsieur."

"Fourteen in the first troop, fifteen in the second, and fifteen
in the third; it is evident they do not count Ernauton, and that
he no longer is one of the Forty-five," said Sainte-Maline to
himself when Loignac had gone.

Sainte-Maline, swollen with pride, fulfilled all his directions
punctually. When he arrived among the Forty-five, the greater
number of them were already preparing for their supper. Thus
the noble Lardille de Chavantrade had prepared a dish of
mutton stewed with carrots and spices, after the method of
Gascony, in which Militor had occasionally aided by trying the
pieces of meat and vegetable with a fork.

Pertinax de Montcrabeau, and the singular servant who spoke
to him so familiarly, were preparing supper for themselves and
six companions, who had each contributed six sous towards it;
each one, in fact, was disposing according to his fancy of the
money of his Majesty Henri III. One might judge of the
character of each man by the aspect of his little lodging. Some
loved flowers, and displayed on their window-sills some fading
rose or geranium; others had, like the king, a taste for pictures;
others had introduced a niece or housekeeper. And M. d'Epernon had told M. de Loignac privately to shut his eyes on these
things. At eight o'clock in winter, and ten in summer, they
went to bed; but always leaving fifteen on guard. As, however,
it was but half-past five when Sainte-Maline entered, he found
every one about, and, as we said, gastronomically inclined.
But with one word he put an end to all this. "To horse,
gentlemen!" said he, and leaving them without another word,
went to explain his orders to MM. de Biran and Chalabre.
Some, while buckling on their belts and grasping their cuirasses,
ate great mouthfuls, washed down by a draught of wine; and
others, whose supper was less advanced, armed themselves with
resignation. They called over the names, and only forty-four,
including Sainte-Maline, answered.

"M. Ernauton de Carmainges is missing," said M. de Chalabre,
whose turn it was to exercise the functions of quarter-master.
A profound joy filled the heart of Sainte-Maline, and a smile
played on his lips—a rare thing with this sombre and envious
man. In fact, Ernauton seemed to him to be finally ruined

by that unexplained absence from an expedition of such importance.

The forty-four set off on their different routes.

CHAPTER XLI

BEL-ESBAT

IT is needless to say that Ernauton, whom Sainte-Maline thought ruined, was, on the contrary, pursuing the course of his unexpected and ascending fortunes. He had gone first to the Hôtel de Guise. There, after having knocked at the great door, which was opened to him with extreme circumspection, he was only laughed at when he asked for an interview with the duchess. Then, as he insisted, they told him that he ought to know that her Highness lived at Soissons, and not at Paris. Ernauton was prepared for this reception, so it did not discourage him.

" I am grieved at her Highness's absence," said he, " for I had a communication of great importance to deliver to her from the Duc de Mayenne."

" From the Duc de Mayenne! Who charged you to deliver it? "

" The duke himself."

" The duke! " exclaimed the porter, with an astonishment admirably affected; " where, then, did he give you that charge? for he is not at Paris either."

" I know that, as I met him on the road to Blois."

" On the road to Blois? " said the porter, a little more attentive.

" Yes; and he there charged me with a message for Madame de Montpensier."

" A message? "

" A letter."

" Where is it? "

" Here," said Ernauton, striking his doublet.

" Will you let me see it? "

" Willingly." And Ernauton drew out the letter.

" What singular ink! " said the man.

" It is blood," said Ernauton, calmly.

The porter grew pale at these words, and at the idea that this blood was perhaps that of M. de Mayenne. At this time, when there was great dearth of ink, and an abundance of blood spil'ed, it was not uncommon for lovers to write to their mistresses, or absent relations to their families, with that fluid.

" Monsieur," said the servant, " I do not know if you will find Madame de Montpensier in Paris or its environs; but go to a house in the Faubourg St. Antoine, called Bel-Esbat, which belongs to the duchess. It is the first on the left hand going to Vincennes, after the convent of the Jacobins. You will be sure to find some one there in the service of the duchess sufficiently in her confidence to be able to tell you where Madame the Duchess is just now."

" Thank you," said Ernauton, who saw that the man either could or would say no more.

He found Bel-Esbat without making any inquiries, rang, and the door opened.

" Enter," said a man, who then seemed to wait for some password; but as Ernauton did not give any, he asked him what he wanted.

" I wish to speak to Madame la Duchesse de Montpensier," replied Ernauton.

" And why do you come here for her? "

" Because the porter at the Hôtel de Guise sent me here."

" Madame the Duchess is neither here nor in Paris."

" Then," said Ernauton, " I will put off till a more auspicious moment acquitting myself of a mission with which M. de Mayenne charged me."

" For Madame the Duchess? "

" Yes."

" From M. le Duc de Mayenne? "

" Yes."

The valet reflected a moment. " Monsieur," said he, " I cannot answer; there is some one else whom I must consult. Please to wait."

" These people are well served," thought Ernauton. " Certainly, they must be dangerous people who think it necessary to hide themselves in this manner. One cannot enter a house of the Guises as you can the Louvre. I begin to think that it is not the true King of France whom I serve."

He looked round him. The courtyard was deserted; but all the doors of the stables were open, as if they expected some troop to enter and take up quarters there. He was interrupted by the return of the valet, who was followed by another.

" Leave me your horse, monsieur," said he, " and follow my comrade; you will find some one who can answer you much better than I can."

Ernauton followed the valet, and was shown into a little

room, where a simply though elegantly dressed lady was seated at an embroidery frame.

"Here is the gentleman from M. de Mayenne, madame," said the servant.

She turned, and Ernauton uttered a cry of surprise.

"You, madame!" cried he, recognising at once, under that third transformation, his page and the lady of the litter.

"You!" cried the lady, in her turn, letting her work drop, and looking at Ernauton. "Leave us," she said to the valet.

"You are of the household of Madame de Montpensier, madame?" said Ernauton, with surprise.

"Yes; but you, monsieur, how do you bring here a message from the Duc de Mayenne?"

"Through a series of circumstances which it would take too long to repeat," replied Ernauton, cautiously.

"Oh, you are discreet, monsieur," said the lady, smiling.

"Yes, madame, whenever it is necessary to be so."

"But I see no occasion for your discretion here; for if you really bring a message from the person you say—Oh, do not look angry! if you really do, I say, it interests me so much that in remembrance of our acquaintance, short though it was, you should tell it to me."

The lady threw into these words all the caressing and seductive grace that a pretty woman can employ.

"Madame," replied Ernauton, "you cannot make me tell what I do not know."

"And still less what you will not tell?"

"Madame, all my mission consists in delivering a letter to her highness."

"Well, then, give me the letter," said the lady, holding out her hand.

"Madame, I believe I had the honour of telling you that this letter was addressed to the duchess."

"But as the duchess is absent, and I represent her here, you may—"

"I cannot, madame."

"You distrust me, monsieur?"

"I ought to do so, madame; but," said the young man with an expression there was no mistaking, "in spite of the mystery of your conduct, you have inspired me, I confess, with very different sentiments."

"Really!" said the lady, colouring a little under Ernauton's ardent gaze.

Ernauton bowed.

" Take care, monsieur ! " said she, laughing, " you are making a declaration of love."

" Yes, madame; I do not know if I may ever see you again, and the opportunity is too precious for me to let it slip."

" Then, monsieur, I understand."

" That I love you, madame? that is easy to understand."

" No, but how you came here."

" Ah, pardon, madame ! but now it is I who do not understand."

" Yes, I understand that wishing to see me again, you invented a pretext to get in."

" I, madame ! a pretext ! you judge me ill. I was ignorant if I should ever see you again, and placed my sole reliance upon chance, which already had twice thrown me in your way; but invent a pretext, I?—never ! I am strange, perhaps; I do not think like all the world."

" Oh, you say you are in love, and you have scruples as to the manner of introducing yourself again to her you love ! It is very fine, monsieur; well, I suspected that you would have scruples."

" Why, madame, if you please? "

" The other day you met me. I was in a litter; you recognised me; and yet you did not follow me."

" Madame, you are confessing you paid some attention to me."

" And why not? Surely the way in which we first met justified my putting my head out of my litter to look after you when you passed. But you galloped away, after uttering an ' Ah ! ' which made me tremble in my litter."

" I was forced to go away, madame."

" By your scruples? "

" No, madame, by my duty."

" Well ! " said the lady, laughing, " I see that you are a reasonable, circumspect lover, who, above all things, fears to compromise himself."

" If you had inspired me with certain fears, there would be nothing astonishing in it. Is it customary that a woman should dress as a man, force the barriers, and come to see an unfortunate wretch drawn to pieces, using meanwhile all sorts of gesticulations utterly incomprehensible? "

The lady grew rather pale, although she tried to smile.

Ernauton went on. " Is it natural also that this lady, after this strange announcement, fearful of being arrested, should fly as though she were a thief—she who is in the service of

Madame de Montpensier, a powerful princess, although not much in favour at court?"

This time the lady smiled again, but ironically. "You are not clear-sighted, monsieur," she said, "in spite of your pretension to be an observer; for with a little sense, all that seems obscure to you would have been clear. Was it not very natural that Madame de Montpensier should be interested in the fate of M. de Salcède, in what he might be tempted to say, what true or false revelations he might utter to compromise the House of Lorraine? And if that was natural, monsieur, was it not also natural that this princess should send some one—some safe, intimate friend—to be present at the execution, and bring her all the details? Well, monsieur, this person was I. Now, do you think I could go in my woman's dress? In fine, now that you know my relation to the duchess, do you think I could remain indifferent to the sufferings of the victim and his possible revelations?"

"You are right, madame; and now I admire as much your logic and talent as I admired your beauty."

"Thank you, monsieur. And now that we know each other, and that everything is explained, give me the letter, since the letter exists, and is not a simple pretext."

"Impossible, madame."

The unknown seemed trying not to grow angry. "Impossible?" she repeated.

"Yes, impossible; for I swore to M. de Mayenne to deliver it only to the duchess herself."

"Say rather," cried the lady, giving way to her irritation, "that you have no letter; that in spite of your pretended scruples, it was a mere pretext for getting in here; that you wished to see me again, and that was all. Well, monsieur, you are satisfied; not only you have effected your entrance, but you have seen me, and have told me you adore me."

"In that, as in all the rest, I have told you the truth, madame."

"Well, so be it. You adore me; you wished to see me; and you have seen me. I have procured you a pleasure in return for a service. We are quits. Adieu!"

"I will obey you, madame; since you send me away, I will go."

"Yes," cried she, now really angry, "but if you know me, I do not know you. You have too much advantage over me. Ah, you think you can enter, on some pretext, into the house of a princess, and go away and say, 'I succeeded in my perfidy!' Ah, monsieur, that is not the behaviour of a gallant man!"

" It seems to me, madame, that you are very hard on what would have been after all only a trick of love, if it had not been, as I have already told you, an affair of the greatest importance and the simplest truth. I put aside all your injurious expressions, and I will forget all I might have said, affectionate or tender, since you are so badly disposed towards me. But I will not go out from here under the weight of your unworthy suspicions. I have a letter from the duke for Madame de Montpensier, and here it is; you can see the handwriting and the address."

Ernauton held out the letter to the lady, but without delivering it. She cast her eyes on it, and cried, " His writing! Blood! "

Without replying, Ernauton put the letter back in his pocket, bowed low, and very pale and bitterly hurt, turned to go. But she ran after him, and caught him by the skirt of his cloak.

" What is it, madame? " said he.

" For pity's sake, pardon me! has any accident happened to the duke? "

" You ask me to pardon you only that you may read this letter; and I have already told you that no one shall read it but the duchess."

" Ah, obstinate and stupid that you are! " cried the duchess, with a fury full of majesty; " do you not recognise me, or rather, could you not divine that I was the mistress? And are these the eyes of a servant? I am the Duchesse de Montpensier; give me the letter."

" You are the duchess? " cried Ernauton, starting back in dismay.

" Yes, I am! Give it to me! I want to know what has happened to my brother."

But instead of obeying, as the duchess expected, the young man, recovering from his first surprise, crossed his arms. " How can I believe you," said he, " when you have already lied to me twice? "

The duchess's eyes shot forth fire at these words; but Ernauton stood firm. " Ah, you doubt still! you want proofs of what I affirm! " she cried, tearing her lace ruffles with rage.

" Yes, madame," replied Ernauton, coldly.

She darted towards the bell, and rang it furiously; a valet appeared.

" What does madame want? " said he.

She stamped her foot with rage. " Mayneville! " she cried; " I want Mayneville! Is he not here? "

" Yes, madame."

" Let him come here."

The valet went; and a minute after Mayneville entered.

" Did you send for me, madame? " said he.

" Madame! And since when am I simply madame? " cried she, angrily.

" Your highness! " said Mayneville, in surprise.

" Good! " said Ernauton, " I have now a gentleman before me; and if he has lied, I shall know what to do."

" You believe then, at last? " said the duchess.

" Yes, madame, I believe, and here is the letter; " and bowing, the young man gave to Madame de Montpensier the letter so long disputed.

CHAPTER XLII

THE LETTER OF M. DE MAYENNE

THE duchess seized the letter, opened it, and read it eagerly, while various expressions passed over her face, like clouds over the sky. When she had finished she gave it to Mayneville to read. It was as follows:

MY SISTER,—I tried to do myself the work I should have left to others, and I have been punished for it. I have received a sword-wound from the fellow whom you know. The worst of it is that he has killed five of my men, and among them Boularon and Desnoises —that is to say, two of my best—after which he fled. I must tell you that he was aided by the bearer of this letter—a charming young man, as you may see. I recommend him to you; he is discretion itself.

One merit which he will have, I presume, in your eyes, my dear sister, is in having prevented my conqueror from killing me, as he much wished, having pulled off my mask when I had fainted, and recognised me

I recommend you, sister, to discover the name and profession of this discreet cavalier; for I suspect him, while he interests me. To my offers of service, he replied that the master whom he served let him want for nothing.

I can tell you no more about him, but that he pretends not to know me. I suffer much, but believe my life is not in danger. Send me my surgeon at once; I am lying like a horse upon straw, the bearer will tell you where.—Your affectionate brother,

MAYENNE.

When they had finished reading, the duchess and Mayneville looked at each other in astonishment. The duchess broke the silence.

" To whom," said she, " do we owe the signal service that you have rendered us, monsieur? "

" To a man who, whenever he can, helps the weak against the strong."

" Will you give me some details, monsieur? "

Ernauton told all he had seen, and named the duke's place of retreat.

Madame de Montpensier and Mayneville listened with interest. When he had finished, the duchess said, " May I hope, monsieur, that you will continue the work so well begun, and attach yourself to our house! "

These words spoken in the gracious tone that the duchess knew so well how to use, were very flattering to Ernauton, after the avowal which he had made; but the young man, putting vanity aside, attributed them to simple curiosity. He knew well that the king, in making it a condition that he should reveal the duchess's place of abode, had some object in view. Two interests contended within him—his love, which he could sacrifice, and his honour, which he could not. The temptation was all the stronger that by avowing his position near the king, he should gain an enormous importance in the eyes of the duchess; and it was not a light consideration for a young man coming straight from Gascony to be important in the eyes of the Duchesse de Montpensier. Sainte-Maline would not have resisted an instant. All these thoughts rushed through Ernauton's mind, and resulted in making him stronger than before.

" Madame," said he, " I have already had the honour of telling M. de Mayenne that I serve a good master, who treats me too well for me to desire to seek another."

" My brother tells me in his letter, monsieur, that you seemed not to recognise him. How, then, if you did not know him, did you use his name to penetrate to me? "

" M. de Mayenne seemed to wish to preserve his incognito, madame; and I therefore did not think I ought to recognise him. And it might have been inconvenient to him that the peasants should know what an illustrious guest they were entertaining. Here there was no reason for secrecy; on the contrary, the name of M. de Mayenne opened the way to you, so I thought that here, as there, I acted rightly."

The duchess smiled, and said, " No one could extricate himself better from an embarrassing question; and you are, I must confess, a clever man."

" I see no cleverness in what I have had the honour of telling you, madame."

" Well, monsieur," said the duchess, impatiently, " I see

clearly that you will tell nothing. You do not reflect that gratitude is a heavy burden for one of my house to bear; that you have twice rendered me a service; and that if I wished to know your name, or rather, who you are—"

" I know, madame, you would learn it easily; but you would learn it from some one else, and I should have told nothing."

" He is always right," cried the duchess, with a look which gave Ernauton more pleasure than ever a look had done before. Therefore he asked no more, but like the gourmand, who leaves the table when he thinks he has had the best bit, he bowed, and prepared to take leave.

" Then, monsieur, that is all you have to tell me? " asked the duchess.

" I have executed my commission, and it only remains for me to present my humble respects to your highness."

The duchess let him go; but when the door shut behind him, she stamped her foot impatiently. " Mayneville," said she, " have that young man followed."

" Impossible, madame. All our household are out; I myself am waiting for the event. It is a bad day on which to do anything else than what we have decided to do."

" You are right, Mayneville; but afterwards—"

" Oh! afterwards, if you please, madame."

" Yes; for I suspect him, as my brother does."

" He is a brave fellow, at all events; and really, we are fortunate—a stranger, an unknown, falling from the sky to render us such a service."

" Nevertheless, Mayneville, have him watched later, at any rate."

" Eh, madame! later I trust we shall have no need to watch any one."

" Come, really, I don't know to-night what I am saying; I have lost my head."

" It is permitted to a general like you, madame, to be preoccupied on the eve of a decisive action."

" That is true. But night is falling, and Valois must be returning from Vincennes."

" Oh! we have time before us; it is not eight o'clock, and our men have not arrived."

" All have the word, have they not? "

" All."

" They are trustworthy? "

" Tried, madame."

" How many do you expect? "

" Fifty; it is more than necessary, for besides them we have two hundred monks as good as soldiers, if not better."

" As soon as our men have arrived, range your monks on the road."

" They are all ready, madame. They will intercept the way; our men will push the carriage towards them; the gates of the convent will be open, and will have but to close behind the carriage."

" Let us sup, then, Mayneville; it will help us to pass the time. I am so impatient that I should like to push the hands of the clock."

" The hour will come; be easy."

" But our men? "

" They will be here; it is hardly eight."

" Mayneville, my poor brother asks for his surgeon. The best surgeon, the best cure for his wound, would be a lock of the Valois's hair; and the man who should carry him that present, Mayneville, would be sure to be welcome."

" In two hours, madame, that man shall set out to find our dear duke in his retreat; he who went out of Paris as a fugitive shall return triumphantly."

" One word more, Mayneville; are our friends in Paris warned?"

" What friends? "

" The Leaguers."

" God forbid, Madame! to tell a *bourgeois* is to tell all Paris. Once the deed is done, remember, we have to send out fifty couriers before it becomes known; then, the prisoner being in a cloister, we can defend ourselves against an army. There will then no longer be any risk in crying from the roof of the convent, ' We have the Valois! ' "

" You are both skilful and prudent, Mayneville. Do you know, though, that my responsibility is great, and that no other woman, in any period, has ever conceived and executed such a project? "

" I know it, madame; therefore I counsel you, trembling with apprehension."

" The monks will be armed under their robes? "

" Yes."

" The soldiers are on the way? "

" They should be there at this moment."

" The *bourgeois* to be notified after the event? "

" Three couriers will attend to that. In ten minutes Lachapelle-Marteau, Brigard, and Bussy-Leclerc will be informed; they will inform the rest."

"Mind you kill those two fellows whom we saw pass, riding at the sides of the carriage; then we can describe what takes place as pleases us best."

"Kill those poor devils, madame! do you think that necessary?"

"Loignac! would he be a great loss?"

"He is a brave soldier."

"A low adventurer, like that other ill-looking fellow who pranced on the left, with his fiery eyes and his black skin."

"Oh, that one I don't care so much about! I don't know him, and I agree with your Highness in disliking his looks."

"Then you abandon him to me?" laughed the duchess.

"Oh, yes, madame! What I said was only for your renown, and the morality of the party that we represent."

"Good, Mayneville, I know you are a virtuous man; and I will sign you a certificate to that effect if you like. You need have nothing to do with it; they will defend the Valois and get killed. To you I recommend that young man."

"What young man?"

"He who just left us; see if he be really gone, and if he be not some spy sent by our enemies."

Mayneville opened the window, and tried to look out. "Oh, what a dark night!" said he.

"An excellent night; the darker the better. Therefore, good courage, my captain."

"Yes, but we shall see nothing."

"God, whom we fight for, will see for us."

Mayneville, who did not seem quite so sure of the intervention of Providence in affairs of this nature, remained at the window looking out.

"Do you see any one?" asked the duchess.

"No, but I hear the tramp of horses."

"It is they; all goes well." And the duchess touched the famous pair of golden scissors at her side.

CHAPTER XLIII

HOW DOM GORENFLOT BLESSED THE KING AS HE PASSED BEFORE THE PRIORY OF THE JACOBINS

ERNAUTON went away with a full heart but a quiet conscience; he had had the singular good fortune to declare his love to a princess, and to cause her, by the important conversation which followed, to forget his declaration just so far that it had worked

no immediate harm, and might bear fruit at some future time.
He had betrayed neither the king, M. de Mayenne, nor himself.
Therefore he was content; but he still wished for many things,
and among others, a quick return to Vincennes, where the king
expected him; then to go to bed and dream.   He set off at full
gallop as soon as he left Bel-Esbat, but he had scarcely gone
a hundred yards when he came on a body of cavaliers who
stretched right across the road.   He was surrounded in a
minute, and half-a-dozen swords and as many pistols were
presented at him.

"Oh!" said Ernauton, "robbers on the road, a league from
Paris!   The devil take the country!   The king has an inefficient
provost; I shall advise him to make a change."

"Silence, if you please!" said a voice that Ernauton thought
he recognised.   "Your sword, your arms! quick!"

And one man seized the bridle of the horse, while two others
stripped him of his arms.

"*Peste!* what clever thieves!" said Ernauton.   "At least,
gentlemen, do me the favour to tell me—"

"Why, it is M. de Carmainges!" said the man who had seized
his sword.

"M. de Pincornay!" cried Ernauton.   "Oh, fie! what a
bad trade you have taken up!"

"I said 'silence!'" cried the voice of the chief; "and take
this man to the *dépôt*."

"But, M. de Sainte-Maline, it is our companion, Ernauton
de Carmainges."

"Ernauton here!" cried Sainte-Maline, angrily; "what is
he doing here?"

"Good-evening, gentlemen," said Carmainges; "I did not,
I confess, expect to find so much good company."

Sainte-Maline remained silent.

"It seems that I am arrested," continued Ernauton; "for I
presume you don't intend to plunder me?"

"The devil!" growled Sainte-Maline; "this is unforeseen."

"By me also, I assure you," said Ernauton, laughing.

"It is embarrassing.   What were you doing here?"

"If I asked you that question, would you answer?"

"No."

"Then let me act as you would."

"Then you will not tell me what you were doing on the
road?"

Ernauton smiled, but made no reply.

"Nor where you were going?"

Ernauton did not answer.

" Then, monsieur, since you do not explain, I must treat you like any other man."

" Do what you please, monsieur; only I warn you, you will have to answer for it."

" To M. de Loignac? "

" Higher than that."

" M. d'Epernon? "

" Higher still."

" Well, I have my orders, and I shall send you to Vincennes."

" That is capital; it is just where I was going."

" I am glad, monsieur, that this little journey pleases you so much."

Two men, pistol in hand, immediately took possession of the prisoner, whom they conducted to two other men about five hundred feet farther on. These did the same with him; so that Ernauton had the society of his comrades even to the courtyard of Vincennes. Here he found fifty disarmed cavaliers, who, looking pale and dispirited, and surrounded by fifty light-horse, were deploring their bad fortune, and anticipating a disastrous ending to an enterprise so well planned. The Forty-five had taken all these men, either by force or cunning, as they had, for precaution, come to the rendezvous either singly, or two or three together at most. Now all this would have rejoiced Ernauton had he understood it, but he saw without understanding. " Monsieur," said he to Sainte-Maline, " I see that you were told of the importance of my mission, and that, fearing some accident for me, you were good enough to take the trouble to escort me hither. Now I will tell you that you were right; the king expects me, and I have important things to say to him. I will tell the king what you have done for his service."

Sainte-Maline grew red and then pale; but he understood, being clever when not blinded by passion, that Ernauton spoke the truth, and that he was expected. There was no joking with MM. de Loignac and d'Epernon; therefore he said, " You are free, M. Ernauton; I am delighted to have been agreeable to you."

Ernauton waited for no more, but began to mount the staircase, which led to the king's room. Sainte-Maline followed him with his eyes, and saw Loignac meet him on the stairs, and make a sign to him to come on. Loignac then descended to see the captives with his own eyes, and pronounced the road perfectly safe and free for the king's return. He knew nothing of the Jacobin convent, and the artillery and musketry of the fathers. But D'Epernon did, being completely informed by Nicolas Poulain. Therefore, when Loignac came and said to his chief, " Monsieur, the roads are free," D'Epernon replied, " Very well; the king orders that the Forty-five Guards form themselves into three compact bodies—one to go before and one on each side of the carriage—so that if there be any firing it may not reach the carriage."

" Very good! " said Loignac, " only I do not see where firing is to come from."

" At the priory of the Jacobins, monsieur, they must close their ranks."

This dialogue was interrupted by the king, who descended the staircase, followed by several gentlemen, among whom Sainte-Maline, with rage in his heart, recognised Ernauton.

" Gentlemen," said the king, " are my brave Forty-five all here? "

" Yes, Sire," said D'Epernon, directing his attention to them.

" Have the orders been given? "

" Yes, Sire, and will be followed."

" Let us go, then! "

The light-horse were left in charge of the prisoners, and forbidden to address a word to them. The king got into his carriage with his naked sword by his side. M. d'Epernon swore, " *Parfandious !* " and gallantly tried his own sword to see whether it moved readily in its scabbard. At nine o'clock they started.

An hour after the departure of Ernauton, M. de Mayneville was still at the window, whence, as we have seen, he had vainly endeavoured to follow the young man's course in the darkness; but after the lapse of that hour he was far less tranquil and hopeful, for none of his soldiers had appeared, and the only sound heard along the silent, black road was the occasional sound of horses' feet on the road to Vincennes. When this was heard, Mayneville and the duchess vainly tried to see what was going on. At last Mayneville became so anxious that he sent off a man on horseback, telling him to inquire of the first body of cavaliers they met. The messenger did not return; the duchess sent another, but neither reappeared.

" Our officer," said the duchess, always hopeful, " must have been afraid of not having sufficient force, and must have kept our men to help him; it is prudent, but it makes one anxious."

" Yes, very anxious," said Mayneville, whose eyes never left the dark and gloomy horizon.

" Mayneville, what can have happened? "

" I will go myself, madame, and find out."

" Oh, no! I forbid that. Who would stay with me? Who would know our friends when the time comes? No, no! stay, Mayneville. One is naturally apprehensive when a secret of this importance is concerned; but really the plan was too well combined, and, above all, too secret not to succeed."

" Nine o'clock!" replied Mayneville, rather to himself than to the duchess. " Well, here are the Jacobins coming out of their convent, and ranging themselves along the walls."

" Listen!" cried the duchess.

They began to hear from afar a noise like thunder.

" It is cavalry!" cried the duchess. " They are bringing him; we have him at last;" and she clapped her hands in the wildest joy.

" Yes," said Mayneville, " I hear a carriage and the gallop of horses."

And he cried out loudly, " Outside the walls, my fathers, outside!"

Immediately the gates of the priory opened, and a hundred armed monks marched out, with Borromée at their head, and took position across the road. Then they heard Gorenflot's voice crying, " Wait for me! wait for me! I must be at the head of the chapter to receive his Majesty worthily."

" Go to the balcony, prior," cried Borromée, " and overlook us all."

" Ah, true! I forgot that I had chosen that place; happily, you are here to remind me, Brother Borromée."

Borromée despatched four monks to stand behind the prior, on the pretence of doing him honour.

Soon the road was illumined by a number of torches, thanks to which the duchess and Mayneville could see cuirasses and swords shining. Incapable of moderation, she cried, " Go down, Mayneville, and bring him to me, bound and attended by guards!"

" Yes, madame; but one thing disquiets me."

" What is it?"

" I do not hear the signal agreed on."

" What use is the signal, since they have him?"

" But they were to arrest him only here, before the priory."

" They must have found a good opportunity earlier."

" I do not see our officer."

" I do."

" Where?"

" See that red plume."

" *Ventrebleu!* that red plume—"

" Well? "

" It is M. d'Epernon, sword in hand."

" They have left him his sword? "

" *Mordieu !* he commands."

" Our people! There has been treason."

" Oh, madame! they are not our people."

" You are mad, Mayneville! "

But at that moment Loignac, at the head of the first body of guards, cried, brandishing his large sword, " Vive le roi! "

" Vive le roi! " replied enthusiastically all the Forty-five, with their Gascon accent. The duchess grew pale and sank down almost fainting. Mayneville, sombre but resolute, drew his sword, not knowing but that the house was to be attacked. The *cortége* advanced, and had reached Bel-Esbat. Borromée came a little forward, and as Loignac rode straight up to him, he immediately saw that all was lost, and determined on his part.

" Room for the king! " cried Loignac. Gorenflot, excited by the cries and by the noise of arms, dazzled by the flaming of the torches, extended his powerful arm and blessed the king from his balcony. Henri saw him, and bowed smilingly; and at this mark of favour Gorenflot gave out a " Vive le roi! " with his stentorian voice. The rest, however, remained mute; they expected a different result from their two months' training. But Borromée, feeling certain, from the absence of the duchess's troops, of the fate of the enterprise, knew that to hesitate a moment was to be ruined, and he answered with a " Vive le roi! " almost as sonorous as Gorenflot's. Then all the rest took it up.

" Thanks, reverend father, thanks! " cried Henri; and then he passed the convent, where his course was to have terminated, like a whirlwind of fire, noise, and glory, leaving behind him Bel-Esbat in obscurity.

From her balcony, hidden by the golden escutcheon, behind which she was kneeling, the duchess saw and examined each face on which the light of the torches fell.

" Oh," cried she, " look, Mayneville! That young man, my brother's messenger, is in the king's service! We are lost! "

" We must fly immediately, madame, now that the Valois is conqueror."

" We have been betrayed! That young man has betrayed us! He knew all! "

The king had already, with all his escort, entered the Porte St. Antoine, which had opened before him and shut behind him.

CHAPTER XLIV

HOW CHICOT BLESSED KING LOUIS XI. FOR HAVING INVENTED POSTING, AND RESOLVED TO PROFIT BY IT

CHICOT, to whom our readers will now permit us to return, after his last adventure went on as rapidly as possible. He well understood that between the duke and himself there would now exist a mortal struggle, which would end only with life. Mayenne, wounded in his body, and still more grievously in his self-love, would never forgive him.

" Come, come ! " said the brave Gascon, hastening on towards Beaugency; " now is the time, if ever, to spend on post-horses the joint contributions of those three illustrious personages called Henri de Valois, Dom Modeste Gorenflot, and Sebastien Chicot."

Skilful as he was in the imitation of all conditions, Chicot immediately assumed the manner of a great lord, as he had assumed previously that of a good *bourgeois*. And never was prince served with more zeal than he, when he had sold Ernauton's horse and had talked for a quarter of an hour with the master of the post. Once in the saddle, he was determined not to stop until he reached a place of safety, and he went as quickly as constant fresh relays of horses would permit. He himself seemed made of iron, and at the end of sixty leagues, accomplished in twenty hours, he felt no fatigue. When, thanks to this rapidity, in three days he reached Bordeaux, he thought he might take breath.

A man can think while he gallops, and Chicot thought much. What kind of prince was he about to find in that strange Henri, whom some thought a fool, others a coward, and all a renegade of small importance? But Chicot's opinion was generally rather different from that of the rest of the world; and he was clever at divining what lay below the surface. Henri de Navarre was to him an enigma, although an unsolved one; but to know that he was an enigma was to have found out much. Chicot knew more of him than others did, in knowing, like the old Grecian sage, that he knew nothing. Therefore, where most people would have gone to speak freely, and with their hearts on their lips, Chicot felt that he must proceed cautiously, and with carefully guarded words.

This necessity of dissimulation was impressed on his mind by his natural penetration, and also by the aspect of the country through which he was passing. Once within the limits of the little principality of Navarre—a country whose poverty was proverbial in France—Chicot, to his great astonishment, ceased to see the impress of that misery which showed itself in every house and on every face in the finest provinces of that fertile France which he had just left. The wood-cutter who passed along, with his arm leaning on the yoke of his favourite ox; the girl with short petticoat and alert step, carrying water on her head; the old man humming a song of his youthful days; the tame bird who warbled in his cage or pecked at his plentiful supply of food; the brown, thin, but healthy children playing about the roads—all said in a language clear and intelligible to Chicot, " See, we are happy here."

Sometimes, hearing the sound of wheels creaking in the ruts, Chicot felt a sudden terror; he recalled the heavy artillery which tore up the roads of France. But at a turn of the road the waggon of a vintager would come to view, full of casks and of children with red faces. Sometimes the barrel of an arquebuse seen behind a hedge, or vines, or fig-trees, made him tremble for fear of an ambush; but it always turned out to be a hunter, followed by his great dogs, traversing the plain, plentiful in hares, to reach the mountain, equally full of partridges and heathcocks. Although the season was advanced, and Chicot had left Paris full of fog and hoar-frost, it was here warm and fine. The great trees, which had not yet entirely lost their leaves, which, indeed, in the south they never lose entirely, threw deep shadows from their reddening tops.

The Béarnais peasants, their caps over one ear, rode about on the little cheap horses of the country, which seem indefatigable, go twenty leagues at a stretch, and never combed, never covered, give themselves a shake at the end of their journey, and go to graze on the first tuft of heath—their only and sufficing repast.

" *Ventre de biche!* " said Chicot; " I have never seen Gascony so rich. I confess the letter weighs on my mind, although I have translated it into Latin. However, I have never heard that Henriot, as Charles IX. called him, knew Latin; so I will give him a free French translation."

Chicot inquired, and was told that the king was at Nérac. He turned to the left to reach this place, and found the road full of people from the market at Condom. He learned—for Chicot, careful in answering the questions of others, was a great questioner himself—that the King of Navarre led a very joyous life, and was always changing from one love to another.

On the road Chicot made acquaintance with a young Catholic priest, a sheep-merchant, and an officer, who had joined company on the road, and were travelling together. This chance association seemed to him to represent Navarre—learned, commercial, and military. The priest recited to him several sonnets which had been made on the loves of the king and the beautiful Fosseuse, daughter of René de Montmorency, Baron de Fosseux.

" Oh! " said Chicot; " in Paris, we believe that the king is mad about Mademoiselle de Rebours."

" Oh! " said the officer, " that was at Pau."

" What! has the king a mistress in every town? "

" Very likely; I know that he was the lover of Mademoiselle de Dayelle, while I was in garrison at Castelnaudary."

" Oh! Mademoiselle Dayelle—a Greek, was she not? "

" Yes," said the priest; " a Cypriote."

" I am from Agen," said the merchant; " and I know that when the king was there he made love to Mademoiselle de Tignonville."

" *Ventre de biche!* " said Chicot; " he is a universal lover. But to return to Mademoiselle Dayelle; I knew her family."

" She was jealous and was always threatening; she had a pretty little poniard, which she kept on her work-table, and one day the king went away and carried the poniard with him, saying that he did not wish any misfortune to happen to his successor."

" And Mademoiselle de Rebours? "

" Oh! they quarrelled."

" Then La Fosseuse is the last? "

" Oh, *mon Dieu!* yes; the king is mad about her—and the more so because she is *enceinte*."

" But what does the queen say? "

" She carries her griefs to the foot of the crucifix," said the priest.

" Besides," said the officer, " she is ignorant of all these things."

" That is not possible," said Chicot.

" Why so? "

" Because Nérac is not so large that it is easy to hide things there."

" As for that," said the officer, " there is a park there containing avenues more than three thousand feet long, bordered by cypresses, plane-trees, and magnificent sycamores; and the shade is so thick it is almost dark in broad daylight. Think what it must be at night."

" And then the queen is much occupied, monsieur," said the priest.

" Occupied? "

" Yes."

" With whom, pray ? "

" With God, monsieur," said the priest, gravely.

" With God? "

" Why not? "

" Ah, the queen is religious? "

" Very religious."

" Nevertheless, there is no mass at the palace, I imagine," said Chicot.

" And you imagine very incorrectly, monsieur. No mass! do you take us for heathens? Learn, monsieur, that if the king goes to church with his gentlemen, the queen hears mass in her private chapel."

" The queen? "

" Yes, yes."

" Queen Marguerite? "

" Yes; and I, unworthy as I am, received two crowns for officiating there twice. I even preached a very good sermon on the text, ' God has separated the wheat from the chaff.' It is in the Bible, ' God will separate; ' but as it is a long time since that was written, I supposed that the thing was done."

" And did the king know about that sermon? "

" He heard it."

" Without annoyance? "

" On the contrary, he applauded it."

" You astound me," said Chicot.

" I must add," said the officer, " that they do something else than hear mass at the palace; they give good dinners—and the promenades! I don't believe that anywhere in France there are more mustaches shown than in the promenades at Nérac."

Chicot had obtained more information than he needed to enable him to lay out his course. He knew Queen Marguerite well, and he knew that if she was blind to these love-affairs, it was because she had some motive for placing a bandage over her eyes."

" *Ventre de biche !* " said he, " these avenues of cypresses, and three thousand feet of shade, make me feel uncomfortable. I am coming from Paris to tell the truth at Nérac, where they have such deep shade that women do not see their husbands walking with other women. *Corbiou !* they will be ready to kill me for troubling so many charming promenades. Happily,

I know the king is a philosopher; and I trust in that. Besides, I am an ambassador, and sacred."

Chicot entered Nérac in the evening, just at the hour of those promenades which occupied so much the King of France and his ambassador. Chicot could satisfy himself in regard to the simplicity of the royal manners by the ease with which he obtained an audience. A valet opened the door of a rustic-looking apartment bordered with flowers, above which was the king's antechamber and sitting-room. An officer or page ran to find the king wherever he might be when any one wished for an audience, and he always came at the first summons. Chicot was pleased with this; he judged the king to be open and candid, and he thought so still more when he saw the king coming up a winding walk bordered with laurels and roses, an old hat on his head, and dressed in a dark-green doublet and grey boots, and with a cup and ball in his hand. He looked gay and happy, as though care never came near him.

"Who wants me?" said he to the page.

"A man who looks to me half courtier, half soldier."

Chicot heard these words and advanced timidly. "It is I, Sire."

"What! M. Chicot in Navarre! *Ventre-saint-gris!* welcome, dear M. Chicot!"

"A thousand thanks, Sire."

"Still alive, thank God!"

"I hope so, at least, dear Sire," said Chicot, transported with happiness.

"Ah, *parbleu!* we will drink together. Really, you make me very happy, M. Chicot; sit there." And he pointed to a grassy bank.

"Oh, no, Sire."

"Have you come two hundred leagues to see me, and shall I leave you standing? No, no; sit down. One cannot talk standing."

"But, Sire, respect—"

"Respect! here in Navarre! You are mad, my poor Chicot."

"No, Sire, I am not mad; I am an ambassador."

A slight frown contracted Henri's brow, but disappeared at once. "Ambassador from whom?"

"From Henri III. I come from Paris and the Louvre, Sire."

"Oh, that is different! Come with me," said the king, rising with a sigh. "Page, take wine up to my chamber—no, to my cabinet. Come, Chicot, I will conduct you."

Chicot followed the king, thinking, "How disagreeable!—to come and trouble this honest man in his peace and his ignorance. Bah! he will be philosophical."

CHAPTER XLV

HOW THE KING OF NAVARRE GUESSES THAT "TURENNIUS" MEANS TURENNE, AND "MARGOTA" MARGOT

THE King of Navarre's cabinet was not very sumptuous, for he was not rich, and did not waste the little he had. It was large, and with his bedroom occupied all the right wing of the château. It was well, though not royally, furnished, and from its windows could be seen the magnificent meadows bordering on the river. Great trees, willows and planes, here and there hid the course of the river, which glanced between, golden in the sunlight, or silver in the light of the moon. This beautiful panorama was terminated by a range of hills, which looked violet in the evening light. The windows on the other side looked upon the court of the château. All these natural beauties interested Chicot less than the arrangements of the room, which was the ordinary sitting-room of Henri.

The king seated himself, with his usual simplicity and his constant smile, in a great armchair of leather with gilt nails, and Chicot, at his command, sat down on a stool similar in material. Henri looked at him smilingly, but with curiosity.

"You will think I am very curious, dear M. Chicot," began the king; "but I cannot help it. I have so long looked on you as dead that in spite of the pleasure your resurrection causes me I can hardly comprehend that you are still alive. Why did you so suddenly disappear from this world?"

"Oh, Sire!" said Chicot, with his usual freedom, "you disappeared from Vincennes. Every one eclipses himself according to his need."

"I recognise by your ready wit that it is not to your ghost I am speaking." Then, more seriously, "But now we must leave wit and speak of business."

"If it does not too much fatigue your Majesty, I am ready."

Henri's eyes kindled. "Fatigue me! It is true I grow rusty here; but I am not fatigued, for I have done nothing. I have to-day exercised my body much, but my mind little."

"Sire, I am glad of that; for, ambassador from a king, your relative and friend, I have a delicate commission to execute with your Majesty."

" Speak quickly; you pique my curiosity."

" Sire—"

" First, your letters of credit. I know it is needless, since you are the ambassador; but I wish to show you that, Béarnais peasant as we are, we know our duty as king."

" Sire, I ask your Majesty's pardon; but all the letter of credit that I had I have drowned in rivers, thrown in the fire, scattered in the air."

" And why so? "

" Because one cannot travel charged with an embassy to Navarre as one travels to buy cloth at Lyon; and if one has the dangerous honour of carrying royal letters, he runs a risk of carrying them only to the tomb."

" It is true," said Henri, " the roads are not very safe, and in Navarre we are reduced, for want of money, to trust to the honesty of the people; but they do not steal much."

" Oh, no, Sire; they behave like lambs or angels. But that is only in Navarre; out of it one meets wolves and vultures around every prey. I was a prey, Sire, so I had both."

" At all events, I am glad to see they did not eat you."

" *Ventre de biche !* Sire, it was not their fault; they did their best, but they found me too tough, and could not get through my skin. But to return to my letter."

" Since you have none, dear M. Chicot, it seems to me useless to return to it."

" I should say that if I have none now, I had one."

" Very good," said Henri, extending his hand; " give it to me, M. Chicot."

" Here is the misfortune, Sire: I had a letter, as I have had the honour to inform your Majesty, and few have ever had a better one."

" You have lost it? "

" I hastened to destroy it, Sire, for M. de Mayenne ran after me to steal it from me."

" Cousin Mayenne? "

" In person."

" Luckily, he does not run fast. Is he still getting fatter? "

" *Ventre de biche !* not just now, I should think."

" Why not? "

" Because, you understand, Sire, he had the misfortune to catch me, and unfortunately got a sword-wound."

" And the letter? "

" He had not a glimpse of it, thanks to my precautions."

" Bravo! your journey is interesting. You must tell me the

details. But one thing disquiets me—if the letter was destroyed for M. de Mayenne, it is also destroyed for me. How, then, shall I know what my brother Henri wrote, if the letter no longer exists?"

"Pardon, Sire; it exists in my memory."

"How so?"

"Sire, before destroying it I learned it by heart."

"An excellent idea, M. Chicot! You will recite it to me, will you not?"

"Willingly, Sire."

"Word for word?"

"Yes, Sire; although I do not know the language, I have a good memory."

"What language?"

"Latin."

"I do not understand you. Was my brother Henri's letter written in Latin?"

"Yes, Sire."

"And why?"

"Ah, Sire, doubtless because Latin is an audacious language —a language which may say anything, and in which Persius and Juvenal have immortalised the follies and errors of kings."

"Kings?"

"And of queens, Sire."

The king began to frown.

"I mean emperors and empresses," continued Chicot.

"You know Latin, M. Chicot?"

"Yes and no, Sire."

"You are fortunate if it is 'yes,' for you have an immense advantage over me, who do not know it. For that reason I have never been able to attend seriously to the Mass, on account of that devilish Latin. Then you know it, do you?"

"They taught me to read it, Sire, as well as Greek and Hebrew."

"That is very convenient, M. Chicot; you are a living book."

"Your Majesty has found the exact word—'a book.' They print something on my memory; they send me where they like; I arrive; I am read and understood."

"Or not understood."

"How so, Sire?"

"Why, if one does not know the language in which you are printed."

"Oh, Sire, kings know everything."

"That is what we tell the people, and what flatterers tell us."

" Then, Sire, it is useless for me to recite to your Majesty the letter which I learned by heart, since neither of us would understand it."

" Is Latin not very much like Italian? "

" So they say, Sire."

" And Spanish? "

" I believe so."

" Then let us try. I know a little Italian, and my Gascon *patois* is something like Spanish; perhaps I may understand Latin without ever having learned it."

" Your Majesty orders me to repeat it, then? "

" I beg you, dear M. Chicot."

Chicot began—

" FRATER CARISSIME,—Sincerus amor quo te prosequebatur germanus noster Carolus Nonus, functus nuper, colet usque regiam nostram et pectori meo pertinaciter adhæret."

" If I am not mistaken," said Henri, interrupting, " they speak in this phrase of love, obstinacy, and of my brother, Charles IX."

" Very likely," said Chicot. " Latin is such a beautiful language that all that might go in one sentence."

" Go on," said the king.

Chicot began again, and Henri listened with the utmost calm to all the passages about Turenne and his wife; only at the word " Turennius," he said, " Does not ' Turennius ' mean Turenne? "

" I think so, Sire."

" And ' Margota ' must be the pet name which my brothers gave to their sister Marguerite, my beloved wife."

" It is possible," said Chicot; and he continued his letter to the end without the king's face changing in the least.

" Is it finished? " asked Henri, when he stopped.

" Yes, Sire."

" It ought to be superb."

" I think so also, Sire."

" How unfortunate that I understood only two words, ' Turennius ' and ' Margota! ' "

" An irreparable misfortune, Sire, unless your Majesty decides on having it translated by some one."

" Oh, no! you yourself, M. Chicot, who were so discreet in destroying the autograph, you would not counsel me to make this letter public? "

" But I think that the king's letter to you, recommended to

me so carefully, and sent to your Majesty by a private hand, must contain here and there good things from which your Majesty might derive some advantage."

" Yes, but to confide these good things to any one, I must have great confidence in him."

" Certainly."

" Well, I have an idea. Go and find my wife Margota. She is learned, and will understand it if you recite it to her; then she can explain it to me."

" That is an excellent plan."

" Is it not? Go!"

" I will, Sire."

" Mind not to alter a word of the letter."

" That would be impossible, Sire. To do that I must know Latin."

" Go, then, my friend."

Chicot received directions for finding Madame Marguerite, and went away more convinced than ever that the king was an enigma.

CHAPTER XLVI

THE AVENUE THREE THOUSAND FEET LONG

THE queen inhabited the other wing of the château. The famous avenue began at her very window, and her eyes rested only on grass and flowers. A native poet (Marguerite, in the provinces as in Paris, was always the star of the poets) had composed a sonnet about her.

" She wishes," said he, " by all these agreeable sights to chase away painful memories."

Daughter, sister, and wife of a king as she was, Marguerite had indeed suffered much. Her philosophy, although more boasted of than that of the king, was less solid, for it was due only to study, while his was natural. Therefore, philosopher as she was, or rather, tried to be, time and grief had already begun to leave their marks on her countenance. Still she was remarkably beautiful. With her joyous yet sweet smile, her brilliant and yet soft eyes, Marguerite was still an adorable creature. She was idolised at Nérac, whither she brought elegance, joy, and life. She, a Parisian princess, supported patiently a provincial life; and this alone was a virtue in the eyes of the inhabitants. Every one loved her, both as queen and as woman.

Full of hatred for her enemies, but patient that she might avenge herself better; feeling instinctively that under the mask of carelessness and long-suffering worn by Henri de Navarre he had a bad feeling towards her—she had accustomed herself to replace by poetry, and by the semblance of love, relatives, husband, and friends.

No one, excepting Catherine de Médicis, Chicot, or melancholy ghosts returned from the realms of death, could have told why Marguerite's cheeks were often so pale, why her eyes often filled with tears, or why her heart often betrayed its melancholy void. Marguerite had no more confidants; she had been betrayed too often.

However, her belief that Henri had a hostile feeling towards her was instinctive only, and came rather from the consciousness of her own faults than from his behaviour. He treated her like a daughter of France, always spoke to her with respectful politeness or grateful kindness, and was always the husband and friend.

When Chicot arrived at the place indicated to him by Henri, he found no one; Marguerite, they said, was at the end of the famous avenue. When he had gone about two thirds of its length, he saw at the end, in an arbour covered with jasmine, clematis, and broom, a group covered with ribbons, feathers, velvets, and swords. Perhaps all this finery was slightly old-fashioned, but for Nérac it was brilliant; and even Chicot, coming straight from Paris, was satisfied with the *coup d'œil*.

As a page of the king preceded Chicot, the queen, whose eyes wandered here and there with the continual restlessness of melancholy hearts, saw the colours of Navarre and called to him. "What do you want, D'Aubiac?" she asked.

"Madame, a gentleman from Paris, an envoy from the Louvre to the King of Navarre, and sent by his Majesty to you, desires to speak to your Majesty."

A sudden flush passed over Marguerite's face, and she turned quickly. Chicot was standing near; Marguerite left the circle, and waving an adieu to the company, advanced towards the Gascon.

"M. Chicot!" she cried in astonishment.

"Here I am, at your Majesty's feet," said he, "and find you ever good and beautiful, and queen here, as at the Louvre."

"It is a miracle to see you here, monsieur; they said you were dead."

" I pretended to be so."

" And what do you want with us, M. Chicot? Am I happy enough to be still remembered in France? "

" Oh, madame," said Chicot, smiling, " we do not forget queens of your age and your beauty. The King of France even writes on this subject to the King of Navarre."

Marguerite coloured. " He writes? "

" Yes, madame."

" And you have brought the letter? "

" I have not brought it, madame, for reasons that the King of Navarre will explain to you, but learned it by heart and repeated it."

" I understand. This letter was important, and you feared to lose it, or have it stolen."

" That is the truth, madame; but the letter was written in Latin."

" Oh, very well; you are aware that I know Latin."

" And the King of Navarre, does he know it? "

" Dear M. Chicot, it is very difficult to find out what he does or does not know. If one can believe appearances, he knows very little of it, for he never seems to understand when I speak to any one in that language. Then you told him the purport of the letter? "

" It was to him it was addressed."

" And did he seem to understand? "

" Only two words."

" What were they? "

" ' Turennius ' and ' Margota.' "

" ' Turennius ' and ' Margota ' ? "

" Yes; those two words were in the letter."

" Then what did he do? "

" He sent me to you, madame."

" To me? "

" Yes, saying that the letter contained things of too much importance to be confided to a stranger, and that it was better to take it to you, who are the most beautiful of learned ladies, and the most learned of beautiful ones."

" I will listen to you, M. Chicot, since such are the king's orders."

" Thank you, madame; where does your majesty wish me to deliver it? "

" Come to my cabinet."

Marguerite looked earnestly at Chicot, who, through pity for her, had let her have a glimpse of the truth. The poor woman felt the need of a support, of a last return to love perhaps, before encountering the trial that awaited her. She turned towards a gentleman in the group, and said, " M. de Turenne, your arm to the château. Precede us, M. Chicot."

CHAPTER XLVII

MARGUERITE'S CABINET

MARGUERITE'S cabinet was fashionably furnished; and tapestries, enamels, china, books, and manuscripts in Greek, Latin, and French, covered all the tables; while birds in their cages, dogs on the carpet, formed a living world round Marguerite.

The queen was a woman to understand Epicurus—not in Greek only; she occupied her life so well that from a thousand griefs she drew forth a pleasure.

Chicot was invited to sit down in a beautiful armchair of tapestry, representing a Cupid scattering a cloud of flowers; and a page, handsome and richly dressed, offered to him refreshment. He did not accept it, but as soon as the Vicomte de Turenne had left them, began to recite his letter. We already know this letter, having read it with Chicot, and therefore think it useless to follow the Latin translation. Chicot spoke with the worst accent possible, that Marguerite might be slower in understanding it; but she understood it perfectly, and could not hide her rage and indignation. She knew her brother's dislike to her, and her mind was divided between anger and fear. But as he concluded, she decided on her part.

" By the holy communion," said she, when Chicot had finished, " my brother writes well in Latin! What vehemence! what style! I should never have believed him capable of it. But do you not understand it, M. Chicot? I thought you were a good Latin scholar."

" Madame, I have forgotten it; all that I remember is that Latin has no article, that it has a vocative, and that ' head ' is of the neuter gender."

" Really! " said some one, entering noiselessly and merrily. It was the King of Navarre. " ' Head ' is of the neuter gender, M. Chicot? Why is it not masculine? "

" Ah, Sire, I do not know; it astonishes me as much as it does your Majesty."

" It must be because it is sometimes the man, sometimes the woman, that rules, according to their temperaments."

" That is an excellent reason, Sire."

" I am glad to be a more profound philosopher than I thought. But to return to the letter. Madame, I burn to hear news from the court of France, and M. Chicot brings them to me in an unknown tongue. Otherwise—"

" Otherwise? " repeated Marguerite.

" Otherwise, I should be delighted, *ventre-saint-gris !* You know how much I like news, and especially scandalous news, such as my brother, Henri de Valois, so well knows how to repeat." And Henri de Navarre sat down, rubbing his hands.

" Come, M. Chicot," the king continued, with the manner of a man preparing to enjoy himself, " you have repeated that famous letter to my wife, have you not? "

" Yes, Sire."

" Well, my dear, tell me what that famous letter contains."

" Do you not fear, Sire, that the Latin is a bad prognostic? " said Chicot.

" Why so? " asked the king. Then, turning towards his wife, " Well, madame? "

Marguerite hesitated for a moment, as if recalling one by one the phrases that had fallen from Chicot's lips. " Our messenger is right, Sire," she said, when her examination was finished, and her course decided upon; " the Latin is a bad sign."

" What ! " said Henri, " does the letter contain anything disagreeable—from your brother, who is so clever and polite? "

" Even when he had me insulted in my litter, as happened near Sens, when I left Paris to rejoin you, Sire."

" When one has a brother whose own conduct is irreproachable," said Henri, in an indefinable tone between jest and earnest—" a brother a king, and very punctilious—"

" He ought to care for the true honour of his sister and of his house. I do not suppose, Sire, that if your sister, Catherine d'Albret, occasioned some scandal, you would have it published by a captain of the guards."

" Oh, I am like a good-natured *bourgeois*, and not a king; but the letter, the letter ! since it was addressed to me, I wish to know what it contains."

" It is a perfidious letter, Sire."

" Bah ! "

" Oh, yes, and which contains more calumnies than are necessary to embroil a husband with his wife, and a friend with his friends."

" Oh, oh ! embroil a husband with his wife ! you and me, then ? "

" Yes, Sire."

" And in what way, my dear? "

Chicot was on thorns; he would have given much, hungry as he was, to be in bed without supper. " The storm is about to burst," thought he.

" Sire," said Marguerite, " I much regret that your Majesty has forgotten your Latin."

" Madame, of all the Latin I learned, I remember but one phrase — '*Deus et virtus æterna*,' — a singular assemblage of masculine, feminine, and neuter, which my professor never could explain except by the Greek, which I understand still less than I do Latin."

" Sire, if you did understand, you would see in the letter many compliments to me."

" But how could compliments embroil us, madame? For as long as your brother pays you compliments, I shall agree with him; if he speaks ill of you, I shall understand his policy."

" Ah! if he spoke ill of me, you would understand it? "

" Yes; he has reasons for embroiling us, which I know well."

" Well, then, Sire, these compliments are only an insinuating prelude to calumnious accusations against your friends and mine."

After boldly uttering these words, Marguerite awaited a contradiction. Chicot lowered his head; Henri raised his shoulders.

" Come, my dear," said the king, " you have understood the Latin none too well, after all; such an evil intention cannot be in my brother's letter."

Although Henri uttered these words in gentle and pleasant tones, Marguerite shot at him a glance of defiance. " Understand me to the end, Sire," she said.

" God is my witness that I ask nothing better," replied Henri.

" Do you want your followers or not, Sire? " said she.

" Do I want them? What a question! What should I do without them, and reduced to my own resources? "

" Well, Sire, the king wishes to detach your best servants from you."

" I defy him! "

" Bravo, Sire! " said Chicot.

" Yes," said Henri, with that apparent candour with which to the end of his life he deceived people, " for my followers are attached to me through love, and not through interest; I have nothing to give them."

"You give to them all your heart and your faith, Sire; it is the best return a king can make his friends."

"Yes, my dear; well?"

"Well, Sire, have more faith in them."

"*Ventre-saint-gris!* I shall not lose faith in them till they compel me to; that is to say, till they forfeit it."

"Well, Sire, the attempt is made to show that they have deserved to lose it, that is all."

"Ah! but how?"

"I cannot tell you, Sire, without compromising—" and she glanced at Chicot.

"Dear M. Chicot," said Henri, "pray wait for me in my cabinet; the queen has something particular to say to me."

CHAPTER XLVIII

THE EXPLANATION

To get rid of a witness whom Marguerite believed to know more of Latin than he admitted, was already a triumph, or at least a pledge of security for her; for alone with her husband, she could give whatever translation of the Latin she pleased.

Henri and his wife were, then, left together alone. He had on his face no appearance of disquietude or menace; decidedly he could not understand Latin.

"Monsieur," said Marguerite, "I wait for you to interrogate me."

"This letter preoccupies you much, my dear; do not alarm yourself thus."

"Sire, it is because that letter is, or should be, an event. A king does not in this way send a messenger to a brother king without reasons of the highest importance."

"Well, my dear, let us leave it for the present; have you not something like a ball this evening?"

"Yes, Sire," said Marguerite, astonished, "but that is not extraordinary; you know we dance nearly every evening."

"I have a great chase for to-morrow."

"Each our pleasure, Sire; you love the chase, I the dance."

"Yes, my dear; and there is no harm in that," said Henri, sighing.

"Certainly not; but your Majesty sighed as you said it."

"Listen to me, madame; I am uneasy."

" About what, Sire? "

" About a current report."

" A report! your Majesty uneasy about a report? "

" What more simple—since this report may annoy you? "

" Me? "

" Yes, you."

" Sire, I do not understand you."

" Have you heard nothing? "

Marguerite began to tremble. "I am the least curious woman in the world," said she; " I hear nothing but what is cried in my very ears. Besides, I think so little of reports, that I should not listen to them if I heard them."

" It is then your opinion, madame, that one should despise these reports? "

" Absolutely, Sire; particularly kings and queens."

" Why so, madame? "

" Because, as every one talks of us, we should have too much to do if we listened to them all."

" Well, I believe you are right, my dear; and I am about to furnish you with an excellent opportunity of exercising your philosophy."

Marguerite believed that the decisive moment had come, and rallied all her courage. " So be it, Sire," said she.

Henri began in the tone of a penitent who has some great sin to acknowledge. " You know the great interest I take in Fosseuse? "

" Ah! " cried Marguerite, triumphantly, seeing he was not about to accuse her. " Yes, yes; the little Fosseuse, your friend."

" Yes, madame."

" My lady-in-waiting? "

" Yes."

" Your passion, your love."

" Ah! you speak like one of the reports you were abusing just now."

" It is true, Sire, and I ask your pardon," said Marguerite, smiling.

" My dear, you are right. Public report often lies, and we sovereigns have great reason to establish this theorem as an axiom. *Ventre-saint-gris!* Madame, I believe I am talking Greek; " and he burst into loud laughter.

Marguerite perceived irony in that laughter, and especially in the subtle glance which accompanied it. Slightly uneasy, she replied, " Well, and Fosseuse? "

" She is ill, my dear; and the doctors do not understand her malady."

" That is strange, Sire. Fosseuse, who you say has always remained chaste; Fosseuse, who, according to you, would have resisted a king, had a king spoken love to her—Fosseuse, that flower of purity, that limpid crystal, ought to allow the eye of science to search her joys and her sorrows."

" Alas! it is not so," said Henri, sadly.

" What! " cried the queen. " Is she not a flower of purity? "

" I do not say that," replied Henri, drily. " God forbid that I accuse any one! I mean that she persists in hiding the cause of her illness from the doctors."

" But to you, Sire, her confidant, her father? "

" I know nothing, or at least wish to know nothing."

" Then, Sire," said Marguerite, who now believed that she had to confer instead of asking a pardon—" then, Sire, I do not know what you want, and wait for you to explain."

" Well, then, my dear, I will tell you. I wish you—but it is asking a great deal."

" Speak on, Sire."

" To have the goodness to go to Fosseuse."

" I go to visit this girl whom every one says has the honour of being your mistress—a thing which you do not deny! "

" Gently, gently, my dear. On my word, you will make a scandal with your exclamations; and really I believe that will rejoice the court of France, for in the letter from my brother-in-law that Chicot repeated to me, there were these words, ' quotidie scandalum,' which must mean ' daily scandal.' It is not necessary to know Latin to understand that. It is almost French."

" But, Sire, to whom did these words apply? "

" Ah! that is what I am unable to understand; but you, who know Latin, can help me to find out."

Marguerite coloured up to her ears, while with his head down and his hand in the air, Henri appeared to search innocently to what person in his court the " quotidie scandalum " could apply. " Well, monsieur," said she, " you wish me to take a humiliating step for the sake of peace; and for the sake of peace I will comply."

" Thanks, my dear, thanks."

" But what is the object of this visit? "

" It is very simple, madame."

" Still, you must tell me, for I am not clever enough to guess it."

" Well! you will find Fosseuse among the ladies-of-honour, sleeping in their room; and they, you know, are so curious and indiscreet that one cannot tell to what extremity Fosseuse may be reduced."

" But then she fears something? " cried Marguerite, with a burst of anger, and hatred. " She wishes to hide herself? "

" I do not know. All I know is that she wishes to leave the room of the maids-of-honour."

" If she wishes to hide, let her not count on me. I may shut my eyes to certain things, but I will never be an accomplice in them," said Marguerite. She then awaited the effect of her ultimatum.

But Henri seemed not to have heard. He had resumed that thoughtful attitude which Marguerite had noticed a moment before. " ' *Margota*,' " he murmured, " ' *Margota cum Turennio*.' Ah! those are the names I was seeking, madame—' *Margota cum Turennio*.' "

Marguerite grew crimson. " Calumnies, Sire! " she cried. " Are you going to repeat calumnies to me? "

" What calumnies? " replied he, with the most natural air. " Do you find any calumny in it? It is a passage from my brother's letter—' *Margota cum Turennio conveniunt in castello nomine Loignac*.' Decidedly I must get this letter translated."

" Leave this comedy, Sire," said Marguerite, tremblingly, " and tell me at once what you want from me."

" Well, I wish, my dear, that you would separate Fosseuse from the other girls, and having given her a chamber by herself, that you would send her a discreet doctor—your own, for example."

" Ah! I see what it is," cried the queen—" Fosseuse the paragon is near her *accouchement*."

" I do not say so, my dear; it is you who affirm it."

" It is so, monsieur; your insinuating tone, your false humility, prove it to me. But there are sacrifices that no man should ask of his wife. Take care of Fosseuse yourself, Sire; it is your business. And let the trouble fall on the guilty, not on the innocent."

" The guilty ! Ah ! that makes me think of the letter again."

" How so? "

" Guilty is ' *nocens*,' is it not? "

" Yes."

" Well, there was that word in the letter—' *Margota cum Turennio, ambo nocentes, conveniunt in castello nomine Loignac*.'

Mon Dieu! how I regret that my knowledge is not as great as my memory is good!"

"'*Ambo nocentes*,'" repeated Marguerite, in a low voice, and turning very pale; "he understands, he understands!"

"'*Margota cum Turennio, ambo nocentes*,'" repeated Henri. "What the devil could my brother mean by '*ambo*'? *Ventre-saint-gris!* my dear, it is astonishing that you who know Latin so well have not yet explained it to me."

"Sire, I have already had the honour to tell you—"

"Eh, *pardieu!*" the king broke in, "there now is '*Turennius*' walking under your windows, and looking up as if he expected you. I will call to him to come up; he is very learned, and he will explain it to me."

"Sire, Sire! be superior to all the calumniators of France."

"Oh, my dear, it seems to me that people are not more indulgent in Navarre than in France; you yourself were very severe about poor Fosseuse just now."

"I severe?"

"Yes; and yet we ought to be indulgent here, we lead such a happy life—you with your balls, and I with my chase."

"Yes, yes, Sire; you are right. Let us be indulgent."

"Oh, I was sure of your heart, my dear."

"You know me well, Sire."

"Yes. Then you will go and see Fosseuse?"

"Yes, Sire."

"And separate her from the others?"

"Yes, Sire."

"And send her your doctor?"

"Yes, Sire."

"And no nurse. Doctors are reticent by profession, nurses are babblers by habit."

"That is true."

"And if, unluckily, what you say were true, and she had been weak; for women are frail—"

"Well, Sire, I am a woman, and know the indulgence due to my sex."

"Ah, you know all things, my dear; you are in truth a model of perfection, and—"

"And?"

"And I kiss your hands."

"But believe, Sire, that it is for the love of you alone that I make this sacrifice."

"Oh, yes, my dear; I know you well, madame, and my brother of France also—he who says so much of you in this letter, and adds, '*Fiat sanum exemplum statim, atque res certior eveniet.*' Doubtless, my dear, it is you who give this good example." And Henri kissed the cold hand of Marguerite. Then, turning on the threshold of the door, he said, "Say everything kind from me to Fosseuse, and do for her as you have promised me. I set off for the chase; perhaps I shall not see you till my return, perhaps never—those wolves are wicked beasts. Come and let me embrace you, my dear."

Then he embraced Marguerite almost affectionately, and went out, leaving her stupefied with all she had heard.

CHAPTER XLIX

THE SPANISH AMBASSADOR

THE king rejoined Chicot, who was still agitated with fears as to the explanation. "Well, Chicot," said Henri, "do you know what the queen says?"

"No."

"She pretends that your cursed Latin will disturb our peace."

"Oh, Sire, forget it, and all will be at an end. It is not with a piece of spoken Latin as though it were written; the wind carries away the one, fire cannot sometimes destroy the other."

"I! I think of it no more."

"That is right."

"I have something else to do, faith, than to think of that."

"Your Majesty prefers amusing yourself?"

"Yes, my son," said Henri, somewhat annoyed by the tone in which Chicot had uttered these words—"yes, my Majesty prefers to amuse himself."

"Pardon, but perhaps I annoy your Majesty."

"Eh! my son," said Henri, shrugging his shoulders, "I have already told you that here it is not as at the Louvre; here we do everything openly—love, war, and politics."

"The first more than the last two, do you not, Sire?"

"Faith! yes; I confess it, my dear friend. This country is so fine, and its women so beautiful."

"Oh, Sire, you forget the queen; can the Navarrese women be more pleasing and beautiful than she is? If they are, I compliment them."

"*Ventre-saint-gris!* you are right, Chicot. And that I should forget that you are an ambassador, and represent King Henri III.; and that he is the brother of Marguerite; and that consequently, before you, I ought to place her before every one! But you must excuse my imprudence, I am not accustomed to ambassadors."

At this moment the door of the room opened, and D'Aubiac announced, " The ambassador from Spain." Chicot gave a start which made the king smile.

" Upon my word! " said Henri, " that is a contradiction that I did not expect. The ambassador from Spain! and what the devil can he want here? "

" Yes," said Chicot; " what the devil does he want here? "

" We shall soon know; perhaps our Spanish neighbour has some frontier dispute to settle with us."

" I will retire," said Chicot. " This is doubtless a real ambassador from his Majesty Philip II., while I—"

" The ambassador from France give place to Spain, and that in Navarre! *Ventre-saint-gris!* that shall not be. Open that library door, Chicot, and go in there."

" But from there I shall hear all, in spite of myself."

" And you shall hear all, *morbleu!* I have nothing to hide. By the way, have you nothing more to say to me from your king? "

" Nothing at all, Sire."

" Very well, then, you have nothing to do but to see and hear, like all other ambassadors, and the library will do excellently for that purpose. Look with all your eyes, and listen with all your ears, my dear Chicot. D'Aubiac, let the ambassador enter."

Chicot hastened to his place of concealment, and drew the tapestry close.

When the preliminaries consecrated to the details of etiquette were over, and Chicot, in his place of concealment, had satisfied himself that the Béarnais well understood how to give an audience, the ambassador said, " Can I speak freely to your Majesty? "

" You may, monsieur."

" Sire, I bring the answer from his Catholic Majesty."

" An answer," thought Chicot; " then there was a question."

" An answer to what? " said Henri.

" To your proposals of last month."

" Faith! I am very forgetful! please to recall to me what they were."

" About the encroachments of the Lorraine princes."

" Yes, I remember, particularly those of M. de Guise; go on, monsieur."

" Sire, the king, my master, although solicited to sign a treaty of alliance with Lorraine, has regarded an alliance with Navarre as more loyal, and—to speak plainly—more advantageous."

" Yes, let us speak plainly," said Henri.

" I will be frank with your Majesty, for I know my master's intentions with regard to you."

" May I also know them? "

" Sire, my master will refuse nothing to Navarre."

Chicot bit his fingers to convince himself that he was not dreaming.

" Since he will refuse me nothing, let us see what I can ask," said Henri.

" Whatever your Majesty pleases."

" The devil! "

" If your Majesty will speak openly and frankly."

" *Ventre-saint-gris!* everything! that is embarrassing."

" Shall I announce his Majesty the King of Spain's proposal? "

" I listen."

" The King of France treats the Queen of Navarre as an enemy; he repudiates her as a sister, and covers her with opprobrium. All this—but I beg your Majesty's pardon for touching on so delicate a subject—"

" Go on."

" All this, then, is public."

" Well, monsieur, what are you aiming at in this? "

" It is consequently easy for your Majesty to repudiate as a wife her whom her brother disclaims as a sister."

Henri looked towards the tapestry, behind which Chicot, with staring eyes, awaited, trembling, what should follow.

" The queen being repudiated," continued the ambassador, " the alliance between the King of Navarre and the King of Spain is concluded; the King of Spain will give the infanta, his daughter, to your Majesty, and he himself will marry Madame Catherine de Navarre, your Majesty's sister."

A movement of pride shook Henri, while Chicot shuddered with terror. The one saw his star rising, radiant like the morning sun; the other saw the sceptre and the fortune of the Valois ready to decline and fall.

For an instant there was profound silence; and then Henri said, " The proposal, monsieur, is magnificent, and crowns me with honour."

" His Majesty," said the negotiator, who already counted on an enthusiastic acceptance, " proposes only one condition."

" Ah, a condition! that is but just; let me hear it."

" In aiding your Majesty against the Lorraine princes—that is to say, in opening to your Majesty a way to the throne—my master desires to facilitate by your alliance the safety of Flanders, which the Duc d'Anjou is already attacking. Your Majesty will understand that it is pure preference on my master's part for you over the Lorraine princes, since MM. de Guise, his natural allies, as Catholic princes, make of themselves a party against the Duc d'Anjou in Flanders. Now, this is the only condition, which you must think reasonable. His Majesty the King of Spain, allied to you by a double marriage, will help you to—" the ambassador seemed to seek for the right word—" to succeed to the King of France, and you will guarantee Flanders to him. I may, then, knowing your Majesty's wisdom, now regard the negotiation as happily terminated."

Henri took two or three turns up and down the cabinet. " This, then," said he at last, " is the answer you were charged to bring me? "

" Yes, Sire."

" Nothing else? "

" Nothing else, Sire."

" Well! I refuse the offer of the King of Spain."

" You refuse the hand of the infanta! " cried the Spaniard, with a start, as though he had received a sudden wound.

" It would be a great honour; but I cannot think it a greater one than that of having married a daughter of France."

" No; but that alliance brought you nearly to the tomb, and this will bring you to the throne."

" An incomparable piece of good fortune, monsieur, I know; but I will never buy it with the blood and honour of my future subjects. What, monsieur! I draw the sword against the King of France, my brother-in-law, for the Spaniards! I arrest the standard of France in its career of glory! I kill brothers by brothers' hands! I bring the stranger into my country! No, monsieur; I asked the King of Spain for aid against the Guises, who wish to rob me of my inheritance, but not against the Duc d'Anjou, my brother-in-law; not against Henri III., my friend; not against my wife, sister of my king. You will aid the Guises, you will say, and lend them your support. Do so, and I will let loose on you and on them all the Protestants of Germany and France. The King of Spain wishes to reconquer Flanders, which is slipping from him; let him do what his father, Charles V., did, and ask a free passage to go and claim his title of first *bourgeois* of Ghent, and Henri III., I am certain, will grant it to him, as François I. did. I wish for the throne of France, says his Catholic Majesty; it is possible, but I do not need him to aid me in getting it. I will do that for myself, once it is vacant, in spite of all the kings in the world. Adieu, then, monsieur. Tell my brother Philip that I am grateful for his offers, but cannot believe for a moment that he thought me capable of accepting them. Adieu, monsieur."

The ambassador was stupefied. He stammered, " Take care, Sire! the good understanding between two neighbours may be destroyed by a hasty word."

" Monsieur, understand this: King of Navarre or king of nothing, it is all one to me. My crown is so light that I should scarcely feel the difference if it slipped off; besides, I believe I can guard it. Therefore, once more, adieu, monsieur, and tell the king your master that I have greater ambitions than he dreams of." And the Béarnais, becoming once more, not himself, but what he generally seemed to be, conducted the ambassador with a courteous smile to the door.

CHAPTER L

THE POOR OF HENRI DE NAVARRE

CHICOT remained plunged in profound surprise. Henri lifted the tapestry, and striking him on the shoulder, said, " Well, Maître Chicot, how do you think I managed? "

" Wonderfully, Sire; and really, for a king who is not accustomed to ambassadors—"

" It is my brother Henri who sends me these ambassadors."

" How so, Sire? "

" If he did not incessantly persecute his poor sister, others would not dream of it. Do you believe that if the King of Spain had not heard of the public insult offered to the queen, when a captain of the guards searched her litter, he would have proposed to me to repudiate her? "

" I see with pleasure, Sire," replied Chicot, " that all attempts will be useless, and that nothing can interrupt the harmony that exists between the queen and yourself."

" Oh, my friend, the interest they have in making us quarrel is too clear."

" I confess to you, Sire, that I am not so penetrating as you are."

" Doubtless Henri would be delighted if I repudiated his sister."

" Why so? Pray explain to me. *Peste!* I didn't think I was coming to so good a school."

" You know they forgot to pay me my wife's dowry, Chicot."

" I guessed as much, Sire."

" This dowry was to consist of three hundred thousand golden crowns and some towns—among others, Cahors."

" A pretty town, *mordieu!* "

" I have claimed, not the money, but Cahors."

" *Ventre de biche!* Sire, in your place, I should have done the same."

" And that is why—do you understand now? "

" No, indeed, Sire."

" That is why they wish me to quarrel with my wife and repudiate her. No wife, no dowry, no three hundred thousand crowns, no Cahors. It is one way of eluding a promise, and Henri is clever in laying snares."

" You would like much to hold Cahors, Sire."

" Doubtless; for after all, what is my kingdom of Béarn? A poor little principality, so clipped by the avarice of my mother-in-law and brother-in-law that the title of " king " attached to it is ridiculous."

" While Cahors—"

" Cahors would be my rampart—the safeguard of my religion."

" Well, Sire, go into mourning for Cahors; for whether you break with Madame Marguerite or not, the King of France will never give it to you, and unless you take it—"

" Oh, I would soon take it if it was not so strong, and, above all, if I did not hate war."

" Cahors is impregnable, Sire."

" Oh, impregnable! But if I had an army, which I have not—"

" Listen, Sire. We are not here to flatter each other. To take Cahors, which is held by M. de Vesin, one must be a Hannibal or a Cæsar; and your Majesty—"

" Well? " said Henri, with a smile.

" Has just said that you do not like war."

Henri sighed, and his eyes flashed for a minute; then he said, " It is true that I have never drawn the sword, and perhaps never shall. I am a king of straw, a man of peace; but by a singular contrast, I like to think of warlike things—that is in my blood. Saint Louis, my ancestor, pious by education and gentle by nature, became on occasion a brave soldier and a skilful swordsman. Let us talk, if you please, of M. de Vesin, who is a Cæsar and a Hannibal."

"Sire, pardon me if I have wounded or annoyed you. I spoke only of M. de Vesin to extinguish every trace of the mad expectation which youth and ignorance of affairs might have allowed to spring up in your heart. Cahors, you see, is so well guarded because it is the key of the south."

"Alas! I know it well. I wished so much to possess Cahors that I told my poor mother to make it a *sine quâ non* of our marriage. See, I am speaking Latin now. Cahors, then, was my wife's dowry. They owe it to me—"

"Sire, to owe and to pay—"

"Are two different things, I know. So your opinion is that they will never pay me?"

"I fear not."

"The devil!"

"And frankly—"

"Well?"

"They will be right, Sire."

"Why so?"

"Because you did not know your part of king. You should have got it at once."

"Do you not, then, remember the tocsin of St. Germain l'Auxerrois?" said Henri, bitterly. "It seems to me that a husband whom they try to murder on the night of his marriage might think less of his dowry than of his life."

"Yes; but since then, Sire, we have had peace and—excuse me, Sire—you should have profited by it, and instead of making love, have negotiated. It is less amusing, I know, but more profitable. I speak, Sire, as much for my king as for you. If Henri de France had a strong ally in Henri de Navarre, he would be stronger than any one; and if the Protestants and Catholics of France and Navarre would unite in a common political interest, they would make the rest of the world tremble."

"Oh, I do not aspire to make others tremble, so long as I do not tremble myself. But if I cannot get Cahors, then, and you think I cannot—"

"I think so, Sire, for three reasons."

"Tell them to me, Chicot."

"Willingly. The first is that Cahors is a town of good productiveness, which Henri III. will prefer to keep for himself."

"That is not very honest."

"It is very royal, Sire."

"Ah! it is royal to take what you like?"

" Yes, that is called acting like a lion; and the lion is the king of beasts."

" I shall remember what you have just told me, Chicot, if ever I become king. Now, your second reason."

" Madame Catherine—"

" Oh! does my good mother Catherine still mix in politics? "

" Always; and she would rather see her daughter at Paris than at Nérac—near her than near you."

" You think so? Yet she does not love her daughter to distraction."

" No; but Madame Marguerite serves you as a hostage, Sire."

" You are cunning, Chicot. Devil take me if I thought of that! But you may be right. Yes, yes! a daughter of France would be a hostage in case of need. Well? "

" Well, Sire, in diminishing one's resources, you diminish the attractiveness to him of any particular dwelling-place. Nérac is a very pleasant place, with a charming park, and avenues such as can be found nowhere else. But Madame Marguerite, deprived of resources, would become weary of Nérac and long for the Louvre."

" I prefer your first reason, Chicot," said Henri, shaking his head.

" Then I pass to the third. Between the Duc d'Anjou, who seeks to make a throne for himself in Flanders, MM. de Guise, who wish for a crown, and shake that of France, and his Majesty the King of Spain, who wishes for universal monarchy, you hold the balance and maintain a certain equilibrium."

" I—without weight? "

" Precisely. If you became powerful—that is to say, heavy —you would turn the scale. You would be no longer a counterpoise, but a weight."

" Ah! I like that reason, and it is admirably argued. This is the explanation of my situation? "

" Complete."

" And I, who did not see all this, and went on hoping! "

" Well, Sire, I counsel you to cease to hope."

" Then I must do for this debt of the King of France what I do for those of my farmers who cannot pay their rent; I put a P against their names."

" Which means 'paid'? "

" Yes."

" Put two P's, Sire, and give a sigh."

" So be it, Chicot. You see I can live in Béarn, even without Cahors."

" I see that, and also that you are a wise and philosophical king. But what is that noise? "

" Noise! where? "

" In the courtyard, I think."

" Look out the window."

" Sire, there are below a dozen of poorly clothed people."

" Ah! they are my poor," said the king, rising.

" Your Majesty has his poor? "

" Doubtless; does not God recommend charity? If I am not a Catholic, Chicot, I am a Christian."

" Bravo, Sire! "

" Come, Chicot, we will give alms together, and then go to supper."

" Sire, I follow you."

" Take that purse lying on the table near my sword; do you see? "

" They went down, but Henri seemed thoughtful and pre-occupied. Chicot looked at him, and thought, " What the devil made me talk politics to this brave prince, and make him sad? Fool that I was! "

Once in the court, Henri approached the group of mendicants. There was a dozen men unlike in stature, features, and dress. An ordinary spectator would have taken them for tramps. An observer would have seen that they were gentlemen in disguise. Henri took the purse from the hands of Chicot and made a sign. All the mendicants appeared to understand that sign. They came forward and saluted Henri with an air of humility, which did not preclude a glance full of intelligence at the king. Henri replied by a motion of the head. Then, putting his fingers into the purse, which Chicot held open, he took out a piece.

" Do you know that it is gold, Sire? " said Chicot.

" Yes, my friend, I know."

" *Peste !* you are rich."

" Do you not see that each of these pieces serves for two? On the contrary, I am so poor that I am forced to cut my pistoles in two to make them go round."

" It is true," said Chicot, with surprise. " They are half-pieces, with fantastic designs."

" Oh, I am like my brother Henri, who amuses himself in cutting out images. I amuse myself with clipping my ducats."

" Nevertheless, Sire, it is an odd method of giving charity," said Chicot, who suspected some hidden mystery.

" What would you do? "

" Instead of cutting each piece, I would give it entire, and would say, ' This is for two.' "

" They would fight, and I should do harm instead of good."

Henri then took one of the pieces, and placing himself before the first beggar, looked at him inquiringly.

" Agen," said the man.

" How many ? " asked Henri.

" Five hundred."

" Cahors ; " and he gave him the piece and took a second.

The man bowed and withdrew.

The next advanced and said, " Auch."

" How many ? "

" Three hundred and fifty."

" Cahors ; " and he gave him his piece.

" Narbonne," said the third.

" How many ? "

" Eight hundred."

" Cahors ; " and he gave him his piece.

" Montauban," said the fourth.

" How many ? "

" Six hundred."

" Cahors."

Each one in this way pronounced a name, received a piece of gold, and mentioned a number, which altogether amounted to about eight thousand. To each of them Henri replied, " Cahors," without varying the tone of his voice in uttering that word. The distribution finished, there were no longer half-pieces in the purse, nor beggars in the court.

" That is all, Sire ? " asked Chicot.

" Yes ; I have finished."

" Sire, am I permitted to be curious ? "

" Why not ? Curiosity is natural."

" What did these beggars say, and what the devil did you reply ? "

Henri smiled.

" Indeed," continued Chicot, " all is mysterious here."

" Do you think so ? "

" Yes ; I have never seen alms given in that way."

" It is the custom at Nérac. You know the proverb, ' Every town has its own customs.' "

" A singular custom, Sire."

" No ; nothing is more simple. Each of those men came from a different city."

" Well, Sire ? "

" Well, that I may not always give to the same, they each tell me the name of their town, so that I can distribute my benefits equally among all the unfortunates in my kingdom."

" Yes, Sire; but why did you answer ' Cahors '?"

" Ah!" cried Henri, with a most natural air of surprise. " Did I say ' Cahors '?"

" *Parbleu!*"

" You think so?"

" I am sure of it."

" It must have been because we had been talking so much about it. I wish for it so much that I must have spoken of it without meaning to do so."

" Hum!" said Chicot, suspiciously, " and then there was something else."

" What! something else?"

" A number that each one pronounced, all of which added together made more than eight thousand."

" Ah! as to that, Chicot, I did not understand it myself; unless, as the beggars are divided into corporations, they named the number of members belonging to each—which seems to me probable."

" Sire, Sire!"

" Come and sup, my friend; nothing enlightens the mind like eating and drinking. Let us go to table, and you shall see that if my pistoles are cut, my bottles are full."

Then, passing his arm familiarly through Chicot's, the king went back to his room, where supper was served. Passing by the queen's room, he glanced at it, and saw no light.

" Page," said he, " is not her Majesty at home?"

" Her Majesty is gone to see Mademoiselle de Montmorency, who is ill."

" Ah, poor Fosseuse!" said Henri; " it is true; the queen has such a good heart! Come to supper, Chicot."

CHAPTER LI

THE TRUE MISTRESS OF THE KING OF NAVARRE

THE repast was joyous. Henri seemed no longer to have any weight either on his heart or his mind, and he was an excellent companion. As for Chicot, he concealed as well as he could the uneasiness he had felt since the coming of the Spanish ambassador and the scene with the mendicants. He endeavoured to drink little and keep cool, to observe everything; but this Henri would not allow. However, Chicot had a head of iron; and as for Henri, he said he could drink these wines of the country like milk.

"I envy you," said Chicot, to the king; "your court is delightful, and your life pleasant."

"If my wife were here, Chicot, I would not say what I am about to say; but in her absence I will tell you that the best part of my life is that which you do not see."

"Ah, Sire, they tell indeed fine tales of you!"

Henri leaned back in his chair to laugh. "They say that I reign more over my female than my male subjects, do they not?" said he.

"Yes, Sire; and it astonishes me."

"Why so?"

"Because, Sire, you have much of that restless spirit which makes great kings."

"Ah, Chicot, you are wrong. I am lazy, and all my life proves it. If I have a love to choose, I take the nearest; if a wine, the bottle close to my hand. To your health, Chicot!"

"Sire, you do me honour," said Chicot, emptying his glass.

"Thus," continued the king, "what quarrels in my household!"

"Yes, I understand; all the ladies-in-waiting adore you, Sire."

"They are my neighbours, Chicot."

"Then, Sire, it might result from this that if you lived at St. Denis instead of Nérac, the king might not live very tranquilly."

"The king! what do you say, Chicot? Do you think I am a Guise? I wish for Cahors, it is true, because it is near to me, still following my system."

"*Ventre de biche!* Sire, this ambition for things within the reach of your hand resembles much that of Cæsar Borgia, who gathered together a kingdom, city by city, saying that Italy was an artichoke to be eaten leaf by leaf."

"This Cæsar Borgia was not a bad politician, it seems to me, my friend."

"No, but he was a very dangerous neighbour and a bad brother."

"Ah! would you compare me to the son of a pope—me, a Huguenot chief?"

"Sire, I compare you to no one."

"Why not?"

" I believe he would be wrong who should liken you to any other than yourself. You are ambitious, Sire."

" Here is a man determined to make me want something," cried Henri.

" God forbid, Sire! I desire with all my heart, on the contrary, that your Majesty should want nothing."

" Nothing calls you back to Paris, does it, Chicot? "

" No, Sire."

" Then you will pass some days with me? "

" If your Majesty does me the honour to wish for my company, I ask nothing better than to give you a week."

" So be it; in a week you will know me like a brother. Drink, Chicot."

" Sire, I am no longer thirsty," said Chicot, who had given up all hopes of seeing the king take too much.

" Then I will leave you; a man should not stay at table when he does nothing. Drink, I tell you."

" Why, Sire? "

" To sleep better. Do you like the chase, Chicot? "

" Not much, Sire; and you? "

" Passionately—since I lived at the court of Charles IX."

" Why did your Majesty do me the honour to ask me? "

" Because I hunt to-morrow, and count on taking you with me."

" Sire, it would be a great honour; but—"

" Oh! this chase is calculated to gladden the eyes and the heart of every man of the sword. I am a good hunter, Chicot, and I wish you to see me to advantage. You wish to know me, you say? "

" *Ventre de biche!* Sire, it is one of my strongest wishes, I confess."

" Well, that is a side on which you have never yet studied me."

" Sire, I am at your orders."

" Good! then it is settled. Ah! here is a page to disturb us."

" Some important business, Sire? "

" Business at table! You think you are still at the court of France, my dear Chicot. Learn one thing—at Nérac, when we have supped, we go to bed."

" But this page? "

" Well, cannot he come for anything but business? "

" Ah, I understand; and I will go to bed."

Chicot rose; the king did the same, and took his arm. This haste to send him away appeared suspicious to Chicot; and he determined not to leave the room if he could help it.

" Oh, oh!" said he, tottering, " it is astonishing, Sire."

The king smiled. " What is astonishing?"

" *Ventre de biche !* my head turns; while I sat still it was all very well, but when I rise—"

" Bah!" said Henri, " we only tasted the wine."

" You call that tasting, Sire? You are a drinker, and I do you homage, as to my superior."

" Chicot, my friend," said Henri, endeavouring to make out by one of his keen glances whether Chicot was really drunk or was pretending, " the best thing you can do is to go to bed."

" Yes, Sire; good-night, Sire."

" Good-night, Chicot."

" Yes, Sire, you are right; the best thing Chicot can do is to go to bed." And he lay down on the floor.

Henri glanced towards the door, and then, approaching him, said, " You are so drunk, my poor Chicot, that you have taken my floor for your bed."

" Chicot does not mind little things."

" But I expect some one."

" For supper; yes, let us sup—" And Chicot made a fruitless effort to rise.

" *Ventre-saint-gris !* how quickly you get drunk! But go along, *mordieu !* she is getting impatient."

" She! who?"

" The lady I expect."

" A lady; why did you not say so, Henriquet? Ah, pardon! I thought I was speaking—to the King of France. He has spoiled me, that good Henriquet. Ah! I will go."

" You are a gentleman, Chicot. Now go quickly."

Chicot rose and went stumbling to the door.

" Adieu, dear friend," said Henri; " adieu, and sleep well."

" And you, Sire?"

" Sh!"

" Yes, yes—sh!" and he opened the door.

" You will find the page in the gallery, who will show you your room."

" Thank you, Sire." And Chicot went out, after saluting with as low an inclination as a drunken man could make. But as soon as the door closed behind him every trace of drunkenness disappeared; he took three steps forward, and suddenly return-ing he placed his eye to the large keyhole. Henri was already opening the door to the unknown, whom Chicot, with the curiosity of an ambassador, wished by all means to see. Instead of a woman, it was a man who entered. The man took off his hat, and Chicot saw the noble but severe face of Duplessis-Mornay—the rigid and vigilant counsellor of Henri de Navarre.

"Ah!" thought Chicot, "this will annoy our lover more than I did."

But Henri's face showed only joy; and after locking the door, he sat down eagerly to examine some maps, plans, and letters, which his minister had brought him. The king then began to write and to mark the maps.

"Oh! this is the way Henri de Navarre makes love," thought Chicot.

At this moment he heard steps behind him, and afraid of being surprised, he turned hastily away, and seeing the page, asked for his room.

"Come with me, if you please, monsieur," said D'Aubiac, "and I will show you the way;" and he conducted Chicot to the second story, where a room had been prepared for him.

Chicot began to understand the King of Navarre. Therefore, instead of going to sleep, he sat sombre and thoughtful on his bed, while the moon shed its silver light over stream and meadows.

"Henri is a real king; and he conspires," thought Chicot. "All this palace, park, town—the whole province—is a focus of conspiracy. All the women make love, but it is political love; and all the men live in the hope of a future. Henri is clever; his talent borders on genius; and he is in communication with Spain, the land of deceit. Who knows if even his noble answer to the ambassador was not a farce, and if he did not communicate with him by some sign unknown to me? Henri has spies. Those beggars were nothing more nor less than gentlemen in disguise. Those pieces of gold, so artistically cut, were pledges of recognition—rallying signs.

"Henri feigns to care for nothing but love and pleasure, and then passes his time working with Mornay, who never sleeps, and does not know what love means. Queen Marguerite has lovers, and the king knows it, and tolerates them, because he has need of them, or of her—perhaps of both. Happily, God, in giving him the genius for intrigue, did not add to it that of war, for they say he is afraid of the noise of musketry, and that when he was taken, when quite young, to battle, he could not stay more than a quarter of an hour in the saddle. It is lucky, for if he had the arm, as well as the head, this man might do anything.

"There is indeed the Duc de Guise, who has both; but he has the disadvantage of being known as brave and skilful, so that every one is on guard against him, while no one fears the Béarnais. I alone have seen through him. Well, having seen through him, I have no more to do here, so while he works or sleeps I will go quietly out of the city. There are not many ambassadors, I think, who can boast of having fulfilled their mission in one day, as I have. So I will leave Nérac, and gallop till I am in France." And he began to put on his spurs.

CHAPTER LII

CHICOT'S ASTONISHMENT AT FINDING HIMSELF SO POPULAR IN NÉRAC

CHICOT, having taken his resolution, began to prepare his little packet. "How much time will it take me," thought he, as he did so, "to carry to the king intelligence of what I have seen, and of what, consequently, I fear? Two days to arrive at a city whence the governor can send couriers—Cahors, for example, of which Henri de Navarre thinks so much. Once there I can rest, for after all, a man must rest some time. I will rest, then, at Cahors, and the horses can run for me. Come, then, Chicot, speed and patience! You thought you had accomplished your mission, and you are but halfway through it."

Chicot now extinguished the light, opened his door softly, and went out on tiptoe. He had hardly gone four steps in the antechamber before he kicked against something. This something was a page lying on a mat outside the chamber, who, awaking, said, "Good-evening, M. Chicot, good-evening."

Chicot recognised D'Aubiac. "Eh, good-evening, M. d'Aubiac," said he. "But get out of the way a little, I beg. I want to go for a walk."

"Ah, but it is forbidden to walk by night in the château."

"Why so?"

"Because the king fears robbers, and the queen lovers."

"The devil!"

"None but robbers or lovers want to walk at night, when they ought to be sleeping."

"However, dear M. d'Aubiac," said Chicot, with his most charming smile, "I am neither the one nor the other. I am an ambassador, very tired from having talked Latin with the queen, and supped with the king. Let me go out, then, my friend, for I want a walk."

"In the city, M. Chicot?"

" Oh, no! in the gardens."

" *Peste !* that is still more forbidden than in the city."

" My little friend, you are very vigilant for your age. Have you nothing to occupy yourself with? "

" No."

" You neither gamble nor fall in love? "

" To gamble one must have money, M. Chicot; and to be in love, one must find a woman."

" Assuredly," said Chicot; and feeling in his pocket, he drew out ten pistoles and slipped them into the page's hand, saying, " Seek well in your memory, and I bet you will find some charming woman, to whom I beg you to make some presents with this."

" Oh, M. Chicot! " said the page, " it is easy to see that you come from the court of France; you have manners to which one can refuse nothing. Go, then, but make no noise."

Chicot went on. He glided like a shadow into the corridor, and down the staircase; but at the bottom he found an officer sleeping on a chair, placed right against the door, so that it was impossible to pass.

" Ah! little brigand of a page," murmured Chicot, " you knew this and didn't tell me."

Chicot looked round him to see if he could find no other way by which he could escape with the assistance of his long legs. At last he saw what he wanted; it was an arched window, of which the glass was broken. He climbed up the wall with his accustomed skill, and without making more noise than a dry leaf in the autumn wind; but, unluckily, the opening was not big enough, so that when he had got his head and one shoulder through, and had taken away his foot from its resting-place on the wall, he found himself hanging between heaven and earth, without being able either to advance or retreat.

He began then a series of efforts, of which the first result was to tear his doublet and scratch his skin. What rendered his position more difficult was his sword, of which the handle would not pass, making a hook by which Chicot hung on to the sash. He exerted all his strength, patience, and industry to unfasten the clasp of his shoulder-belt; but it was just on this clasp that his body leaned, so that he was obliged to change his manœuvre. He succeeded in passing his hand behind his back and drawing his sword from its sheath. The sword once drawn, it was easy —thanks to that angular frame—to find an interstice through which the hilt would pass; the sword therefore fell first on the flagstones, and Chicot now managed to get through after it.

All this, however, was not done without noise, and Chicot, on rising, found himself face to face with a soldier.

" Ah, *mon Dieu!* have you hurt yourself, M. Chicot? " said he.

Chicot was surprised, but said, " No, my friend, not at all."

" That is very fortunate. There are not many people who could accomplish such a feat without breaking their heads; in fact, no one but you could do that, M. Chicot."

" But how the devil did you know my name? "

" I saw you to-day at the palace, and asked who was the gentleman that was talking with the king."

" Well! I am in a hurry; allow me to pass."

" But no one goes out of the palace by night; those are my orders."

" But you see they do come out, since I am here."

" Yes, but—"

" But what? "

" You must go back, M. Chicot."

" Oh, no! "

" How! no? "

" Not by that way, at all events; it is too troublesome."

" If I were an officer instead of a soldier, I would ask you why you came out so; but that is not my business, which is only that you should go back again. Go in, therefore, M. Chicot, I beg you."

And the soldier said this in such a persuasive tone that Chicot was touched. Consequently he put his hand in his pocket and drew out ten pistoles.

" You must understand, my friend," said he, " that as I have torn my clothes in passing through once, I should make them still worse by going back again, and should have to go naked, which would be very indecent in a court where there are so many young and pretty women; let me go, then, to my tailor." And he put the money in his hand.

" Go quickly, then, M. Chicot," said the man.

Chicot was in the street at last. The night was not favourable for flight, being bright and cloudless, and he regretted the foggy nights of Paris, where people might pass close to one another unseen. The unfortunate ambassador had no sooner turned the corner of the street than he met a patrol. He stopped of his own accord, thinking it would look suspicious to try to pass unseen.

" Oh, good-evening, M. Chicot! " said the chief; " shall we

reconduct you to the palace? You appear to have lost your way."

"It is very strange," murmured Chicot, "every one knows me here." Then aloud, and as carelessly as he could, "No, Cornet, I am not going to the palace."

"You are wrong, M. Chicot," replied the officer, gravely.

"Why so, monsieur?"

"Because a very severe edict forbids the inhabitants of Nérac to go out at night, except in cases of urgent necessity, without permission and without a lantern."

"Excuse me, monsieur, but this edict cannot apply to me, who do not belong to Nérac."

"But you are at Nérac. 'Inhabitant' means living at; now you cannot deny that you live at Nérac, since I see you here."

"You are logical, monsieur. Unfortunately, I am in a hurry; make an exception to your rule, and let me pass, I beg."

"You will lose yourself, M. Chicot; Nérac is a strange town. Allow three of my men to conduct you to the palace."

"But I am not going to the palace, I tell you."

"Where are you going, then?"

"I cannot sleep well at night, and then I always walk. Nérac is a charming city, and I wish to see it, to study it."

"My men shall conduct you where you please, M. Chicot. Holloa! three men!"

"Oh, monsieur, I would rather go alone."

"You will be assassinated by thieves."

"I have my sword."

"Ah, true; then you will be arrested for bearing arms."

Chicot, driven to despair, drew the officer aside, and said, "Come, monsieur, you are young; you know what love is— an imperious tyrant."

"Doubtless, M. Chicot."

"Well, Cornet, I have a certain lady to visit."

"Where?"

"In a certain place."

"Young?"

"Twenty-three years old."

"Beautiful?"

"As the graces."

"I felicitate you, M. Chicot."

"Then you will let me pass?"

"Why, it seems to me that it is a case of urgent necessity."

"'Urgent' is the very word, monsieur."

"Go on, then."

" And alone? you know I cannot compromise—"

" Of course not; pass on, M. Chicot."

" You are a gallant man, Cornet. But how did you know me?"

" I saw you at the palace with the king. By the way, in what direction are you going?"

" Towards the Agen gate. Am I not in the right road?"

" Yes, go straight on; I wish you success."

" Thank you;" and Chicot went on more light and joyous than ever. But before he had taken a hundred steps he met the watch.

" *Peste !* this town is well guarded," thought Chicot.

" You cannot pass!" cried the provost, in a voice of thunder.

" But, monsieur, I want—"

" Ah, M. Chicot, is it you? In the streets in this cold?" asked the officer.

" Ah, decidedly it must be a bet," thought Chicot; and bowing, he tried to pass on.

" M. Chicot, take care!" said the provost.

" Take care of what?"

" You are going wrong; you are going towards the gates."

" Precisely."

" Then I arrest you, M. Chicot!"

" Not so, monsieur; you would be very wrong."

" However—"

" Approach, monsieur, that your soldiers may not hear."

The man approached.

" The king has given me a commission for the lieutenant of the Agen gate."

" Ah!"

" That astonishes you?"

" Yes."

" It ought not, since you know me."

" I know you from having seen you at the palace with the king."

Chicot stamped his foot impatiently. " That should prove to you that I possess the king's confidence."

" Doubtless; go on, M. Chicot, and execute your commission."

" Come," thought Chicot, " I advance slowly; but I do advance. *Ventre de biche !* here is a gate; it must be that of Agen. In five minutes I shall be out."

He arrived at the gate, which was guarded by a sentinel walking up and down, his musket on his shoulder.

" My friend, will you open the gate for me?" said Chicot.

"I cannot, M. Chicot," replied the man, "being only a private soldier."

"You also know me?" cried Chicot, in a rage.

"I have that honour, M. Chicot; I was on guard at the palace this morning, and saw you talking with the king."

"Well, my friend, the king has given me a very urgent message to convey to Agen; open the postern for me."

"I would with pleasure, but I have not the keys."

"And who has them?"

"The officer for the night."

Chicot sighed. "And where is he?"

The soldier rang a bell to wake his officer.

"What is it?" said he, passing his head through a window.

"Lieutenant, it is a gentleman who wants the gate opened."

"Ah, M. Chicot," cried the officer, "I will be down in a moment."

"What! does every one know me?" cried Chicot. "Nérac seems a lantern, and I the candle."

"Excuse me, monsieur," said the officer, approaching, "but I was asleep."

"Oh, monsieur, that is what night is made for; will you be good enough to open the door? Unluckily, I cannot sleep, for the king—doubtless you also are aware that the king knows me?"

"I saw you talking with his Majesty to-day at the palace."

"Of course!" growled Chicot. "Well, the king has sent me on a commission to Agen; this is the right gate, is it not?"

"Yes, M. Chicot."

"Will you please to have it opened?"

"Of course. Anthenas, open the gate quickly for M. Chicot."

Chicot began to breathe; the gate creaked on its hinges—the gate of paradise to Chicot, who saw beyond it all the delights of liberty. He saluted the officer cordially, and advanced towards the gate. "Adieu," said he; "thank you."

"Adieu, M. Chicot! a pleasant journey! But stay one moment; I have forgotten to ask for your pass," cried he, seizing Chicot by the sleeve to stop him.

"What! my pass?"

"Certainly, M. Chicot; you know what a pass is? You understand that no one can leave a town like Nérac without a pass, particularly when the king is in it."

"And who must sign this pass?"

"The king himself; so if he sent you he cannot have forgotten to give you a pass."

"Ah, you doubt that the king sent me?" cried Chicot, with

flashing eyes, for he saw himself on the point of failing, and had a great mind to kill the officer and sentinel, and rush through the gate.

" I doubt nothing you tell me; but reflect that if the king gave you this commission—"

" In person, monsieur."

" All the more reason, then. If he knows you are going out, I shall have to give up your pass to-morrow morning to the governor."

" And who is he? "

" M. de Mornay, who does not jest with disobedience, M. Chicot."

Chicot put his hand to his sword, but another look showed him that the outside of the gate was defended by a guard who would have prevented his passing if he had killed the officer and sentinel.

" Well," said Chicot to himself, with a sigh, " I have lost my game! " and he turned back.

" Shall I give you an escort, M. Chicot? " said the officer.

" No, thank you."

Chicot retraced his steps, but he was not at the end of his griefs. He met the chief of the watch, who said, " What! have you finished your commission already, M. Chicot? *Peste!* how quick you are! "

A little farther on the cornet cried to him, " Well, M. Chicot, what of the lady? Are you content with Nérac? "

Finally, the soldier in the courtyard said, *"Cordieu!* M. Chicot, the tailor has not done his work well; you seem more torn than when you went out."

Chicot did not feel inclined to climb back through the window, and he lay down before the door and pretended to sleep; but by chance, or rather by charity, the door was opened, and he returned into the palace. Here he saw the page, who said, " Dear M. Chicot, shall I give you the key to all this? "

" Yes, serpent," murmured Chicot.

" Well, the king loves you so much he did not wish to lose you."

" And you knew, brigand, and never told me? "

" Oh, M. Chicot, impossible! It was a state secret."

" But I paid you, knave."

" Oh, dear M. Chicot, the secret was worth more than ten pistoles."

Chicot returned to his room in a rage.

CHAPTER LIII

THE KING'S MASTER OF THE HOUNDS

ON leaving the king, Marguerite had gone directly to the apartment of the maids of honour. On the way thither she had called for her doctor, Chirac, who had a room at the château, and with him she had visited the poor Fosseuse, who, pale and curiously regarded by those about her, was complaining of pains in her stomach—unwilling, so great was her suffering, to answer questions or accept relief.

Fosseuse was at this time about twenty-one years of age—a tall, handsome woman, with blue eyes, light hair, and a supple and graceful form. For three months she had not left her room; she had complained of a lassitude which compelled her to lie down, and beginning by reclining on a lounge, she had finally taken to her bed.

Chirac began by dismissing the bystanders, and taking possession of the patient, he remained alone with her and the queen.

Fosseuse, terrified by these preliminaries, to which the expression on the faces of Chirac and the queen, the one impassive and the other cold, lent a certain solemnity, raised herself on her pillow and stammered her thanks for the honour done her by the queen her mistress.

Marguerite was paler than Fosseuse; for wounded pride is more painful than cruelty or sickness.

Chirac felt the young girl's pulse in spite of her resistance. " Where is your pain? " he asked, after a moment's examination.

" In my stomach, monsieur," replied the poor child; " but that would be nothing if I could only have peace of mind."

" What do you mean, mademoiselle? " asked the queen. Fosseuse burst into tears.

" Do not be troubled, mademoiselle," continued Marguerite. " His Majesty asked me to come and cheer you up."

" Oh how kind, madame! "

Chirac let fall the sick girl's hand, saying, " I know now what your trouble is."

" You know? " murmured Fosseuse, trembling.

" Yes, we know that you must be suffering very much," added Marguerite.

Fosseuse was still in terror at finding herself thus at the mercy of science and jealousy, both so unsympathetic.

Marguerite made a sign to Chirac, who left the room. Then the fear of Fosseuse turned to trembling, and she was near fainting away.

" Mademoiselle," said Marguerite, " although for some time you have treated me as a stranger, and although I have been told every day of the wrong you have done me—"

" I, madame? "

" Do not interrupt me, if you please. Although you have aspired to a fortune beyond your reasonable ambitions, the friendship which I bore you and that which I have vowed to the maids of honour one of whom you are, urges me to be of service to you in your present misfortune."

" Madame, I swear to you—"

" Make no denials—I have already too much sorrow; do not wreck your honour and mine. I say mine, for I have almost as much interest in your honour as you yourself can have, since you belong to me. Mademoiselle, tell me all, and I will assist you as would a mother."

" Oh, madame! madame! do you then believe what they say? "

" Take care not to interrupt me, mademoiselle, for it seems to me time presses. I would say that Monsieur Chirac, who knows the nature of your sickness (you recall his words spoken without hesitation) is at this moment in the ante-chamber announcing to all, that the contagious disease prevalent in the country has reached the palace, and that you are threatened with an attack. Nevertheless, I will take you—there is time yet—to Mas-d'Agenois, which is a house quite remote from the residence of the king my husband; we shall be there alone or nearly so. The king is setting out with his attendants upon a hunting expedition, which he says will keep him away for several days; we will not leave Mas-d'Agenois until after your confinement."

" Madame! madame! " exclaimed La Fosseuse, red with shame and grief, " if you believe all that is reported of me, leave me alone to die a miserable death! "

" You show no gratitude for my generosity, mademoiselle, and you also reckon too much upon the friendship of the king, who has begged me not to abandon you."

" The king! the king has said—"

" Do you doubt what I say, mademoiselle? If I did not understand the symptoms of your sickness, if I did not divine from your suffering that the crisis is near, I might perhaps have faith in your denials."

Just then, as if to justify the queen, the poor Fosseuse, attacked by a terrible pain, fell back livid and palpitating upon the bed.

Marguerite regarded her for a while, without anger, also without pity.

" Do you still expect me to believe your denials, made-moiselle? " she said at last to the poor girl, as soon as the latter was able to rise, showing, as she did so, a countenance so distracted and tearful as would have melted Catherine herself.

At this moment, as if God had taken pity on the unfortunate girl, the door opened, and the King of Navarre entered hastily. Henri, who had not the same reasons as Chicot for sleeping, had not slept. After having laboured an hour with Mornay, and made all his arrangements for the chase so formally announced to Chicot, he had hastened to the pavilion of the maids of honour.

" Well, how is it? " said he as he came in; " is my child Fosseuse still suffering? "

" Do you not see, madame," cried the young girl at the sight of her lover, and strengthened by the succour his arrival brought, " do you not see that the king has said nothing; and that I am right in denying? "

" Monsieur," interrupted the queen, turning toward Henri, " put an end, I beg you, to this humiliating struggle. I think I understood that your Majesty had honoured me with your confidence, and disclosed to me mademoiselle's condition. Apprise her therefore that I know all, so that she can no longer doubt my assertions."

" My child," said Henri, with an emotion which he did not attempt to conceal, " do you persist in your denial? "

" The secret is not mine, Sire," replied the courageous child, " and so long as I had not received from your lips permission to tell all—"

" My child Fosseuse is brave, madame," said Henri. " Pardon her, I beg you; and you, my child, must place perfect confidence in the kindness of your queen; the acknowledgment concerns me, and I take it upon myself; " and Henri took Marguerite's hand and pressed it warmly.

Just then a sharp pain again attacked the young girl; yielding yet a second time to the tempest and bent like a lily, she bowed her head with a dull moan.

Henri was moved to the very depths of his heart as he looked on that pale brow, those eyes wet with tears, those damp, streaming locks; as he beheld, standing in drops upon the temples and lips of Fosseuse, the sweat of that anguish which

is kindred to agony. He threw himself passionately toward
her with outstretched arms. " Fosseuse, dear Fosseuse," he
murmured, falling on his knees by her bed.

Marguerite, stern and silent, went to cool her burning brow
upon the glass of the window panes.

Fosseuse had sufficient strength to raise her arms and place
them around the neck of her lover; then she put her lips to his,
thinking that she was about to die, and that in this last, this
supreme kiss went out to Henri her soul and her farewell. Then
she fell back unconscious.

Henri, as pale as she, still and voiceless like her, let her head
fall upon the sheet on her bed of agony, which seemed almost
as if it were her winding-sheet.

Marguerite drew near this group, in which pain of body was
combined with anguish of spirit.

" Rise, monsieur, and let me fulfil the duty you have imposed
upon me," she said with dignity. And as Henri seemed disturbed
at this manifestation, and half rose upon his knees, " Oh, do not
fear, monsieur," she said; " since my pride alone is wounded I
am strong; were my heart involved I could not answer for myself;
but happily my heart is not concerned in this matter."

Henri raised his head. " Madame? " he said.

" Not another word, monsieur," said Marguerite, extending her
hand, " or I shall believe that your indulgence has been the result
of calculation. We will agree together as brother and sister."

Henri led her to Fosseuse, whose icy fingers he placed in
Marguerite's burning hand.

" Go, Sire, go," said the queen; " set out for the chase.
The more persons you take away with you, the more will you
shield from curious inquiry the bed of—mademoiselle."

" But," said Henri, " I saw no one in the ante-chambers."

" No, Sire," replied Marguerite smiling, " they think the plague
is here. Hasten, therefore, to seek your pleasures elsewhere."

" Madame," said Henri, " I depart and will go to hunt for
us both." And he cast a last tender glance at the still unconscious Fosseuse, and then darted out of the room. Once in the
ante-chambers, he shook his head as if to cast from his brow
the last sign of disquietude; then with a smile upon his face,
that shrewd smile peculiar to him, he went up to find Chicot,
who, as we have said, was sleeping with clenched fists.

" Eh! eh! comrade, get up, get up! it is two o'clock in the
morning."

" Ah, *diable !* " said Chicot. " You call me comrade, Sire;
do you take me for the Duc de Guise perchance? "

As it happened, Henri, in speaking of the Duc de Guise, was accustomed to call him his comrade.

"I take you for my friend," he said.

"And you make me prisoner—me, an ambassador! Sire, you violate the law of nations."

Henri began to laugh. Chicot, who was especially a man of wit, could not help joining in the merriment.

"You are mad. *Diable!* why did you wish to leave here? Are you not treated well?"

"Too well, *ventre de biche!* too well; my position here seems to be like that of a goose fattening in a farmyard. Everybody says, 'Little, little Chicot, how fine he is! but they cut his wings, and keep him shut up.'"

"Chicot, my good fellow," said Henri, shaking his head, "never fear; you are not fat enough for my table."

"Eh! Sire," said Chicot, raising his head, "you are very merry this morning; what, then, is the news?"

"Ah, I will tell you; I am about to set out for the chase, you see, and that always makes me merry. Come, out of bed, comrade, out of bed!"

"What! am I to go with you, Sire?"

"You shall be my historiographer, Chicot."

"I am to keep count of the shots?"

"Exactly."

Chicot shook his head.

"Well, what is the matter?" asked the king.

"Well, I have never seen such high spirits without anxiety."

"Bah!"

"Yes, it is like the sun when—"

"Well?"

"When, Sire, rain, lightning, and thunder are not far distant."

Henri stroked his beard, smiled, and answered: "If a storm arises, Chicot, my cloak is large, and you will be protected." He then went toward the antechamber, while Chicot began to dress, muttering meanwhile to himself.

"My horse!" cried the king; "and have Monsieur de Mornay notified that I am ready."

"Ah! Monsieur de Mornay is to be the master of hounds for this chase?" asked Chicot.

"Monsieur Mornay is my sole reliance, Chicot," replied Henri. "The King of Navarre is too poor to indulge in specialties. I have one man only."

"Yes, but he is a good one," sighed Chicot.

PART SECOND

CHAPTER I

HOW THEY HUNTED THE WOLF IN NAVARRE

CHICOT, as he glanced over the preparations for departure, could not help remarking to himself in a low voice that the hunting equipments of King Henri of Navarre were much less sumptuous than those of King Henri of France.

A dozen or fifteen gentlemen only, among whom he recognised the Vicomte de Turenne, the object of matrimonial contentions, formed the entire suite of his Majesty.

Moreover, as these gentlemen were rich only in appearance—as they were not possessed of revenues sufficient to warrant superfluous expenditures, or even to provide always the means for expenditures that were not superfluous—nearly all of them wore helmets and cuirasses instead of the hunting-garb in vogue at that period; so that Chicot was led to ask if the wolves in the forests of Gascony defended themselves with muskets and artillery.

Henri heard the question, although it was not directly addressed to him. He drew near to Chicot and touched him on the shoulder.

"No, my son," he replied; "the wolves of Gascony have neither muskets nor artillery; but they are fierce beasts, well supplied with claws and teeth. They draw the huntsmen into thickets, where the garments of the pursuers are likely to be torn by branches and thorns. Now, it is easy enough to tear a coat of silk or of velvet, or even a jacket of strong cloth or of leather; but a cuirass is not to be torn."

"That is a reason, to be sure," growled Chicot; "but it is not a very good one."

"What would you have?" said Henri; "it is the only one I can give you."

"I suppose, then, that I must put up with it."

"That, indeed, is the best thing you can do, my son."

"So be it, then."

"That 'So be it' sounds as if you were not quite satisfied," said Henri, laughing; "are you angry with me for routing you out to follow this chase?"

"Faith! yes."

"So, then, you are finding fault?"

"Is it forbidden?"

"No, my friend, no; fault-finding is current money in Gascony."

"Well, Sire, you must remember," replied Chicot, that I am no hunter; and since I have no occupation, poor idler that I am, I must amuse myself in some way while you and the rest are licking your chops as you scent already the fine wolves that a dozen or fifteen of you are going to run down."

"Ah, yes," said the king, still amused by Chicot's satirical observations; "first you object to the dress of the huntsmen, and now you jeer at their number. Laugh away, laugh away, my dear Chicot."

"Oh, Sire!"

"I must say, however, that you are not very considerate, my son; Béarn is not so large as France. Over there the king is always attended to the chase by a company of two hundred huntsmen; while here, on the other hand, I am obliged to set out with a paltry dozen, as you have so generously pointed out."

"Yes, Sire."

"But," continued Henri, "you may think I am boasting, Chicot; ah, well, think so if you will; sometimes it happens here, as never happens to the king of France, that the gentlemen of the country round about, hearing that I intend setting out for the chase, leave their houses, their castles, and all their affairs, and come to join me; so that, really, Chicot, I sometimes have a quite respectable escort."

"You will see, Sire," said Chicot, "that I shall not have the good fortune to witness a spectacle like that. Indeed, Sire, I fear that I have come at an unlucky time."

"Who knows?" replied Henri, with his bantering laugh.

When, after leaving Nérac, going out by the gates of the city, they had ridden in the open country about half an hour, suddenly Henri exclaimed to Chicot, at the same time shading his eyes by putting his hands above them to serve as a visor:

"Look! look! I am not mistaken, I think."

"What is it?" asked Chicot.

"Look yonder, by the barriers of the Bourg de Moiras: are they not horsemen that I see?"

Chicot raised himself in his stirrups.

"Indeed, Sire," he said, "I believe you are right."

" And I am sure of it."

" Horsemen, yes," said Chicot, looking with more attention—" but huntsmen, no."

" Why not? "

" Because they are armed like Amadis or Roland," replied Chicot.

" Ah, what matters the dress, my dear Chicot? You have seen already that we are not particular as to that."

" But I see at least two hundred men there."

" Ah, that is a good number."

Chicot began to feel very curious. He had really named too low a number, for the group before them consisted of two hundred and fifty men, who came silently and joined their party. Each man was well armed and mounted, and they were led by a gentleman who come and kissed Henri's hand with much devotion. They forded the river Gers. Between the Gers and the Garonne they met a second troop, of one hundred men. The chief approached Henri, and appeared to excuse himself for not bringing a larger number of huntsmen. Henri accepted his excuses and offered him his hand. They continued their march, and reached the Garonne. As they had crossed the Gers they crossed the Garonne; only as the Garonne is deeper than the Gers, they lost their footing and were obliged to swim a distance of thirty or forty feet. Nevertheless, against all expectation they reached the farther bank without accident.

" Tudieu! " said Chicot; " what exercises, then, are you practising, Sire? When you have bridges above and below, you dip your cuirasses in the water like that? "

" My dear Chicot," said Henri, " we are savages here, and you must pardon us. You know that my late brother Charles called me his boar. Now, the boar—but you are not a hunter, and know nothing about it—the boar never goes out of his way; he goes straight on. Having his name, I imitate him, and go straight on. I find a river in my way; I cross it. A city rises before me; I eat it."

That pleasantry of the Béarnais evoked great bursts of laughter around him. M. de Mornay alone, always by the side of the king, made no noise in laughing. He limited himself to compressing his lips, which was with him a sign of extravagant hilarity.

" Mornay is in good humour to-day," said the Béarnais, joyously, to Chicot. " He has just laughed at my pleasantry."

Chicot asked himself at which of the two he ought to laugh—whether at the master, so happy in amusing his servant, or at the servant, so hard to be amused. But his deepest feeling was one of astonishment.

About a half-league beyond the Garonne three hundred horsemen, concealed in a pine-forest, appeared to Chicot. " Oh, oh, monseigneur! " he said in a low tone to Henri, " are not these enemies, who have heard of your chase, and wish to oppose it? "

" No, my son, you are wrong. They are friends from Puymirol."

" *Tudieu !* Sire, you will have more men in your escort than trees in your forest."

" Chicot, I really believe the news of your arrival must have spread through the country, and all these people have come from the four corners of the province to welcome the ambassador from France."

Chicot had too much intelligence not to see that for some time past Henri had been making fun of him. He was disconcerted by that observation, but not offended.

At the end of the day they reached Muroy, where the gentlemen of the country gave a grand supper to the king, in which Chicot took his part enthusiastically, as it had not been deemed necessary to stop on the road for anything so unimportant as dinner, and he had eaten nothing since he had left Nérac.

Henri had the best house in the town. Half the troop slept outside the gates, the other half in the street where the king was.

" When are we to begin the hunt? " asked Chicot of Henri, as he was undressing.

" We are not yet in the territory of the wolves, my dear Chicot."

" And when shall we be? "

" Curious ! "

" Not so, Sire. But you understand, one likes to know where he is going."

" You will know to-morrow, my son. Meanwhile, lie down there on those cushions on my left. Here is Mornay snoring already at my right."

" *Peste !* " said Chicot; " he makes more noise asleep than awake."

" It is true he is not very talkative; but see him at the chase ! "

Day had hardly appeared when a great noise of horses awoke Chicot and the King of Navarre. An old gentleman, who wished to serve the king himself, brought to Henri bread and honey, with spiced wine. Mornay and Chicot were served by

servants of the old gentleman.   The repast finished, the " boot-
and-saddle " was sounded.

" Come, come! " said Henri, " we have a long day's work
before us.   To horse, gentlemen! to horse! "

Chicot saw with astonishment that five hundred horsemen
had swelled the train during the night.

" Sire! " cried he, " you have an army."

" Wait! " replied Henri.

At Lauzerte, six hundred men came and ranged themselves
behind the cavaliers.

" Foot-soldiers! " cried Chicot.

" Nothing but beaters," said the king.

Chicot frowned and spoke no more.   Twenty times his eyes
turned towards the country, and the idea of flight presented
itself to him.   But Chicot had his guard of honour, doubtless as
ambassador of the King of France, and so well was he recommended to this guard that he could not make a movement that
was not repeated by ten men.   This annoyed him, and he said
so to the king.

" The devil! " said Henri; " it is your own fault.   You tried
to run away from Nérac, and I am afraid you will try it again."

" Sire, if I give my word as a gentleman not to do so? "

" That will do."

" Besides, I should be wrong to do so."

" How so? "

" Yes; for if I stay, I believe I shall see curious things."

" I am of your opinion, my dear Chicot."

At this moment they were going through the town of Montcuq,
and four field-pieces took their place in the army.

" I return to my first idea," said Chicot, " that the wolves in
this country are different from others, and are differently
treated—with artillery, for instance."

" Ah! you have noticed that? " said Henri; " it is a mania
of the people of Montcuq.   Since I gave them these four pieces
they take them about everywhere."

" Well, Sire, shall we arrive to-day? "

" No, to-morrow."

" To-morrow morning or evening? "

" Morning."

" Then," said Chicot, " it is at Cahors that we are to hunt,
is it not, Sire? "

" It is in that direction," replied Henri.

" But, Sire, you who have infantry, cavalry, and artillery to
hunt wolves with, should also have taken the royal standard,

and then the honour to the wolves would have been complete."

"We have not forgotten it, Chicot, *ventre-saint-gris!* only it is left in the case for fear of soiling it. But if you wish to see it, and know under whose banner you march, you shall see it."

"No, no, it is useless; leave it where it is."

"Well, be easy; you will see it before long."

They spent the second night at Catus very much as they had spent the night before. From the moment Chicot had given his word of honour not to escape, they paid him no further attention. He took a turn through the village, and visited the advanced posts. On all sides troops of a hundred, a hundred and fifty, two hundred men, came to join the army. That night the foot-soldiers came in.

"It is fortunate that we are not going on to Paris," said Chicot; "we should arrive with a hundred thousand men."

The next morning, by eight o'clock, they were before Cahors, with one thousand foot soldiers and two thousand horse. They found the city in a state of defence, M. de Vesin having heard rumours of the advance.

"Ah!" said the king, "he is warned; that is very annoying."

"We must lay siege in due form, Sire," said Mornay; "we expect still about two thousand men, and that is enough."

"Let us assemble the council," said M. de Turenne, "and begin the trenches."

Chicot listened to all this in amazement. The pensive and almost pitiful air of Henri alone reassured him, for it confirmed his suspicions that he was no warrior.

Henri let every one give his opinion and remained meanwhile as mute as a fish. All at once he raised his head, and said in a commanding tone, "Gentlemen, this is what we must do. We have three thousand men; and you say you expect two thousand more, Mornay?"

"Yes, Sire."

"That will make five thousand. In a regular siege we should lose one thousand or fifteen hundred men in two months; their death would discourage the others; and we should lose a thousand more in retreating. Let us sacrifice five hundred men at once, and take Cahors by assault."

"What do you mean, Sire?" said Mornay.

"My dear friend, we will go straight to the nearest gate. We shall find a fosse in our way, which we will fill with fascines; we may leave two hundred men on the road, but we shall reach the gate."

" And then, Sire? "

" Then we will break it down with petards and go in. It will not be difficult."

Chicot looked at Henri, astonished. " Yes," he grumbled, " coward and braggart—true Gascon; is it you who will place the petard under the gate? "

At that moment, as if he had heard Chicot's *aside*, Henri added, " Let us not lose time, gentlemen; the feast will grow cold. Forward! and let all who love me follow! "

Chicot approached M. de Mornay. " Well, Monsieur the Count," said he, " do you all want to be cut to pieces? "

" Oh! we take our chance."

" But the king will get killed."

" Bah! he has a good cuirass."

" But he will not be foolish enough to go into danger, I suppose? "

Mornay shrugged his shoulders and turned on his heel.

" After all, I like him better asleep than awake, snoring than speaking; he is more polite," said Chicot.

CHAPTER II

HOW HENRI DE NAVARRE BEHAVED IN BATTLE

THE little army advanced to a position near the town; then they breakfasted. The repast over, two hours were given for the officers and men to rest. Henri was very pale, and his hands trembled visibly, when at three o'clock in the afternoon the officers appeared under his tent.

" Gentlemen," said he, " we are here to take Cahors; therefore we must take it, since we have come here for that purpose. But it is necessary to take Cahors by force—by force, do you understand? "

" Not bad," thought Chicot; " and if his gesture did not belie his words, one could hardly ask for anything better even from M. Crillon."

" Marshal de Biron," continued Henri, " who has sworn to hang every Huguenot, is only forty-five leagues from here, and doubtless a messenger is already despatched to him by M. de Vesin. In four or five days he will be on us, and as he has ten thousand men with him, we should be taken between the city and him. Let us, then, take Cahors before he comes, that we may receive him well. Come, gentlemen, I will put myself at your head, and let the blows fall as thick as hail! "

The men replied to this speech by enthusiastic cries.

"A good phrase-maker, Gascon still," said Chicot to himself. "How fortunate it is that one doesn't talk with his hands! *Ventre de biche!* the Béarnais would have stammered finely. Let us see him at the work."

As they were setting off, the king said to Chicot, "Pardon me, friend Chicot; I deceived you by talking of wolves, hunting, and such things. But you see Henri will not pay me his sister's dowry, and Margot cries out for her dear Cahors. One must do what one's wife wants, for the sake of peace. Therefore I am going to try and take Cahors, my dear Chicot."

"Why did she not ask you for the moon, Sire, as you are such a complaisant husband?"

"I would have tried for it, Chicot, I love my dear Margot so much!"

"You will have quite enough to do with Cahors, and we shall see how you will get out of it."

"Ah, yes, the moment is critical and very disagreeable. Ah! I am not brave, and my nature revolts at every musket-shot. Chicot, my friend, do not laugh too much at the poor Béarnais, your compatriot and friend. If I am afraid, and you find it out, tell no one."

"If you are afraid?"

"Yes."

"Are you, then, *afraid* of being afraid?"

"I am."

"But then, *ventre de biche!* why the devil do you undertake such a thing?"

"Why, I am compelled to."

"M. de Vesin is a terrible man."

"I know it well."

"Who gives quarter to no one."

"You think so, Chicot?"

"I am sure of it; red plume or white, he will not care; he will cry, 'Fire!'"

"You say that for my white feather, Chicot."

"Yes, Sire; and as you are the only one who wears a plume of that colour—"

"Well?"

"I would take it off."

"But I put it on that I might be recognised."

"Then you will keep it?"

"Yes, decidedly." And Henri trembled again as he said it.

"Come, Sire," said Chicot, who did not understand this

difference between words and gestures, " there is still time; do not commit a folly. You cannot mount on horseback in that state."

" Am I, then, very pale, Chicot? "

" As pale as death, Sire."

" Good."

" Why good? "

" Yes, I understand myself."

At this moment the noise of cannon and a furious fire of musketry was heard; it was M. de Vesin's reply to the summons to surrender given by Mornay.

" Eh! " said Chicot, " what do you think of this music, Sire? "

" It makes me devilishly cold in the marrow of my bones," replied Henri. " Here, my horse! my horse! " he cried.

Chicot looked and listened, unable to understand him. Henri mounted, and then said,—

" Come, Chicot, get on horseback too; you are not a warrior either, are you? "

" No, Sire."

" Well, come, we will go and be afraid together; come and see the firing, my friend. A good horse here, for M. Chicot! "

Henri set off at full gallop, and Chicot followed him. On arriving in front of his little army, Henri raised his visor, and cried, " Out with the banner! out with the new banner! "

They drew off the case, and the new banner, with the double escutcheon of Navarre and Bourbon, floated majestically in the air; it was white, and had chains of gold on one side, and *fleur de lis* on the other.

" There is a banner," said Chicot to himself, " which will be badly torn up, I am afraid."

At this moment, and as if in response to Chicot's thought, the cannon of the fortifications thundered, and opened a lane through the infantry within ten feet of the king.

" *Ventre-saint-gris!* did you see, Chicot? " said the king, whose teeth chattered.

" He will be ill," thought Chicot.

" Cursed body! " murmured Henri; " ah! you fear, you tremble! Wait! wait! I will give you something to tremble for." And striking his spurs into his horse, he rushed onward before cavalry, infantry, and artillery, and arrived at a hundred feet from the place, red with the fire of the batteries which thundered from above. There he kept his horse immovable for ten minutes, his face turned towards the gate of the city, and crying, " The fascines! *ventre-saint-gris!* the fascines! "

Mornay had followed him, sword in hand, and then came Chicot, wearing a cuirass, but without drawing his sword; behind them the young Huguenot gentlemen, crying, "Vive Navarre!" Each brought a fascine, which he threw in, and the fosse was soon filled. Then came the artillery; and with the loss of thirty or forty men they succeeded in placing their petards under the gate. The shot whistled like a whirlwind of iron round Henri's head, and twenty men fell in an instant before his eyes. "Forward!" cried he; and rushing on through the midst of the fire, he arrived just as the soldiers had fired the first petard. The gate was broken in two places. The second petard was lighted, and a new opening was made in the wood; but twenty arquebuses immediately passed through, vomiting balls on the soldiers and officers, and the men fell like mowed grass.

"Sire," cried Chicot, "in Heaven's name, retire!"

Mornay said nothing; he was proud of his pupil, but from time to time he tried to place himself before him. Suddenly Henri felt the damp on his brow, and a cloud passed over his eyes.

"Ah, cursed nature," cried he, "it shall not be said that you have conquered!" Then, jumping off his horse, "An axe!" he cried, and with a vigorous arm he struck down wood and iron. At last a beam gave way, and a part of the gate and a portion of the wall fell, and one hundred men rushed to the breach, crying, "Navarre! Navarre! Cahors is ours!"

Chicot had not left the king; he was with him under the arch of the gateway when he entered among the first, and at each discharge he saw him shudder and lower his head.

"*Ventre-saint-gris!* did you ever see such a coward, Chicot?" said Henri, furious.

"No, Sire, I have never seen a coward like you."

The soldiers of M. de Vesin now tried to dislodge Henri and his advanced guards, who received them sword in hand; but the besieged were the strongest, and succeeded in forcing Henri and his troops back beyond the fosse.

"*Ventre-saint-gris!*" cried the king, "I believe my flag retreats; I must carry it myself." And snatching it from the hands of those who held it, he raised it aloft, and was the first to re-enter, half enveloped in its folds. "Be afraid, then!" said he, "tremble now, then, poltroon!" The balls whistled round him, and with a sharp sound struck his armour and pierced the flag. MM. de Turenne, Mornay, and a thousand others were in that open gate following the king. The cannon were silent, and the battle was fought hand to hand. Above all the uproar M. de Vesin's voice was heard crying, " Barricade the streets! let trenches be dug, and the houses garrisoned! "

" Oh! " cried M. de Turenne, " the siege of the city is over, my poor Vesin." And as he spoke he fired at him and wounded him in the arm.

" You are wrong, Turenne," cried M. de Vesin, " there are twenty sieges in Cahors; so if one is over, there are nineteen to come."

M. de Vesin defended himself during five days and nights from street to street and from house to house. Fortunately for the rising fortunes of Henri de Navarre, he had counted too much on the walls and garrison of Cahors, and had neglected to send to M. de Biron.

During these five days and nights, Henri commanded like a captain and fought like a soldier, slept with his head on a stone, and awoke sword in hand. Each day they conquered a street or a square, which each night the garrison tried to retake. On the fourth night the enemy seemed willing to give some rest to the Protestant army. Then it was Henri who attacked in his turn. He forced an intrenched position, but it cost him seven hundred men. MM. de Turenne and Mornay, and nearly all the officers, were wounded, but the king remained untouched. To the fear that he had felt at first, and which he had so heroic-ally vanquished, succeeded a feverish restlessness, a rash audacity. All the fastenings of his armour were broken, as much by his own efforts as by the blows of the enemy. He struck so vigorously that he always killed his man. When this last post was forced, the king entered into the enclosure, followed by the eternal Chicot, who, silent and sad, had for five days seen growing at his side the phantom of a monarchy destined to destroy that of the Valois.

" Well, Chicot, what do you think of it? " said Henri, raising his visor, and as if he wished to read the soul of the poor ambassador.

" Sire," murmured Chicot, sadly, " I think that you are a real king."

" And I, Sire, that you are too imprudent," said Mornay, " to put up your visor when they are firing at you from all sides."

As Mornay spoke, and as if to emphasise his words, the king was surrounded by a dozen sharpshooters belonging to the governor's private troop. They had been placed in ambush by M. de Vesin, and aimed low and with exactness. One ball struck off a plume from Henri's helmet; his horse was killed by another, and Mornay's had his leg broken. The king fell, and ten swords were raised above him. Chicot, alone unhurt, leaped from his horse, threw himself before the king, and whirling his sword round to keep off the nearest, helped Henri up and gave him his own horse, saying, " Sire, you will testify to the King of France that if I drew the sword against him, I have at any rate hurt no one."

" *Ventre-saint-gris !* you must be mine, Chicot!" cried Henri. " You shall live and die with me."

" Sire, I have but one service to follow—that of my king. His star diminishes, but I shall be faithful to his adverse fortunes. Let me serve and love him as long as he lives, Sire. I shall soon be alone with him; do not envy him his last servant."

" Chicot, you will be always dear to me, and after Henri de France you will have Henri de Navarre for a friend."

" Yes, Sire," said Chicot, simply, kissing his hand.

The siege was soon over after this. M. de Vesin was taken, and the garrison surrendered. Then Henri dictated to Mornay a letter, which Chicot was to carry to the King of France. It was written in bad Latin, and finished with these words, " *Quod mihi dixisti profuit multum. Cognosco meos devotos; nosce tuos. Chicotus cætera expediet,*" which means, " What you told me was very useful. I know my faithful followers; know yours. Chicot will tell you the rest."

" And now, friend Chicot," said Henri, " embrace me; but take care not to soil yourself, for, *mordieu !* I am as bloody as a butcher. Take my ring, and adieu, Chicot; I keep you no longer. Gallop to France; you will make a success at the court by telling all you have seen."

CHAPTER III

WHAT WAS TAKING PLACE AT THE LOUVRE ABOUT THE TIME CHICOT ENTERED NÉRAC

THE necessity of following Chicot to the end of his mission has kept us a long time away from the Louvre. The king, after having passed so bravely through his adventurous return from Vincennes, experienced that retrospective emotion which sometimes is felt by the bravest heart after the danger is over. He entered the Louvre without saying anything, made his prayers longer than usual, forgetting to thank the officers and guards who had delivered him from his peril. Then he went to bed, astonishing his valets by the rapidity of his toilet; and D'Epernon, who remained in his room to the last, expecting thanks at least, went away in a very bad humour. At two o'clock every one slept in the Louvre.

The next day Henri took four *bouillons* in bed instead of two, and then sent for MM. de Villequier and d'O to come to his chamber to work on a new financial edict. The queen received the order to dine alone; but it was added that in the evening the king would receive. All day he played with Love, saying, every time that the animal showed his white teeth, " Ah, rebel! you also want to bite me; you also attack your king? but every one is doing that to-day."

Then Henri, with as much apparent effort as Hercules put forth in subduing the Nemean lion, conquered that monster as large as his fist, saying with unspeakable satisfaction, " Conquered, Maître Love! conquered, infamous Leaguer! conquered, conquered, conquered! " His secretaries of State were somewhat astonished at all this, particularly as he said nothing else, and signed everything without looking at it. At three o'clock in the afternoon he asked for D'Epernon. They replied that he was reviewing the light-horse; then he inquired for Loignac, but he also was absent. He asked for lunch, and while he ate, had an edifying discourse read to him, which he interrupted by saying to the reader, " Was it not Plutarch who wrote the life of Sylla? "

" Yes, Sire," said the reader, much astonished at being interrupted in his pious reading by this profane question.

" Do you remember that passage where the historian recounts how the dictator avoided death? "

The reader hesitated. " Not precisely, Sire; it is a long time since I read Plutarch."

At this moment the Cardinal de Joyeuse was announced.

" Ah, here is a learned man; he will tell me at once! " cried the king.

" Sire," said the cardinal, " am I fortunate enough to arrive at a seasonable moment? It is a rare thing in this world."

" Faith! yes; you heard my question? "

" Your majesty asked, I think, in what manner and under what circumstances Sylla narrowly escaped death? "

" Precisely; can you answer me, Cardinal? "

" Nothing more easy, Sire."

" So much the better."

" Sylla, who had killed so many men, never risked his life but in combats; did your Majesty mean in one of those? "

" Yes; in one of those combats I think I recollect he was very near death. Open a Plutarch, cardinal—there should be one there, translated by Amyot—and read me the passage where he escaped the javelins of his enemies, thanks to the swiftness of his white horse."

" Sire, there is no need of opening Plutarch for that; the event took place in the combat with Teleserius the Samnite, and Lamponius the Lucanian."

" You are so learned, my dear cardinal!"

" Your Majesty is too good."

" Now explain to me how this Roman lion, who was so cruel, was never molested by his enemies."

" Sire, I will reply to your Majesty in the words of this same Plutarch."

" Go on, Joyeuse."

" Carbo, the enemy of Sylla, said often, ' I have to fight at once a lion and a fox who inhabit the soul of Sylla, but it is the fox who gives me most trouble.' "

" Ah! it was the fox? "

" Plutarch says so, Sire."

" And he is right, cardinal. But speaking of combats, have you any news of your brother? "

" Of which brother, Sire? Your Majesty is aware that I have four."

" Of the Duc d'Arques, my friend, in short."

" Not yet, Sire."

" If M. d'Anjou, who always plays the fox, will only play the lion a little for once."

The cardinal did not reply, so Henri, signing to him to remain, dressed himself sumptuously, and passed into the room where the court waited for him. He entered, looking full of good humour, kissed the hands of his wife and mother, paid all sorts of compliments to the ladies, and even offered them confectionery.

" We were uneasy about your health, my son," said Catherine.

" You were wrong, madame; I have never been better."

" And to what happy influence do you owe this amelioration, my son? "

" To having laughed much, madame."

Every one looked astonished.

" Laughed! you can laugh much, my son; then you are very happy? "

" It is true, madame."

" And about what were you so much amused? "

" I must tell you, mother, that yesterday I went to Vincennes."

" I knew it."

" Oh, you knew it! well, my people told me, before my return, of an enemy's army whose muskets shone on the road."

" An enemy's army on the road to Vincennes? "

" Yes, mother."

" And where? "

" In front of the Jacobins, near the house of our good cousin."

" Near Madame de Montpensier's? "

" Precisely so, near Bel-Esbat. I approached bravely, to give battle, and I perceived—"

" What, Sire? " cried the queen, in alarm.

" Reassure yourself, madame. I perceived an entire priory of good monks, who presented arms to me with acclamations."

Every one laughed, and the king continued, " Yes, you are right to laugh. I have in France more than ten thousand monks, of whom I will make, if necessary, ten thousand musketeers; then I will create a Grand Master of the Tonsured Musketeers, and give the place to you, cardinal."

" Sire, I accept."

The ladies now, according to etiquette, rose, and bowing to the king, retired. The queen followed with her ladies-of-honour. The queen-mother remained; the king's gaiety was a mystery that she wished to fathom.

" Cardinal," said the king, " what has become of your brother, Bouchage? "

" I do not know, Sire."

" What! you do not know? "

" No; I never see him now."

A grave, sad voice from the end of the room said, " Here I am, Sire."

" Ah, it is he! " cried Henri. " Approach, count, approach! "

The young man obeyed.

" *Mon Dieu !* " cried the king, " he is no longer a man but a shade."

" Sire, he works hard," said the cardinal, stupefied himself at the change in his brother during the last week. He was as pale as wax, and looked thin and wan.

" Come here, young man," said the king. " Thanks, cardinal, for your quotation from Plutarch; in a similar case I shall apply to you again."

The cardinal saw that Henri wished to be left alone with his brother, and took his leave.

There only remained the queen-mother, D'Epernon, and Bouchage. The king beckoned to the last, and said, " Why do you hide thus behind the ladies? Do you not know it gives me pleasure to see you? "

" Your kind words do me honour, Sire," said the young man, bowing.

" Then how is it that we never see you here now? "

" If your Majesty has not seen me, it is because you have not deigned to cast an eye on the corner of the room. I am here every day regularly. I never have failed, and never will as long as I can stand upright; it is a sacred duty to me."

" And is it that which makes you so sad? "

" Oh! your Majesty cannot think so? "

" No, for you and your brother love me, and I love you. Apropos, do you know that poor Anne has written to me from Dieppe? "

" I did not, Sire."

" Yes; but you know he did not like going."

" He confided to me his regrets at leaving Paris."

" Yes; but do you know what he said? That there was a man who would have regretted Paris much more; and that if I gave you this order you would die."

" Perhaps, Sire."

" He said yet more, for your brother talks fast when he is not sulky; he said that if I had given you such an order you would have disobeyed it."

" Your Majesty was right to place my death before my disobedience; it would have been a greater grief to me to disobey than to die, and yet I should have disobeyed."

" You are a little mad, I think, my poor count," said Henri.

" I am quite so, I believe."

" Then the case is serious."

Joyeuse sighed.

" What is it? Tell me."

Joyeuse tried to smile. " A great king like you, Sire, would not care for such confidences."

" Yes, Henri, yes; tell me. It will amuse me," said the king.

" Sire, you deceive yourself," said Joyeuse, haughtily; " there is nothing in my grief that could amuse a noble heart."

The king took the young man's hand. " Do not be angry, Bouchage," said he; " you know that your king also has known the griefs of an unrequited love."

" I know it, Sire, formerly."

" Therefore I feel for your sufferings."

" Your Majesty is too good."

" Not so; but when I suffered what you suffer no one could aid me, because no one was more powerful than myself, whereas I can aid you."

" Sire? "

" And consequently hope soon for an end of your sorrows."

The young man shook his head.

" Bouchage, you shall be happy, or I shall no longer call myself the King of France! " cried Henri.

" Happy! alas, Sire, it is impossible," said the young man, with a bitter smile.

" And why so? "

" Because my happiness is not of this world."

" Henri, your brother, when he went, recommended you to my friendship. I wish, since you consult neither the experience of your father nor the wisdom of your brother the cardinal, to be an elder brother to you. Come, be confiding, and tell me all. I assure you, Bouchage, that for everything except death my power and love shall find you a remedy."

" Sire," replied the young man, falling at the king's feet, " do not confound me by the expression of a goodness to which I cannot reply. My misery is without remedy, for it is my misery which makes my only happiness."

" Bouchage, you are mad. You will kill yourself with fancies."

" I know it well, Sire."

" But," cried the king, impatiently, " is it a marriage you wish for? "

" Sire, my wish is to inspire love. You see that the whole world is powerless to aid me in this. I alone can obtain it for myself."

" Then why despair? "

" Because I feel that I shall never inspire it."

" Try, try, my child! you are young and rich. Where is the woman that can resist at once beauty, youth, and wealth? There is none, Bouchage."

" How many persons in my place would bless your Majesty for the great kindness with which you overwhelm me! To be loved by a king like your Majesty is almost equal to being loved by God."

" If you wish to be discreet, and tell me nothing, do so. I will find out, and then act. You know what I have done for your brother—I will do as much for you. A hundred thousand crowns shall not stop me."

Bouchage seized the king's hand, and pressed his lips to it.

"May your Majesty ask one day for my blood, and I will shed it to the last drop to show you how grateful I am for the protection that I refuse!"

Henri III. turned on his heel angrily. "Really," said he, "these Joyeuses are more obstinate than a Valois. Here is one who will bring me every day his long face and his eyes circled with black. How delightful that will be! there are already so many gay faces at court."

"Oh, Sire, I will smile so, when I am here, that every one shall think me the happiest of men."

"Yes, but I shall know the contrary, and that will sadden me."

"Does your Majesty permit me to retire?" asked Bouchage.

"Go, my child, and try to be a man."

When he was gone the king approached D'Epernon, and said, "Lavalette, have money distributed this evening to the Forty-five, and give them holiday for a night and a day to amuse themselves. By the Mass! they saved me, the rascals—saved me like Sylla's white horse."

"Saved?" said Catherine.

"Yes, mother."

"From what?"

"Ah, ask D'Epernon."

"I ask you, my son."

"Well, madame, our dear cousin, the sister of your good friend, M. de Guise—oh, do not deny it! you know he is your good friend—laid an ambush for me."

"An ambush?"

"Yes, madame, and I narrowly escaped imprisonment or assassination."

"By M. de Guise?"

"You do not believe it?"

"I confess I do not."

"D'Epernon, my friend, relate the adventure to my mother. If I go on speaking and she goes on shrugging her shoulders, I shall get angry, and that does not suit my health. Adieu, madame! cherish M. de Guise as much as you please, but I would advise you not to forget Salcède."

CHAPTER IV

RED PLUME AND WHITE PLUME

It was eight in the evening; and the house of Robert Briquet, solitary and sad-looking, formed a worthy companion to that mysterious house of which we have already spoken to our readers. One might have thought that these two houses were yawning in each other's face. Not far from there the noise of brass was heard, mingled with confused voices, vague murmurs and squeaks.

It was probably this noise that attracted a young and handsome cavalier, with a violet cap, red plume, and grey mantle, who, after stopping for some minutes to listen, went on slowly and pensively towards the house of Robert Briquet. Now, this noise of brass was that of saucepans; these vague murmurs, those of pots boiling on fires, and of spits turned by dogs; those cries, those of M. Fournichon, host of the Brave Chevalier, and of Madame Fournichon, who was preparing her rooms. When the young man with the violet cap had well looked at the fire, inhaled the smell of the fowls, and peeped through the curtains, he went away, then returned to resume his examinations. He continued to walk up and down, but never passed Robert Briquet's house, which seemed to be the limit of his walk. Every time that he arrived at this limit he found there, like a sentinel, a young man of about his own age, with a black cap, a white plume, and a violet cloak, who, with frowning brow and his hand on his sword, seemed to say, " Thou shalt go no farther." The young man with the red plume—he whom we first mentioned—took twenty turns before observing this, so preoccupied was he. Certainly he saw a man walking up and down like himself; but as the man was too well dressed to be a robber, he never thought of disquieting himself about him. But the other, on the contrary, looked more and more black at each return of the young man with the red plume, till at last the latter noticed it and began to think that his presence there must be annoying to the other; and wondering for what reason, he looked first at Briquet's house, then at the one opposite, and seeing nothing, turned round and resumed his walk from west to east, while the other walked from east to west. This continued for about five minutes, until, as they once again came face to face, the young man with the white plume walked straight up against the other, who, taken unawares, with difficulty saved himself from falling.

"Monsieur," cried he, "are you mad, or do you mean to insult me?"

"Monsieur, I wish to make you understand that you annoy me much. It seems to me that you might have seen that without my telling you."

"Not at all, monsieur; I never see what I do not wish to see."

"There are, however, certain things which would attract your attention, I hope, if they shone before your eyes;" and he drew his sword as he spoke, which glittered in the moonlight.

The young man with the red plume said quietly, "One would think, monsieur, that you had never drawn a sword before, you are in such a hurry to attack one who does not defend himself."

"But who will defend himself, I hope."

"Why so?" replied the other, smiling. "And what right have you to prevent me from walking in the street?"

"Why do you walk in this street?"

"*Parbleu!* because it pleases me to do so."

"Ah! it pleases you?"

"Doubtless; are you not also walking here? Have you a licence from the king to keep to yourself the Rue de Bussy?"

"What is that to you?"

"A great deal, for I am a faithful subject of the king and would not disobey him."

"Ah! you laugh!"

"And you threaten!"

"Heaven and earth! I tell you that you annoy me, monsieur, and that if you do not go away willingly I will make you."

"Oh, oh! we shall see."

"Yes, we shall see."

"Monsieur, I have particular business here. Now, if you will have it, I will cross swords with you, but I will not go away."

"Monsieur, I am Comte Henri du Bouchage, brother of the Duc de Joyeuse. Once more, will you yield me the place, and go away?"

"Monsieur," replied the other, "I am the Vicomte Ernauton de Carmainges. You do not annoy me at all, and I do not ask you to go away."

Bouchage reflected a moment, and then put his sword back in its sheath. "Excuse me, monsieur," said he; "I am half mad, being in love."

" And I also am in love, but I do not think myself mad for that."

Henri grew pale. " You are in love? " said he.

" Yes, monsieur."

" And you confess it? "

" Is it a crime? "

" But with some one in this street? "

" Yes, for the present."

" In Heaven's name, tell me who it is! "

" Ah! M. du Bouchage, you have not reflected on what you are asking me; you know a gentleman cannot reveal a secret of which only half belongs to him."

" It is true; pardon, M. de Carmainges; but in truth, there is no one so unhappy as I am under heaven."

There was so much real grief and eloquent despair in the words that Ernauton was profoundly touched. " Oh, *mon Dieu!* I understand," said he; " you fear that we are rivals."

" I do."

" Well, monsieur, I will be frank."

Joyeuse grew pale again.

" I," continued Ernauton, " have an appointment."

" An appointment? "

" Yes."

" In this street? "

" Yes."

" Written? "

" Yes, in very good writing."

" A woman's? "

" No, a man's."

" What do you mean? "

" What I say. I have an invitation to a meeting with a woman, written by a man; it seems she has a secretary."

" Ah! go on, monsieur."

" I cannot refuse you, monsieur. I will tell you the tenor of the note."

" I listen."

" You will see if it is like yours."

" Oh, monsieur, I have no appointment, no note."

Ernauton then drew out a little paper. " Here is the note, monsieur," said he. " It would be difficult to read it to you by this obscure light; but it is short, and I know it by heart, if you will trust to me."

" Oh! entirely."

" This is it, then: ' M. Ernauton, my secretary is charged by me to tell you that I have a great desire to talk with you for an hour; your merit has touched me.' I pass over another phrase still more flattering."

" Then you are waited for? "

" No, I wait, as you see."

" Are they to open the door to you? "

" No, to whistle three times from the window."

Henri, trembling all over, placed one hand on Ernauton's arm, and with the other pointed to the opposite house.

" From there? " said he.

" Oh, no! from there," said Ernauton, pointing to the Brave Chevalier.

Henri uttered a cry of joy. " Then you are not going to this house? "

" By no means; the note said positively, 'hostelry of the Brave Chevalier.' "

" Oh! a thousand thanks, monsieur," said he; " pardon my incivility—my folly. Alas! you know that to a man who really loves there exists but one woman; and seeing you always return to this house, I believed that it was here you were waited for."

" I have nothing to pardon, monsieur; for really, I thought for a moment that you had come on the same errand as myself."

" And you had the incredible patience to say nothing! Ah! you do not love! you do not love! "

" Faith! I have no great rights as yet; and I awaited some light on the matter before allowing myself to be annoyed. These great ladies are so capricious, and a hoax is so amusing."

" Oh, M. de Carmainges, you do not love as I do; and yet—"

" Yet what? "

" You are more fortunate."

" Ah! they are cruel in that house? "

" M. de Carmainges, for three months I have loved like a madman her who lives there; and I have not yet had the happiness of hearing the sound of her voice."

" The devil! you are not far advanced. But stay! "

" What is it? "

" Did not some one whistle? "

" Indeed, I think I heard something."

A second whistle was now distinctly heard in the direction of the Brave Chevalier.

" Monsieur the Count," said Ernauton, " you will excuse me for taking leave, but I believe that is my signal."

A third whistle sounded.

" Go, monsieur," said Joyeuse; " and good luck to you! "

Ernauton made off quickly, while Joyeuse began to walk back more gloomily than ever.

" Now for my accustomed task," said he; " let me knock as usual at this cursed door which never opens to me." And while saying these words he advanced trembling towards the door of the mysterious house.

CHAPTER V

THE DOOR OPENS

On arriving at the door of the house, poor Henri was seized by his usual hesitation. " Courage! " said he to himself. But before knocking, he looked once more behind him, and saw the bright light shining through the windows of the hostelry.

" There," said he, " enter, for love and joy, those who are invited almost without desiring; why have I not a tranquil and careless heart? Perhaps I also might enter there, instead of vainly trying here."

Ten o'clock struck. Henri lifted the knocker, and struck once, then again. " There," said he, listening—" there is the inner door opening, the stairs creaking, the sound of steps approaching—always so, always the same thing." And he knocked again. " There," said he, " he peeps through the trellis-work, sees my pale face, and goes away, always without opening. Adieu, cruel house, until to-morrow." And he turned to go; but scarcely had he taken two steps, when the key turned in the lock, and to his profound surprise, the door opened, and a man stood bowing on the threshold. It was the same whom we have seen before in his interview with Robert Briquet.

" Good-evening, monsieur," said he, in a harsh voice, but whose sound appeared to Bouchage sweeter than the song of birds.

Henri joined his hands and trembled so much that the servant put out a hand to save him from falling, with a visible expression of respectful pity.

" Come, monsieur," said he, " here I am; explain to me, I beg, what you want."

" I have loved so much," replied the young man, " that I do not know whether I still love; my heart has beat so fast that I do not know whether it still beats."

" Will it please you, monsieur, to sit down and talk to me? "

" Oh, yes! "

" Speak, then, monsieur, and tell me what you desire."

" My friend, you already know. Many times, you know, I have waited for you and surprised you at the turn of a street, and have offered you gold enough to enrich you, had you been the greediest of men. At other times I have threatened you; but you have never listened to me, and have always seen me suffer without seeming to pity me. To-day you tell me to speak—to express my wishes; what, then, has happened, *mon Dieu ?* "

The servant sighed. He had evidently a pitying heart under a rough covering. Henri heard this sigh, and it encouraged him. " You know," he continued, " that I love, and how I love. You have seen me pursue a woman and discover her, in spite of her efforts to avoid me; but never in my greatest grief has a bitter word escaped me, nor have I given heed to those violent thoughts which are born of despair and the fire of youth."

" It is true, monsieur; and in this my mistress renders you full justice."

" Could I not," continued Henri, " when you refused me admittance, have forced the door, as is done every day by some lad, tipsy or in love? Then, if but for a minute, I should have seen this inexorable woman, and have spoken to her."

" It is true."

" And," continued the young count, sadly, " I am something in this world; my name is great as well as my fortune. The king himself protects me; just now he begged me to confide to him my griefs and to apply to him for aid."

" Ah! " said the servant, anxiously.

" I would not do it," continued Joyeuse; " no, no, I refused all, to come and pray at this door with clasped hands—a door which never yet opened to me."

" Monsieur the Count, you have indeed a noble heart, and are worthy to be loved."

" Well, then, he whom you call worthy, to what do you condemn him? Every morning my page brings a letter; it is refused. Every evening I myself knock at the door; and I am disregarded. You let me suffer, despair, die in the street, without having the compassion for me that you would have for a dog that howled. Ah! this woman has no woman's heart; she does not love me. Well! one can no more tell one's heart to love than not to love. But one may pity the unfortunate who suffers, and give him a word of consolation—may reach out a hand to save him from falling; but no, this woman cares not for my sufferings. Why does she not kill me, either with a refusal from her mouth, or with a dagger-stroke? Dead, I should suffer no more."

"Monsieur the Count," replied the man, "the lady whom you accuse is, believe me, far from having the hard, insensible heart you think. She has seen you; she has understood what you suffer, and feels for you the warmest sympathy."

"Oh, compassion, compassion!" cried the young man; "but may that heart of which you boast some day know love—love such as I feel! and if in return for that love she is offered compassion, I shall be well avenged."

"Monsieur the Count, not to reply to love is no proof that one has never loved. This woman has perhaps felt the passion more than ever you will—has perhaps loved as you can never love."

"When one loves like that, one loves for ever," cried Henri, raising his eyes to heaven.

"Have I told you that she no longer loves?"

Henri uttered a doleful cry, and broke down as if he had been struck with death. "She loves!" he cried. "Ah, *mon Dieu !*"

"Yes, she loves; but be not jealous of the man she loves, Monsieur the Count, for he is no longer of this world. My mistress is a widow."

These words restored hope and life to the young man. "Oh!" he cried, "she is a widow, and recently; the source of her tears will dry up in time. She is a widow; then she loves no one, or only a shadow—a name. Ah! she will love me. Oh, *mon Dieu !* all great griefs are calmed by time. When the widow of Mausolus, who had sworn an eternal grief at her husband's tomb, had exhausted her tears, she was cured. Regrets are a malady, from which every one who survives comes out as strong as before."

The servant shook his head.

"This lady, Monsieur the Count, has also sworn an eternal fidelity to the dead; but I know her, and she will keep her word better than the forgetful woman of whom you speak."

"I will wait ten years if necessary; since she lives I may hope."

"Oh, young man, do not reckon thus! She has lived, you say. Yes, so she has; not a month or a year—she has lived seven years. But do you know why, with what purpose, to fulfil what resolution she has lived? You hope that she will console herself; never, Monsieur the Count, never! I swear it to you—I, who was but the servant of him who is dead, and yet shall never be consoled."

" This man so much regretted, this husband—"

" It was not her husband, it was her lover, Monsieur the Count; and a woman like her whom you unfortunately love has but one lover in her life."

" My friend," cried Joyeuse, " intercede for me."

" I! Listen, Monsieur the Count. Had I believed you capable of using violence towards my mistress, I would have killed you long ago with my own hand. If on the contrary I could have believed that she would love you, I think I should have killed her. Now, Monsieur the Count, I have said what I wished to say; do not seek to make me say more, for on my honour—and although not a nobleman, my honour is worth something—I have told you all I can."

Henri rose with death in his soul. " I thank you," said he, " for having had compassion on my misfortunes; now I have decided."

" Then you will be calmer for the future, Monsieur the Count; you will go away and leave us to a destiny that is worse than yours, believe me."

" Yes, be easy; I will go away, and for ever."

" You mean to die? "

" Why not? I cannot live without her."

" Monsieur the Count, believe me, it is bad to die by your own hand."

" Therefore I shall not choose that death; but there is for a young man like me a death which has always been reckoned the best—that received in defending one's king and country."

" If you suffer beyond your strength; if you owe nothing to those who survive you; if death on the field of battle is offered to you—die, Monsieur the Count. I should have done so long ago had I not been condemned to live."

" Adieu, and thank you," replied Joyeuse. And he went away rapidly, throwing a heavy purse of gold at the feet of the servant.

CHAPTER VI

HOW A GREAT LADY LOVED IN THE YEAR 1586

THE whistles which Ernauton had heard were really his signal. Thus, when the young man reached the door, he found Dame Fournichon on the threshold, waiting for her customers with a smile, which made her resemble a mythological goddess painted by a Flemish painter; and in her large white hands she held a golden crown, which another hand, whiter and more delicate, had slipped in, in passing. She stood before the door, so as to bar Ernauton's passage. " What do you want, monsieur? " said she to him.

" Were not three whistles given from one of those windows just now? "

" Yes."

" Well, they were to summon me."

" You? "

" Yes."

" On your honour? "

" As a gentleman, Dame Fournichon."

" Enter, then, monsieur, enter."

And happy at having a client after her own heart, fit for that ill-fated Rose-tree of Love which had been supplanted by the Brave Chevalier, the hostess conducted Ernauton up the stairs herself. A little door, vulgarly painted, gave access to a sort of antechamber, which led to a room, furnished, decorated, and carpeted with rather more luxury than might have been expected in this remote corner of Paris; but this was Madame Fournichon's favourite room, and she had exercised all her taste in its adornment.

When the young man entered the antechamber, he smelled a strong aromatic odour, the work, doubtless, of some susceptible person, who had thus tried to overcome the smell of cooking exhaled from the kitchen. On opening the door, he stopped for an instant to contemplate one of those elegant female figures which must always command attention, if not love. Reposing on cushions, enveloped in silk and velvet, this lady was occupied in burning in the candle the end of a little stick of aloes, over which she bent so as to inhale the full perfume. By the manner in which she threw the remainder of the branch in the fire, and pulled her hood over her masked face, Ernauton perceived that she had heard him enter; but she did not turn.

" Madame," said the young man, " you sent for your humble servant; here he is."

" Ah! very well," said the lady; " sit down, I beg, M. Ernauton."

" Pardon, madame; but before anything I must thank you for the honour that you do me."

" Ah! that is civil, and you are right; but I presume you do not know whom you are thanking, M. de Carmainges."

" Madame, you have your face hidden by a mask and your hands by gloves; I cannot, then, recognise you—I can but guess."

" And you guess who I am? "

" She whom my heart desires, whom my imagination paints young, beautiful, powerful, and rich—too rich and too powerful for me to be able to believe that what has happened to me is real, and that I am not dreaming."

" Had you any trouble in entering here? " asked the lady, without replying directly to the words which had escaped from the full heart of Ernauton.

" No, madame; the admittance was easier than I could have thought."

" Yes, all is easy for a man; it is so different for a woman. What were you saying to me, monsieur? " added she, carelessly, and pulling off her glove to show a beautiful hand, at once plump and taper.

" I said, madame, that without having seen your face, I know who you are, and without fear of making a mistake, may say that I love you."

" Then you are sure that I am she whom you expected to find here? "

" My heart tells me so."

" Then you know me? "

" Yes."

" Really! you, a provincial, only just arrived, you already know the women of Paris? "

" In all Paris, madame, I know but one."

" And that is myself? "

" I believe so."

" By what do you recognise me? "

" By your voice, your grace, and your beauty."

" My voice—perhaps I cannot disguise it; my grace—I may appropriate the compliment; but as for my beauty, it is veiled."

" It was less so, madame, on the day when, to bring you

into Paris, I held you so near to me that your breast touched my shoulders, and I felt your breath on my neck."

" Then, on the receipt of my letter, you guessed that it came from me? "

" Oh, no, madame, not for a moment; I believed I was the subject of some joke, or the victim of some error, and it is only during the last few minutes that seeing you, touching you—" and he tried to take her hand, but she withdrew it.

" Enough! " said the lady; " the fact is that I have committed a great folly."

" In what, madame? "

" In what? You say that you know me, and still ask? "

" Oh, it is true, madame, that I am very insignificant and obscure in comparison with your Highness."

" *Mon Dieu!* monsieur, pray be silent! Have you no sense? "

" What have I done? " cried Ernauton, frightened.

" You see me in a mask; if I wear a mask it is probably with the design of disguising myself—and yet you call me ' your Highness.' "

" Ah, pardon me, madame! " said Ernauton; " but I believed in the discretion of these walls."

" It appears you are credulous."

" Alas! madame, I am in love."

" And you are convinced that I reciprocate this love? "

Ernauton rose, piqued. " No, madame," replied he.

" Then what do you believe? "

" I believe that you have something important to say to me, and that not wishing to receive me at the Hôtel de Guise, or at Bel-Esbat, you preferred a secret interview in this isolated place."

" You thought that? "

" Yes."

" And what do you think I could have to say to you? " asked the lady, rather anxiously.

" How can I tell? Perhaps something about M. de Mayenne."

" Had you not already told me all you knew of him? "

" Perhaps, then, some question about last night's event."

" What event? Of what do you speak? " asked the lady, visibly agitated.

" Of the panic experienced by M. d'Epernon and the arrest of those Lorraine gentlemen."

" They arrested some Lorraine gentlemen? "

" About twenty, who were found upon the road to Vincennes."

" Which is also the road to Soissons, where M. de Guise holds his garrison. Ah, M. Ernauton, you, who belong to the court, can tell me why they arrested these gentlemen."

" I belong to the court? "

" Certainly."

" You know that, madame? "

" Ah! to find our your address, we were forced to make inquiries. But what resulted from all this? "

" Nothing, madame, to my knowledge."

" Then why did you think I should wish to speak of it? "

" I am wrong again, madame."

" From what place are you, monsieur? "

" From Agen."

" What, you are a Gascon! and yet are not vain enough to suppose that when I saw you at the Porte St. Antoine, on the day of Salcède's execution, I liked your looks? "

Ernauton reddened and looked confused.

The lady went on. " That I met you in the street, and found you handsome? "

Ernauton grew scarlet.

" That, afterwards, when you brought me a message from my brother, I liked you? "

" Madame, I never thought so, I protest."

" Then you were wrong," said the lady, turning on him two eyes which flashed through her mask.

Ernauton clasped his hands. " Madame, are you mocking me? " cried he.

" Faith! no. The truth is that you pleased me."

" *Mon Dieu!* "

" But you yourself dared to declare your love to me."

" But then I did not know who you were, madame; and now that I do know, I humbly ask for pardon."

" Oh! " cried the lady, " say all you think, or I shall regret having come."

Ernauton fell on his knees.

" Speak, madame! speak, that I may be sure this is not all a dream, and perhaps I shall dare to answer."

" So be it. Here are my projects for you," said the lady, gently pushing Ernauton back, while she arranged the folds of her dress: " I fancy you, but I do not yet know you. I am not in the habit of resisting my fancies; but I never commit follies. Had we been equals, I should have received you at my house and studied you before I hinted at my feelings; but as that was impossible, I was driven to this interview. Now you know what to do. Be worthy of me; it is all I ask."

Ernauton exhausted himself in protestations.

"Oh, less warmth, M. de Carmainges, I beg! it is not worth while," she replied carelessly. "Perhaps it was only your name that pleased me; perhaps it is a caprice, and will pass away. However, do not think yourself too far from perfection, and begin to despair. I cannot endure those who are perfect; I adore those who are devoted. Continue to be devoted; I allow you, handsome cavalier."

Ernauton was beside himself. This haughty language, those voluptuous movements, that proud superiority, that frank unreserve, of a person so illustrious, plunged him into extremes of delight and terror. He seated himself near the proud and beautiful lady, and then tried to pass his arm behind the cushions on which she reclined.

"Monsieur," said she, "it appears you have heard but not understood me. No familiarity, if you please; let us each remain in our place. Some day I will give you the right to call me yours; but this right you have not yet."

Ernauton rose, pale and angry. "Excuse me, madame," said he; "it seems I commit nothing but follies. I am not yet accustomed to the habits of Paris. Among us in the provinces, two hundred leagues from here, when a woman says, 'I love,' she loves, and does not hold herself aloof, or take pretexts for humiliating the man at her feet. It is your custom as a Parisian, and your right as a princess. I accept it, therefore; only I have not been accustomed to it. The habit, doubtless, will come in time."

"Ah! you are angry, I believe," said the duchess, haughtily.

"I am, madame, but it is against myself; for I have for you, madame, not a passing caprice, but a real love. It is your heart I seek to obtain, and therefore I am angry with myself for having compromised the respect that I owe you, and which I will change into love only when you command me. From this moment, madame, I await your orders."

"Come, come! do not exaggerate, M. de Carmainges; now you are all ice, after being all flame."

"It seems to me, however, madame—"

"Eh, monsieur! never say to a woman that you will love her in the way you prefer—that is clumsy; show her that you will love her in the way she prefers—"

"That is what I have said, madame."

"Yes, but not what you have thought."

"I bow to your superiority, madame."

"A truce to politeness; I do not wish to play the princess. Here is my hand; take it. It is that of a simple woman."

Ernauton took this beautiful hand respectfully.

"Well!" said the duchess.

"Well?"

"You do not kiss it! Are you mad, or have you sworn to put me in a passion?"

"But just now—"

"Just now I drew it away, while now I give it to you."

Ernauton kissed the hand, which was then withdrawn.

"You see," said he—"another lesson. You make me jump from one extreme to the other. In the end fear will kill passion. I shall continue to adore you on my knees, it is true; but I shall have for you neither love nor confidence."

"Oh! I do not wish that, for you would be a sad lover, and it is not so that I like them. No, remain natural; be yourself, M. Ernauton, and nothing else. I have caprices. Oh, *mon Dieu!* you told me I was beautiful; and all beautiful women have them. Do not fear me; and when I say to the too impetuous Ernauton, 'Calm yourself,' let him consult my eyes and not my voice."

At these words she rose. It was time, for the young man had seized her in his arms, and his lips touched her mask; but through this mask her eyes darted a light, cold and white, like the ominous light that precedes a tempest. That look so affected Carmainges that he let fall his arms, and all his ardour was extinguished.

"Well," said the duchess, "we will see. Decidedly, you please me, M. de Carmainges."

Ernauton bowed.

"When are you free?" she asked carelessly.

"Alas! very rarely, madame."

"Ah! your service is fatiguing, is it not?"

"What service?"

"That which you perform near the king. Are you not some kind of guard to his Majesty?"

"I form part of a body of gentlemen, madame."

"That is what I mean. They are all Gascons, are they not?"

"Yes, madame."

"How many are there? Some one told me; but I forget."

"Forty-five."

"What a singular number!"

"I believe it was chance."

" And these forty-five gentlemen never leave the king you say? "

" I did not say so, madame."

" Ah! I thought you did; at least, you said you had very little liberty."

" It is true, I have very little; because by day we are on service near the king, and at night we stay at the Louvre."

" In the evening? "

" Yes."

" Every evening? "

" Nearly."

" What would have happened, then, this evening, if your duty had kept you? I, who waited for you, ignorant of the cause of your absence, should have thought my advances despised."

" Ah, madame, to see you I will risk all, I swear to you! "

" It would be useless and absurd; I do not wish it."

" But then— "

" Do your duty; I will arrange, who am free and mistress of my time."

" What goodness, madame! "

" But you have not explained to me," said the duchess, with her insinuating smile, " how you happened to be free this evening, and how you came."

" This evening, madame, I was thinking of asking permission of Loignac, our captain, who is very kind to me, when the order came to give a night's holiday to the Forty-five."

" And on what account was this leave given? "

" As recompense, I believe, madame, for a somewhat fatiguing service yesterday at Vincennes."

" Ah! very well."

" Therefore to this circumstance I owe the pleasure of seeing you to-night at my ease."

" Well! listen, Carmainges," said the duchess, with a gentle familiarity which filled the heart of the young man with joy; " this is what you must do, whenever you think you shall be at liberty,—send a note here to the hostess, and every day I will send a man to inquire."

" Oh, *mon Dieu!* madame, you are too good! "

" What is that noise? " said the duchess, laying her hand on his arm.

Indeed, a noise of spurs, of voices, of doors shutting, and joyous exclamations, came from the room below, like the echo of an invasion. Ernauton looked out.

"It is my companions," said he, "who have come here to celebrate their holiday."

"But by what chance do they come here,—to this hostelry where we happen to be?"

"Because it is just here, madame, that we each had a rendezvous on our arrival; and on the happy day of their entry in Paris my friends conceived an affection for the wine and the cooking of M. Fournichon—and some of them, too, for madame's rooms."

"Oh!" said the duchess, with a significant smile, "you speak very knowingly of those rooms, monsieur."

"It is the first time, upon my honour, that I have entered them, madame. But you—you who have chosen them?" he ventured to add.

"I chose (and you will easily understand that) the most deserted part of Paris—a place near the river, where no one was likely to recognise me, or suspect that I could come; but, *mon Dieu!* how noisy your companions are!"

Indeed, the noise was becoming a perfect storm. All at once they heard a sound of footsteps on the little staircase which led to their room, and Madame Fournichon's voice crying from below, "M. de Sainte-Maline! M. de Sainte-Maline!"

"Well!" replied the young man.

"Do not go up there, I beg!"

"And why not, dear Madame Fournichon? Is not all the house ours to-night?"

"Not the turrets."

"Bah! they are part of the house," cried five or six voices.

"No, they are not; they are private. The turrets are mine—do not disturb my tenants."

"I also am your tenant; do not disturb me, Madame Fournichon," replied Sainte-Maline.

"Sainte-Maline!" murmured Ernauton, anxiously; for he knew the man's audacity and wickedness.

"For pity's sake!" cried Madame Fournichon.

"Madame," replied Sainte-Maline, "it is midnight, and at nine all fires ought to be extinguished; there is a fire now in your turret, and I must see what disobedient subject is transgressing the king's edicts." And he continued to advance, followed by several others.

"*Mon Dieu!* M. de Carmainges," cried the duchess, "will those people dare to enter here?"

"I am here, madame; have no fear."

" Oh, they are forcing the doors ! " she cried.

Indeed, Sainte-Maline rushed so furiously against the door that, being very slight, it was at once broken open.

CHAPTER VII

HOW SAINTE-MALINE ENTERED INTO THE TURRET, AND WHAT FOLLOWED

ERNAUTON's first thought when he saw the door of the ante-chamber fly open was to blow out the light.

" M. de Sainte-Maline," cried the hostess, " I warn you that the persons whom you are troubling are your friends."

" Well, all the more reason to present our compliments to them," cried Perducas de Pincornay, in a tipsy voice.

" And what friends are they ?   We will see ! " cried Sainte-Maline.

The good hostess, hoping to prevent a collision, glided among them, and whispered Ernauton's name in Sainte-Maline's ear.

" Ernauton ! " cried Sainte-Maline, aloud, for whom this revelation was oil instead of water thrown on the fire, " that is not possible."

" And why so ? " asked Madame Fournichon.

" Yes, why so ? " repeated several voices.

" Oh, because Ernauton is a model of chastity, and a medley of all the virtues.   No, you must be wrong, Madame Fournichon. It cannot be Ernauton who is shut in there."   And he approached the second door, to treat it as he had the first, when it was opened and Ernauton appeared on the threshold with a face which did not announce that patience was one of the virtues which, according to Sainte-Maline, he practised so religiously.   " By what right has M. de Sainte-Maline broken down that first door ? " he asked.   " And having broken that, does he mean to break this ? "

" Ah, it is he, really ; it is Ernauton ! " cried Sainte-Maline. " I recognise his voice ; but as to his person, devil take me if I can see in this darkness of what colour he is ! "

" You do not reply to my question, Monsieur," said Ernauton. Sainte-Maline began to laugh noisily, which reassured some of his comrades, who were thinking of retiring.

" I spoke.   Did you not hear me, M. de Sainte-Maline ? " said Ernauton.

" Yes, monsieur, perfectly."

" Then what have you to say? "

" We wished to know, my dear friend, if it was you up here."

" Well, monsieur, now you know it, leave me in peace."

" *Cap de Diou !* have you become a hermit? "

" As for that, monsieur, permit me to leave you in doubt, if you are in doubt."

" Ah! bah! " cried Sainte-Maline, trying to enter, " are you really alone? Ah, you have no light—bravo! "

" Gentlemen," said Ernauton, in a lofty tone, " I know that you are drunk, and I forgive you; but there is a limit even to the patience that one owes to men beside themselves. Your joke is over; do me the favour to retire."

" Oh, oh, retire! how you speak! " said Sainte-Maline.

" I speak so that you may not be deceived in my wishes; and I repeat, gentlemen, retire, I beg."

" Not before we have been admitted to the honour of saluting the person for whom you desert our company. M. de Montcrabeau," continued Sainte-Maline, " go down and come back with a light."

" M. de Montcrabeau," cried Ernauton, " if you do that, remember it will be a personal offence to me."

Montcrabeau hesitated.

" Good," replied Sainte-Maline, " we have our oath, and M. de Carmainges is so strict that he will not infringe discipline. We cannot draw our swords against one another; therefore, a light, Montcrabeau, a light! "

Montcrabeau descended, and in five minutes returned with a light, which he offered to Sainte-Maline.

" No, no! " said he; " keep it. I shall perhaps want both hands." And he made a step forward.

" I take you all to witness," cried Ernauton, " that I am insulted without reason, and that in consequence "—suddenly drawing his sword—" I will bury this sword in the breast of the first man who advances."

Sainte-Maline, furious, was about to draw his sword also. But before he had time to do so, the point of Ernauton's was on his breast, and as he advanced a step without Ernauton's moving his arm, Sainte-Maline felt the iron on his flesh, and drew back furious; but Ernauton followed him, keeping the sword against his breast. Sainte-Maline grew pale. If Ernauton had wished it, he could have pinned him to the wall; but he slowly withdrew his sword.

" You merit two deaths for your insolence," said he; " but the oath of which you spoke restrains me, and I will touch you no more. Let me pass. Come, madame, I answer for your free passage."

Then appeared a woman whose head was covered by a hood, and her face by a mask, and who took Ernauton's arm tremblingly. The young man sheathed his sword, and as if he were sure of having nothing further to fear, crossed the antechamber filled with his companions, who were at the same time anxious and curious. Sainte-Maline had recoiled as far as the landing, stifling with rage at the deserved affront he had received in the presence of his companions and the woman unknown. He understood that all would be against him if things should remain as they were between Ernauton and himself. That conviction urged him on to a last extremity. He drew his dagger as Ernauton passed by him. Did he mean to strike Ernauton, or only to do what he did? No one knew; but as they passed, his dagger cut through the silken hood of the duchess and severed the string of her mask, which fell to the ground. This movement was so rapid that in the half-light no one saw or could prevent it. The duchess uttered a cry; Sainte-Maline picked up the mask and returned it to her, looking now full in her uncovered face. " Ah! " cried he, in an insolent tone, " it is the beautiful lady of the litter. Ernauton, you get on fast."

Ernauton stopped and half drew his sword again; but the duchess drew him on, saying, " Come on, I beg you, M. Ernauton! "

" We shall meet again, M. de Sainte-Maline," said Ernauton; " and you shall pay for this, with the rest."

" Good! good! " said Sainte-Maline; " you keep your account, and I will keep mine, and some day we will settle both."

Carmainges heard, but did not even turn; he was entirely devoted to the duchess, whom he conducted to her litter, guarded by two servants. Arrived there, and feeling herself in safety, she pressed Ernauton's hand, and said, " M. Ernauton, after what has just passed—after the insult against which, in spite of your courage, you could not defend me, and which might be repeated—we can come here no more. Seek, I beg of you, some house in the neighbourhood to sell or to let. Before long you shall hear from me."

" Must I now take leave of you, madame? " said Ernauton, bowing in token of obedience to the flattering orders he had just received.

" Not yet, M. de Carmainges; follow my litter as far as the

new bridge, lest that wretch who recognised in me the lady of the litter, but did not know me for what I am, should follow to find out my residence."

Ernauton obeyed, but no one watched them. When they arrived at the Pont Neuf, which then merited the name, as it was scarcely seven years since Ducerceau had built it, the duchess gave her hand to Ernauton, saying, " Now go, monsieur."

" May I dare to ask when I shall see you again, madame? "

" That depends on the length of time which you take in executing my commission; and your haste will be a proof to me of your desire to see me again."

" Oh, madame, I shall not be idle."

" Well, then, go, Ernauton."

" It is strange," thought the young man, as he retraced his steps; " I cannot doubt that she likes me, and yet she does not seem the least anxious as to whether or not I get killed by that brute of a Sainte-Maline. But, poor woman, she was in great trouble, and the fear of being compromised is, particularly with princesses, the strongest of all sentiments."

Ernauton, however, could not foreget the insult he had received, and he returned straight to the hostelry. He was naturally decided to infringe all orders and oaths, and to finish with Sainte-Maline; he felt in the humour to fight ten men if necessary. This resolution sparkled in his eyes when he reached the door of the Brave Chevalier. Madame Fournichon, who expected his return with anxiety, was standing trembling in the doorway. At the sight of Ernauton she wiped her eyes, as if she had been crying, and throwing her arms round the young man's neck, begged for his pardon, in spite of her husband's representations that as she had done no wrong she had no occasion to ask pardon. Ernauton assured her that he did not blame her at all; that it was only her wine that was in fault. This was an opinion which the husband could comprehend, and for which he thanked Ernauton by a nod of the head.

While this was taking place at the door, all the rest were at table, where they were warmly discussing the previous quarrel. Many frankly blamed Sainte-Maline; others abstained, seeing the frowning brow of their comrade. They did not attack with any less enthusiasm the supper of M. Fournichon, but they discussed as they ate.

" As for me," said Hector de Biran, in a loud tone, " I know that M. de Sainte-Maline was wrong, and that had I been Ernauton de Carmainges, M. de Sainte-Maline would be at this moment stretched on the floor instead of sitting here."

Sainte-Maline looked at him furiously.

" Oh, I mean what I say," continued he; " and stay, there is some one at the door who appears to agree with me."

All turned at this, and saw Ernauton standing in the doorway, looking very pale. He descended from the step, as the statue of the commander from his pedestal, and walked straight up to Sainte-Maline firmly but quietly.

At this sight several voices cried, " Come here, Ernauton; come this side, Carmainges. There is room here."

" Thank you," replied the young man; " but it is near M. de Sainte-Maline that I wish to sit."

Sainte-Maline rose; and all eyes were fixed on him. But as he rose, his face changed its expression.

" I will make room for you, monsieur," said he, gently; " and in doing so address to you my frank and sincere apologies for my stupid aggression just now; I was drunk—forgive me."

This declaration did not satisfy Ernauton; but the cries of joy that proceeded from all the rest indicated to him that he ought to appear satisfied, and that he was fully vindicated. At the same time a glance at Sainte-Maline showed him that the latter was more to be distrusted than ever.

" The scoundrel is brave, however," said Ernauton to himself. " If he yields now, it is to pursue some odious plan which suits him better."

Sainte-Maline's glass was full, and he filled Ernauton's.

" Peace! peace!" cried all the voices.

Carmainges profited by the noise, and leaning towards Sainte-Maline, with a smile on his lips, so that no one might suspect the sense of what he was saying, whispered, " M. de Sainte-Maline, this is the second time that you have insulted me without giving me satisfaction; take care, for at the third offence I will kill you like a dog."

And the two mortal enemies touched glasses as though they had been the best friends.

CHAPTER VIII

WHAT WAS TAKING PLACE IN THE MYSTERIOUS HOUSE

WHILE the hostelry of the Brave Chevalier—the abode, apparently, of the most perfect concord—with closed doors and open cellars, showed through the openings of the shutters the light of its candles and the mirth of its guests, an unaccustomed movement took place in that mysterious house of which our readers have as yet seen only the outside.

The servant was going from one room to another, carrying packages, which he placed in a valise. These preparations over, he loaded a pistol, examined his poniard, then suspended it, by the aid of a ring, to the chain which served him for a belt, to which he attached, besides, a bunch of keys, and a book of prayers bound in black leather.

While he was thus occupied, a step, light as that of a shadow, came up the staircase; a woman, pale and ghostlike under the folds of her white veil, appeared at the door; and a voice, sad and sweet as the song of a bird in the wood, said, " Rémy, are you ready? "

" Yes, madame, I am waiting only for your valise, to place it with mine."

" Do you think these valises will go easily on our horses? "

" Oh, yes, madame! but if you have any fear, I can leave mine; I have all I need there."

" No, no, Rémy, take all that you want for the journey. Oh, Rémy! I long to be with my father. I have sad presentiments, and it seems an age since I saw him."

" And yet, madame, it is but three months—not a longer interval than usual."

" Rémy, you are such a good doctor; and you yourself told me, the last time we left him, that he had not long to live."

" Yes, doubtless; but it was only a dread, not a prediction. Sometimes death seems to forget old men, and they live on as though by the habit of living; and often, besides, an old man is like a child, ill to-day and well to-morrow."

" Alas! Rémy, like the child also, he is often well to-day and dead to-morrow."

Rémy did not reply, for he had nothing that was really reassuring to say; and silence succeeded for some minutes.

" At what hour have you ordered the horses? " said the lady, at last.

" At two o'clock."

" And one has just struck."

" Yes, madame."

" No one is watching outside? "

" No one."

" Not even that unhappy young man? "

" Not even he." And Rémy sighed.

" You say that in a strange manner, Rémy."

" Because he also has made a resolution."

" What is it? "

" To see us no more; at least, not to try to see us any more."

" And where is he going? "

" Where we are all going—to rest."

" God give it him eternally! " said the lady, in a cold voice; " and yet—"

" Yet what, madame? "

" Had he nothing to do in this world? "

" He had to love, if he had been loved."

" A man of his name, rank, and age, should think of his future."

" You, madame, are of an age, rank, and name little inferior to his, and you do not look forward to a future."

" Yes, Rémy, I do," cried she, with a sudden flashing of the eyes; " but listen! is that not the trot of a horse that I hear? "

" Yes, I think so."

" Can our guide have arrived already? "

" It is possible; but in that case he is an hour too early."

" He stops at the door, Rémy."

Rémy ran down, and arrived just as three hurried blows were struck on the door.

" Who is there? " said he.

" I," replied a trembling voice—" I, Grandchamp, the baron's valet."

" Ah, *mon Dieu!* Grandchamp, you at Paris! Wait till I open the door; but speak low! " and Rémy opened the door. " Whence do you come? " he asked in a low voice.

" From Méridor."

" From Méridor? "

" Yes, dear M. Rémy—alas! "

" Come in! come in! *mon Dieu!* "

" Well," cried the lady from the top of the stairs, " are they our horses, Rémy? "

" No, madame." Then, turning to the old man, " What is it, Grandchamp? "

" You do not guess? "

" Alas! I do; but in Heaven's name, do not announce that news suddenly! Oh, what will she say? "

" Rémy," said the voice again, " you are talking to some one? "

" Yes, madame."

" I thought I knew the voice."

" Indeed, madame—how can we manage, Grandchamp? Here she is! "

The lady now appeared at the end of the corridor. " Who is there? " she asked. " Is it Grandchamp? "

" Yes, madame, it is I," replied the old man, sadly, uncovering his white head.

" Grandchamp, you! Oh, *mon Dieu!* my presentiments were true; my father is dead? "

" Indeed, Madame, Méridor has no longer a master."

Pale, but motionless and firm, the lady received the blow without flinching. Rémy went to her and gently took her hand.

" How did he die? Tell me, my friend," said she.

" Madame, Monsieur the Baron, who could no longer leave his armchair, was struck a week ago by a third attack of apoplexy. He muttered your name for the last time, then ceased to speak, and soon was no more."

Diane thanked the old servant with a gesture, and without saying more returned to her chamber.

" So she is free at last," murmured Rémy. " Come, Grandchamp, come."

Diane's chamber was on the first story, and looked only into a courtyard. The furniture was sombre, but rich. The hangings, in Arras tapestry, represented the death of our Saviour; a *prie-Dieu* and stool in carved oak, a bed with twisted columns, and tapestries like those on the walls were the sole ornaments of the room. Not a flower, no gilding, but in a frame of black was contained a portrait of a man, before which the lady now knelt down, with dry eyes, but a sad heart. She fixed on this picture a long look of indescribable love. It represented a young man about twenty-eight years old, lying half naked on a bed. From his wounded breast the blood still flowed; his right hand hung mutilated, and yet it still held a broken sword; his eyes were closed as though he were about to die; paleness and suffering gave to his face that divine character which the faces of mortals assume only at the moment of leaving life for eternity. Under the portrait, in letters red as blood, was written, " Aut Cæsar aut nihil." The lady extended her arm towards the portrait, and addressed it as if she were speaking to a god,—

" I had begged thee to wait, although thy soul must have thirsted for vengeance; and as the dead see all, thou hast seen, my love, that I lived only not to kill my father, else I would have died after you. Then, you know, on your bleeding corpse I uttered a vow to give death for death, to exact blood for blood; but I should have burdened with a crime the white head of the venerable old man who called me his innocent child. Thou hast waited, beloved, and now I am free. The last tie which bound me to earth is broken. I am all yours, and now I am free to come to you." She rose on one knee, kissed the hand which seemed to project from the frame, and then continued, "I can weep no more; my tears have dried up in weeping over your tomb. In a few months I shall rejoin you; and you then will reply to me, dear shade, to whom I have spoken so often without reply."

Diane then rose, and seating herself in her chair, murmured, "Poor father!" and then fell into a profound reverie. At last she called Rémy. The faithful servant soon appeared. "Here I am, madame," said he.

"My worthy friend, my brother—you, the last person who knows me on this earth—say adieu to me."

"Why so, madame?"

"Because the time has come for us to separate."

"Separate!" cried the young man. "What do you mean, madame?"

"Yes, Rémy. My project of vengeance seemed to me noble and pure while there remained an obstacle between me and it, and I contemplated it only from a distance. But now that I approach the execution of it; now that the obstacle has disappeared—I do not draw back, but I do not wish to drag with me into crime a generous and pure soul like yours; so you must leave me, my friend."

Rémy listened to the words of Diane with a sombre look. "Madame," he replied, "do you think you are speaking to a trembling old man? Madame, I am but twenty-six; and snatched as I was from the tomb, if I still live, it is for the accomplishment of some terrible action—to play an active part in the work of Providence. Never, then, separate your thoughts from mine, since we both have the same thoughts, sinister as they may be. Where you go I will go; what you do I will aid in—or if in spite of my prayers you persist in dismissing me—"

"Oh!" murmured the young woman, "dismiss you! What a word, Rémy!"

"If you persist in that resolution," continued the young man, "I know what I have to do, and all for me will end with two blows with a poniard—one in the heart of him whom you know, and the other in my own."

"Rémy! Rémy!" cried Diane, "do not say that. The life of him you threaten does not belong to you; it is mine—I have paid for it dearly enough. I swear to you, Rémy, that on the day on which I knelt beside his dead body"—and she pointed to the portrait—" on that day I approached my lips to the lips of that open wound, and those lips trembled and said to me, ' Avenge me, Diane! avenge me!' "

" Madame—"

" Rémy, I repeat, it was not an illusion; it was not a fancy of my delirium. The wound spoke—it spoke, I tell you—and I still hear it murmuring, ' Avenge me, Diane! avenge me!' "

The servant bent his head.

" Therefore, I repeat, vengeance is for me, and not for you; besides, for whom and through whom did he die? By me and through me."

" I must obey you, madame, for I also was left for dead. Who carried me away from the midst of the corpses with which that room was filled? You. Who cured me of my wounds? You. Who concealed me? You, you; that is to say, the half of the soul of him for whom I would have died so joyously. Order, then, and I will obey, provided that you do not order me to leave you."

" So be it, Rémy; you are right—nothing ought to separate us more."

Rémy pointed to the portrait. " Now, madame," said he, " he was killed by treason—it is by treason that he must be revenged. Ah! you do not know one thing: to-night I have found the secret of the *aqua tofana*—that poison of the Médicis and of René the Florentine."

" Really? "

" Come and see, madame."

" But where is Grandchamp? "

" The poor old man has come sixty leagues on horseback; he is tired out, and has fallen asleep on my bed."

" Come, then," said Diane; and she followed Rémy.

CHAPTER IX

THE LABORATORY

Rémy led the lady into a neighbouring room, and pushing a spring which was hidden under a board in the floor, and which, opening, disclosed a straight dark staircase, gave his hand to Diane to help her to descend. Twenty steps of this staircase, or rather ladder, led into a dark and circular cave, whose only furniture was a stove with an immense hearth, a square table, two rush chairs, and a quantity of phials and iron boxes. In the stove a dying fire still gleamed, while a thick black smoke escaped through a pipe entering the wall; from a still placed on the hearth filtered a liquid, yellow as gold, into a thick white phial. Diane looked round her without astonishment or terror; the ordinary impressions of experience seemed to be unknown to her, who lived only in the tomb. Rémy lighted a lamp, and then approached a well hollowed out in the cave, attached a bucket to a long cord, let it down into the well, and drew it up full of a water as cold as ice and as clear as crystal.

" Approach, madame," said he.

Diane drew near. In the bucket he let fall a single drop of the liquid contained in the phial, and the entire mass of the water instantly became yellow; then the colour evaporated, and the water in ten minutes became as clear as before. The fixedness of Diane's gaze alone showed with what profound interest she followed this operation. Rémy looked at her.

" Well? " said she.

" Well, madame," said he; " now dip in that water, which has neither smell nor colour, a flower, a glove, or a handkerchief; soak it into scented soap; pour some of it into the pitcher from which one will take it to cleanse his teeth, his hands, or his face—and you will see, as was seen at the court of Charles IX., the flower stifle by its perfume, the glove poison by its contact, the soap kill by its introduction into the pores of the skin. Pour a single drop of this pure oil on the wick of a lamp or candle, and for an hour the candle or lamp will exhale death, and burn at the same time like any other."

" You are sure of what you say, Rémy? "

" All this I have tried. See these birds who can no longer sleep, and have no wish to eat; they have drunk of water like this. See this goat who has browsed on grass wet with this same water; he moves and totters. Vainly now shall we restore him to life and liberty; his life is forfeited, unless indeed Nature should reveal to his instinct some of those antidotes to poison which animals know, although men do not."

" Can I see this phial, Rémy? "

" Yes, madame, presently."

Rémy then separated it from the still with infinite care, then corked it with soft wax, tied the top up in cloth, and then presented it to Diane. She took it, held it up to the light, and after looking at it, said, " It will do; when the time arrives, we will choose gloves, lamp, soap, or flowers, as convenient. Will the liquor keep in metal? "

" It eats it away."

" But then perhaps the bottle will break? "

" I think not. See the thickness of the crystal; besides, we can enclose it in a covering of gold."

" Then, Rémy," said the lady, " you are satisfied, are you not? " and something like a smile touched her lips.

" More than ever, madame; to punish the wicked is to use the sacred prerogative of God."

" Listen, Rémy! I hear horses; I think ours have arrived."

" Probably, madame—it is about the time; but I will go and send them away."

" Why so? "

" Are they not now useless? "

" Instead of going to Méridor, we will go into Flanders. Keep the horses."

" Ah, I understand! " and Rémy's eyes gave forth a flash of sinister joy. " But Grandchamp; what can we do with him? " said he.

" He has need of repose. He shall remain here, and sell this house, which we require no longer. But restore to liberty that unhappy animal, whom you were forced to torture. As you say, God may care for its recovery."

" This furnace, and these stills? "

" Since they were here when we bought the house, why not let others find them here after us? "

" But these powders, essences, and acids? "

" Throw them in the fire, Rémy."

" Go away, then, or put on this glass mask."

Then, taking precautions for himself, he blew up the fire again, poured in the power—which went off in brilliant sparks, some green and some yellow—and the essences, which, instead of extinguishing the flame, mounted like serpents of fire into the pipe, with a noise like that of distant thunder.

" Now," said Rémy, " if any one discovers this cave, he will only think that an alchemist has been here; and though they still burn sorcerers, they respect alchemists."

" And besides," said the lady, " if they should burn us, it would be justice, Rémy, it seems to me—for are we not poisoners? and provided I have only finished my task, I should not mind that sort of death more than any other. The ancient martyrs mostly died in that way."

At this moment they heard knocking.

" Here are our horses, madame," said Rémy; " go up quickly, and I will close the trap-door."

Diane obeyed, and found Grandchamp, whom the noise had

awakened, at the door. The old man was not a little surprised to hear of his mistress's intended departure, who informed him of it without telling him where she was going. " Grandchamp, my friend," said she, " Rémy and I are going to accomplish a pilgrimage on which we have long determined; speak of this journey to none, and do not mention my name to any one."

" Oh, I promise you, madame! " replied the old servant; " but we shall see you again? "

" Doubtless, Grandchamp—if not in this world, in the next. But, by the way, Grandchamp, this house is now useless to us." Diane drew from a drawer a bundle of papers. " Here are the title-deeds; let or sell this house. If in the course of a month you do not find a tenant or purchaser, abandon it and return to Méridor."

" But if I find some one, how much am I to ask? "

" What you please, Grandchamp."

" Shall I take the money to Méridor? "

" Keep it for yourself, my good Grandchamp."

" What, madame! such a sum? "

" Yes, I owe it to you for your services; and I have my father's debts to pay as well as my own. Now, adieu."

Then Diane went upstairs, cut the picture from the frame, rolled it up, and placed it in her valise.

When Rémy had tied the two valises with leather thongs, and had glanced into the street to see that there were no lookers-on, he aided his mistress to mount. " I believe, madame," said he, " that this is the last house in which we shall live so long."

" The last but one, Rémy."

" And what will be the other? "

" The tomb, Rémy."

CHAPTER X

WHAT MONSEIGNEUR FRANÇOIS, DUC D'ANJOU, DUC DE BRABANT, AND COMTE DE FLANDRE, WAS DOING IN FLANDERS

OUR readers must now permit us to leave the king at the Louvre, Henri de Navarre at Cahors, Chicot on the road, and Diane in the street, to go to Flanders to find M. le Duc d'Anjou, recently named Duc de Brabant, and to whose aid we have seen sent the Grand Admiral of France—Anne, Duc de Joyeuse.

At eighty leagues from Paris, towards the north, the sound

of French voices and the French banner floated over a French camp on the banks of the Scheldt. It was night; the fires, disposed in an immense circle, bordered the stream, and were reflected in its deep waters. From the top of the ramparts of the town the sentinels saw shining, by the bivouac-fires, the muskets of the French army. This army was that of the Duc d'Anjou. What he had come to do there we must tell our readers; and although it may not be very amusing, yet we hope they will pardon it in consideration of the warning—so many people are dull without announcing it.

Those of our readers who have read *Marguerite de Valois* and *La Dame de Monsoreau*, already know the Duc d'Anjou—that jealous, egotistical, ambitious prince, who, born so near to the throne, to which every event seemed to bring him nearer, had never been able to wait with resignation until death should clear for him an open way to it. Thus he had desired the throne of Navarre under Charles IX., then that of Charles IX. himself, then that of his brother Henri III. For a time he had turned his eyes towards England, then governed by a woman, and to possess this throne he had sought to marry this woman, although she was Elizabeth, and was twenty years older than himself. As to this matter Destiny was beginning to smile on him—if marriage with the daughter of Henry VIII. might be considered a smile of Fortune. This man, who, cherishing ambitious desires through all his life, had been unable even to defend his liberty, who had seen slain (perhaps had slain) his favourites, La Mole and Coconnas, and had villanously sacrificed Bussy, the bravest of his gentlemen—all without gain, and with great injury to his fame—this outcast of fortune found himself at the same time overwhelmed with the favour of a great queen, till then inaccessible to human affection, and exalted by a people to the highest rank that they could confer. Flanders offered him a crown, and Elizabeth had given him her ring. He had seen his brother Henri embarrassed in his quarrel with the Guises, and had joined their party; but he had soon discovered that they had no other aim than that of substituting themselves for the Valois. He had then separated himself from them, although not without danger; besides, Henri III. had at last opened his eyes, and the duke, exiled or something like it, had retired to Amboise.

It was then that the Flemings opened their arms to him. Tired of Spanish rule, decimated by the Duke of Alva, deceived by the false peace of John of Austria, who had profited by it to retake Namur and Charlemont, the Flemings had called in

William of Nassau, Prince of Orange, and had made him
Governor-General of Brabant. A few words about this man,
who held so great a place in history, but who will make only a
brief appearance here.

William of Nassau was then about fifty years of age. He
was the son of William called the Old, and of Julienne de
Stolberg, cousin of that René of Nassau killed at the siege of
Dizier. He had from his youth been brought up in principles
of reform, and had a full consciousness of the greatness of his
mission. This mission, which he believed he had received from
heaven, and for which he died like a martyr, was to found the
Republic of Holland, and in that he was successful. When very
young, he had been called by Charles V. to his court. Charles
was a good judge of men, and often the old emperor, who supported the heaviest burden ever borne by an imperial hand,
consulted the child on the most delicate matters connected with
the politics of Holland. The young man was scarcely twenty-
four when Charles confided to him, in the absence of the famous
Philibert Emmanuel of Savoy, the command of the army in
Flanders. William showed himself worthy of this high confidence; he held in check the Duc de Nevers and Coligny, two
of the greatest captains of the time, and under their eyes fortified
Philippeville and Charlemont. On the day when Charles V.
abdicated, it was on William of Nassau that he leaned to
descend the steps of the throne, and he it was who was charged
to carry to Ferdinand the imperial crown which Charles had
resigned.

Then came Philip II., and in spite of his father's recommenda-
tions to him to regard William as a brother, the latter soon
found that Philip II. was one of those princes who do not wish
to have intimate friends. This strengthened in his mind the
great idea of freeing Holland and Flanders, which he might
never have endeavoured to carry into effect if the old emperor,
his friend, had remained on the throne.

Holland, by his advice, demanded the dismissal of the foreign
troops. Then began the bloody struggle of the Spaniards to
retain the prey which was escaping from them; and then passed
over this unhappy people the vice-royalty of Margaret of
Austria and the bloody consulship of the Duke of Alva; then
was organised that struggle, at once political and religious,
which began with the protest of the Hôtel Culembourg, and
which demanded the abolition of the Inquisition in Holland;
then advanced that procession of four hundred gentlemen,
walking in pairs, and bearing to the foot of Margaret's throne

the general desire of the people, as summed up in that protest. At the sight of these gentlemen, so simply clothed, Barlaimont, one of the counsellors of the duchess, uttered the word " Gueux," which, taken up by the Flemish gentlemen, so long designated the patriot party. From this time William began to play the part which made him one of the greatest political actors of the world. Constantly beaten by the overwhelming power of Philip II., he constantly rose again, always stronger after his defeats,—always organising a new army to replace the scattered one, and always hailed as a liberator.

In the midst of these successions of moral triumphs and physical defeats, William learned at Mons the news of the massacre of St. Bartholomew. It was a terrible wound, which went almost to the heart of the Low Country; Holland and that portion of Flanders which was Calvinistic lost by that wound the bravest blood of their natural allies—the Huguenots of France.

William retreated from Mons to the Rhine, and waited for events. Events are rarely false to noble causes. Some of the Gueux were driven by a contrary wind into the port of Brille, and seeing no escape, and pushed by despair, took the city which was preparing to hang them. This done, they chased away the Spanish garrison, and sent for the Prince of Orange. He came; and as he wished to strike a decisive blow, he published an order forbidding the Catholic religion in Holland, as the Protestant faith was forbidden in France.

At this manifesto war again broke out. The Duke of Alva sent his own son Frederic against the revolters, who took from them Zutphen, Nardem, and Haarlem; but this check, far from discouraging them, seemed to give them new strength. All took up arms, from the Zuyder Zee to the Scheldt. Spain began to tremble, recalled the Duke of Alva, and sent as his successor Louis de Requesens, one of the conquerors at Lepanto.

Then began for William a new series of misfortunes: Ludovic and Henry of Nassau, who were bringing him aid, were surprised by one of the officers of Don Louis near Nimègue, defeated, and killed; the Spaniards penetrated into Holland, besieged Leyden, and pillaged Antwerp. All seemed desperate, when Heaven came once more to the aid of the infant republic. Requesens died at Brussels.

Then all the provinces, united by a common interest, drew up and signed, on November 8, 1576—that is to say, four days after the sack of Antwerp—the treaty known under the name of the Treaty of Ghent, by which they engaged to aid one another in delivering their country from the yoke of the Spaniards and other foreigners.

Don John reappeared, and with him the woes of Holland; in less than two months Namur and Charlemont were taken. The Flemings replied, however, to these two checks by naming the Prince of Orange Governor-General of Brabant.

Don John died in his turn, and Alexander Farnèse succeeded him. He was a clever prince, charming in his manners, which were at once gentle and firm, a skilful politician, and a good general. Flanders trembled at hearing that soft Italian voice call her friend, instead of treating her as a rebel. William knew that Farnèse would do more for Spain with his promises than the Duke of Alva with his punishments. On January 29, 1579, he made the provinces sign the Treaty of Utrecht, which was the fundamental basis of the rights of Holland. It was then that, fearing he should never be able to accomplish alone the freedom for which he had been fighting for fifteen years, he offered to the Duc d'Anjou the sovereignty of the country, on condition that he should respect their privileges and their liberty of conscience. This was a terrible blow to Philip II., and he replied to it by putting a price of twenty-five thousand crowns on the head of William. The States-General, assembled at the Hague, then declared Philip deposed from the sovereignty of Holland, and ordered that henceforth the oath of fidelity should be taken to them.

The Duc d'Anjou now entered Belgium, and was received by the Flemings with the distrust with which they regarded all foreigners. But the aid of France promised by the French prince was so important to them that they gave him a favourable reception, in appearance at least. Philip's promise, however, bore its fruits, for in the midst of a fête, a pistol-shot was heard. William fell, and was believed dead; but Holland still had need of him. The ball of the assassin had only gone through his cheeks. He who had discharged the pistol was Jean Jaureguy, the precursor of Balthazar Gérard, as Jean Chatel was to be the precursor of Ravaillac.

From all these events there came to William a sombre sadness, lighted rarely by a pensive smile. Flemings and Hollanders respected that dreamer as they would have respected a god; for they perceived that in him, and in him alone, was all their future. And when they saw him approach, enveloped in his long cloak, his brow covered by his hat, his elbow in his left hand, his chin in his right hand, men stood aside to make room for him, and mothers, with a sort of religious superstition pointed him out to their children, saying, "My son, look at the Silent Man."

The Flemings then, on William's advice, elected François, Duc de Brabant, Sovereign Prince of Flanders. Elizabeth of England saw in this a method of reuniting the Calvinists of Flanders and France to those of England; perhaps she dreamed of a triple crown. William, however, took care to hold the Duc d'Anjou in check, and to counteract the execution of any design which would have given him too much power in Flanders. Philip II. called the Duc de Guise to his aid, on the strength of a treaty which had been entered into by him with Don John of Austria. Henri de Guise consented, and it was then that Lorraine and Spain sent Salcède to the Duc d'Anjou to assassinate him; but Salcède, as we know, was arrested and put to death without having carried his project into execution.

François advanced but slowly, however, in Flanders, for the people were more than half afraid of him; he grew impatient, and determined to lay siege to Antwerp, which had invited his aid against Farnèse, but which when he wished to enter had turned its guns against him. This was the position of the Duc d'Anjou on the day after the arrival of Joyeuse and his fleet.

CHAPTER XI

PREPARATIONS FOR BATTLE

THE camp of the new Duc de Brabant was situated on the banks of the Scheldt; and the army, although well disciplined, was agitated by a spirit easy to understand.

Indeed, many Calvinists assisted the duke, not from sympathy with him, but in order to be as disagreeable as possible to Spain and to the Catholics of France and England; they fought rather from self-love than from conviction or devotion, and it was certain that, the campaign once over, they would abandon their leader or impose conditions on him. With regard to these conditions, the duke always gave them to understand that when the time came he should be ready, and was constantly saying, "Henri de Navarre made himself a Catholic, why should not François de France become a Huguenot?" On the opposite side, on the contrary, there existed a perfect unity of feeling, a cause definitely established—the cause of ambition and wrath.

Antwerp had intended to surrender at her own time and on her own conditions. All at once they saw a fleet appear at the

mouth of the Scheldt, and they learned that this fleet was
brought by the Grand High Admiral of France, to aid the Duc
d'Anjou, whom they now began to look upon as their enemy.
The Calvinists of the duke were little better pleased than the
Flemings at the sight. They were very brave but very jealous;
and they did not wish others to come and clip their laurels,
particularly with swords which had slain so many Huguenots
on the day of the Saint Bartholomew. From this proceeded
many quarrels, which began on the very evening of their arrival,
and continued all the next day. From their ramparts the
Antwerpians had every day the spectacle of a dozen duels
between Catholics and Protestants; and as many dead were
thrown into the river as a battle might have cost the French.
If the siege of Antwerp, like that of Troy, had lasted nine years,
the besieged would have needed to do nothing but look at the
assailants, who would certainly have destroyed themselves.
François acted the part of mediator, but encountered enormous
difficulties; he had made promises to the Huguenots, and could
not offend them without offending at the same time all Flanders.
On the other hand, to offend the Catholics sent by the king to
aid him would be most impolitic. The arrival of this reinforce-
ment, on which the duke himself had not reckoned, filled the
Spaniards and the Guises with rage. It was indeed something
to the Duc d'Anjou to enjoy at the same time that double
satisfaction. But he could not so manage all parties but that
the discipline of his army suffered greatly.

Joyeuse, who we know had never liked the mission, was
annoyed to find among these men such antagonistic opinions.
He felt instinctively that the time for success was past, and
both as an idle courtier and as a captain, grumbled at having
come so far only to meet with defeat. He declared loudly that
the Duc d'Anjou had been wrong in laying siege to Antwerp.

The Prince of Orange, who had treacherously advised the
siege, had disappeared when the advice was followed, and no
one knew what had become of him. His army was in garrison
in the city, and he had promised to the Duc d'Anjou the support
of that army. Nevertheless, there was no rumour of any
division between William's soldiers and the Antwerpians, and
no news of a single duel among the besieged had come to gladden
the besiegers since they had fixed their camp before the place.

What Joyeuse specially urged in his opposition to the siege
was that to possess a great city with its own consent was a real
advantage; but for the Duc d'Anjou to take by assault the
second capital of his future states was to expose himself to the

dislike of the Flemings; and Joyeuse knew the Flemings too well not to feel sure that if the duke did take Antwerp, sooner or later they would revenge themselves with usury. This opinion he did not hesitate to declare in the duke's tent the very night on which we have introduced our readers to the French camp.

While the council was held among his captains, the duke was lying on a couch and listening, not to the advice of the admiral, but to the whispers of Aurilly. This man, by his cowardly compliances, his base flatteries, and his continual assiduities, had kept himself in favour with the prince. With his lute, his love-messages, and his exact information about all the persons and all the intrigues of the court; with his skilful manœuvres for drawing into the prince's net whatever prey he might wish for—he had made a large fortune, while he remained to all appearance the poor lute-player. His influence was immense because it was secret.

Joyeuse, seeing the duke talking to Aurilly, stopped short. The duke, who had after all been paying more attention than he seemed to be, asked him what was the matter.

"Nothing, monseigneur. I am only waiting until your highness is at liberty to listen to me."

"Oh, but I do listen, M. de Joyeuse. Do you think I cannot listen to two persons at once, when Cæsar dictated seven letters at a time?"

"Monseigneur," said Joyeuse, with a glance at the musician, "I am no singer, to need an accompaniment when I speak."

"Very good, duke; be quiet, Aurilly. Then you disapprove of my *coup de main* on Antwerp?"

"Yes, monseigneur."

"I adopted this plan in council, however."

"Therefore, monseigneur, I speak with much hesitation, after so many distinguished captains." And Joyeuse, courtier-like, bowed to all. Many voices were instantly raised to agree with the admiral.

"Comte de Saint-Aignan," said the prince to one of his bravest colonels, "you are not of the opinion of M. de Joyeuse?"

"Yes, monseigneur, I am."

"Oh, I thought as you made a grimace—"

Every one laughed but Joyeuse, who said, "If M. de Saint-Aignan generally gives his advice in that manner, it is not very polite, that is all."

"M. de Joyeuse," replied Saint-Aignan, quickly, "his highness is wrong to reproach me with an infirmity contracted

in his service. At the taking of Cateau-Cambrésis I received a
blow on the head; and since that time my face is subject to
nervous contractions, which occasion those grimaces of which
his highness complains. This is not an excuse that I give you,
M. de Joyeuse; it is an explanation," said the count, proudly.

"No, monsieur," said Joyeuse, offering his hand, "it is a
reproach that you make; and you are right."

The blood mounted to the face of Duc François. "And
to whom is this reproach addressed?" said he.

"To me, probably, monseigneur."

"Why should Saint-Aignan reproach you, whom he does not
know?"

"Because I believed for a moment that M. de Saint-Aignan
cared so little for your highness as to counsel you to assault
Antwerp."

"But, cried the prince, "I must settle my position in the
country. I am Duc de Brabant and Comte de Flandre in
name, and I must be so in reality. This William, who is gone
I know not where, spoke to me of a kingdom. Where is this
kingdom? In Antwerp. Where is he? Probably in Antwerp
also. Therefore we must take Antwerp, and we shall know
how we stand."

"Oh, monseigneur, you know it now, or you are, in truth, a
worse politician than I thought you. Who counselled you to
take Antwerp? The Prince of Orange, who disappeared at the
moment of taking the field; the Prince of Orange, who, while
he made your highness Duc de Brabant, reserved for himself
the lieutenant-generalship of the duchy; the Prince of Orange,
whose interest it is to destroy the Spaniards by you, and you
by the Spaniards; the Prince of Orange, who will replace you,
who will succeed you, if he does not already; the Prince of
Orange—oh, monseigneur, in following his counsels you have
but annoyed the Flemings. Let a reverse come, and all those
who do not dare to look you now in the face will run after you,
like those timid dogs who run after those who fly."

"What! you imagine that I can be beaten by wool-merchants
and beer-drinkers?"

"These wool-merchants and these beer-drinkers have given
plenty to do to Philippe de Valois, the Emperor Charles V.,
and Philip II., who were three princes placed sufficiently high,
monseigneur, for the comparison not to be disagreeable to you."

"Then you fear a repulse?"

"Yes, monseigneur, I do."

"You will not be there, M. de Joyeuse."

" Why not? "

" Because you can hardly have such doubts of your own bravery as already to see yourself flying before the Flemings. In any case reassure yourself; these prudent merchants have the habit, when they march to battle, of cumbering themselves with such heavy armour that they would never catch you if you did run."

" Monseigneur, I do not doubt my own courage. I shall be in the front; but I shall be beaten there, as the others who are behind will be."

" But your reasoning is not logical, M. de Joyeuse; you approve of my taking the smaller places? "

" I approve of your taking those that do not defend themselves."

" And then I am to draw back from the great city because she talks of defending herself? "

" Better than to march on to destruction."

" Well, I will not retreat."

" Your highness must do as you like; and we are here to obey."

" Prove to me that I am wrong."

" Monseigneur, see the army of the Prince of Orange. It was yours, was it not? Well, instead of sitting down before Antwerp with you, it is in Antwerp, which is very different. William, you say, was your friend and counsellor; and now you not only do not know where he is, but you believe him to be changed into an enemy. See the Flemings. When you arrived they were pleased to see you; now they shut their gates at sight of you, and prepare their cannon at your approach, not less than if you were the Duke of Alva. Well, I tell you, Flemings and Dutch, Antwerp and Orange, only wait for an opportunity to unite against you, and that opportunity will be when you order your artillery to fire."

" Well, we will fight at once Flemings and Dutch, Antwerp and Orange."

" No, monseigneur; we have but just men enough to attack Antwerp, supposing we have only the inhabitants to deal with; and while we are engaged in the assault, William will fall on us with his eternal eight or ten thousand men, always destroyed and always reappearing, by the aid of which he has kept in check during ten or twelve years the Duke of Alva, Requesens and the Duke of Parma."

" Then you persist in thinking that we shall be beaten? "

" Without fail."

" Well, it is easy for you to avoid it, M. de Joyeuse," said the prince, angrily. " My brother sent you here to aid me, but I may dismiss you, saying that I do not need aid.''

" Your highness may say so; but I would not retire on the eve of a battle."

A long murmur of approbation greeted the words of Joyeuse; the prince understood that he had gone too far. " My dear admiral," said he, rising, and embracing the young man, " you will not understand me. Yet it seems to me that I am right, and especially because in the position I occupy I cannot openly admit that I have made a mistake. You reproach me with my errors—I know them. I have been too jealous of the honour of my name, and wished too much to prove the superiority of the French army; and I have been wrong. But the evil is done; we are before armed men—before men who now refuse to yield what they themselves offered. Am I to yield to them? To-morrow they would begin to retake, bit by bit, what I have already conquered. No! the sword is drawn; let us strike, or they will strike first. That is my opinion."

" When your highness speaks thus," said Joyeuse, " I will say no more. I am here to obey you, and will do so with all my heart, whether you lead me to death or victory; and yet— but I will say no more."

" Speak."

" No, I have said enough."

" No, I wish to hear."

" In private, then, if it please your highness."

All rose and retired to the other end of the spacious tent.

" Speak," said François.

" Monseigneur may care little for a check from Spain—a check which will render triumphant those drinkers of Flemish beer, or this double-faced Prince of Orange; but will you bear so patiently the laughter of M. de Guise? "

François frowned.

" What has M. de Guise to do with it? " said he.

" M. de Guise tried to have you assassinated, monseigneur; Salcède confessed it at the torture. Now, if I mistake not, M. de Guise plays a great part in all this, and he will be delighted to see you receive a check before Antwerp, or even perhaps to obtain, for nothing, that death of a son of France for which he had promised to pay so dearly to Salcède. Read the history of Flanders, monseigneur, and you will see that the Flemings are in the habit of enriching their soil with the blood of princes, and of the best French warriors."

The duke shook his head.

" Well, Joyeuse," said he, " I will give, if it must be, to the cursed Lorraine the joy of seeing me dead, but not that of seeing me flying. I thirst for glory, Joyeuse; for alone among those of my name, I have still my battles to win."

" You forget Cateau-Cambrésis, monseigneur."

" Compare that with Jarnac and Moncontour, Joyeuse, and then reckon up how far I am behind my beloved brother Henri. No, no; I am no kinglet of Navarre—I am a French prince." Then, turning to the others, who were standing apart, he said, " Gentlemen, the assault is still resolved on. The rain has ceased; the ground is good. We will make the attack this night."

Joyeuse bowed. " Will your highness give full directions? We wait for them," said he.

" You have eight vessels, without counting the admiral's ship, have you not, M. de Joyeuse? "

" Yes, monseigneur."

" You will force the line; the thing will be easy, the Antwerpians having only merchant-vessels in the port; then you will draw near to the quay. If the quay is defended, you will bombard the town, while attempting a landing with your fifteen hundred men. Of the rest of the army I will make two columns —one to be commanded by M. de Saint-Aignan, the other by myself. Both will attempt an escalade by surprise, at the moment when the first cannon-shot is fired. The cavalry will remain in position, in case of a repulse to protect the retreating columns. Of these three attacks, one must surely succeed. The first column which gains the ramparts will fire a rocket to let the others know."

" But one must think of everything, monseigneur," said Joyeuse; " and supposing all three attacks should fail? "

" Then we must gain the vessels under the protection of our batteries."

All bowed.

" Now, gentlemen, silence! " said the duke. " Wake the sleeping troops, and embark with order; but let not a shot reveal our design. You will be in the port, admiral, before the Antwerpians suspect your intention. We shall go along the left bank, and shall arrive at the same time as yourself. Go, gentlemen, and good courage; our former good luck will not fail to follow us over the Scheldt."

The captains left the prince's tent, and gave their orders with the indicated precautions.

CHAPTER XII

MONSEIGNEUR

MEANWHILE the Antwerpians did not quietly contemplate the hostile preparations of the Duc d'Anjou, and Joyeuse was not wrong in attributing to them all possible hostility. Antwerp was like a beehive at night, calm on the exterior, but within full of movement and murmur. The Flemings in arms patrolled the streets, barricaded their houses, and fraternised with the battalions of the Prince of Orange, of whom part were already in garrison there, while the other part entered the city in fractions.

When all was ready for a vigorous defence, the Prince of Orange, on a dark, moonless night, entered the city quietly, and went to the Hôtel de Ville, where his confidants had everything ready for his reception. There he received all the deputies of the *bourgeoisie*, passed in review the officers of the paid troops, and communicated his plans to them, the chief of which was to profit by this movement of the Duc d'Anjou to break with him. The duke had done just what William wished to bring him to, and he saw with pleasure this new competitor for the sovereignty ruin himself, like the others.

William would have taken the offensive, but the governor objected, and determined to wait for the arrival of monseigneur. Then all eyes were directed to a large clock; and every one seemed to require of it that it should hasten the coming of the personage so impatiently expected.

Nine o'clock in the evening sounded, and the uncertainty became real anxiety, scouts having protested that they had seen a movement in the French camp. A little flat boat had been sent on the Scheldt to reconnoitre; the Antwerpians, less disturbed by the movements on land than by those on the water, wished to gain definite intelligence in regard to the French fleet. The boat had not yet returned.

"Gentlemen," said the Prince of Orange to the Antwerpians, "monseigneur will keep us waiting till Antwerp is taken and burned; the city can then learn what difference there is between the French and the Spaniards."

These words were not calculated to reassure the civil officers, and they looked at one another with much emotion. At that moment a spy, who had gone as far as St. Nicolas, returned, saying that he had neither seen nor heard anything indicating the approach of the person expected.

"Gentlemen," cried William, "you see we wait in vain; let us attend to our own affairs. It is good to have confidence in superior talents; but you see that before all things we must rely on ourselves."

He had hardly finished speaking when the door of the hall opened, and a valet appeared and announced "Monseigneur." Immediately a man, tall and imperious-looking, wearing with supreme grace the cloak which entirely enveloped him, entered the hall, and saluted courteously those who were there. But at the first glance his eye, proud and piercing, sought out the prince in the midst of his officers. He went straight up to him and offered him his hand, which the prince pressed with affection, and almost with respect. They called each other "Monseigneur." After this the unknown took off his cloak. He was dressed in a buff doublet, and had high leather boots. He was armed with a long sword, which seemed to make part of himself, so easily it hung, and with a little dagger, which was passed through his belt. His boots were covered with mud and dust, and his spurs were red with the blood of his horse. He took his place at the table.

"Well, where are we?" asked he.

"Monseigneur," replied William, "you must have seen, in coming here, that the streets were barricaded?"

"I saw that."

"And the houses loopholed?"

"I did not see that; but it is a good plan."

"And the sentries doubled?"

"Does not monseigneur approve of these preparations for defence?" said a voice, in a tone of anxious disappointment.

"Yes, but I do not believe that in our circumstances it will be useful; it fatigues the soldier and disquiets the *bourgeois*. You have a plan of attack and defence, I suppose?"

"We waited to communicate them to monseigneur," said the burgomaster.

"Speak, then."

"Monseigneur arrived rather late, and I was obliged to act meanwhile," said William.

"And you did right, monseigneur; besides, whatever you do you do well. But I have not lost my time on the road either."

"We know by our spies," said the burgomaster, "that a movement is preparing in the French camp. They are making ready for an attack; but as we do not know on which side it will come, we have disposed the guns so that they may be equally distributed over the whole rampart."

"That is wise," replied the unknown, with a slight smile and a sly glance at William, who remained silent.

"We have done the same with our civic guards; they are spread over the whole wall, and have orders to run at once to the point of attack. However, it is the opinion of the greater number of our members that the French meditate anything but a feigned attack."

"And what purpose would that serve?"

"To intimidate us, and induce us to admit them amicably."

The stranger looked again at the Prince of Orange, who listened to all this with an indifference which almost amounted to disdain.

"And yet," said an anxious voice, "this evening have been seen in the camp what looked like preparations for attack."

"Mere suspicions," said the burgomaster; "I examined the camp myself with an excellent spy-glass. The men were preparing for sleep, and the duke was dining in his tent."

The unknown threw another glance at the prince, and fancied that this time he returned a slight smile.

"Gentlemen," said the unknown, "you are in error; a regular assault is preparing against you, and your plans, however good, are incomplete."

"But, monseigneur—"

"Incomplete in this, that you expect an attack, and have prepared to meet it."

"Certainly."

"Well, it is you who will make the attack, not wait for it, if you will trust to me."

"Ah!" cried William, "that is talking!"

"At this moment," said the stranger, who saw that he might reckon on the prince's support, "the ships of M. de Joyeuse are getting ready."

"How do you know that, monseigneur?" cried many voices together.

"I know it," replied he.

A murmur of doubt was half-uttered, but the stranger caught it.

"Do you doubt it?" asked he, in the tone of a man accustomed to control all fears, prejudices, and self-loves.

"We do not doubt it if your highness says it; but if you will permit us to observe—"

"Speak."

"That if it were so we should have had tidings of it."

"How so?"

" By our spy."

At this moment another man entered the hall, and came forward respectfully.

" Ah, it is you, my friend," said the burgomaster.

" Myself, monsieur," replied the man.

" Monseigneur," said the burgomaster, " it is the man whom we sent to reconnoitre."

At the word " Monseigneur," not addressed to the Prince of Orange, the new-comer made a movement of surprise and joy, and advanced quickly to see better him who was designated by this title. He was one of those Flemish sailors of whom the type is so recognisable, being marked—with a square head, blue eyes, short neck, and broad shoulders; he crushed in his large hands his woollen cap, and as he advanced he left behind him a watery track, for his clothes were dripping.

" Oh! here is a brave man who has come back swimming," said monseigneur, looking at the man with his accustomed air of authority.

" Yes, monseigneur, yes; and the Scheldt is broad and rapid," said the sailor, eagerly.

" Speak, Goes, speak! " said monseigneur, knowing how a sailor would prize being thus called by his name.

Thus from that minute Goes addressed himself to the unknown exclusively; although, having been sent by another, it was to him that he should have given an account of his mission.

" Monseigneur," said he, " I set out in my smallest boat, and passed, by giving the word, through all our ships, and reached those cursed French. Ah! pardon, monseigneur."

The stranger smiled and said, " Never mind, I am but half French, so shall be but half cursed."

" Then monseigneur pardons me? "

The unknown nodded; and Goes continued, " While I rowed in the dark with my oars wrapped in cloth, I heard a voice crying, ' Boat ahoy! what do you want? ' I thought it was to me that the question was addressed, and was about to reply something or other, when I heard some one cry behind me, ' Admiral's boat!' "

The unknown looked at the officers with an expression which meant, " What did I tell you? "

" At the same moment," continued Goes, " I felt a shock. My boat was swamped, and I fell into the water; but the waves of the Scheldt knew me for an old acquaintance, and threw me up again. It was the admiral's boat taking M. de Joyeuse on board, and which had passed over me; God only knows how I was not crushed or drowned!"

"Thanks, brave Goes, thanks!" said the Prince of Orange, putting a purse into his hand. However, the sailor seemed to wait for his dismissal from the stranger, who gave him a friendly nod, which he apparently valued more than the prince's present.

"Well," said monseigneur to the burgomaster, "what do you say of this report? Do you still doubt that the French are preparing, and do you believe that it was to pass the night on board that M. de Joyeuse was leaving the camp for his ship?"

"But you are a diviner, then, monseigneur?" cried the *bourgeois*.

"Not more than monseigneur the Prince of Orange, who is in all things of my opinion, I am sure. But I, like him, was well informed, and know well those on the other side, so that I should have been much astonished had they not attacked to-night. Then be ready, gentlemen, for if you give them time, the attack will be serious."

"These gentlemen will do me the justice to admit," said the prince, "that before your arrival I held exactly the same language to them that you now do."

"But," said the burgomaster, "how does monseigneur think the French will begin the attack?"

"Here are the probabilities. The infantry is Catholic. It will fight separately; that is to say, it will attack on one side. The cavalry is Calvinist; it also will fight separately. Two sides. The navy is under M. de Joyeuse, who comes from Paris. The court knows with what aim he has set out. He will want his share of battle and glory. Three sides."

"Then let us form three corps," said the burgomaster.

"Make only one, gentlemen, with all your best soldiers, and leave any of whom you may be doubtful in close fight, to guard your walls. Then with this body make a vigorous sally when François least expects it. They mean to attack; let them be anticipated, and attacked themselves. If you wait for their assault you are lost, for no one equals the French in an attack, as you, gentlemen, have no equals in defending your towns on the field of battle."

The Flemings looked radiant.

"What did I say, gentlemen?" said William.

"It is a great honour," said the unknown, "to have been, without knowing it, of the same opinion as the greatest captain of the age."

Both bowed courteously.

"Then," continued the unknown, "it is settled; you will make a furious sortie on the infantry and cavalry. I trust that your officers will so conduct it as to defeat your enemies."

"But their vessels?" cried the burgomaster. "They will force our barrier; and as the wind is north-west, they will be in our city in two hours."

"You have yourselves six old vessels and thirty boats at Ste. Marie; that is a mile off, is it not? That is your maritime barricade across the Scheldt."

"Yes, monseigneur, that is so. How do you know all these details?"

Monseigneur smiled. "I know them, as you see. It is there the fate of the battle lies."

"Then," said the burgomaster, "we must send aid to our brave seamen."

"On the contrary, you may dispose otherwise of the four hundred men who are there. Twenty brave, intelligent, and devoted men will suffice."

The Antwerpians opened their eyes in surprise.

"Will you," continued monseigneur, "destroy the French fleet at the expense of your six old vessels and thirty boats?"

"Hum!" said the Antwerpians, looking at one another, "our vessels are not so old."

"Well, price them," said the stranger, "and I will pay you their value."

"See," said William, softly, to him, "the men against whom I have to contend every day. Were it not for that, I should have conquered long ago."

"Come, gentlemen," continued the stranger, "name your price, but name it quickly. I will pay you in bills on yourselves, which I trust you will find good."

"Monseigneur," said the burgomaster, after a few minutes' deliberation with the others, "we are merchants, and not lords; therefore you must pardon some hesitation, for our souls are not in our bodies, but in our counting-houses. However, there are circumstances in which, for the general good, we know how to make sacrifices. Dispose, then, of our ships as you like."

"Faith! monseigneur," said William, "you have done wonders. It would have taken me six months to obtain what you have obtained in ten minutes."

"This, then, is my plan, gentlemen," said monseigneur: "the French, with the admiral's galley at their head, will try to force a passage. Make your line long enough, and from all your boats let the men throw grappling-irons; and then, having made fast the enemy's ships, set fire to all your own boats, having previously filled them with combustible materials, and let your men escape in one reserved for the purpose."

" Oh," cried William, " I see the whole French fleet burning."

" Yes, the whole. Then no more retreat by sea, and none by land, for at the same time you must open the sluices of Malines, Berchem, Lier, Duffel, and Antwerp. Repulsed by you, pursued by your open dikes, enveloped on all sides by these waters unexpectedly and rapidly rising—by this sea, which will have a flow, but no ebb—the French will be drowned, overwhelmed, destroyed."

The officers uttered a cry of joy.

" There is but one drawback," said the prince.

" What is it, monseigneur? " asked the unknown.

" That it would take a day to send our orders to the different towns, and we have but an hour."

" And an hour is enough."

" But who will instruct the flotilla? "

" It is done."

" By whom? "

" By me. If these gentlemen had refused to give it to me, I should have bought it."

" But Malines, Lier, Duffel? "

" I passed through Malines and Lier, and sent a sure agent to Duffel. At eleven o'clock the French will be beaten; at one they will be in full retreat; at two Malines will open its dikes, Lier and Duffel their sluices, and the whole plain will become a furious ocean, which will drown houses, fields, woods, and villages, it is true, but at the same time will destroy the French so utterly that not one will return to France."

A silence of admiration and almost of terror followed these words; then all at once the Flemings burst into applause. William stepped forward towards the unknown, and holding out his hand, said, " Then, monseigneur, all is ready on our side? "

" All; and stay—I believe on the side of the French also." And he pointed to an officer who was entering.

" Gentlemen," cried the officer, " we have just heard that the French are marching towards the city."

" To arms! " cried the burgomaster.

" To arms! " cried all.

" One moment, gentlemen," cried monseigneur; " I have to give one direction more important than all the rest."

" Speak! " cried all.

"The French will be surprised; it will not be a combat, nor even a retreat, but a flight. To pursue them you must be lightly armed. No cuirasses, *morbleu!* It is your cuirasses, in which you cannot move, which have made you lose all the battles you have lost. No cuirasses, gentlemen! We will meet again in the combat. Meanwhile, go to the place of the Hôtel de Ville, where you will find all your men in battle array."

"Thanks, monseigneur," said William; "you have saved Belgium and Holland."

"Prince, you overwhelm me."

"Will your highness consent to draw the sword against the French?" asked the prince.

"I will arrange so as to fight against the Huguenots," replied the unknown, with a smile which his sombre companion might have envied.

CHAPTER XIII

FRENCH AND FLEMINGS

AT the moment when the members of the council left the Hôtel de Ville, the officers went to put themselves at the head of their troops, and execute the orders they had received. At the same time the artillery thundered. This artillery surprised the French in their nocturnal march, by which they had hoped to surprise the town; but instead of stopping their advance, it only hastened it. If they could not take the city by surprise, they might, as we have seen the King of Navarre do at Cahors, fill up the moats with fascines and burst open the gates with petards.

The cannon from the ramparts continued to fire, but in the darkness took scarcely any effect; and after having replied to the cries of their adversaries, the French advanced silently towards the ramparts with that fiery intrepidity which they always show in attack. But all at once gates and posterns opened, and from all sides poured out armed men, if not with the fierce impetuosity of the French, with a firmness which rendered them massive as a rolling wall. It was the Flemings, who advanced in close ranks and compact masses, above which the cannon continued to thunder, although with more noise than effect. Then the combat began, hand to hand, foot to foot, sword to sword; and the flash of pistols lighted up faces red with blood. But not a cry, not a murmur, not a complaint, was heard; and the Flemings and French fought with equal rage. The Flemings were furious at having to fight, for fighting was neither their profession nor their pleasure; and the French were furious at being attacked when they meant to have taken the initiative.

While the combat was raging violently, explosions were heard near Ste. Marie, and a light rose over the city, like a crest of flames. It was Joyeuse attacking and trying to force the barrier across the Scheldt; and he would soon penetrate into the city—at least, so the French hoped. But it was not so. Joyeuse had weighed anchor and sailed, and was making rapid progress, favoured by the west wind. All was ready for action; the sailors, armed with their boarding-cutlasses, were eager for the combat; the gunners stood ready with lighted matches; while some picked men, axe in hand, stood ready to jump on the hostile ships and destroy the chains and cords.

The eight ships advanced in silence, disposed in the form of a wedge, of which the admiral's galley formed the point. Joyeuse himself had taken his first lieutenant's place, and was leaning over the bowsprit, trying to pierce the fogs of the river and the darkness of the night. Soon, through this double obscurity, he saw the barrier extending itself darkly across the stream; it appeared deserted, but in that land of ambushes, there seemed something terrifying in this desertion. However, they continued to advance, watching the barrier, scarcely ten cable-lengths off; they approached nearer and nearer, and yet not a single *qui vive ?* struck on their ears. The sailors saw in this silence only a carelessness which pleased them; but their young admiral, more far-seeing, feared some ruse.

At last the prow of the admiral's ship entered between the two ships which formed the centre of the barrier, and pushing them before it, made the whole line, the parts of which were fastened by chains, bend inwardly, without breaking, so that the French fleet was flanked by it on either side. Suddenly, as the bearers of the axes received the order to board and cut the chains, grappling-irons, thrown by invisible hands, seized hold of the French vessels. The Flemings had forestalled the intended movement of the French. Joyeuse believed that his enemies were offering him a mortal combat, and he accepted it with alacrity. He also threw grappling-irons, and the two lines of ships were firmly bound together. Then, seizing an axe, he was the first to jump on a ship, crying, " Board them ! board them ! " All his crew followed him, officers and men uttering the same cry; but no cry replied to them, no force opposed their advance. Only they saw three boats full of men gliding silently over the water like three sea-birds.

The assailants rested motionless on the ships which they had conquered without a struggle. All at once Joyeuse heard under his feet a crackling sound; and a smell of sulphur filled the air. A thought crossed his mind, and he ran and opened a hatchway; the vessel was burning, A cry of " To our ships! " sounded through all the line. Each climbed back again more quickly than he had descended; but Joyeuse this time was the last. Just as he reached his galley the flames burst out over the whole bridge of boats, like twenty volcanoes, of which each ship or boat was the crater. The order was instantly given to cut the ropes and break the chains and grappling-irons, and the sailors worked with the rapidity of men who knew that their safety depended on their exertions. But the work was immense; perhaps they might have detached the grappling-irons thrown by the enemy on their ships, but they had also to detach those which they themselves had thrown.

All at once twenty explosions were heard, and each of the French ships trembled to its centre. It was the cannon that defended the barrier, and which, fully charged and then abandoned by the Antwerpians, exploded as the fire gained on them, breaking everything in their direction. The flames mounted like gigantic serpents along the masts, rolled themselves round the yards, then, with their forked tongues, came to lick the sides of the French vessels.

Joyeuse, with his magnificent armour covered with gold, giving calmly, and in an imperious voice, his orders in the midst of the flames, looked like a fabulous salamander covered with scales, which on every movement threw off a shower of sparks. But the explosions became louder than ever; the gun-room had taken fire, and the vessels themselves were bursting.

Joyeuse had done his best to free himself, but in vain; the flames had reached the French ships, and showers of fire fell about him. The Flemish barrier was broken, and the French ships, burning, drifted to the shore. Joyeuse saw that he could not save his ships, and he gave orders to lower the boats, and land on the left bank. This was quickly done, and all the sailors were embarked to a man before Joyeuse left his galley. His coolness seemed to communicate itself to all the rest, and every man landed with a sword or an axe in his hand. Before he had reached the shore, the fire reached the magazine of his ship, which blew up, lighting the whole horizon.

Meanwhile, the artillery from the ramparts had ceased, not

because the combat had abated, but because it was so close that it was impossible to fire on enemies without firing on friends also. The Calvinist cavalry had charged, and done wonders. Before the swords of its cavaliers a pathway opened; but the wounded Flemings pierced the horses with their large cutlasses. In spite of this brilliant charge, a little confusion showed itself in the French columns, and they kept their ground only, without advancing, while from the gates of the city new troops continually poured out. All at once, almost under the walls of the city, a cry of "Anjou! France!" was heard behind the mass of the Antwerpians. Joyeuse, to whom a horse had been brought, and his fifteen hundred sailors, armed with hatchets and cutlasses, had fallen suddenly on the Flemings. They had to avenge their fleet in flames, and two hundred of their companions burned or drowned.

No one could manage his long sword better than Joyeuse— every blow cut open a head; every thrust took effect. The group of Flemings on which he fell were destroyed like a field of corn by a legion of locusts. Delighted with their first success, the sailors continued to push on. Meantime the Calvinist cavalry, surrounded by troops, began to lose ground; M. de Saint-Aignan's infantry, however, kept their place.

The French prince had seen the burning of the fleet, and heard the reports of the cannon and the explosions, without suspecting it could be anything but a fierce combat which must terminate in victory for Joyeuse; for how could a few Flemish ships fight against the French fleet? He expected, then, every minute a diversion on the part of Joyeuse, when the news was brought to him that the fleet was destroyed, and that Joyeuse and his men were fighting in the midst of the Flemings. He now began to feel very anxious; the fleet was a means of retreat, and the safety of the army depended upon it. He sent orders to the Calvinist cavalry to try a fresh charge; and men and horses, almost exhausted, rallied to attack the Antwerpians afresh. The voice of Joyeuse was heard in the midst of the battle, crying, "Hold firm, M. de Saint-Aignan! France! France!" and, like a reaper cutting a field of corn, he whirled his sword and cut down a harvest of men. The delicate favourite, the Sybarite, seemed to have put on with his cuirass the strength of a Hercules; and the infantry, hearing his voice above all the noise, and seeing his sword flashing, took fresh courage, and like the cavalry, made a new effort, and returned to the combat.

But now the person that had been called Monseigneur came

out of the city on a beautiful black horse. He wore black armour, and was followed by five hundred well-mounted horsemen, whom the Prince of Orange had placed at his disposal. By a parallel gate came out William himself, with a picked body of infantry who had not yet appeared. Monseigneur hastened where he was most wanted; that is to say, where Joyeuse was fighting, with his sailors.

The Flemings recognised him, and opened their ranks, crying joyfully, "Monseigneur! monseigneur!" Joyeuse and his men saw the movement, heard the cries, and all at once found themselves opposed to that new body of men, which had appeared as if by enchantment. Joyeuse pushed his horse towards the black knight, and their swords met. Joyeuse was confident in his armour and his skill with the sword; but all his thrusts were skilfully parried, and one of those of his adversary touched him, and in spite of his armour, drew some drops of blood from his shoulder.

"Ah!" cried the young admiral, "this man is a Frenchman, and what is more, he has studied fencing under the same master as I have."

At these words the unknown turned away, and tried to find a new antagonist.

"If you are French," cried Joyeuse, "you are a traitor, for you fight against your king, your country, and your flag."

The unknown replied by attacking Joyeuse with fresh fury; but now Joyeuse was on his guard, and knew with what a skilful swordsman he had to deal. He parried two or three thrusts with as much skill as fury, and it was now the stranger who made a step back.

"See," cried Joyeuse, "what one can do fighting for one's country! A pure heart and a loyal arm suffice to defend a head without a helmet, a face without a visor;" and he threw his helmet far from him, displaying his noble and beautiful head, with eyes sparkling with pride, youth, and anger. His antagonist, instead of replying, or following the example given, uttered a dull roar, and struck at his bare head.

"Ah!" cried Joyeuse, parrying the blow, "I said you were a traitor; and as a traitor you shall die!" And pressing upon him with rapid thrusts, he penetrated an opening in the visor of the unknown. "Ah! I shall kill you," cried the young man. "I shall remove the helmet, which so well protects and hides you; and I will hang you to the first tree that I see."

The unknown was about to return the attack, when a cavalier who had come up leaned over and said in his ear,

" Monseigneur, no more skirmishing; your presence is wanted over there."

Glancing towards the point indicated, the unknown saw the Flemings giving way before the Calvinist cavalry. " Yes," cried he, " those are the men I wanted to meet."

At this moment a troop of cavalry fell on Joyeuse and his sailors, who, wearied by ceaseless blows with their giant arms, made their first step in retreat. The black cavalier profited by this movement to disappear in the confusion and darkness.

A quarter of an hour later the French began to give way. M. de Saint-Aignan tried to retreat in good order, but a last troop of two thousand infantry and five hundred horse came out fresh from the city, and fell on this harassed and already retreating army. It was the old band of the Prince of Orange, which had fought in turn against the Duke of Alva, Don John, Requesens, and Alexander Farnèse. In spite of the coolness of the chiefs and the bravery of many, a frightful rout ensued.

At this moment the unknown fell again on the fugitives, and once more met Joyeuse with his marines, one half of whom he had left on the field of battle. The young admiral was mounted on his third horse, two having been killed under him. His sword was broken; and he had taken from a wounded sailor a heavy boarding-axe, which he whirled round his head with the greatest apparent ease. From time to time he turned and faced his enemy, like the wild boar who cannot make up his mind to fly, and turns desperately on his hunter. The Flemings, who by monseigneur's advice had fought without cuirasses, were active in the pursuit, and gave no rest to the Angevin army. Something like remorse seized the unknown at the sight of this disaster.

" Enough, gentlemen ! " cried he, in French; " to-night they are driven from Antwerp, and in a week will be driven from Flanders. Ask no more of the God of battles."

" Ah, he is French ! " cried Joyeuse; " I guessed it, traitor ! Ah, be cursed, and may you die the death of a traitor ! "

This furious imprecation seemed to disconcert the unknown more than a thousand swords raised against him; he turned, and, conqueror as he was, fled almost as rapidly as the conquered. But this retreat of a single man had no effect on the Flemings; yet fear, which is contagious, seized upon the entire French army, and the soldiers began to fly like madmen. The horses went fast, in spite of fatigue, for they also seemed to be under the influence of fear; the men dispersed to seek a shelter, and in a few hours the army, as an army, existed no longer. This was the time when the dikes were to be opened. From Lier to Termonde, from Haesdonck to Malines, every little river, swollen by its tributaries, every canal, overflowed, and spread over the flat country its contingent of furious water.

Thus, when the fugitive French began to stop, having tired out the enemy; when they had seen the Antwerpians return at length towards the town, followed by the soldiers of the Prince of Orange; when those who had escaped from the carnage of the night believed themselves saved, and stopped to breathe for an instant, some with a prayer, and others with a curse— then a new enemy, blind and pitiless, was let loose upon them; an enemy with the swiftness of the wind and the impetuosity of the sea. And yet, notwithstanding the imminence of the danger which began to surround them, they had no suspicion of it. Joyeuse had commanded his sailors, now reduced to eight hundred, to make a halt; they were the only persons who had preserved some order, the Comte de Saint-Aignan having vainly tried to rally his foot-soldiers.

The Duc d'Anjou, at the head of the fugitives, mounted on an excellent horse and accompanied by a single servant, pushed forward without appearing to think of anything.

" He has no heart," cried some.

" His coolness is magnificent," said others.

Some hours of repose, from two to six in the morning, restored to the infantry the strength to continue their retreat; but provisions were wanting. As for the horses, they seemed more fatigued than the men, and could scarcely move, for they had eaten nothing since the day before.

The fugitives hoped to gain Brussels, where the duke had many partisans, although they were not free from anxiety as to their reception. At Brussels, which was about eight leagues off, they would find food for the famishing troops, and a place of security from which to resume the campaign at a more favourable time. At that time no one foresaw the frightful moment when the ground would give way under the feet of the unhappy soldiers; when mountains of water would beat them down and roll over their heads; and that the remains of so many brave men would be borne on muddy waters to the sea, or would be stopped on the way to fertilise the fields of Brabant.

M. d'Anjou breakfasted in a peasant's hut, between Hèboken and Heckhout. It was unoccupied, but a fire still burned in the grate. The soldiers and officers wished to imitate their chief, and spread themselves about the two villages we have named, but found with a surprise mingled with terror that every house was deserted and that the inhabitants had carried away their provisions. M. de Saint-Aignan, who had aided them in their search, now called to the officers, " March on, gentlemen ! "

" But we are tired and dying with hunger, general."

" Yes, but you are alive; and if you remain here another hour you will be dead. Perhaps it is already too late."

M. de Saint-Aignan knew nothing; but he suspected some great danger. They went on; but two or three thousand men straggled from the main body, or worn out with fatigue, lay down on the grass, or at the foot of a tree, wearied, desolate, and despairing. Scarcely three thousand able men remained to the Duc d'Anjou.

CHAPTER XIV

THE TRAVELLERS

WHILE these disasters—the forerunners of a still greater one— were taking place, two travellers, mounted on excellent horses, left Brussels on a fine night, and rode towards Malines. They rode side by side, without any apparent arms but a large Flemish knife, of which the handle appeared in the belt of one of them. They rode on, each occupied with thoughts perhaps the same, without speaking a word. They looked like those commercial travellers who at that time carried on an extensive trade between France and Flanders. Whoever had met them trotting so peaceably along the road would have taken them for honest men, anxious to find a bed after their day's work. However, it was only necessary to overhear a few sentences of their conversation—when they made any conversation—to abandon any such opinion suggested by their appearance. They were about half a league from Brussels, when the taller of them said, " Madame, you were quite right to set off to-night. We shall gain seven leagues by it, and shall probably arrive at Malines by the time the result of the attack on Antwerp is known. In two days of short marches—and you must take easy stages—we shall reach Antwerp."

The person who was called Madame, in spite of her male costume, replied in a voice calm, grave, and sweet, " My friend, believe me, God will tire of protecting this wicked prince, and will strike him cruelly. Let us hasten to put our projects into execution, for I am not one of those who believe in fatality; and I think that men have perfect freedom in will and deed.

If we leave his punishment to God, and do not act ourselves, it was not worth while living so unhappily until now."

At this moment a blast of north wind, cold and biting, swept across the plain.

" You shiver, madame," said the other traveller. " Take your cloak."

" No, thank you, Rémy. I no longer feel pain of body or mind."

Rémy rode on silently, only now and then stopping and looking back.

" You see no one behind us? " asked his companion, after one of these halts.

" No one, madame."

" That cavalier whom we met at Valenciennes, and who inquired about us, after looking at us so curiously? "

" I do not see him, madame."

" But I fancied I saw him again near Mons."

" And I, madame, am sure I saw him just before we entered Brussels."

" Brussels? "

" Yes; but he must have stopped there."

" Rémy," said Diane, drawing near him, as if even on that lonely road she feared to be overheard, " did he not seem to you like (in figure, at least, for I did not see his face) that unhappy young man? "

" Oh, no, madame, not at all; and besides, how could he have guessed that we had left Paris, and were travelling along this road? "

" But he found us out when we changed our house in Paris."

" No, madame, I am sure he did not follow us; and indeed I believe he had resolved on a desperate course as regards himself."

" Alas, Rémy! every one has his own share of suffering. I trust God will console this poor youth."

Rémy replied with a sigh; and they went on with no other sound than that of their horses' feet on the hard road. Two hours passed thus. Just as they were about to enter Vilvoorden, Rémy turned his head, for he heard the sound of horses' feet behind them. He stopped and listened, but could see nothing. His eyes uselessly tried to pierce through the darkness of the night, and as he no longer heard any sounds, they rode on and entered the town.

" Madame," said he, " if you will take my advice, you will stay here. Daylight will soon appear; the horses are tired; and you yourself need repose."

" Rémy, you are anxious about something."

" Yes, about your health, madame. Believe me, a woman cannot support so much fatigue. I can scarcely do so myself."

" As you please, Rémy."

" Well, then, enter that narrow street. I see a light at the end of it, which must proceed from an inn. Be quick, I beg you!"

" You have heard something?"

" I thought I heard a horse's feet. I am not sure; but I will stay behind a minute to find out."

The lady, without replying, went on, and Rémy got off his horse and let him follow her, while he hid himself behind an immense post and waited.

The lady knocked at the door of the inn, behind which, according to the hospitable custom of the country, watched, or rather slept, a maid-servant. The girl woke up and received the traveller pleasantly, and then opened the stable-door for the two horses.

" I am waiting for my companion," said Diane; " let me sit by the fire. I shall not go to bed until he comes."

The servant threw some straw to the horses, shut the stable-door, then returned to the kitchen, put a chair by the fire, snuffed the candle with her fingers, and went to sleep again.

Meanwhile Rémy was watching for the arrival of the traveller whose horse he had heard. He saw him enter the town and go on slowly, and seeming to listen; then, seeing the inn, he appeared to hesitate whether to go there or to continue his journey. He stopped close to Rémy, who laid his hand on his knife.

" It is he again," thought Rémy, " and he is following us. What can he want?"

After a minute the traveller murmured in a low voice, " They must have gone on, and so will I;" and he rode forward.

" To-morrow we will change our route," thought Rémy. And he rejoined Diane, who was waiting impatiently for him.

" Well," said she, softly, " are we followed?"

" There is no one; I was wrong. You may sleep in perfect safety, madame."

" I am not sleepy, Rémy."

" At least have supper, madame; you have scarcely eaten anything."

" Willingly, Rémy."

They reawakened the poor servant, who got up as good-humouredly as before, and hearing what they wanted, took from the cupboard a piece of salt pork, a cold leveret, and some

pastry, which she set before them, together with a frothing jug
of Louvain beer.

Rémy sat down with Diane, who drank half a glass of beer,
and ate a piece of bread. Rémy did the same, and then they
both rose.

"Are you not going to eat any more?" asked the girl.

"No, thank you; we have done."

"Will you not eat any meat? Is it not good?"

"I am sure it is excellent, but we are not hungry."

The girl clasped her hands in astonishment at this strange
abstinence; it was not thus she was used to see travellers eat.
Rémy threw a piece of money on the table.

"Oh," said the girl, "I cannot charge all that! Six farthings
would be all your bill."

"Keep it all, my girl," said Diane; "it is true my brother
and I eat little, but we pay the same as others."

The servant became red with joy; and at the same time
tears of compassion filled her eyes, so sadly were those words
spoken.

"Tell me, my girl," said Rémy, "is there any cross-road
from here to Malines?"

"Yes, monsieur, but it is very bad, while the regular road
is a very fine one."

"Yes, my child, I know that; but we wish to travel by the
other."

"Oh, I told you, monsieur, because, as your companion is a
lady, the road would not do for her."

"Why not?"

"Because to-night a great number of people will cross the
country to go to Brussels."

"To Brussels?"

"Yes; it is a temporary emigration."

"For what reason?"

"I do not know; they had orders."

"From whom—the Prince of Orange?"

"No; from monseigneur."

"Who is he?"

"I do not know, monsieur."

"And who are the emigrants?"

"The inhabitants of the country and of the villages which
have no dikes or ramparts."

"It is strange."

"We ourselves," said the girl, "are to set out at daybreak,
as well as all the other people in the town. Yesterday, at

eleven o'clock, all the cattle were sent to Brussels by canals and cross-roads; therefore, on the road of which you speak there must be great numbers of horses, carts, and people."

" I should have thought the great-road better for all that."

" I do not know; it was the order."

" But we can go on to Malines, I suppose ? "

" I should think so, unless you will do like every one else, and go to Brussels."

" No, no, we will go on at once to Malines," said Diane, rising, " open the stable, if you please, my good girl."

" Danger every way," thought Rémy; " however, the young man is before us." And as the horses had not been unsaddled, they mounted again, and the rising sun found them on the banks of the Dyle.

CHAPTER XV

EXPLANATION

THE danger that Rémy braved was a real one, for the traveller, after having passed the village and gone on for a quarter of a league without seeing any one before him, made up his mind that those whom he sought had remained behind in the village. He would not retrace his steps, but lay down in a field of clover; having made his horse descend into one of those deep ditches which in Flanders serve as divisions between the properties, he was able to see without being seen. This young man, as Rémy knew, and Diane suspected, was Henri du Bouchage, whom a strange fatality threw once more into the presence of the woman he had determined to avoid. After his conversation with Rémy on the threshold of the mysterious house—that is to say, after the loss of all his hopes—he had returned to the Hôtel Joyeuse, quite decided to put an end to a life which he felt to be so miserable, and as a gentleman, and one who had his name to keep untarnished, he decided on the glorious suicide of the field of battle.

Therefore, as they were fighting in Flanders, and his brother had a command there, Henri, on the following day, left his hotel twenty hours after the departure of Diane and Rémy. Letters from Flanders announced the intended attack on Antwerp, and Henri hoped to arrive in time for it. He pleased himself with the idea that he should die sword in hand, in his brother's arms, under a French flag, and that his death would be talked about until the sound even reached the solitude in which the mysterious lady lived. Noble follies! glorious yet sad dreams!

Just as—full of these thoughts—Henri came in sight of Valenciennes, from whose church tower eight o'clock was sounding, he perceived that they were about to close the gates. He pushed on, and nearly overturned on the drawbridge a man who was fastening the girths of his horse. Henri stopped to make excuses to the man, who turned at the sound of his voice, and then quickly turned away again. Henri started, but immediately thought, " I must be mad—Rémy here, whom I left four days ago in the Rue de Bussy; here now, without his mistress? Really, grief must be turning my brain and making me see everything in the form of my own fancies." And he continued his way, convinced that his idea had been pure fancy. At the first inn that he came to he stopped, gave his horse to a servant, and sat down on a bench before the door, while they prepared his bed and supper. But as he sat there he saw two travellers approaching, and this time he saw more clearly.

" Now," murmured he, " I do not dream, and still I think I see Rémy. I cannot remain in this uncertainty; I must clear up my doubts."

He got up and ran down the road after them, but they had disappeared. Then he went to all the inns and questioned the servants, and after much search discovered that two cavaliers had been seen going towards a small inn in the Rue du Beffroi. The landlord was just shutting the doors when Henri entered. While the man offered him rooms and refreshment he looked round, and saw on the top of the staircase Rémy going up, lighted by a servant; of his companion he saw nothing. At the head of the staircase Rémy paused. The count, on recognising him distinctly, had uttered an exclamation, and Rémy had turned round. On seeing that face, made so remarkable by the scar it carried, and that expression full of anxiety, Henri no longer had any doubt; and being too much moved to take any action at the moment, he withdrew, asking himself with a horrible sinking of the heart why Rémy had left his mistress and was travelling without her; for Henri had been so occupied in identifying Rémy that he had scarcely looked at his companion. The next morning he was much surprised to learn that the two travellers had obtained from the governor permission to go out; and that, contrary to all custom, the gates had been opened for them. Thus, as they had set out at one o'clock, they had six hours' start of him. Henri put his horse to the gallop and passed the travellers at Mons. He saw Rémy; but Rémy would need to be a sorcerer to know him, for he had on a soldier's greatcoat and rode another horse. Nevertheless, Rémy's companion, at a word from him, turned away his head before Henri could see his face. But the young man did not lose courage; he watched them to their inn, and then questioning, with the aid of an irresistible auxiliary, learned that Rémy's companion was a very handsome but very silent and sad-looking young man.

Henri trembled. " Can it be a woman? " he asked.

" It is possible," replied the host. " Many women travel thus disguised just now, to go and rejoin their lovers in Flanders; but it is our business to see nothing, and we never do."

Henri felt heart-broken at this explanation. Was Rémy indeed accompanying his mistress dressed as a cavalier; and was she, as the host suggested, going to rejoin her lover in Flanders? Had Rémy lied when he spoke of an eternal regret? Was this fable of a past love, which had clothed his mistress for ever in mourning, only his invention to get rid of an importunate watcher?

" If it be so," cried Henri, " the time will come when I shall have courage to address this woman and reproach her with all the subterfuges which lower her whom I had placed so high above all ordinary mortals; and seeing nearer this brilliant envelope of a common mind, perhaps I shall fall of myself from the height of my illusions and my love."

And the young man tore his hair in despair at the thought of losing the love which was killing him; so true is it that a dead heart is better than an empty one. So he continued to follow them, and to wonder at the cause which took to Flanders at the same time as himself these two beings so indispensable to his existence.

At Brussels Henri had gathered information as to the Duc d'Anjou's intended campaign. The Flemings were too hostile to the duke to receive well a Frenchman of distinction, and were too proud of their position to refrain from humiliating a little this gentleman who came from France and questioned them in a pure Parisian accent, which at that period seemed ridiculous to the Belgians. Henri began to conceive serious fears with reference to this expedition in which his brother was to bear so prominent a part, and he resolved in consequence to push on rapidly to Antwerp. It was a constant surprise to him to see Rémy and his companion, in spite of their desire not to be seen, continue to follow the same road as himself.

Henri, now hidden in the clover-field, felt certain of seeing the face of the young man who accompanied Rémy, and thus putting an end to all his doubts. As they passed, unsuspicious of his proximity, Diane was occupied in braiding up her hair, which she had not dared to untie at the inn.

Henri recognised her, and nearly fainted. The travellers passed on, and then anger took, in Henri's mind, the place of the goodness and patience he had exercised while he believed Rémy and the lady sincere towards him. After the protestations of Rémy, this journey seemed to him a species of treason.

When he had recovered a little from the blow, he rose, shook back his beautiful light hair, and mounted his horse, determined no longer to take those precautions that respect had made him hitherto observe; and he began to follow the travellers openly, and with his face uncovered. No more cloak nor hood, no more stops and hesitation; the road belonged to him as to them; and he rode on, regulating the pace of his horse by that of theirs. He did not mean to speak to them, but only to let them see him. Rémy soon perceived him, and seeing him thus openly advance without any further attempt at concealment, grew troubled; Diane noticed it and turned also. "Ah!" said she, "is it not that young man, Rémy?"

Rémy, still trying to reassure her, said, "I do not think so, madame. As well as I can judge by the dress, it is some young Walloon soldier, going probably to Amsterdam, and passing through the theatre of war to seek adventures."

"I feel uneasy about him, Rémy."

"Reassure yourself, madame; had he been really the Comte du Bouchage, he would have spoken to us—you know how persevering he was."

"I know also that he was respectful, Rémy, or I should never have troubled myself about him, but simply told you to get rid of him."

"Well, madame, if he be so respectful, you would have no more to fear from him on this road than in the Rue de Bussy."

"Nevertheless, Rémy, let us change our horses here at Malines, in order to get on faster to Antwerp."

"On the contrary, madame, I should say, do not let us enter Malines at all. Our horses are good; let us push on to that little village which is, I think, called Villebrock. In that manner we shall avoid the town, with its questioners and curious gazers."

"Go on, then, Rémy."

They turned to the left, taking a road hardly made, but which visibly led to Villebrock; Henri also left the road, and turned down the lane, still keeping his distance from them. Rémy's disquietude showed itself in his constantly turning to look behind him.

At last they arrived at Villebrock. Of two hundred houses which this village contained, not one was inhabited; some forgotten dogs and lost cats ran wildly about the solitude, the former calling for their masters by long howls. Rémy knocked at twenty doors, but found no one. Henri, on his side, who seemed the shadow of the travellers, knocked at the first house as uselessly as they had done, then, divining that the war was the cause of this desertion, deferred continuing his journey until the travellers should have decided what to do.

The travellers fed their horses with some corn which they found in an inn, and then Rémy said, " Madame, we are no longer in a friendly country nor in an ordinary situation; we must not expose ourselves uselessly. We shall certainly fall in with some French, Spanish, or Flemish band; for in the present state of Flanders adventures of all kinds must be rife. If you were a man, I should speak differently; but you are a young and beautiful woman, and would run a double risk, for life and honour."

" My life is nothing," said she.

" On the contrary, madame, it is everything. You live for a purpose."

" Well, then, what do you propose? Think and act for me, Rémy."

" Then, madame, let us remain here. I see many houses which would afford us a sure shelter. I have arms; and we will defend or hide ourselves, according as I shall judge that we are strong enough, or too feeble."

" No, Rémy, no! I must go on. Nothing shall stop me; if I had fears, they would be for you."

" We will go on, then."

They rode on, therefore, without another word, and Henri du Bouchage followed.

CHAPTER XVI

THE WATER

As the travellers advanced, the country took a strange aspect; for it was utterly deserted, as well as the towns and villages. Nowhere were the cows to be seen grazing in the meadows, nor the goat perched on the top of the mountain, or nibbling the green shoots of the brier or young vine; nowhere the shepherd with his flock; nowhere the cart with its driver; no foreign merchant passing from one country to another with his pack on his back; no ploughman singing his harsh song or cracking his long whip. As far as the eye could see over the magnificent plains, the little hills, and the woods, not a human figure was to be seen, not a voice to be heard. It seemed like the earth before the creation of animals or men. The only people who animated this dreary solitude were Rémy and his companions, and Henri following behind and preserving ever the same distance. The night came on dark and cold, and the northwest wind whistled in the air, and filled the solitude with its menacing sound.

Rémy stopped his companion, and putting his hand on the bridle of her horse, said, " Madame, you know how inaccessible I am to fear; you know I would not turn my back to save my life; but this evening some strange feeling possesses me, and forbids me to go farther. Madame, call it terror, timidity, panic, what you will, I confess that for the first time in my life I am afraid."

The lady turned. " Is he still there? " she said.

" Oh, I was not thinking of him; think no more of him, madame, I beg of you. We need not fear a single man. No, the danger that I fear, or rather feel, or divine with a sort of instinct, is unknown to me, and therefore I dread it. Look, Madame, do you see those willows bending in the wind? "

" Yes."

" By their side I see a little house; I beg you, let us go there. If it is inhabited, we will ask for hospitality; and if not, we will take possession of it. I beg you to consent, madame."

Rémy's emotion and troubled voice decided Diane to yield; she turned her horse in the direction indicated by him. A few minutes after, they knocked at the door. A stream, which ran into the Nethe,—a little river about a mile off,—bordered with reeds and grassy banks, bathed the feet of the willows with its murmuring waters. Behind the house, which was built of bricks, and covered with tiles, was a little garden, encircled by a quickset hedge.

All was empty, solitary, and deserted; and no one replied to the blows struck by the travellers. Rémy did not hesitate. He drew his knife, cut a branch of willow, with which he pushed back the bolt and opened the door. The lock, the clumsy work of a neighbouring blacksmith, yielded almost without resistance. Rémy entered quickly, followed by Diane; then, closing the door again, he drew a massive bolt, and thus intrenched, seemed to breathe more freely. Feeling about, he found a bed, a chair, and a table in an upper room. Here he installed his mistress, and then, returning to the lower room, placed himself at the window, to watch the movements of Bouchage.

Henri's reflections were as sombre as those of Rémy. "Certainly," said he to himself, "some danger unknown to us, but of which the inhabitants are not ignorant, is about to fall on the country. War ravages the land. Perhaps the French have taken, or are about to assault, Antwerp, and the peasants, seized with terror, have gone to take refuge in the towns."

But this reasoning, however plausible, did not quite satisfy him. Then he thought, "But what are Rémy and his mistress doing here? What imperious necessity drags them towards this danger? Oh, I will know! the time has come to speak to this woman, and to clear away all my doubts. Never shall I find a better opportunity."

He approached the house, and then suddenly stopped, with a hesitation common to hearts in love. "No," said he—"no, I will be a martyr to the end. Besides, is she not mistress of her own actions? And perhaps she does not even know what fable was invented by Rémy. Oh, it is she alone that I hate—he who assured me that she loved no one. But still let me be just. Ought this man to have betrayed his mistress's secrets to me, whom he did not know? No, no! All that remains for me now is to follow this woman to the camp, to see her hang her arms round some one's neck, and hear her say, 'See what I have suffered, and how I love you!' Well, I will follow her there, see what I dread to see, and die of it. It will be trouble saved for the musket or cannon. Alas! I did not seek this. I went calmly to meet a glorious death, and I wished to die with her name on my lips. It is not so to be. I am destined to a death full of bitterness and torture. Well, I accept it."

Then, recalling his days of waiting and his nights of anguish, before the inexorable house, he found that aside from the doubt that gnawed his heart, he was less to be pitied here than at Paris, for now he could at least see her, and sometimes hear the sound of her voice. Fixing his gaze on the chamber that she occupied, he continued, "While I await that death, and while she reposes in that house, I will take these trees for a shelter; and shall I complain—I, who can hear her voice if she speaks, and can see her shadow on the window? Oh, no, no! I do not complain. I am even too happy."

He lay down under the willows, listening with a melancholy impossible to describe to the murmur of the water that flowed at his side. All at once he started. The noise of cannon was brought distinctly to him by the wind.

"Ah!" said he, "I shall arrive too late. They are attacking Antwerp."

His first idea was to rise, mount his horse, and ride on as quickly as possible; but to do this he must leave the lady, and die in doubt, so he remained. During two hours he lay there, listening to the reports. He was far from suspecting that what he heard was his brother's ships blowing up. At last, about two o'clock, all grew quiet.

"Now," thought Henri, "Antwerp is taken, and my brother is a conqueror; but after Antwerp will come Ghent, and then Bruges. I shall not want an occasion for a glorious death. But before I die I must know what this woman wants in the French camp."

He lay still, and had just fallen asleep, when his horse, which was grazing quietly near him, pricked up his ears and neighed loudly. Henri opened his eyes. The animal had his head turned to the breeze, which had changed to the southeast, as if listening.

"What is it, my good horse!" said the young man, rising and patting with his hand the animal's neck. "Have you seen some otter which frightened you, or do you regret the shelter of your stable?"

The animal stood still, looking towards Lier, with his eyes fixed and his nostrils distended, and listening.

"Ah!" said Henri, "it is more serious; perhaps some troops of wolves following the army to devour the corpses."

The horse neighed and began to run forward to the west, but his master caught the bridle and jumped on his back, and then was able to keep him quiet. But in a moment Henri himself began to hear what the horse had heard,—a long murmur, like that of the wind, but more solemn, which seemed to come from several points in a semicircle extending from south to north.

"What is it?" said Henri; "can it be the wind? No, it is the wind which brings this sound, and I hear two sounds distinctly. An army in march, perhaps? But no; I should hear the sound of voices and of regular marching. Is it the crackling of a fire? No, there is no light in the horizon; the heaven seems even to grow darker."

The noise redoubled and became distinct; it was an incessant growling and rolling, as if thousands of cannon were being dragged over a paved road. Henri thought of this. "But no," said he; "there is no paved road near."

The noise continued to increase, and Henri put his horse to the gallop and gained an eminence. "What do I see?" cried he, as he attained the summit. What he saw, his horse had seen before him; for he had only been able to make him advance by furious spurring, and when they arrived at the top of the hill he reared so as nearly to fall backwards. They saw in the horizon an immense band rolling over the plain, and rapidly approaching. The young man looked in wonder at this strange phenomenon, when, looking back to the place he had come from, he saw the plain beginning to be covered with water, and that the little river had overflowed, and was beginning to cover the reeds which a quarter of an hour before had stood up stiffly on its banks.

"Fool that I am," cried he, "I never thought of it. The water! the water! The Flemings have broken their dikes!"

Henri flew to the house, and knocked furiously at the door. "Open! open!" he cried.

No one replied.

"Open, Rémy!" cried the young man, furious with terror; "it is I,—Henri du Bouchage."

"Oh, you need not name yourself, Monsieur the Count," answered Rémy from within, "I recognised you long ago; but I warn you that if you break in the door you will find me behind it, with a pistol in each hand."

"But you do not understand!" cried Henri. "The water! it is the water!"

"No fables, no pretexts, or dishonourable ruses, Monsieur the Count; I tell you that you will only enter over my body."

"Then I will pass over it; but I will enter. In Heaven's name, in the name of your own safety and your mistress's, will you open?"

"No."

Henri looked round him, and perceived an immense stone. He raised it and threw it against the door, which flew open. a ball passed over Henri's head, but without touching him; he jumped towards Rémy, and seizing his other arm, cried, "Do you not see that I have no arms? Do not defend yourself against a man who does not attack. Look! only look!" and he drew him to the window. "Well," said he, "do you see now?" and he pointed to the horizon.

"The water!" cried Rémy.

"Yes, the water! it invades us; see, at our feet, the river overflows, and in five minutes we shall be unable to leave."

"Madame! madame!" cried Rémy.

" Do not frighten her, Rémy; get the horses ready at once.

Rémy ran to the stable, and Henri flew up the staircase. At Rémy's cry Diane had opened her door; Henri seized her in his arms and carried her away as he would have a child. But she, believing in treason or violence, struggled, and clung to the staircase with all her might.

" Tell her that I am saving her, Rémy!" cried Henri.

Rémy heard the appeal just as he arrived with the two horses, and cried, " Yes, yes, madame, he is saving you, or rather, he will save you! Come, for Heaven's sake!"

CHAPTER XVII

FLIGHT

HENRI, without losing time in reasoning with Diane, carried her out of the house, and wished to place her before him on his horse; but she, with a movement of invincible repugnance, glided from his arms, and was received by Rémy, who placed her on her own horse.

" Ah, madame!" cried Henri, " how little you understand my heart! It was not, believe me, for the pleasure of holding you in my arms or pressing you to my heart—although for that favour I would sacrifice my life—but that we ought to fly as quickly as the birds; and look at them, how they fly!"

Indeed, in the scarcely dawning light were seen large numbers of curlews and pigeons, traversing the air with a quick and frightened flight, which in the night, usually abandoned to the silent bat, looked strange to the eye, and sounded sinister to the ear.

Diane did not reply, but rode on without turning her head. Her horse, however, as well as that of Rémy, was fatigued with the long journey, and Henri, as he turned back each moment, saw that they could not keep up with him. " See, madame," said he, " how my horse outstrips yours, and yet I am holding him in with all my strength; for Heaven's sake, madame, while there is yet time, if you will not ride with me, take my horse and leave me yours!"

" No, thank you, monsieur," replied she, in her usual calm voice.

" But, madame," cried Henri, in despair, " the water gains on us! Do you hear? Do you hear?"

Indeed, a horrible crashing was now heard; it was the dike

of a neighbouring village giving way to swell the inundation. Boards and props had yielded; a double row of stakes broke with a noise like thunder; and the water, rushing over the ruins, began to invade an oak wood, of which they saw the tops trembling, and heard the branches cracking as though a flight of demons were passing under the leaves.

The uprooted trees knocking against the stakes, the wood of ruined houses floating on the waters, the distant neighings and cries of horses and men carried away by the inundation, formed a concert of sounds so strange and gloomy that the terror which agitated Henri began to seize also upon Diane. She spurred her horse, and he, as if he understood the danger, redoubled his efforts. But the water gained on them, and before ten minutes it was evident that it would reach them. Every instant Henri stopped to wait for his companions, and cried, "Quicker, madame, for pity's sake! The water comes; here it is!"

It came indeed, foaming and turbulent, carrying away like a feather the house in which they had taken shelter; and majestic, immense, rolling like a serpent, it arrived like a wall behind the horses of Rémy and Diane. Henri uttered a cry of terror, and turned against the water, as though he would have fought it. "You see you are lost!" he screamed. "Come, madame, perhaps there is still time; come with me!"

"No, monsieur," said she.

"In a minute it will be too late; look!" cried he.

Diane turned; the water was within fifty feet of her. "Let my fate be accomplished," said she; "you, monsieur, fly."

Rémy's horse, exhausted, fell, and could not rise again, despite the efforts of his rider.

"Save her in spite of herself!" cried Rémy.

At that moment, as he disengaged himself from the stirrups, the water passed over the head of the faithful servant. His mistress, at this sight, uttered a terrible cry, and jumped off her horse resolved to die with Rémy. But Henri, seeing her intention, dismounted at the same time, seized her round the waist, and remounting, placed her before him, and set off like an arrow.

"Rémy! Rémy!" she cried, extending her arms. A cry was the only answer. Rémy had come up to the surface, and with the indomitable hope which accompanies the dying man to the last, was swimming, sustained by a beam. By his side came his horse, beating the water desperately with his feet; while the water gained on Diane's horse, and some twenty feet in front Henri and Diane flew on the third horse, which was mad with terror.

Rémy scarcely regretted life, since he hoped that his loved mistress would be saved. "Adieu, madame!" he cried. "I go first to him who waits for us, to tell him that you live for—"

He could not finish; a mountain of water rolled over his head.

"Rémy, Rémy!" cried the lady, "I wish to die with you! I will, monsieur, I will go to him! in the name of God, I will!"

She pronounced these words with so much energy and angry authority that the young man unfolded his arms, and let her slip to the ground, saying, "Well, madame, we will all three die here together. It is a joy I had not hoped for."

As he said these words, he stopped his horse, and the water reached them almost immediately; but by a last effort of love, the young man kept hold of Diane's arm as she stood on the ground. The flood rolled over them. It was a sublime spectacle to see the coolness of the young man, whose entire bust was raised above the water, while he sustained Diane with one arm, and with the other guided the last efforts of his expiring horse.

There was a moment of terrible struggle, during which the lady, upheld by Henri, kept her head above water, while with his left hand he kept off the floating wood and the corpses which would have struck against them.

One of the bodies floating past sighed out, "Adieu, madame!"

"Heavens!" cried Henri, "it is Rémy!" And without calculating the danger of the additional weight, he seized him by his sleeve, drew him up, and enabled him to breathe freely. But the exhausted horse now sank in the water to its neck, then to its eyes, and finally disappeared altogether.

"We must die," murmured Henri. "Madame, my life and soul belonged to you."

As he spoke, he felt Rémy slip from him, and he no longer tried to retain him; it was useless. His only care was to sustain Diane above the water, that she at least might die the last, and that he might be able to say to himself in his last moments that he had been able to contend with death for her. All at once a joyful cry sounded at his side; he turned and saw Rémy, who had found a boat. That boat had belonged to the little house where they had taken shelter, and the water had carried it way. Rémy, who had regained his strength, thanks to Henri's assistance, had seized the boat as it floated past. The oars were tied to it, and a boat-hook lay in the bottom. He held out the boat-hook to Henri, who seized it, and drawing

Diane with him, raised her over his shoulders, and passed her
to Rémy, and then climbed in himself. The first rays of the
rising sun showed them the plains inundated, and the boat
swimming like an atom on that ocean covered with wrecks.
Towards the left rose a little hill, completely surrounded by
water, looking like an island in the midst of the sea. Henri
took the oars and rowed towards it, while Rémy, with the boat-
hook, occupied himself in keeping off the beams and wrecks
which might have struck against them. Thanks to Henri's
strength and Rémy's skill, they reached, or rather were thrown
against, the hill. Rémy jumped out, and seizing the chain,
drew the boat towards him. Henri approached to take the
lady in his arms; but she extended her hand, and rising unaided,
stepped on the ground. Henri breathed a sigh. For a moment
he had the idea of throwing himself into the abyss and dying
before her eyes. But an irresistible sentiment chained him to
life so long as he could see that woman, whose presence he had
so long wished for in vain. He drew up the boat and seated
himself a little way from Diane and Rémy. They were saved
from the most menacing danger, for the inundation, however
strong, could never reach to the summit of the hill. Below
them they could see that great angry waste of waters, which
seemed inferior in power only to God himself; and by the
increasing light, they perceived that it was covered with the
corpses of French soldiers and their horses.

Rémy had a wound in his shoulder, where a floating beam
had struck against him; but Diane, thanks to Henri's protection, was free from all injury, although she was cold and
wet. At last they noticed in the horizon on the eastern side
something like fires burning on a height which the water could
not reach. As well as they could judge, they were about a
league distant. Rémy advanced to the point of the hill, and
said that he believed he saw, about a thousand feet from where
they were, a sort of a jetty advancing in a direct line towards
the fires. But they could see nothing clearly, and knew not
well where they were, for though day was dawning, it came
cloudily and full of fog. Had it been clear and under a pure
sky, they might have seen the town of Malines, from which
they were not more than two leagues distant.

"Well, Monsieur the Count," said Rémy, "what do you
think of those fires?"

"Those fires, which seem to you to announce a hospitable
shelter, appear to me to be full of danger."

" And why so ? "

" Rémy," said Henri, lowering his voice, " look at these corpses. They are all French; there is not one Fleming. They announce to us a great disaster. The dikes have been broken to finish the destruction of the French army, if it has been conquered; to nullify the victory, if they have been victors. Those fires are as likely to have been lighted by enemies as by friends, and may be simply a ruse to draw fugitives to destruction."

" Nevertheless, we cannot stay here; my mistress will die of cold and hunger."

" You are right, Rémy; remain here with madame, and I will go to the jetty and return to you with news."

" No, monsieur," said Diane, " you shall not expose yourself alone. We have been saved together; we will live or die together. Rémy, your arm; I am ready."

Each word which she pronounced had so irresistible an accent of authority that no one thought of disputing it. Henri bowed, and walked first.

The water had become more tranquil; the jetty formed with the hill a kind of bay, where the water slept. All three got into the little boat, which was once more launched among the wrecks and floating bodies. A quarter of an hour after, they touched the jetty. They tied the chain of the boat to a tree, landed once more, walked along the jetty for nearly an hour, and then arrived at a number of Flemish huts, among which, in a place planted with lime-trees, were two or three hundred soldiers sitting round a fire, above whom floated the French flag. Suddenly a sentinel, placed about one hundred feet from the bivouac, cried, " Qui vive ? "

" France ! " replied Bouchage. Then, turning to Diane, he said, " Now, madame, you are saved. I recognise the standard of the gendarmes of Aunis—a corps in which I have many friends."

At the cry of the sentinel and the answer of the count several gendarmes ran to meet the new-comers—doubly welcome, in the midst of this terrible disaster, as survivors and compatriots. Henri was soon recognised; he was eagerly questioned, and recounted the miraculous manner in which he and his companions had escaped death. Rémy and Diane had sat down silently in a corner; but Henri brought them and made them come to the fire, for both were still dripping with water. " Madame," said he, " you will be respected here as in your own house. I have taken the liberty of calling you one of my relatives." And without waiting for the thanks of those whose lives he had saved, he went away to rejoin the officers.

The gendarmes of Aunis, of whom our fugitives were claiming hospitality, had retired in good order after the defeat and the retreat of the chiefs. Wherever there is similarity of position and sentiment, and the habit of living together, it is common to find unanimity in execution as well as in thought. It had been so that night with the gendarmes of Aunis; for seeing their chiefs abandon them, they agreed together to draw their ranks closer, instead of breaking them. They therefore put their horses to the gallop, and under the conduct of one of the ensigns, whom they loved for his bravery and respected for his birth, they took the road to Brussels. Like all the actors in this terrible scene, they saw the progress of the inundation, and were pursued by the furious waters, but by good luck found in this spot a position strong both against men and water. The inhabitants, knowing themselves in safety, had not left their homes, and had sent off only their women, children, and old men to Brussels. Therefore the gendarmes met with resistance when they arrived; but death howled behind them, and they attacked like desperate men, triumphed over all obstacles, lost ten men, but established the others, and turned out the Flemings.

Such was the recital which Henri received from them. " And the rest of the army? " he asked.

" Look! " replied the ensign; " the corpses which pass each moment answer your question."

" But—my brother? " said Henri, in a choking voice.

" Alas, Monsieur the Count, we do not know. He fought like a lion, but he survived the battle; as to the inundation I cannot say."

Henri shook his head sadly, then, after a minute's pause, said, " And the duke? "

" Count, the duke fled one of the first. He was mounted on a white horse, with no spot but a black star on the forehead. Well, just now we saw the horse pass among a mass of wrecks; the foot of a rider was caught in the stirrup, and was borne above the water."

" Great God! "

" Great God! " echoed Rémy, who had drawn near and heard the tale.

" One of my men ventured down into the water and seized the reins of the floating horse, and drew it up sufficiently to enable us to see the white boot and gold spur that the duke wore. But the waters were rushing past, and the man was forced to let go to save himself, and we saw no more. We shall not even have the consolation of giving a Christian burial to our prince."

"Dead! he also, the heir to the crown! What a disaster!"

Rémy turned to his mistress, and with an expression impossible to describe, said, "He is dead, madame, you see."

"I praise the Lord, who has spared me a crime," said she, raising her eyes to heaven.

"Yes, but it prevents our vengeance."

"Vengeance belongs to man only when God forgets."

"But you yourself, count," said the ensign to Henri, "what are you about to do?"

The count started. "I?" said he.

"Yes."

"I will wait here till my brother's body passes," replied he, gloomily; "then I will try to draw him to land. You may be sure that if once I hold him I shall not let go."

Rémy looked pityingly at the young man; but Diane heard nothing—she was praying.

CHAPTER XVIII

TRANSFIGURATION

AFTER her prayer Diane rose so beautiful and radiant that the count uttered a cry of surprise and admiration. She appeared to be waking out of a long sleep, of which the dreams had fatigued her and weighed upon her mind; or rather, she was like the daughter of Jairus, called from death and rising from her funeral couch, already purified and ready for heaven. Awakening from her lethargy, she cast around her a glance so sweet and gentle, and filled with angelic kindness, that Henri began to believe he should see her feel for his pain, and yield to a sentiment of gratitude and pity if not of love. While the gendarmes, after their frugal repast, slept about among the ruins, while Rémy himself yielded to sleep, Henri came and sat down close to Diane, and in a voice so low and sweet that it seemed a murmur of the breeze, said, "Madame, you live. Oh, let me tell you all the joy which overflows my heart when I see you here in safety after having seen you on the threshold of the tomb!"

"It is true, monsieur," replied she; "I live through you,

and," she added with a sad smile, "I wish I could say that I am grateful."

"But, madame," replied Henri, with an immense effort, "if it is only that you are restored to those you love?"

"What do you mean?"

"To those you are going to rejoin through so many perils."

"Monsieur, those I loved are dead! Those I am going to rejoin are so also."

"Oh, madame!" cried Henri, falling on his knees, "throw your eyes on me—on me, who have suffered so much and loved so much. Oh, do not turn away! You are young, and beautiful as the angels in heaven. Read my heart, which I open to you, and you will see that it contains not an atom of that love that most men feel. You do not believe me! Examine the past hours; which of them has given me joy, or even hope? yet I have persevered. You made me weep; I drank my tears. You made me suffer; I devoured my sufferings. You drove me to seek death; and I went to meet it without a complaint. Even at this moment, when you turn away your head, when each of my words, burning as they are, seems a drop of iced water falling on your heart, my soul is full of you, and I live only because you live. Just now was I not ready to die with you? What have I asked for? Nothing. Have I touched your hand? Never, but to draw you from a mortal peril. I held you in my arms to draw you from the waves—nothing more. All in me has been purified by the devouring fire of my love."

"Oh, monsieur! for pity's sake do not speak thus to me!"

"Oh, in pity do not condemn me! He told me you loved no one; oh, repeat to me this assurance! It is a singular favour for a man in love to ask to be told that he is not loved; but I prefer to know that you are insensible to all. Oh, madame, you who are the only adoration of my life, reply to me!"

In spite of Henri's prayers a sigh was the only answer.

"You say nothing," continued the count; "Rémy at least had more pity for me, for he tried to console me. Oh, I see you will not reply, because you do not wish to tell me that you came to Flanders to rejoin some one happier than I; and yet I am young, and am ready to die at your feet."

"Monsieur the Count," replied Diane, with majestic solemnity, "do not say to me those things that are said to women; I belong to another world, and do not live in this. Had I seen you less noble, less good, less generous; had I not for you in the bottom of my heart the tender feeling of a sister for a brother—I should say, 'Rise, count, and do not importune with love my ears, which hold it in horror.' But I do not say so, count, because I suffer in seeing you suffer. I say more: now that I know you I will take your hand and place it on my heart, and I will say to you willingly, ' See, my heart beats no more; live near me if you like, and assist day by day, if such be your pleasure, at this painful execution of a body which is being killed by the tortures of the soul.' But this sacrifice, which you would accept as a happiness, I am sure—"

" Oh, yes ! " cried Henri, eagerly.

" Well, this sacrifice I ought to forbid. This very day a change has taken place in my life. I have no longer the right to lean on any human arm—not even on the arm of that generous friend, that noble creature, who lies there, and for a time finds the happiness of forgetfulness. Alas ! poor Rémy," continued she, with the first note of sensibility that Henri had remarked in her voice, " your waking will also be sad. You do not know the progress of my thought; you cannot read in my eyes that you will soon be alone, and that alone I go to God."

" What do you mean, madame? Do you also wish to die? "

Rémy, awakened by the cry of the young count, began to listen.

" You saw me pray, did you not? " said Diane.

" Yes," answered Henri.

" This prayer was my adieu to earth. The joy that you remarked on my face—the joy that fills me even now—is the same you would see in me if the angel of death were to come and say to me, ' Rise, Diane, and follow me.' "

" Diane, Diane ! now I know your name—Diane, cherished name ! " murmured the young man.

" Oh, silence ! " said the young woman; " forget this name which escaped me. No living person has the right to pierce my heart by pronouncing it."

" Oh, madame, do not tell me you are going to die ! "

" I do not say that," she replied in her grave voice. " I say that I am about to leave this world of tears, of hatreds, of bad passions, of vile interests and desires. I say that I have nothing more to do among the beings whom God created my fellow-mortals. I have no more tears in my eyes, no more blood in my heart, no more thought in my mind—since the thought that filled it altogether is dead. I am a worthless offering—for in renouncing the world I sacrifice nothing, neither desires nor hopes; but such as I am I offer myself to my God, and he will accept me—he who has made me suffer so much, and yet kept me from sinking under it."

Rémy, who had heard this, rose slowly, and said, "You abandon me?"

"For God," said Diane, raising her thin white hand to heaven.

"It is true,' said Rémy, sadly; and seizing her hand he pressed it to his breast.

"Oh, what am I by these two hearts?" said Henri.

"You are," replied Diane, "the only human creature, except Rémy, on whom I have looked twice for years."

Henri knelt. "Thanks, madame," said he; "I bow to my destiny. You belong to God; I cannot be jealous of God."

As he rose, they heard the sound of trumpets on the plain, still covered with vapours which were clearing from moment to moment. The gendarmes seized their arms and were on horseback at once.

Henri listened. "Gentlemen," cried he, "those are the admiral's trumpets; I know them. Oh, God, may they announce my brother!"

"You see that you still wish for something," said Diane, "and still love some one. Why, then, should you choose despair, like those who desire nothing—like those who love no one?"

"A horse!" cried Henri. "Who will lend me a horse?"

"But the water is still all around us," said the ensign.

"But you see that the plain is practicable. They must be advancing, since we hear their trumpets."

"Mount to the top of the bank, Monsieur the Count. The sky is clear; perhaps you will see."

Henri climbed up. The trumpets continued to sound at intervals, but were seemingly stationary.

CHAPTER XIX

THE TWO BROTHERS

A QUARTER of an hour after, Henri returned; he had seen a considerable detachment of French troops intrenched on a hill at some distance. Excepting in a large ditch, which surrounded the place occupied by the gendarmes of Aunis, the water had begun to disappear from the plain—the natural slope of the ground in the immediate neighbourhood making the waters run towards the sea—and several points of earth, higher than the rest, began to reappear. The slimy mud brought by the rolling waters had covered the whole country; and it was a sad spectacle to see, as the wind cleared the mist, a number of horsemen stuck in the mud, and trying vainly to reach either of the hills. From the other hill, on which the flag of France waved, their cries of distress had been heard, and that was why the trumpets had sounded. The gendarmes now sounded their cornets, and were answered by the firing of muskets in joyful recognition.

About eleven o'clock the sun appeared over this scene of desolation, drying some parts of the plain, and rendering practicable a kind of road. Henri, who tried it first, found that it led by a *détour* from where they were to the opposite hill, and he believed that though his horse might sink to a certain extent, he would not sink altogether. He therefore determined to try it, and recommending Diane and Rémy to the care of the ensign, set off on his perilous way. At the same time that he started, they could see a cavalier leave the opposite hill, and, like Henri, try the road. All the soldiers seemed trying to stop him by their supplications. The two men pursued their way courageously, and soon perceived that their task was less difficult than had been feared. A small stream of water, escaped from a broken aqueduct, washed over the path, and little by little was clearing away the mud. The cavaliers were within two hundred feet of each other.

" France ! " cried the one who came from the opposite hill, at the same time raising his hat, which had a white plume in it.

" Oh, it is you ! " cried Henri, with a burst of joy.

" You, Henri ! you, my brother ! " cried the other.

And they set off as quickly as their horses could manage to go, and soon, among the frantic acclamations of the spectators on each side, embraced long and tenderly. Immediately, all—gendarmes and light-horse, Huguenots and Catholics—rushed along the road, pioneered by the two brothers. Soon the two camps were joined, and there, where they had thought to find death, nearly three thousand Frenchmen cried, " Thank God ! " and " Vive la France ! "

" Gentlemen," said a Huguenot officer, " it is ' Long live the admiral ! ' you should cry, for it is to M. de Joyeuse alone that we now owe the happiness of embracing our countrymen."

Immense acclamations followed this speech. The two brothers talked for some time, and then Joyeuse asked Henri if he had heard news of the duke.

" It appears he is dead," replied Henri.

" Is that certain ? "

" The gendarmes saw his horse drowned, and a rider, whose head was under water, dragged by the stirrup."

" It has been a sad day for France," said Joyeuse. Then, turning to his men, he said, " Come, gentlemen, let us not lose time. Once the waters have retired, we shall probably be attacked. Let us intrench ourselves until the arrival of news and food."

" But, monseigneur," said a voice, " the horses have eaten nothing since four o'clock yesterday, and are dying with hunger."

" We have corn in our encampment," said the ensign, " but what shall we do for the men? "

" Oh! " said Joyeuse, " if there be corn, that is all I ask; the men must live like the horses."

" Brother," said Henri, " I want a little conversation with you."

" Go back to your place; choose a lodging for me, and wait for me there."

Henri went back.

" We are now in the midst of an army," said he to Rémy; " hide yourselves in the lodging I will show you, and do not let madame be seen by any one."

Rémy installed himself with Diane in the lodging pointed out. About two o'clock the Duc de Joyeuse entered, with his trumpets blowing, lodged his troops, and gave strict injunctions to prevent disorder. He distributed barley to the men, and hay to the horses, and to the wounded some wine and beer which had been found in the cellars, and himself, in sight of all, dined on a piece of black bread and a glass of water. Everywhere he was received as a deliverer with cries of gratitude.

" Now," said he to his brother, when they were alone, " let the Flemings come, and I will beat them, and even, if this goes on, eat them; for in truth I am very hungry, and this is miserable stuff," added he, throwing into a corner the piece of bread which in public he had been eating so enthusiastically. " But now, Henri, tell me how it happens that I find you in Flanders when I thought you in Paris."

" My brother," said Henri, " life became insupportable to me at Paris, and I set out to join you in Flanders."

" All from love? " asked Joyeuse.

" No, from despair. Now, Anne, I am no longer in love; my passion is sadness."

" My brother, permit me to tell you that you have chosen a miserable woman. Virtue that cares not for the sufferings of others is barbarous—is a want of Christian charity."

" Oh, my brother, do not calumniate virtue."

" I do not calumniate virtue, Henri; I accuse vice, that is all.

I repeat that this is a miserable woman, and not worth all the torments she makes you suffer. Oh, *mon Dieu !* in such a case you should use all your strength and all your power, Henri. In your place, I should have taken her house by assault, and then herself; and when she was conquered, and came to throw her arms round my neck and say, ' Henri, I adore you,' I should have repulsed her, and said, ' You do well, madame; it is your turn. I have suffered enough for you—to suffer also.' "

Henri seized his brother's hand. " You do not mean a word of what you say," said he.

" Yes, on my honour."

" You, so good, so generous ! "

" Generosity with heartless people is folly."

" Oh, Joyeuse, Joyeuse, you do not know this woman ! "

" No, I do not wish to know her."

" Why not ? "

" Because she would make me commit what others would call a crime, but which I should call an act of justice."

" Oh, my good brother, how happy you are not to be in love ! But, if you please, let us leave my foolish love, and talk of other things."

" So be it; I do not like to talk of your folly."

" You see we want provisions."

" Yes; and I have thought of a way to obtain them."

" What is it ? "

" I cannot leave here until I have certain news of the army— for the position is good, and I could defend myself against five times our number; but I can send out a body of scouts, and they will bring news, and provisions also, for Flanders is a fine country."

" Not very, brother."

" I speak of it as God made it, and not men, who eternally spoil the works of God. Do you know, Henri, what folly this prince has committed—what this unlucky François has lost through pride and precipitation? His soul is gone to God, so let us be silent; but in truth he might have acquired immortal glory and one of the most beautiful kingdoms in Europe, while he has, on the contrary, aided no one but William of Orange. But do you know, Henri, that the Antwerpians fought well ? "

" And you also, so they say, brother."

" Yes, it was one of my good days; and besides there was something that excited me."

" What was it ? "

" I met on the field of battle a sword that I knew."

" French? "

" Yes, French."

" In the ranks of the Flemings? "

" At their head, Henri; this is a secret which forms a sequel to Salcède's business."

" However, dear brother, here you are safe and sound, to my great joy. But I, who have done nothing yet, must do something also."

" And what will you do? "

" Give me the command of your scouts, I beg."

" No, it is too dangerous, Henri; I would not say so before strangers, but I do not wish you to die an obscure death. The scouts may meet with some of those rascally Flemings who fight with flails and scythes; you kill a thousand of them, and the last cuts you in two or disfigures you. No, Henri; if you will die, let it be a more glorious death than that."

" My brother, grant me what I ask, I beg; I promise you to be prudent, and to return here."

" Well, I understand."

" What? "

" You wish to try if the fame of a brave action will not soften the heart of this ferocious tigress. Confess that that is what makes you insist on it."

" I will confess it if you wish, brother."

" Well, you are right. Women who resist a great love sometimes yield to a little noise."

" I do not hope that."

" If you do it without this hope, you are mad. Henri, seek no more reasons for this woman's refusal than that she has neither eyes nor heart."

" You give me the command, brother? "

" I must, if you will have it so."

" Can I go to-night? "

" It is absolutely necessary, Henri; you understand that we cannot wait long."

" How many men do you give me? "

" A hundred; not more. I cannot weaken my force here, you know, Henri."

" Fewer, if you like, brother."

" No, I would wish to give you double. Only promise me, on your honour, that if you meet with more than three hundred men, you will retreat instead of getting killed."

" My brother," said Henri, smiling, " you sell your glory very dear."

"Then I will neither sell nor give it to you; and another officer shall command."

"My brother, give your orders and I will execute them."

"You will only engage with equal, double, or triple forces—not with more?"

"I swear it."

"Very well; now, what men would you like to take?"

"Let me take one hundred of the gendarmes of Aunis; I have plenty of friends there, and can choose whom I like."

"That will do."

"When shall I set out?"

"At once. Take one day's rations for the men, and two for the horses. Remember, I want speedy and certain news."

"I go, brother; are there any other orders?"

"Do not spread the news of the duke's death; let it be believed he is here. Exaggerate my strength, and if you find the duke's body, although he was a bad man and a poor general, yet as he belonged to the royal House of France, have it put in an oak coffin and brought back by your men, that he may be buried at St. Denis."

"Good, brother; now is this all?"

"All! but promise me once more, Henri, you are not deceiving me—you will not seek death?"

"No, brother. I had that thought when I came to join you; but I have it no longer."

"And when did it leave you?"

"Three hours ago."

"On what occasion?"

"Excuse me, brother."

"Of course, Henri; your secrets are your own."

"Oh, how good you are, brother!"

And the young men, once more embracing each other, separated, not without turning to salute each other with smiles and gestures.

CHAPTER XX

THE EXPEDITION

HENRI, full of joy, hastened to Diane and Rémy. "Get ready; in a quarter of an hour we set out," said he. "You will find two horses saddled at the door of the little wooden staircase leading to this corridor; join my suite and say nothing."

Then, going out on the balcony, he cried, "Trumpet of the gendarmes, sound the call!"

The call was quickly heard; and all the gendarmes ranged themselves round the house.

"Gendarmes," said Henri, "my brother has given me, for the time, the command of your company, and has ordered me to set out to-night to obtain provisions and information as to the movements of the enemy; and one hundred of you are to accompany me. The mission is dangerous, but necessary for the safety of all. Who are willing to go?"

The whole three hundred offered themselves.

"Gentlemen," said Henri, "I thank you all. You have rightly been called the example to the army, but I can take only one hundred; and as I do not wish to choose, let chance decide. Monsieur," continued he, to the ensign, "draw lots, if you please."

While this procedure was going on, Joyeuse gave his last instructions to his brother. "Listen, Henri," said he; "the country is drying, and there is a communication between Conticq and Rupelmonde; you will march between a river and a stream —the Scheldt and the Rupel. I trust that there will be no necessity for you to go as far as Rupelmonde to find provisions. My men took three peasants prisoners; I give one of them to you for a guide. But no false pity; at the least appearance of treason shoot him without mercy."

He then tenderly embraced his brother, and gave the order for departure. The one hundred men drawn by lots were ready, and the guide was placed between two, with pistols in their hands, while Rémy and his companion mingled with the others. Henri gave no directions about them, thinking that curiosity was already quite sufficiently aroused about them, without augmenting it by precautions more dangerous than salutary. He himself did not stay by them, but rode at the head of his company. Their march was slow, for often the ground nearly gave way under them, and they sank in the mud. Sometimes figures were seen flying over the plain; they were peasants who had been rather too quick in returning to their homes, and who fled at the sight of the enemy. Sometimes, however, they were unfortunate Frenchmen, half dead with cold and hunger, who, in their uncertainty whether they were to meet with friends or enemies, preferred to wait for daylight to continue their painful journey.

They made two leagues in three hours, which brought the adventurous band to the banks of the Rupel, along which a stony road ran. But here danger succeeded to difficulty; two

or three horses lost their footing on the slimy stones, and rolled
with their riders into the still rapid waters of the river. More
than once also, from some boat on the opposite bank, shots were
fired, and one man was killed at Diane's side. She manifested
regret for the man, but no fear for herself. Henri in these
different circumstances showed himself to be a worthy captain
and true friend; he rode first, telling all the men to follow in
his steps, trusting less to his own sagacity than to that of the
horse his brother had given him. Three leagues from Rupelmonde the gendarmes came upon six French soldiers sitting
by a turf-fire; the unfortunates were cooking some horse-flesh—
the only food they had had for two days. The approach of the
gendarmes caused great trouble among the guests at this sad
feast. Two or three rose to fly; but the others stopped them,
saying, " If they are enemies, they can but kill us, and all will
be over."

" France! France! " cried Henri.

On recognising their countrymen, the soldiers ran to them,
and received from them cloaks and something to drink; they
were also allowed to mount behind the valets, and in this manner
they accompanied the detachment. Half a league farther on
they met four men of the fourth light-horse, with, however,
only one horse; they were also welcomed.

At last they arrived on the banks of the Scheldt. The night
was dark; and the gendarmes found two men who were trying,
in bad Flemish, to obtain from a boatman a passage to the other
side, which he refused. The ensign, who understood Dutch,
advanced softly, and heard the boatman say, " You are French,
and shall die here; you shall not cross."

" It is you who shall die, if you do not take us over at once,"
replied one of the men, drawing his dagger.

" Keep firm, monsieur," cried the ensign, " we will come to
your aid."

But as the two men turned at these words, the boatman
loosened the rope, and pushed rapidly from the shore. One of
the gendarmes, however, knowing how useful this boat would
be, went into the stream on his horse and fired at the boatman,
who fell. The boat was left without a guide, but the current
brought it back again towards the bank. The two strangers
seized it at once and got in. That haste to isolate themselves
astonished the ensign. " Gentlemen," said he, " who are you,
if you please? "

" Gentlemen, we are marine officers; and you are gendarmes
of Aunis, apparently."

" Yes, gentlemen, and very happy to have served you; will you not accompany us? "

" Willingly."

" Get into the waggons, then, if you are too tired to follow us on foot."

" May we ask where you are going? " said one.

" Monsieur, our orders are to push on to Rupelmonde."

" Take care," he replied; " we did not cross the river sooner, because this morning a detachment of Spaniards passed, coming from Antwerp. At sunset we thought we might venture, for two men inspire no disquietude; but you, a whole troop—"

" It is true; I will call our chief."

Henri approached, and asked what was the matter.

" These gentlemen met this morning a detachment of Spaniards following the same road as ourselves."

" How many were they? "

" About fifty."

" And does that stop you? "

" No; but I think it would be well to secure the boat, in case we should wish to cross the river. It will hold twenty men, and in five trips, leading the horses by the bridle, the operation would be completed."

" Good! let us keep the boat. There should be some houses at the junction of the Scheldt and Rupel? "

" There is a village," said a voice.

" We will go there. The angle formed by the junction of two rivers is a good position. Gendarmes, forward! Let two men descend the stream with the boat while we go along the bank."

" We will bring the boat if you will let us," said one of the two officers.

" If you wish it, gentlemen; but do not lose sight of us, and come to us in the village."

" But if we abandon the boat some one will take it? "

" You will find ten men waiting, to whom you can deliver it."

" It is well," said one, and they pushed off from the shore.

" It is singular," said Henri; " but I fancy I know that voice."

An hour after, they arrived at the village, which was occupied by the fifty Spaniards; but they, taken by surprise, made little resistance. Henri had them disarmed and shut up in the strongest house in the village, and left ten men to guard them. Ten more were sent to guard the boat, and ten others placed as sentinels, with the promise of being relieved in an hour. Henri then decided that they should take supper by twenties, in the house opposite to that in which the Spanish prisoners were confined. The supper for the first fifty or sixty was ready. It was that of the party they had captured. Henri chose a separate room for Rémy and Diane. He then placed the ensign at table with seventeen men, telling him to invite the two naval officers when they arrived. He next went out to look for accommodation for the rest of the men; and when he returned in half an hour he found them waiting supper for him. Some had fallen asleep on their chairs; but his entrance roused them. The table, covered with cheese, pork, and bread, with a pot of beer by each man, would have had a tempting appearance even to men who had not been in want for twenty-four hours. Henri sat down and told them to begin. " By the way," said he, " have the strangers arrived? "

" Yes; there they are at the end of the table."

Henri looked and saw them in the darkest part of the room.

" Gentlemen," said he, " you are badly placed, and I think you are not eating."

" Thanks, Monsieur the Count," said one, " we are very tired, and more in need of rest than food. We told your officers so, but they insisted, saying that it was your orders that we should sup with you. We feel the honour; but if, nevertheless, instead of keeping us longer, you would give us a room—"

" Is that also the wish of your companion? " said Henri; and he looked at this companion, whose hat was pushed down over his eyes, and who had not yet spoken.

" Yes, Count," replied he, in a scarcely audible voice.

Henri rose, walked straight to the end of the table, while every one watched his movements and astonished look. " Monsieur," said he, to the one who had spoken first, " do me a favour."

" What is it, Monsieur the Count? "

" Tell me if you are not Aurilly's brother, or Aurilly himself? "

" Aurilly! " cried all.

" And let your companion," continued Henri, " raise his hat a little and let me see his face, or else I shall call him monseigneur, and bow before him." And as he spoke, he bowed respectfully, hat in hand. The officer took off his hat.

" Monseigneur le Duc d'Anjou! " cried all. " The duke, living! "

" Faith! gentlemen," replied he, " since you will recognise your conquered and fugitive prince, I shall not deny myself to you any longer. I am the Duc d'Anjou."

" Vive monseigneur! " cried all.

CHAPTER XXI

PAULUS EMILIUS

" Oh, silence, gentlemen! " said the prince; " do not be more content than I am at my good fortune. I am enchanted not to be dead, you may well believe; and yet if you had not recognised me, I should not have been the first to boast of being alive."

" What, monseigneur! " cried Henri, " you recognised me, you found yourself among a troop of Frenchmen, and would have left us to mourn your loss, without undeceiving us? "

" Gentlemen, besides a number of reasons which made me wish to preserve my incognito, I confess that I should not have been sorry, since I was believed to be dead, to hear what funeral oration would have been pronounced over me."

" Monseigneur! "

" Yes; I am like Alexander of Macedon. I make war like an artist, and have as much self-love; and I believe I have committed a fault."

" Monseigneur," said Henri, lowering his eyes, " do not say such things."

" Why not? The pope only is infallible, and since Boniface VIII., even that has been disputed."

" See to what you exposed us, monseigneur, if any of us had given his opinion on this expedition, and it had been blamed."

" Well, why not? Do you think I have not blamed myself— not for having given battle, but for having lost it? "

" Monseigneur, this goodness frightens me; and will your highness permit me to say that this gaiety is not natural? I trust your Highness is not suffering."

A terrible cloud passed over the prince's face, making it as black as night. " No," said he, " I was never better, thank God, than now, and I am glad to be among you all."

The officers bowed.

" How many men have you, Bouchage? " asked he.

" One hundred, monseigneur."

" Ah! a hundred out of ten thousand; that is like the defeat at Cannæ. Gentlemen, they will send a bushel of your rings to Antwerp; but I doubt if the Flemish beauties could wear them, unless they had their fingers pared by their husbands' knives, which, I must say, cut well."

" Monseigneur," replied Henri, " if our battle was like the

battle of Cannæ, at least we are more lucky than the Romans, for we have preserved our Paulus Emilius!"

"On my life, gentlemen, the Paulus Emilius of Antwerp was Joyeuse; and doubtless, to preserve the resemblance with his heroic model to the end, your brother is dead, is he not, Bouchage?"

Henri felt wounded at this cold question.

"No, monseigneur, he lives," replied he.

"Ah, so much the better!" said the duke, with his icy smile. "What! our brave Joyeuse lives! Where is he, that I may embrace him?"

"He is not here, monseigneur."

"Ah! wounded?"

"No, monseigneur; he is safe and sound."

"But a fugitive like me, wandering, famished, and ashamed. Alas! the proverb is right: 'For glory, the sword; after the sword, blood; after blood, tears.'"

"Monseigneur, I am happy to tell your highness that my brother has been fortunate enough to save three thousand men, with whom he occupies a large village about seven leagues from here, and I am acting as scout for him."

The duke grew pale. "Three thousand men! he has saved three thousand men! He is a Xenophon, and it is very fortunate for me that my brother sent him to me. It is not the Valois who can take for their motto 'Hilariter.'"

"Oh, monseigneur!" said Henri, sadly, seeing that this gaiety hid a sombre and painful jealousy.

"It is true, is it not, Aurilly?" continued the duke. "I return to France like François after the battle of Pavia. 'All is lost but honour.' Ah, ah! I have discovered a motto for the House of France."

A sad silence received these levities, more terrible than sobs.

"Monseigneur," said Henri, "tell me how the tutelary genius of France saved your highness."

"Oh, dear count, the tutelary genius of France was at that moment occupied with something doubtless of more importance, and I had to save myself."

"And how, monseigneur?"

"By my legs."

No smile welcomed this pleasantry, which the duke would certainly have punished with death if uttered by another.

"Yes, yes," he continued; "how we ran! Did we not, my brave Aurilly?"

"Every one," said Henri, "knows the calm bravery and

military genius of your highness, and we beg you not to distress us by attributing to yourself faults which you have not. The best general is not invincible, and Hannibal himself was conquered at Zama."

"Yes, but Hannibal had won the battles of Trebia, Thrasymene, and Cannæ, while I have only won that of Cateau-Cambrésis; it is not enough to sustain the comparison."

"But monseigneur jests when he says he ran away."

"No, I do not. *Pardieu!* do you see anything there to jest about, Bouchage?"

"Could any one have done otherwise?" said Aurilly.

"Hold your tongue, Aurilly! ask the shade of Saint-Aignan if it was necessary to run away."

Aurilly hung his head.

"Ah! you others do not know the history of Saint-Aignan. I will tell it to you. Imagine, then, that when the battle was declared to be lost, he assembled five hundred horse, and instead of flying like the rest, came to me and said, 'We must attack them, monseigneur.' 'What! attack?' said I. 'You are mad, Saint-Aignan; they are a hundred to one.' 'Were they a thousand to one, I would attack them,' replied he, with a hideous grimace. 'Attack if you please,' said I; 'I do not.' 'Give me your horse, and take mine,' said he. 'Mine is fresh; yours is not. And as I do not mean to fly, any horse is good enough for me.' And then he took my white horse and gave me his black one, saying, 'Prince, that horse will go twenty leagues in four hours if you like.' Then, turning to his men, he cried, 'Come, gentlemen, follow me, all those who will not turn their backs;' and he rode towards the enemy with a second grimace, more frightful than the first. He thought he should have met men, but he met water instead, and Saint-Aignan and his paladins were lost. Had he listened to me, instead of performing that act of useless foolhardiness, we should have had him at this table, and he would not have been making, as he probably now is, a third grimace still uglier than the other two."

A thrill of horror ran through the assembly.

"This wretch has no heart," thought Henri. "Oh, why do his misfortune and his birth protect him from the words I long to say to him?"

"Gentlemen," said Aurilly, in a low voice—for he felt the effect these words had produced—"you see how monseigneur is affected; do not heed what he says, for since his misfortune I think he really has moments of delirium."

"And so," continued the duke, emptying his glass, "that is how Saint-Aignan is dead and I am alive. However, in dying, he did me a last service—for it was believed, as he rode my horse, that it was I who was dead; and this belief spread not only among the French, but among the Flemings, who consequently ceased their pursuit. But reassure yourselves, gentlemen, we shall have our revenge, and I am mentally organising the most formidable army that ever existed."

"Meanwhile, monseigneur," said Henri, "will your highness take the command of my men? It is not fit that I should continue to command in presence of a son of France."

"So be it; and, first, I order every one to sup, particularly you, Bouchage—you have eaten nothing."

"Monseigneur, I am not hungry."

"In that case, return to visit the posts. Tell the chiefs that I live, but beg them not to rejoice too openly until we gain a better citadel, or rejoin the army of our invincible Joyeuse; for I confess I do not wish to be taken now, after having escaped from fire and water."

"Monseigneur, you shall be strictly obeyed, and no one shall know excepting ourselves that we have the honour of your company among us."

"And these gentlemen will keep the secret?" said the duke, looking round.

All bowed, and Bouchage went out.

As we have seen, it required but a moment for this vagabond, this fugitive, this conquered runaway, to become again proud, careless, and imperious. To command a hundred men or a hundred thousand men, was still to command.

While Bouchage executed his orders with the best grace he could, François asked questions. He was astonished that a man of the rank of Bouchage had consented to take the command of this handful of men, and of such a perilous expedition. The duke was always suspicious, and asked questions therefore, learning that the admiral had yielded only to his brother's earnest request. It was the ensign who gave this information—he who had been superseded in his command by Henri himself, as Henri had been by the duke.

The prince fancied he detected a slight irritation in this man's mind against Bouchage; therefore he continued to interrogate him. "But," said he, "what was the count's reason for soliciting so earnestly such a poor command?"

"First, zeal for the service, no doubt."

"First! what else?"

" Ah, monseigneur, I do not know."

" You deceive me; you do know."

" Monseigneur, I can give only, even to your highness, public reasons."

" You see," said the duke, turning to the others, " I was quite right to hide myself, gentlemen, since there are in my army secrets from which I am excluded."

" Ah, monseigneur," said the ensign, " you misunderstand me; there are no secrets but those which concern M. du Bouchage. Might it not be, for example, that while serving the general interests, he might have wished to render a service to some friend or relative by escorting him? "

" Who here is a friend or relative of the count? Tell me, that I may embrace him."

" Monseigneur," said Aurilly, mixing in the conversation, " I have discovered a part of the secret. This relative whom M. du Bouchage wished to escort is—a lady."

" Ah, ah! why did they not tell me so frankly? That dear Henri—it is quite natural. Let us shut our eyes to the relative, and speak of her no more."

" You had better not, monseigneur, for there seems a great mystery."

" How so? "

" Yes, the lady, like the celebrated Bradamante, about whom I have so often sung to your highness, disguises herself in the dress of a man."

" Oh, monseigneur," cried the ensign, " M. du Bouchage seems to me to have a great respect for this lady, and probably would be very angry at any indiscretion."

" Doubtless, monsieur; we will be as mute as sepulchres— as mute as poor Saint-Aignan; only, if we see the lady, we will try not to make grimaces at her. Where is this lady, Aurilly? "

" Upstairs."

" Upstairs! what! in this house? "

" Yes, monseigneur; but hush! here is M. du Bouchage."

" Hush! " said the prince, laughing.

CHAPTER XXII

THE DUC D'ANJOU SEARCHES HIS MEMORY

HENRI, as he entered, could hear the ill-omened laugh of the prince, but he had not lived enough with him to know the danger that always lurked in his laugh. He could see also, by the uneasiness manifest on the faces of some, that the duke had entered on a hostile conversation in his absence, which had been interrupted by his return. But he could not suspect the subject of the conversation, and no one dared to tell him in the duke's presence. Besides, the duke, who had already formed his plan, kept Henri near him until all the other officers were gone. He then changed the distribution of the posts. Henri had established his quarters in that house, and had intended to send the ensign to a post near the river; but the duke now took Henri's place, and sent him where the ensign was to have been. Henri was not astonished, for the river was an important point. Before going, however, he wished to speak to the ensign, and recommend to his care the two persons under his protection, and whom he was forced for the time to abandon. But at the first word that Henri began to speak to him the duke interposed. "Secrets?" said he, with his peculiar smile.

The ensign had understood, when too late, the fault he had committed. "No, monseigneur," he replied, "Monsieur the Count was only asking me how much powder we had left fit to use."

The answer had two aims—the first, to turn away the duke's suspicions, if he had any; and the second, to let Bouchage know that he could count on a friend in him.

"Ah!" said the duke, forced to seem to believe what he was told.

And as he turned to the door, the ensign whispered to Henri, "The prince knows you are escorting some one."

Henri started, but it was too late. The duke remarked the start, and as if to assure himself that his orders were executed, he proposed to Henri to accompany him to his post—a proposition to which Henri was obliged to consent. He wished to warn Rémy to be on his guard, but it was impossible; all he could do was to say to the ensign, "Watch well over the powder; watch it as I would myself, will you not?"

"Yes, Monsieur the Count," replied the young man.

On the way the duke said to Bouchage, " Where is this powder that you speak of? "

" In the house we have just left, your highness."

" Oh, be easy, then, Bouchage; I know too well the importance of such an article in our situation, to neglect it. I will watch over it myself."

They said no more until they arrived. The duke, after giving Henri many charges not to leave his post, returned. He found Aurilly wrapped in an officer's cloak, sleeping on one of the seats in the dining-room. The duke woke him. " Come," said he.

" Yes, monseigneur."

" Do you know what I mean? "

" Yes; the unknown lady—the relative of M. du Bouchage."

" Good; I see that the faro of Brussels and the beer of Louvain have not clouded your intellect."

" Oh, no, monseigneur, I am more ingenious than ever."

" Then call up all your imagination, and guess."

" Well, I guess that your highness is curious."

" Ah, *parbleu!* I always am; but what is it that piques my curiosity just now? "

" You wish to know who is the brave creature who has followed the MM. de Joyeuse through fire and water? "

" You have just hit it, ' per mille pericula Martis!' as Margot would say. By the way, have you written to her, Aurilly? "

" To whom, monseigneur? "

" To my sister Margot."

" Was I to write to her? "

" Certainly."

" About what? "

" To tell her that we are beaten, ruined, and that she must look out for herself, since Spain, disembarrassed of me in the north, will fall on her in the south."

" Ah, true."

" You have not written? "

" No, monseigneur."

" You slept? "

" Yes, I confess it; but even if I had thought of it, with what could I have written? I have here neither pen, paper, nor ink."

" Well, seek. ' Quære et invenies,' as it is written."

" How in the devil am I to find all that in the hut of a peasant, who probably did not know how to write? "

" Seek, stupid! if you do not find that, you will find—"

" What? "

" Something else."

"Oh, fool that I was!" cried Aurilly. "Your highness is right—I am stupid; but I am very sleepy, you see."

"Well, keep awake for a little while, and since you have not written, I will write; only go and seek what is necessary. Go, Aurilly, and do not come back till you have found it; I will remain here."

"I go, monseigneur."

"And if in your researches you discover that the house is picturesque—you know how I admire Flemish interiors, Aurilly?"

"Yes, monseigneur."

"Well, call me."

"Immediately, monseigneur; be easy."

Aurilly rose, and with a step light as that of a bird, went up the staircase. In five minutes he returned to his master.

"Well?" asked the latter.

"Well, monseigneur, if I may believe appearances, the house is devilishly picturesque."

"How so?"

"*Peste!* monseigneur, because one cannot get in to look."

"What do you mean?"

"I mean that it is guarded by a dragon."

"What foolish joke is this?"

"Oh, monseigneur, it is unfortunately not a foolish joke, but a sad truth. The treasure is on the first floor, in a room in which I can see light under the door."

"Well?"

"Well! before this door lies a man wrapped in a grey cloak."

"Oh, oh! M. du Bouchage puts a gendarme at the door of his mistress?"

"It is not a gendarme, monseigneur, but some attendant of the lady or of the count."

"What kind of a man?"

"Monseigneur, it was impossible to see his face; but I could distinctly see a large Flemish knife in his belt, and his hand on it."

"It is amusing; go and waken the fellow."

"Oh, no, monseigneur!"

"Why not?"

"Why, without considering what the Flemish knife might do to me, I am not going to amuse myself with making mortal enemies of MM. de Joyeuse, who stand so well at court. If you had been king of this country, it might have passed; but now you must be gracious, above all, with those who saved you, and

the Joyeuses have saved you.   They will say so, whether you do
or not."

" You are right, Aurilly, and yet—and yet—"

" I understand.   Your highness has not seen a woman's face
for fifteen mortal days.   I do not speak of the kind of animals
who live here; they are males and females, but do not deserve
to be called men and women."

" I wish to see this mistress of Bouchage; I wish to see her!
Do you understand, Aurilly? "

" Well, monseigneur, you may see her—but not through the
door."

" So be it; then I will see her through the window."

" Ah, that is a good idea! and I will go and look for a ladder
for you."

Aurilly glided into the courtyard, and under a shed found
what he wanted.   He manœuvred it among horses and men so
skilfully as to wake no one, and placed it in the street against
the outer wall.   It was necessary to be a prince, and sovereignly
disdainful of vulgar scruples, to dare in the presence of the
sentinel, who walked up and down before the door, to accomplish
an action so audaciously insulting to Bouchage.   Aurilly felt
this, and pointed out the sentinel, who, now observing, called
out " Qui vive? "

François shrugged his shoulders and walked up to him.   " My
friend," said he, " this place is the most elevated spot in the
village, is it not? "

" Yes, monseigneur," said the man, recognising him; " and
were it not for those lime-trees, we could see over a great part of
the country."

" I thought so; and therefore I have brought a ladder," said
the duke.   " Go up, Aurilly, or rather, let me go up; I will see
for myself."

" Where shall I place it? " said the hypocritical follower.

" Oh, anywhere; against that wall, for instance."

The sentinel walked off, and the duke mounted the ladder,
Aurilly standing at the foot.

The room in which Henri had placed Diane was matted, and
had a large oaken bed with serge curtains, a table, and a few
chairs.   Diane, whose heart seemed relieved from an enormous
weight since she had heard the false news of the duke's death,
had, almost for the first time since the hour in which she was
informed of her father's death, eaten something more substantial
than bread, and drunk a little wine.   After this she grew sleepy,
and Rémy had left her, and was sleeping outside her door, not

because he had the least apprehension, but because such had been his habit ever since they had left Paris.

Diane herself slept with her elbow on the table and her head leaning on her hand. A little lamp burned on the table and illumined that interior which, on the first view, seemed so calm and peaceful, and in which a tempest had been stilled which was about to be aroused again. In the glass sparkled the Rhenish wine scarcely touched by Diane. She, with her eyes closed, her eyelids veined with azure, her mouth slightly opened, her hair thrown back, looked like a sublime vision to the eyes that were violating the sanctity of her retreat. The duke, on perceiving her, could hardly repress his admiration, and leaned over to examine every detail of her ideal beauty. But all at once he frowned, came down two or three steps with a kind of nervous precipitation, and leaning back against the wall, crossed his arms and appeared to reflect. Aurilly watched him as he stood there, with a dreamy air, like a man trying to recall something forgotten. After a few minutes he remounted and looked in again, but apparently without succeeding in the discovery he sought, for the same shadow rested on his brow, and the same uncertainty remained in his glance. While he was in the midst of his researches, Aurilly called out eagerly from the foot of the ladder, "Quick! quick! monseigneur, come down! I hear steps."

The duke came down, but slowly, still searching his memory.

"It was time," said Aurilly.

"Whence comes the sound?"

"From there," said Aurilly, pointing to a dark street. "But the sound has ceased; it is some spy watching us."

"Remove the ladder."

Aurilly obeyed; and the prince seated himself on a stone bench near the door of the house. However, no one appeared, and they heard no more noise.

"Well, monseigneur, is she beautiful?" said Aurilly, on his return.

"Very beautiful," said the prince, abstractedly.

"What makes you sad, then? Did she see you?"

"No, she was asleep."

"Then what is the matter?"

"Aurilly, it is strange, but I have seen that woman somewhere."

"You recognise her, then?"

"No, I could not think of her name; but her face gave me a fearful shock. I cannot tell how it is; but I believe I did wrong to look."

"However, just on account of the impression she has made on you, we must find out who she is."

"Certainly we must."

"Seek well in your memory, monseigneur; is it at court you have seen her?"

"No, I think not."

"In France, Navarre, Flanders?"

"No."

"A Spaniard perhaps?"

"I do not think so."

"An English lady, one of Queen Elizabeth's?"

"No, she should be connected with my life in a more intimate manner; I think that she appeared to me in some terrible scene."

"Then you would have recognised her at once; you have not seen many such scenes."

"Do you think so?" said the duke, with a gloomy smile. "Now," continued he, "that I am sufficiently master of myself to analyse my sensations, I feel that this woman is beautiful, but with the beauty of death—beautiful as a shade, as a figure in a dream; and I have had two or three frightful dreams in my life, which left me cold at the heart. Well, now I am sure that it was in one of those dreams that I saw that woman."

"Your highness is not generally so susceptible; if I did not feel the weight of watching eyes from yonder street, I would mount in my turn and look."

"Faith! you are right, Aurilly. What does it matter whether we are watched or not? Get the ladder; place it, and go up and look."

Aurilly had already taken some steps forward to obey his master, when a hasty step was heard, and Henri's voice, crying, "Alarm, monseigneur! alarm!"

"You here?" said the duke, while Aurilly bounded back to his side; "you here, count? On what pretext have you left your post?"

"Monseigneur," replied Henri, firmly, "your highness can punish me if you think proper; meanwhile, my duty was to come here, and I came."

The duke glanced towards the window. "Your duty, Count? Explain that to me," said he.

"Monseigneur, horsemen have been seen on the Spanish side of the river, and we do not know whether they are friends or enemies."

"Numerous?" asked the duke, anxiously.

" Very numerous, monseigneur."

" Well, count, no false bravery; you have done well to
return. Awake the gendarmes and let us decamp; it will be
the most prudent plan."

" Doubtless, monseigneur; but it will be necessary, I think,
to warn my brother."

" Two men will do."

" Then I will go with a gendarme."

" No, no, Bouchage; you must come with us. *Peste !* it is
not at such a moment that I can part with a defender like you."

" When does your highness set out? " said Henri, bowing.

" At once, count."

" Holloa, some one! " cried Henri.

The young ensign came out immediately from the dark street.
Henri gave his orders, and soon the place was filled with
gendarmes preparing for departure. Among them the duke
talked with his officers. " Gentlemen," said he, " the Prince
of Orange is pursuing me, it seems; but it is not proper that a
son of France should be taken prisoner. Let us, therefore,
yield to numbers, and fall back upon Brussels. I shall be sure
of life and liberty while I remain among you."

Then, turning to Aurilly, " You remain," said he. " This
woman cannot follow us. Joyeuse will not dare to bring her
with him in my presence. Besides, we are not going to a ball,
and the race we shall run would fatigue a lady."

" Where are you going, monseigneur? "

" To France; I think my business is over, here."

" But to what part of France? Does monseigneur think it
prudent to return to court? "

" No; I shall stop at one of my châteaux—Château-Thierry,
for example."

" Has your highness decided on that? "

" Yes; Château-Thierry suits me in all respects; it is a good
distance from Paris, about twenty-eight leagues, and I can
watch from there MM. de Guise, who are half the year at
Soissons. So bring the beautiful unknown to Château-Thierry."

" But, monsieur, perhaps she will not be brought."

" Nonsense; since Bouchage accompanies me, and she follows
him, it will be quite natural."

" But she may wish to go somewhere else, if she sees that
I wish to bring her to you."

" I repeat that it is not to me that you are to bring her, but
to the count. Really, one would think it was the first time you
had aided me in such circumstances. Have you money? "

" I have the two *rouleaux* of gold that you gave me when you left camp."

" Well, by any and every method, bring me the lady to Château-Therry; perhaps when I see her nearer I shall recognise her."

" And the man also? "

" Yes, if he is not troublesome."

" But if he is? "

" Do with him what you would do with a stone which is in your way—throw him into a ditch."

" Good, monseigneur."

While the two conspirators formed their plans, Henri went up and woke Remy. Rémy knocked at the door in a peculiar manner, and it was almost immediately opened by Diane. Behind Rémy she perceived Henri.

" Good-evening, monsieur," said she, with a smile which had long been foreign to her face.

" Oh, pardon me, madame," said Henri, " for intruding on you; but I come to make my adieux."

" Your adieux, count? You are going? "

" To France, madame."

" And you leave us? "

" I am forced to do so; my duty is to obey the prince."

" The prince! is there a prince here? " asked Rémy.

" Yes, M. le Duc d'Anjou, who was believed dead, and who has been miraculously saved, has joined us."

Diane uttered a terrible cry, and Rémy turned as pale as though he had been suddenly struck with death.

" Repeat to me," stammered Diane, " that the Duc d'Anjou is living; that the Duc d'Anjou is here."

" Had he not been here, madame, and ordered me to follow him, I should have accompanied you to the convent into which you tell me you are about to retire."

" Yes, yes," said Rémy; " the convent; " and he put his finger on his lip.

" I would have accompanied you the more willingly, madame," said Henri, " because I fear that you may be annoyed by the prince's people."

" How so? "

" Yes; I believe that he knows there is a lady here; and he thinks, doubtless, that she is a friend of mine."

" And what makes you think so? "

" Our young ensign saw him place a ladder against this window, and look in."

"Oh!" cried Diane; "*mon Dieu ! mon Dieu !*"

"Reassure yourself, madame; he heard him say that he did not know you. Besides, the duke is going to set off at once; in a quarter of an hour you will be alone and free. Permit me to salute you with respect, and to tell you once more that till my last sigh my heart will beat for you and with you. Adieu, madame, adieu." And the count, bowing, took two steps back.

"No, no!" cried Diane, wildly, "no, God cannot have done this! No, God had killed that man; he cannot have brought him to life again! No, monsieur, you must be wrong; he is dead!"

At this moment, as if in reply, the duke's voice was heard calling from below, "Count, we are waiting for you."

"You hear him, madame," said Henri. "For the last time, adieu."

And pressing Rémy's hand, he flew down the staircase. Diane approached the window trembling, and with a convulsive shudder, like the bird fascinated by the serpent of the Antilles. She saw the duke on horseback, and the light of the torches held by the gendarmes fell on his face.

"Oh, he lives! the demon lives!" murmured she; "and we must live also. He is setting out for France; so be it, Rémy, we also must go to France."

CHAPTER XXIII

HOW AURILLY EXECUTED THE COMMISSION OF THE DUC D'ANJOU

To the confusion occasioned by the departure of the troops a profound silence succeeded. When Rémy believed the house to have been entirely deserted, he went down to prepare for his departure and that of Diane; but on opening the door of the room below, he was much surprised to see a man sitting by the fire with his face turned towards him. The man was evidently watching for Rémy's departure, although on seeing him he assumed an appearance of profound indifference. Rémy approached, according to his custom, with a slow, halting step, and uncovering his head, bald like that of an old man. The other had the fire behind him, so that Rémy could not distinguish his features. "Pardon, monsieur," said he, "I thought myself alone here."

" I also," replied the man; " but I see with pleasure that I shall have companions."

" Oh! very sad companions, monsieur; for except an invalid young man whom I am taking back to France—"

" Ah," said Aurilly, affecting the good-fellowship of a sympathising *bourgeois*, " I know what you mean."

" Really? "

" Yes; you mean the young lady."

" What young lady? "

" Oh, do not be angry, my good friend. I am the steward of the House of Joyeuse. I rejoined my young master by his brother's order, and at his departure the count recommended to my good offices a young lady and an old servant, who were returning to France after following him to Flanders."

As he thus spoke, he approached Rémy with a smiling and affectionate look. By that movement he came within the light of the lamp, so that all its brightness shone on him. Rémy then was able to see him. But instead of advancing, in his turn, towards his interlocutor, Rémy took a step backwards, and a feeling like that of horror appeared for a moment on his mutilated face.

" You do not reply. One would say you were afraid of me," said Aurilly, with his most agreeable expression.

" Monsieur," replied Rémy, affecting a broken voice, " pardon a poor old man, whom his misfortunes and his wounds have rendered timid and suspicious."

" All the more reason, my friend, for accepting the help and support of an honest companion; besides, as I told you just now, I speak on the part of a master who must inspire you with confidence."

" Assuredly, monsieur," replied Rémy, who however still moved back.

" You leave me," said Aurilly.

" I must consult my mistress. I can decide nothing, you understand."

" Oh, that is natural; but permit me to present myself. I will explain to her my directions in all their details."

" No, no; thank you! Madame is perhaps asleep; and her sleep is sacred to me."

" As you wish. Besides, I have told you what my master told me to say."

" To me? "

" To you and the young lady."

" Your master, M. le Comte du Bouchage, you mean? "

" Yes."

" Thank you, monsieur."

When he had shut the door, all the appearances of age vanished except the bald head, and Rémy mounted the staircase with a rapidity and vigour so extraordinary that one would think the old man, sixty years of age—as he had appeared a moment before—had suddenly become a young man of twenty-five.

" Madame, madame! " cried he, in an agitated voice.

" Well, what is it, Rémy. Is not the duke gone? "

" Yes, madame, but there is a demon here a thousand times worse—a demon on whom, for six years, I have daily called down Heaven's vengeance, as you have on his master."

" Aurilly? "

" Yes, Aurilly; the wretch is below, forgotten by his infernal accomplice."

" Forgotten, do you say, Rémy? Oh, you are wrong! you, who know the duke, know that he never leaves to chance any evil deed, if he can do it himself. No, no, Rémy! Aurilly is not forgotten, but left here for some bad design, believe me! "

" Oh, about him, madame, I can believe anything."

" Does he know me? "

" I do not think so."

" And did he recognise you? "

" Oh, madame! " said Rémy, with a sad smile, " no one recognises me."

" Perhaps he knows who I am? "

" No, for he asked to see you."

" I am sure he must have suspicions."

" In that case nothing is more easy; and I thank God for pointing out our path so plainly. The village is deserted; the wretch is alone. I saw a poniard in his belt; but I have a knife in mine."

" One moment, Rémy. I do not ask the life of that wretch of you, but before you kill him, let us find out what he wants of us; perhaps we may make his evil intentions useful. How did he represent himself to you, Rémy? "

" As the steward of M. du Bouchage, madame."

" You see he lies; therefore he has some reason for lying. Let us find out his intentions, and conceal our own."

" I will act as you wish, madame."

" What does he ask now? "

" To accompany us."

" In what character? "

" As the count's steward."

" Tell him that I accept."

" Oh, madame ! "

" Add that I am thinking of going to England, where I have relatives, but have not quite decided. Lie as he does, Rémy; to conquer we must fight with equal arms."

" But he will see you? "

" I will wear my mask; besides, I suspect he knows me."

" Then if he knows you, there must be a snare."

" The way to guard against it is to pretend to fall into it."

" But—"

" What do you fear? We can but die; are you not ready to die for the accomplishment of our vow? "

" Yes, but not to die without vengeance."

" Rémy," cried Diane, her eyes sparkling with wild excitement, " be easy; we will be revenged—you on the servant, and I on the master."

" Well, madame, then so be it."

And Rémy went down, but still hesitating. The brave young man had felt in spite of himself, at the sight of Aurilly, that nervous shudder that one feels at the sight of a reptile; he wished to kill him because he feared him. But as he went down, his resolution returned, and he determined, in spite of Diane's opinion, to interrogate Aurilly, to confound him, and if he discovered that he had any evil intentions, to kill him on the spot. Aurilly waited for him impatiently. Rémy advanced, armed with an unshakable resolution, but his words were quiet and calm. " Monsieur," said he, " my mistress cannot accept your proposal."

" And why not? "

" Because you are not the steward of M. du Bouchage."

Aurilly grew pale. " Who told you so? " said he.

" No one; but M. du Bouchage, when he left, recommended to my care the person whom I accompany, and never spoke of you."

" He saw me only after he left you."

" Lies, monsieur—lies."

Aurilly drew himself up; Rémy appeared to him to be an old man.

" You speak in a singular tone, my good man," said he, frowning. " Take care! you are old, and I am young; you are feeble, and I am strong."

Rémy smiled, but did not reply.

" If I wished ill to you or your mistress," continued Aurilly, " I have but to raise my hand."

" Oh!" said Rémy, " perhaps I was wrong, and you wish to do her good."

" Certainly I do."

" Explain to me, then, what you desire."

" My friend, I will make your fortune at once, if you will serve me."

" And if not? "

" In that case, as you speak frankly, I will reply as frankly that I will kill you. I have full power to do so."

" Kill me!" said Rémy. " But if I am to serve you, I must know your projects."

" Well, you have guessed rightly, my good man; I do not belong to the Comte du Bouchage."

" Ah! and to whom do you belong? "

" To a more powerful lord."

" Take care! you are lying again."

" Why so? "

" There are not many families above the House of Joyeuse."

" Not even the House of France? "

" Oh, oh!"

" And see how they pay," said Aurilly, sliding into Rémy's hand one of the *rouleaux* of gold.

Rémy shuddered at the touch of that hand, and took a step back; but controlling himself, he said, " You serve the king? "

" No, but his brother, the Duc d'Anjou."

" Oh, very well! I am the duke's most humble servant."

" That is excellent."

" But what does monseigneur want? "

" Monseigneur," said Aurilly, attempting again to slip the gold into Rémy's hand, " is in love with your mistress."

" He knows her, then? "

" He has seen her."

" Seen her! when? "

" This evening."

" Impossible; she has not left her room."

" No, but the prince, by his conduct, has shown that he is really in love."

" Why, what did he do? "

" Took a ladder and climbed to the balcony."

" Ah! he did that? "

" Yes; and it seems she is very beautiful."

" Then you have not seen her? "

" No; but from what he said I much wish to do so, if only to judge of the exaggeration to which love brings a sensible mind. So, then, it is agreed; you will aid me?" and he again offered him the gold.

"Certainly I will, but I must know what part I am to play," said Rémy, repulsing his hand.

"First, tell me, is the lady the mistress of M. du Bouchage or of his brother?"

The blood mounted to Rémy's face. "Of neither," said he; "the lady upstairs has no lover."

"No lover! But then she is a morsel for a king—a woman who has no lover! *Morbleu!* Monseigneur, we have found the philosopher's stone."

"Then," said Rémy, "what does M. le Duc d'Anjou want my mistress to do?"

"He wants her to come to Château-Thierry, where he is going at his utmost speed."

"This is, upon my word, a passion very quickly conceived."

"That is like monseigneur."

"I only see one difficulty," said Rémy.

"What is that?"

"That my mistress is about to embark for England."

"The devil! this, then, is where you must try to aid me."

"How?"

"By persuading her to go in an opposite direction."

"You do not know my mistress, monseigneur; she is not easily persuaded. Besides, even if she were persuaded to go to Château-Thierry instead of England, do you think she would yield to the prince?"

"Why not?"

"She does not love him."

"Bah! one always loves a prince of the blood."

"But if Monseigneur le Duc d'Anjou suspects my mistress of loving M. du Bouchage, or M. de Joyeuse, how did he come to think of carrying her off from him she loved?"

"My good man," said Aurilly, "you have trivial ideas, and it appears that we have difficulty in understanding each other; so I will not discuss the matter. I have preferred kindness to violence, but if you force me to change my plans, well! I will change them."

"What will you do?"

"I told you I had full powers from the duke to kill you and carry off the lady."

"And you believe you could do it with impunity?"

"I believe all my master tells me to believe. Come, will you persuade your mistress to come to France?"

" I will try; but I can answer for nothing."

" And when shall I have the answer? "

" I will go up at once and see what I can do."

" Well, go up; I will wait. But one last word; you know that your fortune and life hang on your answer? "

" I know it."

" That will do; I will go and get the horses ready."

" Do not be in too great a hurry."

" Bah! I am sure of the answer; no one is cruel to a prince."

" I fancied that happened sometimes."

" Yes, but very rarely."

While Rémy went up, Aurilly proceeded to the stables without feeling any doubt as to the result.

" Well! " said Diane, on seeing Rémy.

" Well, madame, the duke has seen you."

" And—"

" And he loves you."

" Loves me! but you are mad, Rémy."

" No; I tell you that he—that man—that wretch, Aurilly, told me so."

" But then he recognised me? "

" If he had, do you think that Aurilly would have dared to present himself and talk to you of love in the prince's name? No, he did not recognise you."

" Yes, you must be right, Rémy. So many things have passed through that infernal brain in six years that he has forgotten me. Let us follow this man."

" But this man will recognise you."

" Why should his memory be better than his master's? "

" Oh, it is his business to remember, while it is the duke's to forget. How could he live if he did not forget? But Aurilly will not have forgotten; he will recognise you, and will denounce you as an avenging shade."

" Rémy, I thought I told you I had a mask, and that you told me you had a knife."

" It is true, madame; and I begin to think that God is assisting us to punish the wicked." Then, calling Aurilly from the top of the staircase, " Monsieur," said he.

" Well? " replied Aurilly.

" My mistress thanks M. du Bouchage for having provided thus for her safety, and accepts with gratitude your obliging offer."

" It is well," said Aurilly; " the horses are ready."

" Come, madame, come," said Rémy, offering his arm to Diane.

Aurilly waited at the bottom of the staircase, lantern in hand, all anxiety to see the lady.

" The devil! " he murmured, " she has a mask. But between here and Château-Thierry the silk cords will be worn out—or cut."

CHAPTER XXIV

THE JOURNEY

THEY set off. Aurilly affected good-fellowship with Rémy, and showed to Diane the greatest respect. But it was easy for Rémy to see that these manifestations of respect were not without a motive. Indeed, to hold the stirrup of a woman when she mounts or dismounts; to watch each of her movements with solicitude; to let slip no opportunity for picking up her glove— is the rôle of a lover, a servant, or a spy. In touching Diane's glove Aurilly saw her hand, in clasping her cloak he peeped under her mask, in holding her stirrup he invoked a chance which might make her show that face which the duke had not been able to recognise, but which he doubted not he should be able to.

But Aurilly had to deal with one as skilful as himself. Rémy claimed the right to perform his ordinary services to Diane, and seemed jealous of Aurilly; while Diane herself, without appearing to have any suspicions, begged Aurilly not to interfere with the services which her old attendant was accustomed to render to her. Aurilly was then reduced to hoping for rain or sun to make her remove her mask; but neither rain nor sun had any effect, and whenever they stopped Diane took her meals in her own room. Aurilly tried looking through the keyholes; but Diane always sat with her back to the door. He tried to peep through the windows; but there were always thick curtains drawn, or if none were there, cloaks were hung up to supply their place. Neither questions nor attempts at corruption succeeded with Rémy, who always declared that his mistress's will was his.

" But these precautions are, then, taken only on my account? " said Aurilly.

" No, for everybody."

" But M. d'Anjou saw her; she was not hidden then."

" Pure chance; but it is just because he did see her that she is more careful than ever."

Days passed on, and they were nearing their destination; but Aurilly's curiosity had not been gratified. Already Picardy appeared to the eyes of the travellers.

Aurilly began to lose patience, and the evil instincts of his nature to gain the ascendant. He began to suspect some important secret under all this mystery. One day he remained a little behind with Rémy, and renewed his attempts at seduction, which Rémy repulsed as usual.

" But," said Aurilly, " some day or other I must see your mistress."

" Doubtless," said Rémy; " but that will be when she likes, and not when you like."

" But if I employ force? "

" Try," said Rémy, while a lightning glance, which he could not repress, shot from his eyes.

Aurilly tried to laugh. " What a fool I am! " said he. " What does it matter to me who she is? At least, she is the person whom the duke saw? "

" Certainly."

" And whom he told me to bring to Château-Thierry? "

" Yes."

" Well, that is all that is necessary! It is not I who am in love with her, it is monseigneur; and provided that you do not seek to escape—"

" Do we appear to wish to do so? "

" No."

" And she so little desires to do so that were you not here we should continue our way to Château-Thierry; if the duke wishes to see us, we wish also to see him."

" That is capital," said Aurilly. " Would your mistress like to rest here a little while? " continued he, pointing to a hostelry on the road.

" You know," said Rémy, " that my mistress never stops but in towns."

" Well, I, who have made no such vow, will stop here a moment; ride on, and I will follow."

Rémy rejoined Diane.

" What was he saying? " she asked.

" He expressed his constant desire—"

" To see me? "

" Yes."

Diane smiled under her mask.

"Be on your guard," said Rémy; "he is furious."

"He shall not see me; I am determined that he shall not, and that is to say, he cannot."

"But once we are at Château-Thierry, must he not see your face?"

"What matter, if the discovery come too late? Besides, the duke did not recognise me."

"No, but his follower will. All these mysteries which have so annoyed Aurilly for a week had not existed for the prince; they had not excited his curiosity or awakened his remembrance, while for a week Aurilly has been seeking, imagining, suspecting. Your face will strike on a memory fully awakened, and he will recognise you at once if he has not done so already."

At this moment they were interrupted by Aurilly, who had taken a cross-road and come suddenly upon them in the hope of surprising some words of their conversation. The sudden silence which followed his arrival proved to him that he was in the way, and he therefore rode behind them.

From that moment Aurilly's plan was formed. He instinctively feared something, as Rémy had said; but his floating conjectures never for an instant approached the truth. In order the better to carry out his plan, he appeared to have renounced his curiosity, and showed himself the most accommodating and joyous companion possible during the rest of the day. Rémy remarked this change not without anxiety.

The next day they started early, and at noon were forced to stop to rest the horses. At two o'clock they set off again, and went on without stopping until four. A great forest, that of La Fère, was visible in the distance. It had the sombre and mysterious aspect of our northern forests, so imposing to southern natures, to whom, beyond all things, heat and sunshine are necessary; but it was nothing to Rémy and Diane, who were accustomed to the thick woods of Anjou and Sologne. But they exchanged glances as if they understood that there the event awaited them which from the moment of their departure had threatened them. It might have been about six o'clock in the evening when they entered the forest, and half an hour later the day was nearly at an end. A high wind whirled about the leaves and carried them towards a lake, along the shore of which the travellers were journeying. Diane rode in the middle, Aurilly on the right, and Rémy on the left. No other human being was visible under the sombre arches of the trees.

From the long extent of the road, one might have thought it one of those enchanted forests under whose shade nothing can live, had it not been for the hoarse howling of the wolves waking up at the approach of night. All at once Diane felt that her saddle, which had been put on by Aurilly, was slipping. She called Rémy, who jumped down, and began to tighten the girths. At this moment Aurilly approached Diane, and while she was occupied, cut the strings of silk which fastened her mask. Before she had divined the movement, or had time to put up her hand, Aurilly seized the mask, and looked full at her. The eyes of these two met in fierce encounter; no one could have said which of them looked most pale and menacing. Aurilly let the mask and his dagger fall, and clasping his hands, cried, " Heavens and earth! Madame de Monsoreau!"

" It is a name which you shall repeat no more," cried Rémy, seizing him by the girdle, and dragging him from his horse. Both rolled on the ground together, and Aurilly stretched out his hand to reach his dagger.

" No, Aurilly; no!" said Rémy, placing his knee on his breast.

" Le Haudoin!" cried Aurilly; " oh, I am a dead man!"

" That is not yet true," said Rémy, placing his hand on the mouth of the wretch who struggled under him, " but will be in a moment." With his right hand he drew his knife from its sheath. " Now," said he, " Aurilly, you are right; now indeed you are dead!" and the blade disappeared in the throat of the musician, who uttered an inarticulate gasp.

Diane, with haggard eyes, half turned on her saddle, and leaning on the pommel, shuddering, but pitiless, had not turned her head away from this terrible spectacle. However, when she saw the blood spurt out from the wound, she fell from her horse as though she were dead.

Rémy did not occupy himself with her at that terrible moment, but searched Aurilly, took from him the two *rouleaux* of gold, then tied a stone to the neck of the corpse, and threw it into the lake. He then washed his hands in the water, took in his arms Diane, who was still unconscious, placed her again on her horse, and mounted his own, supporting his companion. Aurilly's horse, frightened by the howling of the wolves, which began to draw nearer, had fled into the woods.

When Diane recovered, she and Rémy, without exchanging a single word, continued their route towards Château-Thierry.

CHAPTER XXV

HOW KING HENRI III. DID NOT INVITE CRILLON TO BREAKFAST,
AND HOW CHICOT INVITED HIMSELF

THE day after that on which the events that we have just related had taken place in the forest of La Fère, the King of France left his bath at about nine in the morning. His *valet de chambre*, after having rolled him in a blanket of fine wool, and sponged him with that thick Persian wadding which looks like the fleece of a sheep, had given him over to the barbers and dressers, who in their turn gave place to the perfumers and courtiers. When these last had gone, the king sent for his steward, and ordered something more than his ordinary broth, as he felt hungry that morning. This good news spread joy throughout the Louvre, and the smell of the viands was already beginning to be perceptible, when Crillon, colonel of the French guards, entered to take his Majesty's orders.

" Faith! my good Crillon," said the king, " watch as you please over my safety, but do not force me to play the king. I am quite joyful and gay this morning; I feel as if I weighed but an ounce, and could fly away. I am hungry, Crillon; do you understand that, my friend? "

" I understand it very well, Sire, for I am very hungry myself."

" Oh! you, Crillon," said the king, laughing, " are always hungry."

" Not always, Sire. Your Majesty exaggerates—only three times a day."

" And I about once a year, when I receive good news."

" *Harnibieu!* it appears that you have received good news, Sire? So much the better, for it is becoming rare, it seems to me."

" Not at all, Crillon; but you know the proverb."

" Ah, yes—' no news is good news.' I do not trust to proverbs, and least of all to that one. You have no news from Navarre, then? "

" None—a proof that they are asleep."

" And from Flanders? "

" Nothing."

" A proof that they are fighting. And from Paris? "

" Nothing."

" A proof that they are making plots."

"Or children, Crillon. Speaking of children, Crillon, I think I am going to have a child."

"You, Sire?" cried Crillon, astonished.

"Yes; the queen dreamed last night that she was *enceinte*."

"Well, I am happy to hear that your Majesty is hungry this morning. Adieu, Sire."

"Go, my good Crillon."

"*Harnibieu!* Sire, since your Majesty is so hungry, you ought to invite me to breakfast with you."

"Why so, Crillon?"

"Because they say your Majesty lives on air, and the air of the times is very bad. Now I should have been happy to be able to say, 'These are all pure calumnies; the king eats like every one else.'"

"No, Crillon, no; let them believe as they do. It makes me blush to eat like a simple mortal in the presence of my subjects. Remember this, Crillon—a king ought always to remain poetical, and only show himself in a noble manner. Thus, for example, do you remember Alexander?"

"What Alexander?"

"Alexander Magnus. Ah! you do not know Latin, I remember. Well, King Alexander loved to bathe before his soldiers, because he was so well-made, handsome, and plump that they compared him to Apollo and even to Antinoüs."

"Oh, oh! Sire, you would be devilishly in the wrong to bathe before yours, for you are very thin, my poor king."

"Brave Crillon, go," said Henri, striking him on the shoulder. "You are an excellent fellow, and do not flatter me. You are no courtier, my old friend."

"That is why you do not invite me to breakfast," replied Crillon, laughing good-humouredly, and taking his leave contentedly, for the tap on the shoulder consoled him for not getting the breakfast. When he had gone, the breakfast was laid at once. The steward had surpassed himself.

A certain partridge soup, with a *purée* of truffles and chestnuts, attracted the king's attention, after he had eaten some fine oysters. Thus the ordinary broth, that faithful old friend of the king, implored vainly from its golden basin; it was neglected. The king began to attack the partridge soup, and was at his fourth mouthful, when a light step near him made the floor creak, and a well-known voice behind him said sharply, "A plate!"

The king turned. "Chicot!" he cried.

"Himself."

And Chicot, falling at once into his old habits, sat down in a chair, took a plate and a fork, and began on the oysters, picking out the finest without saying a word.

" You here! you returned," cried Henri.

" Hush! " said Chicot, with his mouth full; and he drew the soup towards him.

" Stop, Chicot! that is my dish."

Chicot divided it equally, and gave the king half. Then he poured himself some wine, passed from the soup to a *pâté* made of tunny-fish, then to stuffed crab, swallowed as a finish the royal broth, then, with a great sigh, said, " I am no longer hungry."

" *Par la mordieu!* I hope not, Chicot."

" Ah, good-morning, my king. How are you? You seem to me very gay this morning."

" Am I not, Chicot? "

" You have quite a colour; is it your own? "

" *Parbleu!* "

" I compliment you on it."

" The fact is, I feel very well this morning."

" I am very glad of it. But have you no little titbits left for breakfast? "

" Here are cherries which were preserved by the ladies of Montmartre."

" They are too sweet."

" Nuts stuffed with raisins."

" Bah! they have left the stones in the raisins."

" You are not content with anything."

" Well! really, on my word, everything degenerates, even cooking, and you begin to live very badly at your court."

" Do they live better at that of the King of Navarre? "

" Well! I do not say no."

" Then there must be great changes."

" Ah, you do not know how right you are, Henriquet."

" Tell me about your journey; that will amuse me."

" Willingly; that is what I came for. Where shall I begin? "

" At the beginning. How did you make your journey? "

" Oh! delightfully."

" And met with no disagreeable adventures — no bad company? "

" Oh, who would dream of annoying an ambassador of his most Christian Majesty? You calumniate your subjects, my son."

" I asked," said the king, flattered by the tranquillity that reigned in his kingdom, " because you had no official character, and might have run some risk."

" I tell you, Henriquet, that you have the most charming kingdom in the world. Travellers are nourished gratis; they are sheltered for the love of God; they walk on flowers; and as for the wheel-ruts, they are carpeted with velvet and fringed with gold. It is incredible, but true."

" Then you are content? "

" Enchanted."

" Yes, yes; my police is well organised."

" Marvellously; I must do them justice."

" And the roads are safe? "

" As that of paradise; one meets upon them only little angels, who pass singing the praises of the king."

" Chicot, we are returning to Virgil."

" To what part? "

" To the Bucolics—' O fortunatos nimium ! ' "

" Ah ! very well; but why this exception in favour of plough-men, my son? "

" Alas ! because it is not the same in towns."

" The fact is, Henri, that the towns are the centres of corruption."

" Judge of it. You go five hundred leagues without accident, while I go only to Vincennes, three-fourths of a league, and narrowly escape assassination by the way."

" Oh ! bah ! "

" I will tell you about it, my friend; I am having it written. Without my Forty-five Guardsmen I should have been a dead man."

" Truly ! where did it take place? "

" You mean, where was it to have taken place ? "

" Yes."

" At Bel-Esbat."

" Near the convent of our friend Gorenflot? "

" Precisely."

" And how did he behave under the circumstances ? "

" Wonderfully, as usual. Chicot, I do not know if he had heard any rumour; but instead of snoring in bed, he was up in his balcony, while all his convent kept the road."

" And he did nothing else ? "

" Who ? "

" Dom Modeste."

" He blessed me with a majesty peculiar to himself, Chicot."

" And his monks? "

" They cried, ' Vive le roi ! ' tremendously."

" And were they not armed ? "

" They were completely armed, which was a wonderful piece of thoughtfulness on the part of the worthy prior; and yet this man has said nothing, and asked for nothing. He did not come the next day, like D'Epernon, to search my pockets, crying, ' Sire, something for having saved the king!'"

" Oh, as for that, he is incapable of it; besides, his hands would not go into your pockets."

" Chicot, no jests about Dom Modeste. He is one of the greatest men of my reign; and I declare that on the first opportunity I will give him a bishopric."

" And you will do well, my king."

" Remark one thing, Chicot," said the king, assuming his oracular style: " a great man from the ranks of the people is complete; we gentlemen, you see, inherit in our blood certain vices and virtues. Thus, the Valois are cunning and subtle, brave but idle; the Lorraines are ambitious, greedy, and intriguing; the Bourbons are sensual and circumspect, without ideas, force, or will—look at Henri, for example. When Nature, on the contrary, suddenly forms a man, born of nothing, she uses only her finest clay; so your Gorenflot is complete."

" You think so? "

" Yes; learned, modest, cunning, and brave, you could make of him what you liked—minister, general, or pope."

" Pray stop, Sire. If the brave man heard you, he would burst his skin, for in spite of what you say, Dom Modeste is very vain."

" You are jealous, Chicot."

" I! Heaven forbid! Jealous!"

" I am but just; noble blood does not blind me. ' Stemmata quid faciunt?' "

" Bravo! and you say, then, Henri, that you were nearly assassinated? "

" Yes."

" By whom? "

" By the League, *mordieu !* "

" How does the League get on? "

" Always the same."

" Which means that it grows daily."

" Oh, political bodies never live which grow big too young. They are like children, Chicot."

" Then you are content, my son? "

" Nearly so."

" You are happy? "

" Yes, Chicot, and I am very glad to see you return."

" ' Habemus consulem factum,' as Cato said."

" You bring good news, do you not? "

" I should think so."

" You keep me in suspense."

" Where shall I begin? "

" I have already said at the beginning; but you always wander from the point. You say that the journey was good? "

" You see I have returned whole."

" Yes; then let me hear of your arrival in Navarre. What was Henri doing when you arrived? "

" Making love."

" To Margot? "

" Oh, no! "

" It would have astonished me had it been so; he is always unfaithful to his wife, the rascal! Unfaithful to a daughter of France! Luckily, she pays him back. And when you arrived, what was the name of Margot's rival? "

" Fosseuse."

" A Montmorency. Come, that is not so bad for a bear of Béarn. They spoke here of a peasant, a gardener's daughter."

" Oh, that is very old."

" Then he is faithless to Margot? "

" As much as possible."

" And she is furious? "

" Enraged."

" And she revenges herself? "

" I believe so."

Henri rubbed his hands joyfully.

" What will she do? " cried he, laughing. " Will she move heaven and earth, bring Spain on Navarre, Artois and Flanders on Spain? Will she call in her little brother Henriquet against her little husband Henriot, eh? "

" It is possible."

" You saw her? "

" Yes."

" Then they execrate each other? "

" I believe that in their hearts they do not adore each other."

" But in appearance? "

" They are the best friends in the world."

" Yes; but some fine morning some new love will embroil them completely."

" Well, this new love has come."

" Bah! "

" Yes, on my honour; but shall I tell you what I fear? "

" Yes."

" That this new love, instead of embroiling, will reconcile them."

" Then there is a new love, really? "

" Oh, *mon Dieu !* yes."

" Of Henri's? "

" Of Henri's."

" For whom? "

" You wish to know all, do you not? "

" Yes, Chicot, tell me all about it."

" Well, my son, then I must go back to the beginning."

" Go back, but be quick."

" You wrote a letter to the Béarnais."

" Well? "

" And I read it."

" What do you think of it? "

" That if it was not delicate, at least it was cunning."

" It ought to have embroiled them? "

" Yes, if Henri and Margot had been an ordinary, commonplace couple."

" What do you mean? "

" I mean that Henri is no fool."

" Oh! "

" And that he guessed."

" Guessed what? "

" That you wished to make him quarrel with his wife."

" That was clear."

" Yes; but what was less clear was your object in doing so."

" Ah, the devil! the object— "

" Yes, this cursed Béarnais thought your aim was to make him quarrel with his wife, that you might not have to pay her dowry."

" Oh! "

" *Mon Dieu*, yes! that is what got into the head of that devil of a Béarnais."

" Go on, Chicot," said the king, beginning to look annoyed.

" Well, scarcely had he guessed that when he became as you are at this moment—sad and melancholy; so much so that he hardly thought of Fosseuse."

" Bah! "

" Yes, really; and then he conceived that other love I told you of."

" But this man is a Turk—a pagan. And what did Margot say? "

"This time, my son, you will be astonished. Margot was delighted."

"But what is the name of this new mistress?"

"Oh, she is a beautiful and strong person, capable of defending herself, if she is attacked."

"And did she defend herself?"

"Oh, yes!"

"So that Henri was repulsed?"

"At first."

"And afterwards?"

"Oh, Henri is obstinate; he returned to the charge."

"So that?"

"So that he captured her."

"How?"

"By force."

"By force?"

"Yes, with petards."

"What the devil are you telling me?"

"The truth."

"Petards! Who is this belle that is taken with petards?"

"It is Mademoiselle Cahors."

"Mademoiselle Cahors!"

"Yes, a large and beautiful girl, who has one foot on the Got and the other on the hills, and whose guardian is, or rather was, M. de Vesin, a brave gentleman, and one of your friends."

"*Mordieu!*" cried Henri, furiously, "my city! he has taken my city!"

"Why, you see, Henri, you would not give it to him after having promised it, and he was obliged to take it. But, by the way, here is a letter that he asked me to deliver into your own hand."

And Chicot, drawing out a letter, gave it to the king. It was the one which Henri had written after taking Cahors, and which finished with these words, "Quod mihi dixisti profuit multum. Cognosco meos devotos; nosce tuos. Chicotus cætera expediet." Which meant, "What you told me was very useful. I know my faithful followers; know yours. Chicot will tell you the rest."

CHAPTER XXVI

HOW, AFTER RECEIVING NEWS FROM THE SOUTH, HENRI RECEIVED NEWS FROM THE NORTH

THE king, highly exasperated, could hardly read the letter which Chicot gave to him. While he deciphered the Latin with every sign of impatience, Chicot, before a great Venetian mirror, which hung over a gilt table, was admiring the infinite grace of his own person under his military dress.

"Oh, I am betrayed!" cried Henri, when he had finished the letter. "The Béarnais had a plan, and I never suspected it."

"My son," said Chicot, "you know the proverb, 'There is no worse water than still water'?"

"Go to the devil with your proverbs!"

Chicot went to the door as if to obey.

"No, remain."

Chicot stopped.

"Cahors taken!" continued Henri.

"Yes, and very well done too."

"Then he has generals and engineers?"

"No, he is too poor for that. He could not pay them; he does it all himself."

"He fight!" said Henri, disdainfully.

"I do not say that he rushes into it with enthusiasm. No, he resembles those people who try the water before they bathe; he just dips the ends of his fingers with a little shudder, which augurs badly, then his breast. All this takes him about ten minutes, and then he rushes into action, and through fire, like a salamander."

"The devil!"

"And I assure you, Henri, the fire was hot there."

The king rose and walked up and down the room. "Here is a misfortune for me," he cried. "They will laugh at it; they will sing about it. *Mordieu!* it is lucky I thought of sending the promised aid to Antwerp. Antwerp will compensate for Cahors; the north will blot out the disaster in the south."

"Amen!" said Chicot, plunging his hands into the king's confectionery-box to finish his dessert.

At this moment the door opened, and the usher announced, "M. le Comte du Bouchage."

"Ah," cried Henri, "I told you so; here is news. Enter, count, enter."

The usher opened the door, and Henri du Bouchage entered slowly and bent a knee to the king.

"Still pale and sad," said the king. "Come, friend, take a holiday air for a little while, and do not tell me good news with a doleful face. Speak quickly, Bouchage, for I want to hear. You come from Flanders?"

"Yes, Sire."

"And quickly?"

"As quickly, Sire, as a man can ride."

"You are welcome. And now, what of Antwerp?"

"Antwerp belongs to the Prince of Orange."

"To the Prince of Orange?"

"Yes, to William."

"But did not my brother attack Antwerp?"

"Yes, Sire; but now he is travelling to Château-Thierry."

"He has left the army?"

"Sire, there is no longer an army."

"Oh," cried the king, sinking back in his armchair, "but Joyeuse—"

"Sire, my brother, after having done wonders with his marines, after having conducted the whole of the retreat, rallied the few men who escaped the disaster, and made them an escort for M. le Duc d'Anjou."

"A defeat!" murmured the king. But all at once, with a strange look, "Then Flanders is lost to my brother?"

"Absolutely, Sire."

"Without hope?"

"I fear so, Sire."

The clouds gradually cleared from the king's brow. "That poor François!" said he, smiling. "He is unlucky in his search for a crown. He missed that of Navarre; he has stretched out his hand for that of England, and has touched that of Flanders. I would wager, Bouchage, that he will never reign, although he desires it so much. And how many prisoners were taken?"

"About two thousand."

"How many killed?"

"At least as many; and among them M. de Saint-Aignan."

"What! poor Saint-Aignan dead!"

"Drowned."

"Drowned! Did you throw yourselves into the Scheldt?"

"No, the Scheldt threw itself upon us."

The count then gave the king a description of the battle, and of the inundation. Henri listened silently. When the recital was over, he rose, and kneeling down on his *prie-Dieu*, said some prayers, and then returned with a perfectly calm face.

"Well," said he, "I trust I bear things like a king; a king supported by the Lord is really more than a man. And you, count, since your brother is saved, like mine,—thank God!—smile a little."

"Sire, I am at your orders."

"What do you ask as payment for your services, Bouchage?"

"Sire, I have rendered no service."

"I dispute that; but at least your brother has."

"Immense, Sire."

"He has saved the army, you say, or rather its remnants?"

"There is not a man left who does not say that he owes his life to my brother."

"Well, Bouchage, my will is to extend my benefits to both, and I only imitate in that Him who made you both rich, brave, and handsome; besides, I should imitate those great politicians who always rewarded the bearers of bad news."

"Oh!" said Chicot, "I have known men hanged for bringing bad news."

"That is possible," said the king; "but remember the senate that thanked Varro."

"You cite Republicans, Valois; misfortune makes you humble."

"Come, Bouchage, what will you have? What would you like?"

"Since your Majesty does me the honour to speak to me so kindly, I will dare to profit by your goodness. I am tired of life, Sire, and yet have a repugnance to shortening it myself, for God forbids it, and all the subterfuges that a man of honour employs in such a case are mortal sins. To get one's self killed in battle, or to let one's self die of hunger, or to forget how to swim in crossing a river, are travesties of suicide through which God sees very clearly; for you know, Sire, our most secret thoughts are open to God. I renounce the idea, therefore, of dying before the term which God has fixed for my life; and yet the world fatigues me, and I must leave it."

"My friend!" said the king.

Chicot looked with interest at the young man, so beautiful, so brave, so rich, and yet speaking in this tone of despair.

"Sire," continued the count, "everything that has happened to me for some time has strengthened my resolution. I wish to throw myself into the arms of God, who is the sovereign consoler of the afflicted, as he is at the same time sovereign master of the happy. Deign, then, Sire, to facilitate my entrance into a religious life, for my heart is sad unto death."

The king was moved at this doleful request. "Ah! I understand," said he; "you wish to become a monk, but you fear the probation."

"I do not fear the austerities, Sire, but the time they leave one in indecision. No, what I wish is, not to mitigate the trials that may be imposed on me—for I do not hope to withdraw my body from physical suffering, or my soul from moral privations—it is to remove from both every pretext for a return to the past; it is, in a word, to make spring from the ground that grating which will separate me for ever from the world, and which, under ecclesiastical regulations, is formed as slowly as a hedge of thorns."

"Poor boy!" said the king. "I think he will make a good preacher; will he not, Chicot?"

Chicot did not reply. Bouchage continued, "You see, Sire, that it is with my own family that the struggle will take place, and with my relatives that I shall meet with the greatest opposition. My brother the cardinal, at once so good and so worldly, will find a thousand reasons to urge against it. At Rome your Majesty is all-powerful. You have asked me what I wish for, and promised to grant it; my wish is this, obtain from Rome permission for me to dispense with my novitiate."

The king rose, smiling, and taking the count's hand, said, "I will do what you ask, my son. You wish to serve God, and you are right; he is a better master than I am."

"A fine compliment you are paying him!" murmured Chicot, between his mustache and his teeth.

"Well, let it be so," continued the king; "you will be directed according to your wishes, dear count, I promise you."

"Your Majesty overwhelms me with joy," cried the young man, kissing Henri's hand as though he had made him duke, peer, or Marshal of France. "Then it is settled?"

"On my word as a king and a gentleman."

Bouchage's face brightened; something like a smile of ecstasy passed over his lips. He bowed respectfully to the king and took leave.

"What a happy young man!" said Henri.

"Oh," said Chicot, "you need not envy him; he is not more doleful than yourself."

"But, Chicot, he is going to give himself up to religion."

"And who the devil prevents you from doing the same? I

know a cardinal who will give all needed dispensations, and he has more interest at Rome than you have. Do you not know him? I mean the Cardinal de Guise."

" Chicot! "

" And if the tonsure disquiets you (for it is rather a delicate operation) the prettiest hands and the prettiest scissors— golden scissors, faith!—will give you this precious symbol, which would raise to three the number of the crowns you will have worn, and will justify the device, ' Manet ultima cœlo.' "

" Pretty hands, do you say? "

" Yes, do you mean to abuse the hands of Madame de Montpensier? How severe you are upon your subjects! "

The king frowned, and passed over his eyes a hand as white as those spoken of, but certainly more tremulous.

" Well! " said Chicot, " let us leave that, for I see that the conversation does not please you, and let us return to subjects that interest me personally."

The king made a gesture, half indifferent, half approving.

" Have you heard, Henri," continued Chicot, " whether those Joyeuses carried off any woman? "

" No."

" Have they burned anything? "

" What? "

" How should I know what a great lord burns to amuse himself?—the house of some poor devil, perhaps."

" Are you mad, Chicot? Burn a house for amusement in my city of Paris! "

" Oh, why not? "

" Chicot! "

" Then they have done nothing of which you have heard the noise or seen the smoke? "

" Why, no."

" Oh! so much the better! " said Chicot, drawing a long breath, like a man much relieved.

" Do you know one thing, Chicot? " said Henri.

" No, I do not."

" It is that you have become wicked."

" I? "

" Yes, you."

" My sojourn in the tomb had sweetened me, but your presence, great king, has destroyed the effect."

" You become insupportable, Chicot; and I now attribute to you ambitious projects and intrigues of which I formerly believed you incapable."

"Projects of ambition! I ambitious! Henriquet, my son, you used to be only foolish, now you are mad; you have progressed."

"And I tell you, M. Chicot, that you wish to separate from me all my old friends, by attributing to them intentions which they have not, and crimes of which they have never thought; in fact, you wish to monopolise me."

"I monopolise you! what for? God forbid! you are too tiresome, without counting the difficulty of pleasing you with your food. Oh, no, indeed! Explain to me whence comes this strange idea."

"You began by listening coldly to my praises of your old friend, Dom Modeste, to whom you owe much."

"I owe much to Dom Modeste? Good!"

"Then you tried to calumniate the Joyeuses, my true friends."

"I do not say no."

"Then you launched a shaft at the Guises."

"Ah! you love them now; you love all the world to-day, it seems."

"No, I do not love them; but as just now they keep themselves close and quiet, and do not do me the least harm, I do not fear them, and I cling to all old and well-known faces. All these Guises, with their fierce looks and great swords, have never done me any harm, after all, and they resemble—shall I tell you what?"

"Do, Henri; I know how clever you are at comparisons."

"They resemble those perch that they let loose in the ponds to chase the great fish and prevent them from growing too fat; but suppose that the great fish are not afraid?"

"Well?"

"Then the teeth of the perch are not strong enough to get through their scales."

"Oh, Henri, my child, how subtle you are!"

"While your Béarnais—"

"Well, have you a comparison for him also?"

"While your Béarnais, who mews like a cat, bites like a tiger."

"Well, my son, I will tell you what to do—divorce the queen and marry Madame de Montpensier. Was she not once in love with you?"

"Yes, and that is the source of all her menaces, Chicot; she has a woman's spite against me, and she provokes me now and then. But happily I am a man, and can laugh at it."

As Henri finished these words, the usher cried at the door, "A messenger from M. le Duc de Guise for his Majesty."

" Is it a courier or a gentleman? " asked the king.

" It is a captain, Sire."

" Let him enter; he is welcome."

CHAPTER XXVII

THE TWO COMPANIONS

CHICOT, at this announcement, sat down, and turned his back to the door; but the first words pronounced by the duke's messenger made him start. He opened his eyes. The messenger could see nothing but the eye of Chicot peering from behind the chair, while Chicot could see him altogether.

" You come from Lorraine? " asked the king of the new-comer, who had a fine and warlike appearance.

" Not so, Sire; I come from Soissons, where Monsieur the Duke, who has not left the city for a month, gave me this letter to deliver to your Majesty."

The messenger then opened his buff coat, which was fastened by silver clasps, and drew from a leather pouch lined with silk, not one letter, but two; for they had stuck together by the wax, and as the captain advanced to give the king one letter, the other fell on the carpet. Chicot's eyes followed the messenger, and saw the colour spread over his cheeks as he stooped to pick up the letter he had let fall. But Henri saw nothing; he opened his own letter and read, while the messenger watched him closely.

" Ah, Maître Borromée," thought Chicot, " so you are a captain, and you give only one letter to the king, when you have two in your pocket. Wait, my darling, wait! "

" Good," said the king, after reading the duke's letter with evident satisfaction. " Go, captain, and tell M. de Guise that I am grateful for his offer."

" Your Majesty will not honour me with a written answer? "

" No, I shall see the duke in a month or six weeks, and can thank him myself."

The captain bowed and went out.

" You see, Chicot," then said the king, " that M. de Guise is free from all machinations. This brave duke has learned the Navarre business, and he fears that the Huguenots will raise their heads, for he has also ascertained that the Germans are about to send reinforcements to Henri. Now, guess what he is about to do."

As Chicot did not reply, Henri continued, " Well! he offers me the army that he has just raised in Lorraine to watch Flanders, and says that in six weeks it will be at my command, with its general. What do you say to that, Chicot? "

No answer.

" Really, my dear Chicot," continued the king, " you are as absurdly obstinate as a Spanish mule; and if I happen to convince you of some error, you sulk—yes, sulk."

Not a sound came to contradict Henri in this frank opinion of his friend. Now, silence displeased Henri more than contradiction. " I believe," said he, " that the fellow has had the impertinence to go to sleep. Chicot! " continued he, advancing to the armchair; " reply when your king speaks."

But Chicot could not reply, for he was not there; and Henri found the armchair empty.

He looked all round the room; but Chicot was not to be seen. The king was seized with a sort of superstitious shudder; it sometimes came into his mind that Chicot was a supernatural being, a diabolic incarnation—of a good kind, it was true, but still diabolical.

He called Nambu the usher, and questioned him, and he assured his Majesty that he had seen Chicot go out five minutes before the duke's messenger left; that he had gone out with the light and careful step of a man who does not wish his movements to be observed.

" Decidedly," thought Henri, " Chicot was vexed at being in the wrong. How ill-natured men are, even the best of them! "

Nambu was right; Chicot had crossed the antechambers silently, but still he was not able to keep his spurs from sounding, which made several people turn, and bow when they saw who it was.

The captain came out five minutes after Chicot, went down the steps across the court, proud and delighted at the same time—proud of his person, and delighted that the king had received him so well, and without any suspicions of M. de Guise. As he crossed the drawbridge, he heard behind him steps which seemed to be the echo of his own. He turned, thinking that the king had perhaps sent some message to him, and great was his stupefaction to see behind him the demure face of Robert Briquet. It may be remembered that the first feeling of these two men towards each other had not been exactly sympathetical. Borromée opened his mouth, and paused, and in an instant was joined by Chicot.

" *Corbœuf !* " said Borromée.

" *Ventre de biche !* " cried Chicot.

" The *bourgeois !* "

" The reverend father! "

" With that helmet! "

" With that buff coat! "

" I am surprised to see you."

" I am delighted to meet you again."

And they looked fiercely at each other; but Borromée, quickly assuming an air of amiable urbanity, said, " *Vive Dieu !* you are cunning, Maître Robert Briquet."

" I, reverend father? and why do you say so? "

" When you were at the convent of the Jacobins, you made me believe you were only a simple *bourgeois.* You must be ten times more cunning and more valiant than a lawyer and a captain together."

" Ah! " replied Chicot, " and what must we say of you, Seigneur Borromée? "

" Of me? "

" Yes, of you."

" And why? "

" For making me believe you were only a monk. You must be ten times more cunning than the pope himself; but you took me in the snare."

" The snare? "

" Yes, doubtless. Under that disguise you spread a snare. A brave captain like you does not change his cuirass for a frock without grave reasons."

" With a soldier like you, I will have no secrets. It is true that I have certain personal interests in the convent of the Jacobins; but you? "

" And I also; but hush! "

" Let us converse a little about it."

" I am quite ready."

" Do you like good wine? "

" Yes, when it *is* good."

" Well, I know a little inn, which I think has no rival in Paris."

" And I know one also. What is yours called? "

" The Corne d'Abondance."

" Ah! " said Chicot, with a start.

" Well, what is it? "

" Nothing."

" Do you know anything against this house? "

" Not at all."

" You know it? "

" Not the least in the world, and that astonishes me."

" Shall we go there, comrade? "

" Oh, yes, at once! "

" Come, then."

" Where is it? "

" Near the Porte Bourdelle. The host appreciates well the difference between the palate of a man like you and the throat of every thirsty passer-by."

" Can we talk there at our ease? "

" In the cellar, if we wish."

" And without being disturbed? "

" We will close the doors."

" Come," said Chicot, " I see that you are a man of resources, and as well acquainted with wine-rooms as with convents."

" Do you think I have an understanding with the host? "

" It looks like that to me."

" Faith! no; this time you are wrong. Maître Bonhomet sells me wine when I want it, and I pay when I can; that is all."

" Bonhomet! upon my word, that is a name that promises well."

" And keeps its promise. Come, my friend, come! "

" Oh, oh! " said Chicot to himself. " Now I must choose among my best grimaces, for if Bonhomet recognises me at once, it is all over."

CHAPTER XXVIII

THE CORNE D'ABONDANCE

THE way along which Borromée led Chicot, never suspecting that he knew it as well as himself, recalled to our Gascon the happy days of his youth. How many times had he in those days, under the rays of the winter sun, or in the cool shade in summer, sought out this house, towards which a stranger was now conducting him! Then a few pieces of gold, or even of silver, jingling in his purse, made him happier than a king; and he gave himself up to the delightful pleasures of laziness, having no mistress in his lodgings, no hungry child on the threshold, no relatives suspicious and grumbling behind the window. Then he used to sit down carelessly on the wooden bench, waiting for Gorenflot, who however was always punctual to the time fixed for dinner; and then he used to study, with intelligent curiosity, Gorenflot in all the varying phases of drunkenness. Soon the great street of St. Jacques appeared to his eyes, the cloister of St. Benoît, and nearly in front of that the hostelry of the Corne d'Abondance, rather dirty, and rather dilapidated, but still shaded by its planes and chestnuts, and embellished inside by its pots of shining copper and brilliant saucepans, looking like imitations of gold and silver, and bringing real gold and silver into the pockets of the innkeeper. Chicot bent his back until he seemed to have lost five or six inches of his height, and making a most hideous grimace, prepared to meet his old friend Bonhomet. However, as Borromée walked first, it was to him that Bonhomet spoke, and he scarcely looked at Chicot, who stood behind. Time had left its traces on the face of Bonhomet, as well as on his house. Besides the wrinkles, which seem to correspond on the human face to the cracks made by time on the front of buildings, Maître Bonhomet had assumed airs of great importance since Chicot had seen him last. These, however, he never showed much to men of a warlike appearance, for whom he had always a great respect.

It seemed to Chicot that nothing was changed excepting the tint of the ceiling, which from grey had turned to black.

" Come, friend," said Borromée, " I know a little nook where two men may talk at their ease while they drink. Is it unoccupied? " continued he, turning to Bonhomet.

Bonhomet answered that it was, and Borromée then led Chicot to the little room so well known to those of our readers who have been willing to waste their time in reading *La Dame de Monsoreau*.

" Now," said Borromée, " wait here for me while I avail myself of a privilege granted to the *habitués* of this house, and which you can use in your turn when you are better known here."

" What is that? "

" To go to the cellar and choose the wine we are to drink."

" Ah! a fine privilege! Go, then."

Borromée went out. Chicot followed him with his eye, and as soon as the door closed behind him went to the wall and raised a picture, representing Credit killed by bad debtors, behind which was a hole, through which he could see into the public room. Chicot knew this hole well, for he had made it himself. " Ah, ah! " he said; " you lead me to an inn which you are accustomed to frequent; you take me to a room where you think I cannot see or be seen—and in that room there is a hole, thanks to which you cannot make a movement without my seeing it. Come, come, my captain, you are not bright."

On looking through, Chicot perceived Borromée, after placing his finger on his lips as a sign of caution, saying something to Bonhomet, who seemed to acquiesce by a nod of the head. By the movement of the captain's lips, Chicot, an expert in such matters, understood him to say, "Serve us in that room; and whatever noise you may hear, do not come in." After this Borromée took a light, which was always kept burning in readiness, and descended to the cellar. Then Chicot knocked on the wall in a peculiar manner. On hearing this knock, which seemed to recall to him some remembrance deeply rooted in his heart, Bonhomet started, looked up, and listened. Chicot knocked again impatiently, like a man surprised that his first summons is not obeyed. Bonhomet ran to the little room, and found Chicot standing there with a threatening face. At this sight, Bonhomet, who, like the rest of the world, had believed Chicot dead, uttered a cry, for he thought he saw his ghost.

"Since when," said Chicot, "has a person like me been obliged to call twice?"

"Oh, dear M. Chicot, is it you or your shade?" cried Bonhomet.

"Whichever it be, since you recognise me, I hope you will obey me."

"Oh, certainly, dear M. Chicot."

"Then, whatever noise you hear in this room, and whatever takes place here, do not come until I call you."

"Your directions will be the easier to obey, since they are exactly the same as your companion has just given to me."

"Yes, but if he calls, do not come; wait until I call."

"I will, M. Chicot."

"Good! now send away every one else from your inn, and in ten minutes let us be as free and as solitary here as if we came to fast on Good Friday."

"In ten minutes, M. Chicot, there shall not be a soul in the hotel excepting your humble servant."

"Go, Bonhomet; you have retained all my esteem," said Chicot, majestically.

"Oh, *mon Dieu! mon Dieu!*" said Bonhomet, as he retired, "what is about to take place in my poor house?"

As he went, he met Borromée, returning from the cellar with his bottles. "You understand?" said the latter; "in ten minutes, not a soul in the establishment."

Bonhomet made a sign of obedience and retired to the kitchen to consider how he should obey that double injunction of his two formidable patrons.

Borromée returned to the room, and found Chicot waiting for him with a smile on his lips.

We do not know how Bonhomet managed, but when the ten minutes had expired, the last customer was crossing the threshold of the door, muttering, " Oh, oh! the weather is stormy here to-day; we must avoid the storm."

CHAPTER XXIX

WHAT HAPPENED IN THE LITTLE ROOM

WHEN the captain re-entered the room with the basket in his hand containing a dozen bottles, he was received by Chicot with a face so open and smiling that Borromée almost regarded him as a simpleton. Borromée was in haste to uncork his bottles, but his haste was nothing to Chicot's; thus the preparations were soon made, and the two companions began to drink. At first, as though their occupation was too important to be interrupted, they drank in silence. Chicot uttered only these words, " Upon my word, this is good Burgundy."

They drank two bottles in this way.

" *Pardieu!*" murmured Borromée, to himself, " it is a singular chance that I should light on such a drunkard as this."

At the third bottle Chicot raised his eyes to heaven, and said, " Really, we are drinking as though we wished to intoxicate ourselves."

" It is so good," replied Borromée.

" Ah! it pleases you. Go on, friend! I have a strong head."

And each of them emptied another bottle. The wine produced on them opposite effects; it unloosened Chicot's tongue, and tied that of Borromée.

" Ah!" murmured Chicot, " you are silent; then you doubt yourself."

" Ah!" said Borromée, apart, " you chatter; then you are getting tipsy." Then he asked Chicot, " How many bottles does it take you? "

" For what? "

" To get lively."

" About four."

" And to get tipsy? "

" About six."

" And dead drunk? "

" Double."

" Gascon! " thought Borromée, " he stammers already, and has only drunk four. Come, then, we can go on," said he, and he drew out a fifth for Chicot and a fifth for himself.

But Chicot remarked that of the bottles ranged beside Borromée some were half full, and others two thirds; not one was empty. This confirmed him in his suspicions that the captain had bad intentions with regard to him. He rose to receive the fifth bottle as Borromée presented it, and staggered as he did so."

" Oh! " said he, " did you feel it? "

" What? "

" The shock of an earthquake."

" Bah! "

" Yes. *Ventre de biche!* fortunately the hostelry of the Corne d'Abondance is solid, although it is built on a pivot."

" What! built on a pivot? "

" Doubtless, since it turns."

" True! " said Borromée, " I felt the effects, but did not guess the cause."

" Because you are not a Latin scholar, and have not read the *De Natura Rerum*. If you had, you would know that there is no effect without a cause."

" Well, my dear captain—for you are a captain like me, are you not? "

" Yes, from the points of my toes to the roots of my hair."

" Well, then, my dear captain, tell me, since there is no effect without a cause, as you say, what was the cause of your disguise? "

" What disguise? "

" That which you wore when you came to visit Dom Modeste."

" How was I disguised? "

" As a *bourgeois*."

" Ah! true."

" Tell me that, and you will begin my education in philosophy."

" Willingly, if you will tell me why you were disguised as a monk. Confidence for confidence."

" Agreed," said Borromée.

" You wish to know, then, why I was disguised? " said Chicot, with an utterance which seemed to grow thicker and thicker.

" Yes, it puzzles me."

" And then you will tell me? "

" Yes, that was agreed."

" Ah! true; I forgot. Well, the thing is very simple; I was a spy for the king."

" A spy? "

" Yes."

" Is that, then, your profession? "

" No, I am an amateur."

" What were you watching there? "

" Every one. Dom Modeste himself, then Brother Borromée, little Jacques, and the whole convent."

" And what did you discover, my friend? "

" First, that Dom Modeste is a great fool."

" It does not need to be very clever to find that out."

" Pardon me; his Majesty Henri III., who is no fool, regards him as one of the lights of the Church, and is about to make a bishop of him."

" So be it. I have nothing to say against that promotion; on the contrary, it will give me a good laugh. But what else did you discover? "

" I discovered that Brother Borromée was not a monk, but a captain."

" Ah! you discovered that? "

" At once."

" Anything else? "

" I discovered that Jacques was practising with the foils in preparation for practice with the sword; and that he aimed at a target in preparation for aiming at a man."

" Ah! you discovered that? " said Borromée, frowning. " And did you discover anything else? "

" Oh, give me something to drink, or I shall remember nothing."

" Remember that you are beginning your sixth bottle," said Borromée, laughing.

" So I am getting tipsy! " said Chicot; " I don't pretend I am not. Did we come here, then, to philosophise? "

" We came here to drink. '

" Let us drink, then." And Chicot filled his glass.

" Well," said Borromée, " now do you remember? "

" What? "

" What else you saw in the convent."

" Well, I saw that the monks were really soldiers, and instead of obeying Dom Modeste, obeyed you."

" Ah, truly; but doubtless that was not all? "

" No; but more to drink, or my memory will fail me." And

as his bottle was empty, he held out his glass to Borromée, who filled it from his own. Chicot emptied his glass without taking breath.

"Well, now do you remember."

"Oh, yes, I should think so."

"Well, what else?"

"I saw that there was a plot."

"A plot!" cried Borromée, turning pale.

"Yes, a plot."

"Against whom?"

"Against the king."

"Of what nature?"

"To try to carry him off."

"And when was that to be done?"

"When he should be on his way from Vincennes."

"*Tonnerre!*"

"What did you say?"

"Nothing. And you discovered that?"

"Yes."

"And warned the king?"

"*Parbleu!* that was what I came for."

"Then it was you who caused the failure of the project?"

"Yes, I."

"*Massacre!*" murmured Borromée between his teeth.

"What did you say?"

"I said that you have good eyes, friend."

"Bah!" said Chicot, stammering, "I have seen something else still. Pass me one of your bottles, and I will astonish you when I tell you what I have seen."

Borromée hastened to comply with Chicot's desire. "Let me hear," said he; "astonish me."

"In the first place, I have seen M. de Mayenne wounded."

"Bah!"

"No wonder; he was on my route. And then I have seen the taking of Cahors."

"What! the taking of Cahors?"

"Certainly. Ah, captain, it was a grand thing to see, and a brave man like you would have been delighted."

"I do not doubt it. You were, then, near the King of Navarre?"

"Side by side, my friend, as we are now."

"And you left him?"

"To announce this news to the King of France."

"Then you have been at the Louvre?"

" Yes, just before you."

" Then, as we have not left each other since, I need not ask you what you have done since our meeting at the Louvre."

" On the contrary, ask; for upon my word, that is the most curious of all."

" Tell me, then."

" Tell, tell!" said Chicot. " *Ventre de biche!* it is very easy to say, ' Tell.' "

" Make an effort."

" One more glass of wine, then, to loosen my tongue—quite full; that will do. Well, I saw, comrade, that when you gave the king the Duc de Guise's letter, you let another fall."

" Another!" cried Borromée, starting up.

" Yes, it is there." And having tried two or three times with an unsteady hand, he put his finger on the buff doublet of Borromée, just where the letter was. Borromée started as though Chicot's finger had been a hot iron, and had touched his skin instead of his doublet.

" Oh, oh!" said he, " there is but one thing wanting."

" What is that?"

" That you should know to whom the letter is addressed."

" Oh, I know quite well," said Chicot, letting his arms fall on the table; " it is addressed to the Duchesse de Montpensier."

" Blood of Christ! I hope you have not told that to the king."

" No; but I will tell him."

" When?"

" When I have had a nap." And he let his head fall on his arms.

" Ah! you know that I have a letter for the duchess?"

" I know that," stammered Chicot, " perfectly."

" Then as soon as you can walk you will go to the Louvre?"

" I will go to the Louvre."

" You will denounce me?"

" I will denounce you."

" Is it not a joke?"

" What?"

" That you will tell the king after your nap."

" Not at all. You see, my dear friend," said Chicot, half raising his head and looking sleepily at Borromée, " you are a conspirator, and I am a spy; you have a plot, and I denounce you. We each follow our business. Good-night, captain." And Chicot laid his head down again, so that his face was completely hidden by his hands, while the back of his head was protected by his helmet.

" Ah!" cried Borromée, looking with flaming eyes at his companion, " ah, you will denounce me, dear friend? "

" As soon as I awake, dear friend; it is agreed."

" But you will not awake!" cried Borromée; and at the same time he made a furious blow with his dagger on the back of his companion, thinking to pierce him through and nail him to the table. But he had not reckoned on the shirt of mail which Chicot had carried away from the priory. The dagger broke upon it like glass, and for the second time Chicot owed his life to it.

Before Borromée had time to recover from his astonishment Chicot's right arm sprang out as if moved by a spring, described a semi-circle, and delivered a fist-blow weighing five hundred pounds in the face of Borromée, who rolled bleeding and stunned against the wall. In a second he was up again; in another second he had his sword in hand.

Those two seconds had sufficed for Chicot to draw his sword also and prepare himself. He seemed to shake off, as if by enchantment, all the fumes of the wine, and stood with a steady hand to receive his adversary. The table, like a field of battle, covered with empty bottles, lay between them and served as a rampart for both. But the blood flowing down his face infuriated Borromée, who lost all prudence and sprang towards his enemy, approaching as near as the intervening table would permit.

" Dolt!" cried Chicot, " you see that it is decidedly you who are drunk, for you cannot reach me across the table, while my arm is six inches longer than yours, and my sword as much longer than your sword; and here is the proof." As he spoke, he stretched out his arm with the quickness of lightning and pricked Borromée in the middle of the forehead. Borromée uttered a cry, more of rage than of pain, and as he was a man of great courage, attacked with double fury.

Chicot, however, still on the other side of the table, took a chair and quietly sat down. " *Mon Dieu!*" he said, shrugging his shoulders, " how stupid these soldiers are! they pretend to know how to manage their swords, and any *bourgeois*, if he liked, could kill them like flies. Ah, now you want to put out my eye! And now you mount on the table; that alone was wanting. *Ventre de biche!* take care, donkey! upward strokes are dangerous, and if I wished, see, I could spit you like a lark." And he pricked him with his sword in the stomach, as he had already done in the forehead.

Borromée roared with anger, and leaped from the table to the floor.

"That is as it should be," said Chicot; "now we are on the same level, and we can talk while we are fencing. Ah, captain, captain, and so we sometimes try our hand a little at assassination in our spare moments, do we?"

"I do for my cause what you do for yours," said Borromée, now brought back to seriousness, and terrified in spite of himself by the ominous fire which gleamed in Chicot's eyes.

"Now that is talking," said Chicot; "and yet, my friend, it is with no little pleasure I find that I am a better hand than you are. Ah, that was not bad!"

Borromée had just made a lunge at Chicot which had slightly touched his breast.

"Not bad, but I know the thrust; it is the very same you showed little Jacques. I was just saying, then, that I have the advantage of you, for I did not begin this quarrel, however anxiously disposed I might have been to do so. More than that, even, I have allowed you to carry out your project by giving you all the latitude you required, and at this very moment even, I act only on the defensive, because I have something to propose to you."

"Nothing," cried Borromée, exasperated at Chicot's imperturbability, "nothing!" And he gave a thrust which would have run the Gascon completely through the body if the latter had not, with his long legs, sprung back a step, which placed him out of his adversary's reach.

"I am going to tell you what this arrangement is, all the same, so that I shall have nothing left to reproach myself for."

"Hold your tongue!" said Borromée; "hold your tongue! it will be useless."

"Listen," said Chicot; "it is to satisfy my own conscience. I have no wish to shed your blood, you understand; and I don't want to kill you until I am driven to extremes."

"Kill me, kill me, I say, if you can!" exclaimed Borromée, exasperated.

"No, no; I have already once in my life killed another such swordsman as you are; I will even say a better swordsman than you. *Pardieu!* you know him; he also was one of Guise's retainers—a lawyer too."

"Ah, Nicolas David!" said Borromée, terrified by the precedent, and again placing himself on the defensive.

"Exactly so."

"It was you who killed him?"

"Oh, yes, with a pretty little thrust which I will presently show you, if you decline the arrangement I propose."

"Well, let me hear what the arrangement is."

"You will pass from the Duc de Guise's service to that of the king, without, however, leaving that of the duke."

"In other words, I am to become a spy like yourself?"

"No, for there will be a difference; I am not paid, but you will be. You will begin by showing me the Duc de Guise's letter to Madame la Duchesse de Montpensier; you will let me take a copy of it, and I will leave you quiet until another occasion. Well, am I not considerate?"

"Here," said Borromée, "is my answer."

Borromée's reply was a *coupé sur les armes* so rapidly dealt that the point of his sword slightly touched Chicot's shoulder.

"Well, well," said Chicot, "I see I must positively show you Nicolas David's thrust. It is very simple and pretty." And Chicot, who had up to that moment been acting on the defensive, made one step forward, and attacked in his turn.

"This is the thrust," said Chicot; "I make a feint in *quarte basse.*" And he did so.

Borromée parried and gave way; but after this first step backwards, he was obliged to stop, as he found that he was close to the partition.

"Good! precisely so. You parry in a circle; that's wrong, for my wrist is stronger than yours. I catch your sword in mine, thus. I return to the attack by a *tierce haute ;* I fall upon you, so, and you are hit,—or rather you are a dead man!"

In fact, the thrust had followed, or rather had accompanied, the demonstration, and the slender rapier, penetrating Borromée's chest, had glided like a needle completely through him, penetrating deeply, and with a dull sound, the wooden partition behind him.

Borromée flung out his arms, letting his sword fall to the ground. His eyes became fixed and injected with blood; his mouth opened wide; his lips were stained with a red foam; his head fell on his shoulder with a sigh, which sounded like a death-rattle; then his limbs refused their support, and his body, as it sunk forward, enlarged the aperture of the wound, but could not free itself from the partition, supported as it was by Chicot's terrible wrist, so that the unfortunate man, like a gigantic moth, remained fastened to the wall, which his feet kicked convulsively.

Chicot, cold and impassive as he always was in positions of great difficulty, especially when he had a conviction at the bottom of his heart that he had done everything his conscience could require of him,—Chicot, we say, took his hand from his sword, which remained in a horizontal position, unfastened the captain's belt, searched his doublet, took the letter, and read the address, " Duchesse de Montpensier."

All this time the blood was welling copiously from the wound, and the agony of death was depicted on the features of the wounded man. " I am dying! I am dying!" he murmured. " Oh, Heaven! have pity on me!"

This last appeal to the divine mercy, made by a man who had most probably rarely thought of it until this moment of his direst need, touched Chicot's feeling. " Let us be charitable," he said; " and since this man must die, let him at least die as quietly as possible." He then advanced towards the partition, and by an effort withdrew his sword from the wall, and supported Borromée's body, to prevent it from falling heavily. This precaution, however, was useless; the approach of death had been rapid and certain, and had already paralysed the dying man's limbs. His legs gave way beneath him; he fell into Chicot's arms, and then rolled heavily on the floor. The shock of his fall made a stream of blood flow from his wound, with which the last remains of life ebbed away.

Chicot then went and opened the door of communication, and called Bonhomet. He had no occasion to call twice, for the innkeeper had been listening at the door, and had successively heard the noise of tables and stools, the clashing of swords, and the fall of a heavy body. Now, the worthy Maître Bonhomet had, particularly after the confidence which had been reposed in him, too extensive an experience of the character of gentlemen of the sword in general, and of that of Chicot in particular, not to have understood, step by step, what had taken place. The only thing of which he was ignorant was which of the two adversaries had fallen.

It must however be said in praise of Maître Bonhomet that his face assumed an expression of real satisfaction when he heard Chicot's voice, and when he saw that it was the Gascon, who, safe and sound, opened the door. Chicot, whom nothing escaped, remarked the expression of his countenance, and was inwardly pleased at it.

Bonhomet tremblingly entered the apartment. " Ah, good Jesus!" he exclaimed, as he saw the captain's body bathed in blood.

" Yes, my poor Bonhomet," said Chicot; " this is what we have come to. Our dear captain here is very ill, as you see."

" Oh, my good M. Chicot! my good M. Chicot!" exclaimed Bonhomet, ready to faint.

" Well, what? " inquired Chicot.

" It is very unkind of you to have chosen my inn for this execution. Such a handsome captain too! "

" Would you sooner have seen Chicot lying there, and Borromée alive? "

" No! oh, no! " cried the host, from the very bottom of his heart.

" Well, that would have happened, however, had it not been for a miracle of Providence."

" Really? "

" Upon the word of Chicot. Just look at my back, for it pains me a good deal, my dear friend." And he stooped down before the innkeeper, so that both his shoulders might be on a level with the host's eye.

Between the two shoulders the doublet was pierced through; and a spot of blood as large and round as a silver crown-piece reddened the edges of the hole.

" Blood! " cried Bonhomet, " blood! Ah, you are wounded!"

" Wait! wait! " And Chicot unfastened his doublet and his shirt. " Now look," he said.

" Oh, you wore a cuirass! What a fortunate thing, dear M. Chicot! and you say that the ruffian wished to assassinate you."

" The devil! it hardly seems likely I should amuse myself by giving a dagger-thrust between my own shoulders. Now, what do you see? "

" A link broken."

" That dear captain was in good earnest, then. Is there much blood? "

" Yes, a good deal under the links."

" I must take off the cuirass, then," said Chicot.

Chicot took off his cuirass, and bared the upper part of his body, which seemed to be composed of nothing but bones, muscles spread over the bones, and skin merely covering the muscles.

" Ah, M. Chicot! " exclaimed Bonhomet, " you have a wound as large as a plate."

" Yes, I suppose the blood has spread; there is what doctors call ecchymosis. Give me some clean linen, pour into a glass equal parts of good olive oil and wine dregs, and wash that stain for me."

" But, dear M. Chicot, what am I to do with this body? "

" That is not your affair."

" What! not my affair? "

" No. Give me some ink, a pen, and a sheet of paper."

" Immediately, dear M. Chicot," said Bonhomet, as he darted out of the room.

Meanwhile Chicot, who probably had no time to lose, heated at the lamp the point of a small dagger, and cut in the middle of the wax the seal of the letter. This being done, and as there was nothing else to retain the despatch, Chicot drew it from its envelope, and read it with the liveliest marks of satisfaction. Just as he had finished reading it, Maître Bonhomet returned with the oil, the wine, the paper, and the pen.

Chicot arranged the pen, ink, and paper before him, sat down at the table, and turned his back with stoical indifference towards Bonhomet for him to operate upon. The latter understood the pantomime, and began to rub it.

However, as if, instead of irritating a painful wound, some one had been tickling him in the most delightful manner, Chicot, during the operation, copied the letter from the Duc de Guise to his sister, and made his comments thereon at every word. The letter was as follows:—

DEAR SISTER,—The expedition from Antwerp has succeeded for everybody, but has failed as far as we are concerned. You will be told that the Duc d'Anjou is dead; do not believe it—he is alive.

He lives, you understand; and that is the whole question. There is a complete dynasty in those words; those two words separate the House of Lorraine from the throne of France better than the deepest abyss could do it.

Do not, however, make yourself too uneasy about that. I have discovered that two persons whom I thought were dead are still living, and there is a great chance of death for the prince while those two persons are alive.

Think, then, only of Paris; it will be time enough for the League to act six weeks hence. Let our Leaguers know that the moment is approaching, and let them hold themselves in readiness.

The army is on foot; we number twelve thousand sure men, all well equipped; I shall enter France with it, under the pretext of engaging the German Huguenots, who are going to assist Henri de Navarre. I shall defeat the Huguenots, and having entered France as a friend, I shall act as a master.

" Oh, oh! " cried Chicot.

" Did I hurt you, dear M. Chicot? " said Bonhomet, discontinuing his frictions.

" Yes, my good fellow."

" I will rub more softly; don't be afraid."

Chicot continued:—

P.S.—I entirely approve your plan with regard to the Forty-five; only allow me to say, dear sister, that you will be conferring a greater honour on those fellows than they deserve.

" Ah, the devil ! " murmured Chicot, " this is getting obscure."
And he read it again :—

I entirely approve your plan with regard to the Forty-five.

" What plan? " Chicot asked himself.

Only allow me to say, dear sister, that you will be conferring a
greater honour on those fellows than they deserve.

" What honour? "
Chicot resumed :—

Than they deserve.—Your affectionate brother, H. DE LORRAINE.

" At all events," said Chicot, " everything is clear, except the
postscript. Very good! we will look after the postscript, then."

" Dear M. Chicot," Bonhomet ventured to observe, seeing
that Chicot had finished writing, if not thinking,—" dear M.
Chicot, you have not told me what I am to do with this corpse."

" That is a very simple affair."

" For you, who are full of imagination, it may be; but
for me? "

" Well! suppose, for instance, that that unfortunate captain
had been quarrelling with the Swiss guards or the *reîtres*, and
had been brought to your house wounded, would you have
refused to receive him? "

" No, certainly not, unless indeed you had forbidden me,
dear M. Chicot."

" Suppose that, having been placed in that corner, he had,
notwithstanding the care and attention you had bestowed upon
him, departed this life while in your charge, it would have been
a great misfortune, and nothing more, I suppose? "

" Certainly."

" And instead of incurring any blame, you would deserve to
be commended for your humanity. Suppose, again, that while
he was dying this poor captain had mentioned the name, which
you know very well, of the prior of Les Jacobins St. Antoine? "

" Of Dom Modeste Gorenflot? " exclaimed Bonhomet, in
astonishment.

" Yes, of Dom Modeste Gorenflot. Very good! You will go
and inform Dom Modeste of it. Dom Modeste will hasten here
with all speed; and as the dead man's purse is found in one of
his pockets—you understand it is important that the purse
should be found; I mention this merely by way of advice—and
as the dead man's purse is found in one of his pockets, and this
letter in the other, no suspicion whatever can be entertained."

" I understand, dear M. Chicot."

" In addition to which, you will receive a reward instead of being punished."

" You are a great man, dear M. Chicot. I will run at once to the priory of St. Antoine."

" Wait a minute! did I not say there was the purse and the letter? "

" Oh, yes! and you have the letter in your hand."

" Precisely."

" I must not say that it has been read and copied? "

" *Pardieu!* it is precisely if this letter reaches its destination intact that you will receive a recompense."

" The letter contains a secret, then? "

" In such times as the present there are secrets in everything, my dear Bonhomet." And Chicot, with this sententious reply, again fastened the silk under the wax of the seal by making use of the same means as before. He then fastened the wax so artistically that the most experienced eye would not have been able to detect the slightest crack, after which he replaced the letter in the pocket of the dead man, had the linen, which had been steeped in the oil and wine, applied to his wound by way of a cataplasm, put on again the coat of mail next to his skin, his shirt over his coat of mail, picked up his sword, wiped it, thrust it into the scabbard, and withdrew. He returned again, however, saying, " If, after all, the story which I have invented does not seem satisfactory to you, you can accuse the captain of having thrust his own sword through his body."

" A suicide? "

" Well, that doesn't compromise any one, you understand."

" But they won't bury the unfortunate man in holy ground."

" Pooh! " said Chicot, " will that be giving him much pleasure? "

" Why, yes, I should think so."

" In that case, do as you like, my dear Bonhomet. Adieu." Then returning a second time, he said, " By the way, I pay, since he is dead." And Chicot threw three golden crowns on the table; and then, placing his forefinger on his lips, in token of silence, he departed.

CHAPTER XXX

THE HUSBAND AND THE LOVER

IT was with no inconsiderable emotion that Chicot again recognised the Rue des Augustins, so quiet and deserted, the angle formed by the block of houses which preceded his own, and lastly, his own dear house itself, with its triangular roof, its worm-eaten balcony, and its gutters ornamented with water-spouts. He had been so afraid that he should find nothing but an empty space in the place of the house; he had so strongly apprehended that he should see the street blackened by the smoke of a conflagration—that the street and the house appeared to him miracles of neatness, loveliness, and splendour.

Chicot had concealed the key of his beloved house in the hollow of a stone which served as the base of one of the columns by which his balcony was supported. At the period we are now writing about, any kind of key belonging to a chest or piece of furniture equalled in weight and size the very largest keys of our houses of the present day. The door-keys, therefore, following the natural proportions, were equal in size to the keys of our modern cities. So Chicot had considered the difficulty which his pocket would have in accommodating the happy key, and had hidden it in the spot we have indicated. It must be confessed that he felt a slight shudder creeping over him as he plunged his fingers in the hollow of the stone. This shudder was succeeded by a feeling of the most unmixed delight when the cold of the iron met his hand—for the key was actually in the place where he had left it.

It was precisely the same with regard to the furniture in the first room he came to; the same too with the small board which he had nailed to the joist; and lastly, the same with the thousand crowns, which were still slumbering in their oaken hiding-place.

Chicot was not a miser—quite the contrary, indeed. He had very frequently thrown gold about broadcast, thereby allowing the ideal to triumph over the material, which is the philosophy of every man who is of any value; but no sooner had the mind momentarily ceased to exercise its influence over matter (in other words, whenever money was no longer needed, nor sacrifice requisite); whenever, in a word, the senses temporarily regained their influence over Chicot's mind, and whenever his mind allowed the body to live and to take enjoyment—gold, that principal, that unceasing, that eternal source of animal delights, reassumed its value in our philosopher's eyes; and no one knew better than he did into how many delicious particles that inestimable totality which people call a crown is subdivided.

"*Ventre de biche!*" murmured Chicot, sitting down in the middle of his room, after he had removed the flagstone, and with the small piece of board by his side, and his treasure under his eyes—"*ventre de biche!* that excellent young man is a most invaluable neighbour, for he has made others respect my money, and has himself respected it too; in sober truth, such an action is wonderful in such times as the present. *Mordieu!* I owe some thanks to that excellent young fellow, and he shall have them this evening."

Thereupon Chicot replaced the plank over the joist, the flagstone over the plank, approached the window, and looked towards the opposite side of the street.

The house still retained that grey and sombre aspect which the imagination sometimes bestows upon certain buildings whose character it knows.

"It cannot yet be their time for retiring to rest," said Chicot. "And besides, those neighbours, I am sure, are no great sleepers; so let us see."

He descended his staircase, crossed the road—forming, as he did so, his features into their most amiable and gracious expression—and knocked at his neighbour's door. He remarked the creaking of the staircase, the sound of a hurried footstep, and then waited long enough to feel warranted in knocking again.

At this fresh summons the door opened, and the outline of a man appeared in the gloom.

"Thank you, and good-evening," said Chicot, holding out his hand; "here I am back again, and I am come to return you my thanks, my dear neighbour."

"I beg your pardon?" inquiringly observed a voice, in a tone of disappointment, the accent of which greatly surprised Chicot. At the same moment the man who had opened the door drew back a step or two.

"Stay! I have made a mistake," said Chicot; "you were not my neighbour when I left, and yet I know who you are."

"And I know you too," said the young man.

"You are M. le Vicomte Ernauton de Carmainges."

"And you are the Shade."

"Really," said Chicot, "I am quite bewildered."

" Well, and what do you want, monsieur? " inquired the young man, somewhat churlishly.

" Excuse me, but I am interrupting you perhaps, my dear monsieur? "

" No, only you will allow me to ask you what you may want."

" Nothing, except that I wished to speak to the master of this house."

" Speak, then."

" What do you mean? "

" I am the master of the house, that is all."

" You? since when, allow me to ask? "

" The devil! since three days ago."

" Good! the house was for sale, then? "

" So it would seem, since I have bought it.

" But the former proprietor? "

" No longer lives here, as you see."

" Where is he? "

" I don't know."

" Come, come! let us understand each other," said Chicot.

" There is nothing I should like better," replied Ernauton, with visible impatience; " only let us do so without losing any time."

" The former proprietor was a man between five-and-twenty and thirty years of age, but who looked as if he were forty."

" No; he was a man about sixty-five or sixty-six years old, who looked his age quite."

" Bald? "

" No, on the contrary, with a forest of white hair."

" He had an enormous scar on the left side of the head, had he not? "

" I did not observe the scar, but I did a good number of wrinkles."

" I cannot understand it at all," said Chicot.

" Well," resumed Ernauton, after a moment's silence, " what did you want with that man, my dear Monsieur the Shade? "

Chicot was on the point of stating what he had come to say; suddenly, however, the mystery of the surprise which Ernauton had exhibited reminded him of a certain proverb very dear to all discreet people. " I wished to pay him a neighbourly visit," he said, " that is all."

In this way Chicot did not tell a falsehood, and yet admitted nothing.

" My dear monsieur," said Ernauton, politely, but reducing

considerably the opening of the door, which he held half closed,
" I regret I am unable to give you more precise information."

" Thank you, monsieur," said Chicot; " I must look elsewhere, then."

" But," continued Ernauton, as he gradually closed the door,
" that does not prevent my congratulating myself upon the
chance which has brought me again into personal communication
with you."

" You would like to send me to the devil, I believe," murmured
Chicot to himself, as he returned bow for bow.

However, as notwithstanding this mental reply, Chicot, in his
preoccupation, forgot to withdraw, Ernauton, enclosing his face
between the door and the doorway, said to him, " I wish you a
very good-evening, monsieur."

" One moment, M. de Carmainges," said Chicot.

" Monsieur, I exceedingly regret that I am unable to wait,"
replied Ernauton; " but the fact is, I am expecting some one
who will come and knock at this very door, and this person will
be angry with me if I do not show the greatest possible discretion
in receiving him."

" That is quite sufficient, monsieur; I understand," said
Chicot. " I am sorry to have been so importunate, and I now
retire."

" Adieu, dear Monsieur the Shade."

" Adieu, excellent M. Ernauton." And as Chicot drew back
a step, he saw the door quietly shut in his face. He listened
to satisfy himself whether the suspicious young man was watching his departure, but he heard Ernauton's footsteps as he
ascended the staircase; he therefore returned to his own house
without uneasiness, and shut himself up in it, thoroughly
determined not to interfere with his new neighbour's habits,
but in accordance with his usual custom, equally resolved not
to lose sight of him altogether.

In fact, Chicot was not a man to slumber on a circumstance
which seemed to him of any importance, without having handled
and dissected it with the patience of a skilled anatomist. In
spite of himself—and it was an advantage or a defect of his
organisation—every material impression that his mind received
presented itself by its salient features for analysis, in such a
manner that poor Chicot's brain was driven to an immediate
examination.

Chicot, whose mind up to that moment had been occupied
with that phrase of the Duc de Guise's letter—namely, " I
entirely approve your plan with regard to the Forty-five,"—

consequently abandoned that phrase, the examination of which he promised himself to return to at a later period, in order that he might forthwith thoroughly exhaust this new subject of pre-occupation, which had just taken the place of the older one.

Chicot reflected that nothing could be more singular than to see Ernauton installing himself, as if he were its master, in that mysterious house whose inhabitants had suddenly disappeared. And the more so, since to these original inhabitants a phrase of the Duc de Guise's letter relative to the Duc d'Anjou might possibly have some reference. That was a chance which deserved attentive consideration; and Chicot was in the habit of believing in providential chances. He developed, even, whenever he was begged to do so, some very ingenious theories on the subject.

The basis of these theories was an idea which in our opinion was quite as good as any other; it was as follows: chance is God's reserve. The Almighty never communicates that reserve except in momentous circumstances, particularly since he has observed that men are sagacious enough to study and foresee the chances which may befall them in accordance with natural causes and regularly organised principles of existence. More-over, God likes to counteract the combinations of the proud, whose past pride he has already punished by drowning them, and whose future pride he will punish by burning them. God, then, we say, or rather Chicot said, is pleased to counteract the combinations of the proud by means with which they are unacquainted, and whose intervention they cannot foresee.

This theory, as may be perceived, includes some very specious arguments, and might possibly furnish some very brilliant theses; but the reader, anxious, as Chicot was, to know what Carmainges's object was in that house, will feel obliged to us for pausing in their development.

Chicot, then, reflected that it was strange to see Ernauton in the very house where he had seen Rémy. He considered it was strange for two reasons: first, because of the entire ignorance in which the two men lived with respect to each other, which led to the supposition that there must have been an inter-mediary between them unknown to Chicot; and secondly, because the house must have been sold to Ernauton, who possessed no means of purchasing it.

" It is true," said Chicot, installing himself as comfortably as he could in his usual place of observation—" it is true that the young man pretends he is expecting a visit, and it is probable that the expected visitor is a woman. In these days women are rich and indulge in caprices. Ernauton is handsome, young, and graceful; he has taken some one's fancy; a rendezvous has been arranged; and he has been directed to purchase this house; he has bought the house, and has accepted the rendezvous.

"Ernauton," continued Chicot, "lives at court; it must be some lady belonging to the court, then, with whom he has this affair. Poor fellow, will he love her? Heaven preserve him from such a thing! he is going to fall headlong into that gulf of perdition. Very good! ought I not to read him a moral lecture thereupon?—a moral lecture doubly useless and ten times stupid; useless because he won't understand it, and even if he did understand it, would refuse to listen to it; stupid, because I should be doing far better to go to bed, and to think a little about that poor Borromée.

"On this latter subject," continued Chicot, who had suddenly become thoughtful, "I perceive one thing; namely, that remorse does not exist, and is only a relative feeling. The fact is, I do not feel any remorse at all for having killed Borromée, since the manner in which M. de Carmainges's affair occupies my mind makes me forget that I have killed the man; and if he, on his side, had nailed me to the table as I nailed him to the wainscot, he would certainly have had no more remorse than I have myself at the present moment."

Chicot had reached so far in his reasonings, his inductions, and his philosophy, which had consumed a good hour and a half altogether, when he was drawn from his train of thought by the arrival of a litter proceeding from the direction of the inn of the Brave Chevalier. This litter stopped at the threshold of the mysterious house. A veiled lady alighted from it, and disappeared within the door, which Ernauton held half open.

"Poor fellow!" murmured Chicot, "I was not mistaken, and it was indeed a lady he was waiting for; and so now I shall go to bed." Whereupon he rose, but remained motionless, although standing up. "I am mistaken," he said. "I shall not be able to go to sleep; but I maintain what I was saying—that if I don't sleep it will not be remorse which will prevent me, it will be curiosity; and that is so true that if I remain here in my observatory, my mind will be occupied with but one thing, and that is the question which of our noble ladies honours the handsome Ernauton with her affection. Far better, then, to remain where I am; since if I went to bed, I should certainly get up again to return here." And thereupon Chicot resumed his seat.

An hour had nearly passed away—and we cannot state

whether Chicot was engaged in thinking of the unknown lady or of Borromée, whether he was occupied by curiosity or tormented by remorse—when he fancied he heard the gallop of a horse at the end of the street. And in fact, a cavalier, wrapped in his cloak, made his appearance immediately.

The cavalier drew up in the middle of the street, and seemed to be looking about him to see where he was. He then perceived the group which was formed by the litter and its bearers. He drove his horse against them. He was armed, for the rattling of his sword against his spurs could be distinctly heard. The bearers of the litter seemed desirous of barring his passage; but he addressed a few words to them in a low tone of voice, and not only did they withdraw with every mark of respect, but one of them, as the rider sprang to the ground from his horse, even received the bridle from his hand. The unknown advanced towards the door and knocked loudly.

" Well," said Chicot, " I was right in remaining, after all; my presentiments, which told me that something was going to take place, have not deceived me. Here is the husband, poor Ernauton; we shall presently see something serious. If, however, it be the husband, he is very kind to announce his return in so riotous a manner."

Notwithstanding the magisterial manner in which the unknown thundered at the door, some hesitation seemed to be shown in opening it.

" Open! " cried he who was knocking.

" Open! open! " repeated the bearers.

" There is no doubt it is the husband," resumed Chicot; " he has threatened the men that he will have them whipped or hanged, and they have declared themselves on his side. Poor Ernauton, he will be flayed alive! Oh, oh! I shall not suffer such a thing, however," added Chicot. " For in fact," he continued, " he assisted me; and consequently, when an opportunity presents itself, I ought to help him. And it seems to me that the opportunity has now arrived, or it never will arrive."

Chicot was resolute and generous, and curious into the bargain; he unfastened his long sword, placed it under his arm, and hurriedly ran down the staircase. He knew how to open his door noiselessly, which is an indispensable piece of knowledge for any one who may wish to listen with advantage. He glided under the balcony, then behind a pillar, and waited.

Hardly had Chicot installed himself, when the door opposite was opened, as soon as the unknown had whispered a word through the keyhole; and yet he did not venture beyond the threshold. A moment afterwards the lady appeared within the doorway. She took hold of the cavalier's arm, who led her to the litter, closed the door of it, and then mounted his horse.

" There is no doubt on the subject," said Chicot; " it is the husband—a good-natured fellow of a husband after all, since he does not think it worth his while to explore the house in order to be revenged on my friend Carmainges."

The litter then moved off, the cavalier walking his horse beside the *portière*.

" *Pardieu !* " said Chicot, " I must follow those people and learn who they are, and where they are going; I shall at all events draw some solid counsel from my discovery for my friend Carmainges."

Chicot accordingly followed the *cortége*, observing the precaution, however, of keeping in the shadow of the walls, and taking care that the noise made by the footsteps of the men and of the horses should render the sound of his own inaudible. His surprise was by no means slight when he saw the litter stop at the door of the Brave Chevalier. Almost immediately afterwards, as if some one had been on the watch, the door was opened.

The lady, still veiled, alighted, entered, and mounted to the turret, the window of the first story of which was lighted. The husband followed her, both being respectfully preceded by Dame Fournichon, who carried a light in her hand.

" Decidedly," said Chicot, crossing his arms on his chest, " I cannot understand a single thing of the whole affair."

CHAPTER XXXI

SHOWING HOW CHICOT BEGAN TO UNDERSTAND THE PURPORT OF M. DE GUISE'S LETTER

CHICOT fancied that he had already seen somewhere the figure of this courteous cavalier; but his memory, having become a little confused during his journey from Navarre, where he had met with so many different persons, did not, with its usual facility, furnish him with the cavalier's name on the present occasion.

While, concealed in the shade, he was interrogating himself, with his eyes fixed upon the lighted window, as to the object of this lady and gentleman's interview at the Brave Chevalier, our worthy Gascon, forgetting Ernauton in the mysterious house, observed the door of the hostelry open; and in the stream of light which escaped through the opening, he perceived something resembling the dark outline of a monk's figure. The outline in question paused for a moment to look up at the same window at which Chicot had been gazing.

" Oh, oh! " he murmured; " if I am not mistaken, that is the frock of a Jacobin friar. Is Maître Gorenflot so lax, then, in his discipline as to allow his sheep to go strolling about at such an hour of the night as this, and at such a distance from the priory? "

Chicot kept his eye upon the Jacobin, who was making his way along the Rue des Augustins; and something seemed instinctively to assure him that he should, through this monk, discover the solution of the problem which he had up to that moment been vainly endeavouring to ascertain.

Moreover, in the same way that Chicot had fancied he had recognised the figure of the cavalier, he now fancied he could recognise in the monk a certain movement of the shoulder, and a peculiar military movement of the hips, which belong only to persons in the habit of frequenting fencing-rooms and gymnastic establishments. " May the devil seize me," he murmured, " if that frock yonder does not cover the body of that little miscreant whom I wished them to give me for a travelling-companion, and who handles his arquebuse and foil so cleverly! "

Hardly had the idea occurred to Chicot, when, to convince himself of its value, he stretched out his long legs, and in a dozen strides rejoined the little fellow, who was walking along, holding up his frock above his thin and sinewy legs, in order to move more rapidly. This was not very difficult, however, inasmuch as the monk paused every now and then to glance behind him, as if he was going away with great difficulty and with feelings of profound regret. His glance was invariably directed towards the brilliantly lighted windows of the hostelry.

Chicot had not gone many steps before he felt sure that he had not been mistaken in his conjectures. " Holloa, my little master! " he said; " holloa, my little Jacquot! holloa, my little Clement! Halt! " And he pronounced this last word in so thoroughly military a tone that the monk started at it.

" Who calls me? " inquired the young man, rudely, with something rather antagonistic than cordial in his tone of voice.

" I! " replied Chicot, drawing himself up in front of the monk; " I! don't you recognise me? "

" Oh, M. Robert Briquet! " exclaimed the monk.

" Myself, my little man. And where are you going like that, so late, darling child? "

" To the priory, M. Briquet."

" Very good; but where do you come from? "

" I? "

" Of course, little libertine."

The young man started. " I don't know what you are saying, M. Briquet," he replied; " on the contrary, I have been sent with a very important commission by Dom Modeste, who will himself assure you that such is the case, if there be any occasion for it."

" Gently, gently, my little Saint Jerome. We take fire like a match, it seems."

" And not without reason, too, when one hears such things said as you were saying just now."

" The devil! when one sees a frock like yours leaving a tavern at such an hour—"

" A tavern! I! "

" Oh, of course not; the house you left just now was not the Brave Chevalier, I suppose? Ah, you see I have caught you! "

" You were right in saying that I left that house, but it was not a tavern I was leaving."

" What! " said Chicot; " is not the hostelry of the Brave Chevalier a tavern? "

" A tavern is a house where people drink, and as I have not been drinking in that house, that house is not a tavern for me."

" The devil! that is a subtle distinction, and I am very much mistaken if you will not some day become a very forcible theologian; but at all events, if you did not go into that house to drink, what did you go there for? "

Clement made no reply, and Chicot could read in his face, notwithstanding the darkness of the night, a resolute determination not to say another word.

This resolution annoyed our friend extremely, for it had become a habit with him to know everything.

It must not be supposed that Clement showed any ill feeling by his silence; for, on the contrary, he had appeared delighted to meet in so unexpected a manner his learned fencing-master, Maître Robert Briquet, and had given him the warmest reception that could be expected from that close and rugged character.

The conversation had completely ceased. Chicot, for the purpose of starting it again, was on the point of pronouncing the name of Brother Borromée; but although Chicot did not feel any remorse, or fancied he did not feel any, he could not summon up courage to pronounce that name.

His young companion, still preserving the same unbroken silence, seemed as if he were awaiting something; it seemed too as if he considered it a happiness to remain as long as possible in the neighbourhood of the hostelry of the Brave Chevalier.

Robert Briquet tried to speak to him about the journey which the boy had for a moment entertained the hope of making with him. Jacques Clement's eyes glistened at the words " space " and " liberty." Robert Briquet told him that in the countries through which he had just been travelling the art of fencing was held greatly in honour; he added with an appearance of indifference that he had even brought away with him several wonderful passes and thrusts.

This was placing Jacques upon slippery ground. He wished to know what these passes were; and Chicot, with his long arm, indicated a few of them upon the arm of the little monk.

But all these delicacies and refinements on Chicot's part in no way affected little Clement's obstinate determination; and while he endeavoured to parry these unknown passes, which his friend Maître Robert Briquet was showing him, he preserved an obstinate silence with respect to what had brought him into that quarter.

Thoroughly annoyed, but keeping a strong control over himself, Chicot resolved to try the effect of injustice; injustice is one of the most powerful provocatives ever invented to make women, children, and inferiors speak, whatever their nature or disposition may be. " It does not matter," he said, as if he returned to his original idea—" it does not matter; you are a delightful little monk! but that you visit hostelries is certain, and what hostelries too!—those where beautiful ladies are to be found. And you stop outside in a state of ecstasy before the window, where you can see their shadow. Oh, little one, little one! I shall tell Dom Modeste all about it."

The bolt hit its mark—even more exactly than Chicot had supposed it would; for when he began, he did not suspect that the wound had been so deep.

Jacques turned round like a serpent that had been trodden on. " That is not true," he cried, crimson with shame and anger. " I don't look at women."

" Yes, yes," pursued Chicot; " on the contrary, there was an exceedingly pretty woman at the Brave Chevalier when you left it, and you turned round to look at her again; and I know that you were waiting for her in the turret, and I know too that you spoke to her." Chicot proceeded by the inductive process.

Jacques could not contain himself any longer. " I certainly have spoken to her!" he exclaimed. " Is it a sin to speak to women? "

" No, when one does not speak to them of one's own accord, and yielding to the temptation of Satan."

" Satan has nothing whatever to do with the matter; it was absolutely necessary that I should speak to that lady, since I was desired to hand her a letter."

" Desired by Dom Modeste? " cried Chicot.

" Yes, go and complain to him now if you like."

Chicot, bewildered, and feeling his way as it were in the dark, perceived at these words a gleam of light traversing the obscurity of his brain.

" Ah! " he said, " I knew it perfectly well."

" What did you know? "

" What you did not wish to tell me."

" I do not tell my own secrets, and for a greater reason, the secrets of others."

" Yes, but to me."

" Why should I tell them to you? "

" You should tell them to me because I am a friend of Dom Modeste; and for another reason you should tell them to me because—"

" Well? "

" Because I know beforehand all you could possibly have to tell me."

Jacques looked at Chicot and shook his head with an incredulous smile.

" Very good! " said Chicot, " would you like me to tell you what you do not wish to tell me? "

" I should indeed."

Chicot made an effort. " In the first place," he said, " that poor Borromée—"

A dark expression passed across Jacques's face. " Oh! " said the boy, " if I had been there—"

" Well! if you had been there? "

" The affair would not have turned out as it did."

" Would you have defended him against the Swiss with whom he got into a quarrel? "

" I would have defended him against every one."

" So that he would not have been killed? "

" Either that, or I should have got myself killed along with him."

" At all events, you were not there, so that the poor devil breathed his last in an obscure tavern, and in doing so pronounced Dom Modeste's name; is not that so? "

" Yes."

" Whereupon the people there informed Dom Modeste of it? "

" A man, seemingly scared out of his wits, who threw the whole convent into consternation."

" And Dom Modeste sent for his litter, and hastened to the Corne d'Abondance? "

" How do you know that? "

" Oh, you don't know me yet, my boy; I am somewhat of a sorcerer, I can tell you."

Jacques drew back a couple of steps.

" That is not all," continued Chicot, who, as he spoke, began to see clearer by the light of his own words; " a letter was found in the dead man's pocket."

" A letter; yes, precisely so."

" And Dom Modeste charged his little Jacques to carry that letter to its address."

" Yes."

" And the little Jacques ran immediately to the Hôtel de Guise."

" Oh! "

" Where he found no one—"

" *Bon Dieu !* "

" But M. de Mayneville."

" *Misericorde !* "

" And M. de Mayneville conducted Jacques to the hostelry of the Brave Chevalier."

" M. Briquet! M. Briquet! " cried Jacques, " if you know that—"

" Eh, *ventre de biche !* you see very well that I know it," exclaimed Chicot, feeling triumphant at having disentangled this secret, which was of such importance for him to learn, from the provoking intricacies in which it had been at first involved.

" In that case," returned Jacques, " you see very well, M. Briquet, that I am not guilty."

" No," said Chicot, " you are not guilty in act nor in omission, but you are guilty in thought."

" I! "

" I suppose there is no doubt you think the duchess very beautiful? "

" I ! "

" And you turned round to look at her again through the window."

" I ! "   The young monk coloured and stammered out, " Well, it is true; she is exactly like a Virgin Mary which was placed over the head of my mother's bed."

" Oh," muttered Chicot, " how much those people lose who are not curious! "

And thereupon he made little Clement, whom from this moment he held in his power, tell him all he had himself just told him, but this time with the details, which he could not possibly otherwise have known.

" You see," said Chicot, when he had finished, " what a poor fencing-master you had in Brother Borromée."

" M. Briquet," said little Jacques, " one ought not to speak ill of the dead."

" No; but confess one thing."

" What? "

" That Borromée did not make such good use of his sword as the man who killed him."

" True."

" And now that is all I had to say to you. Good-night, Jacques; we shall meet again soon, and if you like—"

" What, M. Briquet? "

" Why, I will give you lessons in fencing for the future."

" Oh, I shall be most thankful."

" And now off with you, my boy, for they are waiting for you impatiently at the priory."

" True; true! Thank you, M. Briquet, for having reminded me of it." And the little monk disappeared, running as fast as he could.

Chicot had a reason for dismissing his companion. He had extracted all he wished to learn from him, and on the other hand there still remained something further for him to learn elsewhere. He returned, therefore, as fast as he could, to his own house. The litter, the bearers, and the horse were still at the door of the Brave Chevalier. He regained his place of observation without making a noise. The house opposite to his own was still lighted up, and from that moment all his attention was directed towards it.

In the first place, Chicot observed, by a rent in the curtain, Ernauton walking up and down, apparently waiting with great impatience. He then saw the litter return, saw Mayneville leave, and lastly, he saw the duchess enter the room in which

Ernauton, palpitating and throbbing rather than breathing, impatiently awaited her return.

Ernauton kneeled before the duchess, who gave him her white hand to kiss. She then raised the young man from the ground, and made him sit down before her at a table which was most elegantly served.

"This is very singular," said Chicot. "It began like a conspiracy, and finishes by a rendezvous. Yes," he continued, "but who appointed this rendezvous? Madame de Montpensier."

And then, as a fresh light flashed through his brain, he murmured, "'I entirely approve your plan with regard to the Forty-five; only allow me to say, dear sister, that you will be conferring a greater honour on those fellows than they deserve.' *Ventre de biche !*" he exclaimed; "I return to my original idea —it is not a love-affair, but a conspiracy. Madame la Duchesse de Montpensier is in love with M. Ernauton de Carmainges; let us watch over this love-affair of Madame the Duchess."

And Chicot watched until midnight had long passed, when Ernauton hastened away, his cloak concealing his face, while Madame la Duchesse de Montpensier returned to her litter.

"Now," murmured Chicot, as he descended his own staircase, "what is that chance of death which is to deliver the Duc de Guise from the presumptive heir of the crown? Who are those persons who were thought to be dead, but are still living? *Mordieu !* I shall trace them before long."

CHAPTER XXXII

THE CARDINAL DE JOYEUSE

YOUTH has its obstinate resolutions, both as regards good and evil in the world, which are by no means inferior to the inflexibility of purpose of maturer years.

When directed towards good purposes, instances of this dogged obstinacy of character produce what are termed the great actions of life, and impress on the man who enters life an impulse which bears him onward, by a natural course, towards a heroism of character of one kind or another.

In this way Bayard and Du Guesclin became great captains, from having been the most ill-tempered and most intractable children that ever existed; in the same way, too, the swineherd whom nature had made the herdsman of Montalte, and whose genius had converted him into Sixtus Quintus, became a great pope, because he had persisted in performing his duties as a swineherd in an indifferent manner.

Again, in the same way were the worst Spartan natures displayed in heroic directions, after beginning with persistence in dissimulation and cruelty.

We have now to sketch the portrait of a man of an ordinary stamp; and yet more than one biographer would have found in Henri du Bouchage, at twenty years of age, the materials for a great man.

Henri obstinately persisted in his love and in his seclusion from the world. As his brother had begged, and as the king had required him to do, he remained for some days closeted alone with his one enduring thought; and then, when that thought had become more and more fixed and unchangeable in its nature, he one morning decided to pay a visit to his brother the cardinal—an important personage, who, at the age of twenty-six, had already for two years past been a cardinal, and who from the archbishopric of Narbonne had passed to the highest degree of ecclesiastical dignity, a position to which he was indebted as much to his noble descent as to his powerful intellect.

François de Joyeuse, whom we have already introduced to enlighten Henri de Valois respecting the doubt he had entertained with regard to Sylla—François de Joyeuse, young and worldly-minded, handsome and witty, was one of the most remarkable men of the period. Ambitious by nature, but circumspect by calculation and position, François de Joyeuse could assume as his device, " Nothing is too much," and justify his device.

The only one, perhaps, of all those who belonged to the court —and François de Joyeuse was attached to the court in a very especial manner—he had been able to create for himself two means of support out of the religious and lay thrones to which he in some way approximated, as a French gentleman, and as a prince of the Church.   Sixtus protected him against Henri III.; Henri III. protected him against Sixtus.   He was an Italian at Paris, Parisian at Rome, magnificent and able everywhere.

The sword alone of Joyeuse the grand admiral gave the latter more weight in the balance; but it might be inferred from certain smiles of the cardinal that if those temporal arms failed him which the hand of his brother, refined and admired as he was, wielded so successfully, he himself knew not only how to use, but also how to abuse, the spiritual weapons which had been intrusted to him by the sovereign head of the Church.

The cardinal, François de Joyeuse, had very rapidly become a wealthy man—wealthy in the first place from his own patrimony, and then from his different benefices. At that period the Church was richly endowed—very richly endowed, even; and when its treasures were exhausted, it knew the sources, which at the present day are exhausted, whence to renew them.

François de Joyeuse therefore lived in the most magnificent manner. Leaving to his brother all the pageantry and glitter of a military household, he crowded his salons with priests, bishops, and archbishops; he gratified his own peculiar fancies. On his attaining the dignity of cardinal, as he was a prince of the Church, and consequently superior to his brother, he had added to his household pages, according to the Italian fashion, and guards, according to that which prevailed at the French court. But these guards and pages were used by him as a still greater means of enjoying liberty of action. He frequently ranged his guards and pages round a huge litter, through the curtains of which his secretary passed his gloved hand, while he himself, on horseback, his sword by his side, rode through the town disguised with a wig, an enormous ruff round his neck, and horseman's boots, the sound of which delighted him beyond measure.

The cardinal, then, lived in the enjoyment of the greatest consideration, for in certain elevated positions in life, human fortunes are absorbing in their nature, and as if they were composed of adhesive particles, oblige all other fortunes to attend on and follow them like satellites; and on that account, therefore, the recent and marvellous successes of his brother Anne reflected on him all the brilliancy of those achievements. Moreover, as he had scrupulously followed the precept of concealing his mode of life, and of dispensing and diffusing his mental wealth, he was known only on the better sides of his character, and in his own family was accounted a very great man—a happiness which many sovereigns, laden with glory and crowned with the acclamations of a whole nation, have not enjoyed.

It was to this prelate that the Comte du Bouchage betook himself after his explanation with his brother, and after his conversation with the King of France; but as we have already observed, he allowed a few days to elapse, in obedience to the injunction which had been imposed on him by his elder brother, as well as by the king.

François resided in a beautiful mansion in that part of Paris called La Cité. The immense courtyard was never quite free from cavaliers and litters; but the prelate, whose garden was immediately contiguous to the bank of the river, allowed his courtyards and his antechambers to become crowded with courtiers. And as he had a mode of egress towards the river-bank, and a boat close thereto which conveyed him without any disturbance as far and as quietly as he chose, it not unfrequently happened that the courtiers uselessly waited to see the prelate, who availed himself of the pretext of a serious indisposition, or a rigid penance, to postpone his reception for the day. For him it was a realisation of Italy in the bosom of the capital of the King of France; it was Venice embraced by the two arms of the Seine.

François was proud, but by no means vain; he loved his friends as brothers, and his brothers nearly as much as his friends. Five years older than Bouchage, he withheld from him neither good nor evil counsel, neither his purse nor his smile. But as he wore his cardinal's costume with wonderful effect, Bouchage thought him handsome, noble, almost formidable, and accordingly respected him more, perhaps, than he did the brother who was older than either of them. Henri, with his beautiful cuirass, and the glittering accessories of his military costume, tremblingly confided his love-affairs to Anne, while he would not have dared to confess himself to François.

However, as Henri proceeded to the cardinal's hotel, his resolution was taken—he would frankly address the confessor first, and the friend afterwards. He entered the courtyard, which several gentlemen were at that moment leaving, wearied with having solicited, without obtaining, the favour of an audience. He passed through the antechambers, salons, and then the more private apartments. He had been told, as others had, that his brother was engaged in conference; but the idea of closing any of the doors before Bouchage never occurred to any of the attendants.

Bouchage therefore passed through all the apartments until he reached the garden—a true garden of a Roman prelate, luxurious in its shade, coolness, and perfume, such as at the present day may be found at the Villa Pamphile or the Palace Borghese.

Henri paused under a group of trees. At this moment the gate close to the river-side rolled on its hinges, and a man shrouded in a large brown cloak passed through followed by a person in a page's costume. The man, perceiving Henri, who was too absorbed in his reverie to think of him, glided through the trees, avoiding the observation either of Bouchage or of any one else.

Henri paid no attention to this mysterious entry; and it was only as he turned round that he saw the man entering the apartments. After he had waited about ten minutes, and as he was about to enter the house for the purpose of interrogating one of the attendants with the view of ascertaining at what hour precisely his brother would be visible, a servant, who seemed to be in search of him, observed his approach, and advancing in his direction, begged him to have the goodness to pass into the library, where the cardinal awaited him.

Henri complied with this invitation, but not very readily, as he conjectured that a new contest would result from it; he found his brother the cardinal engaged, with the assistance of a *valet de chambre*, in trying on a prelate's costume, a little worldly-looking, perhaps, in its shape and fashion, but elegant and becoming in its style.

" Good morning, count," said the cardinal; " what news have you ? "

" Excellent news, as far as our family is concerned," said Henri. " Anne, you know, has covered himself with glory in that retreat from Antwerp, and is alive."

" And, thank God ! you also, Henri, are safe and sound ? "

" Yes, my brother."

" You see," said the cardinal, " that God has his designs in regard to us."

" I am so full of gratitude to God, my brother, that I have formed the project of dedicating myself to his service. I am come to talk seriously to you upon this project, which is now well matured, and about which I have already spoken to you."

" Do you still keep to that idea, Bouchage ? " said the cardinal, allowing a slight exclamation to escape him, which was indicative that Joyeuse would have a struggle to encounter.

" I do."

" But it is impossible, Henri," returned the cardinal; " have you not been told so already ? "

" I have not listened to what others have said to me, my brother, because a voice stronger than mine, which speaks within me, prevents me from listening to anything which would turn me away from God."

" You cannot be so ignorant of the things of this world, Henri," said the cardinal, in his most serious tone of voice, " to believe that the voice you allude to was really that of the

Lord; on the contrary—I assert it positively too—it is altogether a feeling of a worldly nature which addresses you. God has nothing to do in this affair; do not abuse that Holy Name, therefore, and, above all, do not confound the voice of Heaven with that of earth."

"I do not confound, my brother; I only mean to say that something irresistible in its nature hurries me towards retreat and solitude."

"So far, so good, Henri; we are now making use of proper expressions. Well, my dear brother, I will tell you what is to be done. Taking what you say for granted, I am going to render you the happiest of men."

"Thank you! oh, thank you, my brother!"

"Listen to me, Henri. You must take money, a couple of attendants, and travel through the whole of Europe in a manner befitting a son of the house to which we belong. You will see foreign countries—Tartary, Russia, even the Laplanders, those fabulous peoples whom the sun never visits; you will become absorbed in your thoughts, until the devouring germ which is at work in you becomes either extinct or satiated; and after that, you will return to us again."

Henri, who had been seated, now rose, more serious than his brother had been. "You have not understood me, monseigneur," he said.

"I beg your pardon, Henri; you made use of the words 'retreat' and 'solitude.'"

"Yes, I did so; but by 'retreat' and 'solitude' I meant a cloister, and not travelling; to travel is to enjoy life still. I wish almost to suffer death, and if I do not suffer it, at least to live near it."

"That is an absurd thought, allow me to say, Henri; for whoever, in point of fact, wishes to isolate himself, is alone everywhere. But the cloister let it be. Well, then, I understand that you have come to talk to me about this project. I know some very learned Benedictines, and some very clever Augustines, whose houses are cheerful, adorned with flowers, attractive, and agreeable in every respect. Amid the works of science and art you will pass a delightful year, in excellent society—which is of no slight importance, for one should avoid lowering one's self in this world; and if at the end of the year you persist in your project, well, then, my dear Henri, I will not oppose you any further, and will myself open the door which will peacefully conduct you to everlasting rest."

"Most certainly you still misunderstand me, my brother,"

replied Bouchage, shaking his head, " or I should rather say your generous intelligence will not comprehend me. I do not wish for a cheerful residence or a delightful retreat, but a rigorously strict seclusion, as gloomy as the grave itself. I intend to pronounce my vows—vows which will leave me no other distraction than a grave to dig, a long prayer to say."

The cardinal frowned, and rose from his seat. " Yes," he said, " I did perfectly understand you; and I endeavoured by opposition, without set phrases or discussion, to combat the folly of your resolutions. But you force me to it; listen to me."

" Ah!" said Henri, despondently, " do not try to convince me; it is impossible."

" Brother, I will speak to you in the name of God, in the first place—of God, whom you offend in saying that this wild resolution comes from him. God does not accept sacrifices hastily made. You are weak, since you allow yourself to be conquered by a first disappointment; how can God be pleased to accept a victim as unworthy as that you offer?"

Henri started at his brother's remark.

" Oh, I shall no longer spare you, Henri—you, who never consider any of us," returned the cardinal; " you, who forget the grief which you will cause our elder brother, and will cause me too—"

" Forgive me," interrupted Henri, whose cheeks were dyed with crimson—" forgive me, monseigneur; but is the service of God, then, so gloomy and so dishonourable a career that all the members of a family are to be thrown into distress by it? You, for instance, my brother, whose portrait I observe suspended in this room, with all this gold, these diamonds, this purple around you—are you not both the delight and honour of our house, although you have chosen the service of God, as my eldest brother has chosen that of the kings of the earth?"

" Boy, boy!" exclaimed the cardinal, impatiently, " you will make me believe your brain is turned. What! will you venture to compare my residence to a cloister? my hundred attendants, my outriders, the gentlemen of my suite, and my guards, to a cell and a broom, which are the only arms and the sole wealth of a cloister? Are you mad? Did you not just now say that you repudiate these superfluities—necessary to me—these pictures, these precious vases, pomp, and distinction? Have you, as I have, the desire and hope of placing on your brow the tiara of Saint Peter? That indeed is a career, Henri; one presses forward in it, struggles in it, lives in it. But as for you, it is the miner's pick, the Trappist's spade, the grave-digger's tomb, that you desire—utter abandonment of life, of pleasure, of hope. And all that—I blush with shame for you, a man— all that, I say, because you love a woman who loves you not. You do foul injustice to your race, Henri, most truly."

" Brother ! " exclaimed the young man, pale as death, while his eyes blazed with kindling fire, " would you sooner have me blow out by brains, or plunge in my heart the sword I have the honour to wear by my side? *Pardieu !* monseigneur, if you, who are cardinal and prince besides, will give me absolution for so mortal a sin, the affair will be so quickly done that you shall have no time to complete your odious and unworthy thought that I am capable of dishonouring my race, which— God be praised !—a Joyeuse will never do."

" Come, come, Henri ! " said the cardinal, drawing his brother towards him, and pressing him in his arms; " come, dear child, beloved by all, forgive, and be indulgent towards those who love you. I have personal motives for entreating you. Listen to me; we are all happy—a rare thing here below—some through satisfied ambition, some by reason of the blessings of every kind with which God has crowned our lives. Do not, I implore you, Henri, cast the mortal poison of the retreat you speak of upon our family happiness. Think how our father will be grieved at it; think, too, how all of us will bear on our countenances the dark reflection of the mortification you are about to inflict upon us. I beseech you, Henri, to allow yourself to be persuaded. The cloister will not benefit you. I do not say that you will die there, for, misguided man, your answer will be a smile, which alas ! would be only too intelligible for me. No, believe me, the cloister is more fatal to you than the tomb. The tomb annihilates but life itself; the cloister annihilates intelligence. The cloister bows the head, instead of raising it to heaven; the cold, humid atmosphere of the vaults passes by degrees into the blood and penetrates the very marrow of the bones, changing the cloister recluse into another granite statue in the convent. My brother, my dear brother, take heed ! We have but few years; we have but one period of youth. Well, the beautiful years of your youth will pass as they are passing; for you are under the empire of a great grief. But at thirty years of age you will have become a man; the vigour of maturity will have then arrived; it will hurry away with it all that remains of your worn-out sorrow, and then you will wish to live again. But it will be too late; you will have grown melancholy, ugly, miserable; passion will have been extinguished in your heart; the bright light of your eye will have become quenched. They whose society you seek will flee you as a whited sepulchre, whose dark-some depths repel every glance. Henri, I speak as a friend, seriously, wisely; listen to me."

The young man remained unmoved and silent. The cardinal hoped that he had touched his feelings, and had shaken his resolution.

" Try some other resource, Henri. Carry this poisoned shaft which rankles in your bosom into all places—into the midst of noise, into festive scenes; sit with it at banquets. Imitate the wounded deer, which flees through the thickets and brakes and forests, in its efforts to draw out from its body the arrow which is rankling in the wound; sometimes the arrow falls."

" For pity's sake," said Henri, " do not persist any more! What I solicit is not the caprice of a moment, or the decision of an hour; it is the result of a laborious and painful determination. In Heaven's name, therefore, my brother, I adjure you to accord me the favour I solicit!"

" And what is the favour you ask?"

" A dispensation, monseigneur."

" For what purpose?"

" To shorten my novitiate."

" Ah! I knew it, Bouchage. You are worldly-minded even in your rigorousness, my poor boy. Oh, I know very well what reason you are going to give me! Yes, you are indeed a man of the world; you resemble those young men who offer themselves as volunteers, and eagerly seek fire, balls, and blows, but care not for working in the trenches, or for sweeping out the tents. There is some resource left yet, Henri. So much the better! so much the better!"

" Give me the dispensation I ask; I entreat you on my knees."

" I promise it to you; I will write to Rome for it. It will be a month before the answer arrives; but in exchange, promise me one thing."

" Name it."

" That you will not during this month's postponement reject any pleasure or amusement which may be offered to you; and if a month hence, you still entertain the same projects, Henri, I will give you this dispensation with my own hand. Are you satisfied now, and have you nothing further to ask me?"

" No, I thank you; but a month is a long time, and delays are killing me."

" In the meantime, and in order to change your thoughts, will you object to breakfast with me? I have some agreeable companions this morning." And the prelate smiled in a

manner which the most worldly disposed favourites of Henri
III. would have envied.

"Brother!" said Bouchage, resisting.

"I will not accept any excuse; you have no one but myself
here, since you have just arrived from Flanders, and your own
house cannot be in order just yet."

With these words the cardinal rose, and drawing aside a
portière which hung before a large cabinet sumptuously
furnished, he said, "Come, countess, let us persuade M. le
Comte du Bouchage to stay with us."

At the very moment, however, when the cardinal drew aside
the *portière*, Henri had observed, half reclining upon the
cushions, the page who had with the gentleman entered the gate
adjoining the banks of the river; and in this page, before even
the prelate had announced her sex, he had recognised a woman.
An indefinable sensation, like a sudden terror, or an overwhelming feeling of dread, seized him; and while the worldly cardinal
advanced to take the beautiful page by the hand, Henri du
Bouchage darted from the apartment, and so quickly, that when
François returned with the lady, smiling with the hope of
winning a heart back again to the world, the room was empty.

François frowned; then, seating himself before a table covered
with papers and letters, he hurriedly wrote a few lines. "May
I trouble you to ring, dear countess," he said, "since you have
your hand near the bell?"

The page obeyed, and a *valet de chambre* in the confidence of
the cardinal appeared.

"Let a courier start on horseback, without a moment's loss
of time," said François, "and take this letter to the grand
admiral at Château-Thierry."

CHAPTER XXXIII

NEWS FROM AURILLY

On the following day the king was working at the Louvre with
the superintendent of finances, when an attendant entered to
inform his Majesty that M. de Joyeuse, the eldest son of that
family, had just arrived, and was waiting for him in the large
audience-chamber, having come from Château-Thierry with a
message from M. le Duc d'Anjou.

The king precipitately left the business which occupied him, and ran to meet a friend whom he regarded with so much affection.

A considerable number of officers and courtiers were present in the cabinet; the queen-mother had arrived that evening, escorted by her maids-of-honour, and these light-hearted ladies were suns always attended by satellites.

The king gave Joyeuse his hand to kiss, and glanced with a satisfied expression around the assembly.

In the angle of the entrance door, in his usual place, stood Henri du Bouchage, rigorously discharging his service and the duties which were imposed on him. The king thanked him and saluted him with a friendly motion of the head, to which Henri replied by a profound reverence.

These silent communications made Joyeuse turn his head and smilingly look at his brother, without, however, saluting him in too marked a manner, for fear of violating etiquette.

" Sire," said Joyeuse, " I am sent to your Majesty by M. le Duc d'Anjou, recently returned from the expedition to Flanders."

" Is my brother well, Monsieur the Admiral? " inquired the king.

" As well, Sire, as the state of his mind will permit. However, I will not conceal from your Majesty that he appears to be suffering greatly."

" He must need something to change the current of his thoughts after his misfortune," said the king, delighted at the opportunity of proclaiming the check which his brother had met with, while appearing to pity him.

" I believe he does, Sire."

" We have been informed that the disaster was most severe."

" Sire—"

" But that, thanks to you, a considerable part of the army was saved. Thanks, Monsieur the Admiral, thanks! Does poor M. d'Anjou wish to see us? "

" Most anxiously so, Sire."

" In that case we will see him. Are not you of that opinion, madame? " said Henri, turning towards Catherine, whose heart was wrung with feelings the expression of which her face determinedly concealed.

" Sire," she replied, " I should have gone alone to meet my son; but since your Majesty condescends to join with me in this mark of kind consideration, the journey will be a party of pleasure for me."

" You will accompany us, gentlemen," said the king to the

courtiers. "We will set off to-morrow, and I shall sleep at Meaux."

"Shall I at once announce this excellent news to monseigneur, Sire?"

"Not so. What! leave me so soon, Monsieur the Admiral? Not so, indeed. I can well understand that a Joyeuse must be loved and sought after by my brother; but we have two of them, thank God! Bouchage, you will start for Château-Thierry, if you please."

"Sire," said Henri, "may I be permitted, after having announced your Majesty's visit to Monseigneur le Duc d'Anjou, to return to Paris?"

"You may do as you please, Bouchage," said the king.

Henri bowed, and advanced towards the door. Fortunately, Joyeuse was watching him narrowly.

"Will you allow me to say one word to my brother," he inquired.

"Do so; but what is it?" said the king in an undertone.

"The fact is that he wishes to use the utmost speed to execute the commission, and to return again immediately, which happens to interfere with my projects, Sire, and with those of the cardinal."

"Away with you, then, and rate this love-sick swain most roundly."

Anne hurried after his brother, and overtook him in the antechambers. "Well!" said he, "you are setting off very eagerly, Henri."

"Of course, my brother!"

"Because you wish to return here soon again?"

"That is quite true."

"You do not intend, then, to stay any time at Château-Thierry?"

"As little as possible."

"Why so?"

"Where others are amusing themselves is not my place."

"On the contrary, Henri, it is precisely because Monseigneur le Duc d'Anjou is about to give some fêtes to the court that you should remain at Château-Thierry."

"It is impossible."

"Because of your wish for retirement, and of the austere projects you have in view?"

"Yes."

"You have been to the king to solicit him to grant you a dispensation?"

" Who told you so? "

" I know it to be the case."

" It is true; I have been to him."

" You will not obtain it."

" Why so, my brother? "

" Because the king has no interest in depriving himself of such a devoted servant as you are."

" My brother the cardinal, then, will do what his Majesty will be disinclined to do."

" And all that for a woman! "

" Anne, I entreat you, do not persist any further."

" Ah, do not fear that I shall begin again; but, once for all, let us to the point. You set off for Château-Thierry. Well, instead of returning as hurriedly as you seem disposed to do, I wish you to wait for me in my apartments there; it is a long time since we have lived together. I particularly wish to be with you again, you understand."

" You are going to Château-Thierry to amuse yourself, Anne, and if I were to remain there I should poison all your pleasures."

" Oh, not at all! I resist, and am of a happy temperament —quite fitted to drive away your melancholy."

" Brother—"

" Permit me, count," said the admiral, with an imperious air of command; " I am the representative of our father here, and I enjoin you to wait for me at Château-Thierry. You will find out my apartments, which will be your own also; they are on the ground-floor, looking out on the park."

" If you command me to do so, my brother," said Henri, with a resigned air.

" Call it by what name you please, count, desire or command; but await my arrival."

" I will obey you, my brother."

" And I am persuaded that you will not be angry with me for it," added Joyeuse, pressing the young man in his arms.

The latter withdrew from the fraternal embrace somewhat ungraciously perhaps, ordered his horses, and immediately set off for Château-Thierry. He hurried thither with the anger of a vexed and disappointed man; that is to say, he pressed his horses to the top of their speed.

The same evening he was slowly ascending, before nightfall, the hill on which Château-Thierry is situated, with the river Marne flowing at its foot. At his name, the doors of the château flew open before him; but as far as an audience was concerned, it was more than an hour before he could obtain it. The prince, some told him, was in his apartments; others said he was asleep; he was practising music, the *valet de chambre* supposed. No one, however, among the attendants could give a positive reply.

Henri persisted, in order that he might no longer have to think of his service on the king, and might abandon himself to his melancholy thoughts unrestrained. By reason of his persistence, and because it was well known that he and his brother were on the most intimate terms with the prince, Henri was ushered into one of the salons on the first floor, where the prince at last consented to receive him.

Half an hour passed away; and the shades of evening insensibly closed in. The heavy and measured footsteps of the Duc d'Anjou resounded in the gallery; and Henri, on recognising them, prepared to discharge his mission with the accustomed formal ceremonies. But the prince, who seemed much hurried, quickly dispensed with these formalities on the part of his ambassador by taking him by the hand and embracing him. "Good-day, count," he said; "why should they have given you the trouble to come and see a poor defeated general?"

"The king has sent me, monseigneur, to inform you that he is exceedingly desirous of seeing your highness, and that in order to enable you to recover from your fatigue, his Majesty will himself come and pay a visit to Château-Thierry, to-morrow at the latest."

"The king will be here to-morrow!" exclaimed François, with a gesture of impatience, but recovering himself immediately. "To-morrow, to-morrow," he resumed; "why, the truth is that nothing will be in readiness, either here or in the town, to receive his Majesty."

Henri bowed, as one whose duty it had been to transmit an order, but who was not charged to comment upon it.

"The extreme haste in which their Majesties are to see your royal highness has not allowed them to think of the embarrassment they may cause."

"Well, well!" said the prince, hurriedly, "it is for me to make the best use of the time I have at my disposal. I leave you therefore, Henri; thanks for the alacrity you have shown, for you have travelled fast, I perceive. Go and take some rest."

"Your highness has no other orders to communicate to me?" Henri inquired respectfully.

"None. Go and lie down. You shall dine in your own apartments. I hold no reception this evening; I am suffering, and ill at ease. I have lost my appetite, and cannot sleep, which makes my life a sad, dreary one, which, you understand, I do not choose to inflict upon any one else. By the way, you have heard the news? "

" No, monseigneur; what news? "

" Aurilly has been eaten up by the wolves."

" Aurilly? " exclaimed Henri, with surprise.

" Yes, yes! devoured! It is singular how every one who comes near me dies a violent death. Good-night, count; may you sleep well! " And the prince hurried away rapidly.

CHAPTER XXXIV

DOUBT

HENRI descended the staircase, and as he paseed through the antechambers, observed many officers of his acquaintance, who ran forward to meet him, and with many marks of friendship offered to show him the way to his brother's apartments, which were situated in one of the corners of the château. It was the library which the duke had given Joyeuse to occupy during his residence at Château-Thierry.

Two salons, furnished in the style of François I., communicated with each other, and terminated in the library, the latter apartment looking out on the gardens. The admiral's bed had been put up in the library. Joyeuse was of an indolent, yet of a cultivated, turn of mind. If he stretched out his arm he laid his hand on science; if he opened the windows he could enjoy the beauties of nature. Finer and superior organisations require more satisfying enjoyments; and the morning breeze, the songs of birds, or the perfumes of flowers, added fresh delight to the triplets of Clément Marot, or to the odes of Ronsard.

Henri determined to leave everything as it was, not because he was influenced by the poetic sybaritism of his brother, but on the contrary through indifference, and because it mattered little to him whether he was there or elsewhere.

But as the count, in whatever frame of mind he might be, had been brought up never to neglect his duty or respect towards the king or the princes of the royal family of France, he inquired particularly in what part of the château the prince had resided since his return.

By mere accident Henri met with an excellent cicerone in the person of the young ensign whose indiscretion had, in the little village in Flanders where we represented the personages in this tale as having halted for a short time, communicated the count's secret to the prince. This ensign had not left the prince's side since his return, and could impart to Henri very accurate information.

On his arrival at Château-Thierry, the prince had at first entered upon a course of reckless dissipation. At that time he occupied the state apartments of the château, had receptions morning and evening, and was engaged during the day in stag-hunting in the forest; but since the intelligence of Aurilly's death, which had reached the prince from a source unknown, he had retired to a pavilion situated in the middle of the park. This pavilion, which was an almost inaccessible retreat except to the intimate associates of the prince, was hidden from view by the dense foliage of the surrounding trees, and could hardly be perceived above their lofty summits, or through the thick foliage of the hedges.

It was to this pavilion that the prince had retired two days before. Those who did not know him well said that it was Aurilly's death which had made him betake himself to this solitude; while those who were well acquainted with his character maintained that he was carrying out in this pavilion some base or infamous plot, which some day would be revealed to light.

A circumstance which rendered either of these suppositions much more probable was that the prince seemed greatly annoyed whenever a matter of business or a visit summoned him to the château; and so decidedly was this the case that no sooner had the visit been received, or the matter of business been despatched, than he returned to his solitude, where he was waited upon only by the two old *valets de chambre* who had been present at his birth.

" Then," observed Henri, " the fêtes will not be very gay if the prince continue in this humour."

" Certainly," replied the ensign, " for every one will know how to sympathise with the grief of the prince, smitten in his pride and in his affections."

Henri continued his interrogatories without intending it, and took a strange interest in doing so. The circumstance of Aurilly's death, whom he had known at the court, and whom he had again met in Flanders; the indifference with which the prince had announced the loss he had met with; the strict seclusion in which it was said the prince had lived since his death—all this seemed to him, without his being able to assign a reason for his belief, a part of that mysterious and darkened web wherein, for some time past, the events of his life had been woven.

" And," inquired he of the ensign, " it is not known, you say, how the news of Aurilly's death reached the prince? "

" No."

" But surely," he insisted, " people must talk about it? "

" Oh, of course," said the ensign; " true or false, you know, people always will talk."

" Well, then, tell me what it is."

" It is said that the prince was hunting under the willows close beside the river, and that he had wandered away from the others who were hunting also—for everything he does is by fits and starts, and he becomes as excited in the field as at play, or under fire, or under the influence of grief—when suddenly he was seen returning with an expression of consternation. The courtiers questioned him, thinking that it was nothing more than a mere incident of the hunting-field. He held two *rouleaux* of gold in his hand. ' Can you understand this, messieurs? ' he said in a hard, dry voice. ' Aurilly is dead; Aurilly has been eaten by the wolves.'

" Every one immediately exclaimed.

" ' Nay, indeed,' said the prince; ' may the devil take me if it be not so! The poor lute-player had always been a far better musician than a horseman. It seems that his horse ran away with him, and that he fell into a pit, where he was killed. The next day a couple of travellers who were passing close to the pit discovered his body half eaten by the wolves; and a proof that the affair actually did happen as I have related it, and that robbers have nothing whatever to do with the whole matter, is that here are two *rouleaux* of gold which he had about him, and which have been faithfully restored.'

" Now, since no one had been seen to bring these two *rouleaux* of gold," continued the ensign, " it is supposed that they had been handed to the prince by the two travellers, who, having met and recognised his highness on the banks of the river, had announced the intelligence of Aurilly's death."

" It is very strange," murmured Henri.

" And what is more strange still," continued the ensign, " is that it is said—can it be true, or is it merely an invention? —it is said, I repeat, that the prince was seen to open the little gate of the park close to the chestnut-trees, and that something like two shadows passed through the gate. The prince, then, has introduced two persons into the park—probably the two travellers. It is since that time that he has retired into his pavilion, and we have been able to see him only by stealth."

"And has no one seen these two travellers?" asked Henri.

"As I was proceeding to ask the prince the pass-word for the night, for the sentinels on duty at the château, I met a man who did not seem to me to belong to his highness's household; but I was unable to observe his face, the man having turned aside as soon as he perceived me, and having drawn the hood of his coat over his eyes."

"The hood of his coat, do you say?"

"Yes; the man looked like a Flemish peasant, and reminded me, I hardly know why, of the person by whom you were accompanied when we met out yonder."

Henri started. The observation seemed to him in some way connected with the profound and absorbing interest with which the story inspired him. To him, too, who had seen Diane and her companion confided to Aurilly, the idea occurred that the two travellers who had announced to the prince the death of the unfortunate lute-player were acquaintances of his own.

Henri looked attentively at the ensign. "And when you fancied you recognised this man, what was the idea that occurred to you, monsieur?" he inquired.

"I will tell you what my impression was," replied the ensign; "however, I will not pretend to assert anything positively. The prince has not, in all probability, abandoned his idea with regard to Flanders. He therefore maintains spies in his employ. The man with the woollen overcoat is a spy, who on his way hither may have become acquainted with the accident which had happened to the musician, and may thus have been the bearer of two pieces of intelligence at the same time."

"That is not improbable," said Henri, thoughtfully; "but what was this man doing when you saw him?"

"He was walking beside the hedge which borders the parterre —you can see the hedge from your windows—and was going towards the conservatories."

"You say, then, that the two travellers—for I believe you stated there were two—"

"Others say that two persons were seen to enter; but I saw only one, the man in the overcoat."

"In that case, then, you have reason to believe that the man in the overcoat, as you describe him, is living in the conservatories?"

"It is not unlikely."

"And have these conservatories a means of exit?"

" Yes, count, towards the town."

Henri remained silent for some time. His heart was throbbing violently; for these details, which were apparently matters of indifference to him, who seemed throughout the whole of this mystery as if he were gifted with the power of prevision, were, in reality, full of the deepest interest for him.

Night had in the meantime closed in, and the two young men were conversing together without any light in Joyeuse's apartments. Fatigued by his journey, oppressed by the strange events which had just been related to him, unable to struggle against the emotions which they had aroused in his breast, the count had thrown himself on his brother's bed and mechanically directed his gaze towards the deep blue heavens above him, which seemed studded with diamonds.

The young ensign was seated on the ledge of the window, and voluntarily abandoned himself to that listlessness of thought, to that poetic reverie of youth, to that absorbing languor of feeling, which the balmy freshness of evening inspires.

A deep silence reigned throughout the park and the town; the gates were closed; the lights were kindled by degrees; the dogs in the distance were barking in their kennels at the servants on whom devolved the duty of shutting up the stables in the evening.

Suddenly the ensign rose to his feet, made a sign of attention with his hand, leaned out of the window, and then, calling in a quick, low tone to the count, who was reclining on the bed, said, " Come! come! "

" What is the matter? " Henri inquired, arousing himself by a strong effort from his revery.

" The man! the man! "

" What man? "

" The man in the overcoat! the spy! "

" Oh! " exclaimed Henri, springing from the bed to the window, and leaning on the ensign.

" Stay! " continued the ensign; " do you see him yonder? He is creeping along the hedge. Wait a moment; he will show himself again. Now look towards that spot which is illuminated by the moon's rays—there he is! there he is."

" Yes."

" Do you not think he is a sinister-looking fellow? "

" Sinister is the very word," replied Bouchage, in a gloomy voice.

" Do you believe he is a spy? "

" I believe nothing, and I believe everything."

" See! he is going from the prince's pavilion to the conservatories."

" The prince's pavilion is in that direction, then? " inquired Bouchage, indicating with his finger the direction from which the stranger appeared to be proceeding.

" Do you see that light whose rays are trembling through the leaves of the trees? "

" Well? "

" That is the dining-room."

" Ah! " exclaimed Henri, " see, he makes his appearance again."

" Yes, he is no doubt going to the conservatories to join his companion. Did you hear that? "

" What? "

" The sound of a key turning in the lock."

" It is singular," said Bouchage; " there is nothing unusual in all this, and yet—"

" And yet you tremble, do you not? "

" Yes," said the count; " but what is that? "

The sound of a bell was heard.

" It is the signal for the supper of the prince's household. Are you going to join us at supper, count? "

" No, I thank you, I do not require anything; and if I should feel hungry, I will call for what I may need."

" Do not wait for that, monsieur; but come and amuse yourself in our society."

" No, it is impossible."

" Why so? "

" His royal highness almost directed me to have what I should need served to me in my own apartments; but do not let me delay you."

" Thank you, count, good-evening; do not lose sight of our ghost."

" Oh, rely upon me for that! unless," added Henri, who feared he might have said too much—" unless, indeed, I should be overtaken by sleep, which seems more than probable, and a far more wholesome occupation than that of watching shadows and spies."

" Certainly," said the ensign, laughingly, as he took leave of Bouchage.

As soon as the ensign had left the library, Henri darted into the garden.

" Oh! " he murmured, " it is Rémy! it is Rémy! I should know him again in the darkness of hell." And the young man, as he felt his knees tremble beneath him, buried his burning forehead in his cold damp hands. "Great Heaven!" he cried, "is not this rather a phantasy of my poor fevered brain, and is it not written that in my slumbering and in my waking moments, day and night, I shall ever see those two figures who have made so deep and dark a furrow in my life? Why," he continued, like a man who finds it necessary to convince himself—"why, indeed, should Rémy be here in this château while the Duc d'Anjou is here? What is his motive in coming here? What can the Duc d'Anjou possibly have to do with Rémy! And why should he have left Diane—he, who is her constant companion? No, it is not he."

Then again, a moment afterwards, a conviction, thorough, profound, instinctive, overcame his doubts. "It is he! it is he!" he murmured in despair, leaning against the wall to save himself from falling.

Just as Henri was giving expression to this controlling, unconquerable idea, the sharp sound of the lock was again heard; and although the sound was almost imperceptible, his overexcited senses detected it. An indefinable shudder ran through the young man's whole frame; again he listened with eager attention. So profound a silence reigned around him on every side that he could hear the throbbings of his own heart. A few minutes passed away without anything he expected making its appearance. In default of seeing, however, his ears told him that some one was approaching; he heard the sound of the gravel under advancing footsteps. Suddenly the straight black line of the hedge seemed broken; he imagined he saw upon this dark background a group still darker moving along.

"It is he returning again," murmured Henri. "Is he alone, or is some one with him?"

The group advanced from where the silver light of the moon had illuminated a space of open ground. It was at the moment when, advancing in the opposite direction, the man in the overcoat crossed this open space, that Henri fancied he recognised Rémy. This time Henri observed two shadows very distinctly; it was impossible he could be mistaken. A death-like chill struck to his heart and seemed to have turned it to marble.

The two shadows walked quickly along, although with a firm step. The first was dressed in a woollen overcoat; and at that second apparition, as at the first, the count was sure that he recognised Rémy.

The second, who was completely enveloped in a large cloak of masculine apparel, defied every attempt at recognition; and yet beneath that cloak Henri thought he could detect what no human eye could have possibly seen. He could not suppress a groan of despair; and no sooner had the two mysterious personages disappeared behind the hedge than the young man darted after them, and stealthily glided from one group of trees to another, in the wake of those whom he was so anxious to discover. " Oh! " he murmured, as he stole along, " do I not indeed deceive myself? *Mon Dieu!* is it possible? "

CHAPTER XXXV

CERTAINTY

HENRI glided along the hedge on the side which was thrown into deep shade, taking care to make no noise either on the gravel or against the trees. Obliged to walk carefully, and while walking to watch over every movement he made, he could not perceive anything. And yet, by his style, his dress, his walk, he was still sure that he recognised Rémy in the man who wore the overcoat. Conjectures, more terrifying for him than realities, arose in his mind with regard to this man's companion.

The road which they were following, and which was bounded by a row of elms, led to a high hawthorn hedge and a wall of poplars, which separated from the rest of the park the pavilion of the Duc d'Anjou, and enveloped it as with a curtain of verdure, in the midst of which, as has been already observed, it was completely concealed in an isolated corner of the grounds of the château. There were several beautiful sheets of water, shaded groves through which winding paths had been cut, and venerable trees, over the summits of which the moon was shedding its streams of silver light, while underneath the gloom was thick, dark, and impenetrable.

As he approached this hedge, Henri felt that his heart was on the point of failing him. In fact, to transgress so boldly the prince's orders, and to abandon himself to a course of conduct as indiscreet as it was rash, was the act, not of a loyal and honourable man, but of a mean and cowardly spy, or of a jealous man driven to extremities. But when, in opening the gate which separated the greater from the smaller park, the man he followed moved in such a way that his features were revealed, and he perceived that these features were indeed those of Rémy, the count's scruples vanished, and he resolutely advanced at all hazards. Henri found the gate closed. He leaped over the railings, and then continued his pursuit of the prince's two strange visitors, who still hurried onward. Another cause of terror was soon added, for the duke, on hearing the footsteps of Rémy and his companion upon the gravel-walk, made his appearance from the pavilion. Henri threw himself behind the largest of the trees and waited.

He could not see anything, except that Rémy made a very low salutation, that Rémy's companion courtesied like a woman instead of bowing like a man, and that the duke, seemingly transported with delight, offered his arm to the latter as he would have offered it to a woman. Then all three advanced towards the pavilion, disappeared under the vestibule, and the door closed behind them.

"This must end," said Henri; "and I must seek a more convenient place, where without being seen I can see everything that may happen."

He decided in favour of a clump of trees situated between the pavilion and the wall, from the centre of which the waters of a fountain gushed forth—an impenetrable place of concealment, for it was not likely that in the night-time, with the freshness and humidity which would naturally be found near this fountain, the prince would seek the vicinity of the water and the thickets. Hidden behind the statue with which the fountain was ornamented, standing at his full height behind the pedestal, Henri was enabled to see what was taking place in the pavilion, the principal window of which was wide open before him. As no one could, or rather as no one was likely, to penetrate so far, no precautions had been taken.

A table was laid, sumptuously served with the richest viands, and with rare wines in bottles of costly Venetian glass. Two seats only at this table awaited two guests. The duke approached one of the chairs; then, leaving the arm of Rémy's companion, and pointing to the other seat, he seemed to request that the cloak might be thrown aside, as although it might be very serviceable for an evening stroll, it became very inconvenient when the object of the stroll was attained, and when that object was a supper.

Thereupon the person to whom the invitation had been addressed, threw the cloak upon a chair, and the dazzling blaze of the torches lighted up, without a shadow on their loveliness, the pale and majestically beautiful features of a woman whom the terrified eyes of Henri immediately recognised. It was the lady of the mysterious house in the Rue des Augustins, the wanderer in Flanders; it was that Diane whose gaze was as mortal as the thrust of a dagger. On this occasion she wore the apparel of her own sex, and was richly dressed in brocaded silk; diamonds blazed on her neck, in her hair, and on her wrists. In that attire she appeared still paler than before, and in the light which shone from her eyes it almost seemed as if the duke had, by the employment of some magical means, evoked the ghost of this woman, rather than the woman herself. Had it not been for the support afforded by the statue round which he had thrown his arms, colder even than the marble itself, Henri would have fallen backwards into the basin of the fountain.

The duke seemed intoxicated with delight; he fixed his passionate gaze upon this beautiful creature, who had seated herself opposite to him, and who hardly touched the dishes which had been placed before her. From time to time François leaned across the table to kiss one of the hands of his pale and silent guest, who seemed as insensible to his kisses as if her hand had been sculptured in alabaster, which, for transparency and whiteness, it so much resembled. Henri raised his hand to his forehead, and with it wiped away the death-like sweat which dropped from it, and asked himself, " Is she alive or dead? "

The duke tried his utmost efforts and displayed all his powers of eloquence to soften the rigid beauty of Diane's face. Rémy, the only attendant—for the duke had sent every one away—waited on them both, and occasionally, lightly touching his mistress with his elbow as he passed behind her chair, seemed to revive her by the contact, and to recall her to life, or rather to the position in which she was placed.

Thereupon a bright flush spread over her whole face, her eyes sparkled, she smiled as if some magician had touched a secret spring in this intelligent automaton, and by the operation of some mechanism had drawn light to her eyes, colour to her cheeks, and a smile to her lips. Then she relapsed into immobility. The prince, however, approached her, and by the passionate tone of his conversation succeeded in warming into animation his new conquest. Then Diane, who occasionally glanced at the face of a magnificent clock suspended over the prince's head, against the wall opposite to where she was seated, seemed to make an effort over herself, and keeping the smile upon her lips, took a more active part in the conversation.

Henri, concealed in his leafy covert, wrung his hands in despair, and cursed the whole creation, from the women whom God had made to God who had created him. It seemed to him monstrous and iniquitous that this woman, so pure and rigidly inflexible, should yield herself so unresistingly to the prince because he was a prince, and abandon herself to love because it was offered within the precincts of a palace. His horror at Rémy was such that he could have slain him without remorse, in order to see whether so great a monster had the blood and heart of a man in him. In such paroxysms of rage and contempt did Henri pass the time during the supper which to the Duc d'Anjou was so full of rapture and delight.

Diane rang. The prince, inflamed by wine, and by his passionate discourse, rose from the table to embrace her. Every drop of blood curdled in Henri's veins. He put his hand to his side to see if his sword were there, and then thrust it into his breast in search of a dagger. Diane, with a strange smile, which most assuredly had never until that moment had its counterpart on any face, stopped the duke as he was approaching her.

" Will you allow me, monseigneur," she said, " before I rise from the table, to share with your royal highness one of those tempting-looking peaches? "

And with these words she stretched out her hand towards a basket of gold filagree-work, in which twenty peaches were tastefully arranged, and took one. Then, taking from her girdle a beautiful little knife, with a silver blade and a handle of malachite, she divided the peach into two portions, and offered one of them to the prince, who seized it and carried it eagerly to his lips, as though he would thus have kissed Diane's.

This impassioned action produced so deep an impression on the duke that a cloud seemed to obscure his sight at the very moment he bit into the fruit. Diane looked at him with her clear, steady gaze and her immovable smile. Rémy, leaning his back against a pillar of carved wood, also looked on with a gloomy expression of countenance.

The prince passed one of his hands across his forehead, wiped away the perspiration which had gathered there, and swallowed the piece that he had bitten. This perspiration was most probably the symptom of a sudden indisposition; for while Diane ate the other half of the peach, the prince let fall on his plate what remained of the portion he had taken, and with difficulty rising from his seat, seemed to invite his beautiful companion to accompany him into the garden in order to enjoy the cool night air.

Diane rose, and without pronouncing a word, took the duke's arm, which he offered her. Rémy watched them, especially the prince, whom the air seemed completely to revive. As she walked along, Diane wiped the small blade of her knife on a handkerchief embroidered with gold, and restored it to its shagreen sheath. In this manner they approached the clump of trees where Henri was concealed.

The prince, with a passionate gesture, pressed his companion's arm against his heart. " I feel better," he said, " and yet I hardly know what heavy weight seems to press down on my brain; I love too deeply, madame, I perceive."

Diane plucked several sprigs of jasmine and of clematis, and two beautiful roses from among those which bordered the whole of one side of the pedestal of the statue behind which Henri was shrinking, terrified.

" What are you doing, madame? " inquired the prince.

" I have always understood, monseigneur," she said, " that the perfume of flowers was the best remedy for attacks of giddiness; I am gathering a bouquet, with the hope that if presented by me it will have the magical effect which I wish it to have." But while she was arranging the flowers, she let a rose fall from her hand, which the prince eagerly hastened to pick up.

The movement that François made was rapid, but not so rapid, however, but that it gave Diane sufficient time to pour upon the other rose a few drops of a liquid contained in a small gold bottle which she drew from her bosom. She then took from his hand the rose which the prince had picked up, and placing it in her girdle, said, " That one is for me; let us change." And in exchange for the rose which she received from the prince's hand, she held out the bouquet to him.

The prince seized it eagerly, inhaled its perfume with delight, and passed his arm around Diane's waist. But this latter action in all probability completely overwhelmed the already troubled senses of the prince, for his knees trembled under him, and he was obliged to seat himself on a bank of green turf, beside which he happened to be standing.

Henri did not lose sight of these two persons, and yet he had a look for Rémy also, who in the pavilion awaited the termination of this scene, or rather seemed to devour every minute incident of it. When he saw the prince totter, he advanced towards the threshold of the pavilion. Diane, perceiving François stagger, sat down beside him on the bank.

The giddiness from which François suffered continued on this occasion longer than on the former. The prince's head was resting on his chest. He seemed to have lost all connection in his ideas, and almost the perception of his own existence; and yet the convulsive movement of his fingers on Diane's hand seemed to indicate that he was instinctively pursuing his wild dream of love. At last he slowly raised his head, and his lips being almost on a level with Diane's face, he made an effort to touch those of his lovely guest; but as if unobservant of the movement, she rose from her seat. "You are suffering, monseigneur," she said; "it would be better if we were to go in."

"Oh, yes, let us go in!" exclaimed the prince, in a transport of joy; "yes, come; thank you!"

And he arose, staggering, to his feet; then, instead of Diane leaning on his arm, it was he who leaned on Diane's arm. And, thanks to this support, walking with less difficulty, he seemed to forget fever and giddiness too, for suddenly drawing himself up, he in an unexpected manner pressed his lips on her neck. She started as if instead of a kiss, she had received the impression of a red-hot iron.

"Rémy!" she exclaimed, "a torch! a torch!"

Rémy immediately returned to the dining-room, and lighted, by the candle on the table, a torch which he took from a small round table, and then, hurrying to the entrance to the pavilion, and holding the torch in his hand, he cried out, "Here is one, madame."

"Where is your highness going?" inquired Diane, seizing the torch and turning her head aside.

"Oh, we will return to my own room; and you will lead me, I venture to hope, madame?" replied the prince, in a frenzy of passion.

"Willingly, monseigneur," replied Diane, and she raised the torch in the air, and walked before the prince.

Rémy opened, at the end of the pavilion, a window through which the fresh air rushed inwards in such a manner that the flame and smoke of the torch which Diane held were carried back towards François's face, which happened to be in the very current of the air. The two lovers, as Henri considered them, proceeded in this manner, crossing a gallery, to the duke's own room, and disappeared behind a *portière*.

Henri had observed everything that had taken place with increasing fury, and yet this fury was such that it almost deprived him of life. It seemed as if he had no strength left except to curse the fate which had imposed so cruel a trial upon him. He had left his place of concealment, and in utter despair, his arms hanging by his side, and with a haggard gaze, he was on the point of returning, half dead, to his apartments in the château when suddenly the hangings behind which he had seen Diane and the prince disappear were thrown aside, and Diane herself rushed into the supper-room, and took hold of Rémy, who, standing motionless, seemed only to be awaiting her return. "Quick! quick!" she said to him; "all is finished!" And they both darted into the garden, as if they had been drunk, or mad, or raging with passion.

No sooner did Henri observe them, however, than he recovered all his strength. He hastened to place himself in their way; and they came upon him suddenly in the middle of the path, standing erect, his arms crossed, and more terrible in his silence than any one could ever have been in his loudest menaces. Henri's feelings had indeed arrived at such a pitch of exasperation that he would readily have slain any man who would have ventured to maintain that women were not monsters sent from hell to corrupt the world. He seized Diane by the arm and stopped her suddenly, notwithstanding the cry of terror which she uttered, and notwithstanding the dagger which Rémy put to his breast, and which even grazed his flesh. "Oh, doubtless you do not recognise me," he said furiously, grinding his teeth. "I am that simple-hearted young man who loved you, and whose love you would not return, because for you there was no future, but merely the past. Ah, beautiful hypocrite that you are, and you, foul liar, I know you at last—I know and curse you. To the one I say, I despise you; to the other, I shrink from you with horror."

"Make way!" cried Rémy, in a strangled voice; "make way, young fool, or if not—"

"Be it so," replied Henri; "finish your work, and slay my body, wretch, since you have already destroyed my soul."

"Silence!" muttered Rémy, furiously, pressing the blade of his dagger more and more against Henri's breast.

Diane, however, violently pushed Rémy aside, and seizing Bouchage by the arm, she drew him straight before her. She was lividly pale; her beautiful hair streamed over her shoulders; the contact of the hand on Henri's wrist affected him with a coldness like that of a corpse. "Monsieur," she said, "do not rashly judge of the affairs of God. I am Diane de Méridor, the mistress of M. de Bussy, whom the Duc d'Anjou miserably allowed to perish when he could have saved him. Eight days since, Rémy slew Aurilly, the duke's accomplice; and the prince himself I have just poisoned with a peach, a bouquet, and a torch. Move aside, monsieur! move aside, I say, for Diane de Méridor, who is on her way to the convent of the Hospitalières!" With these words, and letting Henri's arm fall, she took hold of that of Rémy, as he waited by her side.

Henri fell on his knees, following the retreating figures of the two assassins, who disappeared, like an infernal vision, behind the thick copse. It was not till fully an hour afterwards that Bouchage, overpowered with fatigue and overwhelmed with terror, with his brain on fire, was able to summon sufficient strength to drag himself to his apartment; nor was it until after he had made the attempt nearly a dozen times that he succeeded in escalading the window. He took a few steps in his chamber and staggered to his bed, on which he threw himself. Every one was sleeping quietly in the château.

CHAPTER XXXVI

FATALITY

THE next morning, about nine o'clock, the beautiful rays of the sun were glistening like gold on the gravelled walks of Château-Thierry. Numerous gangs of workmen, who had the previous evening been directed to be in attendance, had been actively at work from daybreak upon the preparations in the park, as well as in the decoration of the apartments destined to receive the king, whose arrival was momentarily expected. As yet nothing was stirring in the pavilion where the duke reposed, for he had on the previous evening forbidden his two old servants to awaken him. They were to wait until he summoned them. Towards half-past nine two couriers rode at full speed into the town, announcing his Majesty's approach. The civic authorities, the governor, and the garrison formed themselves in ranks on either side of the road, leaving a passage for the royal procession. At ten o'clock the king appeared at the foot of the hill; he had mounted his horse when they had taken their last relays. It was an opportunity of which he always availed himself, especially when entering towns, as he was a good rider. The queen-mother followed him in a litter; fifty gentlemen belonging to the court, richly clad and well mounted, followed in their suite. A company of the guards, commanded by Crillon himself, a hundred and twenty of the Swiss, and as many of the Scotch guards, commanded by Larchant, and all the members of the royal household who accompanied the king in his excursions, mules, coffers, and domestic servants, formed a numerous army, the files of which followed the windings of the road leading from the river to the summit of the hill. At length the *cortége* entered the town, amid the ringing of the church-bells, the roar of cannon, and bursts of music. The acclamations of the inhabitants were enthusiastic, for a visit from the king was of so rare occurrence at that time that seen thus closely, he seemed to be a living embodiment of divine right. The king, as he progressed through the crowd, looked on all sides for his brother, but in vain. He found only Henri du Bouchage waiting for him at the gate of the château.

When once within the château, Henri III. inquired after the health of the Duc d'Anjou from the officer who had assumed the high distinction of receiving the king.

" Sire," replied the latter, " his highness, during the last few days, has been residing in the pavilion in the park, and we have not yet seen him this morning. It is most probable, however, that as he was well yesterday, he is well also to-day."

" This pavilion is in a very retired part of the park, it seems," said Henri, in a tone of displeasure, " since the sound of the cannon does not seem to have been heard."

" Sire," one of the duke's two aged attendants ventured to remark, " his highness did not perhaps expect your Majesty so soon."

" Old fool," growled Henri, " do you think, then, that a king presents himself in that way at other people's residences, without giving them notice? M. le Duc d'Anjou has been aware of my intended arrival since yesterday." And then, afraid of casting a gloom over those around him by a grave or sullen countenance, Henri, who wished to appear gentle and amiable at the expense of his brother François, exclaimed, " Well, then, since he has not come to meet us, we will go to meet him."

" Show us the way there," said Catherine, from the litter.

All the escort followed the road leading to the old park. At the very moment that the guards, who were in advance, approached the hedge, a shrill and piercing cry rent the air.

" What is that? " said the king, turning towards his mother.

" *Mon Dieu!* " murmured Catherine, endeavouring to read the faces of those around her; " it is a cry of distress or despair."

" My prince! my poor master! " cried François's other aged attendant, appearing at the window, and exhibiting signs of the most passionate grief. Every one hastened towards the pavilion, the king himself being hurried along with the others. He arrived at the moment when they were raising from the floor the Duc d'Anjou's body, which his *valet de chambre*, having entered without authority, in order to announce the king's arrival, had just perceived lying on the carpet of the bedroom. The prince was cold and stiff, and it was only by a strange movement of the eyelids and a nervous contraction of the lips that it could be observed he was still alive. The king paused at the threshold of the door, and those behind him followed his example.

"This is an ugly omen," he murmured.

"Do not enter, my son, I implore you," said Catherine to him.

"Poor François!" said Henri, delighted at being sent away, and thus being spared the spectacle of that agony.

All the company followed the king as he withdrew.

"Strange! strange!" murmured Catherine, kneeling down by the side of the prince, or rather of his inanimate body, no one being in the room with her but the two old servants; and while the messengers were despatched in every quarter of the town to find the prince's physician, and a courier galloped off to Paris to hasten the attendance of the king's physicians, who had remained at Meaux with the queen, Catherine, with less knowledge, very probably, but not with less perspicacity than Miron himself could possibly have shown, examined the symptoms of that singular malady which had struck down her son so suddenly. She had experience, the Florentine; in the first place, therefore, she interrogated calmly, and without confusing them, the two attendants, who were tearing their hair and wringing their hands in the wildest despair.

Both the attendants replied that the prince had returned on the previous evening about nightfall, after having been disturbed at an inconvenient hour by M. du Bouchage, who had arrived with a message from the king. They added that when the audience had terminated, which had been held in the château itself, the prince had ordered a delicate supper to be prepared, and had desired that no one should venture to approach the pavilion without being summoned; and lastly, that he had given the strictest injunctions not to be awakened in the morning, and that no one should enter without a positive summons.

"He probably expected a visit from a lady?" observed the queen-mother, inquiringly.

"We think so, madame," replied the valet, respectfully; "but we could not discreetly assure ourselves of the fact."

"But in removing the things from the table, you must have seen whether my son had supped alone?"

"We have not yet removed the things, madame, since the orders of monseigneur were that no one should enter the pavilion."

"Very good!" said Catherine; "no one, then, has been here?"

"No one, madame."

"You may go."

And Catherine was now left quite alone in the room. Leaving the prince lying on the bed where he had been placed, she immediately began the minutest investigation of each symptom, and of each of the traces to which her attention was directed as the result of her suspicions or apprehensions. She had remarked that François's forehead was of a bistre colour, his eyes were bloodshot and encircled with blue lines, his lips marked with furrows, like the impression which burning sulphur leaves on living flesh. She observed the same sign upon his nostrils and upon the sides of the nose.

"Now let me look carefully," said Catherine, gazing about her on every side. The first thing she remarked was the candlestick in which the candle which Rémy had lighted the previous evening had burned away. "This candle has burned a long time," she said, "and shows that François was a long time in this room. Ah, here is a bouquet lying on the carpet!" She picked it up eagerly; and then, remarking that all its flowers were still fresh, with the exception of a rose, which was blackened and dried up, "What does this mean?" she said. "What has been poured on the leaves of this flower? If I am not mistaken, I know a liquid which withers roses in this manner." She threw aside the bouquet, shuddering as she did so. "That explains to me the state of the nostrils and the manner in which the flesh of the face is affected; but the lips?"

Catherine ran to the dining-room. The valets had spoken the truth, for there was nothing to indicate that anything on the table had been touched since the previous evening's repast had been finished. Upon the edge of the table lay the half of a peach, in which the impression of a row of teeth was still visible. Catherine examined this with special attention. The fruit, usually of a rich crimson near the core, had become black like the rose, and was discoloured by violet and brown spots. The corrosive action was more especially visible upon the part which had been cut, and particularly so where the knife must have passed. "This explains the state of the lips," she said; "but François had bitten only one piece out of this peach. He did not keep the bouquet long in his hand, for the flowers are still fresh. The evil may yet be repaired, for the poison cannot have penetrated very deeply. And yet if the evil be merely superficial, why should this paralysis of the senses be so complete, and why indeed should the decomposition of the flesh have made so much progress? There must be more that I have not seen." And as she spoke, Catherine again looked all round her, and observed, hanging by a silver chain to its pole, the red and blue parrot to which François was so attached. The bird was dead, stiff, and the feathers of its wings rough and erect.

Catherine again looked closely and attentively at the torch which she had once before already narrowly inspected, to satisfy herself that by its having burned out complete, the prince had returned early in the evening.

"The smoke!" said Catherine to herself; "the smoke! The wick of that torch was poisoned; my son is a dead man!" She called out immediately; and the chamber was in a minute filled with attendants and officers of the household.

"Miron, Miron!" cried some of them.

"A priest!" exclaimed the others.

But Catherine had in the meantime placed to the lips of François one of the small bottles which she always carried in her alms-bag, and narrowly watched her son's features to observe the effect of the antidote she applied.

The duke immediately opened his eyes and mouth; but no glance of intelligence gleamed in his eyes, no voice or sound escaped from his lips.

Catherine, in sad and gloomy silence, withdrew from the apartment, beckoning to the two attendants to follow her, before they had as yet had an opportunity of communicating with any one. She then led them into another chamber, where she sat down, fixing her eyes closely and watchfully on their faces. "M. le Duc d'Anjou," she said, "has been poisoned some time during his supper last evening; and it was you who served the supper."

At these words the two men turned as pale as death. "Torture us, kill us, if you will," they said, "but do not accuse us."

"Fools that you are! do you suppose that if I suspected you, that would not already have been done? You have not yourselves, I know, assassinated your master, but others have killed him; and I must know who the murderers are. Who has entered the pavilion?"

"An old man, wretchedly clothed, whom monseigneur has seen during the last two days."

"But the woman?"

"We have not seen her. What woman does your Majesty mean?"

"A woman has been here, who made a bouquet—"

The two attendants looked at each other with an expression

of such simple surprise that Catherine recognised their innocence in that single glance.

"Let the governor of the town and the governor of the château be sent for," she said.

The two valets hurried to the door.

"One moment!" exclaimed Catherine, fixing them to the threshold by this brief command. "You only and myself are aware of what I have just told you; I shall not breathe a word about it. If any one learns it, therefore, it will be from or through one of you; on that very day both your lives shall be forfeited. Now, go!"

Catherine interrogated the two governors with more reserve. She told them that the duke had received from some person or persons a distressing intelligence which had deeply affected him; that that alone was the cause of his illness; and that if the duke had an opportunity of putting a few further questions to the persons again, he would in all probability soon recover from the alarm into which he had been thrown.

The governors instituted the minutest search in the town, the park, the environs; but no one knew what had become of Rémy and Diane. Henri alone knew the secret, and there was no danger of his betraying it.

Throughout the whole day, the terrible news, commented upon, exaggerated, and mutilated, circulated through Château-Thierry and the province; every one explained, according to his own individual character and disposition, the accident which had befallen the duke. But no one, except Catherine and Bouchage, ventured to acknowledge that the chance of saving the duke's life was hopeless.

The unhappy prince did not recover either his voice or his senses—in short, he ceased to give any sign of intelligence.

The king, who was immediately beset with the gloomiest fancies, which he dreaded more than anything, would very willingly have returned to Paris; but the queen-mother opposed his departure, and the court was obliged to remain at the château.

Many physicians arrived. Miron alone divined the cause of the illness, and formed an opinion upon its serious nature and extent; but he was too good a courtier to confess the truth, especially after he had consulted Catherine's looks. He was questioned on all sides, and he replied that the Duc d'Anjou certainly had suffered from some seriously disturbing cause, and had been subjected to some violent mental shock. In this way he avoided compromising himself, which is a very difficult matter in such a case. When Henri III. required him to answer affirmatively or negatively to his question, "Will the duke live?" he replied, "I will answer your Majesty in three days."

"And when will you tell me?" said Catherine, in a low voice.

"You, madame, are very different; I answer you unhesitatingly."

"Well?"

"Your Majesty has but to interrogate me."

"On what day will my son die, Miron?"

"To-morrow evening, madame."

"So soon?"

"Ah, madame," murmured the physician, "the dose was by no means a slight one."

Catherine placed one of her fingers on her lips, looked at the dying man, and repeated in an undertone this sinister word "Fatality."

CHAPTER XXXVII

LES HOSPITALIÈRES

THE count had spent a terrible night, in a state bordering on delirium and death. Faithful, however, to his duty, as soon as he had heard the king's arrival announced, he rose and received him at the gate, as we have said; but no sooner had he presented his homage to his Majesty, saluted respectfully the queen-mother, and pressed the admiral's hand, than he shut himself up in his own room, not to die, but to carry determinedly into execution his long-cherished project, which nothing could any longer interfere with.

Towards eleven o'clock in the morning, therefore—that is to say, as soon as, immediately after the terrible news had circulated that the Duc d'Anjou's life was in imminent danger, every one had dispersed, leaving the king completely bewildered by this new event—Henri went and knocked at his brother's door, who, having passed a part of the previous night travelling, had just retired to his own room.

"Ah! is that you?" asked Joyeuse, half asleep. "What is the matter?"

"I have come to bid you farewell, my brother," replied Henri.

"Farewell! What do you mean? Are you going away?"

"Yes, I am going away, brother; and nothing need keep me here any longer, I presume."

"Why nothing?"

"Of course, since the fêtes at which you wished me to be present will not take place, I may now consider myself as freed from my promise."

"You are mistaken, Henri," replied the grand admiral; "I have no greater reason for permitting you to leave to-day than I had yesterday."

"So be it, my brother; but in that case, for the first time in my life, I shall have the misfortune to disobey your orders, and to fail in the respect I owe you—for from this very moment I declare to you, Anne, that nothing shall restrain me any longer from taking religious vows."

"But the dispensation which is expected from Rome?"

"I can await it in a convent."

"You must positively be mad to think of such a thing!" exclaimed Joyeuse, as he rose, with stupefaction depicted on his countenance.

"On the contrary, my dear and honoured brother, I am the wisest of you all, for I alone know what I am about."

"Henri, you promised us a month."

"Impossible."

"A week longer, then."

"Not an hour."

"You are suffering so much, then, poor boy?"

"On the contrary, I have ceased to suffer; and that is why the evil is without a remedy."

"But, at all events, this woman is not made of bronze; her feelings can be worked upon. I will undertake to persuade her."

"You cannot do impossibilities, Anne; besides, even were she to allow herself to be persuaded now, it is *I* who could no longer consent to love her."

"Well, that is quite another matter."

"Such is the case, however, my brother."

"What! if she were now willing, would you be indifferent? Why, this is sheer madness."

"Oh, no, no!" exclaimed Henri, with a shudder of horror; "nothing can any longer exist between that woman and myself."

"What does this mean?" inquired Joyeuse, with marked surprise. "And who, then, is this woman? Come, tell me, Henri; you know very well that we have never had any secrets from each other."

Henri feared that he had said too much, and that in yielding to the feeling which he had just exhibited, he had opened a door by which his brother would be able to penetrate the terrible secret which he kept imprisoned in his breast. He therefore fell into an opposite extreme; and as it happens in such cases, in order to recall the imprudent words which had escaped him, he pronounced others which were more imprudent still. "Do not press me further," he said; "this woman will never be mine, since she belongs to God."

"Folly! mere idle tales! This woman a nun! She has deceived you."

"No, no! this woman has not spoken falsely; she is now an Hospitalière. Do not let us speak any further of her; and let us respect those who throw themselves at the feet of the Lord."

Anne had sufficient power over himself not to show the delight this revelation gave him. He continued, "This is something new, for you have never spoken to me about it."

"It is indeed quite new, for she has only recently taken the veil; but I am sure that her resolution, like my own, is irrevocable. Do not therefore seek to detain me any longer, but embrace me, as you love me. Permit me to thank you for all your kindness, for all your patience, and for your unceasing affection for a poor heart-broken man, and farewell!"

Joyeuse looked his brother full and steadily in the face; he looked at him like one whose feelings had overcome him, and who relied upon a display of feeling to persuade another. But Henri remained unmoved at this exhibition of emotion on his brother's part, and replied only by the same mournful smile.

Joyeuse embraced his brother, and allowed him to depart. "Go," he said apart; "all is not yet finished, and whatever speed you make, I shall soon have overtaken you." He went to the king, who was taking his breakfast in bed, with Chicot sitting by his side.

"Good-day! good-day!" said the king to Joyeuse; "I am very glad to see you, Anne. I was afraid you would lie in bed all day, you indolent fellow. How is my brother?"

"Alas! Sire, I do not know; I am come to speak to you about mine."

"Which one?"

"Henri."

"Does he still wish to become a monk?"

"More so than ever."

"And will he take the vows?"

"Yes, Sire."

"He is quite right too."

"How so, Sire?"

"Because men go straight to heaven that way."

"Oh!" said Chicot to the king, "men go much faster still by the way your brother is taking."

"Will your Majesty permit me to ask a question?"

"Twenty, Joyeuse, twenty. I am as melancholy as I can possibly be at Château-Thierry, and your questions will distract my attention a little."

"You know all the religious houses in the kingdom, Sire, I believe?"

"As well as I do the coats-of-arms."

"What is that which goes by the name of Les Hospitalières, Sire?"

"It is a very small, highly distinguished, very strict, very severe order, composed of twenty ladies, canonesses of St. Joseph."

"Do they take the vows there?"

"Yes, as a matter of favour, and upon a presentation from the queen."

"Should I be indiscreet if I were to ask your majesty where this order is situated?"

"Not at all; it is situated in the Rue du Chevet St. Landry, in the Cité, behind the gardens of Notre-Dame."

"In Paris?"

"Yes."

"Thank you, Sire."

"But why the devil do you ask me that? Has your brother changed his mind, and instead of turning a Capuchin friar, does he now wish to become one of the Hospitalières?"

"No, Sire, I should not think he would be so mad, after what your Majesty has done me the honour to tell me; but I suspect he has had his head turned by some one belonging to that order, and I should like to discover who this person is, and speak to her."

"*Par la mordieu!*" said the king, with a self-satisfied expression, "some seven years ago I knew the superior of that convent, who was an exceedingly beautiful woman."

"Well, Sire, it may perhaps be the very one."

"I cannot say; since that time, I too, Joyeuse, have assumed religious vows myself, or nearly so, indeed."

"Sire," said Joyeuse, "I entreat you to give me, at any rate, a letter to this lady, and leave of absence for two days."

"You are going to leave me?" exclaimed the king; "to leave me all alone here?"

"Oh, ungrateful king!" said Chicot, shrugging his shoulders, "am I not here?"

" My letter, if you please, Sire," said Joyeuse.

The king sighed, but wrote it, notwithstanding. " But you cannot have anything to do at Paris? " said Henri, handing the note to Joyeuse.

" I beg your pardon, Sire; I ought to escort, or at least to watch over my brother."

" You are right; away with you, but return as quickly as you can."

Joyeuse did not wait for this permission to be repeated; he quietly ordered his horses, and having satisfied himself that Henri had already set off, galloped all the way until he reached his destination.

Without even changing his dress, the young man went straight to the Rue du Chevet St. Landry. At the end of this street was the Rue d'Enfer, and parallel with it the Rue des Marmouzets.

A dark and venerable-looking house, behind whose walls the lofty summits of a few trees could be distinguished, with a few barred windows and a wicket gate—such was the exterior appearance of the convent of the Hospitalières. Upon the keystone of the arch of the porch an artisan had rudely engraved these Latin words with a chisel:—

MATRONÆ HOSPITES.

Time had partially destroyed both the inscription and the stone.

Joyeuse knocked at the wicket, and had his horses led away to the Rue des Marmouzets, fearing that their presence in the street might attract too much attention. Then, knocking at the entrance gate, he said, " Will you be good enough to go and inform Madame the Superior that M. le Duc de Joyeuse, Grand Admiral of France, wishes to speak to her on behalf of the king? "

The face of the nun who had made her appearance behind the gate blushed beneath her veil, and she shut the gate. Five minutes afterwards, a door was opened, and Joyeuse entered a room set apart for the reception of visitors. A beautiful woman of lofty stature made Joyeuse a profound reverence, which the admiral returned gracefully and respectfully.

" Madame," said he, " the king is aware that you are about to admit, or that you have already admitted, among the number of the inmates here, a person with whom I must have an interview. Will you be good enough to place me in communication with that person? "

" Will you tell me the name of the lady you wish to see, monsieur? "

" I am not acquainted with it."

" In that case, then, monsieur, how can I accede to your request? "

" Nothing is easier. Whom have you admitted during the last month? "

" You tell me too precisely, or with not sufficient precision, who this person is," said the superior; " and I am unable to comply with your wish."

" Why so? "

" Because during the last month I have received no one here until this morning."

" This morning? "

" Yes, Monsieur the Duke, and you can understand that your own arrival, two hours after hers, has too much the appearance of a pursuit for me to grant you permission to speak to her."

" I implore you, madame! "

" Impossible, monsieur."

" Will you only let me see this lady? "

" Impossible, I repeat. Although your name was sufficient for the doors of this house to be thrown open before you, yet in order to speak to any one here, except indeed to myself, a written order from the king is necessary."

" Here is the order you require, madame," replied Joyeuse, producing the letter that Henri had signed.

The superior read it and bowed. " His Majesty's will shall be obeyed," she said, " even when it is contrary to the will of God." And she advanced towards the court-yard of the convent.

" You now perceive, madame," said Joyeuse, courteously stopping her, " that I have right on my side; but I fear committing an error, and abusing the permission I have received from the king. Perhaps the lady may not be the one I seek; will you be kind enough to tell me how she came here, why she came, and by whom she was accompanied? "

" All that is useless, Monsieur the Duke," replied the superior; " you are in no error, for the lady who arrived only this morning, after having been expected for the last two weeks—this lady, who was recommended by one who possesses the greatest authority over me, is indeed the person with whom M. le Duc de Joyeuse must wish to speak." With these words the superior made another reverence to the duke and disappeared. Ten minutes afterwards she returned, accompanied by an

Hospitalière, whose veil completely covered her face. It was Diane, who had already assumed the dress of the order.

The duke thanked the superior, offered a chair to her companion, himself sat down, and the superior left the room, closing with her own hands the doors of the gloomy apartment.

"Madame," said Joyeuse, without any preface, "you are the lady of the Rue des Augustins, that mysterious person with whom my brother, M. le Comte du Bouchage, is so passionately and madly in love."

The Hospitalière bowed her head in reply, but did not open her lips.

To Joyeuse this affectation seemed uncivil. He was already badly disposed towards his interlocutor, and continued, "You cannot have supposed, madame, that it is sufficient to be beautiful, or to appear beautiful, while you have no heart lying hidden beneath that beauty, while you inspire a wretched and despairing passion in the heart of a young man of my name, and then one day calmly tell him, 'So much the worse for you if you possess a heart; I have none, nor do I wish for any.'"

"That was not my reply, monsieur; and you have been incorrectly informed," said the Hospitalière, in so noble and touching a tone of voice that Joyeuse's anger was in a moment subdued.

"The actual words are immaterial, madame, when their sense has been conveyed. You have rejected my brother, and have reduced him to despair."

"Innocently, monsieur; for I have always endeavoured to keep M. de Bouchage at a distance."

"That is termed the art of coquetry, madame; and the result proves the fault."

"No one has the right to accuse me, monsieur; I am guilty of nothing. You are angry with me; I shall say no more."

"Oh, oh!" said Joyeuse, gradually working himself into a passion, "you have been the ruin of my brother, and you fancy you can justify yourself with this irritating majesty of demeanour. No, no! the steps I have taken must show you what my intentions are. I am serious, I assure you; and you see by the trembling of my hands and lips that you will need some good arguments to move me."

The Hospitalière rose. "If you come here to insult a woman," she said with the same calm self-possession, "insult me, monsieur; if you have come to induce me to change my opinion, you are wasting your time, and can withdraw."

" Ah, you are no human creature!" exclaimed Joyeuse, exasperated; " you are a demon!"

" I have answered already; I will reply no further. Since that is not sufficient, I shall withdraw." And the Hospitalière moved towards the door. Joyeuse stopped her.

" One moment! I have sought you for too long a period to allow you to leave me in this manner; and since I have succeeded in meeting with you; since your insensibility has confirmed me in the idea which had already occurred to me, that you are an infernal creature, sent hither by the enemy of mankind to destroy my brother—I wish to see that face whereon the bottomless pit has written its blackest traces; I wish to behold the fire of that fatal gaze which bewilders men's minds. Approach, Satan!"

And Joyeuse, making the sign of the cross with one hand, by way of exorcism, with the other tore aside the veil which covered the face of the Hospitalière; the latter, silent and impassive, free from anger or ill-feeling, fixed her sweet and gentle gaze upon him who had so cruelly outraged her, and said, " Oh, Monsieur the Duke, what you have just done is unworthy a gentleman."

Joyeuse was struck to the heart. Her gentleness quenched his wrath; her beauty overturned his reason.

" Oh, madame," he murmured, after a long silence, " you are indeed beautiful, and truly must Henri have loved you. Surely, Heaven can have bestowed upon you loveliness such as you possess only that you might shed it like perfume upon an existence devoted to your own."

" Monsieur, have you not conversed with your brother? If you have done so, he cannot have thought it expedient to make you his confidant; otherwise, he would have told you that I have done what you say—I have loved. I shall never love again; I have lived, and have now only to die."

Joyeuse had not taken his eyes from Diane's face; and the soft and gentle expression of her gaze penetrated the inmost recesses of his being. Her look had destroyed all the baser material in the admiral's heart; the pure metal alone was left, and his heart seemed rent asunder, like a crucible which had been riven by the fusion of metal. " Yes, yes!" he repeated in a still lower voice, and continuing to fix upon her a gaze from which the fire of his fierce anger had disappeared—" yes, yes! Henri must have loved you. Oh, madame, for pity's sake, on my knees I implore you to love my brother!"

Diane remained cold and silent.

"Do not reduce a family to despair; do not sacrifice the future prospects of our race! Be not the cause of the death of one from despair, of the others from regret!"

Diane, still silent, continued to look sorrowfully on the suppliant bending before her.

"Oh," exclaimed Joyeuse, madly, pressing his hand against his heart, "have mercy on my brother! have mercy on me! I am burning! that look consumes me! Adieu, madame, adieu!"

He sprang to his feet like a man bereft of his senses, unfastened, or rather tore open the door of the room where they had been conversing, and, bewildered and almost beside himself, fled from the house towards his attendants, who were awaiting him at the corner of the Rue d'Enfer.

CHAPTER XXXVIII

HIS HIGHNESS MONSEIGNEUR LE DUC DE GUISE

On Sunday, the 10th of June, towards eleven o'clock in the day, the whole court were assembled in the apartment leading to the cabinet in which, since his meeting with Diane de Méridor, the Duc d'Anjou was dying by slow but sure degrees. Neither the science of the physicians, nor his mother's despair, nor the prayers which the king had desired to be offered up, had averted the fatal termination. Miron, on the morning of this 10th of June, assured the king that all chance of recovery was hopeless, and that François d'Anjou would not outlive the day. The king pretended to display extreme grief, and turning towards those who were present, said, "This will fill my enemies full of hope."

To which remark the queen-mother replied, "Our destiny is in the hands of God, my son."

Whereupon Chicot, who was standing humbly and reverently near Henri III., added in a low voice, "Let us help God when we can, Sire."

Nevertheless, the dying man, towards half-past eleven, lost both colour and sight; his mouth, which up to that moment had remained open, became closed; the flow of blood which for several days past had terrified all who were near him, like the bloody sweat of Charles IX. at an earlier period, had suddenly ceased, and hands and feet became cold. Henri was sitting beside the head of the couch whereon his brother was extended. Catherine was standing in the recess in which the bed was placed, holding her dying son's hand in hers.

The Bishop of Château-Thierry and the Cardinal de Joyeuse repeated the prayers for the dying, which were joined in by all who were present, kneeling, and with clasped hands. Towards midday, the dying man opened his eyes; the sun's rays broke through a cloud and inundated the bed with a flood of light. François, who up to that moment had been unable to move a single finger, and whose mind had been obscured like the sun, which had just reappeared, raised one of his arms towards heaven with a movement of terror. He looked all round the room, heard the murmuring of the prayers, perceived his weakness, and understood his situation—perhaps because he already looked into that obscure and sinister world whither go certain souls on leaving the earth. He uttered a loud and piercing cry, and struck his forehead with a force which made every one tremble. Then, knitting his brows, as if he had solved in his thought one of the mysteries of his life, he murmured, " Bussy! Diane! "

This latter name had been overheard by none but Catherine, so weakened had the dying man's voice become before pronouncing it. With the last syllable of that name François d'Anjou breathed his last sigh.

At this very moment, by a singular coincidence, the sun, which had gilded with its rays the royal arms of France and the golden *fleur de lis,* was again obscured; so that the *fleurs de lis,* which had been so brilliantly illuminated but a moment before, became as dull as the azure ground which they had but recently studded with constellations almost as resplendent as those whereon the eye of the dreamer rests in his upward gaze towards heaven.

Catherine let her son's hand fall. Henri III. shuddered, and leaned tremblingly on Chicot's shoulder, who shuddered too, but from a feeling of awe which every Christian feels in the presence of the dead.

Miron placed a golden spatula on François's lips; after a few seconds, he looked at it carefully and said, " Monseigneur is dead."

Whereupon a deep prolonged groan arose from the antechamber, as an accompaniment to the psalm which the cardinal murmured, " Cedant iniquitates meæ ad vocem deprecationis meæ."

" Dead! " repeated the king, making the sign of the cross as he sat in his *fauteuil ;* " my brother, my brother! "

" The sole heir of the throne of France," murmured Catherine, who, having left the bed whereon the corpse was lying, had placed herself beside the only son who now remained to her.

" Oh," said Henri, " this throne of France is indeed large for a king without issue. The crown is indeed large for a single head. No children! no heirs! Who will succeed me? "

Hardly had he pronounced these words when a loud noise was heard on the staircase and in the halls. Nambu hurriedly entered the death-chamber, and announced, " His Highness Monseigneur le Duc de Guise."

Struck by this reply to the question which he had addressed to himself, the king turned pale, rose, and looked at his mother. Catherine was paler than her son. At the announcement of the horrible misfortune to her race which chance predicted, she grasped the king's hand, and pressed it, as if to say, " There lies the danger; but fear nothing, I am near you."

The son and mother, under the influence of the same terror and the same menace, had comprehended each other.

The duke entered, followed by his officers. He entered, holding his head loftily erect, although his eyes ranged from the king to the death-bed of his brother with a glance not free from a certain embarrassment.

Henri III. stood up, and with that supreme majesty of carriage which on certain occasions his singularly poetic nature enabled him to assume, checked the duke's further progress by a kingly gesture, and pointed to the royal corpse upon the bed, the covering of which was in disorder from his brother's dying agonies.

The duke bowed his head, and slowly fell on his knees. All around him, too, bowed their heads and bent their knees. Henri III., together with his mother, alone remained standing, and bent a last look, full of pride, upon those around him. Chicot observed this look, and murmured in a low tone of voice, " Dejiciet potentes de sede et exaltabit humiles " (" He will put down the mighty from their seat, and will exalt the humble.")

POSTSCRIPT

A few words with reference to the principal characters in *The Forty-five* are necessary to complete the story.

Diane de Monsoreau, having taken the vows at the convent of the Hospitalières, survived the Duc d'Anjou only two years. Of Rémy, her faithful companion, we hear no more. He disappeared without leaving a trace behind him.

History, however, informs us more fully as to the others. The Duc de Guise, having at last broken into open rebellion against Henri III., was so far successful that with the aid of the League he compelled the king to fly from Paris. A hollow reconciliation was, however, patched up between them, the Duc de Guise stipulating that he should be appointed lieutenant-general of the kingdom; but no sooner had the king returned to the Louvre than he determined on the assassination of the duke. He sounded Crillon, the leader of the Forty-five, on the subject, but this noble soldier refused to have anything to do with it, offering, however, to challenge the duke to single combat. Loignac was less scrupulous, and we know the result. The Duc de Guise and his brother the cardinal were both murdered. Ten days after this event, Catherine de Médicis, the queen-mother, died, regretted by none.

The Parisians, exasperated by the murder of the Duc de Guise, declared his brother, the Duc de Mayenne, the head of the League, and rose against the king, who was again obliged to fly. He begged the King of Navarre for aid, who promptly responded to the call, and they were shortly before Paris with a united army of Catholics and Huguenots. Henri III. was, however, pursued by the relentless hate of the clever and unscrupulous Duchesse de Montpensier. She worked so skilfully on the fanatical mind of the young Jacobin friar, Jacques Clement, that he undertook the death of the king. He entered the camp with letters for Henri, whom he stabbed while reading them. The king died August 2, 1589, after having declared Henri de Navarre his successor.

Of the subsequent life and adventures of Chicot, unfortunately nothing authentic is known.

TRANSLATOR.